STRANGLE

By

Michael Disney

A novel set around and amidst The Battle of the Atlantic, the most titanic, the most ruthless and the most momentous battle in all of history.

COPYRIGHT PAGE

© 2021   Michael Disney

Published by Kindle Direct Publishing

ISBN: 9798507528677

THE BATTLE OF THE ATLANTIC

"... the U-boats and the convoy escorts would shortly be locked in a deadly ruthless series of fights in which no mercy would be expected and little shown. Nor would one battle , or weeks or months of fighting decide the issue. It would be decided by which side could endure the longer; by whether the stamina and strength of purpose of the crews on the Allied escort vessels and aircraft, watching and listening all the time for the hidden enemy, outlasted the willpower of the U-boat crews , lurking in the darkness or the depths, fearing the relentless tap of the Asdic, the unseen eye of the radar and the crash of the depth-charges. It depended on whether the men of the Merchant Navy, themselves almost powerless to defend their precious cargoes of fuel, munitions and food, could stand the strain of waiting day after day and night after night throughout the long slow passages for the rending detonation of the torpedoes, which could send their ships to the bottom in a matter of seconds, or explode their cargoes in a searing sheet of flame from which there could be no escape. It was a battle between men, aided certainly by all the instruments and devices which science could provide, but still one that would be decided by the skill and endurance of men, and by the intensity of moral purpose which inspired them. In all the long history of sea warfare there has been no parallel to this battle…… "

Taken from *"The War at Sea,1939—1945"* by Captain SW Roskill: HMSO, 1956, Vol II, p 355.

Dedicated to the memory of the brave sailors **on both sides**, many of whom lost their lives, in the most titanic, most momentous, and yet liitle known battle in all of history. They don't even have a memorial!

c

STRANGLE.   By Michael Disney

TABLE OF CONTENTS

CHAPTER 1

DARTMOUTH

1925

Sometimes the storm approaches as a great thunderhead, frightening, unmistakable in its malicious intent. At others it begins as no more than a puff of vapour, a playful billow of cumulus in the summer sky. And so it was here.

The fishing boat made toward the distant shore of Devon, rolling giddily in a beam sea. The two fishermen, father and son, stood in the stern sheets gutting their catch, tossing the offal to be fought over by a flock of herring gulls screaming in their wake.

"Hey dad – what's that to starboard?"

The older man held his hand against the sea glare but failed to see what his son had.

"Looks like a body to me" : the son leapt forward to the wheelhouse, throttled back and spun the wheel.

"Ar she does" The father shouted: "I kin see the life-jacket."

As his son brought the vessel expertly alongside he moved forrard to get the boathook, and hook on to the orange life-preserver.

"It's one of the they cadets from the naval college, and he looks gorne to me; more blue than white."

"Give over talking dad, let's heave him aboard."

The two men, powerful though they were, struggled to lift the sodden corpse over the gunnel and down onto the deck.

The son knelt and felt the boy's neck:

"He's still got a pulse, very weak though . Ee's unconscious. E'll be gorne soon."

"They don't last long in this cold April water."

The fishermen, working at desperate speed, stripped the boy naked, dragged him into the forepeak cabin, and laid him on to a bunk.

"Get us to the quayside as fast as you can, and radio ahead for an ambylance." the father instructed, tearing off his fisherman's rubber apron and vigorously towelling the skinny little body with his own guernsey. Then, looking around as if embarrassed, he tore off most of the rest of his own clothes, climbed into the bunk and enfolded the boys weakening body inside his own. It was all a man could do, a desperate remedy, as old as seafaring itself.

"No you can't take him!" The hospital doctor was furious.

"But we've got a perfectly equipped sickbay at the college." protested the naval lieutenant who had come to collect the cadet.

"I dare say you have. And you must have got a perfectly equipped torture chamber there too."

"What on earth…"

"That lad's body is covered with beatings, bruisings and scars. He's even got cigarette burns on his genitals – and not just one or two. I would say he's been systematically tortured for 2 to 3 weeks – before ending up as near as dead in the sea."

"But he belongs to the Navy – I've been commanded to take him back."

"You touch him and I'll have every newspaper in the land hounding your damned college. I've already reported the matter to the police: they've seen the marks on his body, they've interviewed the two fishermen who rescued him and the inspector says this could be attempted murder – and I agree. Now be off Lieutenant and tell your commandant. The poor little wretch – and he's not out of the wood yet – belongs to the Law now and *not , definitely not to the Royal Navy*! If I have anything to do with it there will be an Inquiry into this affair that will shake the whole Land."

There was an Inquiry. In 1925 the last thing the Navy could afford, with all the financial cutbacks, was a national scandal. So the Admiralty dispatched its most diplomatic senior officer – Commodore Percy Noble – down to Dartmouth to see what he could do.

His first act was to contact the boy's father– who had come down from Birmingham to be by his son's bed. It turned out that they were past shipmates, having served briefly together on the battleship *Lion* in Scapa Flo during the Great War.

Noble explained to the other six naval officers who made up the internal Navy Inquiry:
"The father was a Chief Petty Officer gunner with 21 years service before his compassionate discharge at the end of 1918. His wife died in the 'flu epidemic and he went home to Birmingham to bring up his eight-year-old son. He is a very angry man of course, and quite rightly so. But he has long fond memories of his Navy days and he won't damage us unless he has to. But he's no fool; on the contrary. Somehow – and God knows how – we have to get him on to our side."
"Now gentlemen" he looked around a table at the other officers in their navy uniforms with the world-famous plain gold rings on their sleeves: "Who's going to start? If none of you knows what is behind this ugly incident, then you will all be to blame."
"I think Instructor-Lieutenant Swallow should speak first Commodore." the commandant replied.
"Very well. Swallow?"
"About a month ago or so I set the second-year cadets an essay- project for debate: 'What will the future battleship be like?' It's the normal thing because it really engages their minds. I marked their essays – a mixed bag as you would expect. But one stood out; it was 'The battleship has no future' . It was by the cadet Sturdee who is now in hospital. I had no idea of course, but the essay seemed so remarkable to me – and to one of two of the other instructors – that I asked him to come out in front of the class and talk about it – which he did with great self-confidence and skill. I have his essay here." He offered it to Commodore Noble.
Noble opened the exercise book then closed it again thoughtfully: "Later. I'll read it later. Please tell us lieutenant what did Cadet Sturdee have to say?".
"It was all about dive-bombing sir, a mathematical analysis of a dive bomber attacking a battleship – now, and 10 years ahead, when Sturdee supposes aircraft will be much faster than they are today."
"As they will be," the Commodore admitted regretfully. "As they will be. Pray continue."
"Cadet Sturdee first proved mathematically that a bomb released at high-speed would penetrate any feasible armour plating on a deck light enough not to capsize the battleship.

And he did so using a most ingenious argument. He bypassed all the engineering details simply pointing out that the kinetic energy of the bomb's motion could easily melt through 6 inches, even 12 inches of armour plate. After all, that energy does have to go somewhere: it cannot just disappear."

"You were convinced?"

"Well, yes. It was bloody clever – yet obvious once pointed out. That's often the sign of really sound science."

"Pray continue."

"The second part of his argument concerned the probable ineffectiveness of anti-aircraft fire directed against determinedly-handled bombers diving on the warship from astern or aquarter. He used reasonable figures for accuracy, for aiming-off etcetera and it did seem the attacker had a fair chance of hitting the ship with the bomb."

"Fair chance?"

"He couldn't be too precise about that."

"I bet." came from some voice around the table.

"Ah yes, but you see the had a master argument to overcome the doubts and imprecisions. He pointed out the dive bomber costs only £1000 whereas a Dreadnought class battleship costs £10 million. The ship could be faced with not one but with swarms of dive bombers."

The naval officers temporarily forgot they were at an official enquiry and argued heatedly among themselves about the boy's thesis before the Commodore recalled them to order:

"Gentlemen, gentlemen ; it's not our reaction which matters surely. What was the reaction of the other cadets to Sturdee?"

"Well at first they thought he was foolish; had made some elementary blunder. They laughed at him but he shot them down one by one, and none too gently either. Sturdee has never been short of conceit where his mathematics is concerned. You know he's one of Jackie Fisher's 'scholarship-boys' – the intake from the so-called 'talented lower classes' ."

Noble groaned theatrically: "It could hardly get any worse could it? One can see the newspaper headlines – particularly in the redder rags. But there's a long road between unpopularity and attempted murder, a much shorter road between snobbery and sadistic bullying. You must have questioned all the cadets gentlemen – what have they got to say? And what am I going to tell the poor boy's father?"

A week later, in lodgings thoughtfully paid for by the Navy, the father found out. The two men, Noble looking like a benevolent clergyman in a dark suit, the other like a pirate with his spade beard, sat with a bottle of gin between them and negotiated – all charm on the surface, all jagged reefs underneath.

"Every cadet witness clammed up, though we've questioned them all repeatedly. A complete conspiracy of silence." Noble shrugged his shoulders : "It is their beastly code of honour – the bully's license."

"Somebody's got to pay."

"Oh they will, they will. But your boy hasn't helped has he?"

"He's as 'honourable' as anyone." The ex-petty- officer sounded bitter. "More, I dare say. because he's come up through the hawse-pipe."

4

"You know Giles is wasted at the college – wasted as a naval officer? They all say so, and after reading his essay I agree. We need to get him into a good school and then on to a top university science department."

There was long silence while both men apparently savoured their gin.

"We?" The father was guarded.

"Well naturally…". Noble waved his hands : "The Navy would be foolish not to sponsor such a clever boy. His brains might one day make the difference."

"It was a near run thing last time Commodore."

"Exactly. Exactly so. We'd be feathering our nest while providing for Giles."

"I'd want him to go to the best school in the Midlands."

"Which is?"

"King Edwards High School ,Birmingham."

The Commodore wrote in his diary : "I feel sure that can be arranged. But will the boy agree – to leave Dartmouth I mean?"

"Poor little devil didn't stand a chance did he? Coming here I mean? I feel guilty myself now. Me in the Navy and all. What else did I know? So of course I influenced him. He was forced into following my footsteps – well meant like. Now I can see he's very angry. If he's going to go he'll want others punished too."

"It's hardly punishment for him – never that."

"*Ee* might see it that way." The father emphasised his first syllable.

"Well we've already agreed to expel every cadet who was in that patrol launch that he 'fell' out of. That's eight. And all twelve in his dormitory – who must have been complicit in his bullying. Altogether that's sixteen boys who've lost their careers – and their dreams."

"Serves 'em all bloody right!"

"I agree. But we'll have to deal with some very angry parents too."

"None more angry than me."

"No that's certainly true. What about it Sturdee? "

"I'll talk to him, Commodore. I'll talk to him, though this time he'll have to decide; not me again. But I reckon he'll be glad to see the back of this bloody place. Must've broke his heart what they done. He idolized the Andrew."

CHAPTER 2
SUFFOLK
1940/41

On his return from two years of postdoctoral research in Germany, Sturdee registered with the Directorate of Scientific Manpower, signed the Official Secrets Act, and was posted to Bawdsey Manor, a large country- house on a remote stretch of the Suffolk coast.

He found himself in a situation perfectly suited both to his talents and his temperament. He and half a dozen other young scientists, working under their youthful boss Dr Taffy Bowen, had been assigned the task of developing the very first airborne radar system. The technical difficulties were so formidable that only brash and brilliant young men unused to failure would have seriously attempted this impossible task – and only then when the stakes were so very high. As Winston Churchill the new Prime Minister had to put it: "We are fighting for the survival of Christian civilisation ." The Luftwaffe , having been defeated by day in the Battle of Britain, was now terror-bombing Britain's cities by night – hundreds of bombers dropping thousands of high-explosive and incendiary bombs on factories, dockyards, railway-marshalling-yards, city centres, housing estates and practically anywhere between Glasgow and Plymouth where they could wreak destruction, death or terror. Unless a means could quickly be found to locate and destroy those night bombers, surrender seemed inevitable. Radar had won the Battle of Britain so why not the terrible battle for the night? Not only were airborne radars needed to direct night fighters, but also to find U-boats at sea, because the other battle the British were losing comprehensively was that most terrible struggle of all – the Battle of the Atlantic. To maintain itself and fight a war Britain needed one million tons of imports a week, brought in by 1000 cargo vessels a month. And yet in some months U-boats was sending 200 of her precious ships so the bottom. It was hoped an airborne radar would locate these sea-wolves and drive them beneath the surface where they would be too slow to do much harm.

Unfortunately, the existing radar was of the low-frequency, long wavelength kind which required 200-foot-high aerials to transmit its outgoing signals and pick up the incoming returns. Fitting such monstrous apparatus in a plane was out of the question, whereas aerials of lesser size would squirt the precious radiation in all manner of unwanted directions – not least towards the ground from which it would bounce back up and drown the much weaker signals from an enemy bomber or submarine. But somehow or other – by brilliance, by persistence or luck , the problem , or rather set of problems, had to be overcome.

Brilliant young scientists relish nothing more than a problem which most of their seniors reckon to be intractable. And so it was at Bawdsey Manor. Taffy Bowen's airborne radar team had a whale of a time spinning mad ideas, arguing, trying things out, learning, failing, and occasionally making progress. And somehow, in between all the science, they managed to fit in swimming, tennis, shooting rabbits for the pot, sailing, drinking in local pubs and racing about on their motorbikes, while flying was of course an almost daily part of their job. Fighter Command's Martlesham Heath aerodrome nearby was the base for all their airborne trials.

War or no , Sturdee had never been so happy. He was sharing a house with good and merry companions and realising how important having a scientific challenge would be throughout his life. The big Suffolk skies stimulated his oil painting, as they had stimulated Constable's – who had been born nearby. He bought an ancient two-berth sailing yawl, the '*Pelican*', in which, with his crew, usually one of his radar mates, he was exploring the maze of channels, sandbanks and swatch-ways which made up the Suffolk coast – a pastime requiring navigational skills of an order he would hardly have acquired as a naval officer. Lying half asleep at night his mind would drift out over the running tide as it swept through the Oaze Deep or the East Swin and out past the Gunfleet Sands.

His role in the airborne interception, or AI team as they were known, was crucial. He designed the aerials that would fit in aircraft to try and get something like the beam-shape which each mission required: a narrow beam looking ahead and upward to locate bombers, a fan beam looking down on to the water at either side for U-boats. It involved a deal of higher mathematics, a lot of specialised knowledge, and the intuition which came only with experience. 'Something like' was the operative phrase because the aircraft aerials were way too small to provide precision. Avoiding the interference from the ground returns was a huge headache. Each radar-set the Bawdsey group produced was only as good as its aerial design, Giles' aerial design. He and the resident electronic genius Hanbury Brown worked hand in glove to refine a set which, although far from perfect, allowed night fighter crews, in favourable conditions, to occasionally pick up a bomber from 2 miles astern. It was a start – sufficient to convince the authorities to up their manpower and resources.

Then, out of the blue the following order came by motorcycle dispatch rider direct from the Admiralty but countersigned by the Scientific Manpower Director:

Dr Sturdee,
You will proceed forthwith to headquarters Commander in Chief Western Approaches, Derby House, Liverpool and there report to Capt. Mansfield. The matter is confidential. A first class railway warrant for the journey is attached.

Sturdee protested to everyone, especially the station commandant A.P.Rowe: "They can't order me a about like this. I am a civilian, not a bloody matelot. What do they mean? There's not even a return railway warrant. I'm being press-ganged."

Official enquiries confirmed that the order had come from very high up, with the result that the angry young scientist found himself at Ipswich railway station early next morning bound for London and on to Liverpool.

It turned out to be a horror of a journey which Sturdee was never to forget all his life. Overnight bombings had brought about chaos and cancellations. Seats there were none and every compartment and corridor was packed with travelling servicemen and their heavy kitbags. Food and drink were non-existent. He sat on his upturned suitcase in the corridor for 16 hours, during seven of which the train never moved from a siding near Stafford. No one knew for certain why, but it probably had to do with a heavy air raid the previous night on Crewe Junction. By the time he finally reached his destination Sturdee was exhausted – and in no doubt about the chaos into which his country was descending: "If this is what the Germans can do in three months, may God help us a year from now!" he thought.

Liverpool had been blitzed during the night so he had to walk through rubble-strewn streets to Headquarters Western Approaches at Derby House. Captain Mansfield was brusque but understanding: "You look bushed. Here's a chitty for our wardroom mess. Get a meal and get your head down. Admiral Noble will probably send for you tomorrow morning."
"Who is Admiral Noble?"
"Admiral Sir Percy Noble – Commander-in-Chief Western Approaches. I'm surprised you don't know him? He certainly remembers you."
Sturdee was in no mood to be charmed by any Admiral let alone one who had dragged him across England on such a horrendous journey. But, in spite of all, he was. For all his gold lace and medal ribbons Percy Noble had the look of a kindly grandfather who knew all about mutinous young men, and rather liked them. There was also a stillness and depth to him that spoke to Giles of intellect and wisdom : "He looks like a university Vice-Chancellor ought to look " he thought "But they never do."
After the initial pleasantries, including enquiries about Giles's father, who was serving as chief gunner aboard an armed merchant cruiser, the admiral ushered him into an armchair at the side of the room and took one opposite:
"I am sorry about the press-gang technique – but these are special days. You are of course free to return to Suffolk at any time. But I would like you to hear me out first; then consider the matter at your leisure. I very badly need your help. Do you remember this?"
He handed Giles an ancient exercise book with 'Britannia Naval College Dartmouth' embossed on the cover.

"Good Lord! " Sturdee exclaimed. "It's the one I wrote that wretched battleship essay in. Here it is…. No I don't want to look at it – it makes me feel faint – physically sick." He handed it back as if it was poisonous.

"I'm sorry. Would you like a glass of water?"

"No no…… I wasn't prepared… put all that behind me…"

"I understand you've had a very distinguished career since? Physics, Birmingham University – then a doctorate of philosophy, then further fellowships to the best physics departments in Germany. You are a radar man now they tell me?"

"Yes – thank you. Dad did tell me that the Navy paid for all my scholarships and the Fellowship at Göttingen. I'm sorry I had forgotten your actual name– it must be a Freudian slip."

"No matter. But no regrets? "

"Leaving the Navy was the best thing I ever did."

"I rather thought it might be. And your father was a wise man to see it that way."

There was a moments silence. The admiral rose: "Come with me".

Sturdee had never seen a larger map in his life, a map of the entire Atlantic from Britain to the USA, from Greenland to Gibraltar and the Caribbean. The size of almost half a tennis court it occupied the entire wall or what might once have been a very tall gymnasium. From where they stood they could watch Wrens perch on high ladders on rails , moving pieces about on the map. Below them rows of naval and air-force officers sat at desks covered with telephones, watching the game, occasionally intervening.

"Those are our convoys " the Admiral pointed "Green for Fast, Red for Slow. Nearly 1000 ships at sea. And those black Gothic crosses are U-boat contacts. Those are Royal Navy Escort Groups – those Canadian. Those yellow counters mark recent sinkings. You can see Slow convoy SC261 bound for Halifax, lost two more ships during the night, that's 6 since she left Liverpool. She's got no air escort out there in the mid-Atlantic and a wolf-pack on her tail. There is nothing I can do about it."

"Do you control it all from here?"

"The Admiralty have an identical plot in Whitehall. The Canadians run the western one-third. Now look down there." he pointed to Brittany: "Huge new U-boat pens invulnerable to our bombs have been built at Brest, Lorient and La Palice . We never expected to be attacked from that direction. We were planning to fight this battle in the North Sea. Now it's out there in mid-Atlantic, way beyond range of our destroyer escorts. Hitler's Type VII U-boats have a range of 7500 miles without refuelling."

"The scale of the whole thing is breath-taking."

"Yes. Here is where the war will eventually be won or lost, never mind what goes on in other theatres. Two ruthless beasts, Nazi Germany and the Royal Navy– are literally strangling the life out of one another. We have barely let them have a single cargo since the day war broke out. For all his boasting Mr Hitler will be feeling the pinch – or rather his people will. Imagine living for years without coffee, tobacco, tea, even cotton for fresh underclothes, not to say oil and rubber."

"What about us? "

"Yes indeed. We are far more dependent on imports than Germany: one million tons a week, that's 250 shiploads a month, just to keep going. That is half what we expect in peacetime. The fall of France denied us all the channel ports including London. They're too vulnerable to bombing attack. The same applies to the Bristol Channel – Avonmouth, Cardiff, Swansea. Everything, literally everything is now coming in through the North-Western Approaches, to Liverpool and the Clyde"

"That sounds impossible. Impossible!"

"The side that is going to win this war is going to have to do many impossible things before it's decided. And not make mistakes. That's where you might come in."

"Me?" Sturdee sounded shocked.

"An analytical brain like yours could make a real difference. Not battleships and dive bombers this time – but U-boats and escort vessels – wolf-packs versus convoys. You see I'm putting together the very best Staff I can. Their Lordships are highly supportive right now, they know just how crucial we are going to be. Lose the North-Western Approaches and we've lost everything. Britain could then starve within months – capitulate within weeks. Do you know we import two thirds of all our food? While he was here last week the PM Mr Churchill told me the only thing which keeps him awake at nights is the U-boat menace."

"When you think of all the other things he's got on his plate …"

"Yes exactly. Well it was he, indirectly, who made me think of you – and your essay. He had his personal scientific adviser with him, Professor Lindemann."

"Oh yes, the infamous 'Prof'."

"The PM trusts Lindemann. It was he who went through all our numbers and gave a digest to Churchill. That is what I am desperately going to need: someone with a lightning brain, an analytical mind, and sound judgement. He will keep his fingers on the pulse of this ocean battle – tell me instantly where we are losing, where we are winning. Of course I could ask for someone through the usual channels – but would I trust him – as I believe I could trust you? Personal trust counts so much in battle. The wrong man could lose the Atlantic for me – and for all of us."

The two men stared up of the great green plot . A wren rolled a ladder sideways across the map, climbed the rungs and moved an Eastbound Fast convoy south of Iceland just a little toward Scotland.

"Have we got a chance?" Sturdee asked.

Noble took a long time before replying: "I would say it's going to be touch and go. That's why your decision Sturdee could be important. Right now the Germans have the technology on their side – their magnificent U-boats. But they've only got about 50 for now with one third at sea – far too few to clinch the issue. We are in an even worse state with regard to convoy escort vessels – but we have the broad

Atlantic on our side. We ought to be able to sneak most of our convoys across that vasty deep without them ever being located."

"It doesn't look like that now."

"I'm afraid it doesn't. We lost nearly 200 ships last month alone, that's 700,000 tons." Giles winced.

On the long and awful train journey back to Suffolk Giles occupied his time doing convoy calculations He could no more help himself than a crossword addict. He drew a 3000 by 1000-mile rectangle to represent the Atlantic battlefield, infested it with a flotilla of 20 U-boats, there being only one in three on station at any one time, and asked what the chances were of a ship travelling independently, being spotted. Assuming a visible range of about 10 miles he found that about one in every five ships would be located and probably sunk by the much faster U-boats. In the long run such odds were hopeless. A convoy of say 50 ships straggling over several square miles would obviously be easier to see than an individual vessel – by a factor of three Giles reckoned. But there would be 50 times less convoys than ships! Most U-boats would never find a convoy and only one convoy in 100 would be spotted!

The change-about was so magic that Sturdee couldn't believe his figures at first. But eventually he realised that he'd only re-discovered why birds flock and fish shoal. By doing so they didn't fend off their predators – but they reduced their chances as individuals of ever being killed. The rare hawk who did manage to find the flock could only pick off one bird. The rare U-boat that did manage to locate a convoy would only have enough loaded torpedo tubes to attack one cargo vessel. It was so obvious to see in retrospect, had been so hard for the Royal Navy to see in prospect. In 1917 Lord Jellicoe the First Sea Lord had almost conceded defeat in the Atlantic before turning to the convoy and nearly instant salvation. Convoying offended the Royal Navy 's Nelsonian offensive spirit – it was slinking out of sight instead of doing battle. Sturdee sat by the train window watching the grim industrial landscape of the potteries sliding slowly by. Nothing gave his mathematical brain greater satisfaction than a simple calculation which disclosed a previously concealed truth. With its convoys Britain ought to be winning the Battle of the Atlantic – decisively. Instead it seemed to be losing. He got his pen out and his slide-rule, and began all over again, but this time looking at the ocean battle from the U-boats' point of view .

Back at Bawdsey Giles confided in his most trusted friend there, Hanbury Brown, who responded:

"I can see the attraction Giles. You could play God like that swine Lindemann from Oxford. Next to Churchill he must carry more weight in Britain than anybody. Look how he interfered in the Tizard Committee – almost put an end to Britain's radar research. If Churchill had been Prime Minister back then we would surely have lost the Battle of Britain. I don't trust him – he is a German – and what is worse, a vegetarian."

"But seriously?"

Hanbury Brown looked at his friend speculatively:

"It sounds to me as if anyone in that position could win the U-boat war – or lose it. Science has to be the major player out there on the grey Atlantic – asdic , radar, search and avoidance strategies, depth charging, aerial reconnaissance... You can't leave all that to crusty old shellbacks who probably trained in the days of sail. And you'd be good at it, very good Giles. For a start, as a result of your German experience, you respect the enemy. That's rare, and bloody important here."

"I respect their science."

Hanbury broke into a smile: "Anyway you can't go Giles. We need your aerial expertise here. You're irreplaceable right now. Others will be able to do Noble's job. If you walk out on us now we won't get airborne radar. That would be treachery to us, to Taffy and your country. Anyway airborne radar could be key to the Atlantic."

Hanbury's advice agreed so neatly with his own inclinations that Sturdee wrote to Noble declining his invitation, explaining where his priorities must for now lie. But some instinct prevented him posting the letter over the weekend.

On Monday Taffy Bowen called the group together for an important announcement. He had a huge grin on his face and an even more emphatic Swansea lilt in his voice than normal:

"Well boys we're going to win this bluttie war."

Enjoying the suspense he opened a small cardboard box to reveal a scruffy looking device which looked more than anything like a round copper snuffbox with copper pipes sticking out of it:

"Or rather this ingenious contrivance is going to win it for us."

"What is it?" Hanbury asked.

" It's the answer to all our prayers boys. Two fellows at Birmingham University came up with it – Randall and Boot."

"I know them." Giles exclaimed.

"They call it a 'Cavity Magnetron'. It can generate very short radar waves, down to 2 centimetres in wavelength – and here's the point – with a power output 1000 times greater than any previous klystron or valve."

They all stared at the crudely wrought copper miracle, trying to work out the implications. Eventually Hanbury said:

"We could build an airborne radar round that which would fit in a suitcase."

"And the range would be fantastic... almost unlimited !"

"And we could use a proper dish antenna with a clean beam and no side-lobes " someone else added.

"And with no ground- returns ..." Hanbury broke in. " We could generate a thousand times stronger signal, but pick up a thousand times weaker returns. A factor of a million.........",

"I told you Boys, this is going to win the blutty war." Taffy grinned round at them. "But here is the bad news: they're moving us out of here to some godforsaken air-station near Dundee in Scotland. Bawdsey is too close to the German Coast. If the Nazis raided by here they might get their hands on this beauty." He patted the Cavity Magnetron.

It took Sturdee less than 24 hours to realise that his specialised skills with aerials were now redundant. All those makeshift dipoles and Yagis would be replaced by nifty little parabolic dishes that could be nodded and rotated as necessary – centimetric radar would project clean beams in any required direction.

He telegraphed his acceptance to Noble, sold the *Pelican* for a song: crated up most of his possessions for the duration of the war, held a party in the pub for his friends, scrounged as many petrol coupons as he could and set off cross-country on his BSA motorbike for Liverpool .

CHAPTER 3
LIVERPOOL

Sturdee hated everything about his new life . He hated the Navy, he hated Liverpool, he hated the hostel he was living in, he hated the bombing which ruined every night's sleep, he hated his job – if you could call it a job – he hadn't a soul to talk to – and he hated himself for having given up his wonderful work on radar for a position where he hadn't even got a desk to call his own and where the majority of his naval colleagues – if you could call them that – regarded him with a mixture of impatience and suspicion. And, to crown it all, someone else had filled in much of his Times crossword while he had been waiting in the canteen queue to collect his treacle - tart and custard. It was the very last straw – he wanted to cry – or pull somebody's hair.

"Who filled in my bloody crossword?" He glared at the naval officers who mostly made up his table. One frowned at him as if at a naughty child, the rest carried on with their discussion of convoy tactics.

"Come on; who the Hell did this?" He pointed to his newspaper. That got their attention:

"Some of us " A lieutenant commander said, looking pointedly at Sturdee's civilian clothing "Are trying to win a war. Who the hell cares about your silly little crossword. Grow up man!"

Sturdee felt like a fool. An elderly four-ringer, a Captain, leant forward:

"There was a young woman here moments ago. I think I saw her with your crossword."

It wasn't fair. Not only had he had his crossword pinched but now he had to feel ashamed about it.

"Ah, here she comes." The captain pointed as a striking young woman sat down opposite Sturdee and tucked into her treacle-tart.

"Oh dear" she was looking at him: "You look so cross and upset. I suppose it's your crossword. I couldn't help myself."

"You've done almost a third of it." Sturdee felt close to tears once again.

"It's a terrible habit I've got." the woman explained, as if she was rather proud of herself. "It infuriated my dad – he was a crossword addict. The only time he gave me a really good hiding was when I filled in his favourite Observer crossword."

"Well he didn't smack you hard enough!" Sturdee snapped at the offender who angrily looked up as though she might throw her pudding at him, but then thought better of it. She clearly had a hearty appetite.

"I'm sorry" Sturdee flushed too : "I shouldn't have said that. It's just that I'm having such a miserable time at the moment: I don't know anybody in Liverpool. I've spoken to almost no one in three weeks. The only thing to keep me sane in my wretched hostel at night is to lie on the dormitory bed, try to shut out the world, and do the crossword. And now…"

"Poor thing." She reached out her hand and put it on his wrist "I felt just like you when I first arrived here. I can make it up to you. How would you like a fresh egg for breakfast?"

Conversation stopped around them. In 1941 a fresh egg was a miracle.

"Are you serious?"

"I should have thought a third of the Times crossword was worth at least one fresh egg."

"More like two." Sturdee smiled

"All right two then. I'll bring them to lunch tomorrow. Same time." She stood up

"Actually I don't have anywhere to cook an egg." The naval officers watching the drama looked disappointed.

The young woman tore a page out of her notebook and wrote on it:

"If you come to this address at eight tomorrow I'll be feeding my lodger his breakfast. You can have your own then."

"Lucky devil." one of the sailors commented as the young woman made off: "She could cook my breakfast any morning."

Much to his surprise Sturdee found himself riding his motorbike up the driveway of a large Victorian mansion next morning. Summoned by a pull on the colossal mechanical doorbell yesterday's young woman opened the 10-foot-high door in her apron.

"So you came." she said, holding out a hand "My name is Joan by the way, Joan Duff. Come in and meet Maurice."

Maurice, a very distinguished looking man of about 60 with thick white hair was sitting at the kitchen table in his braces reading a newspaper propped up against the teapot :

"Ah yes" he said waving to a chair "The young man who has come to collect his payoff. You should know better than to leave the crossword anywhere near Joan; she is a terror. Polishes them all off in about 10 minutes flat. Don't you my dear? She spoils it for the rest of us. I've had to give them up. She was giving me an inferiority complex. So, what is your game? You can tell us while Joan boils your eggs. Help yourself to toast – but go easy on the marge – it's all we've got left until Monday."

"I'm a scientist – sort of."

"You don't sound very sure." Joan interjected from the gas stove.

"Well I am – I'm a theoretical physicist, Giles Sturdee is my name by the way. But the post I am supposed to be filling at the moment is hardly scientific – not in the strict sense."

"What do you do all day my boy? I suppose I can't have an egg Joannie?"

"No you can't Maurice; and don't 'Joannie' me. But if you catch up on your digging schedule today you can have one tomorrow."

"I'm supposed to advise the Admiral on scientific matters; anything he asks me – or I can think up for myself. What about you?"

"They have dug me up – or rather dug me out of premature retirement. I used to be in a historian – now in the Ministry of War Transport for the duration– working with Joan. I used to be her boss. Now it's the other way round."

Two perfect brown eggs in orange eggcups appeared before Sturdee:

"Four minutes exactly." Joan said "Top them and see if they are to your taste. Both laid this very morning. And don't listen to Maurice. He's a very distinguished historian, the world expert on Blockade. You should read his book some time: I read it at a sitting. Now I'm off to work; there is a big convoy due in this evening. I will no doubt see you again in the canteen Giles. Why don't you stay on and talk to Maurice if you're lonely. Maurice is a great talker – but he has been known to listen occasionally. No don't thank me!" She kissed the older man on the forehead: "Now don't forget the digging Maurice – you promised." And was gone.

"What a woman!" Maurice said pouring them both more tea "That's what comes of having four brothers to look after."

"Four?"

"And three are working out of Liverpool at present – as RNVR officers on convoy escort vessels, the fourth is a merchant skipper working out of Australia. Her mother sent Joan up here from Essex to provide them with a home when they are ashore, which isn't often. She's rented this great pile from some shipowners – who had the good sense to move inland, well away from the bombing."

"It does seem a bit excessive."

" Twenty-seven rooms would you believe – many for servants. But the attraction for Joan was a huge garden – nearly 3 acres. She's turning it into a small-holding. Chickens already, ducks, pigs... but above all onions. Do you realise you can't buy an onion for love or money in Britain? They all used to come in from Brittany or the Channel Islands – all occupied now by the bloody Jerries. If we can grow a few tons of onions this summer we can use them for barter and live like kings – eggs every day, bacon, pork-sausages..." Sturdee found himself salivating.

" The trouble is..." Maurice sighed. "All the bloody hard work involved. As part of my rent I have contracted to dig up the entire tennis lawn before April. Look..." He pointed to the callouses on his hands."

"She's quite a tartar then... Joan?"

"She's quite a girl all round" Maurice retorted. "Do you know that right now she's probably the second most important person in Liverpool – after your Admiral Noble. She operates the daily schedule of goods trains running in and out of the port – a fiendishly complex task in the circumstances – what with the bombing and the dislocation of the railway system further inland. Churchill came down to give us a pep talk recently. He said if we can't unload and load ships promptly it won't matter whether we win or lose the Battle of the Atlantic."

"I hadn't thought of that."

"Nobody anticipated that most of our ports would be closed by enemy bombing. Do you know everything that used to come in and out through London, Southampton, Bristol, Cardiff, Dover, Newcastle… has all got to come through Liverpool and Glasgow now; one million tons a week– that is 250 ships in – and 250 out. That is at least 1000 trainloads a week – at least. Right now Joan is responsible for the Liverpool half."

"But surely…"

"She is too young you mean? Of course, she is, but there's nobody else around who can hold so many facts and figures in their heads at once and who can re-organise things in a matter of hours when a crucial wharf or junction gets bombed. Of course we are developing a system – but for the moment it is Joan Duff. She is my contribution to the war effort."

"How do you mean?"

"She came to me as a casual clerk. Quite by accident I found out her astonishing capabilities. You saw her murder your crossword. Well you should see her with a complex timetable after a nightmare bombing raid. I loaded more and more of the responsibility onto her… do you realise that the government has drafted 60,000 more stevedores up here from London? Right now *this* is the Battle for Britain."

"I never realised…"

" Scarcely anybody does– outside the Cabinet. We daren't let anyone know – especially Hitler – how desperate our situation really is. If he was to switch even more of his bombing effort from London onto Liverpool and Glasgow we could seize up entirely – starve within a matter of months – capitulate long before that. This war is going to be won or lost by blockade – like the last war and the Napoleonic war before that. It is just a matter of who cracks first – Germany or Britain. Hitler must be in dire straits himself – where is he getting the oil, the rubber, the nickel, the aluminium, the tobacco, the phosphates to fight this war? One of us is going to crack soon – in a matter of months."

Sturdee got up and paced about the ugly Victorian kitchen with its shit-coloured linoleum and its two dozen bells for summoning the long departed servants:

"I still find it hard to believe that Joan Duff – she can't be 30 – is holding the fort for us – against Hitler. It doesn't make sense."

"No it doesn't I agree–but exceptional circumstances call for exceptional people. I once knew a chap called Faulkner who had memorised the entire

British railway timetable. You could ask him how to get from Bude in Cornwall to Godmanchester starting on a Sunday afternoon – and he'd get it right every time– every bloody time I tell you. Look at the incredibly brave chaps now defusing unexploded bombs – many of them were physics-masters – or electricians a mere few months ago apparently. I've lived long enough Sturdee to come across some extraordinary people. Joan doesn't realise how exceptional she is. Left school at 15, not enough money in the family to educate the girls – it all went on the boys. Worked in offices in London – then worked in Paris – later in Rome. After this war she will probably marry her young man – if he survives – have babies – and sink back into obscurity."

"Does she have a young man?" Sturdee felt vaguely cheated.

" Not disappointed, are you? Yes, she has; an Australian bomber pilot. But he's just been posted to the Far East – probably for the duration. So the field might be clear for a new aspirant for Joan's affections. But he'd have to be very special – if only to show up well against her five brothers. The one I met – second-in-command of a corvette – was pretty formidable. Look, I've got to go out and get on with my digging. You can help me if you like. I bet we can find another spade. And I'm sure it'll impress Joan."

The two men, working yards apart, dug steadily all day, meanwhile talking. It was Professor Maurice Picton's thesis that most Britons, deliberately or otherwise, misunderstood their own history: " They controlled the continent and built up their own empire, almost entirely by blockading their rivals: we don't want to admit it Sturdee – because it's a pretty heinous thing to do – starving helpless women and children into submission. We can do it, as nobody else can, because of our geographical position off the end of the European peninsula – and because we've corked up the Mediterranean at Gibraltar."

"Nobody told us that at school."

"They don't do they, but sophisticated modern societies have become increasingly dependent on imports and therefore vulnerable to naval blockade. Napoleon had nowhere else to go so he invaded Russia in 1812 – bringing about his own downfall a year later. France had been strangled by a close blockade from the Mediterranean to the Baltic for over 15 years. Scarcely a Frenchman had had a cup of coffee, or a French woman new cotton underclothes, in all that time. How can you go on claiming to be the great Emperor in such circumstances? He had to find a way out of the Royal Navy's stranglehold. Likewise, in 14/18. We always hear about the Great War in the trenches. But that was a sideshow. The Germans nearly starved in the awful Turnip Winter of 16/17. No German civilian had a proper diet after that. And when the German soldiers made a last desperate attack in the spring of 18, they were too ill-fed and under-supplied to keep it up for long. When they overran our trenches and found them littered with what they regarded as luxuries – coffee, tinned-meat and decent tobacco for instance, they knew the game was up. And do you know we maintained the blockade long after the Armistice was signed?"

"No I didn't."

"It was a vindictive and foolish thing to do – as I said in my book – and no small part of the reason we are at war once again. But of course nobody wanted to hear. I was naïve enough to believe that writing history was about telling the truth."

"What is it about then?"

"As far as I can see Sturdee it's mostly about supplying myths that will make people feel good about themselves. Its propaganda after-the-fact. What American wants to know that they cheated and wiped out the Red Indians; what Frenchmen to know that France has lost war after war after war; what Brit to know that they acquired empire by starving the Germans, the French, the Spaniards, the Dutch – and so on?"

By dark they'd virtually finished the lawn. Both men were sore and exhausted – but pleased with one another. As they sat over tea in the kitchen Picton said:

"How would you like to come and live here at Duff House? Joan needs to let more of the bed-rooms out to lodgers – but she's choosy and wants the right sort of people."

"What are the right sort?"

"Mostly people who her brothers will approve of, people with brains who are fighting the Germans. Above all people who will make her smallholding work. I could put in a good word for you after your efforts today. Look at your hands – blisters everywhere. She will approve of that."

"Well – it would certainly be a huge step up from my hostel. I'm desperate for some peace and quiet – and a room of my own. And there'd be you for company."

"And Joan, don't forget." Picton smiled at Sturdee who blushed. "I can see you're sweet on her. But don't get your hopes too high my lad . Joan's the faithful sort if I'm not mistaken. Do you want me to put it in a word?"

Sturdee nodded.

"Be off with you then. It will come better if you're not here when she gets home. And think of something you could contribute to her smallholding. How about a side-car on your motorbike – useful for transporting farm produce. She might really go for that! Maurice smiled again: "The quickest way to a small-holder's heart."

CHAPTER 4
WESTERN APPROACHES

Any intention Sturdee may have had to desert the Navy vanished as the seriousness of Britain's situation sank in. For the first time in 900 years his country stood in danger of imminent defeat, its island status promising not protection – but death by starvation. Foolishly it had come to rely on imports even for its basic diet – now it looked like having to pay the price. The wholesale sinking of its merchant fleet out on the Atlantic, the bombing of its docks, the gradual strangulation of its railway system – any one could bring the nation to its knees. No hysterical propaganda, no amount of Churchillian oratory could alter the one appalling fact: the country that had ruthlessly built an empire through blockading its rivals was now dying slowly by the very same garotte. Even the colossal Spanish Armada had posed no such threat as the armada of U-boats now increasing around her shores, sinking hundreds of thousands of tons of shipping a month.

Desperately wanting to help was one thing, being able to do anything effective quite another. Each week that passed only emphasised Sturdee's colossal ignorance of everything to do with his task; submarine warfare in general and convoying in particular. He had come to admire Noble from a distance and would love to have repaid the trust which the admiral had placed in him – but there was nothing he could think of, absolutely nothing. He realised that, after Churchill, Noble must be the most harassed man in Britain. In post for only three months he was trying to build a system as it was being bombed and torpedoed to bits around him. Apparently he had gone out with a convoy destroyer himself – and discovered total chaos. One by one the escort vessels have been detached by the Admiralty to hunt down possible U-boat contacts leaving the convoy of 50 to the protection of a single destroyer, the one with Noble on board. No wonder morale both within the merchant fleet and the Royal Navy stood in grave danger of disintegration.

"Morale is my first priority" Noble explained on the one occasion he been able to spare Sturdee a few minutes: "Everybody has to be convinced that we can win this submarine war – as we won the last one. But that conviction will only come if we can build a system based on mutual trust – one with information travelling freely upwards and sideways as well as down. There is little opportunity to talk things through out on the sea – it has got to happen right here ashore: I want everybody talking to everybody else, everybody feeling that their ideas will be heard – at the highest level if necessary. As usual the side that will win will be the side which can learn from its mistakes the fastest. And I am determined that side will be us."

The admiral had added as they parted: "By the way Sturdee I'm not expecting any instant miracles from you. Take your time. I like to think there's one person at least on my staff who does have the time to ponder things through deeply and dispassionately when the rest of us are too busy to think clearly. Consider that your main role for now…. Here is a draft of my new 'Western Approaches Convoy Instructions'; if you have any comments, send them up the line."

Sturdee had asked the admiral for only two things: office space and an 'oppo' , somebody he could argue with. He had explained:
"Nearly every scientist needs an intellectual equal to argue with, someone who can spot the weaknesses in his ideas. I certainly do. Thinking aloud is essential for me I find."
"I'll do what I can," Noble had promised: "But he'll probably have to be a sailor not a scientist."

The arrival of Noble's appointee Tony Loader, a career naval lieutenant with a new artificial right - hand, quickly livened up Sturdee's working life. Tall, energetic and irreverent, Loader certainly enjoyed arguing – and taking charge of Sturdee, who was two years his junior:
"We can't live here - old boy. I've sorted out something around the corner. Not exactly Admiralty House – but our very own."
Loader's 'very own' turned out to be an ex dry-cleaning shop, its windows blown out by a bomb and then stoutly boarded up:
"No point in putting in new glass– won't last a week. We'll be very cosy here. We'll partition the downstairs into two offices, one for each of us. There's a kitchen upstairs – and an office for the girl."
"What girl?"
"I requisitioned a Wren ;Wren Jones. Typing and all that kind of thing. I suppose she can do all that – but actually I chose her for her gorgeous bottom: incomparable – but I need to have a closer look, much closer for preference. Are you a bum man yourself?"
Sturdy blushed
"A virgin by God!" Loader sounded delighted: "We will have to do something about that old chap. I'll arrange for a pretty little wren to be about next time we have a blitz. They cling on like billy-oh when they're frightened – very grateful for a little comforting here and there – especially there – if you know what I mean."

And so matters were arranged – as they usually were when Loader was in charge. They had to do most of the shop-fitting for themselves, and all of the furniture removal, but a phone from Derby House was installed and Wren Jones duly arrived with her typewriter and her posterior – which fully lived up – so he claimed – to Loaders extravagant expectations.

"So what do we do now boss? You're the great thinker – so Sir Percy told me. And my job is, so I understand, to piss in your occasional vanilla pudding?"

As Sturdee was coming to appreciate, the Battle of the Atlantic was dominated by two factors: distance and speed. The Battlefield was 3000 nautical miles long, stretching from Liverpool to New York, first along the Great Circle rout, then back down again past Labrador and the coast of Newfoundland. Approximately 1000 miles wide it offered Britain no less than that 3 million Square miles in which to hide its ships, while it posed Germany a corresponding challenge to find them. A lookout in the conning tower searching about, even on a clear day, could command only 500 square miles and so might search for a month without spotting potential prey. Success or failure might well depend on ruse, intelligence or espionage.

Speed entered the equation in many ways, but most particularly in the speed of the U-boats relative to their merchant victims. Running on its diesel engines at 17 knots a surfaced U-boat had twice the speed of a convoy and could pass ahead of it in the distance by day, then speed back through its clumsy ranks by night, firing torpedoes from close range as it went. On the other hand a submerged U-boat, depending on its batteries, could make barely 4 knots, half the speed of a convoy. It was unlikely to torpedo any ship, unless that vessel happened to pass within periscope range. A bold U-boat Commander would thus submerge only as a last resort when he was under attack, either by escort vessels or aircraft. And even then he might prefer to take his chance on the surface, particularly at night, because with their low profiles submarines were very hard to see and even harder to hit with gunfire. And, unfortunately for the Royal Navy, its Corvettes were too slow to catch surfaced U-boats, while it's 30-knot destroyers were often too short of fuel to undertake prolonged chases On the other hand the much higher speed and altitude of an escorting aircraft meant that it could patrol 20 times the area that escort vessels could in the same time, spotting U-boats both far ahead and far astern of a convoy, driving them to submerge and lose contact. The problem was of course that patrol aircraft didn't have the range to reach most of the vast Atlantic.

Convoy was by no means an obvious remedy against U-boat attack – after all it offered the attacker a juicy basket of targets which a salvo of torpedoes could scarcely miss. At least so reasoned the Admiralty in the First World War. Only after 395 of its merchant ships – comprising 881,000 tons –were sunk in

April 1917 alone , was the Admiralty forced to change its mind and turn to convoying as a desperate last resort in a losing battle – so Sturdee read in Maurice Picton's fascinating book on Blockade. Its success had come as a surprise to almost everyone, including its strongest advocates. However even its sceptics couldn't argue with the numbers: it was found that an unaccompanied ship was 20 times more likely to be sunk than one in convoy. Maurice had quoted Churchill in his 1923 Account of the war: "The size of the sea is so vast that the difference between the size of a Convoy and the size of a single ship shrinks in comparison almost to insignificance. There was in fact very nearly as good a chance of a convoy of 40 ships in close order slipping unperceived between patrolling U-boats as there was of a single ship; and each time that happened, 40 ships escaped instead of one. Here was the key to the success of the convoy system against U-boats. The concentration of ships greatly reduced the number of targets in a given area and this made it more difficult for submarines to locate their prey. Moreover, the convoys were more easily controlled and could be quickly deflected by wireless from areas known to be dangerous at any given moment. Finally, the destroyers, instead of being dissipated on patrol over wide areas, were concentrated at the point of hostile attack, and the opportunities for an offensive action frequently arose."

So the point of convoy, as Sturdee came to realise, was more concealment than outright protection. If the convoy escort-group, comprised of half a dozen destroyers and corvettes, managed to sink a U-boat well and good, but a truly successful convoy was one which never encountered the enemy. As Noble wisely put it at the head of his 'Western Approaches Convoy Instructions: "The safe and timely arrival of the convoy at its destination is the primary object of the escort." Convoying benefited from the same principle as birds flocking or fish shoaling. A hawk could kill and eat only one victim at a time. A U-boat could fire only one salvo of torpedoes before retiring from the battle to re-load its tubes.

Now comfortably settled in the house where Joan had assigned him a large bedroom overlooking the conservatory and the erstwhile tennis lawn, Sturdee could sleep properly – because the nightly bombings seldom strayed so far inland from the docks. With some peace and privacy at last he could think deeply about the submarine war. As a start he had constructed what he called the 'Corden 'Model'. It was a very simple mathematical model of the Battle of The Atlantic which attempted to estimate the relative importance of various factors which might decide the final outcome. It assumed that Admiral Doenitz would station a cordon or cordons of U-boats across the thousand-mile width of the battlefield to intercept convoys. It assumed that a successful interceptor would then shadow the convoy and summon up R reinforcement by radio. The $(R+1)$ U-boats would then make a Wolfpack attack on the N merchant vessels in the convoy – which the E escort vessels of the Escort-group would attempt to protect. A fraction K of all of these attacks would lead to sinkings and a further fraction D of the torpedoed sailors would be drowned. In addition Sturdee assumed that signal-intelligence wireless deciphers might increase the effectiveness of that U-boat cordon by a factor e if used by the enemy – or decrease it but by another factor e-prime if used by ourselves, as it had been so successfully in the First World War when Room 40 at the Admiralty had decrypted so many German signals – including the infamous Zimmerman Telegram that had eventually brought the United States into that war. By making plausible guesses and values for the various factors involved Sturdee hoped to make an appreciation of the battle to come which might be of some assistance to the admiral, and which might also influence his own future plans. He wrote out a copy of this Appreciation and gave it to Tony Loader for comment.

As he should have anticipated, Joan had driven a very hard bargain over his tenancy agreement. In addition to his newly acquired second hand side-car – which he omitted to tell Joan was Maurice's idea, not his own – he had contracted to build a pigsty by mid-June and to supply the entire household with firewood throughout the winter.

"I told you" Maurice chortled "She can see you're sweet on her. She will have no mercy henceforth."

"D….Don't be ridiculous" Sturdee stuttered, unable to conceal a half blush.

Joan's plans were certainly taking shape. The onion-seeds, brought over from America by one of those sea-going brothers, had germinated in the conservatory , and were being replanted out on the tennis lawn in tens of thousands. Joan – who stoutly believed in prayer – prayed every day against an unseasonal frost and ordered all her tenants to do likewise. One of her brothers, back home from the Atlantic for a few days leave, was set to work building an Anderson air-raid shelter in the orchard. A dozen ducklings had arrived, Aylesburys and Khaki-Runners, while Maurice was employed in converting a bomb crater in the garden into a pond for them. A vicious cockrell had been purchased in the hope that he would do his patriotic duty by the hens. Joan herself was digging up the kitchen garden and replanting it with all manner of vegetables from runner beans to King Edward potatoes.

"Everyone else can starve." she announced "We won't. We've got 60 apple trees, including 10 cookers, a dozen pears, a dozen plums and four cherries. The pigs can live on the windfalls. Come the summer I'm going to get you boys bottling like billy-oh if I can just find enough preserving jars. And there's a whole stand of raspberry- canes, as well as blackcurrants and gooseberries. And if only I can get my hands on a plough I know where I can borrow a draught-horse. We could then put down at least another acre of late potatoes–and swedes for the pigs. We don't want to have to slaughter them all at once."

"Well I'm not slaughtering them," Maurice protested "I like pigs."

"In that case you won't get any of the pork or ham – not even the black puddings, the jellied trotters, or the chitterlings. We can't have any shirkers in this establishment – can we Giles?"

"I suppose not." Sturdee rather liked pigs too.

"I shan't care." Maurice boasted.

"Oh yes you will – when the time comes. I've seen you salivating over your ham and parsley-sauce. Which reminds me, we ought to plant a herb garden. Who is going to volunteer for that? What about you Maurice? Herbs don't have to be slaughtered – at least not the ones I know about."

"She's not usually this short tempered " Maurice confided in Sturdee : "She's under terrible strain at the Ministry just now. There is scarcely a train leaving that doesn't have to be rescheduled, whilst our sidings and shunting-yards are full to bursting. But how long she can keep it up one can't say. We've got to do everything we can to humour her meanwhile. But you know Giles I think deliverance is on the way."

"The Yanks?"

"Good Lord no! If they ever come into this war – which I doubt – it will be entirely for their own ends – or to do us British down. Look what they did – or rather didn't do–in the last show. When they finally did turn up late in 1918 they were without any field-guns so they couldn't really fight. Nor would they fight under allied command – as if they knew anything of modern war. And then President Wilson had the bloody nerve to try and hijack the peace conference."

"Then who?"

"I rather think that Mr Hitler himself will be coming to our rescue."

"What?" Giles was astounded.

"I was thinking of his options – in a Napoleonic sort of way. If he can't break the Royal Navy blockade – and there is no sign of that so far – then he's got to break out in some other direction. He's not got the natural resources – oil in particular – to fight a long war against Britain – with all of the resources of the Empire behind us. He has really only got two choices: invade Russia and go for the oil in the Caucuses: or to cross the Mediterranean via Sicily, take Suez and go on to take our own oilfields in Persia. It's obvious when you think about it."

"I don't see how that is going to help us."

" Well either way he'll need every bomber he's got. And that will be a relief for Liverpool – and Joan . I rather think he'll cross the Med – from Sicily with his pal Mussolini's support, move eastwards into Egypt – then, when he's beaten us, move quickly on to the Middle Eastern oilfields. With those in his hands the world will be his oyster: India – or up into the Caucasus – who could stop him?"

"It does sound… rather fanciful."

"Not really – not after all of Europe fell to his forces in a matter of weeks. We've got a couple of weak armoured divisions in Egypt– anyway they 've got their hands full with the I-ties. No Giles you watch my words; Mr Hitler is up to something. He's gone too quiet of late. If you care to take a bet the I'll put £20 on it. When the fighting season starts Hitler will unleash his panzers. Care to take me on – at evens ? My historian's instinct tells me I'll win."

CHAPTER 5

FIRST IMPRESSIONS

At the shop next morning Sturdee went into Loader's office to see what he had made of his Appreciation. Loader tossed the paper dismissively back at him:

"If you ask me, San Fairy Ann."

"San…?"

"Ca va ne rien. It's Frog for a load of poppycock."

"I see." Sturdee's intestines contracted.

"Well you did ask old man."

"I am disappointed in you Loader. You're not going to be of any use to me."

"Don't worry old cock – I won't be a millstone. I have made an appointment to see Captain Mansfield, Noble's Chief of Staff, this afternoon. I'm sure you can find somebody more suitable – more malleable if you like."

"Perhaps you'd like to explain your objections? At least it might pass the time of day. We've got nothing else on this morning."

"Wouldn't know where to start."

" Why not start with what infuriates you most of all." Sturdee sat down opposite Loader and stared at him direct: " I'm sure you're not entirely lost for words."

"Very well then. You asked for it Sturdee. The idea that some swot who's never been to sea can tell sailors how to win a naval battle is sickening … No that's not the word… It's preposterous."

"So, you disagree with Sir Percy?"

"No… Yes… Well No. I thought this paper would be about technical matters like radar – things a boffin might know about. Instead it's all about strategy and tactics – about which you know nothing Sturdee. I'm sure the admiral will agree – if he ever gets to read it."

"Actually no."

"Actually No what?"

"The Admiral wouldn't. He wants me to think about every aspect of the U-boat War. He was quite specific."

"That makes no sense to me."

"Obviously not. But why don't you think – instead of giving way to a gust of emotion?"

"For instance?"

"For instance, convoying in itself. In the last war was it the Admiralty which came up with the idea? No it wasn't! It was forced upon Jellicoe by Lloyd George – who hadn't been to sea either."

"That old chestnut…". Loader waved his one good arm in dismissal.

The argument between the two men gradually grew more heated. Sturdee was angered to think that he was being treated as he had been by the other cadets at Dartmouth once more, while Loader, having already lost his right hand in the U-boat war was damned if he was going to be lectured to by a civilian. Eventually a wide-eyed Wren Jones came downstairs in an attempt to keep the peace.

Sturdee got up in disgust:

"You can tell Captain Mansfield this afternoon that I need somebody more intelligent to do your job Loader – who thinks before he loses his temper. If anybody wants me Gwen, I'll be back from Gladstone Dock after lunch."

Next morning Loader appeared in Sturdee's office:

"Can I sit down old man?

"You can old man." Sturdee emphasised the last two words: "When can I expect your replacement?"

"Not immediately it would appear."

A long Silence ensued.

"Look Sturdee, Mansfield gave me a flea in the ear. Told me the C-in- C would be most disappointed. That there must be some trifle in your paper worth picking up on. And if I couldn't find that something he threatened to reappoint me out to Stornoway – as a billeting officer. Can you imagine me among all those sheep-shaggers? "

Sturdee couldn't help smirking: "What do you want me to do?"

"We can give things a second chance, couldn't we?"

"We could I suppose, we could. But only if you show the right attitude. I don't want you to agree with me Loader . Quite the contrary. But I want you to give reasons I can argue with, not simply air your prejudices. I am a scientist, not a bloody psychiatrist. If there are weaknesses in my arguments, I want to know exactly what they are – before I present them to Noble. You can disagree with me as much as you like – but you've got to give reasons, supply evidence. Noble listens to everyone – take a leaf out of his book. If you bloody can't do that you might as well go to Stornoway. Here – take my Appreciation back, and come back with a reasoned response – however unfavourable."

Next day Loader was back to his ebullient self: "I stayed up with your paper nearly all night – I did manage to find something of value at least – which Noble will want to hear about."

"Oh – what's that?"

"I'd rather go through things systematically Sturdee – getting matters straight in my mind as I go."

"Okay. Fire away."

Loader sat down and opened the appreciation. He was learning, not very successfully, to write with his left hand.

"As I understand it Sturdee you are suggesting that Doenitz will need a cordon of 100 U-boats actually at sea in order to intercept all our convoys?"

"That's Doenitz's estimate, not mine. It allows for a separation of 10 miles between two neighbouring submarines."

"Sounds about right" Loader conceded "Allowing for bad weather and darkness. At present he's way short of that: only 10 or 20 out on patrol they say."

"Which means that about 90 percent of our convoys should be getting through his cordon undetected."

"Which also checks with the facts" Loader conceded "And you are estimating that to win he needs to sink 200 ships – or 800,000 tons – every month?"

"That is Sir Percy's estimate – not mine. He would then have sunk half our Merchant Marine within a year – and all of it within two."

"But somewhere Sturdee – ah yes here, you have calculated that an individual U-boat will find for itself only one convoy a month. So even if it manages to sink one ship from that convoy , with only 20 U-boats at sea, that's only 20 sinkings a month; only 10% of the necessary score."

"Yes, but if all our ships were travelling independently, each U-boat would spot , and probably sink, 20 ships a month, for a total of 400. Hence the colossal benefit of convoy."

"No argument there old cock. You then go on to say that the only hope the Jerrys have at present is for a U-boat, once it has spotted a convoy, to shadow it and call up reinforcements. And if the cordon is separated 10 miles apart that means about one reinforcing U-boat will arrive every hour."

"Yes."

"So, it is all a question of how many hours a shadower can keep in contact with the convoy, right? If it is for R hours that's R reinforcements to the Wolfpack? Can't argue with that."

"And, then when the pack attacks you assume that an average U-boat will make K kills– In other words will torpedo K cargo vessels. Right?"

"Right."

There was a long silence while Loader read on through several pages:

"Then Sturdee you go on to include other factors... the number of escort vessels per convoy... the number of drownings per sinking... the effects of signal intelligence – I suppose that's code breaking and stuff?"

"Yes that's right. Clearly that could benefit either side – depending on which has the best wireless code. And which the best codebreakers. In the last war that was the British. In this case it could well be the Germans."

"God forbid! "

"The enemy has set up this code breaking organisation call B-Dienst apparently – Germany has much better mathematicians than we do."

"And then you put all the numbers together and come up with this equation which you call the 'Commander-in-Chief's Equation' ".

Loader looked up Sturdee:

"I don't mind admitting Giles that this is what got my goat the first time round... working out victory or defeat like a grocer adding up his bill. No room for courage, for morale, for enterprise... for chance.... The Royal Navy doesn't work like that. It never has. Haven't you ever heard of the Nelson Touch? Lay yourself alongside the enemy and damn the odds. And it has worked for 300 years. If we'd thought like you do, we'd probably be an offshore province of France– like Jersey on a somewhat larger scale."

"Well that's what Noble has hired me for , to supply him with the numbers, not to make the tactical decisions. And that's what my Commander-in-Chief's Equation is intended to do. It summarises a lot of thinking in a short, sharp, memorable way. It's a sort of mnemonic. Read it out."

Loader looked back down at the script:

"For the Royal Navy to be winning K times R times U times D times E must be less than one. KRUDE equals crude."

"In essence" Sturdee translated "It means that as Doenitz increases U – the number of his U-boats on patrol, we have to reduce their individual kill ratios K, and their shadowing capacity, their ability to call up reinforcements – R. Doesn't that make common sense? I should have thought it was bloody obvious."

"May be but it doesn't tell you how to reduce those factors – which is surely the important thing. And anyway, as you admit yourself Giles, it leaves out two absolutely key factors – U-boat sinkings and air power. An analysis of antisubmarine warfare which ignores the sinking of U-boats is almost a contradiction in terms ."

Sturdee got to his feet and paced round his side of Loaders desk:

"I thought I'd made myself clear. But evidently not. We don't seem able to sink U-boats at present, very few anyway, and we don't know why. And air warfare is evolving so rapidly that we can't clearly foresee its consequences for now. So there is no point in mathematically modelling either just yet. But here is the cardinal point Loader: both can only *increase* the Royal Navy's chances of winning eventually and I am estimating that, if we make the right moves, and make them fast enough, we can win this U-boat war anyway. Isn't that encouraging?"

"It's certainly surprising old boy – with the dire current sinking-rate and the consequent despondency about."

"I certainly didn't expect it myself – which makes me suspicious. What have I done wrong – or left out? That's your pigeon Loader. We can't show this to the Admiral until we are as near as dammit sure."

It was Loader's turn to get out from behind his desk and think aloud:

"As far as I can see all you're claiming , or *can* claim at this stage, is that Doenitz cannot win with only 50 U-boats in all – 20 on patrol – as he has apparently at present. But in a couple of year's time , in 1943 say, he will have built up to 300, with a full cordon of 100 strung right across the Atlantic from North to South. He will then intercept every one of our convoys. Concealment, the main point of convoy, will then be out of the question. What you are further assuming, implicitly perhaps, is that by then we will have enough escort vessels per convoy to prevent U-boats making successful torpedo attacks and to prevent them from shadowing convoys for long enough to call up effective reinforcements. Isn't that so?"

"Yes… yes it is."

"So, in your eyes Sturdee, it is a straight competition between two putative building programs – Jerry's to build more U-boats. and ours to build more escort vessels? "

"Exactly… Yes. Right. But I didn't put it quite like that in my paper. But it must be so."

"It amounts to saying that if we can build two-thousand-ton long-range escort destroyers faster that he can build 800-ton U-boats, then we can win. I have no idea whether that is the case ; have you?"

"Nope."

"But your optimistic case hinges on that doesn't it Sturdee?"

"It does."

" You could well be right of course. We have a larger naval building capacity than he has – or rather we used to have before the bloody Geddes Axe. And we could have escort vessels built abroad – in Canada or the United States for instance – which he cannot. We will have to do some more research on this. Do you want me to have a go?"

"By all means. It's not in my line anyway. Now what about that other thing, that other useful trifle of mine you said might interest Noble?"

"Ah yes old boy – now that was a surprise." Loader thumbed back through the appraisal: "You say, and I quote: 'Ships cannot avoid their fate – men can. If merchant seaman, particularly those from the neutral nations from which we charter so many ships, refuse to sail, because it looks too dangerous, we will lose the war, irrespective of the sinkings. As we will see next, merchant seamen's morale is more likely to determine the issue of the battle than monthly tonnages sunk.' Now that was an eye-opener!"

"Yes, I was surprised myself."

"You go on to do another one of your calculations. You assume a typical seaman will be called upon to make so many voyages over the course of the whole battle, and if he is to remain at sea he will demand odds of better than 3 to 1 of surviving the war. If the apparent odds fall below that, his morale will crack and he will refuse to sign on again. And we won't be able to do much about it – because in the end he is a free agent, not subject to military discipline." Loader looked up.

"That's about it yes. Naturally what will matter to him will not be losing his ship but losing his life. What proportion of torpedoed merchant seamen drown when their ships go down? That is the ' D' in my calculation. And it is absolutely critical."

"You make a rough estimate that a trained seaman will be called upon to make about 20 transatlantic voyages over the course of the entire battle , which you assume to last for three-years. And then you do something really cunning. You calculate under what circumstances merchant navy morale will crack before sheer sinkings do for us."

"And I find?""

"That if we can rescue at least six out of seven torpedoed seamen we won't have to worry about morale."

"But can we do that?"

"A very good question Giles. I have no more idea than you appear to have. But the water out there in the North Atlantic, particularly in winter, is cold enough to kill in a matter of minutes. So, rescuing six out of seven does seem a tall order. But of course, if the crew get into a lifeboat – or a Carley Raft , they will have a far better chance. I have sent Gwen round to the public library to see if she can find out how many merchant seamen died in World War I. Either way Noble is going to have to know about this. And, of course, most convoys are already accompanied by a rescue vessel – as a matter of common humanity – often a converted trawler. But if you are right it may be the difference between winning this war – or losing it. In that case the Admiralty will have to take a firm hand in the matter. You can't leave it to the shipowners. As I understand it many of them are callous swine anyway – particularly the Greeks. Some of their vessels don't even carry life- boats."

The prejudice against civilians felt by naval officers like Loader was tiresome but understandable. They went to Dartmouth when they were only 13 years old and they were thereafter completely immersed in the mystique and tradition of the Royal Navy. And what a powerful mystique it had – based as it was on a record of unbroken victory stretching back more than 300 years to the Armada. From the Nile to The Saintes, from Copenhagen to Coronel, it had annihilated, literally annihilated every fleet that had dared to challenge it. At Trafalgar– so Sturdee recalled from his own Dartmouth days – Nelson's own ship had lost only 48 men while his enemies had lost 25,000, their blood running out of the scuppers to stain the sea. No wonder the Kaiser's High Seas Fleet had put to sea once and once only – at Jutland–and then fled back to Keil for the duration of the war. From admirals downward, sailors worldwide were terrified of the Royal Navy. And why not. No military instrument in history, not even the Roman army, could boast such an unbroken record of victory after victory.

Intelligent admirals though, like Jackie Fisher and Percy Noble, recognised that tradition alone never had been, and never would be enough. A good part of the navy's success was owed to continual reform and innovation. The Armada had lost because of the Royal Navy's 'Seed guns', the first cast-iron guns in history that could be fired again and again without bursting. But blood and courage made for a better story to tell schoolboys, and so the Navy's innovative tradition was often understated and sometimes forgotten. Thus the verbal battles which shook the dry-cleaning shop just off the Liverpool docks, followed a long tradition of their own. Loader wanted the Appreciation to be as short as possible with nothing in it which might offer a hostage to fortune:

"If Sir Percy buys it then he'll listen to whatever we say in future. But if you put in things like your perishing C-in-C's Equation he will probably write you off as deolali. It is your credibility which is at stake Sturdee."

"Noble is more intelligent than that." Sturdee responded. "He knows this is only an appreciation – and as such, necessarily based on hypothesis. He will certainly have made an appreciation of his own – won't he?"

" Admirals are trained to do that kind of thing – so I believe."

"The value of my appreciation to him is that it comes from right outside the naval officer tradition. Thus it might contain arguments he may have missed – such as my point about Merchant Navy morale. No, I want to leave everything in – that is not demonstrably wrong. And as for my ignorance Loader I am going to have to put that right. If I'm going to tackle the U-boat sinking problem next, I'll have to go to sea in an escort vessel and experience depth-charge attacks at first hand. Do you think Noble would object?"

"I don't see why old boy. It's the kind of thing he does himself. I believe he went out on a Sunderland flying-boat himself last week – on a long-range convoy-escort patrol. A great man our Sir Percy. Not many full admirals do that. He likes to see for himself – and be seen. So he can hardly object to you swanning about the Atlantic. But I foresee a practical difficulty."

"Oh?"

"Most of our convoys at present are avoiding U-boats altogether. You could be out for weeks – and never see a depth-charge dropped in anger."

"I hadn't thought of that."

" It'll do you good though Giles. See life at the sharp end – hideous seasickness, continually wet clothes – nothing to eat for weeks but tinned bully-beef, biscuit and kye – while Gwen and I are tucked up in bed here with a warm hot-water bottle. Do you no end of good old chap. I have a fancy we wouldn't hear so much about 'Commander in Chief's Equations' after that."

A much-edited version of 'Our Appreciation' was sent up to the admiral who summoned Sturdee to see him:

"I liked this Sturdee. Just the kind of perceptive analysis I was hoping from you. We are working on your rescue-ship ideas already. My predecessor in this post had of course instituted such ships already but neither he nor I recognised their possible impact on the outcome of the battle. As it happens the one kind of vessel we have in surplus is the oceangoing trawler. I've ordered more to be fitted out as rescue vessels so that most convoys will have two. As you suggested we looked at the figures – both of this and of the last war. In the first we lost 20,000 merchant sailors in 8 million tons of British shipping lost, or an average of about 10 lost per torpedoing – or about one in eight of every sunken crew. So, we rescued seven in eight – close to the number you are demanding in this. However…" Noble withdrew a hand from his jacket pocket to emphasise the point "Most of our ships lost in that war went down not too far off the coast of Britain – in warmer waters where life-boats could hoist their sails and make land in a matter of days. In this case… God help the poor devils who try their luck up near the Arctic Circle – we've got to do better – much better. I have apprised the Admiralty of this matter. I think we can assume action will be taken with regard to ship's life-boats and so forth – and merchant seamen's morale in general. So well done – very well done Sturdee."

"Lieutenant Loader has proved to be a great help."

"Has he poor devil? He was destined for higher command."

"What about the other stuff in our paper Sir Percy?"

The Admiral paced about, both hands in his jacket pockets, as was the habit with most senior naval officers:

" A lot to think about Sturdee – a lot. By and large I agree with you. The crunch will come in late 42 or early 43. I'm trying to get the cabinet to promise us enough escort vessels by then to discourage U-boats from pressing home successful torpedo attacks; our corvettes are too slow to catch surfaced U-boats. But somebody's had a good idea; to refuel our escort destroyers from a tanker in the convoy. It's never been done before and it might be tricky – but we are working on it. A thirty-five-knot destroyer can cover a lot of sea."

"Do you think they could put off the shadowing U-boats? "

"That of course is the vital question. The problem is as much one of visibility as speed. U-boats lie so low in the water, and make so little wake, that it's damned hard to see them from the bridge of a destroyer – as I know to my cost – especially at night."

"I expect the next generation ten-centimetre wavelength radar will solve our problems there."

"We can only hope so. The present one-and-a-half-meter wavelength sets are not good for much beyond station-keeping at night. Even in moderate weather they can't pick up U-boats as well as the trained human eye. How confident are you about the new radars? It was your field wasn't it?"

"Yes it was. I am not in the loop any longer, but this new short-wave transmitter developed at Birmingham University ought to revolutionise the whole field. As far as U-boats are concerned the night may no longer offer refuge – not if they're surfaced."

"And that is when they're so dangerous. The submerged U-boat is too slow to prove much of a threat. Well let's hope – but not count too many premature chickens."

Sturdee next brought up the matter of U-boat sinkings – or rather the Royal Navy's failure to sink many:

"I was going to suggest that as my next topic for research sir?"

"I agree entirely." the admiral halted in his tracks and gazed down calmly at the shorter man: " It's a sad business Sturdee – very sad. We were hoping so much from our asdic – but it appears to be virtually useless– and we don't know why – have no idea. 'It's affecting morale, on both sides I suspect. We're despondent – the Jerries are cock-a-hoop. And while you're at it ask yourself the question about U-boat morale. What can cause them to throw in the sponge? I suspect it might be the number of U-boat sinkings per successful torpedo attack. If that is the case, then in order to win the Battle of the Atlantic – which is what Winston is calling it now – we have to sink U-boats – we simply have to, and lots of them. And yes of course you can go to sea. I was going to recommended it myself. But seeing that you are a civilian…"

CHAPTER 6
OUT TO SEA

With no mother and no sister and growing up as he had in a series of exclusively male establishments, from boys' schools to university physics - departments, Sturdee had no intimate experience of women, let alone personable and attractive young women like Joan Duff. That meant that sharing a house with her was likely to prove awkward. As he had half admitted to Maurice he had a crush on Joan even before he settled into Duff House, a crush that was growing into an embarrassing and quiet unsuitable obsession. Although she was younger than he was she was a much more forceful personality than he was, she was his landlady and she was much in love with an Australian war-hero about whom she talked incessantly and whose engagement-ring she proudly wore. She adored her father and idolized an older brother David while she had two formidable younger brothers who she seemed to have half brought-up – so Joan had very high standards in men. She was unlikely to be impressed by the calf love of a total innocent like himself – or so he tried to convince himself after a long heart-to-heart with Maurice:

"What's he like – the fiancé?"

"Desmond? He's *'formidable'* as the French say. Tall, broad shouldered, calm, humorous, modest to a fault … almost any girl would be proud to have him as a fiancée, even Joan. Volunteered in Australia on the first day of the war, trained as a bomber pilot in Canada, transferred over to the RAF, flies his own Bristol Blenheim, adored by his crew, already decorated for gallantry…"

"So no chance for me then…" Sturdee sighed despondently.

"I wouldn't quite say that Giles. Women are strange cattle – none stranger than Joan. She is for instance quite strong enough not to need a strong silent man like Desmond. Then Blenheims are death-traps– 'Flying Greenhouses' I believe they're called."

"I wouldn't like him to be killed."

"Wouldn't you? It might be your best chance of getting her; when she's in shock."

"Don't be a rotter Maurice."

" Am I – well perhaps I am. I've got a sweet spot for Joan myself. If I was 30 years younger……. I'd hate to see Joan throw herself away."

" The Great Desmond hardly sounds like that."

"No, but a trifle conventional. Joan's got to become more than a suburban housewife with a fridge and two kids."

"I'll say…"

"Which she never would be with you ."

"No she wouldn't by Jove."

" You just might have the qualities needed to push Joan to her limits –
goodness knows where *they* lie. So don't give up on her entirely. Some women
might consider you quite a catch Giles."

"Oh really…" he sounded surprised.

"But let me give you a bit of sage advice young man. Never let Joan
know you're sweet on her – especially not yet. If you're going to get anywhere
at all with her it'll have to be a case of 'slowlee slowlee catchee Joanee' ."

"I see…" Sturdee sounded doubtful.

"As a university professor it amused me to watch budding romances –
sometimes the most unlikely liaisons – developing among my brighter young
charges. Brains can sometimes be very arousing – sexually I mean. Ask yourself
how attractive Joan would be to you if she spent her time talking about film-
stars… or female adornment."

Whether she appreciated brains or not Joan certainly appreciated practical
achievements and had no time for 'weeds'– a word she had picked up from her
brothers. Sturdee had no idea how to build a pig-sty – or where to get the
necessary materials from – but he wasn't about to let Joan know that. However,
passing a bomb-site one day, the answer became obvious and bricks, timber,
glass and even corrugated iron for the roof, mysteriously arrived at Duff House.
A bag of cement proved much trickier and only appeared after an elaborate
deal over onion-futures. Thank God that the onions, lovingly attended by Joan
and her minions, were thriving in the lengthening hours of spring sunlight.
Picton and Sturdee had hung makeshift bunting between the high wire-netting
round the   tennis-lawn to scare off birds until such time as the onions were big
enough to look after themselves.

The architecture of pigsties turned out to be a good deal higher tech than
Sturdee had anticipated. Being more or less naked, domestic pigs had to be
pampered: good ventilation – but no draughts – and sloping floors to provide
natural drainage so that their bedding remained warm and dry for as long as
possible. The Ministry of Agriculture provided all manner of information-
leaflets for tyros like Joan and Giles, anxious to 'Pig for Victory' as Joan put it.

The air-raid sirens continued to chill the blood whenever the dock areas
caught it, as they did on a regular basis, especially near the full of the Moon.
With Maurice's Anderson shelter completed they dutifully traipsed into the
garden with their blankets and gas-masks when the sirens went off, and then
down into the earth among the sandbags. Hanging the hurricane lantern from a
rafter they tried to sleep on the two tiers of wooden bunks. The damp earth and
wet sand certainly damped the sound of the bombs and even the frenzied
pounding of the Ack-Ack batteries as the Heinkels and Dorniers came over to

be picked up in the beams of anti-aircraft searchlights which swept the skies in all directions.

"I suppose we'll be safer down here," Joan complained "But I feel half in the grave already. If we survive the war I'll never forget the smell down here. Never!"

The others agreed so that it was with more and more reluctance that they vacated the house and took to the shelter, especially when the nights were freezing cold.

"We could sleep in the cellar." Sturdee suggested.

"And be buried alive if the house collapsed on top of us – which it probably would. " Maurice responded.

"I think I'd rather die wrapped up warm and comfortable in my bed." was Joan's opinion . "Look I've I got these ministry-issue rubber ear-plugs. It would all be over before we knew it. This shelter wouldn't protect us from a direct hit would it?"

" Of course not." Maurice agreed "But that is not the point. The statistics show we are ten or twenty times more likely to survive in here than above ground. Despite all the bomb damage, remarkably few people get killed by aerial bombing – if they take shelter."

Their nightly discussion was being echoed in millions of air-raid shelters across the land, with the result that most citizens returned to their houses and slept on the floor under their kitchen or dining-room tables. At Duff House they compromised, depending on the phase of the moon. For a couple of nights either side of full moon they slept in the Anderson, but otherwise, when the sirens rang, they moved down to the family dining-room and made themselves as comfortable as they could under the massive Victorian dining table. With only one candle between them they took it in turns to read to one another. Sturdee chose Dickens's 'Sketches by Boz' and kept the other two in fits of laughter.

"You know there's something about this war" Maurice said "If it wasn't for Mr Hitler I'd be at home alone, bored to death with my own company. Instead , I'm lying under the table with two brilliant young people, being royally entertained. And listening to the crump of bombs going off in the distance. And when we get up tomorrow, we'll all be doing something really worthwhile."

"You're right Maurice" Joan agreed. "That's what I disliked before the war – all the triviality – typing formal letters about a few grubby half-pence here and there … : 'Dear sir , with regard to yours of the 24th instant., etc etcetera ' … Ugh! …... What about you Giles?"

"I suppose I was lucky – being a scientist. There are always exciting and significant things for scientists to do – if they have any ambition."

"What was yours?"

"I was still looking for my very own problem – but I felt I was getting very close – something in between Relativity and Quantum Mechanics."

"I have no idea what either of those phrases means." Joan said.

"Relativity is the modern theory of Space and Time, usually associated with Einstein in the public mind – somewhat inaccurately I have to say. Then Quantum Mechanics describes how matter and radiation behave on the atomic scale – very bizarrely indeed. Subatomic particles such as electrons can be in two places at once."

"Golly" Joan said. "How exciting!"

"Yes – well it is. That's why I spent two years in Germany – first at the University of Göttingen – then in Munich. That was where the theory was largely being developed. I was in amongst all the pioneers… Heisenberg, Schrodinger, Pauli, my own boss Sommerfeld… there were seminars and colloquia several times a week – arguing, arguing , arguing – you never knew what was coming up next. We all felt we were very close to the heart of things. Often I was so excited I couldn't sleep at night. I felt that I had my hand on the door into nature's secrets. One push and…"

"Like Harold Carter at the door to Tutankhamen's tomb." Joan exclaimed.

"Oh no. " Sturdee put her down " Far far more exciting than that. Far more! Tut was only ever going to tell us about some episode in Egyptian history. Quantum Mechanics is a pathway……. to the stars."

"Example?" Joan demanded.

"Okay" Sturdee replied: "Think about the sun and the stars. Where do they get all their energy from – vast amounts of energy, enabling them to go on shining for thousands of millions of years… ? We suspect they get it by burning their hydrogen into helium. But the centre of a star, although its temperature is about ten million degrees, is still far too cool to burn hydrogen – in normal circumstances. But Quantum Mechanics offers a weird way out. I told you an atomic particle can be in two places at once. In that case… a hydrogen atom might be, for part of the time, inside the nucleus of *another* hydrogen atom. It is called 'quantum tunnelling'. In that case the two nuclei might occasionally merge to form helium – and release a vast amount of energy. That's what I was working on – with several other people of course."

Maurice said: "This war must all seem pretty trivial to you Giles."

"I wouldn't say that…though it is certainly far less interesting. Maybe that sounds arrogant; but I do resent having I to give all of that up to worry about U-boats…"

"And onions…" Joan added.

"But we *do* have to fight," Sturdee conceded "Not for Christian civilisation… I'm an atheist. But we do have to fight for civilisation itself. The Nazis were destroying the very fabric of science in their own country; science depends above all on the freedom to think and to communicate freely. And they were stifling that: persecuting many of the finest spirits – particularly Jewish scientists. That's why Einstein fled to New Jersey. that's why my own close colleague Hans Bethe – the 'Starlight Man' – is somewhere in America now. I came back to Britain, reluctantly in many ways I have to say – I was having such a wonderful time in Munich, because Theoretical Physics was dying around me. The best minds – or many of them, were obsessed with fleeing …– to Switzerland, Denmark, America , Britain….. We knew it was all over… the magic moment had gone."

"How sad!" Joan sounded genuinely stricken "Like the end of Viennese music – or French Impressionist painting."

"Do you think it will ever come back?" Picton asked.

"I think about that all the time. " Sturdee replied "You see, so few of us were involved. Could we re-create that magic atmosphere after the war? That's the ambition crystallising in my mind Maurice. If I can find a chair in Physics one day that is what I would try to do – re-light that spark of numinous flame. Make it blaze again in some provincial university… attract the Gods back down to Earth."

There was a loud crump not too far away which made all their huge Victorian windows rattle in their frames. The ack-ack rose to an almost continuous crescendo.

"Wasn't that a land-mine?" Joan asked. " Why do the Jerries drop mines on the land?"

"Because their magnetic-mine campaign has failed." Sturdee explained: "I was peripherally involved in that. Once we had de-gaussed our ships they wouldn't set off the Jerry mines in the approaches to our ports. so they're dropping them on the land instead – using parachutes. They make huge bangs – but are far too inaccurate to be a serious threat. I think it shows they are getting a bit desperate. The bombing campaign is seven months old now – and it hasn't brought us to our knees."

"Not yet." Joan qualified.

"In a few months' time we'll be able to shoot their bombers out of the sky, even at night – using radar."

"Are you sure? " Picton asked, his voice barely decipherable above the cannonade. Sturdee waited for a lull in the bombardment: "As near as dammit. We've made a huge breakthrough in shortwave radar – which will fit in our night-fighters. Then the Heinkels will have to watch out. They'll be lucky to reach London – never mind get all the way up to Liverpool."

"I pray to God you're right Giles " Joan said "We are really creaking under the strain right now. We're not even going to get our absolutely minimum import tonnage ashore this year." Then she added incongruously: "I wish I was a physicist."

Beyond the stark figures for monthly sinkings Sturdee and Loader needed no other urging to realise the challenges they faced. Since the fall of France in May 1940 they read:

June 1940	585,000 tons of merchant shipping sunk
July	387,000 tons
August	397,000 tons
September	448,000 tons
October.	442,000 ton
November.	386,000 tons
December	350,000 tons
January 1941.	320,000 tons
February	403,000 tons

The only news to relieve the gloom was that in March the Navy had somehow managed to sink five U-boats, among them Germany's three greatest tonnage aces : Gunther Prien (U47: 200,000 tons); Joachim Schepker (U99, 230,000 tons) and Otto Kretschmer (U100, 282,000 tons, about 70 ships). Kretschmer had first made his name by penetrating the defences of Scapa Flo– where the Royal Navy kept its Grand Fleet, supposedly safe behind anti-submarine nets, and sinking the battleship *Royal Oak*, before getting clean away. His audacious exploit had echoed around the world's media – seeming to promise for the Kreigsmarine the same spectacular success already enjoyed by Hitler's Wehrmacht and Luftwaffe. Asdic had played some role in these U-boats sinkings though the first contacts had been visual and only one of the three had been sunk with depth-charges, the others by ramming or torpedoes. Britain had of course celebrated – perhaps the corner had been turned at last? But then the sinkings figure came in for April – by far the worst of the war: 687,000 tons or 195 ships lost – within five of the monthly figure Noble considered must lead to eventual defeat.

"We simply can't go on like this." was the universal feeling within Western Approaches Command, and back at Duff House.

"Churchill has sent for Sir Percy" Loader mattered to Sturdee , almost under his breath :   " Christ he's only been in post since February. He is our only hope Giles, he really is. If Churchill's sacks him now we're lost !"

Sturdee tried to find out the source of his colleague's Faith in Admiral Noble – which amounted almost to hero worship – not a sentiment he would have expected in a rough diamond like Loader.

"Well, for a start old man, every junior officer owes him. He it was, as Fourth Sea Lord, who introduced the marriage-allowance for us in 1933. Before that June and I were practically starving."

"I didn't know you were married Tony."

"Was old man, was – but no longer. She took one look at my missing flipper and decided even life with a dentist was preferable. I believe they're emigrating to Argentina for the duration."

"I'm sorry…"

"But that of course is not the real reason. The Navy is full of physical courage. I know, I've seen a British matelot jump over the side into the freezing North Atlantic to rescue a German U-boat man for heaven's sake. But moral courage is another matter. That's much rarer – and Sir Percy is abrim with that. That's why he stood up to the Admiralty on our behalf – and against his own career interest. One knows he will always do that – whatever the pressure. He'll stand up to Churchill even – if he thinks it's right. And that is exactly what we want at this mo'. Exactly! And then he's damned intelligent. When he came to this command he found out what needed to be done in a matter of weeks – and he's doing it."

"What's that?"

"Training old cock – training, training, training. Do you realise that our escort ships have to communicate with each other using flags like Nelson? They're not allowed to use radio for fear of it being picked up by the enemy's listening-stations and giving the convoy position away. And at night they must use signal lamps. Imagine trying to fight off a U-boat pack in half a gale at night using only Morse code sent by telegraph lamp across miles and miles of heaving Atlantic."

"I never imagined…."

"You have to be on the bridge of a destroyer rolling her guts out while trying to read a vital signal from the convoy-commodore eight miles away…"

"How can training make such a difference?"

"By cutting down the need for such communications: if everyone in the escort group knows exactly what the others will do in any given tactical situation then you can almost dispense with flags and lamps. Sir Percy has turned Escort Groups into permanent teams which stick together, train together and fight together. Before him they were temporary aggregations of ships – whose commanders might never have met. Everyone realises it's improved our fighting efficiency hundreds of times over. And Sir Percy has given the authority to the Escort - Commander on the spot. He won't let the Admiralty interfere – despatching escort vessels away from a convoy on wild goose chases, as they used to do before. He must've had a titanic battle with Whitehall to get that through – but he won it thank God . With all that – and his newly issued *Western Approaches Convoy Instructions* – he's welding a half-demoralized collection of odds and sods into a formidable fighting command – with faith in itself – and in eventual victory. Without Sir Percy's innovations we would never have got those three German U-boat aces – never!"

"He sounds quite a commander."

"Oh he is Giles, he is. But it would be so easy to underestimate him. He is understated – not a braggart like Beaverbrook or Churchill. Look what *they* did to Dowding – they sacked him immediately after he'd won the Battle of Britain– and replaced him with Sholto Douglas. God knows why."

"I never knew you to be so passionate Tony."

"You civilians take us professionals for granted – until there's a war. And after we've won the war for you you turn on us – the admirals and generals in particular – and call us Blimps. And that suits politicians like Lloyd George and Churchill – who can then claim all the glory for themselves. The Royal Navy hasn't lost a significant battle in three centuries. Can that be the result of a series of fortunate coincidences?"

"Keep your hair on Loader. I don't want to sack your favourite admiral. I just wanted to know why you hold him in such esteem. Now I know – and you sound as if you are talking sense. I like the cut of Sir Percy's jib myself – otherwise I wouldn't be here. I am his protégé after all. If he goes I'll probably get the push the week afterwards."

"You need to go to sea to really appreciate what he is doing."

"Ah yes that's what I really wanted to talk about Loader.Sitting around here in this bloody office I'm not getting anywhere with the Asdic problem. I need to get to sea – and observe Asdic in operation. But how – and with whom? I don't want to waste my time travelling with a convoy that never sees action – in other words a successful convoy."

There was, it appeared, no easy solution because most convoys were evading U-boat contacts at this time. Doenitz had too few of his grey wolves at sea. All Loader could suggest was a visit to HMS *Western Isles* at Tobermory out on the Isle of Skye. Newly commissioned escort vessels were worked-up there – and put through their Asdic paces against Royal Navy submarines.

"It's pretty damned realistic." Loader claimed.

"It can't be" Sturdee demurred "You told me Asdic was successful in training, but not against real U-boats. There must be something vital missing from those exercises out round Skye. And that vital something could be the very thing we need to identify Tony – the very thing."

"I won't argue old cock – but you could waste the entire summer swanning peacefully around the deep."

As it happened one of Joan's brothers John was on leave for a few days at Duff House. When he wasn't sleeping – which he seemed to do for at least 16 hours every day – he helped Sturdee to finish the pigsty. He was, he explained, the anti-submarine officer aboard the corvette HMS *Pimpernel* now belonging to Captain McIntyre's Escort Group Number Five. When consulted about Sturdee's problem he said: "Well if you're serious about it you'd better get going PDQ."

"Why?"

"Because summer is coming up fast in the North Atlantic – where we go – and the nights get shorter and shorter, and the U-boats – which attack almost exclusively at night nowadays – mostly leave the convoys alone – they go off in search of easier prey – ships travelling independently."

"I never thought of that."

"They've got a lot warier of late – especially after they lost those three aces. Those chaps were fearless – but they paid the price for that. You know it was our group that got 'em?"

"Yes – you were the toast of Liverpool."

"The problem Giles with finding a berth on an escort vessel is that they are grossly overcrowded already. Every time they load some new electronic wizardry on board, we need more wizards to operate it. We are carrying 84 on board Pimpernel already instead of our proper complement of 53. The mess-deck is like a rabbit warren."

"Oh hell! I'm desperate to go."

"Hold on though Giles – you might just be in luck. Our first lieutenant has just gone ashore for a hernia op. I am taking over temporarily, and my berth will be vacant on our next trip. How quickly could you get ready?"

72 hours later Sturdee found himself on the open bridge of His Majesty's Corvette *Pimpernel* as she warped out of Gladstone Dock into the Mersey and then out towards the Irish sea where their New York-bound convoy was gathering. He was both excited and nervous, nervous mainly about seasickness. Corvettes were notorious for their sickening motions – it was said 'they would roll in a heavy dew'.

"Most of us get over it in 4 to 5 days." Duff said " Best thing is to keep busy. If you've got nothing better to do, shadow me. You might pick up some useful guff that way – but don't ask questions. I'll be too bloody busy the next couple of days."

Like his sister Joan, Pinger Duff, as he was known to his shipmates, was a dynamo of energy and self-confidence as he made the Pimpernel and her crew ready for the long voyage ahead.

His first sight of a convoy made an emotional impression on Sturdee he had never expected. 50 or more steamers ranging from oil tankers to cargo tramps, belching smoke and blowing their steam whistles as they manoeuvred into two long columns that then steamed side-by-side slowly down the mine-swept channel out towards the North-West Approaches. Ancient many of them, single funnelled, invariably rusty, their red dusters flying proudly out astern, they represented Britain's hope, Britain's only lifeline. If they could make it Britain, and western civilisation with it, would make it too. But if the sea wolves got them – and they looked so vulnerable with their big slab sides pitching slowly into the growing seas – then all would be lost. They seemed to go on and on forever ahead of the Pimpernel, and astern – and yet the Germans had just sunk four times their number in a single month. Four times! It was beyond his imagination to conceive such devastation: torpedoes slamming into hulls, ships breaking in half and sinking in seconds, munitions exploding, precious cargoes sliding into the depths, oil tankers ablaze, whole crews burning or drowning… all out of sight of the millions – no hundreds of millions who depended on them not just now – but for all of history to come. Sturdee's eyes stung with tears he hastily brushed away. No wonder these men fought with such desperate determination; there had to be at least 5000 seamen in this convoy alone, the population of a small town. And there were 20 other such convoys at sea, from Freetown West Africa to Halifax Nova Scotia: 100,000 men fighting for their lives, for their families and for whatever they believed it. "So this is the Battle of the Atlantic" he thought to himself half aloud, shivering in the North westerly breeze: "I never really knew".

Besides the 50 great ships – which towered out of the water because they were in ballast, that is to say empty, the six escort vessels which were supposed to protect them , looked tiny, like corgis amidst a herd of cows. The four escort destroyers – led by Captain McIntyre in *Walker* , weighed less than 2000 tons apiece, the two Corvettes less than 1000 – while some of the tankers weighed over 15,000. And how flimsy their weapons were: Asdics which didn't seem to work; depth charges that were impotent, radars that sometimes failed to pick up a surfaced U boat less than a mile away – and 4-inch popguns that were wildly inaccurate when fired from the deck of a small vessel pitching and rolling violently amongst the heavy seas. It was just as well, Sturdee thought, that few of the merchantmen would realise just how flimsy their protection was. Had they done so they might not have put to sea. Their only hope at the moment lay in the vastness of the ocean. But once Doenitz had his full cordon of 100 U-boats at sea, even that hope would be gone:

"Before then we've got to learn to sink U-Boats " Sturdee said to a startled lookout as darkness closed in.

He must have slept for several hours because when he woke in the two-berth cabin he shared with 'Guns' *Pimpernel* was rolling and pitching considerably. Feeling nauseous he decided to go back on deck in order to catch a glimpse of the horizon – something steady to settle his brain.

On the bridge it was pitch black– no sign of a star– never mind the horizon. He clung onto the combing, peering into the wind and the smashing of the sea.

"Doctor Sturdee I presume" a deep voice spoke from feet away. Sturdee could see no one.

"The captain" the disembodied voice explained its origin

"I'm sorry, I can't see anything yet. I blinded myself turning on my torch for a few seconds."

"That will kill your night-vision. It should take minutes to come back– an hour to reach full acuity."

"How can the ships keep station in this blackness?"

"The Mark One Eyeball, if looked after, is a wondrous thing. I can see the wake of the steamer about two cables ahead; we're keeping station on that just for now, and on the one in the other column to starboard."

Gradations in the blackness gradually became apparent: the ship from the sea, the sea from the sky; then the captain, and the three other figures on the open bridge – the officer of the watch peering ahead, a starboard look-out by the starboard Oerlikon, his counterpart to port.

"This is total darkness such as we no longer see on land any more." Sturdee remarked "There's always something – even in the blackout. They say we Europeans can't see the universe any more – because we 've buried it in man-made light."

"That is so" the Captain agreed. "I remember nights at sea , south of Capricorn, when every corner of the heavens was a blaze of stars, star-clusters and nebulae… we all became amateur astronomers then. But thank God it's not like that here!"

"Why?"

"U-boats. They're hunters of the night – almost exclusively now. They are so low in the water that they can look up and pick our tall ships out against the stars – whereas, looking down from the bridge, we can't see them. They don't need to submerge: they can slam torpedoes into us with little thought of retaliation."

"I thought you had star shells – 'Snowflake' – artificial illumination."

"Oh yes we have – as you will see if we get attacked. But I sometimes think it is counter-productive – blinds our night-vision while lighting up the sky – enabling the U-boat commanders to see us even better."

"What about radar? I thought you all had it fitted?"

"An excellent device – in principle. But the sets we have can barely pick up a surfaced U-boat even a mile away – especially when there's a sea running – which there invariably is in the North Atlantic. There is too much clutter coming back from the waves. Mind you, they are damned useful for station-keeping on a dark night like this. You can pick up the merchant vessels in the convoy miles away – because they stick up above the waves. Right now our radar technician in the cabinet behind you is our main station-keeper. He'll warn the officer of the watch if we get seriously out of position ; take a look if you like - but I warn you you'll lose your night vision."

"No thanks. It's amazing how much more I can see now."

" Captain McIntyre, our escort-group commander, is a fanatic on night vision. He believes it can win us or lose us this war. He had a boffin come lecture the whole group about it. Apparently human night-vision relies on entirely different mechanisms from the day-time variety. You know all those three U-boats we recently sank were picked up visually first – only one other by radar. The Jerries, McIntyre says, have far better binoculars and night glasses than we do."

"I can believe that" Sturdee said "They've got the Zeiss Company. However, help is on your way. Radar-sets are in the pipeline vastly better than those you have now. My radar friends tell me U-boats will then entirely lose the cloak of darkness. By the way: are we in any danger of U-boats here?"

"Probably not. We're still too close to land. Air patrols out of Northern Ireland will be here at first light. U-boats hate air reconnaissance. It forces them down – to use up their batteries–and they cannot keep up with the convoy then. No, I don't anticipate trouble for another night or two. And all the time we are moving North – where the nights get shorter, thank God."

Sturdee was still on the bridge when a sickly sun , or at least its sickly presence could be sensed above the North-eastern horizon. Pinger Duff had taken over the watch by then and in between taking and issuing flag-signals he explained what was going on:

"We're getting into our seagoing formation: a dozen columns of four or five ships each , separated from each other by about a quarter mile. It minimises the target for U-boats. They usually attack us from ahead. When we're in this formation they can usually get in only one salvo before we are gone. All these flag signals are from the Commodore in charge of the convoy, to the merchant vessels. We are merely acting as a relay station. No radio signals remember – we don't want to give the convoy position away."

Later Sturdee went down to the ward-room below the bridge with Duff and tried to eat some breakfast – fried tinned tomatoes with fried bread – usually one of his favourites. But down below, with no horizon to steady his balance, he began to feel nauseous again and fled back to the bridge. The Corvette's motion, with its relentless eight and a half- second corkscrew, was nothing like his little Pelican.

" Remember Giles. one hand for the ship, and one for yourself." Duff said when he came back up to the bridge "You don't want to break a rib or an arm like so many chaps do on their first trip. We don't carry a doc. Any treatment you get will be from the First Lieutenant – that's me. I've got aspirins, laxatives, and stuff for VD. so, if I was you, I'd keep out of the sick-bay. Now let's get the Asdic going."

By now the convoy had sorted itself out into its oceangoing formation of a dozen short columns spread out side-by-side across 2 miles. Five of the six escort vessels were in line spread out ahead of the convoy with Pimpernel stationed near the centre.

"Without all our Asdics going, sweeping out in front of us, U-boats submerged ahead of us it could get in and among our ships undetected. That's what they used to do, and caused havoc. But in this formation, they can't. That's why they've been forced to operate at night – mostly on the surface."

" Is the Asdic on now?"

"Yep, so, before we go into the cabin, I'll try to explain the principles – in so far as I understand them. I know you're a scientist Giles but you have to be patient."

"Okay."

"Under the bows there's a rotating dome with the gear inside. It projects powerful pulses of sound in a narrow column which points downwards into the water as an angle of about 16° below the horizontal. If it hits something solid like a submarine, part of the sound energy bounces back, and we pick it up. Because sound travels a mile a second in water there is a delay between transmission and reception which we measure – which gives us the range: up to fifteen hundred yards in practice. since we set the direction of the pulse in the first place from up here – and now we have the range, we know the exact position of the U-boat relative to the ship, including its depth. All we have to do then is to go there and drop depth-charges on it."

"Sounds simple."

"It does doesn't it. But there are complications unfortunately."

"I imagine."

"The worst by far is what we call the 'Dead Time'. You see the sound beam is very narrow:– it has to be to be precise. so, as we race towards the U-boat to attack it, our beam, which is fixed in the vertical plane – at 16 degrees as I said, passes above it. So, we lose contact with him completely for a minute or two – the 'Dead Time'. He knows we've lost him because he can't hear our pings any more. That gives him the opportunity to rapidly change his course and depth so that our depth-charges, when we do eventually drop them – miss him. God knows how many we've dropped this last year without a single success – it must be hundreds. It's disheartening I tell you Giles: we are an anti-submarine vessel without an anti-submarine weapon."

They then went into the Asdic cabin, little more than a hutch at the front of the bridge, to meet the leading seaman operator who was crouched intently over his instrument wearing earphones. Without breaking off his search he handed a second pair of phones to Sturdee. Every few seconds the machine emitted a loud ping with in between faint hushing sounds which seemed to come from a vast distance away. Closing his eyes Sturdee could imagine the sound rushing out and down into the depths searching… searching… searching. Occasional odd tinkling sounds came back which might have been anything… fish… currents… bubbles…

Out in the open again Duff explained: "It is a highly skilled business –
requires a hell of a lot of patience. Every few seconds or so he rotates the beam
a few degrees sideways and sends out another Ping. Over and over and over he
and his mates stay at it day and night – sometimes for weeks at a time. Now and
then they get a return –sometimes from whales, from shoals of fish, even from
the bubbles left behind by breaking waves. In bad weather it's difficult to make
any sense of the Asdic at all."

"How does the attack work? "

"If the operator gets a solid return, or better still a series of solid returns,
he informs the officer of the watch and turns on the repeater so everyone on the
ship can hear what is going on over the tannoy system – loud pings going out –
weak ones coming back."

"So that's why you're called Pinger."

"Action stations are called; the captain takes over here on the bridge. The
depth-charge crews close up on the after-deck. The anti-submarine officer–
that's me – usually goes down there too. Come on – let's take a dekko."

From the bridge they scrambled down onto the main deck.

"You be bloody careful here Giles. When she's rolling like this, green
seas sometimes sweep down this deck waist-high. Get caught in one of those
and you could be over the side in a jiffy – or slammed against something hard
and sharp. Wait for the roll to come up – then run like billy-oh. Watch me."

Whenever the corvette rolled over on their side they seemed to be
hanging over the sea as it swept by at ten knots, crested with foam from the
bow wave . Duff peered forrard looking for a clear interval. Then he yelled but
his words were drowned in the wind and sea – as a tide of green water rushed
past them down the deck and over the side.

The vessel heaved up again and Duff staggered down the deck, tottering
from side to side, his arms held out to either flank in order to grab a rail or
stanchion if necessary. Watching him gain the safety of the afterdeck Sturdee
prepared to make the dash himself. But first came a big sea which rushed past
him with the force of an avalanche. Leaving the deck glistening wet in the sun,
the water rushed back over the rail or into the scrappers. His legs were soaked
to the thigh. He'd never reckoned on this – but there was no avoiding the ordeal.

To get a feel for the timing of the ships corkscrew motion he let several
more seas go by before staggering off in pursuit of Duff. His yachting
experience helped him to keep a balance as the wind tore at his clothing. All the
same he was nearly caught by a following sea before Duff grabbed him by his
collar and heaved him up into the shelter of some superstructure.

"You are going to have to really watch it. " Duff yelled in his ear
"You've come to sea without any sea legs. They take weeks to develop."

Panting from his exertions and nervousness, Sturdee could only agree. They scrambled off aft with him clinging to every rail or handhold he could find.

Duff didn't halt until they reached the very stern of the ship, from which, to say the least of it, the views were spectacular. They seemed to be very low – close to the white water which welled up out from their propeller-wash. Sturdee could feel the thrumming of the propeller-shaft shaking beneath his feet. Astern of them 50 black ships spread over several miles pitched in what seemed to him a heavy sea, their bow waves exploding jets of white foam into the cold grey monotony. To port he could pick up an escort destroyer which seemed to be lancing through the waves rather than over them , white water almost burying its bridge and superstructure from sight.

"They were never meant for the open ocean" Duff screamed in his ear "But then neither were we. This battle was supposed to take place in the North Sea – not the bloody North Atlantic. You will see when we run into rough weather – which we surely will."

Sturdee didn't want to see – not at all. This was already quite rough enough for him.

"These " yelled Duff with his hand on large black steel barrel that was like a drum of oil "These are our depth-charges: Type Sevens. Each contains 300 pounds of high explosive – Amatol. And it's fitted with a hydrostatic pistol to detonate it at the pre-set depth – up to 300 feet. To make it sink more rapidly each carries an extra hundred and fifty pounds of iron ballast. Weighing nearly a quarter of a ton each they're absolute pigs to handle, especially in heavy seas. We have to use these derricks to heave them onto the stern rails"

"How many?" Sturdee yelled back into the gale

"Usually in salvos of four at a time, in a diamond-shaped pattern. First one over the stern, then two projected sideways, one from either Thrower – then our last one over the stern – all set at different depths to give us a better chance."

The 'Throwers' turned out to be two massive mortars to port and starboard, each pointing outwards and upwards at 45°, and capable of projecting a depth- charge to a distance of 50 yards from the ship.

"Our crews have to be highly trained – and fucking strong." Duff boasted: "After one salvo they can be ready with four more depth-charges , two in the Throwers , two on the stern rack, in 10 seconds."

"I can't believe that."

"You'll see you if you're lucky. That's what training is for."

"How many depth charges do you carry?"

"40 up here on deck. Usually more below. Don't last long in a U-boat attack. I've chucked the lot overside in less than an hour."

"How fast do they sink?"

"About 15 feet a second. so it takes 20 seconds to get down to 300 feet. We have to allow for that – as well as the much longer Dead-time. That's more room for error; more chance for the bloody U-boat to escape."

As advised Sturdee tried to keep busy, filling up his exercise-book with copious notes. But it didn't work. As the convoy made North-west on its great circle route up towards Iceland, the wind rose , the waves grow taller and steeper, the corvette's motion ever more frantic. On the captain's orders, Sturdee was confined to his bunk – for fear of injuring himself – and there he gave way to seasickness of the most wretched kind, vomiting into a bucket until he felt his guts must come up. 24 hours, 48 hours… 72… it was easy to understand why some poor devils had thrown themselves overboard rather than suffer any longer. The scream of the wind round the bridge superstructure, the rushing of water along the decks outside, the slamming of the bow, the pounding of the stern, the groaning of steel in agony, the sound of rivets working loose….They all multiplied his sense of hopelessness, of matters running away totally out of his control.

"I'm sorry about the stench. I can't seem to stop vomiting." he apologised to his cabin mate 'Guns', a boyish RNVR sub-lieutenant."

"Don't worry old chap. We all have to go through it."

"Is it often like this – the weather I mean?"

"Good Lord yes. This is nothing. The galley fire is still going: we had dried egg and dogs' cocks for breakfast. You should come up here in winter – the waves can get so big one dare not look at them. At least I don't. But somehow the old girl picks up her skirts and gets over'em, she has so far anyway. Corvettes you know are based on whale-chasers – designed to face high latitudes. And it's as bad for the U-boats as it is for us – perhaps worse. They have no freeboard you see."

"Could we be attacked here?"

"Unlikely in this weather I'd say."

Eventually the seas abated, Sturdee's semi-circular canals settled down and his interest in life returned.

"Notice how short the nights have become" John Duff pointed out. "You can understand why the U-boats don't fancy their chances. Just as well because our four destroyers have left us."

"Why?"

"Out of oil. They had to go in to Iceland to refuel. We'll carry on to the MOMP then switch convoys with the Royal Canadian Navy escort group which will take our ships on to Halifax Nova Scotia; we'll take theirs back to the Mersey."

"MOMP?"

"Mid Ocean Meeting Point. And in the mean time we'll have aerial reconnaissance help from an RAF Coastal-Command Catalina squadron based near Reykjavik. That's very welcome because it will keep any would-be shadowing U-boat submerged. Whether the Cats can spot the U-boats I'm not sure – but the U-boats will certainly hear the Cats buzzing about and dive – which is all that matters to us."

"So, I'm not going to get my U-boat battle?"

"Probably not on the way out. But you will get another chance on the way back– I don't hope. In the mean time what do you want to do?"

"Not sure."

"I'm going to inspect the ship from track to keelson – part of the first lieutenant's regular duties. Follow me around if you like – I'll find the time to answer questions."

Sturdee was both impressed and appalled; impressed by how much had been squeezed into such a tiny ship, scarcely larger than a fishing trawler; appalled by the conditions under which the ordinary seaman and stokers were expected to live. The men were crowded into the tiny mess-deck in the forecastle. They slept, if sleep they could, in hammocks suspended from deck above with only an inch between them. The deckhead above leaked abominably in any weather, the ventilation was rudimentary while the hull sweated continuously – with the result that tuberculosis was rife.

"And do you realise Giles the bloody designers put the galley aft. To get any hot food up here to the men it has to be carried over the open deck– and you saw how bloody perilous that could be. They often go without anything hot for weeks! How they stand it I do not know. Every bloody Ordinary seaman aboard deserves a medal for simply going to sea and doing his job. We officers have it so cushy by comparison that it makes me feel ashamed."

Down in the bowels of the little ship they watched the oil-fired steam engine pumping away, delivering nearly 3000 horse-power to the single propeller shaft:

"My God it looks positively Victorian" Sturdee said "I thought it would be a turbine these days?"

"These Corvettes, including their engines, had to be built in small yards at great speed as a matter of national emergency. Anything more complex than a simple reciprocating engine was therefore out of the question. But the engine works, its bloody reliable, it doesn't need graduate engineers, and it gives us a range of 4000 miles on 12 tons of oil a day; we've got less than 3000 shaft horsepower whereas those destroyers have over 30,000 – but they have got no range. Every ship is a compromise. It just has to be better than its opposition. Our real problem is lack of top speed. At 16 ½ knots max. we can't keep up with a surfaced U-boat – which can do 17 ½. They know that. That is why it's vital to have at least one fast escort vessel, usually a destroyer, in every escort group. But they lack the range for the full Atlantic."

"I'd hate to work down here."

"Me too. But stokers are a special breed. In many ships, but not Corvettes, they live separated from the seamen. If we get torpedoed they would stand little chance of getting out of here. Either the boiler will burst, or seawater will rush in. Fortunately, corvettes are too small and too nippy to make easy targets. We can turn on a sixpence – unlike the big oil tankers. The U-boat skippers go for gross tonnage. At 900 tons we're barely worth a torpedo, let alone a salvo. But we have been targeted several times."

Back in the wardroom with a hot cup of Kye – strong Navy cocoa, Sturdee said:

"It was worth coming to sea just to find out how you chaps have to live. I'll never bellyache again – *and* I'll sit on anyone who does. We civilians have no idea what you fellows are having to put up with. No wonder you need your cheap gin and your free rum. I shall even be able to bear your insufferable pride."

"Not mine; I'm RNVR – 'hostilities only'. But I know what you mean. These RN types can't imagine defeat. They know they'll win in the end – whatever the odds. That's what 300 years of unrelenting victory does for you. Men like Noble and McIntyre are a different breed, certainly different from Doenitz and Hitler."

"If they can't sink U-boats they are not going to win this time."

"No – you're damn right there Giles. so that means it's up to me and you. And I don't seem able to sink 'em – try as I may – so old boy it's up to you. Joan says you're damned bloody bright – I've never heard her say that about anyone else before – not even about our dad – and she worships him."

As they approached the MOMP (the 'Mid Ocean Meeting Point') alertness aboard the Pimpernel increased notably:

"You'd be surprised how easy it is for two massive convoys to miss each other out here." John Duff explained "If navigators can't take sun sights or star sights for days or even weeks we will become reliant on dead reckoning, and if each of the two rendezvousing convoys makes an error of 15 miles you can miss each other entirely. And we can't use radio. What would be the point of coming right up here and then giving away our position – two positions in fact?"

The captain, Captain Gay, who turned out to be a very large, bearded ex-merchant-navy Master Mariner, twice the age of his other officers, was constantly on the bridge scanning the horizon.

"The skipper's the Senior Naval Officer for now" Duff explained sotto voce "It's his responsibility, to make the rendezvous."

"What happens if we miss?"

"God knows. It hasn't happened yet – not in my experience. But it would certainly screw up the whole convoy schedule – and the escort groups. Did you hear that Icelandic Catalina buzzing about this morning?"

"No."

"He ought to be able to see the other convoy 50 miles away in this visibility – and give the skipper some help."

"How?"

"Drop a flare in the relevant direction."

Sturdee was on the bridge when the starboard watch sang out triumphantly:

"Smoke bearing Green Four Zero !"

After staring through his binoculars for some time Captain Gay growled "Well done Stubbs." then he yelled to the Yeoman of signals:

"Hoist to Commodore: 'Convoy in sight, Green Four Zero' " .

The convoy altered course and the bridge filled up as most of the officers came to witness the magic moment when 100 ships filled the sea from horizon to horizon.

"Thank God for the Royal Canadian Navy!" Duff said taking his binoculars back from Sturdee: "Without them we'd be sunk. Yet they hardly had a ship of their own three years ago. They built 70 Corvettes in record time, and somehow trained crews to man them. As a result they have taken the whole burden of escort off our shoulders in the Western Atlantic. Bully for them. Look – there is their escort group standing off to larboard – waiting to take over from us. Four corvettes and what looks like an old World-War I destroyer. The skipper will order three cheers for them as we pass by. Then we'll go about and pick up their ships. Look how much lower they are in the water than ours – loaded down to the plimsolls with vital supplies. I can see at least half a dozen big tankers – they will have come up from Trinidad or Venezuela. Then there are 'Reffers', refrigerator-ships with beef from Argentina. Then there are low-slung ore carriers from the Great Lakes – mainly nickel ore and bauxite. When they get torpedoed they go straight down like stones."

Flags flew up and down the signal halyards as the British and Canadian escort groups exchanged charges and reversed directions.

"Tomorrow our escort destroyers will rejoin us out from Iceland," Duff explained as he left the bridge: "Capt McIntyre will take over command of the escort group again and our poor bloody skipper will be able to get some sleep. He's barely been off the bridge for 72 hours poor devil. Where these old chaps get their stamina from I'll never know. Come on, I'll buy you a pink gin to celebrate. I happen to know, first lieutenant's privilege, that there is roast beef and Yorkshire pud for din dins."

Sturdee's appetite, which had come back with a vengeance, made his mouth water.

The Pimpernel's wardroom enjoyed having a fresh face to argue with and make fun of. They were especially intrigued by Sturdee's sojourn in Germany – but rather shocked to discover that he had generally liked Germans:

"Why not?" He tried to explain "They're not so different from us; like a drink and a laugh and they help you if they can."

"Why did you enjoy Germany?" A truculent RN sub-lieutenant wanted to know.

"It wasn't so much Germany itself – as the lifestyle I was leading out there. Take Munich where I spent my last 18 months. I was working in a really civilized university with the some of the cleverest people I've ever met. My boss Professor Sommerfeld owned a ski-lodge and invited us all up there on winter weekends. In the evenings we'd sit around the log-fire drinking glau-wein , singing and arguing about Physics, which was our passion. And in the summer there was Alpine walking and mountaineering. And all around us the most wonderful music and opera. All my landlord's family were musical and played instruments."

"What about the politics?"

"Not being political myself I barely noticed it. Then a friend invited me to go to a Nuremberg rally to hear Hitler."

"Ah, so that's when you found out what a swine he was."

" On the contrary. It was an amazing experience. 100,000 people in the single stadium at night – massed bands – loudspeaker-systems blaring out anthems – orators working the crowd up into a hysterical frenzy – then suddenly complete hush. The lights go out one by one. Complete darkness – a hundred thousand souls waiting in silence. Then a single powerful spotlight comes on – and there in its beam is the Great Man himself driving into the stadium in his open car – arm up at the salute. "Sieg Heil! Sieg Heil!"– 100,000 voices cry out in chorus . Bands crash. The crowd goes wild – temporarily mad. The hairs on my neck literally stand on end. Tears gush from my eyes. I'm on my feet screaming with the rest of them – and so is Hans: "Ein Volk, ein Reich, ein Fuhrer!"

Sturdee could see his audience was shocked:

"It was only on our way back to Munich in Hans's car– that we began to feel ashamed of ourselves, almost sick with shame. We'd been victims of mass hysteria, whipped up by experts using modern technology – massive loud-speaker systems in particular. Not one of you would have been able to resist – any more than we could – not at the time."

"I would." somebody interjected not altogether convincingly.

"Anyway, next day Hans and I analysed ourselves, analysed the whole bizarre experience. Temporarily – and I mean temporarily – we'd been the dupes of Nazi hysteria – and we became angry – mostly with ourselves for being such dopes. It opened our eyes, politically at last; and what we saw we didn't like. And when some of our colleagues were dismissed from the University for " Not being of Aryan origin" we all had to take sides. Hans was so angry that he accepted a post in America – and I came home to fight Hitler."

Sturdee's story started a heated discussion about propaganda in general, and whether Churchill was using it legitimately to whip up the British people. They were, however, even more interested in Sturdee's expert views on radar: "I predict that within twelve months – possibly six –you will have sets capable of picking up surfaced U-boats reliably at a range of 5 miles. Their cloak of darkness will vanish." That set up another passionate debate about what would happen afterwards – how would Doenitz change his tactics?

As the laden convoy rolled and pitched its way South East toward Britain so the nights grew longer and the prospect of a live U-boat attack upon it increased. Relieved of *mal-de-mer* Sturdee could concentrate on the business which had brought him to sea – how to sink U-boats. He'd been flattered indeed thrilled by Joan's faith in his ability to solve the problem – a faith he would now have to justify . He spent much time in the Asdic cabin, listening through the earphones, talking to the operators, reading their logs, writing notes, and making calculations. Understandably they were not encouraged to do three-dimensional trigonometry but to follow drills – "when this happens do that"– and so on. As far as Sturdee could see their failures might stem from four quarters; the Asdic set itself was defective; the drills in which operators had been trained were misconceived; the 'plot' operated by the navigator to calculate exactly where and when depth charges should be dropped, had been incorrectly designed; or finally U-boat hulls were strong enough to resist British depth charges – except at much closer ranges than anticipated.

Trussed onto his bunk, notebook and slide rule on his lap, Sturdee worked through the Possibilities. The Asdic machine itself was in essence so simple any deficiencies would have long since been spotted by the engineers and operator; so he could rule that out for now. The drills in which the operators had been trained were straightforward. They had only to read off and relay on to the navigator the direction, the range and the estimated depth of the target. All those might change as a ship closed in to attack, so the most vital measurements would be the last ones obtained before the Asdic beam moved over and beyond the U-boat, leaving it in the dead zone of undetectability. From the geometry of the beam this final depth- estimate ought to be about one third of the last measured range before the U-boat passed out of the beam. It was so important because upon it the depth settings of the depth-charge detonators – between 50 and 300 feet – would depend. According to the Asdic manual a Type Seven depth-charge was lethal at any distance less than about 40 feet.

So far so good. What worried Sturdee most were what happened to the Asdic measurements next . They were automatically relayed to the plotting table in the navigators Cabin right next door. The plotting table was a crude analogue computer, something like a mechanical slide rule. It was designed to instantly turn incoming measurements into outgoing estimates of direction, range and depth, estimates upon which a commander could base his attack: for instance when to drop his depth charges, and what depth to set them at.

Obviously, there was much room for error in the plotting table design. Sturdee decided to test it out in a series of mock attacks. He would imagine each attack in detail, work out the simulated Asdic measurements with his slide rule, feed them to the plotting table, and see what predictions came out. Would they have agreed with the true position of the imaginary U-boat?

Each simulated attack required hours of intricate calculation. He then gave them to the navigating officer who fed them into his machine. To the officer's delight and Sturdees surprise the Plotting Table always came up trumps.

Sturdee's last hypothesis – underpowered depth charges – was a good deal trickier to work out. He knew nothing about explosives, nothing about submarine hull-strength and not much about fluid dynamics. He imagined that when the charge went off it would deposit vast amounts of heat energy into the surrounding water. The water would instantly evaporate forming an expanding cavity of very high-pressure steam. However, as the cavity expanded its pressure would drop. But if the expanding cavity hit the U-boat hull while the pressure inside the cavity was too high for the hull to withstand, the hull would implode.

Seen in this simple light he realised that he could use Dimensional Analysis because pressure had exactly the same dimensions as energy per unit volume. The energy in the Amatol per pound could be roughly estimated assuming it was much like sugar, which was itself a crude explosive. So, given 300 pounds of Amatol he could estimate the falling pressure in the cavity as it expanded in size: what it would be at 10-foot radius, 20-foot radius and so on.

He was excited by this ingenious calculation done in an hour or two, never having expected to get so far. All he needed to do now was estimate the strength of a U-boat hull .

Basically, the pressure hull of any submarine was a long cylinder with a hemispherical dome at either end. Its strength must come, he realised, from its arch-like qualities. You could take a circular section of the cylinder, imagine the water pressure pressing vertically down on it, resisted by the strength of the steel in the hull pushing back up. As the boat went down the water pressure would rise until the steel could resist no longer and the hull would collapse. Sturdee quickly arrived at the formula for the maximum depth which any boat could reach given his hull radius, its hull thickness, and the properties of its steel. That maximum depth would in turn imply the maximum pressure from a depth charge which the boat could sustain and thus how close the depth-charge would have to explode in order to crack open its hull.

Sturdee was so excited by his ingenious and yet so simple calculation that he couldn't remain in his cabin. He climbed up to the bridge – but there was no one there he could tell. He went aft to the depth-charge deck – but that was deserted too . If only he had had another scientist he could talk to, someone who could appreciate the spare elegance of his argument – Hanbury- Brown, Hans in America or Arnold Sommerfeld his old professor at Munich. Sommerfeld in particular would have enjoyed it.

When eventually he did encounter Duff and tried to explain himself Duff's reaction was:
"So, what's the answer?"
"What answer?"
"Are our depth-charges powerful enough?"
"I haven't calculated that yet."
"Well surely that was the whole point?"
"I suppose it was."
"You really can be a chump Sturdee... Mad scientist and all that..."

To get any further Sturdee needed to know the properties of a U-boat. Unfortunately, they didn't carry a manual on the *Pimpernel* but Duff thought he could recall from his antisubmarine course that the Type Seven U-boat had a pressure hull diameter of about 5 metres and a thickness of 20 millimetres .
"But what kind of steel John?"
"No idea old boy. They never went into that kind of detail."
Unfortunately the Pimpernel didn't carry a qualified engineering officer. Her engine- room staff were supervised by a Chief Engine-room-Artificer who dwelt with the other senior non-commissioned officers, so Sturdee went off aft to the Petty Officers mess to find 'Chiefie'. Chiefie, who was old enough to have been his father, and who had been brought out of retirement for the war, listened carefully. A Plymouth man, or a 'guzzer' as they called them in the Navy because they supposedly guzzled on Cornish pasties and Cornish cream, replied:

"They would almost certainly be made of mild steel. Anything tougher would be hard to weld. I don't know its strength off-hand, but I'm sure I can find it somewhere. When I do I'll send a stoker forrard and leave it with your wardroom steward."

Two hours later Sturdee had the vital figure in his hand: '20 tons per square inch'. He rushed downstairs to his slide-rule and notebook. The lethal range of a British Type-seven depth charge worked out at about 16 feet near the surface and perhaps 25 feet at depth, less than the proclaimed 40 feet, but not dramatically so, particularly considering the crudeness of his own calculations. Depth charge impotence was probably *not* the cause of the Royal Navy's failure to sink U-boats. He was deflated. He'd run out of ideas.

When the Action stations alarm went off it took Sturdee some time to realise where he was. Once he did he leapt out of the bunk, struggled into his life-jacket and shoes and rushed up to the bridge. Overhead dozens of parachute flares had turned night into day, their brilliant white illumination reflecting off the unusually calm sea-surface like moonlight.
"A surfaced U-boat has broken through the Asdic screen from ahead " Duff explained "He torpedoed a 'Reffer'– see her burning out there to starboard – and was coming back through the convoy when *Vanoc* spotted him and gave chase. He dived and *Vanoc* lost contact. We've been ordered to carry out an Asdic search and keep him down at all costs. The convoy's about to execute a big course-change, and we don't want him to see where we're going."

"I can understand that." Sturdee listened to the loud Pings that were being relayed all over the ship's tannoy system. There was no hint of a return signal.
"We've still got a couple of miles to go to his last reported position."
The *Pimpernel* appeared to be racing backwards on a reciprocal course to the main convoy.
"Aren't you going down to the depth-charge deck?"
"Nope. I can press the tit from up here. I prefer to be close to the Asdic operator."
"Contact!" An excited yell came over the tannoy and following the next loud Ping they picked up the faint return echo.
"Contact definite. Green 15 degrees. Range 1000 yards."
The *Pimpernel* heeled slightly as she switched to her new course.
"Slow to 15 knots" the captain ordered.
"Asdic works better at that speed " Duff explained, before shouting into his microphone: "Depth charge crew stand by. Salvo of four, firing from the bridge."
"Moving left two knots" came from the Navigator working with the plotting table.

"U-boats have to keep moving to maintain depth with their hydroplanes " Duff explain.

The Asdic returns were getting louder – the intervals between the out and return Pings noticeably shorter.

"Still moving left two knots. Range is 800 yards. He's deep."

"Port 10. Commence depth charge attack." The captain ordered.

"We'll lose the bugger in a moment" Duff swore: "Our Asdic beam will overrun him."

As if on cue the next Ping had no echo.

"Depth settings 300 feet ". That was the Navigator.

"Standby – depth charge crew. Maximum depth settings."

"There will now be about 49 seconds dead-time" Duff muttered "while we come up to him. Allow 20 seconds after that for the charges to sink .You won't to see anything from here. But if you go to the bridge wing you'll see the Thrower doing its stuff."

Something had gone awry in Sturdee's mind – though he really couldn't think what it was. He moved out to the port wing as if in a trance. something vital had been said or done . What it was he couldn't identify precisely. But it seemed to be mixed up with the trigonometric sines and tangents he'd been calculating earlier in the day Whatever it was he knew it was vital,

"... Six, ...Five... Four... Three,... Two, ... One ... Zero!" the Navigator called out.

Looking astern Sturdee saw one of the big drums roll off the stern rack and drop into their wake. seconds later there was a loud double "Tonk" and the ship shook as two more charges arched up into the sky from their Throwers and splashed into the flame-lit sea fifty yards to either flank. Seconds after that the last of their diamond-shaped salvo rolled off the stern as the depth-charge handlers swung their derricks and begun to frantically re-load the two Throwers.

The whole ship's crew held its breath for what seemed an eternity, until four stunning Thumps announced powerful explosions down in the deep. To Sturdee's disappointment there was no eruption of spray. The flame-lit surface merely seemed to jump for a second before settling back into place .

At that moment he got it: "Range 1000 yards; sine 16 degrees roughly 0.275. So the depth must be 275 yards – 800 feet!!!!!!!!!!"

Now he knew– or thought he knew – why the Royal Navy wasn't sinking U-boats. Yes: that had to be it. surely."

CHAPTER 7.
SUSPECTING THE TRUTH

As soon as the *Pimpernel* docked Sturdee thanked Captain Gay and went round to the dry-cleaning shop. He didn't have his key but Loader let him in:

"Well blow me down" Loader mimicked a West Country pirate "If 'tizzn't our owld peg-leg back from the briny. 'ow wuzzit it me 'arty?"

"Interesting." Sturdee pushed past Loader and into his office:

"Where is Gwen?"

"Upstairs – I believe."

"Surely you must know. Gwen !" He yelled up the staircase

A slightly dishevelled Gwen Jones came down with her dictation pad. Sturdee guessed his two colleagues had been enjoying what was in Loaders louche phrase 'a bit of nookey'.

"We were expecting you old boy – weren't we Gwen?"

"I don't want to repeat myself" Sturdee announced: "But I believe I'm getting somewhere with our problem. I suspect U-boats are diving much deeper than we bargained for"

" How deep?"

"At least 600 feet, possibly deeper."

Loader broke off in mid whistle: "I don't believe it."

"And why not?"

"For a start its way beyond anything our submarines can achieve."

"Which is?"

"Maximum operating depth 250 feet I believe. Why would the Jerries want to go any deeper?

"To get below our depth-charges – that's why . We have a maximum depth setting…"

"… Of 300 feet." Loader interjected "By Jove that would do the trick. But I don't believe it."

"So you said Loader – but belief isn't argument!"

"Well, for a start, how could they know we have 300-foot maximum settings? Their U-boats must've been designed in the 20s or early 30s – long before our depth charges. Then it would cost a bomb in performance characteristics. You can only strengthen the pressure hull with more steel – and more steel weighs – which is not good for submarines which have to eventually surface. To compensate they would have to carry less torpedoes, less crew, less fuel, lesser engines – meaning less speed and endurance."

"Yes, but I calculated their hull strength Tony. If I've got my figures right Type Seven U-boat hulls can withstand 27 atmospheres of pressure – that's 900 feet."

"900 feet!" Loader was incredulous. "Anyway, it's not just the hull Giles. Designers have to worry about stuffing-boxes, periscope-glands, ballast- tank valves, torpedo-tube doors, waterproof hatches… All the inlets and egresses that any submarine must have in its pressure hull. Ensuring the integrity of all those down to 900 feet would probably be impossible – certainly extravagant. And Gwen my dear a stuffing box is *not* what you are thinking – it prevents high-pressure water backing up into the hull via the propeller shaft."

"Then if they can't get to 900 feet Loader why bother to build the hull so thick and so heavy in the first place?"

"Got me there old boy– no wait. It's obvious– to resist our depth- charges."

"That's what I thought." Sturdee stood in triumph and banged on the table: "But don't you see – they go together. If you can build a stronger hull you might as well exploit its depth capabilities – and that is just what U-boat commanders have been doing. They go straight down to 400 feet or more – knowing we can't reach them."

Loader still wasn't convinced – but Sturdee didn't care:

"What I want you two to do is find out everything you can about the depth performance of submarines – our own, and the Germans' – anyone's. Much must be known… tests must have been made – even tests to destruction. I want to know hull materials, hull thicknesses, stuffing box technology, failures… everything. Facts not opinions please. The sooner we can convince the Admiralty the sooner we can get them to modify our depth charges and start sinking U-boats at last. Now I'm going to sleep for 48 hours non-stop."

"Blitzes permitting."

"It'll take some blitz to wake me up after that voyage."

When Sturdee did pull his curtains at last and opened the window he saw below him a tennis court full to brimming with young onions. Maurice – in gumboots and gloves – was bent over, selecting plants for transplantation, and tossing them into a wheelbarrow:

"So, our sailor is home from the sea – the huntsman home from the hill? We both missed that esoteric knowledge and astringent criticism – Joan especially I have to say. I do believe she must be getting quite fond of you Giles. She talked about you enough … worried about you. Absence makes the heart… Perhaps you should go to sea more often. How about a cuppa? Do you know we're selling thousands of our surplus onion-plants…? And reaping an absolute fortune?"

Sturdee tried not to blush when Joan gave him a rather more than sisterly hug on her return from the Ministry. She wanted to know all about his trip and about her brother John.

"I honestly don't know how those men stand it," Giles said "Tiny boats, monstrous waves, cold and wet all the time, alarm after alarm, no sleep, seasickness, cold food – if I see another tinned bully-beef sandwich I'll vomit – and I haven't even mentioned the enemy. Your brothers all understate the horrors of it – probably for your benefit. Don't be fooled. We civilians have no idea what our sailors are going through now – and it's only going to get worse as Doenitz builds up his U-boat fleet. As it was on this trip, we slipped through safely except for one solitary U-boat attack." He described the loss of the refrigerator vessel and the *Pimpernel's* subsequent battle with the U-boat:

"We made a dozen depth-charge attacks; and dropped 50 depth-charges , all to no discernible affect; he was still pinging away."

"So it escaped?"

"A destroyer came to relieve us while we returned to the convoy – but he had no luck either. But – and this is important– I think I know what's been going on. And if I'm right we can do something about it."

He explained his ideas to the other two, swearing them to secrecy.

"You are clever Giles. Didn't I tell you Maurice? I've seen all those mathematical symbols he uses – Greek aren't they? I wish I could understand them."

"I can teach you if you like." Sturdee offered. Joan appeared to think about it:

"Maybe after we've won this ruddy war Giles. In the mean time I've got a lot of stuff for you to do. On Thursday morning I need you to take me out to Ormskirk market on your motorbike. That's a dozen miles inland from here. Now that your pigsty is ready, I need to buy two young pigs – Wessex Saddlebacks if we can get them. I've made a deal with the manager of our ministry canteen: Half a side of bacon in return for two binfulls of swill a week until ready to slaughter."

"How are we going to get the pigs home?"

"In your side-car of course silly."

Joan and Sturdee knew quite a lot about pigs *in theory*– after all they'd been reading about them for weeks in Ministry of Agriculture pamphlets. But they'd never actually encountered one in the flesh, and had no idea how big and strong, how cunning, how determined and bloody-minded they could be when they wanted to.

"You'll nivver get 'em 'ome in that…" the farmer who sold them pointed contemptuously at Sturdee's side-car. "Yer'll need a lurry…"

Staring at the two black-and-white monsters before him Giles was inclined to agree. He and Joan had imagined two sweet little piglets:

"They two weigh more'n five score apiece. They won't tek kindly to being squeezed into that itty-bitty thing. I reckon you'll 'ave a mutiny on yer 'ands missis." He tipped his hat to Joan and vanished into the crowd.

For once in her life Joan looked discomfited.

"Can't we hire a 'lurry'?" Giles asked.

Enquiries quickly established that they could indeed hire a stock-vehicle with driver. But the cost of getting the two pigs all the way to Liverpool would practically wipe out any profits they could expect from rearing them.

"It's a seller's market" Joan said ruefully."

"By the time we beat the Germans Black marketeers will own this country." Sturdee said. "When I think of those poor devils out in the convoys trying to bring home the bacon while these swine line their pockets it makes my blood boil."

"Getting angry won't bring home this particular bacon Giles.".

"No, it won't. But even if we can get the pigs into the sidecar how are we to stop them from leaping out again and killing themselves?"

"By taking thought, " Joan giggled "I have every confidence in you Giles. A man who can defeat the U-boats........."

The shenanigans that followed provided amusement in public bars around Ormskirk for weeks to come. The sight of a city slicker chasing two rebellious pigs in and out between the feet of the onlooking crowd drew roars of laughter as if it was an entertainment specially laid on by ENSA. And when, humiliated in front of Joan, Sturdee finally lost his temper and rugby tackled one of the pigs, there were strong men in the audience who actually cried.

Ordered to get some rope Joan returned with a washing line she'd managed to purchase in a stall and the two of them trussed up the screaming animal until it couldn't move. Sturdee, with the superhuman strength generated by adrenaline and bad temper, heaved the beast across his shoulder, carried it across the market and hurled it into the sidecar head first.

"T'other one's over there mister. " the crowd cried out, wanting a repeat performance. Filthy from head to foot, but with an implacable blaze in his eyes, Sturdee obliged. The second recalcitrant porker, screaming in protest, was slung into the side car on top of the first, Joan mounted the pillion and Sturdee kicked the motor into life. The crowd gave way and cheered as the odd combination gathered way on its long journey towards Liverpool.

Outside the town Sturdee could feel Joan apparently coughing in distress behind him. He pulled into a layby:

"What's wrong?" He was irritated.

"Oh Giles…" she dissolved into hysterical laughter… "You were so angry back there…"

He wanted to slap her for a moment before seeing the funny side himself and following her into hysterics.

Their tribulations were by no means over. The pigs screamed for help whenever they passed through country towns, eliciting some very odds stares. And when no help was forthcoming the pigs evacuated their bowels into Sturdee's new side-car. Joan went into further hysterics which Sturdee followed. And when they did eventually reach Duff House a titanic battle of wills ensued before the two porkers were finally corralled. Indeed, before Maurice could prod and wheedle them into their sty Sturdee and Joan had first to go inside and lie among the new straw emitting what they imagined to be encouraging piggy noises. When Maurice clicked the bolt of the lower door behind the two pigs Joan could restrain herself no longer. She grabbed Sturdee's' two arms and howled with laughter:

"I'll never forget today Giles– never never never! That was better even than when Liz and I went to see the Sistine Chapel."

"It's solved one problem at least" Giles replied

"Oh, what's that?"

"Slaughtering the bastards . I'm looking forward to the day."

Joan burst into more laughter before looking into his eyes. "And how would you do that Giles?"

"I've a mind to borrow one of your brother's bloody great depth charges. They must be capable of blowing up something."

Back at the office Loader met Sturdee with a long face:

"I'm afraid Giles things don't look good for your idea. I have been on the phone almost since you got back. Hardly anyone has got a good word to say for it."

"Go on."

"First I rang people at *HMS Dolphin* – that's submarine headquarters – split between Gosport near Portsmouth and Aberdour in Scotland. They explained that there are three kinds of depth involved . First there is maximum operating depth – the maximum our boats are allowed to reach. It is 250 feet for most modern types and is never exceeded – except by very rare accident. Then there is test-depth – the depth to which a boat is taken just once during its working- up trials – before it is accepted by the Navy. That is invariably 300 feet. The 50 foot difference between that and operating depth provides a margin of safety. Then there is the crushing-depth or collapse-depth as it is more usually known. Normally that can be estimated only by calculation. Submarines have almost certainly been lost to crushing – but their remains have never been recovered. As you can imagine being crushed is not a fate any crew would welcome."

"I can see that."

"Our crews would like to go deeper – particularly those in the Med where the water is so bloody clear that, even submerged, they can sometimes be spotted from the air. But they stay above operating depth for fear of crushing. Apparently you need a good margin because your depth is not always easy to control."

"Why is that?"

"Because a sub's buoyancy depends critically on water temperature and water salinity – which can change rather erratically I gather. Moreover, ballast tanks don't always work with the precision and the speed one would wish."

"Explain."

"Well submarines retain depth control in two ways. For fine control they use hydro-planes – rather like horizontal rudders– or a dolphin's flippers. But they only work when the submarine is moving through the water – and they work slowly. If you want to come up fast you have to do blow your ballast tanks. To do that they keep a supply of very high-pressure air on board– hopefully higher than the water pressure outside – and when they let that into a ballast tank some of the water inside is expelled – lightening the vessel – and up it comes. But if you're not careful you can surface unintentionally. So ballasting is tricky– and has to be used very delicately, another reason why crews are reluctant to go down close to the maximum operating depth. Indeed, HMS Dolphin has no records of boats surviving accidental dives below test depth – that is 300 feet you remember Giles. And our submarines have hulls that are marginally thicker than the Jerries. So, you can see why they laughed when I mentioned 600 feet."

"I see." Sturdee looked truculent.

"However!" Loader sounded more hopeful "You insisted on facts Giles. And here's one. In the 1920s the Admiralty carried out real crushing trials on two obsolete subs; they lowered them into the depths until they imploded. Both reached 600 feet , twice their test depth, before collapsing. You can interpret that both ways of course."

"Ah! So what else did you come up with Tony?"

"Naturally I rang our antisubmarine warfare establishment at Portland. I even spoke to their chief scientist , a Professor somebody. You could talk to him yourself. He… well he snorted. For a start he could see no point in going so deep. It would involve losing too much operational performance – number of torpedoes carried in particular. That is what limits them – that is what more often brings them back in to port than fuel or provisions. And torpedoes are heavy – a ton or so each. The Type VII U-boat carries only 14. You thicken up the hull in a search for more depth – and you could quickly be down to a magazine of only eight . So, one can understand why he snorted Giles – can't one?"

Sturdy wrinkled his nose.

"But anyway, the killer is that one actually measures U-boat depth every time we make an Asdic contact. We have to – in order to get the depth- charge settings. The professor emphasised that. He said 'Go through the Asdic logs' ".

"Ah yes" Sturdee said, getting to his feet "I thought it'd come to that Loader. I dare say the good professor had something to say about how those measurements are made in practice? "

"I wouldn't know. But surely he ought to know what he's talking about?"

"My experience Tony is that no scientist should pay too much attention to authoritative opinions – so often they been proved wrong in the past. Indeed, scientific progress consists very largely in overturning 'received opinion'. It's not that old men are stubborn or foolish …"

"Then what is it?"

"I'm not sure I understand Tony. No one, so far as I can see, really understands the so-called Scientific Method. But important conclusions rarely rely on a single line of argument. They depend on several assumptions, axioms they are called, which may be unconscious. So, if just one such assumption is wrong so will be the conclusions. Our good professor may have imbibed some such false assumption in his youth. I have learned from some very good scientists – both here and in Germany – to follow my own nose – until such time as the evidence is overwhelmingly against. That's probably where I have something to contribute to the Navy. You chaps are raised to respect tradition – and with very good reason I have to admit. But we physicists are the opposite. The whole history of physics this century is radically iconoclastic."

"I'm not sure if I know what that means Sturdee. I wish I did."

There was a long silence between the two men, neither knowing where to go next. Eventually Loader broke the silence: "You have never explained Giles what gave you your depth idea in the first place. That might help."

"Oh, it was pretty obvious really. Nothing clever at all. It's just that I'd been doing a lot of Asdic calculating the day before: nothing elaborate – just schoolboy trigonometry. Do you recall any?"

"Of course. We naval officers need it for navigating."

"I'd forgotten that. Well you know the Asdic beam on a ship points downwards at 16 degrees? The apparatus measures the range of the U-boat– from the time delay of the 'return' and the depth is then the range multiplied by the Sine of 16 degrees. That came up so often in my calculations I'd memorised it: Sine 16 degrees is 0.275, right?"

"If you say so."

"Well when our Asdic man sang out 'Range 1000 yards' over the intercom, subconsciously, not consciously, I must have translated that into 'Depth 275 yards– that's over 800 feet' ."

"Christ!"

"But the penny didn't drop for a few minutes . And even then I had grave doubts. And when I asked the operator afterwards, he didn't know any trig. –

but more important, he said, operators had been warned not to use extreme ranges to calculate depths."

"Why not?"

"Because of the pitching of the vessel. As its bow goes up and down so does the Asdic beam. Thus a shallow U-boat might appear to be much deeper than it really was."

"Or shallower."

"True. But the general point is that Asdic depths are obviously more unreliable at long-range than they are short. Right?"

"Right."

"So, operators are actually trained to use only the shortest-range echoes."

"And? "

"They are the very ones most affected by the dead-time – the disappearance of the U-boat under the beam."

"I see."

"But here's the point Tony: that particular attack took place in conditions of rare, very rare dead calm. So, there was no reason to question the depth estimate at long-range– 275 yards, 800 and odd feet. In fact it was probably far more accurate than the close-range estimate – with all its dead- time."

"I'm beginning to see…"

"But I was still far from convinced. It was only after the attack was over– and I could go back down to my bunk, that I could calculate the U-boat's hull-strength and hence depth-capability. When that also came out above 800 feet, I began to see the light. Mind you I couldn't convince anybody on board – least of all be antisubmarine officer."

"Duff?"

"Yes."

"Why not?"

"For a start he wasn't convinced by my hull-strength calculations. If you ask me, he was too shagged out to concentrate."

"I'm not."

"You?" Sturdee sounded astounded.

"I'm not a complete fool you know Giles."

"It's not that…" Sturdee hastened to explain. "It's that you are generally such a sceptical bugger."

"That's my job isn't it?"

"Yes… I suppose it is… Of course it is."

" So, if you can convince me Giles, we might all be going somewhere; I might be able to convince other naval officers – where a boffin like you couldn't."

It took Sturdee some minutes to see Loader's point:

"Very well Tony. If you can suppress your scepticism for a moment bring your chair round here and we will go through the calculation step-by-step on this pad. Then you can take it away and think about it afterwards."

On the pad Sturdee drew two exact circles one just inside the other:

"That's the cross-section of a U-boat cylindrical pressure-hull."

He tore out the page, took some scissors and cut through the page right across the diameter of the circle. He gave one half of the page to Loader, the other he kept for himself:

"Know what you've got there?"

Loader rotated his piece: "It's a C-shaped sort of semi-circular arch."

"Exactly. And How does an arch work?"

" The load presses down and is resisted by the floor pressing up on the two feet of the arch."

"Good. Now this arch is underwater Tony, deep underwater. So above it let's colour in the water – which is the load pressing down on our arch." He cross- hatched the paper above the arch with his pencil until it reached a surface with waves on it. Loader did likewise.

"Now let's calculate the load. Obviously it's the weight of water above the arch. And that's equal to the depth H, times the spread of the arch D, times the density of water in pounds-per-cubic-foot, times the acceleration of gravity 'g'. Right?"

Loader chewed his pencil thoughtfully.

"Take your time Tony. There's no rush."

"I agree." Loader conceded eventually. "It's the weight crushing down on the arch."

"Which is resisted by these two legs one diameter apart i.e. D apart. Now each arch has thickness T and a strength S – meaning to say it can resist a stress of S tons per square inch before collapsing. Right?"

"Right."

" Now what we have here Tony is precisely the situation of a cylindrical pressure hall pushing back against the surrounding pressure. My half is pushing against yours, yours pushing back against mine. It doesn't matter which is up or which is down because water pressure is always equal in all directions. Right?"

"I guess so."

"So let us ignore my drawing and concentrate on yours. Yours is the upper half of the U-boat hull supporting the weight of the water column above it, which is, as we have agreed, depth H times D times water-density times gravity. That's resisted by two feet of thickness T and strength S, so collapse will only occur when H times D times water-density times g exceeds 2 times S times T. So the maximum depth the hull can withstand is?"

Loader sucked his pencil and then wrote down rather childishly:

"When H exceeds two S times T divided by D times water-density times g."

"Are you sure?"

"I think so. I mean it makes sense doesn't it? If we increase S the strength, or T the thickness, we can go deeper , but if we were to increase the hull diameter D or the density of water or the force of gravity g we couldn't go so deep."

"Yep – that's a good way to think of it. Any other formula wouldn't make sense. Scientists often think that way. "

"So, let's put in the numbers."

"No! I don't want you to do that yet – not yet. First you need to convince yourself, absolutely convince yourself, that this maximum depth formula is right. Take your time. Think about it overnight if necessary. Try to derive it for yourself – without being influenced by me. Only then – if you can so convince yourself – will you believe the numbers which come out of it. I know that from personal experience as a scientist Tony. If I go the other way and arrive at a number I don't like, I'm inclined to go back and cook the books."

When Sturdee got into work next day he was greeted by a furious Loader:

"Christ – what kept you Giles? You're at least three hours late!"

"Since when did we keep office hours? But I'm sorry. Our bloody pigs disappeared last night. We thought they'd been poached by rustlers. But guess what – the police had found them wandering round a shopping centre two miles away. It cost us an arm and a leg to get them home again. And I daresay the bastards will escape again. They evidently enjoyed themselves. You could see it by the smirk on their faces."

"Steady old boy – you mustn't let such things get under your skin."

"Huh – what do you know Loader? Churchill apparently keeps pigs and he says 'Dogs look up to you; cats look down on you – but pigs treat you like equals!' I'll swear these two – Damn and Blast we call them, spend their considerable leisure time planning."

"They have got to you. Gwen and I thought you might have been bombed."

"Anyway, what's the hurry?"

"Ah yes Sturdee. You set me some homework– and I did it. In fact I spent half the bloody night worrying about it – your damned formula. At one point I woke up thinking I'd found a flaw. But no. Fascinating I have to say. Like a crossword – but much more interesting – not to say momentous."

"Well?"

"I'm absolutely convinced – bloody sure it's right Giles. It couldn't be other than it is. Now I want you to give me the numbers."

"Positive?"

"Yes."

"You can't change your mind you know."

"I'm not going to."

"Very well." Sturdee retrieved a file and began copying some figures on to notepaper:

"I'm giving you the numbers in two different sets of units – in pounds and inches, and in kilograms and metres. That way you will get a double check – but both should come to the same answer."

Loader went to his own office while Sturdee went up to the kitchen to make some tea and chat with Gwen.

"Tony – I mean Lieutenant Loader– has set me going through old minutes of the Escort Washout Committee."

"What's that?"

"It's an idea of the admiral's. When escort groups get back, their officers are supposed to all sit round a table, together with members of the admiral's staff, to discuss what happened during their last convoys. It's mainly to see where tactics might be improved or where the Western Approaches Convoy Instructions could be amended. Everyone is very keen on them. Sometimes merchant navy captains are invited to attend. The admiral calls it 'My Brains Trust' ."

"What a great idea." Sturdee sipped his tea while absent-mindedly admiring Wren Jones's breasts. No wonder Loader fancied her. He was surprised to notice that she wore a wedding ring, and immediately felt guilty.

"What did Loader tell you to look for?"

"Anything to do with U-boat depths."

"Any luck?"

"Not much, though this morning I did come across something. Several weeks ago, Escort Group 5 reported a U-boat down below 600 or 700 feet."

"Good heavens!" Sturdee spilt his tea : "Can I see it?"

"If you'd like to wait here sir I'll look for it in my office."

"For God's sake don't call me 'Sir'. I'm younger than Loader. Call me Giles wren…"

"Yes sir… I mean no sir… I mean Giles…"

" I'll call you Gwen – like he does."

"Very well sir … I mean…" She disappeared around the corner in confusion.

"Loader is right about one thing," he thought "She really does have a lovely little bottom". Then he felt ashamed of himself. Married women weren't supposed to have bottoms – at least not bottoms other men could legitimately admire.

When the Wren returned her extract indeed proved relevant. *HMS Walker*, commanded by Captain Donald McIntyre had been escorting a convoy not far off the coast of Derry when it was attacked by a submerged U-boat in broad daylight and one ship was torpedoed and sunk. The weather was warm and sunny, the sea preternaturally calm.

"Now that's important." Sturdee remarked.

Since the U-boat was submerged, and therefore moving slowly, McIntyre instituted an asdic search to the rear of the convoy. Sure enough they picked up a clear asdic contact and went into the attack. But then, in McIntyre's own words: ' To our dismay the contact was lost at 500 yards – much further away than normal. We began to suspect it must be one of those maddening shoals of fish which so often give an echo to our ping . However, when a wider search was made, there was a solid echo with all the characteristics of a submarine under way. Confidence restored, we ran in for another attack but once again contact was lost at 500 yards or so, and when next picked up the target was far from where it was calculated it should be at the time... It was clear we were up against a U-boat with capabilities of deep diving and rapid manoeuvre greater than any with which they had been credited to date. The range at which contact was lost was an indication of the great depth of the target, for the asdic beam was fixed in elevation... To lose contact at 500 yards means the U-boat was some 600 to 700 feet deep... We eventually, to our chagrin, lost contact."

That then followed a transcript of the lengthy discussion in Noble's brains trust which followed McIntyre's report. In essence the entire Trust had proved sceptical. It was pointed out that the meteorological and sea conditions had been most unusual for the North Atlantic. Under such condition, steep gradients of temperature and salinity might build up and divert the normally straight courses of acoustic beams. This was finally accepted – and the discussion had moved on.

"I should have thought," Sturdee muttered to himself. "On a warm day temperature gradients should make U-boats appear shallower – not deeper..."

"Ah there you are Giles! " Loader burst into the room:

"I've done it. I've calculated it both ways – in meters and feet. You're right , absolutely bloody right! U-boats can get below 800 feet. Our boss Gwen is a really smart chap! You wouldn't think so to look at him, would you Gwennie? But he is ; he bloody is. I've a good mind to kiss him – but why don't I kiss you instead."

CHAPTER 8

GOING DEEP

At Duff House Maurice Picton was thrilled by Germany's invasion of the Balkans:

"What did I tell you Sturdee? Our blockade is beginning to work. Hitler had to break out somewhere in search of new supplies, particularly oil. The Rumanian fields at Ploesti will never provide enough. Either he had to go for the Caucasus or for Persia. I'm surprised – it looks like he's opted for the Middle East."

"What are you so happy about? If you ask me it's a disaster for us. He's thrown us out of Greece – I don't know how many ships the Royal Navy has lost evacuating our army from Crete."

"Churchill was a fool to try and defend Greece. But he can't resist disastrous amphibious operations. You'd think he would have learned after Gallipoli."

"Fool or not Maurice, Hitler's now got airfields within reach of the Suez Canal. We could lose the entire Mediterranean, North Africa and with it the Middle East."

"But don't you see Giles– that's it? If he fights a naval battle in the Med he will have to divert U-boat forces out of the Atlantic – where he is short of numbers already – giving us immediate relief."

"I hadn't thought of that."

" Because you're not a military historian Giles. Hitler has forgotten his 'schwerpunkt'– the critical point in any battle. He did it at the Battle of Britain by diverting his attack from our fighter airfields – just as he was about to win – on to London. Now he's done it again. Churchill may be no military commander – but Hitler looks to be even worse. It illustrates an old maxim – "You don't have to be good to win – just better than your adversary'. "

"Well I hope you're right Maurice. After last month's sinkings – nearly 700,000 tons of merchant shipping – we need every tiny bit of help we can get. But I have to say – as a mere scientist – that your theory sounds like academic hocus-pocus to me. It sounds more like we're losing all over the board – both in the Med *and* the Atlantic."

"The dark before the dawn dear boy."

"In the meantime, it's your turn to carry the pig swill. I did it both times yesterday."

The swill arrived by a rag and bone man's horse and cart twice a week. Sturdee hadn't realised but it had to be boiled before it was fit for the pigs to eat. Joan had volunteered for this grisly duty and boiled the swill in a witch's cauldron over a gas ring in the scullery. While it was bubbling the whole back of the house smelt of sour vegetables and rancid meat.

"It has to be done" she explained through a makeshift mask "Otherwise the animals will get dysentery."

For their part Sturdee and Picton had to deliver buckets of the noisome brew down the seventy yards to the sty – morning and evening.".

Despite his initial animosity Sturdee was growing fond of Damn and Blast: their so evident enjoyment of the small pleasures in life, their extroversion, even their humour appealed to an introvert like himself. He whittled them a back-scratcher and would lean over their wall scratching away while they emitted extravagant grunts of appreciation.

"And they are so clean." Joan boasted when she took over the scratcher: "They never mess – except in the corner most distant from their bedding. It's filthy farmers who make filthy pigs. The poor creatures can't help themselves. No more could we in the same circumstances. And how they are growing Giles."

"I know – it means they're going to need more food soon."

"I've got a plan. In the wild, pigs root. Now most of this end of the garden is wild paddock isn't it? The owners used it to browse their horses. So we can put the pigs out to root for themselves most of the day – until the apples and pears start fruiting – when they can feast on windfalls."

"Yes, but how are you going to prevent them getting into your kitchen garden?"

"I've been reading about that. It's a good thing you are a scientist Giles. You will have to construct an electric fence. It doesn't sound difficult – and we could buy materials out of our onion receipts."

Sturdee stifled a protest – unwilling to get into Miss Duff's bad books.

"My brother Gordon can help you. He will be here this Saturday on a whole week's leave."

"I read your note." Noble said to Sturdee and Loader, looking more like a wise old eagle than ever:

"Very interesting idea. It would certainly explain a lot. But is it right – that is the question? I took it with me when I flew down to the Prime Minister's anti-U-boat committee on Wednesday. Thank goodness the sinkings this month are down by almost 200,000 tons, so the PM was in a relatively good mood. Unwisely perhaps I floated your paper as a trial balloon."

"Gosh!" Loader couldn't restrain himself.

"I am sorry to say it didn't float for long. Admiral Sir Max Horton was there; C in C of all our submarines. 'Preposterous!' was the word he used, I'm afraid. And the PM listens to him, as he should where submarines are concerned."

"Did he give any reason?" Sturdee asked.

"Only that British submarines never exceed 300 feet."

"But that is not a good argument."

"Maybe not. But I didn't press the point… at that moment. After all we want the depth-charge design altered as soon as possible. We don't want endless haggling. That requires stronger evidence than you've got at present. Find that Sturdee and I'll go in to bat. How was your trip by the way?"

Sturdee realised the interview was over and bit his tongue.

"What kind of evidence *will* convince them?" Sturdee almost shouted at Loader back in their office.

"Obviously not mathematical formulae old boy. I suppose the capture of a U-boat would deliver the real McCoy. But there's not much chance of that. Even when they abandon ship like Kretchmar and his crew did – they open the seacocks and scuttle the vessel first. Can't blame them can you. I'm sure we'd do the same in the circs. Meantime Gwen is going through all the escort logs. You never know she might still turn up trumps."

"I want to talk to that McIntyre fellow – he carries a lot of weight doesn't he?"

"None more – since he sank their Aces. Let me look at the Escort schedule to find out when he's ashore next."

Captain Donald George Frederick Wyville McIntyre, DSO, RN had a chubby face and eyes that seemed to be looking for the next good laugh. He stood in his cabin on the *Walker*, captain's cap pulled well down over his eyes, hands in his jacket pockets as if he didn't know what to do with them, a common affliction among senior British naval officers so Sturdee had observed:

"What can I do for you Sturdee? The Admiral has mentioned your name – in glowing terms I should say."

"I am sorry to bother you Sir– but it's about the depths U-boats can reach. I have calculated that that they're strong enough to get down below 800 feet, and I understand that you might be the only naval officer who might believe me."

McIntyre stared at Sturdee as if he'd seen a ghost: " Sit down young man. This is a story I want to hear – all of it!. I have always felt there was something fishy about that 'salinity gradient' twaddle. Too bloody pat, too ad hoc, too convenient."

"Have you heard of Ockham's Razor captain?"

"Can't say I have."

"It's a maxim we appeal to all the time in Science. It's invaluable. In essence it says, 'Always pick the simplest hypothesis for preference – because it is far more likely to be right' ."

"I like it." McIntyre growled "I'm an amateur historian you see, exceedingly amateur. But history is all about choosing between alternative hypotheses, and I can see what you're getting at. Losing Asdic contacts at 500 yards means U-boats at depths of more than 700 feet – no nonsense!"

"And picking up Asdic contacts out at more than 1000 yards – in calm seas– implies exactly the same thing. They are a long way down – below our depth-charges. And now I've calculated that their hulls are strong enough to get there."

"You're going have to talk to my Asdic people Coster and Ridley . I really trust them. Time and time again they've been proved right. If they believe U-boats can reach more than seven hundred, and they do, then so do I. After all they've got more experience of successfully hunting U-boats than anybody else in the Kings Navy." He emphasised the word 'successfully'.

"Well he believed us" Sturdee crowed to Loader when he got back to the office. " Says he'd have a quiet word with some ' influential shipmates' – whatever that means."

"A lot I would say."

"Unfortunately, he is being posted to Iceland."

"Oh hell!" Loader was furious "That is the Admiralty Personnel Department losing this war yet again. Don't they bloody understand that keeping successful escort groups and their commanders together is – without question the most vital element in this battle? Sinking one of our own aircraft carriers would be a more sensible thing to do!"

The next couple of months were the most infuriating of Sturdee's life. As a young scientist he had no experience of trying to convince others and no real inclination to do so. When he had completed a piece of scientific research it was written up in a terse technical paper and sent off to a scientific journal. The journal would send it out for refereeing by experts in the field. If they could find nothing wrong with it his work would be published. Whether other scientists read it thereafter – or what they thought about it – was not his concern. At least that was the principle. It was based on the philosophical notion that good ideas should speak for themselves and not require advocacy. As he matured though Sturdee came to realise that such high principles were in practice more often honoured in the breach. The journal editors were very often big beasts out to push their own ideas, their own boys, their own institutes – even their own countries. He'd been particularly shocked to find out that Einstein's famous 1905 paper on Relativity had been rushed through to publication in a German journal without any refereeing and so had pipped into publication an even weightier paper on the same subject from the Frenchman Henri Poincaré. It was supposed among the cognoscenti that this was done so that Germany could claim the glory for Relativity at a time when France and Germany were at daggers drawn over Alsace. Even so, young scientist like himself had not been encouraged to try and advocate their own ideas. It was supposed that in the end Time would issue a wise verdict. But in war there was no time. U-boats were already sinking more than 100 Allied cargo ships a month and German shipyards were delivering 20 more U-boats a month. Britain was only surviving to the present because Doenitz had too few submarines to cordon the Atlantic effectively, with the result that 90% of all Allied convoys were getting through undetected. But all that was about to change – must change for the worse. With 100 U-boats at sea, as he could expect to have by the end of 1942 – Doenitz would intercept every convoy and the whole advantage of the convoy system – that is to say concealment – would be lost. And with it the loss of the Atlantic.

Sturdee would lie in bed at night grinding his teeth in anger and frustration. He, and he alone excepting Loader, knew how to reverse the terrible course of events – but nobody would listen. He had found it would be a trivial matter to alter depth- charge pistols to fire down to 1000 feet. Even a few such depth charges could alter the whole course of the war. Once U-boat commanders heard charges going off far below them they would no longer be tempted to go deep because their hulls would already be stressed, rendering deep charges far more lethal.

If Sturdee was haunted Loader was haunted too because it was naval officers of his own kind who were denying the truth, turning their backs on obvious salvation. In offices, in meetings, even in pubs he tried to persuade them of Sturdee's calculation, but their eyes glazed over.

"One can even see how this whole snafu originated Giles – a typical inter departmental cock up. The Future Requirements people issue an operational request for a new British submarine capable down to 250 feet. The Seamen's Branch said 'To be on the safe side, make that 300 feet'. Then it goes to the Naval Constructor's Office. They don't want to cop any blame if boats get lost, and anyway they're naturally conservative. So, they say 'make that 600'. The amended operational requirement is then issued to industry — to the shipyards that build our submarine – like Vickers Armstrongs. Naturally they play safe as well – not wishing to get into the Navy's bad books, so they add on a further 50% – and what do you finish work with? A submarine strong enough to survive at 900 feet. And I bet it was exactly the same in Germany. It's the bureaucratic caste of mind. It's even sensible in its way."

"Yes, I agree."

"So, everybody's mind is fixated on 250 or at most 300 feet – even the chaps designing our Asdic sets. They know or believe 'U-boats can't survive below 300 feet'. But then what happens when war breaks out? Some poor bloody U-boat commander, beset by depth charges, loses his nerve and takes his boat down to 350 or even 400. He survives. Better still all the mayhem is going on far above his head. He tells his mates and one of them risks 500 – to no ill effect. Soon they are all going down to 5 or 600 and the Royal Navy is completely buggered. I bet that's how it all happened Giles. And when someone sensible like McIntyre says 'Wait a mo' the know-alls come up with ad hoc arguments like ' Salinity gradients'."

"I dare say you're right Tony – it does have a depressingly familiar ring. But I don't see where it's going to get us."

"I can't bloody sleep at night."

"Me neither."

"To think that in this piffling office – this bloody dry-cleaning establishment – we and we alone have the key to winning or losing the Battle of the Atlantic... even the whole bloody war ..." Loader faded into incoherence, appalled by what he felt.

When Hitler attacked Russia on June 22, 1941 Maurice Picton purred like a cat that had found the cream. He said to the other two over breakfast:

"That's more like it chaps. I half suspected his Balkan venture was just a feint."

"Well you never said anything Maurice." Joan was tart.

"Maybe not out loud. But I did hint didn't I Giles?"

Sturdee was noncommittal.

"But anyway, my opinions are beside the point. The fool is now fighting on two fronts – like the Kaiser – and Napoleon before him. What do you think Joan?"

"I can't see that history has any comforts for us. Napoleon may have lost, but the Kaiser won – at least in the East. After Tannenberg in 1917 Russia collapsed."

But the Kaiser collapsed in the end, Tannenberg or no –we shouldn't forget that. What do you think Giles?"

"We've all noticed how the Blitz has markedly dropped off of late. I attributed it to short summer nights. But now we can see the true reason: Hitler is going to need every bomber on the Eastern Front. Won't it make life much easier for you Joan? Our docks and railways should be relatively undisturbed from now on."

"Let's hope so. Gosh, that's almost too good to believe…"

" Sturdee is right" Maurice pronounced, "We're not going to see much of the Luftwaffe for the next few weeks, even months. And there's no guarantee that Hitler will win in the end. Russia is an absolutely gigantic region. It's not a country like France that can be overrun in six weeks…"

A mechanical doorbell above their heads began to ring frantically. They all looked up . "It's the front door" Joan said ."I'll go"

She returned with a naval officer :

"It's a Lieutenant Loader for you Giles."

"Sorry to break in on your domestic bliss old boy, but I thought you ought to know. There is a strong rumour that we've captured a U-boat intact."

"Good heavens!" Sturdee leapt to his feet and, forgetting the security implications, explained to the others:

"You see now we can actually measure how deep a U-boat can dive. After that there can be no argument, and we can fix the depth charge problem. This is just break we were both hoping for."

Down at the dry-cleaning shop Loader was more cautious: "I did say it was only a rumour old boy."

"But such rumours tend to be right?"

"Yes – perhaps not in detail – but in general yes. Though I have thought of a snag."

"Oh what?"

"Their Lordships might want to keep this mum if they can. They won't want the enemy to know; the longer he doesn't know, the more useful secrets we can winkle out of it."

"I suppose so."

"You suppose right, but it all depends on the details of the capture. Did he get off a wireless message before surrendering?."

"But there's no time to waste." Sturdee was insistent. "Every Tom Dick and Harry will want to go over that U-boat with a toothcomb. That could take weeks…"

"Months more likely…"

"But first we've got a find out its depth capability."

"And how do we do that?"

"By taking it down of course – to 600 feet – or even deeper."

"You and who else?" Loader sounded furious.

It didn't take Sturdee long to guess the reason for Loaders reservations. If Sturdee, a civilian, was going to take a U-boat down far below any depth which a Royal Navy submarine had survived, his naval assistant would naturally be expected to go down too. And whereas Sturdee might have complete faith in his strength calculations one could hardly expect a tyro like Loader to risk his life with the same confidence.

Sturdee wrote to the Admiral:

Sir

It is absolutely vital we test out the captured U-boat's depth capability without delay so that our our depth charge pistols can be modified accordingly.

The only way to do that convincingly is to dive a vessel to 600, and preferably to 700 feet. Since I have complete confidence in my own calculations I volunteer to take the vessel down to that depth myself. Whether I could do it on my own I am not competent to judge. But perhaps I could be accompanied by a skeleton crew from the U-boat itself. Like me they would have faith in its diving capability, based on personal experience. If anything were to go wrong it is vital that Lieutenant Loader, who is apprised of the whole complex situation, remain ashore to carry on. May I repeat how urgent this matter is.

Yours sincerely

G Sturdee, PhD.

A few days later Noble sent for him – a more than normally bright twinkle in his eye :

" Your proposal does you credit Sturdee, a man with the courage of his scientific convictions. But I would have expected no less . Alas there are three snags."

"Three?"

"Here is the first" He handed Sturdee a note. It read:

"Sir

I submit that we carry out of depth test on the captured U-boat without delay. The only way to convincingly do so is to take her down to 700 feet and then test all her watertight mechanisms including the periscopes, torpedo tubes and propeller shafts. I volunteer to lead such a test dive, accompanied by a minimum number of other volunteers as required. On no account should Doctor Sturdee be allowed to partake. He is far too valuable to Western Approaches to risk his life at this juncture, though he has signified his intention to volunteer.

Yours sincerely

AJP Loader, Lieutenant RN

"Good Lord!" Sturdee couldn't help smiling:

"What a traitor. But I would expect you to ignore him Sir. This is my pigeon – mine alone. Anyway, with only one hand, he wouldn't be much use."

" Alas Sturdee there are two more objections to your proposal."

"Sir?"

"The first of course is that nobody is going to let you crush the very first U-boat the Navy has managed to get their hands on, my Lords of the Admiralty included. Everyone will want to extract the last ounce of information and intelligence out of this lucky break before handing it over to some suicidal maniac like yourself."

"But Sir…"

"Even the Prime Minister couldn't over-rule their Lordships on a matter as important as this."

"But sir…"

"It's no good arguing Sturdee. You may get your chance eventually, but it might not be for weeks… More probably months."

"But that's ridiculous…"

Sturdees protests tailed off. Evidently Noble was not on his side.

"And there is one other small matter Sturdee – which is not entirely irrelevant.."

"Sir?"

"I am sorry to say" The admiral smiled "Indeed I am *very* sorry to say–that no such captured U-boat actually exists. We did indeed capture U110 – but she sank while under tow. You've been fooled by one of those wartime rumours which, in a climate of secrecy, sometime get entirely out of hand – like those Russian soldiers marching through Belgium in 1914 to the aid of the British Army – 'with snow on their boots' ."

"Oh no!" Sturdee was devastated.

"But you can be sure Sturdee that if we do actually capture such a vessel you will be one of the very first to know."

Admiral Sir Percy Noble positively grinned .

Over supper Joan explained the situation to her two tenants:

"This morning I went out looking for that draft horse that we might borrow to do some ploughing. He's kept in the field not far from here. I found him all right – but guess what – he shares his stable with a young boy – a half-starved little fellow who appears to be living rough. It occurred to me that he could come here and live with us. He could be very useful. When we are out all day he could keep an eye on things – particularly the animals ; he likes animals – he could collect the eggs, boil the swill, help you with your firewood Giles… So on and so on."

"But could we trust him?" Picton asked.

"Your guess is as good as mine. He should be here any moment– if he's is going to come that is. He may be on the run… But it will have to be a unanimous decision by all three of us. Ah there he is." The front door bell rang above their heads.

When Joan returned she was followed into the kitchen by the wildest looking child Sturdee had ever seen. His eyes were those of a hunted animal, his hair stood out in all directions like a chimney sweeps' brush. His toenails were sticking through his shoes. His fingers, moving restlessly, were as thin as claws. His haunted eyes look warily back and forth between the two men.

"Don't worry about them" Joan said "They are my good friends: he's Maurice and that's Giles. I dare say you're hungry – you come and sit here; I've kept you some stew."

"What's your name boy?" Maurice sounded unnecessarily magisterial.

"Arfur" The boy replied defiantly as if he expected contradiction.

"You don't come from round here?"

"Nah" Arfur responded, attacking his stew with a large spoon: "Isle o' Dogs – dahn London way."

"So how come you're in Liverpool?"

"Me dad worked on oil tankers: Dutch Shell. When they closed the depot dahn there 'cos of the bombing we come up here – me and mum. Got a house in Bootle. Then dad got torpedered."

He took the wedge of bread and mopped up the last of the gravy with relish.

"I'm afraid there's no more."

"Very nice missus. Fanks."

"When did you last have some hot food Arthur?" Sturdee wanted to know.

"Sat'day night. I 'ang arahnd the chippy. Sometimes people gives me stuff…"

"How come you're not living at home?"

"Mum – she took up wiv this new feller. 'e don't like me an I don't like 'im. An 'e ain't got a ration book. Uses mine. So, I don't get much grub even when I'm there."

"What a swine!" Sturdee was outraged.

"He must be a deserter." Maurice said.

"Would you like a fresh egg Arthur?"

"Don't mind if I do missis."

"How come you finished in a stable?"

"It's warmer in there than what it is in a bombsite. Ginerally there's straw. And old Gem 'e gives off heat. Pity is 'e usually stands up. When 'e lies dahn we cuddles up close. But 'e won't lie dahn when there's bombs abaht."

"How would you like to come and live with us?" Joan asked, putting three fried eggs in front of Arthur.

"Free eggs!" The boy couldn't believe his luck. He tucked in, not answering her question .

"I mean it." Joan said: "You could have your own room in the top floor."

Arthur finished his eggs , wiped his mouth on his sleeve and put jam on the last of the toast.

"You could even have a fire up there on cold winters nights – couldn't he Giles?"

"Of course he could; especially if helped me cutting firewood. Can you use a chopper?"

" 'course I can. Oo can't?"

"Well then?" Joan insisted.

"Can't leave Old Gem missus , he's me friend and I'm 'is. 'e's got no owner now 'is driver died – what he did last winter. See Gem used to pull a Council milk float. But when he got too old the council puttim out ter grass in that field – wiv two uvver old horses; their drivers looked after 'em. Even got n'allowance fer bran. But when the other two got snitched – fer meat if you ask me, old Gem were left on 'is own. And if I'm not there ee's like to be snitched too; 'orsemeat is vallible these days. I dare say as he's getting nervous on his own. I told him as I'd be back later – but 'e don't allus understand. 'e is over twenty I reckon. I better go missis." The boy stood up.

"But you can't go back there into the cold and dark." Joan protested.

"It's much warmer now than what it was."

"It's still very cold."

"Leave him be Joan." Sturdee intervened. "Arthur knows his own mind, I can see. But I dare say a bit of money would come in handy now and again – wouldn't it Arthur?"

"Depends." The boy sounded suspicious.

"You'd have to earn it of course."

"Course."

"You see we need help – with the animals in particular – don't we Joan: collecting eggs; feeding the ducks and chickens: watching to see the pigs don't get into Joan's vegetables… you call around here breakfast times – when you've nothing better to do – and we'll give you jobs – and pay for the work you did the day before. You might earn 10 bob a week that way."

"Cor!" Arthur looked astounded by the munificence of the sum.

"One could buy an awful lot of fish and chips with ten bob." Maurice ruminated.

"I've had a bloody brilliant idea." Loader burst into Sturdees office.

"I thought I was the one who was supposed to have the ideas, your job to shoot them down.

"Remember Kretschmar's U-boat which McIntyre sank back in March?"

"U 97?"

"Yes. Well McIntyre managed to take off the crew before the vessel sank."

"Well?"

"Don't you see Giles? They'll know how deep U-boats can dive. The answer has been under our noses all the time."

"But how do you get them to talk? We signed the Geneva convention you know Loader."

Loader waved his arms impatiently:

"We don't ask them – we simply isolate the crew and bug their prison. They're bound to talk among themselves – sure to; wouldn't you?"

Such a brilliantly simple trick was bound to work – and it did. Within the month they found that Sturdees calculations had been right. The crew of U 97 had themselves been below 700 feet and they knew of other crews who had survived below 800."

"How did you think of it Tony?"

"It was while we were planning to deep dive that mythical U-boat ourselves. I was thinking of the minimum skeleton crew I would need to take down with me to operate the hydroplanes and ballast tanks : Jerries obviously. How could I get them to cooperate? As you say we couldn't force them. Then I realised – they already knew how deep the bloody things could go. We just had to trick them."

Sturdee and Loader, this time together, wrote a paper on sinking U-boats. Its main points were:

(1)   Depth charges should immediately be fitted with detonator pistols capable of at least 900 feet.

(2)   Early in any depth charge attack at least one depth charge should be launched with the maximum depth setting so that the U-tube commander would know that he had no chance of getting below the depth charges and would thereafter remain at comparatively shallow depth. This would dramatically reduce the volume that had to be blasted.

(3) That the deeper U-boat's can go in theory, the greater the uncertainty in their actual positions. In other words, the total volume that has to be blasted to be reasonably certain of making a kill will unfortunately rise with the cube of the U-boat's depth capability. Had that been 300 feet 10 depth charges might have sufficed on average to make a sinking. But at 600 feet an average of 80 will be needed.

But the critical point of their paper was the last:

(4) In such circumstance it is unreasonable to expect that the normal escort vessels accompanying a convoy would regularly sink U-boats. A depth charge attack employing 80 or more depth charges could take several hours. Detaching escort vessels for that length of time for the attack and for the time needed to catch up with the convoy afterward would leave the convoy unescorted for far too long. This is particularly true of Corvettes which have such low speeds (16 knots) and carry only half (i.e. 40) the number of depth charges generally necessary for success. Therefore, in our opinion, normal escort vessels should concentrate on keeping U-boats 'Down' so that they lose radio contact with each other and with headquarters, and with the convoy – and even corvettes are capable of that. However to actually sink U-boats the Admiralty will need to provide special groups of two or three vessels that can be sent to the support of the convoy under attack, groups with no other responsibility but to remain with a U-tube contact until such time as it is sent to the bottom. We see no reason why most such dedicated attacks won't result in success.'

There was a Postscript with a sting in its tail:

' The extra depth capability of U-boat means that dropping depth charges onto them from the surface is an extremely slow and extravagant way to sink them. It comes about partly because the lethal range of a depth charge is so short (4 to 5 yards). The obvious remedy is to guide a more modest explosive charge close up to a U-boat hull, something which would be affected by an acoustically guided torpedo. As we discus in appendix A such a weapon could be relatively simple and cheap because a submerged U-boat moves very slowly and yet must betray its position because it will have to use acoustically loud propellers to keep its hydrophones in action. When developed such an acoustic torpedo will render the U-boat obsolete overnight. Once it has located a U-boat using asdic, an escort vessel will simply heave an acoustic torpedo overboard and depart, leaving the automaton to its deadly business. The apprehension of being chased down into the depths to be so murdered by a mindless machine could only undermine U-boat morale. The Admiralty should therefore consider putting about rumours of such a torpedo even before it is brought into service. U-boats might then hesitate to press home attacks for fear of such a devilish fate'.

Sturdee and Loader were working quite well together now despite the nasty row they had had over Joan. Loader had started it when Sturdee came in one morning during the crisis over the imaginary captured U-boat:

"You keep that bloody girlfriend of yours away from me in future Sturdee! I won't have her coming in here and lecturing me like a naughty boy. Who the hell does she think she is?"

"What girlfriend? I don't have a girlfriend."

"Huh! " Loader was contemptuous. "The one you bloody live with of course. The one I saw you with the other day."

"That's Joan. She's not my girlfriend, she's my landlady."

"Don't try kidding me Sturdee – what sort of fool do you think I am? For a start land-ladies don't look like Joan – pretty scrumptious I have to say – you're a dark horse there – but more to the point they don't come round and shout at a chap in defence of their tenants – accusing them of risking their lives. She was like an angry mother-bear in defence of her little cub. Anyone would think I was trying to murder you."

"I don't know what you're talking about Loader."

"She seemed to think it was me that persuaded you to take that captured sub down to 700 feet – or rather volunteer to do so."

"Good heavens!" Sturdee was obviously surprised.

"When the truth was I was trying to do the opposite."

"I know. I know Tony. Admiral Noble showed me your note. Thanks by the way. I was going to thank you."

It was Loader's turn to look surprised: "Do you mean to say you didn't know that that spitfire came round here?"

"Joan is not a spitfire."

"You could fool me – and Gwen. She was here as well. Do you want me to fetch her down…"

"No, no…"

Loader looked at Sturdee in some wonder:

" You poor sap. You're such an Innocent. You're living in the same house with a bloody glamorous woman – and you have no idea – I can see that now – you have no idea that she's got designs on you."

"She hasn't" Sturdee protested. "Didn't you see her engagement ring? She is engaged to an Australian bomber pilot – a decorated war hero and a good egg by all accounts."

"I don't doubt you're telling the truth Sturdee. But I know a thing or two about women. They don't always realise who they're in love with – or falling for – any more than we poor bloody men do. But I'd like to bet – in fact I'll put a pony on it at evens – that when your landlady is going off to sleep and thinking of you, she's got more on her mind, or in her heart, than your monthly rental money."

" Don't be ridiculous. You're a sailor Loader – you have even less of an idea about women than I have."

"Take my bet on then."

" Very well. What's more I'll double your Odds to two to one against."

" That'd be stealing sweeties off a baby. No, we'll stick to evens."

Noble was both delighted and depressed by their paper. He was delighted because, as he put it: "At least we know what is going on at last. There's nothing basically wrong with our asdic – on which we so rely; it seems our adversaries have not developed some wonder weapon which must seal our fate – as I sometimes imagined in my darker moments . It's most unfortunate the mere factor of two U-boat hull strength gives rise to a factor of two cubed or eight in depth charge cost – but at least we can understand why and can hope to do something about it, in the long run."

He paused, obviously gathering his thoughts:

"What you are saying in essence though – and I go along with you here – is that we need twice as many capable escort vessels as we did before: one lot to protect convoys, a second lot to sink U-boats – your so-called ' Sinking Groups' – or, as I prefer to call them, 'Support Groups.' But where we are to get them from, and in particular to get them from in time to affect the crux in the battle when it comes in 12 to 18 month's time – I have no idea. Every British yard capable of building escort vessels, and in particular fast ones, has been going flat out since 1938 and is booked up for years ahead. The Canadian yards have done a heroic job of turning out Corvettes – 50 or more – in record time, but they don't have the skills to build destroyers – nor the high-pressure steam turbines necessary to drive them. The Americans have leased us, as you know, 50 very ancient Town-class destroyers which we are fitting with asdic and other modern weaponry – as fast as we can – but there are no more where they came from – and they are anyway marginally effective in mid-Atlantic. So I'm not looking forward to telling the Prime Minister, as I shall have to do now, that we need something like twice as many escort vessels as we did yesterday. I can see the thunderclouds gathering on the poor man's brow. All his forces are clamouring for more arms. The Eighth Army desperately needs more tanks to face Rommel's Tigers in Africa. Bomber Command is losing 5% of its aircraft per sortie over Germany and needs every heavy bomber they can get to maintain, never mind build up, the offensive campaign against German industry that it has been ordered to carry out. Without new aircraft-carriers we could lose the Mediterranean – and then of course the Middle East. The British Army lost all its artillery, its armour and its transport at Dunkirk. Where are their replacements to come from? Then there's the Blitz; we all know about that –and the populance, through Parliament, are understandably clamouring for night-fighters – which presently don't exist, and hundreds of anti-aircraft batteries – with the ammunition to go with them. In addition, we need thousands of radar sets – which haven't yet been designed – let alone built."

"But the Russians…"

"Ah I'm glad you mentioned them Loader. Ostensibly our new allies, they're likely to prove a real headache for the Royal Navy. How are we to keep them in the war? They and their Fifth Column are bellowing for trucks, for tanks, for aircraft, for rubber, for aluminium – for all the very things we most need for ourselves. Everybody agrees that we've got to help them but even if we can find the material how is it to be delivered to the Soviet Union? There is in practice only one hope: by sea around the North Cape of Norway to Archangel and Murmansk. In the strictest confidence I can tell you that the cabinet has already asked the Admiralty to prepare a plan to convoy supplies that way. Can you imagine what a horrendous task that will be? Quite apart from the arctic weather, our ships will have to pass around a German occupied Norwegian coast bristling with aircraft, U-boats and even heavy commerce raiders hiding in its fjords. Preliminary estimates suggest that on average every merchant ship will require at least one escort vessel to stand a chance of getting through."

"Good Lord!"

"Yes Loader – one can see the implications for us. Far from gaining escort vessels for the Western approaches we'll be losing many that we've got now – to supply the Russians."

The two younger men – whose hopes had been so high –were deflated.

"It is no part of my job " The Admiral said "To sow despondency in my command – on the contrary. It is just that I detect an unhealthy degree of hubris in your paper. Through some brilliant research you have indeed identified the problem facing us. I, and everyone in Western Approaches, must be grateful to you for that. If I get the chance I'll mention your names in the PM's U-boat committee. However, you haven't, we haven't identified its practical solution – not yet anyway. Yes we'll get our depth charges modified as a matter of urgency: I've put that in hand already, and I propose to set up an experimental sinking group – or Support Group as I prefer to call it– with two or three destroyers – as soon as I can assemble the right vessels and the right men. We'll need to find out how to get the best out of them. I want you to think about that in more detail – and give me your thoughts. Maybe we won't need twice as many escort vessels? At least I hope not."

"What about the acoustic torpedo?"

"Ah yes Sturdee. I was dancing on air when I read your appendix. It seems it will eventually sound the death of our foe. And I raised the matter with the Prime Minister – and he was excited too. But I'm afraid the news is not good. The underwater weapons people at Portland – who would have to develop it – were not keen at all. They say they are vastly overstretched already – which I can imagine is true – and that your torpedo would take 3 to 5 years to develop into a practical weapon."

" That, I have to say sir, is stuff and nonsense. It's an obvious case of 'Not invented here'. Since they didn't conceive it they don't want to see it work and so they aren't going to cooperate. You see that sort of attitude all the time – especially among second raters. They flubbed the depth charge problem – the 300-foot limit – and they're hopping mad about that – so they are intent on sabotaging the acoustic torpedo."

"Strong words Sturdee."

"I'm sorry – but it's all too obvious. We did enough work on the acoustic torpedo to show it won't be a real technical challenge – far easier than a conventional torpedo."

"Why's that – it sounded quite a technical tour de force to me?"

"It can be slow, it can run off a battery, only needs a short range, needs to carry only a small charge, needs no gyroscopic self-steering, uses a primitive contact detonator, and has a strong, steady and reliable signal – the U-boat propeller – on which to home."

"But the electronics – the Portland people say you have completely underestimated the challenge there."

"What do they know about electronics?" Sturdees sneered " They couldn't even get their dumb pressure pistols right. One of my radar colleagues would design and knock together an electronic self-guidance system in days – certainly weeks. It will be child's play. You only need to wire four passive acoustic sensors– which already exist – to about half a dozen valves and bobs your uncle. Portland's advice should simply never have been sought on the matter. You might as well ask a blacksmith to comment on fighter plane design."

"Well I'm sorry Sturdee. The harm seems to have already been done. From what you say though it's a battle you might refight with some hope of winning. But I am afraid it's a battle you'll have to fight yourself. I'd like to help but it sounds like pure science to me – not admiralty."

CHAPTER 9

ARFUR AND GEM

After Arfur left the house Joan turned on Sturdee:

"You might have backed me up Giles"

" I did, but our Arfur is a man of principle – he won't succumb to female wiles, not even bribery."

"Huh –what about all that money you dangled in front of his nose?"

"That was merely to get him back here. I want him with us as much as you do. With our crops and livestock we need someone on the premises day and night. Food is getting so scarce that rustling is becoming pernicious."

"I read in the newspaper yesterday" Maurice added "Of a couple who had their smallholding stripped bare while they were in church for Sunday matins. The gang apparently used three trucks and half a dozen men. I don't think we can afford to leave the 'Onion plants for sale' notice out on the road Joan. It's an open invitation."

Sturdee said :"I've had an idea of how to get Arfur to stay. I'll show you both after breakfast in the morning."

Being a Victorian mansion Duff House had an extensive collection of outhouses for the numerous staff who must have laboured on the estate. Sturdee took the other two out through the scullery next morning into the yard which ran along the side of the house under the windows of the kitchen, the scullery and the butler's pantry. Using a massive Victorian key he let them into the large building where he kept his motorcycle sidecar.

"What's this?" He asked them.

"It's a garage of course." Picton replied.

"No it isn't. It was built before the motorcar was invented."

"Well it's a coach-house then . It must have been a bloody big coach."

"And what did they use for motive power?"

"Horses."

"Two horses I imagine in this case. That is what the two -acre paddock down the bottom of the garden is for: to keep the family horses."

"I don't see where this is leading." Joan was usually in a hurry in the morning.

"Follow me."

They crossed the yard past the coal-house, the laundry, the servant's lavatory, the tool-shed, and the cycle shed to a larger brick building which was never used because it was stuffed with ancient furniture. Sturdee picked another colossal key from off the ring:

" What do you notice about this door?" he asked, inserting the key in the lock.

"It's double" Maurice replied "Half up, half down."

"It must be a stable" Joan said

"It was indeed. Come inside and look."

"Good heavens" Maurice exclaimed "That's a manger. I haven't seen one of those in ages."

"And that , if I'm not mistaken," Sturdee pointed to a massive trapdoor in the ceiling "Is the hayloft where they kept the fodder and bedding. It would also act to keep the horses warm in winter."

"This place is a terrible fire risk" Joan observed. If we got an incendiary bomb in here it would set off a blaze which we could spread to the main house."

"My thought exactly" Sturdee agreed. "We're going to have to clear it out anyway. I'll chop most of this furniture up for kindling."

"Now I see what you're getting at Giles" Joan sounded triumphant. "Of course! We could put Arfur's old horse in here."

"Yes but who would feed him?"

"He'd feed himself Maurice like he does now. Arfur would let him into our paddock every morning… it badly needs keeping down." Sturdee said.

"I was thinking of putting some geese in there" Joan said

"Fine – go-ahead – there's plenty of grass for all."

"I love a Christmas goose." Maurice sounded hungry.

" Then you can be responsible for them." Joan replied, ever practical.

"I don't mind " Maurice said "Geese make excellent watchmen you know. They cackle like hell when disturbed. The Romans used them all the time – even on their city walls."

"And look what happened to the Romans." Sturdee couldn't resist.

"I've got to go!". Joan announced "Are we all agreed then? If and when Arfur shows up we negotiate with him – or rather I negotiate with him – on the basis of him keeping his old horse in here at night. But he'll have to do his share of work.".

"Yes, and more importantly" Maurice added, always mindful of his stomach "We need to get a hold of his ration-book."

"And his clothes coupons. I'll see to that." Joan added as she rushed back towards the scullery door. "I've got to dash chaps. Don't forget Maurice, it's your turn to cook tonight!"

Since there was no rush for him to get to work Sturdee normally fed the pigs in the mornings. He was just warming their swill in the laundry when he heard the distant ring of the bell. In broad daylight Arfur looked younger and, if anything, even more farouche than the evening before.

"You can watch me feeding Damn and Blast." Sturdee said, as he poured their swill out of the cauldron into two buckets.

"Don't arf pong."

Then, as they were trudging down the garden path towards the paddock:

"Wassat?" Arfur hung back.

"That's the pigs. They always scream when they hear me coming."

"I fort pigs grunted?"

"They do when they're full – not when they're hungry."

"I never seen a live pig Mister."

"Then you have a double treat in store."

As usual Damn and Blast were on their hind legs, trotters on the gate, screaming blue murder.

"Giddown you buggers; I can't get in." Sturdee bonked them on their snouts with the scratcher.

Arfur watched in awe as the two Saddlebacks snuffled and grunted in their trough:
" Cor they'm much bigger'n what I fort."

"And getting bigger by the day. Soon one bucket each won't be enough. You know what they do when they get really hungry? They'll pick up a bucket on the end of their snout and hurl it upwards at the corrugated iron ceiling: enough din to wake the dead – as intended."

"Sounds like they got brains. What they do all day?"

" Not much poor devils – not in this little sty. I imagine they are plotting to get out. And they will when I have completed their electric fence."

At Sturdee's bidding Arfur let out the chickens and ducks and searched their nesting boxes for eggs:

"Cor this'un is warm Mister." he held it in wonder.

Back at the yard Sturdee unlocked the stable door: "What do you reckon this place is Arfur?"

It didn't take the boy long to locate the manger and infer its purposes. Sturdee explained their scheme.

"You mean to say Gem could live in 'ere?" Arfur looked around in wonder.

"Is it large enough for him? He's a big Shire horse isn't he?"

"Oh yerse". The boy nodded his head with certainty "Much warmer in 'ere than where 'e is now."

"And safer. He couldn't be snitched from here. So – if you can come to an arrangement with Joan I dare say this would become Gem's permanent home. Had any breakfast.?"

"Nah, not yet." Arfur sounded as if he had any number of invitations to choose from.

"What are we going to do next?" Loader asked

"I am not sure" Sturdee replied "Think probably. The order in which one does things in science often dictates the outcome. So it's vital to get the order right if one can – but usually one cannot know."

"Sir Percy wants us to look into our Sinking Groups."

"He does – but why do we want to sink U-boats?"

"I should have thought that was obvious."

"Not to me it isn't. If 'the safe and timely arrival of convoys' is our primary objective – as we have been told is the case at present – then sinking U-boats is almost irrelevant. We only have to prevent them finding convoys."

"But if their numbers escalate…?"

"Now you're talking Tony – yes, the more effectively they will find our convoys. But they still have to sink our ships. And that is where U-boat morale comes in. We know already that a small minority of U-boats make most of the sinkings – which suggests that many crews are either incompetent – or more likely – loth to press home their attacks. So U-boat morale may be the key factor. Remember we were going to look into that?"

"We were."

"That's one of the reasons I'm so keen on the acoustic torpedo."

"What a horrible beastly weapon! " Loader shuddered metaphorically "Certainly not cricket! There you are, a brave sub-mariner risking your life for your country – being chased to a horrible death by a lousy box of tricks. Where is the gallantry in that? You don't even have a live opponent to out-wit. You haven't got a hope or a prayer – all you face is certain extermination. In a way I'm glad we're not going ahead with it Giles."

"You can bet your bottom dollar the Nazis won't be so squeamish. I bet they're working on acoustic torpedoes of their own right now. Just imagine a U-boat in convoy firing off a salvo of five such torpedoes at once… five certain victims. Or an escort vessel trying to sink a submerged U-boat – which simply fires off an acoustic torpedo which blows the escort and its crew to smithereens. It's not a matter of 'if' but 'when' Loader. The side with the first acoustic torpedo could win."

"I suppose you're right."

"Imagine what history would say about us: 'Christian civilisation fell because two young admiralty scientists refused to develop acoustic torpedoes. It is believed that a Lieutenant A. Loader was chiefly responsible. He said 'It wouldn't be cricket…'. "

Loader couldn't help laughing.

"But seriously" Sturdee continued "We've got the acoustic torpedo on our plate as well. You heard Noble. As the scientist it's my responsibility now. And he's right. And you know what? I have no idea where to start. Who can I appeal to – who can I argue with? I don't mind telling you it's keeping me awake at night. All I've done so far is write to a former radar colleague of mine – who is it an electronic whizz – to find out if the guidance system is as straightforward as we supposed in our paper. If it is, that might suffice to sink the Portland people."

"Let me know when you hear back."

"Of course".

"In the mean time Giles why don't I have a go at Noble's Sinking Groups? We never said he'd need twice as many escort vessels did we?"

"No; that was his assumption. It might become true if and when all our convoys are being intercepted, but right now it's ten per cent only."

"The trouble is we don't know which ten per cent Giles. If we did we could simply assign the sinking groups to them. It would only need ten per cent more escort vessels."

"Yes, that raises an entirely new issue, Signal Intelligence, SIGINT or code breaking – which we haven't even considered here yet – although it might dictate the final outcome of the battle. How much do the Admiralty know of U-boat intentions – and vice versa? Quite a lot of I imagine – judging from the First World War."

Loader was to get little help with Sinking groups because Sturdee had been diverted into something far more interesting as a result of a conversation with Maurice Picton. They had been arguing about the Romans – of whom Sturdee had an unfashionably low opinion:

"I have never been able to understand how such a lumpish race managed to control the world for 600 years . They contributed almost nothing to science, to mathematics, to philosophy, to sculpture, to literature… while their politics was brutal, primitive and corrupt. On almost every front they took a backwards step from the Greeks."

"Aren't you forgetting their army Giles? That is what earned them their empire – and allowed them to hold it for so long."

"I've never understood that either. What weapons did they have that others did not? They used simple broad-swords and shields like their contemporaries and rivals."

"They had savage discipline. Few people who use the word 'decimate' realise what it meant. It meant every tenth man in any Roman unit which failed would be flogged to death."

"Typical Roman brutality. That doesn't explain how they overcame so-called barbarian armies 10 or even 100 times their size – which they regularly did."

"I seem to remember an article by a man called Lanchester Giles. It was called 'Mathematics in warfare ' or something like that – right up your street. I can't say I understood it in full but it claimed to explain the very problem you're raising. I remember being utterly convinced at the time. As far as I can recall Lanchester claimed that the effectiveness of any fighting force does not rise simply in proportion to its size. On the one hand, as in Roman times, size may be irrelevant whereas today, so he claimed, effectiveness may actually rise with a square of the size – you know twice as big as equals four times as effective as. You really ought to read it Giles. It could be the key to your submarines."

Maurice Picton's remarks had stuck in Sturdees's mind, but it had taken several weeks for a librarian in Liverpool Central Library to locate a copy of the relevant article in ' *Aircraft in Warfare* ' by Frederick William Lanchester – published in 1916.

When Loader chided Sturdee for neglecting their work he was met with:

"Look Tony how would you feel if someone had just persuaded you that the world is round – when all your previous life you have believed to be flat?"

"Shocked I suppose – but excited – Jolly excited and pleased."

"That is exactly my state right now. This man Lanchester," and he tapped the library book. "Has completely opened my eyes. Nothing we do here will ever seem the same. We've been wandering about in the dark. Winning or losing the Battle of the Atlantic could depend on the equations in this book. It's more brilliant than anything I ever read by Einstein or Heisenberg. I hope to God there is no German translation."

"Can't you explain?"

"Not easily – you see it uses calculus – albeit simple schoolboy calculus."

Loader looked crestfallen.

"Let me finish it; I might be able to give you an outline then – when I thoroughly– and I mean thoroughly– understand his principles myself. You see Lanchester was quite simply a genius – a vastly overused word. Do you know he wrote the first book on Aerodynamics? It was so far in advance of its time it it took others in the field 30 years to catch up. He foresaw the importance and role of the aeroplane in war – all in his spare time. He made his fortune out of the motorcar; built the first petrol engine in Britain back in 1893 and invented the hydraulic gearbox."

"… Used in the Lanchester car?."

"Exactly."

"Well hurry up and finish it Sturdee. Don't forget Doenitz is commissioning a new U-boat practically every day. Time is most definitely not on our side."

The arrival at Duff house of Arthur Ostragradski Sugden
–   for so he was named in his ration book – brought in its train many unanticipated consequences. The top floor of the house, hitherto blocked off by a beige door, had to be opened up to find him accommodation. Up two more flights of stairs it consisted of one huge room which ran from the front to the back of the house with windows at either end, and two smaller rooms with a simple gable window each. There were in all, four fireplaces.

"Obviously the servants' quarters." Joan remarked

"It puts a whole new perspective on Victorian social life." Maurice retorted. "Why this colossal room – larger than any downstairs, larger even than the family's withdrawing room? Did they have servants balls up here?"

"More likely they packed in a dozen poor servant girls in here." Sturdee remarked: "Scullery maids, laundresses, nursery maids, housemaids, lady's maids, kitchen maids… With the two separate rooms for the butler and the head cook."

"Do you realise there isn't a loo? " Joan said. "They had to creep down four flights of stairs and then out into the yard in order to go…"

"They didn't have time to go to the loo " Sturdee was cutting. "These poor creatures had to rise at 4 AM to light all 20 fires and prepare meals for the parasites on the lower floors."

"Chamberpots" Maurice retorted "It was all done with chamberpots."

"We'll put Arfur in here." Joan decided ,indicating the lighter of the two small rooms.

"I'm glad you chose that one because I would like to bag the other one as a studio." Sturdee said

"Studio?" Maurice looked quizzical.

"Believe it or not I paint, and the other room has a Northern light."

"I worry that he won't be warm enough up here. Surely we can't trust a child only 12 years old with a fire of his own?"

"I don't know. After all when Herr Hitler is doing his best to drop incendiary bombs on us…"

"It shocked me to find out he was barely twelve" Joan said "I nearly changed my mind when I saw his ration book. At that age school is compulsory. By keeping him away we'd be abetting a felony , or something."

"But if he's at school all day he won't be any use to us." Maurice articulated a thought in all their minds.

"I guessed he was younger than fourteen." Sturdee said "He simply doesn't want to go to school."

"We'd be depriving him of an education" Joan said.

"No we wouldn't." Picton retorted "Between us we could turn him into the best educated urchin in England. Giles could teach him mathematics and science. You could teach English Joan with a smattering of French polish. And I could teach him Literature and History. He'd have to learn because we'd threaten to turn him in to the educational authorities."

"What a swine you are Maurice." Sturdee said "A blackmailer on top of everything else… But you're right though – I mean about his education. He is a very bright lad– far more likely to learn from us than from a government school – especially now when so many of the best teachers are in the forces– or doing war work. Do you know they've called up physics masters to become bomb -disposal officers – pretty much a death sentence?"

"So that's agreed." Joan said "No school for Master Sugden."

"Now that you've reported his mother's boyfriend to the military police…"

"Oh yes" Joan said "I meant to tell you. They rang back yesterday because I might have to act as a witness. He is indeed a deserter– as you guessed Maurice, from the Pioneer Corps. He will be court-martialed."

"Could he be shot?" Sturdee sounded hopeful.

"Alas no, unless he deserted in the face of the enemy" Maurice said "More likely to get ten years hard labour in military prison."

"Huh – we're all undergoing that at present."

"I never knew you thought about my house like that Giles."

"You know what I mean Joan." Sturdee blushed.

"I will give you the benefit of the doubt – this time anyway. But if you are going to leave I'll need a month's notice."

"What about Arfur's mother?" Maurice hastily intervened. "Won't she want him back now?"

"She well might ," Joan said "But I put the fear of God into her. I said I was 'from the Ministry'. I didn't say which ministry…"

The two men laughed out loud.

"What a character you are Joanie." Maurice wiped a tear from the corner of his eye onto the back of his hand: "God help anyone who gets on the wrong side of you…"

"So I'm an ogress? You can give me a month's notice as well Professor Picton." but this time she grinned: "The point is Arfur can decide for himself. Now that I've got his clothes coupons and we cut his hair we can make him look less like a vagrant. Otherwise he could be picked up by the police and sent to a reformatory..."

"Arctic-steak rissole , with boiled nettles" Joan announced as she handed round plates. " One for us and two for Arfur because he doesn't get a cooked lunch."

"So what have you been up to my lad?" Picton asked.

"I wish you wouldn't sound so much like an examining magistrate Maurice. I've told you before, Arfur isn't a potential criminal are you Arthur? He is now a full member of this household – with all the responsibilities and privileges entailed."

"All boys are potential criminals – and not just potential..."

"I never et nettles before."

"Nor yet Arctic Steak, I'll be bound . I suppose it's Whale meat? I thought it tasted a trifle fishy."

"Whales ain't fish" Arfur announced.

"How do you know?"

"Reddit in the newspaper. Said it should be sold in the butchers – not fishmongers."

"So that's what you do when you're supposed to be looking after our property?"

"Got to 'ave me lunch ain't I? Joan makes me sandwiches don't you Joan?"

"Of course I do. Don't you take any notice of him Arfur – he's just a crabby old man. I'm glad you read the newspapers – because we have barely got the time. There might be something important in them that we've missed. From now on that will be your responsibility – won't it Giles?"

"Certainly! We could easily miss something vital – and get into trouble with the police. Blackout precautions for instance, or black-market regulations."

" They want famblies to 'and in their spare saucepans to make Spitfires an' that. They're going to come round collecting – or yer can 'and them in at the perlice station."

"For goodness sake don't hand in any of ours" Joan said. "We've got the bare minimum as it is – all second hand."

"I'm sorry Joan, I can't finish these nettles." Maurice said

"I et all mine. Joan picked them all wiv her own 'ands didn't you Joan? And she got stung. I reckon you should finish 'em off Maurice because they're full o' proteins."

"What are you spluttering and turning red for Sturdee?" Maurice sounded angry

After supper Sturdee went out into the yard with Arfur to say good night to Gem. The old horse , as always, was waiting for them, his head out through the upper stable door:

"I can see why you love him so much Arfur... he's all grace and patience... and wisdom... and kindliness... not like us selfish human beings."

Arfur climbed onto a tomato box and joined in stroking the gigantic Shire who was taller than either of them.

"You know I want to paint him? As soon as I saw his lovely face I wanted to paint it – and I haven't painted for a year – but now my hands are itching for a brush. And that's a good sign – I'll probably make a fair job of it."

"What'll you do with the pitture – when you've finished it?"

"We'll hang it on the wall naturally. And when old old Gem dies I'll give it to you – so you can remember him always."

"I don't want to fink of 'im dying."

"Of course not. Anyway he's quite young. 20 you said? I believe some horses reach thirty. Shall we fill his nose bag?"

Sturdee had found a big old scythe in the tool-shed and used it in the paddock to cut the long green grass ripening in the early summer sun to make hay for Gem, while Joan had tatted together a nosebag out of some old canvas. Both were now heroes in Arfur's eyes.

"'e likes to munch 'e does– specially in the morning."

Sturdee was startled when a large ginger cat leapt onto the top of the stable door beside him and disappeared into the stable.

"Who the hell is that?"

"Ee's nuffink to do wiv me" Arfur was defiant. "I didn't bring him. He muster come later on 'is own because he's a friend of Gem's. Used to live in Gem's old stable. I reckon he sneaks in 'ere – when I'm not looking. I'll shoo 'im away if yer like?"

"It's not me you should worry about – it's Joan. She won't like having a big cat like that about – not with the ducks and chickens…"

"Oh Higgins won't bovver with them; he lives on mice he does. He eats two a day, sometimes free . I seen him catching them down the paddock. Sniffs 'em down a hole then he waits for hours wivout movin'. Then quick as lightning he's on 'em. Anyway he's frightened o' ducks. When he saw his first one 'is hair stood on end, his tail stood up, he arched 'is back – then he run away and up a tree… I couldn't stop laughin'… He ain't forgive me yet."

"I think you'd better let me approach Joan about what's his name."

"Higgins."

"She's talking about rearing day-old chicks in incubators. I dare say Higgins would fancy day-old chicks – for his breakfast."

After Arfur had gone to bed and Joan had gone upstairs to read him another chapter of *Huckleberry Finn* the two men washed the dishes in the butler's pantry:

"I really have to thank you Maurice for your tip about Lanchester. His book has completely revolutionised my thinking about warfare. I can't quite see where it fits into the U-boat battle yet but I am absolutely sure it's going to. Right now I'm worried that the Germans might read it too ."

"You will have to remind me about the salient points Giles. It must be at least 20 years since I read it – and even then I couldn't understand much because he uses so much mathematics. I was in any case only interested in its application to the Roman army – which was my fascination in those days – before I got into Blockade."

"Okay. Lanchester points out that in classical times the main weapon was the broadsword – which had a range not much longer than a man's arm. So when the formations came in to battle with one another the only fighting and killing took place at the interface between the two sides: all remaining troops on the battlefield were powerless to intervene – right?

"I'm beginning to. It is beginning to come back."

"Lanchester asserts that therefore numbers were irrelevant in those days: all that mattered was the relative fighting quality of the individual soldiers on the two sides: it was in essence a number of simultaneous man-to-man battles. The Romans, recognising this, formed the first fully professional army. Roman soldiers trained and practised all day, every day of the year. As a result their swordplay was superior, their arms were much stronger and their stamina much greater than all their opponents'– who were mostly farmers or citizens fighting in a temporary war. That was the Roman secret – professionalism. So provided a Roman unit could fight in formation, never breaking up in to units, it could slice through an enemy army, no matter what its size, like a hot knife through butter. For instance it could head towards and capture the enemy chieftain – or his baggage train: Battle over."

"Yes now I remember Giles – of course." Picton was delighted as he dried his hands on the tea towel: "Amazing to think isn't it that such a colossal episode of history was founded on a simple trick – the professional soldier. You know Gibbon never realised that – he blamed the fall of Rome on Christianity. So far as I know Lanchester was the first man to get it right – and you say he was a mere engineer?"

"Don't be such a snob."

"No, I shouldn't be. Why should historians have all the brains? You know Henri Pirenne maintains that the whole feudal, mediaeval world derived from the invention of the horse stirrup? To resist the Mongolian hordes, who invented it, first the Persians, and then the Europeans, had to develop the heavily armoured knight fighting on the back of a war-horse like that colossus in our stable. Those knights then became a generation of gangsters who took over our society and called themselves 'aristocrats'."

"Lanchester had a very great mind – I'm convinced . As far as I can see he wrote the history of the Second World War 23 years before it even broke out. He's convinced it will be won by air power."

"Well I'm glad to hear that Giles; that history and historians are not entirely irrelevant in our wonderful modern age – even if most of our revered leaders are too ignorant to realise that."

"It is frightening to think isn't it Maurice that the Battle of the Atlantic, and with it – according to Churchill–'the survival of Christian civilisation ' could hinge on some tiny piece of knowledge such as Lanchester's Equation – which one side understands – and the other does not. If you and I hadn't been idly discussing Roman history over supper… I think it started from a crossword clue…"

"Well I find that encouraging – very encouraging Sturdee. If it's true, and I concede that that is a big If– then the most civilized society , the better educated in fact – is most likely to win."

"Don't be too certain that it will be Britain then. I spent two years inside the German university system – and by and large it seemed a good deal more enlightened than our own. For instance, it's not dominated by priest-holes like Oxford and Cambridge – seminaries trying to pretend they're centres of learning."

"Don't start on that hobbyhorse again please Giles. I suspect you're right but knowledge of it isn't going to win this war."

"I suppose not; though Knowledge of Lanchester's Equations might well do so. I am going to make it my mission to see that they do – if indeed they can."

"To change the subject entirely do you notice how our Joan has calmed down of late?"

"I suppose it's the reduction in the bombing– re-routing all those trains."

" Possibly – though It's not all on her shoulders any longer thank God. We've devised a proper management system. But I suspect it's something quite else. Our Joan is a born mother – from her Venus-like figure to her compassionate nature. That girl should have half a dozen kiddies of her own – and look at her– nearly thirty and not even married – nor likely to be for several more years if things go on as they are with a fiancé half the world away. No, it is young Sugden. She's putting her powerful maternal instincts to work on him; he has no idea how lucky he is; no ruddy idea."

When Sturdee barged in to Loader's office next day he was touched to find the naval officer pouring over Lancelot Hogben' s *Mathematics for the Million.* "

"You'll never learn anything out of that twaddle."

"Why not?"

"The man is a pompous fool. Great title, wonderful diagrams by Horrabin… but the text…"

"It's had great reviews."

"I know but I bet none of the reviewers actually learned any maths out of it."

"It says in the blurb that he is a distinguished medical statistician."

"That's a contradiction in terms. No, the man is a fool. He was at my university – Birmingham. Any man who is a dogmatic Marxist – as he is –must be a raving fool – must be ."

" But I thought you were a…"

"A socialist… a pragmatic socialist of the Fabian School. We despise Marxists – and they loathe us, because we've rumbled them."

"I was trying to learn Calculus."

"If you're serious then chuck that tripe away and get Sylvanus P Thompsons 'Calculus Made Easy'. But anyway I don't think you're going to need it – not to understand Lanchester's Equations. I was just coming in to give you a tutorial. They're bloody amazing. Every sailor above the rank of Leading Stoker should have them tattooed on his arm."

"But I thought you said…"

"Never mind that" Sturdee sat down "I'm going to set you a problem Tony which I want you to think about very hard, very hard indeed. If we get to the bottom of this we'll be half way there."

"Fire away."

"I want you to imagine a sea battle – between two sets of modern battleships. Individually the battleships on each side are of identical quality – in firepower, range, speed etc etc. They come together in such a way that every ship on one side can fire upon every ship on the other. The only difference between the two sides is in the number of ships they possess at the beginning of the battle. One side, let's call them the Bigs, has 20 battleships, while the other side – the Smalls– have only ten . Right?"

"Seems straightforward. Sounds a bit like Jutland in 1916."

"So I want you to work out which side will win, and more importantly, how many ships it will have left over after it's sunk all of the enemy's. "

Sturdee got to his fee to return his own room.

"But Giles… it seems obvious…"

"But me no buts. I'm going to give you 48 hours. – I bet you'll still get it wrong."

Two days later he returned to Loader's office. Loader's table was covered in sheets of paper while its owner looked as if he hadn't been sleeping well.

"What's the answer?"

"Well of course the Bigs must win. And I reckon they have ten ships left over after the battle. After all the ships on both sides are equally potent. So if the Big ships sink ten Smalls the Smalls must have sunk ten Bigs.. But I suppose that's too obvious to be right?"

"I don't know about that – but it certainly isn't right Tony. According to Lanchester the Bigs will sink all the ten Smalls but lose only three of their own. They will have 17 of their original fleet of 20 left over. So the correct answer is 17, or slightly more."

Loader looked incredulous.

"I can assure you the answer is 17 or thereabouts – but it isn't obvious is it? I was just as mystified as you now look."

Loader simply shook his head.

"Look Tony, now that you know the right answer I'll give you another 24 hours to see if you can work out how it arises – qualitatively at least. Never mind the exact numbers. And I'm going to give you a big clue. Ask yourself how long the average battleship on each side will survive."

The morning after, Loader definitely looked as if he really hadn't slept:

" I think I get the general idea Giles . Since the Small's ships have twice as much fire directed upon them as the Bigs they only last half as long, and therefore fire off only half as many salvos as the Bigs before they sink. Towards the end of the battle there may be 15 or more big ships raining fire on one poor surviving Small. It would be sunk in a jiffy. But by God it isn't obvious is it?"

"No it isn't. You see in this instance Lanchester's Equations lead to the non-intuitive conclusion that the effectiveness of a fighting force goes up with the *square* of its size: a force twice as large will be four times as effective – and who is going to believe that?"

"Until you understand that businesses about survival-time – then the penny dropped – with a loud clang. I spent the night working out the implications. It makes so much sense of naval history."

"For instance?"

"Well – take our Grand Fleet holed up in Scapa Flow throughout the First World War. Everyone was screaming at Jellicoe to divide it – send half to the Mediterranean . Had he done so he might have had to to face the German High Seas Fleet in the North Sea – with inferior numbers – and have lost in consequence. And if the Mediterranean half of his fleet had then returned it too would've been shot you to bits because of inferior numbers. So Jellicoe was right to keep his 'fleet in being' at Scapa ready for the Jerries to come out of Kiel. And when they did at Jutland in 1916, although the German ships would appear to have been superior – they turned tail and scuttled back to Germany, knowing the numerical odds were against them. And all this was before Lanchester published his article?"

"Yes"

"But doesn't that argue that Admirals recognised the importance of concentration before Lanchester?"

"Yes it does – but only in a general way. Indeed in his article – which you should read – Lanchester argues that Nelson followed the principle at Trafalgar, and Rodney at the Battle of the Saintes even before Nelson. Knowing he was outnumbered Nelson attacked the centre and rear of the Combined Fleet – knowing that their van, in the light winds prevailing , could never get back to help them. So Nelson had local superiority in numbers and crushed them."

"We were of course taught something of that at Dartmouth – but not the overarching principle"

" For that you need Calculus."

"Which I am now definitely going to learn. But where does all this leave us Giles?"

"That I don't yet understand. We both agree that the crux of the battle will be coming in about 18 month's time when Doenitz has his 300 U-boats making a complete cordon across the Atlantic – and we have as many escort- vessels as we can muster. Every one of those convoys can then expect to be detected by the cordon and will have to fight across the ocean with every weapon it can then command. Crucial to the outcome will surely be the ratio of escort-vessel numbers to U-boat numbers, and that is presumably where Lanchester's equations must come in. But the simple example I gave you might not be relevant – might not be relevant at all. It was assumed that every battleship had guns with a range long enough to hit every ship in the enemy fleet: thus total numbers become crucial, and the N-squared rule prevails. But consider an alternative situation when the numbers matter not at all."

Sturdee went through the example of the Roman army, as he had done with Maurice a few days before.

Loader's final question was: "Do you think Jerry understands all this stuff too?"

"I have wondered about that myself. 'Probably yes' is the answer. But would Hitler listen? He doesn't sound the listening type to me."

CHAPTER 10
SECRET CIPHERS

Sturdee and Loader always dreaded the moment when the monthly sinking figures were divulged. They were amazed when the figure for July came in at only 120,000 tons or forty three ships , only 20 percent of the sinkings earlier in the year,.

"Surely it can't only be due to the short summer nights?" Sturdee wondered.

"No way. Last years July figures were a hundred and five ships, and 140 in June – some of the highest for that year." Loader pointed to their list of figures on Sturdee's wall.

"Has Doenitz moved his U-boats elsewhere? The Med for instance?"

"If he had we'd have heard about it from the boys in Gibraltar. U-boats can't get through those straits without ringing loud bells."

"That leaves only one alternative explanation – Sigint – or Signal Intelligence. Either Doenitz has lost his break into our ciphers – or else we've broken into his. We haven't changed our ciphers have we?"

"No, definitely not."

"Then we must've broken into his in a big way. Remember that U-boat we almost captured – but which sunk under tow?

"U110?"

"I reckon we probably snatched its codebook, enabling us to break in."

"Possible I suppose – but the Jerries are very strict about throwing their weighted codebooks overboard before abandoning ship. You were going to look into all his Sigint stuff weren't you Giles ?"

"I was – but it's is all highly classified; top top top secret. Noble had a hell of a job with getting me the necessary security clearance – but according to Mansfield it has just come through. Perhaps I should use it before someone upstairs changes their mind."

Sturdee snatched a lift in Admiral Noble's de Havilland Rapide when Noble flew down to London to attend one of Churchill's 'Battle of the Atlantic Committees'. Armed with a letter of introduction he went to the new bomb-proof Citadel building off Horse Guards Parade where the Admiralty had recently housed its Operational Intelligence Centre (OIC), the nerve centre of all its naval operations.

Commander Rodger Winn RNVR turned out to be a very odd sort of naval officer – he had the twisted back and crippled legs of a polio victim – but he was in charge of the Admiralty's Submarine Tracking Room.

He smiled when Giles turned up:

"From your title – 'Chief Scientist Western Approaches Command' I was expecting a grizzled old professor."

"Oh that? Giles laughed. "As far as I know I'm the *only* scientist in Western Approaches."

"Well then you have a truly important position: Western Approaches is *the* front line in our battle – indeed in this war."

"Don't remind me."

"So what can I do to help?"

"Well we have convinced ourselves at Western Approaches that the crunch will come in 12 to 24 months time, and that we will win – but the one significant unknown is signal intelligence. If the Germans get the upper hand in that then we could still lose. So what I'm groping after is a feeling for that. Are we on top in signal intelligence – as we were in the First World War – and if so will we remain on top? Or are we floundering – and likely to remain so?"

"I'm not sure I'm the person to ask – you'll probably have to go to Station X for that. I'm a user of SIGINT– or ULTRA as it is called, not on originator. I will show you what we do with the Ultra though – and show you how vital it is. Have you heard of Ultra before?"

"No. I've only just obtained my security clearance. I'm a complete novice in this field."

"Very well." Winn made a tent with his fingers and stared at Sturdee through circular horn-rimmed spectacles:

"The first thing you must learn is just how secret Ultra is. It is the biggest British secret of this war – at least I believe it is. You cannot tell anyone a single word about it who hasn't got the same stratospheric level of security-clearance as yourself. Probably Admiral Noble is the only other person in Western Approaches who knows about it. There are 2000 people working here in the Operational Intelligence Centre and only half a dozen or so know about Ultra. Churchill feels it's so important it 'must be surrounded by a bodyguard of lies'."

"Gosh." Sturdee was at a loss for words.

"If you can't keep a secret, if you take a glass too many, or if you're liable to be blackmailed, then you don't want to know about Ultra – not if you are a patriot. Do I make myself clear?"

Sturdee nodded.

"Very well then. Ultra is information garnered from decrypting Nazi radio traffic. There are tens of thousands of wireless operators both here, and across the globe, working for Station Y whose mission it is to record every German radio signal they can pick up. From their army, their air-force , their navy, their governmental and diplomatic services, their meteorological bureaus – and so on and so on. All the messages they don't want us to read are encrypted. They will be sent to Station X at Bletchley Park whose business is decryption – or code breaking as it is vulgarly called."

"You and I" he continued "Are actively interested in naval Enigma – so-called because it is encrypted by the Germans, using a commercial Enigma machine. The operator puts the settings of the day into the machine, then types in his message in plain German text. The machine, using a combination of rotor -wheels and wires, then scrambles all the letters and puts out an entirely different sequence of letters which are then transmitted by radio. It's simple in principle but, to decipher it, if you don't know the Enigma settings of the day, is fiendishly difficult apparently. I've been told there are 100 million million million ways of scrambling the same message."

" Unless" Sturdee said "You know the particular settings for the day, which have presumably been distributed to all users on the net in the form of codebooks?"

"Precisely."

"We guessed, from the pattern of recent sinkings, that Britain must have broken into the Nazi code – possibly as the result of a pinch from U110."

Winn looked uncomfortable: "I didn't realise it was quite as obvious as that. But yes. That's the problem with this deciphered information. If you use too much of it the enemy will guess his code has been compromised – and change it. Let's go downstairs and look at the plot."

Like the one at Derby House Winn's U-boat plot was a colossal map of the Atlantic occupying the whole wall of a room the size and shape of a theatre. As at Derby House Wrens climbed about on tall sliding ladders, moving symbols on the map from place to place.

"It's very like yours." Winn commented "Indeed information is constantly passing back and forth between our plot and Liverpool's by means of teleprinter, but we concentrate more on U-boats, you on shipping. Our task is to try and guess, from U-boat movements, where they're trying to concentrate into wolfpacks, and then re-route your convoys around them. We don't necessarily need decrypts because the Y-station people get a positional fix on every U-boat wireless transmission, and from the movements of several U-boats we can guess the position to which they are converging. Fortunately for us Doenitz's U-boats are rather garrulous."

"So you don't rely on code-breaking?"

"No, not entirely. You can guess quite a lot about a message from its length , it's timing and it's place of origin. But as you can imagine that position can't be very accurate if it is inferred from shore-based bearings taken from hundreds or sometimes thousands of miles away. So of course a decrypted message from a U-boat, giving its course and position is far far better – provided – and that's a big proviso Sturdee – that that information is reasonably current i.e. hours and not days old. Sometimes it takes Station X days or even weeks to decrypt some traffic – in which case it can't be of much use to us.. At the moment we are pretty current. Look up there at HX 147" he pointed to a homebound convoy halfway between Britain and Iceland. "I'm keeping an eye on that U-boat" And he pointed again "And on that other over there because they appear to be moving to a position about one day ahead of it. Should I divert it ? When should I divert it ? And should I divert it North or South? And if I do divert it will that make the Germans suspicious that we've broken their cipher – which indeed we have at the moment? But if I don't divert it our ships – which we could have saved – will go to the bottom."

"I wouldn't like your job Commander."

" Our present Policy is not to use decrypted information – unless we can provide a cover story – part of Churchill's ' bodyguard of lies'. So in this instance I've ordered a

Catalina flying boat out of Iceland to intercept that U-boat there. Because of thick cloud in the area he very likely won't succeed in spotting the U-boat but it's quite probable that the U-boat will hear him and report that to Doenitz. So when I do divert the convoy I will have a cover-story. Doenitz will suppose the Catalina spotted the U-boat using it's radar."

"Real cat and mouse stuff."

"Yes – but who's the mouse, who is the cat? Alas we have far too few long-range aircraft to use that ruse often. There are heart-breaking times when we can watch the convoy steaming straight into the jaws of a pack and we can do nothing to warn them – because we don't have a cover story."

Back in Winn's room they discussed the future. Sturdee gave Winn a copy of the Appreciation he had written for Noble, and gave him a verbal precis.

"Yes I agree" Winn said "At the time when Doenitz has his full cordon of U-boats Ultra, and indeed signal intelligence in general, will lose much of its purpose, because Doenitz will pick up most of our convoys visually. The convoy system – so powerful at the present moment – will lose most of its power of concealment. The battle then will turn into a straight fight between the U-boat packs and your convoy escorts groups – presumably with some help from the air force – Coastal Command"

They're not much help at present."

"No they aren't Sturdee. The top RAF brass are committed to winning the war on their own – using bombers. They give Coastal Command very low priority – particularly with regard to the very long-range aircraft we so badly need. I only hope the Prime Minister's Battle of the Atlantic Committee can force them to change their minds. On the other hand RAF Bomber Command may so disrupt German industry as to prevent Doenitz getting any new U-boats – so the real Battle of the Atlantic might never get fought."

"Do you think the Jerries have broken our own codes?"

Winn said: "I ask myself that question half a dozen times a day. If we can break his ciphers why can't he break ours? After all he's been preparing to fight this war for much longer than we have. Moreover we can't afford to use very sophisticated ciphers where we have to communicate with so many cargo vessels – not only from Britain but from other countries like Greece. I'm particularly worried about BAMS or 'Broadcast to Allied Merchant Ships'– an Admiralty cipher whose name speaks for itself. Coordinated movement among U-boats towards a convoy which none of them can see – would strongly suggest prior intelligence of some kind. And then I'm highly tempted to cry Wolf in order to get the admiralty to change BAMS – and some of its others ciphers. But then, a few days later, the U-boats appear to be operating completely in the dark. Was I mistaken earlier– or is my counterpart in B-dienst in Berlin – that's their codebreaking equivalent of our Station X – playing cat and mouse with me – as I am attempting to play it with him – using that Catalina. Without watertight evidence – which I do not have at present – I dare not cry wolf about our codes. It will be a devil of a job for the Admiralty to change them, so they will be very reluctant to do so."

"I can see your dilemma. But if we've now broken into their Naval Enigma traffic won't we find clues as to their own cipher breaking success?"

"One can only hope so – but if they are cunning they can devise cover stories too."

"I don't know how you sleep at nights Commander."

"Quite often I don't – but my legal training helps. One has to forget a case once the verdict has been reached. There are more miscarriages of justice then one might suppose – absolute certainty is rarely to be found in Law."

"Likewise in science" Sturdee said "We don't like to admit it but we deal in Odds too".

"I'm surprised to hear you say that."

"Most people are, even scientists. People like to believe it's all about dispassionate logic, but as far as I can see it's nothing of the kind. In the end we human beings all have to deal in Odds – even scientists."

"How interesting. I would like to talk about this again. Please drop by when you can. I'm afraid my job doesn't allow me to get away much."

Winn, a fluent German speaker himself, was fascinated by Sturdee's two years in Germany and over lunch he quizzed him closely about it. Although 10 years older than Sturdee the two had much in common: both had wanted to be naval officers but had been frustrated in that ambition – Winn by his polio; both had grown up in King's Norton just outside Birmingham and both had been to the same school, King Edward's Birmingham , though Winn had gone into Law via Cambridge and Harvard. Perhaps because both had an insatiable curiosity they revelled in each other's company and vowed to keep in regular touch. Sturdee told Winn to read both Lanchester and Maurice's book on Blockade.

Winn had arranged for Sturdee to travel to station X in one of the many vehicles which shuttled back between there and the admiralty. Bletchley Park turned out to be a country house, by no means as large or as grand as Bawdsey Manor but inhabited by a rather similar mix of civilians and service personnel bustling about with a preoccupied air. He was eventually picked up from the waiting-room by a tousled looking young man in sports coat and Oxford bags:

"George McVittie" he introduced himself, carefully inspecting Sturdee's pass before shaking hands: "Mathematical astronomer at Kings College London in real life. Here I work mainly on German meteorological ciphers with the aim of breaking into U-boat traffic. I've been deputed to brief you."

"How does that work?" Sturdee wanted to know, as they crossed the lawn towards a collection of temporary wooden buildings.

"This is Hut 8." McVittie said. "Where we try to break U-boat ciphers. Well, everybody needs weather information don't they, not least the German navy. They use their U-boats as seaborne weather stations. The Submarines report in to Berlin's meteorological bureau once or twice a day. And in return they get an Atlantic weather forecast back. Now the point is that no one thinks of weather as a matter of high security – so they can be careless about sending the meteorological stuff about; for instance a weather report in a low-level cipher we have broken may be enciphered, without any change, into a high-level cipher we have not. Snap! We can break straight into the Enigma settings of the high level cipher for that day."

"Ingenious!" Sturdee said.

"Not really – just obvious common sense. And that's mostly how the cipher breaking business works. There are plenty of people here and elsewhere who like to think of us as 'Mathematical geniuses'. There are certainly some very smart people around– for instance Alan Turing and Gordon Welchman in this hut alone. But if you ask me the genius bit is grossly overblown. What I would like to impress upon you Sturdee – so that you can impress it upon your navel pals in return – is the vital importance of *cipher-discipline*. Everybody breaks everybody else's codes at least some of the time – and you know why ? Not by genius but by exploiting the other side's mistakes – usually carelessness. Some clerk in Kiel always signs off his ciphers 'Heil Hitler'– and we've got him – and all the other poor devils on his net. Cipher breaking is, more than anything, a matter of effort. Because we are on the defensive Britain is putting a huge effort into it just now. The Germans are winning so comprehensively that they don't particularly care what we are up to since they've got the initiative. We have to react to them – not the other way round, so we're maybe putting in 10 times the effort of B-dienst in Berlin."

"I never thought about it like that."

"Cipher systems like Enigma may be devised by very ingenious people but they have to be used by very ordinary folk, exhausted people in the heat of battle. They fumble and make mistakes – then we Listeners break in."

"I see."

"And effort counts in another way; speed. Suppose, as a result of meteorological clue, we break into the U-boat cipher for the day. Hundreds, even thousands of cipher messages flood in from Station Y. They all have to be broken into plaintext German, translated into English, analysed by experts, filed and cross correlated with the Index – that's a colossal job in itself, then distributed around the globe so the right operational commands can make use of it. You wouldn't be surprised to find that all that takes 48 hours?"

"No I wouldn't."

"Alas by then much of it would be out of date. The U-boat would have already sunk its prey and got away. That is why speed, and hence effort, is of the essence."

"I can see that."

"Fortunately the PM can see it too. That's why we are at last getting the necessary resources and the people. Turing is trying to mechanise the process by building a machine that works like an Enigma in reverse. We all believe that the key to success will be mechanisation – the faster the machines the better."

"You mentioned 'the Index' – what's that?"

"Ah yes. There are far more people here working on that than actually breaking ciphers – and with good reason. As you would appreciate three independent clues bearing on a particular problem can lead to its watertight solution – where only one clue would be more or less useless. We had a case yesterday. We got a fix on a particular U-boat – call it X. In the Index there are two previous transmissions from X. One gave an earlier position, while the first proved to be a damage report. A clear picture emerged. The U-boat is limping home at very low speed and too damaged to submerge. That info has been sent to Coastal Command who will probably send out an aircraft to sink him when he reaches the Bay of Biscay. Without the Index we wouldn't have been able to assemble the story fast enough to take effective action."

"I can see that."

"And that is why we do all the decryption here under one roof – to exploit the possibilities for cross-referencing information from quite different sources – to draw valuable inferences which might otherwise evade detection. Most of the dandruffy types you see wandering around here have nothing to do with decryption. They are experts of various kinds, mostly from universities, trying to analyse the stuff in the Index. I hear they just shipped in Russian experts to go through the stuff coming in from Hitler's Russian front."

"With such a huge staff here the possibility for a security leaks must be immense?"

"Yes. But we are swarming with spooks too – and everybody works on a 'need to know' basis."

"I don't follow."

"I know what goes on in Hut 8 – but not in the Huts 5 and 6 – and I'm not allowed to ask – without proper authority. So even if I am a spy I can do only limited damage. Your own stratospheric Security classification, high though it is, only permits you to know certain things – but not others. For instance I can tell you all about meteorological 'pinches' but not stolen- codebook 'pinches' because I don't actually know about that stuff myself: I'm not allowed to know. Turing, Welchman and Hugh Alexander do that kind of thing, but they don't know my little secrets."

"Isn't that tricky?"

"Very. Only the boss knows everything and can put people in touch with each other when he judges there is an occasion for it."

"And who is he?"

"Sorry, can't tell you."

"Well" Sturdee smiled: "I suppose I don't really need to know."

"What *do* you really need?"

Sturdee considered for a moment: "First I'd like to know if our own convoy ciphers have been broken by the Jerries. That could be incredibly important for us."

"I can see that." McVittie made a note "I'll look into it and let you know what I can in a day or two."

"If we are broken shouldn't that turn up in your U-boat traffic?"

"It should – but the Jerries are damn good at disguising their intelligence sources. They report that a Focke-Wulf picked up your convoy position – when in truth it was a B-dienst decrypt of an Admiralty cipher."

"Oh God!" Sturdee groaned "Where is the truth ever to be found in this slippery game"?"

"Certain truth will usually evade us. As in Astronomy, probabilities are the most we can generally hope for. You should know that as a scientist yourself!"

"I do." Sturdee nodded "But like a child one can't help hoping for certainty."

"I'm sorry to say you're rarely going to get that from us. I'll be able to tell you that Father Christmas does exist – but with no better than 75% Probability."

"The other thing we desperately need to know" Giles explained "Is about the future. Is our Sigint. going to improve relative to theirs – or vice versa?"

"Again you're barking at the Moon. We wizards at Station X can see no further than 48 hours into the future – and even then with little certainty."

"I know. But at Western Approaches we are obsessed about the big Battle of the Atlantic when Doenitz gets his full complement of U-boats – 100 on station at once. It may lie up to 2 years ahead: we think 1943."

"I can give you my private opinions, such as they are – as long as you treat them as such – give them no official weight ? "

"Okay."

"First then, don't rely on us to win your battle for you. Sigint will rarely get U-boat positions accurate enough for you to find them and sink them. Our receiving stations are far too far away for accurate fixes, while the delays in the decryption system will nearly always permit a U-boat to move away. And if by chance we did have bang-on positions we probably wouldn't release them to you for fear that some fool would use them too directly – and give away the entire Ultra game to the Nazis."

"I can see that – though I hadn't appreciated it before."

"Then again what success we're having could evaporate overnight. The Germans are by no means using the entire encryption potential of the Enigma machine at present. If they get suspicious they can add extra rotors – making what is already hard, virtually impossible."

"Is that so; I didn't realise that."

"We don't like to think about it ourselves. We're all close to a nervous breakdown as it is: some are over the edge already. Indeed if I couldn't turn to astronomy from time to time I'd go mad myself.".

"You worked with Eddington didn't you?"

"He was my supervisor. As mad as the proverbial hatter. I couldn't get away from him fast enough."

"He was one of my heroes. You know I worked on stellar structure and evolution before the war. I loved his book."

"So did a lot of people – but in truth it's full of flaws."

" I didn't know that." Sturdee was genuinely shocked.

"Eddington thinks of himself as a genius – and spends most of his time trying to convince everybody else. You know he's never wrong?"

"No I didn't."

"That alone disqualifies him as a serious scientist."

The two of them talked astrophysics for a while before McVittie returned to the war:

"As I said Sigint will never win the U-boat war because it is, in this context, primarily a defensive and not an offensive weapon. We can help to prevent you losing the war by helping you to divert convoys around suspected U-boat concentrations, but we cannot find U-boats with sufficient precision for you to sink them . You'll have to find other means to do that. As far as you at Western Approaches are concerned we are never going to be Father Christmas."

"I'm beginning to appreciate that – and it is very useful information – very useful."

" On the other hand you mustn't think of us as wizards. You have no doubt heard of the Enigma machine as having 100 million trillion possible settings?"

"I just did yesterday."

"It sounds like a very big number doesn't it?"

"It certainly does."

"Well it isn't – not in this context. It's less than the number of ways you can permute 15 letters together to make a sentence ."

"I don't follow."

"There are 26 different letters in the alphabet, right? Thus the number of possible permutations of 15 letters is 26 to the power of 15 – which is larger than the number of Enigma settings."

"The implication being?"

"One has only to correctly guess 15 letters in an Enigma message – which is sometimes not difficult if you know who is sending it to who – and you'll have all the information needed to break-in – at least in theory."

"Well I'm damned !" Sturdee was delighted.

"I'm telling you this because at present there are only a handful of inspired guessers like me working on Naval Enigma. Now your boss Admiral Noble is a really big beast – a full admiral and commander-in-chief. He ranks way above anybody here, or indeed anyone at OIC where you were yesterday. So if he wanted more effort to go into naval Enigma, he would probably get it – with proportionate results. It wouldn't be magic – but just more plodding but productive guesswork."

" I'll remember that. I'd like to continue but I've got to catch Admiral Noble's plane back to Liverpool. We should keep in touch."

"By all means."

"Why don't you come up to Liverpool one day – and see the sharp end ? "

"I thought you had been bombed practically flat."

"That was in May. We had a blitz lasting eight consecutive nights ."

"Phew!"

"They kept it quiet – for morale reasons– 4,000 people dead. But we haven't had a bomb for weeks.

"I suppose the poor bloody Russians are copping it instead."

"Goodbye McVittie – and thanks."

CHAPTER 11

IN THE DARK

Now that he was in the Ultra circle Sturdee had to constantly watch his tongue – something which, both as a scientist and a human being, he found unnatural and distasteful. For instance there was much that he could no longer discuss with Loader or Picton for fear of letting slip. He explained to Loader:

"In some respects, I wish I hadn't delved so far into Sigint. In some ways you're lucky to be outside. What I can tell you is this: Sigint isn't going to win the Battle of the Atlantic for us, though it may help us not to lose it for now. Yes, we sometimes do break some of their codes – just as they break into ours. But success on both sides is intermittent and unpredictable. And what I hadn't realised is that most Sigint is too out of date to be of much operational use. Let's say it is 12 hours behind. That would be current enough for us to divert a convoy around a gathering U-boat pack but it wouldn't give the current position of a single U-boat with sufficient timeliness or precision for us to sink it. That's the hypothesis on which you and I must work. If we are going to find and sink U-boats we'll mostly have to do so without the aid of Sigint ."

"And in the future?

"I'm afraid your guess is as good as mine – or anybody else's. Doenitz will in any case be able to find our convoys – once he has enough-boats out there – so Sigint will become less important, perhaps much less important than it is now."

"Well at least we know where we stand Giles – not depending on some kind of unreliable magic."

"Exactly my thoughts Tony."

"So where do we go next? RDF– or 'radar' as they're beginning to call it?"

"That's the obvious next port of call. I've got an invitation to go and see my mate Hanbury Brown – he is the expert on ASV– that's Air to Surface Vessel radar. The trouble is he's down in Dorset at a Place called Worth Matravers. Can one find a civilised way of getting down there and back – on a Sunday?"

"I'll see what I can do old boy. We do have a Walrus seaplane. That might get you to Poole Harbour."

Loader's contacts worked, with the result that on a lovely sunny Sunday morning Sturdee found himself in the co-pilot's seat of a single engined Supermarine Walrus amphibian as it droned across Cheshire, the Malvern Hills, and the Welsh Marches.

"What a beautiful island we live in", he thought as they lifted over the Brecon Beacons with the Severn estuary before them and the South Wales coast vanishing into the West , creamy surf breaking on its yellow sandy beaches.

After crossing Gloucestershire, they began to pick out the chalk uplands of high Dorset and the pilot pointed ahead: "Poole harbour" mimicking with his lips

The vast natural harbour with it's a cosy sheltered shallow water presented any number of places to land. The pilot brought them right down until he could judge the wind direction from the waves, turned into the West, and settled downwards at what seemed an alarming speed until they bumped and splashed into the gentle summer surf.

Hanbury Brown, as jovial as ever, but wearing a hearing-aid, met him with an RAF staff-car.

"What on Earth?" Sturdeep pointed to the incongruous aid.

"I'm afraid it's put an end to my high-altitude flying Giles. I was flying in a Beaufighter at 20,000 feet testing our latest night-fighter radar when I must have accidentally pulled out my oxygen tube and passed out. Fortunately, the pilot noticed I'd gone rather quiet so he went into a steep dive. It saved my life but also burst my right eardrum. So, I'm moving into the lower altitude stuff – like ASV which you naval types are interested in. We've solved the night-fighter problem anyway."

"You could have fooled me!"

" Haven't you noticed the fall off in the intensity of the Blitz?"

"Well yes – but I thought that was Hitler's Russian folly."

"Let everyone think that. We don't want the Luftwaffe to know. Last May our Beaufighters , equipped with Mark Four radar, shot down over 100 Jerry bombers."

"Good lord!"

"I thought you'd be pleased to know Giles – after all that work we put in together at Bawdsey Manor. It took a lot of development – but it's paid off in the end. The Beaufighter has got four Hispano-Suiza cannons which can blast a Heinkel or a Dornier to bits in a single bust. But it's all hush-hush for now: we don't want Jerry to develop counter-measures."

"It shows what radar can do. You must be thrilled. You started all this airborne radar off didn't you –with Taffy Bowen – back in 36? "

"Indeed we did. When I see the bomb damage in poor old London I realise I'll never do anything so worthwhile in my life again."

"You should see Liverpool: we were blitzed eight nights in a row in May."

"We heard. But that's unlikely to ever happen again. If Jerry bombers tried to fly right across Britain to your area our Beaufighter boys would get them."

"They used 300 bombers on those raids – every night."

" By the end of this year I suspect we'll be able to shoot down that number every *month*. Now I want to try and help you chaps find U-boats from the air."

"We certainly can't do that now."

"I know. But you know why?"

"Not precisely."

"It's a matter of priorities. Every time we've tried to work on ASV something more urgent has intervened, like night-fighter radar."

"We're going to desperately need something urgently – before 12 months are out. The Battle of the Atlantic is coming to a crux. We're hopeless at sinking U-boats – but if we can keep them down– submerged – they can't keep up with and shadow the convoys. And then they can't call other U-boats to join in their wolfpack attacks."

"And how can we help?"

"All the records seem to suggest that the convoy which has both surface and air escort, rarely gets attacked . So airborne sets which worked out to a distance of 10 or 20 miles, day or night, would be a godsend."

"I don't see why we couldn't manage that – in principle. But your problem will be priorities again. As far as I can see Coastal Command always gets the hind tit where the RAF is concerned. It's a dumping ground for second-rate aircraft and second-rate people."

"Is that so? It certainly hasn't done much for the Battle of the Atlantic so far."

"And now it's got an even bigger rival – Bomber Command."

"How come? Why would bombers need radar?"

"It would appear that Bomber command drops the majority of its bombs 5 miles or more away from its targets."

"Good Lord."

"That's very hush-hush info by the way. The PM practically had a fit when he saw the report. What's the point of bombing Germany, or bombing anything, if you can't do better than that? And we're putting an absolutely massive effort into Bomber Command – for now it's our only way of retaliating against the Nazis ."

"I suppose so."

"But radar may offer a way out Giles. We recently discovered an extraordinary thing: 'corner reflection' – do you know what I mean?"

"No."

"Take three flat mirrors and put them together to make a perfect right-angled corner. Now what happens if you shone a torch into the setup?"

"I don't know."

"The torch beam reflects off the three mirrors one by one and then shines back exactly in the direction from whence it has come."

"Yes, I can imagine that. But so what?"

"If you shine a radar beam into any right-corner you get a very strong return – that's what. And where do you find right corners? In built-up areas, where there are lots of man-made right corners. Thus towns give surprisingly strong radar reflections."

"I am beginning to see."

"A high frequency radar capable of scanning the landscape beneath a bomber would be the perfect mapping device for its navigator. The bomber could see and accordingly bomb its targets accurately even through cloud at night. So Bomber Command is screaming for thousands of sophisticated radars of the very kind you chaps need – now! And the PM might very well go along with them – and the Atlantic will lose out yet again."

"Oh no!"

"But anyway, we are reaching Worth Matravers. It's the headquarters of TRE –the Telecommunications Research Establishment – the up-to-date version of Bawdsey

Manor. I have asked you here today because the superintendent A. P. Rowe has started a remarkable institution, which we've nicknamed the 'Sunday Soviet'. We invite all parties concerned with a new project to discuss it face-to-face: the scientists, the air crews, senior officers, maintenance staff… you name it and the truth finally comes out. Is it doing its job? And if not why not? And how do we fix it? Only thus we found with night fighter radar that it was useless without a complimentary ground-controlled interception set to put the fighter close enough onto the tail of the bomber so that its own radar would work. Then we had to develop aerial tactics so that the fighter could home in without weaving about so much as to lose its target. Then we found the critical parts of set-maintenance – calibration for instance– to make them work reliably. When you can sit down face-to-face and hold a no-holds-barred discussion you can fix things which might otherwise take years – in weeks. I wanted you see to see it at work – it's something you might be able to take back to your own colleagues."

Worth Matravers stood atop the chalk cliffs of Dorset looking out across the English Channel – a'sparkle in the in early August sun. It had obviously been erected in a hurry as part of the Chain Home radar system which had been built around the coast and served so well in the Battle of Britain. It's three very tall radio masts stood over a collection of temporary buildings which would have been conspicuous on the bare chalk downs had they not been camouflaged with netting.

The meeting was interesting enough though it dealt with a kind of radar of no interest to Sturdee. It was remarkable for the robust nature of the discussion, with rank granted no privileges. With the windows wide open and the smells of the sea blowing in Sturdee found it hard to concentrate. He was, he realised, starved of beauty in urban Liverpool and longed to be out on the clifftop, his hair blowing in the breeze, the gulls skimming just overheard as they worked the up-currents rising from the chalk cliff face below. At the lunchbreak he managed to persuade Hanbury to grab a sandwich and the two of them sat cross-legged in the grass atop the cliff and enjoyed a summer neither of them had had the leisure to notice, let alone enjoy, before.
"My God it's peaceful out there." Sturdee waved at the Channel.
"Peaceful is hardly the right word Giles. It's deserted of ships you mean. Jerry aircraft would bomb anything afloat by day, and Jerry E-boats would torpedo anything afloat on it by night. Even inshore fishing vessels get machine-gunned by Messerschmitt 109s."
" It's hard to believe that out there, just over the horizon, Europe lies squirming under the Nazi jackboot."
"Yes, and it's up to people like you and me to defeat them – using our wits. Talking of which I brought my stuff on your Acoustic torpedo."
He took the papers out of his sports-jacket pocket and laid them out on the grass, weighing them down with his penknife.
"While I was in hospital with my ear I spent a couple of weeks on it. A fascinating idea I have to say. Yours?"

"It's obvious really. The Admiralty are desperately worried that the U-boats will use acoustic torpedoes against our ships. But no one had thought of using them against U-boats."

"The perfect application I would say Giles. Submerged U-boats can't move fast so an acoustic torpedo with quite a modest performance could hunt them to destruction. The main problem as I see it is first locking on to the target. You drop the little devil into the briny leaving it to locate its prey on its own?"

"Yes."

"In my scheme is goes down to 50 feet, switches on its four phones and starts executing a spherical orbit – That's to say it goes round and round in three-dimensions, tracing out the surface of a sphere. At some point in that orbit the phones will all be pointing right at the target when all phones should be getting the same signal; right?"

"Yep."

"That is the end of the 'Search' mode, thereafter it automatically switches to the Hunt mode. All it has to do now is keep adjusting the four rudder planes so as to keep the four phone-signals equal, and Bob's your uncle. It's slightly more complex than that but I can do the whole thing with a circuit employing less than 20 valves. With more time I could probably get it down to less than a dozen."

"What happens if it loses the signal?"

"Automatically goes back into Search mode and starts again."

"Seems straightforward."

"It is Giles, it is! Those Porton people were talking through their hats. Here – you could take this circuit diagram to a competent electronic engineer who could check that it makes sense, and then build it in a week. Testing and adjustment might take three months in a big tank. You could use all off-the-shelf components: battery, drive motor, phones, planes, explosives, contact-detonator – the most expensive item would probably be the hundred-pound explosive charge which you specified."

"At present we need about 100 300-lb. weight depth-charges to sink an average U-boat, so this will be 300 times cheaper."

"It would be criminal not to go ahead with it right away. Criminal! It's a thousand times simpler than night fighter radar, and it's difficult to see an effective counter-measure. A U-boat can't turn off its engine can it?"

"Not for more than a few seconds – because then it loses its depth control – which relies on its hydroplanes."

"In a perfect world you'd get this thing into service within six months. But alas… you can't believe the incompetencys we had to suffer since you left us Giles. First they moved us to Dundee – where there were zero facilities – and can you believe it – they left our admin. people back down in Suffolk. So, if you wanted a screwdriver you had to indent for it on a form, post the form down to Bawdsey; they would then send it back – approved if you were lucky – but unfortunately there were no stores in Dundee. I mean it nearly drove us mad. And then, without warning, they moved us down to Saint Athans in Wales – which was if anything even worse. There were no proper workshops so we were installing radar out in the open at temperatures below freezing. Normally Taffy

Bowen would have sorted all that out – but now he's gone to America, and probably won't come back. Did you know?"

"No, I didn't. Surely that's a disaster?"

"He's teaching the Yanks how to build radar. They're setting up a vast laboratory in Massachusetts with five thousand scientists."

"But they're not even on our side! They could betray our secrets to the Jerries."

"We must hope not – but it's a rank gamble if you ask me. Churchill must be hoping that either he or Roosevelt can lure the Americans into the war on our side."

"They're certainly doing more than you would expect of a neutral – Lend- lease and all that."

"That's probably a quid pro quo. We gave them all our scientific and engineering secrets – they give us military aid – like those 50 ancient destroyers."

"Which incidentally are not much cop."

"You know Taffy took the Cavity Magnetron over to the States?"

"But that's like gifting the Crown Jewels – but a thousand times worse!"

"It's a gamble – as I say. If they do come in on our side we'd have all the radars we need. They may not be much cop at research, but when it comes to mass-production they're streets ahead. Combine the two and it's 'Good Night Mr Hitler'. But this isn't going to get your nasty little torpedo built. What you need Giles is a scientific mentor– someone really high up who could push your idea through the committee system. That's the only way to get things done here and now. If we hadn't had access to so Sir Henry Tizard, and Air Marshal Dowding, we wouldn't have got night fighter radar for 5 to 10 years – and I kid you not."

"But I don't have a scientific mentor – not in Britain. You know I went straight to Germany after I got my PhD?"

"Look Giles I'll tell you what I know about the scientific establishment at the very top level – and it's always better to go to the top if you can. As far as I can make out are three people who really matter . First there is Sir Henry Tizard – officially rector of Imperial College London – but also Chairman of any number of wartime scientific committees. It was one of his committees, back in 1935, which got the whole radar thing going and got Chain Home built in time for the Battle of Britain. He it was who persuaded me to go to Bawdsey when I was a grad student at his university. Taffy was another one of his protégés. So Tizzard is a very big beast indeed – but he's badly wounded – fatally perhaps."

"How come?"

"These big beasts have terrible fights with one another, and Tizard took on Lindemann."

"He's Churchill's personal scientific advisor isn't he?"

"Indeed he is Giles, and a very nasty piece of work into the bargain. He's a German, and professor of Physics at Oxford – though no one has a good word to say about his science. He was on the Tizzard's radar committee and tried to obstruct its work at every turn. He had some cock-and-bull idea about using infrared to detect enemy aircraft instead of radio waves. Caused so much trouble that the rest of the Tizard committee all resigned, then re-formed themselves into a new committee, but without Lindemann on it. Lindemann has never forgiven Tizzard for that and hates him like poison. That wouldn't have mattered because Lindemann, or 'Prof'. as he insists on being called, is a scientific dwarf. But then Churchill came to power and 'Prof' is suddenly top of the heap, having the Great man's ear on a daily basis. They go to the same posh country-house weekend parties I believe, and Tizard doesn't. Lindemann's got his sting into both Dowding and Tizard so neither can survive for long."

"My God – what a fool Churchill sounds!"

"Not entirely Giles, not entirely. Winston relies on Lindemann for one very good reason. In the First World War Lindemann performed one of the cleverest and certainly the bravest acts ever by a scientist. He solved the problem of spinning in aircraft. Ever heard of that?"

"Vaguely."

"The early aircraft were so unstable that one in five novice-pilots died when their machines, for no apparent reason – went into a dreaded spin. Even experienced pilots were terrified and helpless when it happened – unable to keep or restore control, condemned to death when their machines spun into the ground at high-speed."

"I remember now."

"Well Lindemann, working at the Balloon Factory– which is now the Royal Aircraft Establishment at Farnborough, developed a theory about spinning ,and how to get out of one. It worked on models but he couldn't ask anyone to put a real aircraft deliberately into a spin and then try to come out of it. But cool as a cucumber– no pilot himself – Lindemann had himself taught to fly – and then tried out the suicidal manoeuvre himself. No parachute in those days remember: cold-blooded courage of the highest order. And his idea worked. Since then every novice pilot has been trained how to get into a spin – and pull out safely again – while aircraft have been redesigned to spin less readily. Tens of thousands of flyers, possibly millions, owe their lives to Lindemann. You can see why Churchill admires and trusts him ."

"I do; that's quite a story."

"The third big beast is Professor PMS or Patrick Blackett, ex Royal Naval officer, fought at Jutland, now professor of particle-physics at Manchester University, bound to get a Nobel Prize one-day for discovering the first anti-particle, the Positron. Worked closely with Tizard on radar. But unfortunately he's a socialist – which has put him into Winston's and Lindemann's bad books. He despises them almost as much as they despise him. I met him once – and he terrified the daylights out of me – grim faced like some flogging headmaster. He enjoys support from Socialists in the cabinet – including Attlee and Bevin ; done some valuable work for Air Marshal Bowhill C-in-C Coastal Command."

"They all seem pretty terrifying to me Hanbury. What do you advise?"

"I don't. All I'm saying is that if you can get one of them on side your torpedo stands a good chance of being made – in time to win your battle. Otherwise… if it was a radar matter and I was in yours shoes, I go to Taffy with a paper; Taffy – if he agreed with me –would go to see Watson-Watt the big chief of radar, and if he agreed he would go to see Tizard. Then if Tizard could get around Lindemann something constructive might be done. To get GCI, such a vital component of night-fighter radar – we had to bypass Watson-Watt because he disagreed with the idea. Almost 2 years was lost that way. Without that debate we might have avoided the Blitz almost entirely."

"My God!" Sturdee was shocked.

"But I'm not blaming the government Giles… all governments must set priorities. No one could have foreseen the precipitate fall of France. All our worst problems, including the blitz, stem from that. The problem is that the priorities have to be set at a very high-level. We underlings cannot appreciate all the alternative pressures such decision-makers are facing. That's why you need a high-level scientific mentor – who *is* aware of those rival calls for resources – to get your little devil actually built. All I can say is 'Good luck'. Now about your air to surface- vessel radar needs?"

Margaret explained the concept of U-boats shadowing convoys in order to call up reinforcements:

"It's the only workable riposte to the convoy system. One U-boat on its own can never take on a well trained Escort Group. So our paramount need Hanbury is to keep those shadowers submerged, then they can't keep up with the convoy – and even if they could they couldn't radio their comrades. It doesn't matter how many U-boats Doenitz gets – if they can't keep in contact they'll be useless. Hence our crying need for airborne radar cover. All the evidence shows that when U-boats see or even hear aircraft coming they dive and stay submerged. The aircraft doesn't even have to attack – the Jerries presume it will call up our escort vessels."

"The last time we looked at ASV Giles at Saint Athans we fitted a meter-wavelength sideways looking system to a Whitley bomber. We had 10 dipole aerials for the transmitter and two Sterba aerials, one each side, for the receiver. The overall power gain was 50 and so we could detect coastlines at 60 miles, ships at 40 and surfaced Submarines at 10 to 15 miles. We called it 'Long range ASV' because it's Range is two and a half times that of the existing Mark One sets fitted in Sunderland flying-boats and Coastal Command Wellingtons. Would that work for you?"

Sturdee took out his fountain pen and did a calculation on the back of his hand:

" Assuming an air speed 150 knots we could scan 3000 square miles of ocean in an of hour. Assuming the effective shadowing region covers 30 x 40 miles we could scan each point of that region every 24 minutes. That's a bit too long – it would allow U-boats to re-surface."

"It won't be easy to increase the radar range in the short-term. You need a faster aircraft."

"Yes. 200 knots would reduce the scan interval to 18 minutes – which is more like it."

"What sort of aircraft are you thinking of?"

"I'm not sure; beggars can't be choosers Hanbury. As you pointed out, Coastal Command usually gets leftovers."

"Well you 'd better make certain they can reach mid-Atlantic because you can be sure that that is where Jerry will eventually station his U-boat cordon."

"I suppose so. We haven't been thinking of aircraft much – too busy with U-boats and depth-charges. Look at this scarlet pimpernel – they thrive on the chalk land."

"Didn't know you were a wildflower type Giles."

"I'm not but I'm a 'beautiful-countryside type' very definitely. All this makes me want to paint again."

"You were very talented Giles. I remember that one you did of the Debden Estuary. Where is it now?"

"God knows. I left it hanging in the canteen at Bawdsey."

"Sure to have been pinched then. It was much admired you know. Don't give up painting will you? It's part of all this beauty and civilisation we're supposed to be fighting for."

"Do you hear that Skylark?" Sturdee held up a hand to his lips.

"Not with this bloody eardrum."

"I'd forgotten."

"But there it is !" Hanbury pointed up in the sky to the West: "Go little one, go! Look after your babies. Never mind this bloody wretched war!"

CHAPTER 12
AIRBORNE

By mid-August Duff House had become a thriving market garden. Its 60 apple trees, 40 pears and dozens of cherries and plums, were beginning to fruit. Arfur had a store on the front lawn facing the road where he sold thousands of onions, fruit of all kinds including blackcurrants, gooseberries and raspberries from Joan's portion of the kitchen garden, potatoes, even some much sought-after tomatoes from the conservatory and summerhouses in Maurice's charge. The hens were laying well, and the geese fattening while the ducks were producing ducklings. Damn and Blast , already weighing 10 score pounds apiece, were half feeding themselves by rooting in the paddock and gobbling windfalls in the orchard. Using Gem to successfully pull a plough had proved to be beyond them, but he call could pull a mower through the paddock to provide his own hay – and the bedding for the pigs. They had also acquired an old cart which Gem could pull about with Arfur at the reins, relieving Sturdee from making local deliveries. Joan had turned the kitchen and scullery into a small factory for bottling fruit and making jam using black-market sugar bought or bartered for with onions.

Picton thought the whole thing had got out of hand: "Who would've thought a woman with a brain like hers would turn into a greengrocer?" he said in disgust "And a bloody farmer. It started out as a modest but sensible attempt to supplement our meagre rations. Now we're slaving from dawn until dusk to feed two dozen people – at least."

"She thinks it's an essential part of the war effort." Sturdee tried to defend her. "And she does distribute half of everything free to schools and hospitals."

"If you ask me she's doing it for fun. She's a natural farmer's wife. When she marries that Desmond fellow she'll turn him into a farmer even if he wants to be an interior decorator."

"What *does* he want to be?"

"No idea – but it doesn't matter – Joan will have him out with a muckrake in no time."

"Do you think she's bossy Maurice?"

"Of course she is – and thank God for it. Sometimes it's the only way to get things done. If it wasn't for Joan Liverpool might have collapsed in May. But as a wife, I'm not sure." He drew an imaginary knife across his throat: "I couldn't handle her – that's certain. Look how she bosses those formidable brothers of hers about."

"But they all seem to adore her."

"That's true – but don't be getting any daft ideas above your station Giles – you haven't got a clue about women. Our Joan is a pedigree racehorse – wonderful in the right hands – experienced hands – but hopeless in the wrong. No,

I can see Joan after the war running a colossal sheep station in the outback of New South Wales, hundreds of thousands of sheep, and 10 times as many acres."

'After the war': they often talked about 'After the war', it was a common preoccupation. Partly it was escapism, but partly it was a determination to see that their efforts and sacrifices wouldn't be wasted, as their parents' had been wasted after the First World War.

"So, what are you going to do Giles – how do you see yourself living after the war?" Maurice had asked him as they were all sitting round the table late one night drinking some of Joan's home-made sloe-gin.

"As I think I told you, I see myself teaching Mathematical Physics in some provincial University – preferably in a lovely part of Britain. After seeing Dorset the other day the Southwest sounds attractive."

"Not many universities down that way." Maurice objected

"There's Bristol and Exeter…"

"Anyway" Joan said, "All that will change after the war… a university education won't just be for the privileged minority."

"I agree" Sturdee said "We couldn't afford an uneducated population any more. That's why we had a bloody depression in the 30s."

"And it's half the reason we've got this much bloodier war." Maurice agreed "If people hadn't been so ignorant of History in the 20s we might have avoided the tragedy of Versailles."

" Wos 'Versailles' ?"Arfur asked. He was drinking home-made apple juice instead of sloe-gin.

"It was a peace conference near Paris in 1919," Joan explained "To make sure there would never be another war."

"But instead of acting wisely" Maurice continued. "The winners – that's us and the French – tried to punish the loser – that was Germany. The Germans almost starved – and vowed to get their revenge – and here we are fighting again. That didn't happen in 1815 after the end of the Napoleonic war – and as a result we had 100 years of peace to follow it. Versailles was a folly of ignorance Arfur – that's why we want you to learn some History – don't we chaps?"

"Or Wales" Sturdee continued at a tangent "There are universities in Cardiff, Swansea, Bangor and Aberystwyth."

"They sound a bit industrial to me old chap." Maurice said

"That's what I thought," Sturdee agreed "But we flew back up from Dorset across Wales – and it looked absolutely enchanting. I got the pilot to take us low over the Gower peninsular – that's near Swansea – and I've never seen coastline so beautiful in my life."

"So, you are going to teach physics at Swansea University," Joan said "But what about the rest of your life Giles – you won't be working all of the time – surely?"

"Of course not. I've got one or two plans.".

"Such as?"

"For one thing I want to build a small wooden sailing cruiser – two or three berths– about 25 feet long – able to get across to France or Ireland. You know I had my own small cruiser down in Suffolk? I absolutely love sailing – I want to do much more. I even thought of sailing across France by canal and river, down into the Mediterranean."

"Can one do that?" Joan sounded amazed.

"It's been done." Sturdee assured her. "Just imagine slinging your hook in to some field in Burgundy and strolling along to the local auberge for a cassoulet…"

"… with a fresh baguette and Roquefort cheese." Joan's eyes sparkled

"… And a divine Beaujolais" Maurice added "Which the locals keep to themselves because 'It doesn't travel well'."

"But wouldn't you have to be rich?" Joan sounded doubtful.

"Rich in Time yes– but not in money. I'd build the boat myself. I've got the plans already from 'Yachting Monthly' magazine. She's a Maurice Griffiths design, hard chine, with two bilge-keels to take the ground when the tide goes out. Sloop rig, three berths, occasional four; a galley of course, and an outboard-motor for when the wind dies. And university lecturers get four months holiday every summer! We could cross France in one summer – then round the coast of Italy the next – lay the boat up for the winter near Venice – and come back … up the Danube…"

"What about your research? " Maurice objected "University vacations are not meant for jaunting about you know."

Sturdee tapped his head: "It will go with me. Don't forget I'm a mathematical physicist. There we'd be on the Seine or the Loire… I'd get an idea, tie up in the shade of some willows and out would come my differential equations. I'd only need the odd textbook. Anyway, why not stop off at French universities along the route? Set up collaborations – give the odd seminar…"

"What about your painting?" Arfur asked

" I'd forgotten that. But of course: I will keep my easel and gear up in the forepeak – and when we came upon some view so utterly beautiful that I couldn't resist, or some gnarled old peasant with his pipe upside down in his mouth, then I'd do an inspired painting. And when we got back to Britain I'd sell the lot – and we'd actually make a small profit on the holiday – so we could go out again the following summer – and the next…"

"And the next…" Arfur added

"… and why come back up the Danube anyway?" Sturdee said: "I've always fancied the Greek islands. When we've rounded the toe of Italy we can head off across the Adriatic for the Ionian Isles . They're gorgeous I've heard. Then when we are tired of paradise and retsina we'll sail South around the Peloponnese until the whole Aegean opens up before us with its many mythic archipelagos – the Sporades, the Cyclades, the Dodecanese….."

"Who is we?" Joan interrupted "You keep on mentioning 'we' ."

"Me and the boat of course," Sturdee replied " But I dare say I could persuade special friends to come out and enjoy the odd week on board with us."

"I'd come." Arfur volunteered.

"So you could," Sturdee agreed : "Why, you'd take up almost no room at all. You could bunk in the forecastle – or have a quarter berth under the chart-table. I could teach you to sail and navigate… Provided your mathematics was good enough. Ah – but I've thought of a snag . You would be no use on board."

"Why not?" Arfur sounded indignant.

"You don't know any French, that's why not. How could you go ashore in France and do the shopping – or ask the way, if you couldn't speak French?"

"And he doesn't want to learn." Joan added "He told me so when I offered to teach him – didn't you Arfur?"

"That was before… 'fore I 'eard abaht his boat. I could chinge me mind."

"I'm afraid you'd have to," Sturdee continued " I couldn't take the responsibility of having a boy on board who could get lost because he couldn't speak the local language – no by gum that *would* be foolish."

"How was the Shag-bat?" Loader asked Sturdee back to their office.

"The what?"

"The 'Shagbat'– that's what the flying-officer types call the Walrus."

"I love her. I want one of my own."

" You'll be lucky; she is the Admiral's means of getting about his command. You know she's amphibious?"

"I noticed some wheels tucked away."

"One day she goes down to London, landing at Hendon Aerodrome; the next he flies out to Tobermory and anchors off the quay. She lands so slowly she can even land on an aircraft-carrier without needing an arrester hook."

"That's amazing."

"You know she was designed by RJ Mitchell at Supermarine – the chap who designed the Spitfire."

"What for?

"Long-range fleet reconnaissance. Shagbats can be catapulted from a battleship ,and even from cruisers, to get an eagle's eye view of the surroundings out to 300 miles. If we'd had just one at Jutland Jellicoe would have sunk the Kaiser's entire High Seas Fleet."

"Then they're exactly what we want to accompany our convoys!" Sturdee was excited.

" Alas there are snags Giles. You need a big ship to catapult one – bigger than any of our current escort vessels. Then when they've completed their missions they must land back on the ocean to be hoisted back aboard their mother ship. You've seen the North Atlantic…"

"Yes; every mission would be a suicide mission…"

"Exactly. The Shagbat was designed for the calm waters and clear skies of the South Pacific. And they're too small to be fitted with radar apparently. So even if you could launch them they wouldn't see much from above the North Atlantic clouds."

Sturdee was deflated. Loader continued:

" They are used for antisubmarine patrols flying out of Northern Ireland. They've been damned useful in the immediate Western Approaches but they can't get out to sea much more than 200 miles. We need to get out a thousand or more."

"Long-range is crucial."

"As it is for our Escort Vessels. Almost none of our fast escort vessels have the range we need in the Atlantic: our destroyers were designed for the North Sea."

"So I understand."

"And our long-range escort vessels – only corvettes at present , are too bloody slow to catch U-boats."

"So, it's the combination of long range and high-speed we need – both in the air and on the sea . That might be impossible? "

" The bloody U-boats have it: 7500 nautical miles and nearly 18 knots. Our only hope apparently is refuelling our faster escort vessels at sea. I know Noble is pressing very hard for that – but it's not easy – not in rotten weather at least ."

"And it always seems to be rotten…"

"Up on the Great Circle route it is."

Sturdee cursed himself for a fool. Yet again he'd neglected something fundamental. He'd assumed that airborne radar would come to their rescue, but if Hanbury hadn't reminded him on the clifftop at Worth Matravers he would have ignored the problem of aircraft range. If Britain didn't have, and couldn't acquire in time, radar-equipped aircraft that could patrol the mid-Atlantic, then that was where Doenitz would station his entire U-boat cordon, and win the decisive battle. If nothing else his lapse of imagination illustrated the weakness of a tiny scientific group like his own. He and Loader couldn't be expected to cover everything. He knew from his civilian experience, and from his time at Bawdsey Manor, that bigger scientific groups were better, if only because they fostered stimulating interactions between scientists with different preoccupations and different skills. For instance if there'd been an airman in his group they surely wouldn't have overlooked the crucial factor of aircraft range. He vowed to canvass Noble for another team member – one from RAF Coastal Command. In the mean time he would have to try and work out the science of flying-range for himself. It could win or lose not only the battle but the entire war.

In any spare moments Loader had put Gwen to plotting on large wallcharts of the Atlantic the positions of every ship sunk by a U-boat, the different charts for the different phases of the war. What was remarkable and thought-provoking about them was the way they differed so much from epoch to epoch. For instance, in the first six months of the war sinkings had taken place in the south-western approaches to the English Channel and the Irish Sea. For most of 1940 they'd switch to the north western approaches between Northern Ireland and Iceland. Latterly the sinkings had scattered themselves all over the eastern Atlantic with concentrations off Gibraltar and Freetown in West Africa. Staring at them every day it was easy to read into them significances they probably didn't deserve. Presumably, like any good admiral, Doenitz was switching his point of attack to where his boats could sink the most at the lowest risk to themselves. After the fall of France they'd driven the British out of the south-western approaches and then followed them around Ireland to the north-west. Their latter switch to mid-Atlantic and beyond presumably testified to this success of convoying out to the MOMP or midocean meeting point where the convoys either dispersed or were taken over by light Canadian escorts. The really angry rash broke out in in the middle South of Cape Farewell – the southern tip of Greenland. It was also, and probably not by coincidence, the very area where it was impossible to provide air cover now – and might be so in future.

Admiral Noble had insisted that the RAF be housed right next to him in Derby House. Number 15 Group of Coastal Command, responsible for the whole North Atlantic, was headed by Air Vice-Marshal Robb whose operational office was next door to Noble's , both looking out through neighbouring windows at the Atlantic Plot on the far side of the giant room. The bitter wrangling between the RAF and Royal Navy which had been going on since they had separated at the end of the First World War had recently been settled by the Cabinet: Coastal Command would remain in the RAF but operational control of its aircraft would go to the admiral commanding the sea-area in question. In his usual tactful way Noble had established friendly relations with his air-staff, so Sturdee didn't feel any hesitation in knocking on their doors ,asking any number of awkward questions and finally organising a flight far out into the Atlantic on a Catalina flying boat. A squadron leader who had recently completed a tour of duty patrolling himself, explained: "Coastal Command has always been the poor cousin within the RAF, partly because it was only formed in 1936. It has the glamour of neither Fighter Command nor Bomber Command so we have never had the privilege of specifying or commissioning our own aircraft – which is ridiculous considering that we have very special needs. Obviously we are not much interested in altitude, but we are very interested in the endurance and range. Why should they give us old crows – that is to say bomber command's hand-me-downs, instead of albatrosses? I don't blame the Royal Navy getting mad at us – or even contemptuous – when we don't have the equipment to do our job. Yes we do let you down. The only decent aircraft we have a present is the Short Brothers Sunderland flying-boat."

"I've seen them patrolling above our convoys when I was at sea. Everyone felt safer when there was a Sunderland around. I don't know whether that was a delusion?"

"You might well ask. We haven't even got a decent anti-submarine weapon yet. Our 100-pound bomb is far too feeble. But we will be getting a version of the Navy's 300-pound depth charge with a nose and fins to give it aerial stability. That should make a big difference."

"What about range?" Sturdee explained his worry about the mid ocean air gap – especially as they moved towards the crux of the battle."

"The Sunderland can patrol for three to four hours out at 600 nautical miles, the others – Whitlys and so on, only out to 300 nautical miles. That indeed leaves a vast gap to the South of Greenland over 1000 miles wide. I don't see how we are ever going to patrol that. Some call it 'The Black Pit'."

"We've got to!" Sturdee slammed one fist into the other "Our figures show that convoys accompanied by air patrols very rarely get attacked. And later, when Doenitz gets his full numbers, air patrols will be our only way to keep his shadowing submarines down and so prevent him building big wolf packs."

"Well I don't know where we're going to get the necessary aircraft . The only thing we have in the pipeline is the American PB-Y Catalina – it's a seaplane with enormous endurance, 20 hours or more. There are some already out in Northern Ireland and some in Iceland."

"Do you think there's any chance I could hitch a lift in one?"

"Doubtful. Every extra bod they have to carry means less fuel and therefore less range. They're pretty sticky about that sort of thing."

Sturdee went directly to Noble to talk about the airgap and Noble introduced him to Air Vice Marshal Robb – who looked like an insignificant pigeon beside the Admiral:

"He's been very useful to me Robb. You might think of borrowing him yourself. He could report directly to you on air-force matters. You understand Sturdee? You two should talk."

Robb was amenable: " My previous boss Air Marshall Bowhill, previous Head of Coastal Command – was a big believer in scientific advisers. In fact he appointed what he calls his ' Operational Research Unit' a few months ago, headed by a Professor Patrick Blackett. Have you heard of them?"

"No sir , but I've heard of Blackett."

"Bowhill put them to work on the Bay of Biscay problem"

"What's that?"

"How can 19 Group sink more – indeed sink *any* U-boats in the Bay? U-boats have to transit the Bay both outward and inward bound from their bases in Brittany. The RAF has set itself the task of sinking them."

Sturdee was going to ask: 'But how is it you are going to find them?' suspecting that the RAF had fallen into the same folly as the Royal Navy in its

Hunting- group days, but decided to let it pass for now. He needed Robb's support.

The Air Vice Marshal listened to Sturdee's request:

"I don't see why not. I'm flying out to our Castle Archdale base next week. You can come with me in the Walrus and I'll try to spirit you aboard one of 209 Squadron's Catalinas. They go out for very long flights – one was out 26 hours during the hunt for the *Bismarck*."

The Fleet Air Arm Walrus flew them out across the Irish Sea and then down through County Fermanagh in the Southwest corner of Northern Ireland. They came down over Enniskillen then down over Lower Loch Erne with all its white seaplanes swinging at anchor. Sturdee had never seen a greener or emptier country in all his life. The water sparkled in the sunlight as they went ashore in a launch, and although he couldn't see it he could smell the sea somewhere close at hand.

The CO of 209 Squadron , who'd been briefed about his mission, introduced him to a Flight Lieutenant Fox who barely looked 20 years old:

"We're happy to have you. I understand you are a radar expert? We can certainly do with better radars. Crafty Fox here will take you. He's scheduled to go out tonight, Met – permitting, to meet a convoy in mid-Atlantic."

"I've got to go out to the kite." The boy-captain announced "We can have a dekko around her in daylight. This afternoon is for some serious kipping. I'd advise you to get your head down too." He waved down a launch.

There were two dozen or so large white flying-boats swinging at their moorings in the sun, fitters up on their high wings servicing their engines.

"K for Ken is a Short Sunderland." The boy wonder pointed, "Pride of the fleet. Ten crew, four Bristol Hercules engines, range of 1800 nautical miles. Known as the Flying Porcupine because it bristles with guns, so Jerry tends to leave them alone. Whoa; here comes one!"

A huge white flying boat came sweeping down towards them, barely above the surface of the lake, its radial engines whispering.

"It's so quiet" Sturdee remarked, noticing the tail-gunner in his tiny turret with twin machine guns poking out beneath the huge tail fin.

"U-boats sometimes don't hear it coming" Fox said, "Gives its rear gunner a chance to press his tit. Alas it's only a machine-gun – can't penetrate the pressure-hull we think. We need explosive cannon-shells for that. Here we are: 'G for George' " he spoke with pride.

"It's certainly an odd-looking machine" Sturdee replied, but then could have bitten off his tongue. "But beautiful too. More beautiful than a Sunderland."

" Do you think so?"

He'd evidently said the right thing

The Catalina consisted of a large straight wing with its fuselage , like a boat, or the the gondola of an airship, hanging underneath it on a pylon. The two engines: close together, projected out ahead of the wing above the cockpit:

"Pratt & Whitney Wasps" The captain boasted" more than a thousand horse-power each. Mind you she's not fast – that wasn't the idea. Some people call her 'The world's fastest Balloon'."

The launch pulled alongside the stern and they climbed aboard through one of the clear plastic blisters which stuck out to port and starboard. Fox remarked: " Wonderful for observation – which after all is our main purpose." They made their way forward through the roomy cabin:

"Wireless operator to port here with the radar operator beside him. We carry three of those to avoid fatigue. On the right here is the navigator's desk. He is by far the most important chap on board. If he can't find the convoy once we get there then we might as well have not taken off. And if he can't find our way home we have to ditch – which means curtains all round in the North Atlantic. I'd be grateful, by the way, if you didn't bother him – he needs all the concentration he can get. This is my seat – that is the co-pilot's. The bombardier-front gunner lies down there forrard , and all three of us keep the watch ahead. That's five pairs of eyes and one radar all searching ahead. Nobody goes to sleep because of those buggers ." He pointed out through the canopy to the propellers just outside, with the engines above: "The din they make will wake a whale. But one can sleep in the four stern bunks . The engineer works back in the pylon, next to the two off-duty crew."

"Fuel?"

"That is up above us in the wing tanks; they put in over 6 tons yesterday. We could carry more – but could we get it into the air? Calm water with little wind is not good for flying-boats. We need strong headwinds and steep waves to knock us up."

"Weapons?""

"We're carrying four one-hundred- pound antisubmarine bombs under the wings. The general opinion is that they're no bloody good. Not much bang, and they go off too deep. More for putting the wind-up Jerry if you ask me. The trouble is we are too slow and too noisy. He's generally dived and gone before we are on top of him."

They were woken at midnight and given breakfast. Sturdee went out to the boat in the launch with the rest of the crew while the captain, the navigator and the

chief WT-man went to a briefing. It was a fine night with a half Moon on the
lapping lake water. A couple of other boats were already revving their engines
preparatory to take-off.

The co-pilot, who looked to be Fox's even younger brother, helped Sturdee
into his flying gear and flotation jacket and settled him down into his own, the co-
pilot's seat.

"It's strictly forbidden – but seeing it's you the skipper said okay. You
mustn't disturb him on take-off. He'll be very busy on his own. We'll be flying
out to sea across the Republic of Ireland."

"Isn't that illegal?"

"Strictly speaking yes. Certainly, Jerry would be furious if he knew. But
the Irish government has created this narrow Donegal Corridor for us which saves
an hour each way. It's the least they can do, seeing all their imports come in on
convoys escorted by us."

Fox arrived and started issuing orders over the intercom. The two engines
burst into deafening life, sending wavelets across the moonlit surface. A fitter
came forward: disappeared into the bombardier's cubbyhole and then appeared
outside Studee's window with a boat-hook in his hand. The boat swung first
one-way than the other as they revved up the two colossal engines in turn. Sturdee
began to feel nervous. What had seemed like an adventure into which he had put
too little thought was now becoming deadly serious. A mere schoolboy was about
to take them far out over the ocean in a complex mass of machinery with
absolutely no room for mechanical or human failure. If they came down in the
Atlantic they could look for nothing better than a cold and miserable death – the
quicker the better. And now he couldn't remember precisely why he had come.

A klaxon sounded, the fitter threw off their mooring and wriggled back
inside. The two engines roared upwards a tone and the boat moved forwards in
between two darkened Sunderlands and towards the flight path. Fox at the wheel
swung his head vigorously back and forth before turning down the flight path
towards the south western reach of Loch Erne. He spoke into his microphone
again then pushed forward the two throttles , holding them to their stops. The
engine noise rose to a crescendo and the boat began to gather way, bobbing up and
down as it went. Looking out of his window Sturdee could see spray flying out
behind the floats near the wing tips. The plane was lifting a bit, climbing onto is
hydrofoil step , but still securely held to the surface by the force of hydrodynamic
suction. A lighted rowing- boat, part of the flare path, flew past.

"Get off you bitch, fly you fucker…"

Sturdee saw the imprecations on Fox's lips , even if he couldn't hear them.

In the moonlight a speedboat shot across the bow in front of them:

"Whomp!" The Catalina hit the speedboat's wake and lifted a couple of
feet into the air. The shuddering beneath them ceased, the air-speed gathered, the

nose began to slowly rise until Sturdee could see that they were just going to surmount the low hills ahead.

As they nosed over the rise they saw the brilliant lights of a town to starboard. Sturdee was shocked for a moment, before he remembered that Eire was a neutral country at peace.

"That's Donegal Town and that's Killibegs Harbour," Fox came through on the intercom: "We're over the ocean already. Thank God for the Donegal Corridor. The old girl took a bit of bouncing to get off there. We've got a hell of a lot of fuel on board." He throttled back to a steady drone:

"115 knots air speed – that's all she can do in cruise. And it's not unusual to get a headwind of 60 knots."

"Christ almighty!" It was Sturdee's turn to swear.

"As you say. We absolutely rely on dead reckoning navigation. No wireless use whatsoever. More than 500 miles out there we've got to hit a tiny little convoy, and this thing might be crabbing at 30° to its true course. The navigator's estimate of wind-speed and direction has to be very nearly perfect. He's going to make a measurement every few minutes for the next few hours. One mistake and we are right in the shit."

Sturdee was incredulous :"How the hell does he do it?

"Using great skill and a vast amount of practice. That's why we don't want you to bother him. Maybe I'll show you myself in the morning. But you can understand why we all call him 'Einstein' ."

"I had no idea…"

"Now I suggest you go aft and get some more shut-eye. There will be absolutely nothing to see for the next 6 to 8 hours – not until we are due to rendezvous with the convoy. I'm going to hand over the boat to George, that's the automatic pilot. He can fly far more accurately than any human – and precise flying is just as important as precise navigation out here. One is obviously no good without the other."

When he awoke it took Sturdee some seconds to recall where he was. The Pratt & Whitney engines groaned steadily on, their noise tolerable in the rear cabin. The boat shook a little from time to time as if it was negotiating an air-pocket. They were presumably only a few hundred feet above the sea. He imagined just below him the ugly grey waves that would have been above him when he'd stood on the corvette's afterdeck. A blown fuse, magneto failure, a temporary blockage in a petrol filter, a failure in the autopilot… and they would be crashing into that hell in a second or two. He tried to imagine the chaos: total darkness; injured crew; fuel-laden wing crushing them down below the surface; icy water rushing into the blisters; the stench of aviation petrol everywhere; instant sea-sickness, shock, the hopelessness of their situation, the impossibility of rescue … That was the reality with which these young man had to live on every ocean reconnaissance. What were the statistics he wondered? How many sorties never returned? What was the life expectancy of a single crew?

To his amazement he picked up the smell of grilling sausage and bacon and shortly afterwards the cabin light came on to reveal one of the fitters with an excellent breakfast comprising cereal, grill, toast and butter and tea:

"It helps to keep the lookouts alert at night," their waiter explained: "It's growing light; Daddy Einstein predicts convoy rendezvous in 30 minute's time. The Skipper wants everyone up forrard staring out."

Standing behind and between the two pilots Sturdee looked down on a colourless featureless seascape of grey upon grey, leaden apart from the occasional breaking crest. They were higher than he'd imagine, just under cloud-base at 1700 feet by the altimeter. Behind him to Starboard the navigator, 10 years older than the rest, was working on his chart with dividers and parallel rulers. To his left a radar operator had his head over the eyepiece of the set. There was a palpable air of tense expectancy:

"Six minutes to contact ." The navigator intoned .

The Catalina droned on . By Sturdee's watch they had been in the air for over 6 and a half hours, and only God and perhaps the navigator knew where the winds had taken them.

"Radar contact expected at 30 nautical miles." The navigator announced.

"No contact. Sea clutter fair to good." the radar operator replied.

"Visual horizon estimated 15 to 20 miles" the co-pilot added.

"This is where the radar is really useful." the captain explained." Not much cop for finding U-boats but it can find a convoy up to 60 miles away even in heavy cloud, or at night."

"Radar contact!" The operator couldn't conceal his excitement "Bearing Port 15; distance 55 nautical miles; Many ships."

"Bloody well done Navigator!" Fox expressed their universal appreciation.

Eventually Sturdee could pick up streaks of black smoke blowing down towards them on the westerly wind. Then a dozen or more columns of black ships, each outlined in a sparkling white wake which streamed astern, filled most of the horizon ahead.

"Prepare recognition signal."

The Cat canted slightly to port as the co-pilot picked up the Aldiss lamp and sighted is on the leading escort vessel at the head of the convoy, evidently a destroyer from the bone in its teeth.

"If we don't signal we're likely to be shot at." Fox explained. "Some of those merchant ships carry guns and they're trigger-happy."

"Recognition signal acknowledged." The co-pilot translated : "Await my instructions."

From the bridge of the destroyer Sturdee could see a single light blinking at them from the bridge of the destroyer.

"Patrol… flanks… and… particularly rear of convoy. U-boat detected in vicinity from radio transmission two hours ago." The co-pilot read it slowly.

"Acknowledge." Fox banked the plane sharply to port: "Action stations! We'll creep up on the bastard from astern . Navigator plot convoy. Coming down to 200 feet."

Some of the ships look massive as they sped by, although they were loaded up to their plimsoll-marks with valuable cargoes for Britain. Sturdee noticed one vessel with a deck cargo of aircraft. Beside the Red Ensign of the Home Fleet he picked out Dutch, Norwegian, Danish, Greek , US and Swedish flags. Crews waved up to them from their bridges, probably relieved to have an aerial escort at last after the long lonely passage of the mid-Atlantic.

They skirted the horizon, leaving the convoy behind, hoping to evade any U-boat lookout.

"Okay chaps, eyes skinned now. Watch your sectors. We're on the convoy's course."

"You're too low Skip if you want to use the radar. All I've got are   bloody sea returns."

"Okay, I'm climbing."

"Contact! Radar :Starboard ten ;range four miles."

"I see him!" Fox yelled   "It's a bloody U-boat fellows. Prepare to attack."

Sturdee saw the submarine ahead, end on, nothing more than the small black conning-tower with spray occasionally jumping up around it. The seaplane dived down again for invisibility, gathering speed.

"I'll come up again at half a mile bombardier."

"Acknowledge. What settings?"

"Wait…

"150 knots Skipper."

"Wait…"

"He's seen us. He's diving."

Sturdee had never expected to actually see a U-boat – but there it was, black shining wet like a dolphin, already submerging, it's 88-mm gun on the foredeck tearing through the water and disappearing, conning-tower empty.

"Bomb gone!"

The U-boat had disappeared astern; they heard machine gun fire from the rear of the plane as the two observers opened fire through their open blisters.

"Climbing. Prepare to mark position with orange smoke float. I'm coming around again."

"Bomb exploded Skipper. U-boat disappeared. No obvious wreckage."

"Keep your eye on the explosion ."

"Wilco."

Apart from some froth there was little to mark the U-boat's last position. Seeing how many depth-charges U-boats could take it seemed very unlikely to Sturdee that their hundred-pound bomb had done any significant damage. The pilot lined up the plane again and began his dive.

"Do you see it?"

"I think so skipper."

"Drop floats when ready."

"Smoke gone!"

"Okay, climbing to one thousand. Prepare to fire three red Very Lights to attract Escort. Keep your eyes open in case the bastard surfaces. If he does we'll bomb him again. And don't forget – where there's one U-boat there may be more! Eyes skinned chaps. That's what we're here for."

In due course an escort vessel came racing up to the U-boat's last position, marked by their several smoke signals. A destroyer, she immediately began an asdic search , quartering back and forth at 15 knots. Sturdee could see depth charge crews closed up on her quarter deck. They climbed up to cloud base from where they could watch both the convoy and the action below."

" Convoy is changing course skipper."

'It would.' Sturdee thought. The escort commander would assume that the U-boat had radioed their present position and course to call up reinforcements. It was vital to keep him down while the convoy escaped in the new direction.

The Cat remained with the convoy for five hours by which time its replacement had arrived from Northern Ireland. During that time the destroyer made an asdic contact and began depth charging. From aloft they watched over 40 depth charges roiling and shuddering the water beneath – to no evident effect.

"He's not much bloody good is he ?" Fox was contemptuous.

Sturdee thought of explaining the depth problem to the airmen but decided, on security grounds, that he could say nothing.

On the way home the adrenaline of the attack gave way to despondency. As the captain put it: "What's the point of coming all the sodding way out here, finding a U-boat, attacking it, and seeing it get away. What good are we doing? We might as well be bombing Germany."

Sturdee had to remind them they'd done 95% of their job:

"You've saved that convoy of over 50 laden ships. Almost certainly they'll get home now unmolested. The chances of a second U-boat finding them are 10 or 20 to 1 against. It would've been nice to sink that U-boat but don't forget that the whole object of the exercise is 'The safe and timely arrival of our ships' – and that you have ensured. If that U-boat had called up 10 or so his mates, as he might well have done over the next 12 hours, it would have been slaughter down there. We could easily have lost 10 or 20 vessels, and their cargoes, with most of their crews."

On their way back the Navigator– who turned out to be a maths master from Barry in South Wales – was even busier than on the way out.

"We'll be short of fuel when we approach Ireland" The co-pilot explained. "This bus won't survive on the open sea, she can't come down on solid ground, and if we land in Eire we'll be interned for the duration, along with the plane. Rules of war. So old Einstein here has got to thread us through that narrow Donegal corridor, a mile or two wide – and probably in the dark. So, we will leave him in peace shall we – unless you fancy several years is an Irish internment camp – miles out in the bogs? We pilots are supposed to learn enough navigation to get us home – in case the real navigator gets shot up – it happens you know. I'll try to demonstrate the gentle art."

The skill in navigating the world's fastest balloon lay in very accurately determining the wind's speed and direction over the sea. Sturdee lay up in the nose and used the bomb-sight to align on a wave-cap on the sea. Then he turned the sight until the cap appeared to move exactly along the drift wires. From the bomb-sight heading he learned to measure the drift. He then did the same with a wave-cap astern, using a special navigator's periscope that fitted down through the floor. If the seaplane made precise turns in between such fixes it was possible to infer the plane's velocity over the sea. But that it would enable them to hit the Donegal Corridor after something like 20 hours over the ocean seemed like an impossible aspiration to Sturdee.

The Pratt & Whitneys droned on. No less than three more hot and tasty meals were served. Sturdee thought of the poor devils down on the corvettes, living on little but bully-beef sandwiches and cocoa. Darkness began to gather ahead of them in the East. Everyone went forward and took a surreptitious look at the petrol gauges, especially when they went past the 18-hour mark.

Sturdee stood out between the pilots and the navigator waiting for land to show up ahead.

"Not much more I can do now," said the Navigator who was called Daddy by the rest of the crew because he was almost 30. "If I could take a star sight I would." He showed Sturdee his bubble-sextant in which the true horizon was replaced by a bubble – as in a spirit level.:

"Our RDF set" – he used the old-fashioned name for radar, "Comes in damned useful at this point. Our Mark-Two set is not much use against U-boats – but it can find coastlines can't it Talbert?"

"If it's bloody there!" The radar operator growled.

"Well it won't have moved much. You can be sure of that." Fox turned to Sturdee : "When are we going to get those Mark 3 sets everyone is talking about? If we're going to sink U-boats we need longer range and faster aircraft, bigger bombs, and above all better radar sets."

"They're in the pipeline I'm told ."

"Lights ahead!" Fox called out.

Sturdee could see the faintest of faint glows up in the sky – reflections of city lights far below.

Later the radar picked up the coastline.

"Right bang on the money again Daddy." Fox said "That's Killibegs Harbour alright though Donegal Town is lost in low cloud. How long have we been out?"

"19 hours 34 so far." Daddy wrote in his notebook.

"Drinks all round for Daddy chaps. He's brought us right through the slot again."

Cheers emanated from all ends of the plane as the engine note began to fall, partly of acclaim, partly of relief.

"God I'm knackered. " the radar operator switched off his set as they lost altitude descending into the Corridor.

"Strap yourselves in chaps . I have requested permission to land. We'll be landing to the West as per usual."

"They've lit the flare path – all three bloody lights."

"They've fired a green. Permission to land."

"Christ I could murder a beer."

"Here we go chaps. I'm taking the kite down. And if you miss the buoy again Spriggs it's pints all-round."

Sturdee stayed on at the Loch Erne base for several days, talking to the airmen and trying to get a feel for the way the battle would turn.

There was no doubt that the Catalina was an old-fashioned aircraft with its elephantine speed and almost non-existent weaponry. If fifty 450-pound directed depth charges were not going to sink a U-boat what chance had a single 100 - pound bomb dropped from a high overhead? And yet the sheer presence of the flying boat out there with a convoy had made all the difference . From its altitude it had immediately spotted the shadowing U-boat , put it down, and helped to keep it down whilst the convoy altered course and made its escape. Indeed, a telephone call to Roger Winn at the Admiralty was informative:

"Yes, we worried about that convoy – several U-boatsd were converging on it under orders from Doenitz's headquarters in Lorient. When the convoy changed course of its own volition they lost it and the convoy got clean away. So your Catalina made a difference I suppose. No I'm afraid the escort didn't sink the U-boat."

So, G for George's patrol illustrated yet again the vital importance of air escort. Because of their speed and height, aircraft could put down shadowing U-boat anywhere near a convoy and so nullify the whole wolf-pack tactic. No matter how ineffective they were as hunters they were indispensable as scarecrows – able to keep the predators at bay. This explained the bone-dry statistics – which went all the way back to the First World War: convoys with both surface and air escorts were seldom if ever attacked. As Doenitz built up his numbers it would become ever more necessary, even vital, to air-patrol the whole of the Atlantic convoy route.

To estimate the nature of that challenge Sturdee traced himself yet another map of the North Atlantic this time inscribed with circles of range surrounding the United Kingdom. The 500-mile circle passed well beyond the West Coast of Ireland. The 1000 mile circle bisected Iceland. The 1500- and 2000-mile circles ran down the east and West coasts of Greenland respectively while the 2500-mile circle touched Newfoundland. With the Catalina as the longest range aircraft available to the Allies, and with the bases in Northern Ireland, Iceland and Newfoundland, they could patrol for two hours or so 800 miles out, but that still left a gap 600 miles wide South-east of Greenland and centred on the meridian at 40° West. That was where Doenitz was going to fight his final battle. Even in good weather every convoy would take three days and three nights to cross it and with 100 U-boats constantly out there on station the German wolfpacks would rip them to pieces. The Allies would lose the Battle of the Atlantic and lose the war. At any one time there would be four convoys in the Gap which meant the Doenitz would be able to concentrate 25 U-boats against each convoy, roughly one U-boat for every two cargo vessels: it would be slaughter. Whole convoys might disappear in a single night – carrying their helpless crew with them because the rescue of so many shipwrecked men at once would be beyond rescue ships and escort vessels as had not been torpedoed themselves.. When the awful news got out some merchant seaman would refuse to put to sea and defeat, final and complete, would come suddenly. And all this, only 12 to 18 months ahead. Unless, and this was the challenge that faced Britain, aircraft could be found that could reach the Gap, patrol those seas, and hold shadowing U-boats down. That was the only putative chink that Sturdee could see in Doenitz's armour. If he couldn't call his wolves in then the helpless ships might still slip by.

The challenge was stark. Britain had not much more than 12 months to develop an aircraft that could fly out 1300 miles from its base, stay on patrol for several hours, find U-boats and attacks them lethally, and then fly back to base again. It was a capability way beyond anything that existed at present. Even the Catalina was 500 miles short in range, the Sunderland 700 and the rest of Coastal Command's raggle-taggle of obsolescent bombers almost 900. In any case none of the available aircraft had a lethal anti-submarine weapon or an effective radar. No wonder Coastal Command had so far failed to sink a single U-boat.

Out at lower Loch Erne Sturdee's confidence that Britain would eventually win, began to evaporate. He had always assumed that radar would eventually prove to be a British trump card. But a radar set on an escort vessel not many feet above the surface would always have its limitations, particularly in range. In daylight it can see no further than that the naked eye, a fact of nature that was unlikely to change by very much. But from the new Mark III 10 cm radars – powered by cavity magnetrons – a Coastal Command aircraft could survey a whole convoy battlefield– if only they could be flown out to the battleground.

The base commander asked Sturdee to give a talk to the aircrew about his research and about the future of radar. A couple of dozen turned up and the talk evolved into a brainstorming session along the lines which Taffy Bowen had organised at Bawdsey Manor. Obsessed as he was about the Air Gap Sturdee brought up the question of whether it would be possible to develop a suitable very long range, or VLR,aircraft in time.

"Why not convert one of those four-engine bombers now coming into service with Bomber Command?" Someone suggested. "Handley Page Halifaxs or Avro Lancasters?"

"But would they have the range ?" Sturdee asked.

"Almost certainly not – not as they are. What range do you want?"

"Well we need 1400 nautical miles just to get from base to the far side of the Gap. Double that to get back – that's 2800. Add six hours patrolling out there at 200 knots and that's 4000 nautical miles altogether."

Several of the aircrew whistled.

"And you should have at least 10% for contingencies – headwinds in particular."

"Say 4,500 Miles then" Sturdee concluded . "Is there any chance whatsoever of attaining that range – because if we can't we might lose this war?"

There was a long silence.

It was broken eventually by one of the squadron CO.s:

"I went on a Lancaster conversion course. I can tell you about its performance."

"Thanks – please do."

"Carrying 2200 gallons of fuel it has a maximum range of 2400 miles. I always remember that it does 1.1 miles to the gallon."

There were groans from the audience.

"Yes – but wait on – that was carrying a bomb load of 6 ½ tons. We wouldn't need to carry more than four depth charges at 250 pounds each. Say half a ton."

"That would allow it to carry six more tons of fuel"

"Aviation fuel weighs 10 pounds a gallon." A flight engineer pointed out.

"So one ton is 220 gallons" Sturdee remarked, getting out his small slide-rule "Six tons 1320 gallons – which is 60% of the original fuel load of 2,220 gallons. That will increase range by 60% – up to 3850 miles – still 700 miles short."

"Ah yes" The squadron CO pointed out" but a bomber that has to fly over Germany would carry a whole lot of extra weight we wouldn't need at sea – armour for instance to protect the crew, and other vital components – against flak. I bet there's a ton of that we could strip out and convert in to feel."

"That's another 220 gallons Sturdee calculated" or 240 miles. That's still gets us only up to 4,100."

"Yes, but we don't need all those ruddy gun-turrets sticking out into the air-flow – the dorsal and ventral turrets in particular.– that's a 10% improvement in both speed and range ."

"That's 4,500 miles by God – exactly what we need!." Somebody said.

"Now are you sure?" Sturdee asked "This is incredibly important. If it's true there is a real chance we could have the very long-range aircraft we need in time for the crux of the battle, but to convert them in time won't be easy. My boss– that's Admiral Noble, and your boss Air Marshall Joubert – would have to go before the Prime Minister's Battle of the Atlantic Committee and convince them without one shred of doubt."

Hubbub broke out among the audience as the young men argued among themselves over the details.

"It's too important to leave this in the air" Sturdee summed up : "I suggest we meet again here tomorrow at 11 – such of you as can come. In the meantime, thoroughly check your figures, and I will try to estimate just how many such VLR aircraft we will need – because that will be vital too. I'll give you those figures tomorrow – and we can argue about them."

When they reconvened, opinion have hardened around the 4,500-mile figure – particularly so when the Halifax bomber turned out to have much the same potential range as the Lancaster.

"After all," somebody pointed out. "It's more a question of combined engine-power than anything else. The more tonnage of fuel you can drag up into the air the further you are going to go. It's the engines, it's always the engines not the airframe. But engines aren't glamorous. It's invariably the airframe that gets the popular press."

"Why don't we need flying boats?" Sturdee asked, to be greeted by a long silence.

"Well you don't want to drag a bloody great boat with the aerodynamic properties of brick shit-house through the air for 4,500 miles."

"And anyway, boats will be no good for dropping depth charges. You can't have bomb-bay doors in a boat and you can't hang 300-pound barrels of explosive in the air-stream under a wing."

"No, that's clear." Sturdee made a note. "Now here is my estimate of the numbers required. At any one time there are 20 convoys at sea in the North Atlantic, ten going one way, ten the other. The 600-mile wide air Gap comprises one fifth of the entire 3000-mile voyage so that means four convoys in the gap at any one time. If each convoy requires 24-hour round the clock air escort, and a single VLRA can patrol for six hours, we need an absolute minimum of 4×4 or 16 in all. But that makes no allowance for servicing, for losses, for rest etc . I reckon we need 64 or about four squadrons, one in Northern Ireland or the Hebrides, one in Iceland, and two in Newfoundland – probably with the Royal Canadian Air Force."

It was pointed out that because of the perpetual fogs off the Newfoundland Grand Banks, and because of the prevailing offshore wind out there, the flying conditions on the Canadian side were much worse and would call for more aircraft and more crew , four squadrons out there instead of two.

Sturdee was able to sum up:

"I would like to thank you all. The whole experience, including my flight, has been a real eye-opener for me. You can have no doubt that your presence circling a convoy is crucial to their success in getting through – absolutely crucial. By holding shadowing U-boats down where they can neither see, communicate, or even keep up, you prevent the assembling of the wolf pack, as G for George did the other day. You will be pleased to hear that, thanks to Crafty Fox and his crew, 55 heavily burdened ships got through entirely unscathed." This was greeted by ironic cheers.

"The fact that you are not as yet sinking U-boats is unfortunate – but is not critical to the course of the battle *for now*. But things will have to change, and will change as better weapons and better radars – which are both in the pipeline and only months away, arrive." This last was greeted by ribald or sceptical remarks.

" 'G for George''s little encounter took place out 700 miles, a range no other aircraft but a Catalina from Loch Erne could manager at present. But a year from now the battle will surely move out another 400 Miles – at least. In that case we will have to do without air escort altogether – which means – at least in my opinion – that we will lose."

" But now you have convinced me that the means to win that coming battle exists – at least in principle: a stripped down four-engined bomber with a range of 4,500 nautical miles. I will do all I can to bring your ideas to the attention of those in higher places, and in particular to Admiral Noble, commander-in-chief Western Approaches, who is responsible to the Admiralty, and to the Prime Minister, for winning the Battle of the Atlantic. But I am only one voice – and a pretty insignificant one at that. Therefore, I suggest, indeed I beg you, to do everything you can, up through your own chain of command, to bring that VLRA into existence *as soon as possible*! If it comes two years from now it will be too late!"

CHAPTER 13
KINDLY LIGHT

"I tell you what Loader, each of my excursions to the front line has proved incredibly valuable. It's all very well trying to answer questions which your boss has set you; but the really crucial questions may be the ones you can only see for yourself. That's certainly true in science. It's seemingly also true in war."

"For instance?"

"We would never have recognised the U-boat depth problem if I hadn't gone out on *Pimpernel* and witnessed an Asdic attack. And now – if I hadn't been to Loch Erne – I wouldn't have seen the vital importance of VLR aircraft– and caught a glimpse of its possible solution. Only airmen could have seen that. But they were not aware how vital it's going to be when the battle reaches its climax in a year or two. How could they? They are not privy to Admiralty strategy. Someone needs to see the whole picture. Ideally that would be Churchill's Battle of the Atlantic Committee – but I doubt that anyone who sits at that high table goes to sea in corvettes any more, or flies in Catalinas."

"Noble does."

"And thank God he does, but he's not a regular member of the committee – he attends only when invited – and in any case he doesn't have the technical background to spot some crucial clues."

"Like U-boat depth capability."

"Or the limitations of Sigint. So one of our jobs Tony is to know something about everything to do with the Battle of the Atlantic. The victor may be the side which first sees that the combination of two opportunities will lead to the winning strategy. That's so often the case in science. Arnold Sommerfeld, my boss in Munich, who was a wonderful scientific mentor, never missed an opportunity to ram that into us."

"Example?"

"One he was fond of quoting was the discovery of Electro-magnetism by the Danish physicist Hans Christian Oersted back in 1820. Oersted had been hired by his government to study storms at sea. He was asked to go through the log books of sea captains who had survived violent storms. Very often they reported that during electrical disturbances their compasses had gone haywire. Now this was surprising to Oersted because, at that time, no one suspected there was any connection between electricity and magnetism. So he went out, bought a battery, and passed a current through a wire juxtaposed to a compass. Dramatic result – the compass needle swung violently. Huge excitement all round the scientific world: electricity and magnetism were related .It led – through the work of Faraday and others – to electric motors, dynamos, telegraphy .– and indeed to the modern world."

"So what did you learn on this trip old boy?"

"So many things it will take me days to tell you. But here's one putative winning combination: short wavelength airborne radar and VLR aircraft. Married together in time for the climactic battle they could prevent Doenitz ever assembling his wolf packs in the mid-Atlantic airgap – by keeping his shadowing U-boats down!"

"Hold your horses old boy . You are going to have to explain all this slowly."

They wrote up Sturdees conclusions – not for Noble, but for his air-force deputy Air Vice Marshal Robb, Commander of Group 15 Coastal Command.

"But why?" Loader wanted to know.

"Because the Admiral made it clear that that was what he wanted. He can't have his pet scientist probing into and possibly criticising Air Force business. That's no way to foster an alliance. Of course I'm hoping Robb will show it to Noble – but that must be his decision. There's so much ill feeling between the RAF and the Navy over Coastal Command that we have to tread carefully. Anyway Robb was very supportive of me. It was he who laid on that Catalina flight. I owe him the courtesy."

"I suppose so."

"If we get this wrong Loader we could actually lose the climactic battle through our own actions."

"Explain."

"Coastal Command is in a very odd situation. Its presence above the convoy makes all the difference. So I think; so better qualified people like McIntyre think; and so do the Statistics – which are rather sparse. As soon as we reached the convoy we spotted its shadowing U-boat – and down he went. While he was down, the convoy changed course – and was never spotted again. But Coastal Command didn't have much substantive to show for it – no sunken U-boat wreckage for example. Thus it is at a big disadvantage relative to Bomber Command – which can show the Prime Minister reconnaissance photos of burning cities or flattened German factories. Thus Coastal Command may never get the resources its true value demands – and in particular it may never get the VLR aircraft equipped with centimetre radar which its vital role will increasingly demand. Even my Catalina crew saw themselves as having failed – because their patrol had nothing substantive to show by the time they landed . The fact that their convoy arrived safely in the Clyde three days later would never have been known to them had I not rung the Admiralty myself. At least an Escort Group can steam proudly into port with its ducklings, knowing that it has ensured 'The safe and timely arrival of its cargo vessels.' All the Catalina crew had to report was an unsuccessful bombing attack on a U-boat. If the airmen concerned cannot see their own value how could we expect the top brass to draw the right conclusions? After all so many of our convoys are anyway getting through unscathed at present – 90% or more – so the statistics needed to make a watertight case for air-escort are simply not available ."

"Ah yes Giles, something new came out while you were away. U-boats have been getting through the Straits of Gibraltar into the Med – maybe a dozen or so, with a similar number into the Baltic. Friend Hitler has been robbing his Atlantic Fleet to support his adventures on land ."

"But that would leave his Atlantic Fleet almost totally depleted..."

"... explaining the dramatically low sinkings in July."

"So as soon as his numbers go up again– as they are bound to do with 20 new U-boats being delivered every month – we can expect the awful sinking totals to resume. My God that's depressing Tony– just when we were taking heart."

Sturdee and Loader agonised over the wording of the VLR aircraft report, knowing that every phrase could potentially win or lose the war. There was a time window of maybe three, certainly less than six months, during which Britain could address the VLR problem. After that it would be too late. If Bomber Command couldn't be forced into coughing up 100 of its precious four-engine bombers to be modified for Coastal Command duties then the Battle of the Atlantic would probably be lost in the mid-ocean Air Gap in a matter of weeks. It was as simple, as terrible as that.

A day after receiving the report Robb sent for Giles:
"Very interesting indeed Sturdee. The fact that we could get 4,500 miles range out of a Lancaster bomber never occurred to me."
"It wasn't me sir. It was your boys who worked that out. I'm only reporting what they said – but we did of course check their numbers."
"Air Marshal Joubert will certainly want to see this urgently – he's my boss. He's the one who will have to fight with Bomber Command over allocating the necessary aircraft."
"And Admiral Noble?"
"But of course. Mind you I would like one or two small changes in the report first – if we can agree."
Robb's suggested changes were cosmetic. One was not. He demanded that special reference to the Lancaster be deleted:
"They are Bomber Command's diamonds. They will never part with those. But if other four-engine bombers will do – as I suspect they might – because – as you say – it's mainly a matter of raw engine power – then we should include those others too – with the appropriate modifications. Jones can help you with that. I'd rather like his name to go on the paper too. Then it will seem like a combined RAF /Royal Navy/ Scientific effort – and therefore could carry more weight. If both Air Marshall Joubert and Admiral Noble will support it then Bomber Harris – chief of Bomber Command – might not get his way– as he usually does with Churchill. I'm sure it will have to go up to that level – because Harris will fight it every step of the way. Every step. He hates parting with a single aircraft –l et alone a four-engine one. He'll probably threaten to resign."

Sturdee was no longer sleeping well at night – an affliction that had never bothered him in his life before. It was all very well telling Loader that they had to learn everything they could about the Battle of Atlantic. Now he knew almost as much as Noble and certainly more than Churchill. He could see the writing on the wall – but unlike them he had no power whatsoever to do anything about it. What did his squeaky little reports matter if he had no means to put them into effect, no means even to defend them against other dissenting scientists. This was brought home to him when Loader threw a dog-eared copy of their depth-charge report on his table with the remark:

"Read the back."

Scrawled on the page in a very angry hand, he read:

"I have been asked to comment on this slipshod and amateur report, especially the section dealing with acoustic torpedoes. The authors appear not to know that the whole question of Asdic Dead time was looked into in great detail by professionals at this and other Admiralty research establishments 18 months ago. The unequivocal recommendation of all concerned was that Royal Navy anti-submarine vessels should all be fitted with forward projecting mortars, slaved to their asdic systems, that will fire explosive projectiles several hundred yards ahead of the vessel, so eliminating the dead time problem entirely. Such systems have already been developed, tested, and are in production. Hedgehog will fire salvos of 24 65-pound contact-fused projectiles up to 300 yards ahead, whilst Squid will fire three much larger 400- pound charges up to 250 yards ahead. Such systems render an anti-submarine acoustic torpedo , as proposed, entirely unnecessary. In any case we have anti-ship acoustic torpedoes under intensive investigation against the day when the Nazis can be expected to deploy them on their U-boats, and we will have to find countermeasures.

May I suggest that amateurish reports of this kind not be allowed to rise so far up the system and waste the time of professionals who are already vastly overworked in their efforts to win the war.

Signed Squiggle, PhD

Senior Principal Scientific Officer.

Scientific Research Superintendent HMS Dolphin. "

Sturdee felt he had been kicked in the stomach. Certainly he had never heard of Hedgehog or Squid when he should have made it his business to find out about them.

"Did you know Tony?"

"Nope. They must be very hush-hush – hence the funny codenames. Naturally the Admiralty wouldn't want the Jerries to know about them a moment too soon. But this character does sound bloody angry doesn't he?"

"What is HMS Dolphin?"

"It's a stone frigate as we call them, an Admiralty shore establishment now based at Dunoon in Scotland. Its job is to develop underwater weapons – including torpedoes and depth-charges."

"I suppose they think we are treading on their toes."

"Well we are Giles, but it serves the buggers right. They should have spotted the depth-charge problem themselves – about 10 years ago."

When he'd had a chance to calm down Sturdee read the acidulous comments once again, and reflected on what they meant . Firstly his acoustic torpedo would never get built if it had the entire admiralty scientific establishment against it – which would seem to be the case already. Secondly – he should have known about Hedgehog and Squid – which, on reflection, did seem sensible weapons. Thirdly, scientists don't get angry when they know they are right. But they do get angry when they've been found out in the wrong. This Doctor Squiggle was evidently very aggrieved. Hedgehog or not, his establishment evidently hadn't known how deep U-boats could go , otherwise Royal Navy depth-charges wouldn't have had restricted depth-settings – which were now being altered as a result of the Sturdee / Loader paper. Thus his accusation of slipshoddiness was as good as a confession of incompetence. And if he and his associates hadn't known how deep U-boats could go – then how could they have designed and tested the mortar systems correctly? It was quite possible that the Royal Navy was heading for another disaster simply because one of its senior scientists didn't have the strength of character to admit a serious mistake. At the very least Hedgehog and Squid would now have to be reappraised by an independent scientific team – and urgently. He must talk to Noble about it.

The real problem , as Hanbury Brown had pointed out in Dorset, was that Sturdee didn't belong to any scientific chain of command. For instance there was no senior scientist to whom he could complain about Squiggle and Hedgehog. Noble had so much on his plate that it wouldn't be right or fair to burden him with squabbles between scientists. He would have to crush Squiggle on his own – but how.

Air Vice Marshall Robb expressed himself very pleased with the amended paper on the VLR problem. With Jones Sturdee had looked into the aerodynamics of aircraft range and come across Bregeut's aircraft-range equation. It was disarmingly simple. The ultimate range depended only on the fraction of the all-up weight made up of fuel, and the aerodynamic cleanliness of the aircraft. Obviously the cleaner the profile and the better the lift- characteristics of its wing, the further a plane would go.

"So it's largely a matter of eliminating drag – getting rid of unnecessary gun turrets and things?" he asked Jones.

"Yes and no" Jones replied. "As I understand it the main source of drag in these big weight-lifting aircraft is Induced Drag. What that is old boy I don't really understand. All they told us was 'It's the drag associated with creating the lift.' "

In his last summer in Munich Sturdee had discovered that one of his colleagues Hans- Pieter was a keen glider-pilot. Intrigued by the idea of flying without a motor he'd enquired whether it was possible to take a flight himself and one weekend Hans-Pieter had taken them down to his gliding club in the foothills of the Alps. There he had been strapped into the front seat of a two-seater and was catapulted 1000 feet into the sky with an instructor behind. From there they'd soared by means of thermals and hill-lift until they'd risen above the summit of the Eiger and the other high mountains of the Bernese Oberland. Sturdee had never been more terrified – or more entranced in his life before. He had vowed to take up the sport himself as soon as he was able, and bought several books on soaring in the meanwhile. One, in German, dealt with aerodynamics and that he consulted on the subject of Induced Drag.

An aircraft remained airborne because its wing left behind a carpet of air which it had deflected downward. A smaller wing would deflect a narrower carpet and so would have to deflect it faster to generate the necessary lift. A wider wing would deflect a wider carpet at a lower and more economic speed. Induced Drag was the Energy needed to generate the descending carpet of air. For a low drag to lift ratio – which is what was wanted for long range – a wide high aspect ratio wing, such as was found on an albatross, or competition glider – was optimal. Armed with this knowledge Sturdee went through the list of four-engine bombers, both British and American, that Coastal Command might acquire on a feasible timescale: the Avro Lancaster, the Handley Page Halifax, the Short Stirling, the Boeing B 17 Flying Fortress, and the Consolidated B-24 Liberator. Of these the last appeared to have much the highest aspect-ratio wings.

"But it's not a very good bomber – from what I've heard." Jones said.

"So much the better," Sturdee replied "The easier it will be to get our hands on it. But what's wrong with it?"

"Not very robust – easily shot down. Slow at high altitude – it had to have superchargers retrofitted to it. Heavy on the pilot – who needs very strong arms. And tends to kill the crew when it crash lands because of its high wing full of fuel collapses on top of them. That's why it is the only one of the five designs which the RAF has never ordered. But the Yanks are planning to mass produce them in vast numbers at the Ford plant near Detroit. Come to think of it we do have a handful – which we inherited from the French."

"None of those defects would ruin its performance as a marine reconnaissance aircraft would they Jones?"

"I suppose not. There's not much flak from U-boats. We don't need high altitude. It will be on autopilot most of the time. And crash landings will mostly be at sea. So you are right Giles. Maybe the B- 24 Liberator might be just what we're looking for – because the Bomber-boys won't want it so much. It might be an unwanted Cinderella – whereas if we asked for Lancasters they'd scream blue murder."

"I've never heard of the 'Consolidated Aircraft Corporation."

"Yes you have. They designed and built your Catalina."

"So they did!"

"They are based in San Diego on the Pacific. That might be why they have an interest in long range and endurance – hence the high aspect ratio wings."

"Yes the Catalina has an enormously long wing. So that's why it can go over 20 hours I suppose. But it's too slow to make a decent anti-submarine aircraft. Does that apply to this Liberator?"

"Not to my knowledge. I believe it cruises at over 200 knots – like the rest of them"

"Better and better. Twenty hours endurance like the Catalina, and a speed of 220 knots gives 4,500 nautical miles range, exactly what we want. And we haven't began to strip it down yet. From this photo it looks to have both dorsal and ventral gun turrets we could dispense with."

"And don't forget the superchargers can go: they eat up fuel."

"So do we nominate the Liberator as the ideal VLR anti- submarine patrol aircraft?"

"Wait on old chap – it's way too early for that. There might be snags. I think we should mention the matter privately to Air Vice Marshal Robb who can pass the tip on to Marshall Joubert. They can then take the credit – if the decision goes that way. And in my experience bosses love to take the credit."

"If it makes them fight harder for our idea, so much the better."

The Battle of the Atlantic was becoming more and more urgently a race against time. Doenitz could expect to have more than 100 U-boats actually out at sea every day of the year. His transatlantic cordon would then be complete so that no ship could expect to get by undetected – and the main purpose of convoy would be undermined. Every one would have to fight its way across surrounded by a ravening pack of wolves .

On the Allied side more escort vessels were coming down the slipways – In particular frigates, vessels bigger and faster than Corvettes, and capable of catching surfaced U-boats. Unlike the destroyers though they had the range to cross the entire Atlantic Ocean. If only they could first find, and second sink U-boats – neither of which they could do at present – the submarines might have a battle on their hands. Then there was radar – so far its performance had been disappointing. The sailors used it for station-keeping at sea, the airmen for finding land, leaving it to the Mark One eyeball to find attacking U-boats at night. But according to Hanbury that technology could only improve as shorter wavelength sets with more powerful transmitters came into service – but when? Once they had lost the cloak of darkness U-boats might become very vulnerable to faster escort vessels – and in particular to the proposed Support groups which would have the time to sit on top of them and blast them to perdition. Those groups would require even more escort vessels – but where were they to come from? Warships were not mere floating boxes that could be mass produced in any old shipyard, they were sophisticated greyhounds packed with gunnery, radar, Asdics, fire-control electronics, optics, high-pressure turbines, watertight bulkheads, torpedoes, anti-aircraft weapons, signalling gear, depth charges, damage control mechanisms, armour… every British and Canadian shipyard capable of the task was already working day and night at breakneck speed to keep up with and even surpass the German output. Everything was building towards a final climax which could only spell catastrophic defeat for one side or the other And it wasn't just weapons that would count but tactics – and in particular the local concentration of force. As Sturdee was coming to understand from studying Lanchester's Equations and naval history, local concentration was everything. Twice as many U-boats as escort vessels concentrated round the convoy could lead, as it had in the case of PQ 17, to the loss of almost all its merchant ships. Twice as many escort vessels as U-boats and no U-boat would stand a chance of pressing home a successful torpedo attack. Concentration by convoy on the one hand, concentration by wolfpack on the other – would decide the issue. The U-boats had no way of preventing the convoys from concentrating, but the Escort forces had one means, in principle, of foiling the concentration of U-boats: air-power. Doenitz wouldn't be able to concentrate his pack towards a convoy unless he could keep a shadowing U-boat on station for a dozen hours or so. But experience showed that a single escort aircraft could stifle that. So everything would come to depend on the provision, by some means or other, of local air cover.

Round and round, day and night the opposing factors in the upcoming battle chased each other around in Sturdee's head: depth charge settings, radar, escort-numbers, refuelling capability, acoustic torpedoes, Hedgehogs, aircraft range, code-breaking, seamen's morale, Asdic, concentration… no wonder he couldn't sleep. He tried exercise. Joan had assigned him responsibility for providing firewood so, with the help of Arfur and Gem he cut down two of the 50 giant poplar trees that surrounded their paddock. Sawed into convenient lengths, they were towed by Gem towards a saw-bench which he'd built with his own hands out of timber which Arfur had filched from a bombsite. Using Gem's enormous strength and a makeshift hoist, lengths of Poplar were dragged onto the bench and cradled in place. Stripped to the waist he sawed the lengths into huge logs that could be further split with a woodman's axe. Arfur and Gem moved these split logs in their cart up to the coach house to dry, and Joan was delighted with the result, absolving Sturdee of any further domestic duties.

Wood cutting certainly provided Sturdee with all the exercise he could wish for – but still he couldn't sleep. Every day seemed like a day lost as the coming Battle of the Atlantic circled round and round in his mind. He'd never been one who could easily switch off, now he couldn't switch off at all.

Joan noticed. She must have seen his light under the door at 3 AM and knocked:
"Are you all right Giles?" She looked charming in a Chinese dragon dressing gown: " Can I get you some cocoa and a home-made gingernut? They helped me to sleep at the height of our railway problems. We could even pinch some of Maurice's Scotch. I'm sure it wouldn't mind."
"I'm sure he would " Sturdee laughed. "But a cocoa would be very welcome. It's this wretched Battle of the Atlantic chasing round in my mind."
"Well you can tell me about it – the non-hush-hush bits anyway. I find talking usually helps. It's not so much what the other person says as enunciating the problem clearly for oneself."
So they sat in the kitchen huddled close to the kitchen rage, drinking cocoa and talking. Joan's advice was:
"You've got too much on your plate Giles. You can't win that battle on your own. All you can do is identify problems and suggest possible solutions. It's up to that admiral of yours and the Prime Minister to put them into effect. They have millions of men at their beck and call while all you have is Tony Loader. And what's more he's not a scientist. So to all intents and purposes you are working entirely on your own. That

can't be either healthy or effective. If you ask me you badly need someone of your kind
, preferably senior, to talk to."

Joan was right of course, she usually was.

"What are the alternatives?" She wanted to know.

"Well there's no one, absolutely no one in Western Approaches. I'm doing what is
coming to be called 'Operational Research' or 'OR'. They were pretty keen on that at
Bawdsey Manor – in fact the term was invented there by the assistant superintendent
A.P. Rowe. They had their own OR group headed by a fellow called Eric Williams.
They did vital work in tying together the radar stations and fighter-control in time for
the Battle of Britain. I took Eric sailing in my boat once."

"So why not contact him?"

"The Bawdsey Manor group was disbanded.".

"Never mind, he won't have vanished."

"That's a good idea Joan. I think I'll try."

"In the mean time you're going to have to take your mind off things. You're
looking exhausted Giles. Why not try that painting you're always talking about?"

"Am I?"

"You promised Arfur to do that painting of Gem. He'd be so so pleased."

Sturdee had always been fond of drawing – especially sailing boats and human
faces. He could knock off a caricature in a few minutes and drew them incessantly, to
the general amusement but not always to that of the sitters themselves. Then when he
went to Bawdsey he found something in the Suffolk light, something in the creeks and
estuaries, something of the ghost of Constable, that suddenly made him want to paint.
He bought an easel, some oil paints and an elementary instruction book and started
painting some of the old sailing-vessels, mostly barges and bawlies that still worked the
tidal creeks of the Debden River and the wider Thames estuary. He found himself
enthralled, so much so that hours would pass between one sip of his tea and the next.
Every brushstroke was challenging, every rare success a thrill. Soon the canvases piled
up around his room until friends asked for them. He did portraits on request and found
they came very easily. He could have made money but charged only for materials.
When he left Bawdsey for Liverpool he put the paintings into storage, never expecting
to see them again. Now he missed painting with a palpable hunger, even more than he
missed his little sailing cruiser 'The Pelican', no doubt rotting up some lonely creek of
the estuary.

Days after his late-night conversation with Joan Sturdee came home late turned on
the light in his room to find his bed covered in painting materials, mostly second-hand
but in good order. He picked up some tubes of oil paint and turned them over in wonder,
set up the easel and mounted a canvas.

When thanked Joan was abrupt:

"It's really a present for Arfur. You promised him Giles. Now get on with it."

Sturdee could understand why Arfur so loved Gem. The old horse positively radiated goodness of spirit, eternal patience, kindness of soul. He walked about the world with a benign smile on his face as if to say 'Aren't we all lucky to be here?' As an adolescent Sturdee had read a great deal of philosophy before coming to believe that most of it was nonsense. One philosopher though he had retained a great respect for and so read from time to time – David Hume from the Scottish Enlightenment who had said. "… no truth appears to me more evident than that beasts are endowed with thought and reason as well as men." And that so appositely fitted Gem. Only a gross fool could fail to see the saintliness of the old Shire Horse that glowed like a kindly light in in a grosser man-made world. It was this kindly light that Sturdee was aching to capture in paint.

He set his easel in the yard outside Gems stable so that Gem could stick his head out over the lower door and watch his portrait in progress, as he liked to watch anything unusual or interesting going on. But that didn't work because Sturdee wanted to paint the head from the side. So Arfur was recruited to stand on a box and talk to his friend, who naturally turned in Arfur's direction most of the time

Sturdees pencil simply flew over the large canvas and without intention Arfur's head got in bottom right looking half up at Gem. Then, using a thin mixture of burnt sienna an outline of the two heads grew into existence almost of its own accord – as if it had been lurking in the air. It was so good, so perfect, caught the two souls in their mingling love so perfectly, that it terrified Sturdee. He knew he wasn't responsible, knew that every brushstroke he added could only diminish the magic. He stepped back several yards cleaning the paint off his hands with the turpentined rag. If he went on and filled it all in he would almost certainly weaken the painting. His luck , his inspiration, call it what you will, couldn't last. On the other hand to stop now would be arrant cowardice, running away in the face of the enemy. He'd never become a proper painter then. He marched back to the easel and began mixing three shades of bay, testing them out in his sketchbook.

"Can I see?"

"No you can't – not until it's finished. And don't talk – not to me. If you have to, talk to Gem."

Using his three biggest brushes, none as big as he would have liked, Sturdee filled in the main areas of contrast in Gem' head and neck, trying not to lose the outlines of his sienna sketch. With smaller brushes he worked on the liquid eye the long eyelashes, the whole so evidently focused on Arfur. Then the big black ears, standing up listening to his little friend.

Then Arfur. For reasons unknown he sketch-painted the boy in a light patina of greenish grey, using the absolute minimum of brushstrokes to suggest his intelligence and his affection for his faithful companion. The thin neck, the tousled hair all grew out of the whole canvas in no more than a dozen carefully placed strokes.

He stood back: "My God it's powerful. But I mustn't push my luck. I can't leave it white though."

He flew at the background, filling it with the thinnest of of cerulean blue as if the two heads were floating in sky. That strengthened the beam of love which lanced between them, the strongest feature on the entire canvus, although it had no physical representation.

Picton came out of the scullery door into the yard

"Bugger off Maurice. I won't be long. I hate being watched."

When he turned back to the canvas he realised it was finished. He looked at his watch – five hours. Of course he could go on adding and adding… Gem's lower neck, the stable doors, Arfur's shoulder… But no… better minimal perfection to disastrous detail. He signed his name 'Sturdee 1941' behind Arfur's head, but in the mid-bay brown he'd used for Gem.

"Alright Arfur – you can look now."

The lad jumped off his box and came round:

"Gor you've got 'im Giles. 'ees loverly. Now he can't never die can 'ee ? But I've gotter 'ave a pee. Shall I fetch Joan and Maurice. I hear'd her coming in."

Maurice stared at the painting, stared at Sturdee then shook his head as if bemused.

Jean also stared at the picture, but for once said nothing; she simply hugged herself and went on staring.

"What you think Joan?" The boy stared anxiously up at her.

"I don't think Arfur. I can feel it – can't you? It's alive. It makes me want to cry – like a new-born baby does. Where did Giles find it?" Then she, wrapped her arms round Arfur nearly asphyxiating the boy.

The night after the painting Sturdee slept soundly. Joan had been right. When he arrived at work Robb sent for him:

"I showed your paper to Air Marshall Joubert yesterday. To say he was mightily impressed would be an understatement. The idea wasn't new to him of course but the argument for it, and the urgency were. He realises it's up to him to persuade the Air Staff , and then the Combined Chiefs of Staff to find candidates. So he's put some of his own staff into looking into the various types and the necessary numbers. He agrees with me – we should keep off Lancasters and concentrate on the less glamorous alternatives – of which your B-24 Liberator could be one. He reckons it might take 3 to 6 months to adapt them for long range duties; the bottle neck might be those new centimetre radars. There's some scheme, not yet agreed to, to mass produce them in America. He was, I'm glad to say, more sanguine than I was about us getting the aircraft themselves than I was . If we only need 100 VLRAs to win the Battle of the Atlantic that's a mere trifle beside the 10,000 or more B-24s they're planning to produce in their Willow Run plant near Detroit. Surely the Prime Minister can't deny us such a trifle. But he's done it before: fobbed us off with Bomber Command's castoffs because he's in thrall to them. He finds their argument that only they can win the war attractive."

"But if we lose the sea battle they'll quickly ran out of bombs and bombers."

"Exactly Sturdee – but that's an argument we still have to fight and win. Which reminds me, Air Marshall Joubert has a very strong message for you."

"For me?"

"For you personally. He's very proud that Coastal Command have poached a Professor Patrick Blackett from General Pile, who is head of Britain's Anti-aircraft Command. Blackett will run, indeed is running Coastal Command's Operational Research section. He's a genius apparently. Have you heard of him?"

"As a scientist yes. He was one of Rutherford's boys – who discovered positrons , or anti-electrons, but I didn't know about his operational research work."

"He came up here in May for a few days and convinced Coastal Command to paint all its aircraft white – harder for U-boats to see apparently."

"I do remember he was one of the three scientists on Tizard's committee – which first stimulated the development of radar back in 1935. So yes – he's a very big shot indeed."

"Well Joubert wants you to get in touch with him immediately. He's planning to use Blackett to help him persuade the Air Staff, and even Churchill, to part with the necessary VLR aircraft. Since you started this particular hare Sturdee, Joubert thinks that you and Blackett should be in very close touch, not rivals getting in one another's way."

"Hardly rivals. He is in a very different league from me sir. Anyway he's working for the Air Force, and I for the Navy – or rather for Admiral Noble."

"Of course, of course. but that's really Joubert's underlying point. We want complete accord between the Air Force and the Navy on this one, between Western Approaches and Coastal Command. Anything less, any hint of disagreement, even at the technical level could lose the VLRA battle and hence the Atlantic."

"My loyalties must always be with Admiral Noble."

"Of course. But he's one hundred per cent with Joubert on this. We spent much of yesterday talking it all through together over the scrambler. He's even written a fulsome letter of recommendation for you to go to Blackett, and I've written one likewise. Speed is of the essence here. The Admiral wants to see you later today… and if you could meet Blackett this week – so much the better."

Sturdee recalled that Blackett was one of the three names suggested by Hanbury as a possible scientific patron for himself, the others being Sir Henry Tizard and Churchill 's own guru Prof Lindemann. He hesitated – knowing none of them. Now it looked as if fate was taking a hand. He rang Hanbury at Farnborough to ask his opinion of Blackett:

"He's a coming man alright. Bound to get a Nobel. Got Rutherford's old chair at Manchester. I've seen him in operation once or twice. Strong opinions, doesn't suffer fools gladly; a good hater so I understand. Served in the Royal Navy as a regular officer in the First World War – fought at Jutland I believe. That gives him an almost unique cachet: ex-naval officers who can win Nobel Prizes are as scarce as hens teeth. So he carries a lot of weight. Not always liked though. A rabid socialist like a lot of those ex-Cambridge types. Makes no secret of his loathing for Lindemann – or his contempt for Churchill. On the other hand he's damn good at gathering very smart people around him who

seem to be fiercely loyal. They did some great work marrying radar to anti-aircraft batteries for General Pile. They were called ' Blacketts Flying Circus' but I haven't encountered them recently."

Blackett sounded pretty frightening – but without someone like that behind him to push some of Sturdee's ideas, like the acoustic torpedo, they would never get anywhere. Noble could push naval matters, but not scientific ones against the unanimous advice of the Admiralty Research Establishments. Then there were matters like the VLR aircraft problem which were neither purely air-force nor purely naval affairs – but somehow vital to both. They needed advocates who could appeal to general principles that transcended interservice rivalries – if they were to be effective and convince politicians at the very highest level. Sturdee thought back to the first world war which Britain had almost lost in 1917 thanks to the combined opposition of the admirals and the shipowners to convoying. A man of his own age and heft would never have been able to convince them whereas a man with Blacketts dual background – and sufficient self-confidence to despise Churchill, could take on anything or anybody.

Noble was his usual intelligent selfless self:

"Of course I don't mind sharing you with Professor Blackett Giles – if that's what it comes to. But I certainly don't want to lose you entirely. You've made a great deal of difference here; I don't' have to tell you that. There's not an officer in Western Approaches headquarters who would want to see you leave. You've struck up a wonderful relationship with Loader and now with Robb. He thinks you're the bee's knees. Most importantly you get the very best out of the crews with which you serve. They know you are on their side, not just snooping. So you're welcome everywhere – and that's not a privilege to be thrown away lightly. At some stage you should go to sea with one of our Escort Group commanders."

"I'd love to Admiral."

"But there's so much for you to do here. I'm looking forward to your paper with Loader on the size of my Support Groups or Sinking Groups as you used to call them."

"It's in hand Admiral. Tony is doing most of the work on that now. He's a real tiger. Would you believe he's teaching himself Calculus?"

"Good for him. I know he thinks the world of you Giles – and that counts in our narrow seagoing family. His fellow officers will take their opinion on scientists, or 'Boffins' as they seem to call them, from him."

"We still have frightful rows."

"Good; that is what he is there for. Now I have got one last thing to say. I'm sorry I couldn't support you more strongly over your Acoustic torpedo idea – but when you become a senior commander you have to select your battles carefully – as you may one-day find out. But here's an idea. How many depth-charges on average do we reckon it's going to take to sink a U-boat?"

"About 100 sir?"

"And what aircraft can carry a hundred depth-charges weighing 300 pounds or more each?"

"None. I hadn't thought…"

" So none of our aircraft are ever going to sink U-boats unless…?"

Sturdee shook his head, not getting the point.

"Unless they can carry one or two of your deadly little acoustic devils. And they could couldn't they? After all they can't be fitted with Hedgehogs or Squids."

"Why didn't I think of that?" Sturdee sounded delighted

"Probably too busy with other things. But wouldn't that provide the watertight case you need to get them built – and urgently?"

"It would – Oh yes it would sir."

"Then Joubert is your man to fight for that. If he can put his explosives right up the spout of the enemy – while Bomber command can only scatter them all over the landscape – it would enormously strengthen his case for VLR aircraft in the Prime Minister's eyes. The two seem made for one another… But don't for goodness sake tell Joubert it was my idea – it might put him off altogether."

The Admiral got to his feet and shook hands:

"Good luck with Professor Blackett Giles. I have written him a very strong letter in your support by the way. So don't let him bully you. I dare say you are every bit as clever as he is."

As it happened Blackett was paying a rare week's visit to his department at Manchester University and agreed to see Sturdee at once. A tall lean figure of a man he looked and acted more like a distinguished Admiral than a professor. In repose his face was gloomy but it occasionally lit up with enthusiasm and warmth. On his desk he had Sturdee's two letters of recommendation one from Noble and one from Robb. He got up to shake hands, towering above Sturdee, the very image of a born leader.

"Do you know I have been trying to get Operational Research into the Admiralty for two years, and you've been doing it very successfully, all on your own. I wish I'd known about you beforehand."

"I'm rather unofficial" Sturdee admitted, sitting down. " It's strictly a private arrangement between Admiral Noble and myself. I'm not sure the Admiralty knows that I exist."

"How do you manage to work so alone?"

"With increasing difficulty." Sturdee replied "I really need other scientific colleagues to argue with as well as a senior scientific patron who carries far more weight than I do. I was thinking of approaching you myself when Joubert rather forced my hand."

"You wouldn't mind cooperating with my group?"

"On the contrary – as long as I can spend 60% of my time on Western Approaches stuff, working for Noble in the Derby House set up."

"At the moment Sturdee your connections are rather better than mine. Next to Alanbrooke – the Chief of the Imperial General Staff, who effectively runs this war whatever Churchill may think, Noble holds the most critical command in Britain – and you are his personal protégé. He thinks very highly of your work ." Blackett tapped Noble's letter. "And Nothing we do, nothing, must interfere with that relationship. Nothing! You may not realise it yet but having your commander's trust is almost everything in Operational Research. Once you forfeit that you might as well move on. Right now I've got an excellent relationship with Joubert – but how long that will last who can tell. He's a very touchy fellow. He showed me your VLRA aircraft paper and it fascinated me. It seems to me we've got to do everything we can to commandeer the necessary four-engine bombers – and fast. I feel that you and I could collaborate on that?"

"Happy to." Sturdee said. "But I'm not sure what more I can contribute. Ideally we'd like much better statistics on the importance of air cover to convoy security. They must actually exist– for the First World War – among Air Ministry files."

"I could put somebody on to that at once." Blackett made a note in the small black pocketbook.

" And of course there's the acoustic torpedo."

"What's that?"

Sturdee went through the whole saga, including Noble's recent suggestion of it as an airborne weapon – without mentioning Noble's name. He gave Blackett a copy of their depth-charge report.

"Sounds like a miracle weapon" Blackett said. "And I have to say that in general I'm sceptical of those. Better to make good use of the weapons one's got than to hope that something revolutionary won't have snags of its own."

"I don't see any other way that VLRA aircraft could carry an effective weapon for sinking submarines" Sturdee argued. "Even ships with Asdic need to drop twenty or more tons of depth-charges to make a single killing. And if VLRAs can't make the occasional kill the U-boats will lose their fear of them, and refuse to dive – which is the whole point."

"My group is doing a lot of work on airborne depth-charge settings just now." Blackett said "It's for the Biscay campaign."

"Oh that." Sturdee couldn't help himself sounding dismissive.

Blackett looked up every inch the admiral being contradicted by a junior officer.

"The Navy's view of that" Sturdee hastily explained " Is that it's a waste of time and resources. It harks back to the old idea of 'hunting U-boats ' which was so fashionable at the beginning of the war but which turned out such a failure. You can't hunt for U-boats – the ocean's far too big , even the Bay of Biscay. If you want to sink U-boats you've got to wait for them to come to you – in the vicinity of the convoy. It was a hard lesson we had to learn in Western Approaches but one which Noble drilled into everyone, and with which everyone in the Navy now agrees. It is ' the safe and timely arrival of the shipping' which matters not sinking U-boats *per se*."

"But U-boats have to concentrate as they leave and return to their Biscay bases" Blackett retorted

" Yes but it's still a colossal area 500 times 500 miles in size. A convoy is only 25 x 25 at most so you are 400 times more likely to encounter a U-boat there; but the glamour boys on the Air Staff don't want to listen. Like Bomber Command they want to win the war all on their own – and as a result they're losing it. Many of our Escort Group commanders say the Biscay campaign is a disgrace – an absolute disgrace."

"I hadn't heard that argument before." Blackett sounded thoughtful.

"That's why we scientists have to see you the whole picture" Sturdee got on his hobbyhorse "Neither our admirals nor our air marshals seem capable of doing so at present. The Battle of the Atlantic transcends any one command. The side which can see it as a whole will win. The side which cannot, will lose."

"You seem very certain. What gives you the right to say that?"

Sturdee hesitated, knowing their relationship was approaching a critical juncture: "Being wrong I suppose, so many times: and having to change my mind when I came to see more of the story . The Battle of the Atlantic is such a huge, multi-dimensional story that is easy to fool oneself through narrowness of focus. Hardly a week goes by when I don't have to reappraise the situation. For instance I made a fool of myself through ignorance of Hedgehog and Squid."

"What are they?"

"There you are professor – vital weapons in the upcoming battle – but as evidently unknown to you as they were to me."

Sturdee described his voyage in the *Pimpernel* and his recent Catalina patrol. Blackett questioned him closely about each, occasionally taking notes.

"I feel so vulnerable" Sturdee said. "Because I have only got one pair of eyes and one pair of ears. The Admiralty needs to have a large Operations Research group looking at the whole picture."

"Precisely my point." Blackett said:. "But they won't buy it – at least not yet – whereas the Air Force is far more willing to listen. It is a question of new boys versus senior prefects. My Lords of the Admiralty think they know it all – what needs have they for us scientists?"

"Noble is not like that."

"Obviously not – a fine man by all accounts, far too fine for Winston. Noble is a gentleman, and not being one himself, Winston can't abide them. You watch – he'll get rid of Noble just as he got rid of his two finest commanders Dowding and Wavell. He prefers bumptious, loudmouthed pot-bellied little men like himself, like Beaverbrook. We can only hope that Herr Hitler is equally obtuse. By the way I see you were in

Göttingen. Pat and I spent a year over there in 25/6. Wonderful days– what did you think of it?"

Sturdee had evidently passed some test, because Blackett was all affability after that. They lunched together in one of the new 'British Restaurants' on black pudding with cabbage and afterwards Blackett took him down into the basement of his laboratory and showed Sturdee where Rutherford and Geiger had discovered the atomic nucleus back in 1913: "Arguably the biggest scientific discovery of the century." Blackett said. "People forget that he did it here in Manchester: not in Cambridge. The British are as snobbish about their science as they are about everything else. If you went to Dartmouth you'll know all about that."

Sturdee shuddered silently in agreement.

Before he left it was agreed that Sturdee would go down to London and give several talks about his work to Blackett's group, and that both groups would exchange all their papers in future.

"In the mean time you can be certain that Joubert will begin agitating for four-engined bombers. If there are any developments on that front I'll let you know Sturdee."

CHAPTER 14
MORALE

Sturdee felt he'd been neglecting his staff of late so he gave Loader, and to a lesser extent Gwen, a detailed account of his encounter with Blackett:

"You and I Tony will go down to London and meet Blackett's Circus. We'll tell them about our work, they'll tell us about theirs. What we're doing is coming to be called 'Operational Research', or OR, and we, apparently, are the only people doing it within the Navy, though there is a lot going on for the Air Force, and even for the Army. Commanders apparently tend to either love it or loathe it. If it helps them to get their own way they of course think it is the bees' knees and boast about their '*backroom boys*'. But if not they refer to us as 'Overgrown schoolboys trying to win a war with slide rules'. We're very lucky apparently in having Admiral Noble's personal encouragement. The rest of the admirals are very huffy. But Blackett thinks things are bound to change. For a start the Prime Minister has his own Rasputin – an ignorant fellow apparently called 'Prof' Lindemann. The only effective defence against him is having a scientific guru of one's own. Blackett reckons Churchill is aiming to get rid of Noble."

"For God sake why?"

"Because he is a gentleman apparently. At least that's Blackett's theory, and Winston hates gentlemen – not being one himself."

"I thought Winnie was a Duke's grand-nephew or something." Loader said.

"That may be, but that doesn't make him a gentleman, merely an aristocrat. According to Blackett Winston's father died of syphilis whilst his mother was one of those American heiresses who sold her body for a title. Blackett is very left-wing – even if he behaves like a Duke himself. I'm not sure we can trust his political opinions. But if it's true that Churchill will try to get rid of our Admiral – we may have to defend him against Rasputin on some high-level committee. It's certainly true that Churchill got rid of Dowding as soon as he'd won the Battle of Britain. Why on Earth would one do that – particularly as it was Dowding who had also organised the development of night- fighter radar which appears to have ended the Blitz? According to Blackett again our dear Prime Minister was trying to deflect any blame for the Blitz onto Dowding's shoulders whilst stealing more of the glory for the Battle of Britain for himself."

"I don't believe it." Gwen said. "Mr Churchill is winning the war – isn't he?"

"He'd certainly like us to think so and it's certainly good for the national morale if we believe him. But according to Blackett – who appears to know all these things – Winnie is drunk three-quarters of the time. The war is actually run by The Chiefs of Staff who meet in committee for three or four hours every day. There's a kind of unwritten agreement that Winnie won't overrule them as long as they maintain the fiction that he's the one in charge. And I suppose that's a wise compromise – a bit like a constitutional monarchy – carried one stage further."

"Don't tell as you believe all that stuff, " Loader said "Otherwise we'll think you're as red as that Blackett."

"I honestly don't know what to believe." Sturdee said. "And none of us will know the truth for at least 25 years. I was simply intrigued by the effrontery of a man who could look down upon Winston Churchill as 'a jumped up little salesman'."

"He sounds like an ass!" Loader said

"Wait until you meet him. He could make an Admiral of the Fleet quake in his shoes. So what have you two been up to while I've been winning the war?"

"As you can see Gwen's been getting the sinking charts up-to-date while I've been looking at sinking groups or 'Support groups' as Admiral Noble prefers to call them – which he is entitled to since he invented them. We simply hijacked them to do our heavy depth-charging – if you remember."

"How's it going?"

"Driving me crazy if you want to know. Just as I come to a conclusion it jumps out of the window and escapes. Sometimes I think we'll need only 10% more escort vessels to form Support groups but as other times 50 %. They can't both be right. I'll go through my figures."

After several days of heated discussion Sturdee conceded:

"We're going round and round in circles Tony. When that happens in science it's often a sign that the wrong question is being asked. The more fundamental question is 'What constitutes victory and what constitutes defeat in the Battle of the Atlantic?'. You will remember earlier that we concluded that we could lose the battle over the question of merchant seamen's morale. If they refuse to put to sea because the chance of them surviving becomes too low, then the battle will be over – and Noble agreed. Perhaps we should now look at the issue from a U-boat man's point of view. It won't be necessary – or feasible – to kill them all. But if we could discourage them from pressing home their attacks on our convoys – because it was becoming too dangerous to try – then we'd have won wouldn't we? No matter how many U-boats are out at sea they'd be ineffective if they avoided our convoys. Right?"

"Right old man."

"It's a question of U-boat morale at some level, at the level of their ordinary seaman, at the level of his commander – or at the level of his commander-in-chief. If any one throws in the towel we'd have won. Do you remember why U-110 surrendered?"

"No."

"Because the sailors on deck refused to go back into her hull. They reckoned there was too much poisonous Chlorine gas down there – leaking from her damaged batteries. And I don't blame them. There can hardly be a more horrible death than Chlorine gas poisoning. The Germans used it against our troops in the trenches."

"The swine!"

"So what we have to tackle next Tony is the U-boat morale problem. I promised Noble we would have a go at it – but I hesitated – simply not knowing where to start. Last night however I had an idea."

"Go on."

"There you are, a U-boat crew resting between patrols at your base in Brittany – waiting for your other mates to return from their Atlantic patrols. If they do then it's okay. But if they mostly do not you begin to worry that the business is becoming too bloody dangerous – practically suicidal. It's unlikely you would mutiny – because the Gestapo would shoot you – but you might vow to no longer press home attacks against heavily defended convoys – as becoming too dangerous. That is what happened back in March, so McIntyre told me, after the Nazis lost their three Aces. After that, convoy attacks simply weren't pressed home with their former bravado. U-boats drifted away in search of easier prey – stragglers and independents."

"I guess that makes sense" Loader agreed "U-boat commanders aren't supermen."

"No they aren't. No more than German air-men were in the First World War . Their flying circuses were admissions of defeat. Instead of slogging it out with our Flying Corps chaps for control of the air above No Man's Land they retreated far behind their own lines and circled in swarms called "circuses" with a so-called Ace like Baron von Richthofen at the bottom . He was invulnerable, protected by all his mates circling above, and so he could go off in search of an unknown Brit actually doing a proper job like artillery-spotting. The Press of course thought of the Aces as heroes – when in fact they were cowards. That is why Dowding discouraged the whole Ace system in Fighter Command – one of the reasons Churchill wanted to sack him apparently."

"Don't start that again Giles for Christ's sake."

"But you get my general point? I assume that if less than 4 out of 5 U-boats return from patrol the whole U-boat force will begin to lose heart. That sets us a definite target. If we can sink better than one in five of all the U-boats at sea at any one time then we are on the way to winning the morale war. Do you buy that?"

There was a long pause while Loader thought, doodling a bunch of bananas with his pencil:

"Yes I think I do ." he finally looked up. "A figure of about one in five sounds right to me. It implies that over the course of a year the odds on a given crew , a given sailor, being killed are about 3 to 1 on. Pretty frightening."

"So how many are out there at present?"

"The best figures from the Admiralty Tracking Room are only about 20 – After Hitler's diversions to the Med and to the Baltic."

" So to be winning we need to be sinking one fifth of 20, or about 4 a month . What are the latest figures?".

Loader looked up at a wallchart and read: "For 1941 so far: zero, zero, five, two: one, three. An average of about two."

"So we're not doing as badly as I thought. If deeper depth charge settings help us to double that number, then we'll be in business."

"I'm encouraged. Bloody good thinking Giles. You *are* a cunning bugger – for all your education."

"Ah but I haven't finished yet – not by a long shot. That is merely one morale consideration. What about the crux of the battle?"

"When there are 100 U-boats on patrol? That means we'll have to sink 20 a month."

"Exactly. That's the magic number. If we can sink more than 20 a month at that stage then we'll win. It's the figure we have to aim for."

"We've never sunk more than five so far."

"But that's because of the relatively small number of U-boats at sea. Things will hot up."

"Both ways." Loader remarked

"But there's more. If monthly sinkings exceed new U-boat builds that's likely to discourage the U-boat Commander-in-chief. And we believe, from intelligence, that their building rate is 20 a month. So the magic figure 20 turns up yet again."

"I'm with you."

"But we could also look at things from an entirely different point of view. Men might be prepared to sacrifice their lives if they felt that sacrifice wasn't in vain. How many of our merchant vessels would a crew have to torpedo first before they felt their sacrifice was worth it? Hazard a guess."

"I don't know. Five perhaps?"

"That was my guess too. Now if we sink more than 20 U-boats month whilst they're sinking no more than 100 of our ships, then the game won't be worth the candle : not to them. So the magic figure of 20 a month turns up yet again."

" So that's it – that's our objective – 20 U-boat sinkings a month Giles. That gives the Support Groups something definite time to aim for. That is what our discussion was lacking before – a definite objective. That's why we were going round in bloody circles. 20 a month. 20!" Loader sounded thoughtful.

"Ah, but there's another morale factor – probably more important than any we've discussed so far. We've agreed that escort vessels and escort aircraft can't expect to be both good sinkers *and* good scarecrows. The Catalina for example is a hopeless sinker but a great scarecrow. If the U-boats can be scared off from pressing home attacks against convoys, who cares whether they get sunk or not? And I reckon that is where our real opportunity will come. The improved 10 -centimetre radars now being fitted to all our escort vessels will make it practically impossible for a U-boat to make a surfaced night attack on a convoy any more – and that is where they've had all their successes, at least against convoys – in the past. I was up all night working this out. With the new Type 271 radar even a Corvette is guaranteed to pick up surfaced U-boat at 7,000 yards or 4 miles – probably five in most conditions. Now imagine you are a U-boat commander who has placed himself ahead of the convoy – as they usually do – on the surface at night. He would expect to race through it from front to rear hoping for enough time to pick a target, take three bearings, compute his offset angle and launch between one and four torpedoes at his target, four being the number of his loaded torpedo-tubes. Right?"

"Right."

"I estimate that that would take him a minimum of 4 to 6 minutes."

"Seems reasonable old boy. To get his aim-off angle right he will need to see the target bearings change by at least 45 degrees."

" But he is moving through the convoy at a combined speed of 17 plus 8 knots so he's only got seven minutes in total within range of potential targets."

Tinker repeated the quick sum and nodded his head in agreement."

" So he's only got time for one attack. In the mean time all the escort- vessel radar antennae will be rotating away – with an effective range of 4 to 5 miles each. Even if there were only four of them the chance of all four missing him for more than a few minutes must be rather small. Then it's going to take another 2 to 3 minutes to launch a star-shell to illuminate him and give chase. So his chances of getting through the combined radar screen and finding the time to make a well-aimed attack become very small, and the more escort vessels there are the lower his chances will be. Then either he will have to flee on the surface at high-speed – hoping there is not a very much faster destroyer after him, or he will have to submerge and face a terrifying depth charge attack. Do you agree?

"Yep.

"So Tony I reckon that after 10 such aborted attacks even a stout hearted U-boat skipper would lose his nerve and give up. I know I would. I would slip astern hoping to pick up a straggler – a merchant ship which, for one reason or another couldn't keep up with the convoy and won't stand a chance."

"Makes sense Giles. Me too."

"Now here is the point. I went through the chances last night. Even if it took an average six minutes for one of the escort vessels to spot the U-boat and fire a star shell at it, the odds on the U-boat launching its torpedoes is less than 1 in 10 with only four escort vessels, and less than 1 in a *thousand* with eight. This last demonstrates the dramatic effect of Escort-Group size. Their combined effectiveness rises exponentially – that is to say multiplicatively – not additively. I hadn't realised that, and it's absolutely crucial! It may be the key to the whole bloody war. Larger Escort groups – when we can afford them, will be lethal to U-boats."

"From what you're saying Giles it sounds as if U-boats won't stand a chance once all our escort vessels have the new 10 centimetre radars fitted – which I believe will be by the end of this year?"

"Not quite. A wolfpack attack could still prove utterly lethal. If ten U-boats suddenly appeared together on your radar screens the Escort Group would be overwhelmed, and many U-boats would launch successful attacks. Hence the crucial importance of detecting any shadowing U-boat."

"Which points once again to the absolute necessity for air escort."

"Even – or especially – in mid-Atlantic ."

At Duff House Sturdee told Joan and Maurice about Blackett and his political opinions.

"Very understandable." Maurice said. "We poor devils who fought in the Great War, hoped that some sense would come out of the slaughter and the sacrifice –'Homes fit for heroes' and all that. Instead, what did we get? Unemployment, wage-cuts and eventually the stock market crash and the long Depression. In the eyes of smart people, Winston Churchill should get much of the blame for that. In 1925, when he was Chancellor of the Exchequer, the silly fool put us back on the gold standard – forcing our export prices up and making much of British industry uncompetitive. The employers, particularly the coal owners, tried to force down wages – and that led to the general strike of 1926. Churchill – and the rest of the crypto-fascists manned the barricades against the poor bloody miners and ship-building workers."

" 'Crypto-fascist', isn't that a bit strong?" Joan said.

"No it isn't. Their bloody newspaper, the London *Times*, owned by Lord Astor, was openly pro-Hitler and pro Mussolini, as well as a proselyte for Appeasement. And they were more than happy to see the poor Socialist government in Spain destroyed by Franco's Fascist gang aided by the Nazis and Mussolini. You can hardly blame smart young people turning hard Left. That seemed to be the only humane direction left open to them. I was tempted to turn that way myself. Britain was rotten with war profiteers and imperialists. But I could read Russian and I knew too much about Lenin and Stalin to be tempted in the end."

"I can't see why Professor Blackett's political opinions need bother Giles – one way or the other." Joan said. " Can he help you win the Battle of the Atlantic or not – surely that's the question."

"If I work with Blackett, and Blackett falls out with Churchill, it won't help Admiral Noble. Churchill thinks he himself is running the Battle of the Atlantic – and perhaps he is."

"I suspect Churchill has other eggs to fry." Picton said. " His strategy is to gradually lure the Yanks into the war by stringing Roosevelt along. I doubt that it will work though."

"Why not?" Joan wanted to know.

"Because America is basically anti-British. I spent a year there at Harvard University which is in Boston, Massachusetts. Boston is the largest Irish city in the world in terms of Irish inhabitants, followed by Chicago, and both are rabidly anti-British. The largest numbers of US immigrants – as we tend to assume – are not British by extraction but German first, then Italian, then Irish. And of course the Americans are after our wealth and power. They made a vast fortune out of us in the First World War and they are making another in this. They want to see us on our knees so they can take over without lifting a finger. You can't blame them – they did it in the First– made a lot of fuss and bother, and came over so late in 1918 – without any field guns, so they couldn't fight mind you – just in time to try and filch the credit. That idiot Woodrow Wilson even tried to dictate the peace – an attempt which ended in disaster."

"I gather you are not pro-American." Sturdee grinned

"I'm not pro – but not anti either. If I was in their shoes I'd probably do the same. But we British have got to keep our eyes open. We've been running the world for too long now to have many friends. The Americans want to pinch our leadership role – at just as little a cost to themselves as possible. The longer we and Germany go on battering each other the better the Yanks will be pleased. I'm not sure Churchill understands that. Being half American himself, but very ignorant of America, he seems to have rose-tinted spectacles where the Yanks are concerned. Unless it's all propaganda of course, like all that pathetic nonsense you see in the papers about Dear old pipe-smoking Uncle Joe. Stalin is a cold-blooded, mass-murdering, secret policeman."

"Nice allies we've got." Joan said. "But we're getting off the subject. Let me ask you a couple of questions about Blackett Giles."

"Go ahead."

"How old is he?"

"About a dozen years older than me I'd guess."

"So if he fought at Jutland as you mentioned he couldn't have been much more than a boy at the time. That hardly qualifies him as a distinguished sailor."

"I suppose not."

"And what did he do that so distinguishes him as a scientist? Are you sure it was really brilliant – or was it mostly luck?"

Sturdee thought for a moment: " His boss Lord Rutherford set him the task of identifying the particles which emerge from nuclear reactions. One of them turned out to be the Positron, which was new."

"Sounds to me as much luck as judgement."

"What's your point Joan?" Picton asked.

"Well I don't think Giles ought to be too impressed by Professor Blackett. What has he done as clever as working out how deep U-boats dive? And, as he himself admitted, he hasn't penetrated the Admiralty yet – whereas Giles has. Sounds as if he needs you Giles – more than you need him. So if it does come down to negotiation you can afford to drive a hard bargain."

Sturdee nodded. He'd never thought of that.

Picton said: "You should listen to her advice Sturdee."

"I do, I do... I wouldn't have gone to see Blackett otherwise. I really do need a scientific patron though – a senior scientist who can fight battles within Whitehall– and really there is not much choice for me now that Taffy Bowen has hopped it for the States; there's no one else I know left. As Joan says 'Damn his politics!' I happen to think Winnie is doing the right thing luring the Yanks into war. We don't want the war to go on – like it did with Napoleon – for 20 years, so we need their production capability, if nothing else. And I don't quite buy your cynical appraisal of their intentions Maurice. Roosevelt is doing everything he can to draw the Americans into the war on our side – and he will succeed within 3 to 6 months. His problem is the primitive nature of United States government with its anti-diluvian constitution and its system of checks and balances. Practically everybody has to agree before war can be declared –

which is perhaps no bad thing in general. In the mean time they've introduced their so-called 'Security Zone' which stretches 2,000 miles eastward from New York – a real joke. They intend to patrol it aggressively and report to us any U-boats they locate there. Then they are supplying us with large amounts of munitions, planes, tanks and guns through the so-called 'Lend Lease program'. British ships are repairing in US Navy Yards. They've taken over the occupation of Iceland from us – releasing 5,000 British troops, and they are establishing bases in Northern Ireland and Scotland preparatory to taking over convoy escort duties in October, sometimes as far East as 25 degrees West. And if necessary I'll tell Blackett that."

"Why does Roosevelt want to enter the war on our side anyway ?" Joan asked.

"Good question." Picton replied. "If you ask me he doesn't fancy the prospect of being left to face Hitler alone. If we fall, so will Russia. Hitler will get his Middle Eastern oil and take India as well as Europe, and the Mediterranean – and Africa. He will then have a hegemon the like of which no one, not even Alexander the Great, could imagine. If he wanted to, Hitler could then bring America to its knees either by blockade – more likely by scientific superiorrity. The Yanks are way behind Europe in science."

'So Roosevelt's policy is primarily there for the protection of the United States – and not ours?"

" Of course – and all the better for that."

"But then you can't argue that Churchill is responsible for it." Joan said.

"I suppose not." Sturdee smiled ruefully.

"Nothing gets past our Joan Giles, I told you. She could have become a very distinguished historian... still could ..."

"Not if she's a farmer's wife in the Australian outback, she won't. Too busy dosing sheep for worms." Sturdee sounded bitter.

Sturdee's feelings for Joan were becoming ever more confused. The more he saw of her the better he liked her and the more he admired her brains. The idea of moving out and never seeing her again was insupportable. At the same time it was difficult to moon over someone you saw over the breakfast table every morning, or standing in the scullery with a knotted duster round her hair stirring pig-swill over the stove with a wooden ladle. He'd read that boys and girls who grew up together in institutions never fell in love – like brothers and sisters did not – and he could well imagine it. On the other hand he'd fallen for Joan before she had become his landlady. And he still felt desperately jealous whenever she read out extracts from her fiancée Des's frequent and, it had to be said, witty letters from the Far East. There could be no doubt but she was growing increasingly fond of himself though. Her face lit up when he appeared and she seemed to like spending her time with him and Arfur. Arfur had become their mutual foster-child. Evenings would often see the three of them together lying either on Arfur's or Giles's bed, reading a book aloud – taking it in turns. Starting with *Huck Finn* and *Tom Sawyer* they'd done *'The Lost World, 'Micah Clarke"* and were now working their way through the Rider Haggard masterpieces *'She'* and *'Alan*

Quartermain'. Sometimes Arfur would light the Hurricane Lamp and insist on them lying among the straw in the stable and sharing their stories with Gem. Particularly when Arfur was reading, the old horse would prick up his ears as if he understood every word. Joan and Arfur also liked to watch Giles painting – or working on his mathematics:

"You look so happy, so wrapped up in it Giles, so lost in another world, that it's good for my soul." Joan said. "All the cares of the world drift away as if I were listening to Evensong. What do you think Arfur ?"

"I fink he looks like Gem of an evening – when e's munching from 'is nose-bag."

Sturdee best loved those moments when it was Joan's turn to read because then he could stare at her lovely face from very close quarters without feeling self-conscious. One day, he knew, he wouldn't be able to help himself. He'd reach across and kiss her. Then everything would be spoiled. He'd have to leave Duff House , losing not only her but Arfur and Maurice too. But was it possible, just possible that she would respond and kiss him back? Often, as he was going off to sleep, he dreamed about such a miracle. It didn't seem entirely impossible. But when he got up next morning and went downstairs there would be Joan striding about, dressed for the day's work, issuing orders like a Sergeant Major. That she would think of kissing him back seemed to him laughable then.

There was no one who he could really talk to about Joan apart from Maurice and Loader. Maurice, from the detachment of old age, affected to find the situation amusing: "It's a contest between brains and contiguity on your side, romantic love and absence on Des's. Joan, I surmise, is a faithful and honest soul who would find it very difficult to betray her plighted troth – almost unimaginable I would say. On the other hand, as I can daily see, she is becoming increasingly enchanted by you Giles. She's never before met a man with a brain almost the equal of her own – and naturally she finds that fascinating. More even than that, she realises you will always carve your own idiosyncratic, even poetic path through life , as you have done already. I was watching her face as you were describing sailing through France: she was a little girl being told her very first fairy story. She knows you will go on telling fairy stories, even living them, all your life. What woman with romantic inclinations, and she is romantic you know – when she's not calculating onion prices – wouldn't be intrigued by a man like you? And young Arfur isn't doing your cause any harm."

"How do you mean?"

"Well he hero-worships you – which is only to be expected at his age. You're the only male role-model of roughly the right age he has got. It's comic to watch at times – but touching. You'll obviously make a good father one day– just what any prospective mother like Joan wants."

Loader on the other hand, had no time for Joan since his run in with her: "She's just keeping you on ice Giles– in case hubby gets shot down. You could be mooning about for years and then the day the war ends she'd vanish like dust. Your life is worth more than that isn't it? The trouble is you're so bloody naïve and innocent – wet behind the ears in fact. You ought to get to know a decent warm-hearted woman."

"Like who?"

"Like Gwen for instance."

"Gwen?" Sturdee was incredulous: "When anyone can see what's going on there behind her husband's back while he's fighting in Egypt!."

"And you think that's terrible?"

"Yes I do – who wouldn't?"

"Any man with a warm heart – and some experience of women."

"That's hypocritical."

"For a virgin who knows bugger all about real life you're a pretty free with your criticisms Sturdee."

"I'm sorry, I didn't mean to be. It's none of my business what you and Gwen get up to. It's just that she can't be mentioned in the same breath as Joan."

" Oh can't she? That shows how little you know. Gwen loves her husband Geraint deeply – has known him since they were kids together growing up together in some Welsh village. She'll go back to him like a shot – lucky bugger – if he survives the war . But she's like lots of women, who once they've started having sex, can't do without it – need a good ronge at least once a week– otherwise they go scatty. And I am the beneficiary just now. By consorting with me, she is remaining faithful to her hubby – she's never going to run off with another man."

"I think you're mad Loader."

"More compliments. Well I forgive you because I know Sturdee you are just plain ignorant. Why don't you sleep with her yourself?"

"With who?"

"With Gwen of course. I know she fancies you – though God knows why. She told me so . It would do you no end of good Giles, it really would. You'd be able to treat that Joan then – as just another woman. Don't you see just how unnatural it is – to still be a virgin at your age?"

"Would you be jealous?"

"Good heavens no. I don't own Gwen – she's happily married – and she doesn't own me. You know sex is just sex old boy– very nice indeed – but nothing to do with what you evidently imagine to be romantic love. Don't you fancy Gwen?"

"She's certainly very attractive."

"You want to see her with her clothes off Giles , she's sensational. I get her to parade round in the all-together while I stare at her. She loves it. She knows her body can't last forever, any more than a rose can bloom. In the mean time it would be a crime to hide it – like locking the Rokeby Venus in a safe, only 10 times worse – no a hundred times worse. No doubt the Rokeby bum is legendary but our Gwen's is even better. Out of the goodness of her heart Gwen likes to make a man happy. If you gave her the chance she'd cook you a delicious meal just to watch you enjoying it. One day she'll do the same for her children. I'd marry her like a shot. But alas she's faithful to Geraint.

Sturdee shook his head: " I don't know what to say Tony. Its all beyond my ken."

167

"Well exactly Sturdee. But it shouldn't be – not at your age. If you don't learn the facts of life soon you will become a menace to yourself and to everybody else. Even if she is no good at doing crosswords our Gwen is more than the equal of your Joan. Any day!"

CHAPTER 15

TO SINK A U-BOAT

Sir Percy called Sturdee and Loader in to discuss their U-boat morale paper:

"Morale is such a difficult topic to pin down – indeed nothing is more, or even half as important. For once Napoleon got it right when he said the moral is to the material as 3 to 1. At least. Our poor sailors are about to face another dreadful winter out there in escort vessels that were never built to take the North Atlantic – never mind in winter. The corvettes were designed for coastal escort mostly in sight of land, the destroyers for the North Sea – which they can cross in the matter of hours, and so take shelter at the approach of any real storm. Now they have to weather storm after storm, their men crowded into wet mess decks – largely without hot food, and mostly in total darkness. The conditions are as appalling as they were in the trenches during the last war, perhaps worse. Quite frankly I don't know how men can stand it – or for how long they can go on. Do either of you?"

Sturdee shook his head.

"I believe two things help sir." Loader ventured. "They know the U-boat men are suffering as well – and they don't want to be the first to crack. The Royal Navy has never cracked first before – it's not going to start now. Then when they come home and see our blitzed-out cities they go to sea again determined to exact revenge. I don't think that kind of feeling could have existed in Britain before. This time it's total war."

"Yes, so the newspapers say. But the Germans must be feeling the same way now that Bomber command is plastering their cities night after night…"

"I hadn't thought of that." Loader admitted

"As I understand it, you two are suggesting that U-boat crew morale will begin to crack when more than one in five U-boats fails to return from each voyage. If my sums are right then in those circumstances the odds of a crew surviving for a whole year would be 3 to 1 against? There would be a 75 per cent chance of being killed?"

"That is correct Admiral." Sturdee agreed.

"Then I think it is a reasonable working supposition. It cannot be all that far out. And if it is true then to win we have to sink one in five of the U-boats at sea. That means four a month at present, and 20 a month when we come to the climactic battle. When you consider that we are sinking only two a month now that seems a dramatic increase."

Noble glanced down at their paper: "The second argument you use concerns the exchange rate between ships torpedoed by them, and U-boats sunk by us. You are suggesting Sturdee that once the ratio of ships to U-boats sunk drops below about five they will become discouraged, their rewards won't be worth the risk?"

"Right sir."

"That's more debatable it seems to me – but it gives much the same answer as before. Seeing they torpedo of order 100 ships a month at present , we need to sink 20 U-boats again?"

"Yes."

"Then you bring up the number of new U-boats being commissioned – again 20 a month. If we can sink more than that, their overall numbers would decline – which won't appeal to Doenitz. He will begin to lose his influence with Hitler. No commander likes to see his forces shrink."

" Finally you bring up an entirely different argument ,which I must say appeals to me, if only because there is some evidence for it already. You feel that U-boat commanders who've been forced to break off their attacks before they've launched their torpedoes, eventually lose heart. That certainly happened after we sunk their three Aces back in March. And most of their commanders nowadays must be novices – with little in the way of experience to give them encouragement. So if the new 10 centimetre radars work anything like as well as we have been promised, they'll spot U-boats surfaced at night long before they can properly launch torpedoes. In other words this is a tactic we ought to succeed with – even if we can't sink 'em. Am I reading you right Giles?"

"Yes Admiral."

"Now there is one further thing here which is implicit, even if you don't spell it out in words. You suggest that the effectiveness of a radar screen goes up exponentially, i.e. dramatically, with the number of vessels in the screen. But the number of escort vessels will in general rise with the number of ships in the convoy. So that raises a very important general question – and one about which I've often wondered: 'What is the optimal size for a convoy?' My Lords of the Admiralty keep insisting that the optimum size is 40 ships – but they give no convincing rationale for their number. I want you to look into it urgently. It could be crucial when the day of reckoning arrives – absolutely crucial. I think I know what the answer is. Let's see if we can independently agree."

"We'll get on that Admiral, immediately after we've finished your Support Group paper."

"Yes, that was my next question. How is that going? I need some answers soon."

"It will be ready in a few days Admiral" Loader promised "But we needed to find out if your views on U-boat morale coincided with ours – which apparently they do."

"Yes, let me summarise on that. If we can, every month, sink one-fifth of the U-boats actually at sea then German morale will crack for three separate reasons: submarining will appear too dangerous; the number of ships torpedoed will be too few to justify the cost in lives; and finally the loss-rate will exceed the building rate – which will lead to a shrinking fleet. You further suggest that even if we cannot sink the requisite number of U-boats we can still demoralise U-boat skippers by forestalling torpedo attacks before their fish are launched. Thank you gentlemen – once again you give me much to think about. By the way Sturdee, how did you get on with Professor Blackett?"

"Well enough Sir; we are going to keep in close touch. For the moment he recommends we carry on much as we are – working directly for you. He and his group are presently taken up with Coastal Command's 'Battle for the Bay of Biscay' ."

"And what do you think of that Sturdee?"

"If you ask me sir it is misconceived and extravagant. It harks back to that obsession for 'Hunting submarines' when Coastal Command should be helping us to harass the ones we already know about – in the vicinity of convoys. What do you think Admiral?"

"I think I'd best keep my views on this delicate matter to myself – for now. What did you tell Blackett?"

"Much what I've just told you sir. I could see he was surprised, but he sounded thoughtful afterwards. I don't think his group has questioned Coastal Command strategy – so far."

"If you ask me" Maurice said over the supper table: "Hitler has missed his chance. The fighting season in northern Europe is over – the roads are turning into quagmires. Snow is covering the landscape. Tanks will become helpless – aircraft will be crippled by low cloud, artillery will run out of ammunition. Any infantry out in the open will freeze to death in hours. So it's all over until next spring – April at the earliest. In the mean time sheer survival will be at a premium. Many will freeze, poor devils – the soldiers and civilians, and millions will starve – perhaps whole populations"

"How dreadful." Joan shuddered And we are the beneficiaries. Had Hitler not attacked Russia in June we'd be on our knees right now also. If the May Blitz on Liverpool had continued for another week or two we wouldn't have been able to unload our convoys. As it was we went down to a weekly import total of a quarter of a million tons as opposed to half a million tons estimated as the absolute minimum needed to continue the war, and over four times less than we took in peacetime. That of course is highly confidential. Had it come out at the time we might have faced calls for capitulation."

"And now?" Sturdee wanted to know.

"We're doing fine. With the blitz over… do you think Hitler will bring his bombers back if he can't use them in Russia for now?"

"He could I suppose" Sturdee said. "But we're ready for them this time. According to Hanbury our night fighters will wipe them out."

"So he really has missed his chance?" Joan asked.

"His U-boats could still win at sea." Picton replied "Couldn't they Giles?"

"They could. Expect the climactic battle in about a year. We have survived 1941 so far only because Hitler diverted U-boats to the Med and into the Baltic. That's a piece of luck that may not continue."

"We've got so much to be thankful for." Joan said. "After the fall of France, less than 18 months ago, it all looked up for our little island. But first the miracle of Dunkirk, then the Battle of Britain, then the Blitzes… We survived them all . I know it's late for the harvest but I think we'll hold a harvest thanksgiving – to say thankyou for everything. Look how much we grew: onions, apples, potatoes, pears, berries…"

"… carrots, hay, plums, cherries, eggs, swedes, beans, peas…" Arfur continued the list.

"We have fed at least 20 people at a time when the country was supposed to be starving."

"Mostly thanks to you Joan." Sturdee said. "I know I wouldn't have lifted a finger – just grumbled – like Maurice."

"We all helped." Joan said "especially Arfur and Gem. Things could've gone wrong. Without God's help the pigs could've died, the chickens could have been stolen, leather-jackets could've eaten the spuds, the onions might not have flourished… so we are going to have a harvest thanksgiving."

So it was arranged. Several war orphans were invited from the orphanage and put under Arfur's care. Using Gem they built a giant bonfire in the paddock. Friends were invited over for the whole day and Sturdee invited Loader and Gwen. Giles strangled a goose and a non-laying hen; Maurice plucked them for Joan to stuff and roast. Bartering led to the appearance of several bottles of alcohol including elderflower champagne, navy rum and sloe- gin. Gwen turned out to be a skilled baker and, with ingredients supplied by Joan, baked a big barrabrith, an apple-tart and mince pies. A roaring fire was lighted in the dining room and the giant table put to its proper use, not for ping-pong, for the very first time.

Shortly after noon the party traipsed down to the paddock and lit the bonfire. Loader served a rum punch with a lot of rum and even more punch. And everybody's face turned bright red, whether from heat or from good cheer it was difficult to say. Joan said a prayer of Thanksgiving – barely audible above the crackle and roar of the fire, before they all sang "For those in peril on the sea" with such force and feeling that the three pigs joined in from their sty in the distance. Then the adults returned to the house, leaving Arfur and his minions to retrieve the potatoes baking in the embers and carry them up later to the kitchen.

Maurice carved the two birds, Gwen portioned out the vegetables, Joan the stuffings and gravies, Loader served more drinks and they all sat down to their harvest banquet. Even with five adults around the table and six children at the other end, there were still vacant chairs in the middle.

After the feast Maurice staggered to his feet, a jam-jar of sloe gin in his hand because there were insufficient glasses to go around:

"My friends, it is my privilege, as the oldest of the company, to offer a choast… a choast… I can't say it properly – but you know what I mean. It was Joan's idea– and a very good one as always – to shelebrate the very great good fortune that has attended us all this pasht year or sho. When France fell the Nazis seemed invinshible – invincible – and that it would be our turn next. But then miracle followed upon apparent miracle: Dunkirk, the Battle of Britain, shurviving the Blitz, Taranto, the shinking of the Bismarck, Barbarossha… And here we are, shtill undefeated. Indeed there is a real proshpect that we will eventually win – unlikely as that sheemed only 12 months ago."

Maurice swilled his sloe gin round and round for a minute and stared into the fire as if looking into the future:

"If we do win it will be because our people have thrown up new leaders to take over from the old – and one of them is sitting at this table. In May , as I'm sure you all remember, we were blitzed eight nights in shuccession. At the time we kept the figures secret – because they were so horrifying. But I can tell you now that over 4,000 of our citizens were killed and 50,000 of our dwellings were destroyed or badly damaged. Worse shtill Liverpool almost ceased to function as a port when its twelve miles of quays were turned into burning rubble. When you realise that over 90per cent of our imports from the Americas come through this shitty, you can appreciate how close we came and collapshe. Somehow we had to unload and reload hundreds and hundreds of ships, and convey their cargoes inland to the resht of our island by rail. But the railways and the shunting yards and locomotive sheds were being bombed as heavily as the docks – so that total paralysis stared us in the face. I know, better than anyone else, because, as a senior civil servant in the Ministry of War Transport here, it was our job to short it out. But we failed. Every emergency called for a new plan. We made a new plan but then the bombs ruined that, and it had to be changed again and again and again. I was in deshpair, we were all in deshpair when that young woman…" He pointed dramatically at Joan. " Took over. In her head she could somehow hold half a dozen train schedules at once, and modify them almost continuously. We stood back and watched in awe. The right rolling stock came alongside the right ships at the right quays and loaded with the right cargos. Trains were somehow put together in the marshalling yards and dispatched all over the country. Liverpool docks began to function again – and therefore sho did Britain. For a week or two back then Joan Duff became a leader as important to our survival as Air Marshall Dowding or Admiral Noble. She won't have it of course – no doubt because she's been brought up to believe she's only a weak woman. A woman she might be – but weak she is not. So I ashk you all, even you children down the end of the table, to stand up with me and raise your glashes and gives thanks to Providence for… Mish Joan Duff."

Joan turned beetroot red, everybody stood, the men banged their approval on the table as the toast was drunk.

Somebody turned off the lights so that only the firelight flickering off the walls illuminated the glowing faces. Loader splashed more gin into Maurice's jar whilst everybody else sat down. The old man sipped again before continuing:

"Thish is a thanksgiving feast, a shelebration of our good fortune. Mr. Churchill says we are fighting for the survival of Christian civilisation. And who am I to argue with him? When we have won , as I am more confident now that we will, we will look back to this deshperate time as the proudest period of our lives. Pershonally, it has been for me, and I hope for some of you, alsho one of the happiest. The war has brought together people who would otherwise never have known one another – wonderful people – and encouraged us to show our better qualities. Even when we were shivering together in that terrible shelter with the bombs raining down, the aerial mines exshploding and the anti- aircraft guns going berserk, I knew I was lucky to be with

Joan, with Giles here, and later with Arfur – not to shay his old horse Gem. We are, like many others, a wartime family brought together by a common enemy, and a common resolve – and all the better for that. Of course I want us to win – and as shoon as poshible – but I do not want to see them leave –and dishappear again into their private lives – of which I will no longer be a part. The most foolish belief on this planet is that men are first and foremost materialistic creatures. As a historian I can assure you that nothing could be further from the truth. Men only decline into materialism when they cannot find a better purpose, a more inshpiring common enterprise. My friends, for all our misfortunes, we are not lacking in that. So we have much to be thankful for at this time. For deliverance from Evil. For the harvest brought safely home. For wonderful friends. For a common purpose under God. Amen."

Noble had always regarded Support Groups – that could be sent to the aid of besieged convoys, as a principle part of his strategy. The question was 'Could they be afforded?' Where were all of the extra escort vessels they needed to come from – when he was desperately short already? That is why he had asked Sturdee to look into the matter, and why he was eager to discuss their paper as soon as it arrived on his desk:

"If you chaps are right we shall need only ten or twenty per cent more escort vessels to get going – and of course we could manage that. But why so few?"

"Because the indications are that Doenitz will always concentrate his boats in very limited areas of the ocean – where he thinks they will have the best chance." Sturdee laid some of Gwen's sinking maps out on the desk in support of his contention. In the first six months most vessels had been torpedoed in the south-western approaches. Then there had been an abrupt switch to the north western approaches. Now most of the sinking ewre taking price place either in mid-Atlantic or off the bulge of West Africa:

"That, we believe is what will give you your chance Sir. There is no need to deploy your Support Groups everywhere – only in the current area of maximum danger."

"That makes sense of course. Every commander tries to concentrate his force to maximum effect. I like your charts. Make sure I have copies."

"Gwen Jones , our Wren, is already making them sir." Loader intervened "We'll keep them up-to-date .Notice how Doenitz is now concentrating his boats – in mid-Atlantic and off Freetown Sierra Leone. Coastal command should plug this last gap immediately."

"I've already been on to Joubert about that."

"So," Sturdee continued: "That is why we have assumed that the climax battle will take place in the mid-Atlantic air gap. That's 600 miles wide, or a fifth of the whole Crossing. If you concentrate all your support groups within that gap then you can do with only one support group for every five escort groups. And we assume you need only half the number of escort vessels in a Support group as in an Escort group Admiral."

"Why?"

"Because it will have a much more limited task: only to sink U-boats already located by the escort groups and submerged by an escort vessel above them on the surface. Once called out by radio, a support group will remain in place until the submarine is destroyed."

"We have reckoned about four ships to a Support group" Loader continued "First because, between them, they will carry 400 depth-charges, enough to sink about four U-boats without replenishment. Two can work together to do the sinking, whilst two others act as guard-ships, protecting their vulnerable colleagues from attack by other U-boats."

"That sounds sensible." Noble agreed.

"But they all need to be fast ships." Sturdee insisted. "Not corvettes. Why? Because the escort vessel cannot remain over the targeted submarine for more than a few hours, leaving its own Escort-group depleted."

"Naturally."

"That means fast Support groups, but it also means the escort groups must be able to find a lot of U-boats, so as to be able to pick and choose help only when there is a Support group within a few hours call."

"I hadn't thought of that." Noble conceded

"It wasn't obvious" Sturdee said. "Until you look into the timing problem: how much time will be wasted by Support groups steaming around trying to find U-boats? On average, the less time wasted steaming about, the less Support groups you will need."

"That's what I need you for Sturdee. We might have got there eventually – probably would – but you've anticipated the problem and considered the consequences. I bet you didn't think about it Loader?"

"I didn't Admiral. These scientists have a different kind of imagination – always asking numerical questions. At least Giles does."

"As it happens Loader we may be able to help you. Ever heard of Huff Duff?"

"No sir."

"It's mumbo-jumbo. designed to disguise 'High Frequency Direction Finding' , or 'HF – DF'. Don't ask me how it works – but it's being developed by the Admiralty Signals Establishment at Haslemere. Any escort vessel fitted with Huff Duff should be able to get an instant and accurate bearing on any U-boat transmitting a radio message within something like 20 miles. U-boats shadowing convoys will be detected immediately, chased, and put down. That's what you wanted – lots of contacts?"

"Exactly Sir ."

"Well you'd better look into it and tell me what you think."

"I will." Sturdee made a note.

"In the mean time I'm going to take a very positive message out of our discussion. We can afford to start forming support groups right now because we are going to need no more than 20 per cent extra escort vessels to do it – perhaps only 10. But they must contain only fast escort vessels, otherwise the Support groups will arrive too late to be of much use."

Noble ticked the points off on his fingers: "Each Support Group should contain close to four fast vessels. They should be deployed only in those areas of the battlefield where the struggle is currently most intense, notably in the Air gaps. They should be summoned by radio – only when they can arrive within a few hours, probably no more than six. Such will be possible only when escort groups can locate plenty of U-boats. To that end new research techniques such as Huff Duff need to be introduced expeditiously – certainly before the climax battle expected in 12 to 18 months time. Provided a typical convoy can pick up two or more U-boats whilst it is crossing the gap then even if there's only one Support group in the gap we should sink over 20 U-boats a month – the number we judge , on morale grounds, will be necessary to bring about victory. Have I left anything out?"

"Only this Admiral," Sturdee replied. "All our numbers are predicated on wolfpack numbers not becoming too large. If a dozen U-boats attack a convoy at once, the arrival of a small Support group. of the kind we have suggested, won't help. The convoy might still be overwhelmed in short order. Hence the importance of air cover to prevent the assemblage of large packs. We must not allow anyone to think that Support groups are an alternative to VLRAs. They are not. They are only an economic tactic for sinking a lot of U-boats. They will not save a convoy once it is attacked by a large and coherent pack."

"Yes I see your point Giles. In all our documents to authority we need to emphasise the urgent need for VLR aircraft up front – that there is no alternative." He jotted away for a minute or two and, then looked up, screwing the top back onto his fountain pen.

"Once again I am grateful to you both. This is not the end of the story of course, far from it. I intend to rewrite the case for Support groups in my own words, taking all your points into account of course, and present it to a conference of my whole staff – you included – and to all of the Escort- group commanders. Assuming their approval, we will immediately form a first experimental Support group to see how it goes and I will go up to my Lords of the Admiralty, and if necessary to Mr Churchill's Battle of the Atlantic committee, to ask for 20 per cent more escort vessels, particularly fast ones. Largely thanks to your numerical work I feel I could do that in good conscience. And I will fight hard – as I will over VLR. But I'm beginning to see real chinks of light at the end of what is still a long dark dangerous tunnel. Deeper depth-charges, better radar, Long range patrol aircraft, Huff Duff – if it comes to anything, Support groups… They're all going to help. Of course the enemy will not be idle – will make his own improvements too, but we've got much to look forward to. And I haven't mentioned Hedgehog have I?"

"No Sir". Sturdee and Loader looked meaningfully at one another.

"It is a new, ahead-firing mortar being built into new escort vessels. I saw an impressive demonstration of it at Portland recently. It fires 24 bombs in a pattern 300 yards ahead of the ship. The bombs are streamlined, sink rapidly and detonate only on contact so you don't have to worry about uncertainties as to the U-boat's depth. There's some worries about the lethality of the bombs, and its accuracy in rough weather– but much is expected of it. At the moment though it's very hush-hush and, because it points up , we are pretending it's an anti dive-bomber weapon. Also, but further into the future, we have a colossal mortar called Squid which will hurl 300-pound depth charges up to 300 yards ahead of the ship, with the depth-setting controlled automatically by a depth-detecting Asdic. But, of course, we must not rely on such untested miracle-weapons – which may well turn out to be useless in practice. Which is why I didn't tell you about them when you were looking into sinking U-boats yourselves. Had I done so you might well have missed your vital insight into the depth capabilities of U-boats."

Sturdee and Loader looked knowingly at one another again, both thinking 'Cunning old devil.'

CHAPTER 16
FLYING CIRCUS

At the end of November Sturdee and Loader flew South in the Walrus with Air Vice Marshal Robb who was on his way to a meeting of Coastal Command top brass at its headquarters at Norwood in South London. Since Blackett's operational research group was based there too it was an opportunity to meet up.

The Walrus landed on the Thames near Greenwich Palace and a brief drive south took them to their destination near Dulwich. Blackett, looking more like an admiral in mufti than a physicist, had assembled his so-called 'flying circus' in a large conference room where he introduced everybody. Sturdee was amazed by the size and calibre of the circus. There must have been a dozen senior scientists, including half a dozen Fellows of the Royal Society, including an old acquaintance from Bawdsey, E.G. Williams, a fierce-looking Welshman built like a wrestler, but with eye-brows like a predatory owl. Blackett opened the meeting:

"We scientists at Norwood have no doubt as to the value of OR, and more importantly neither do the commanders of Coastal command – first Air Chief Marshall Bowhill , and now his successor Air Chief Marshall Joubert. But other senior commanders are not similarly convinced, and in particular the Royal Navy – which, as always, carries the main responsibility for defending Britain – is resistant to the whole idea. Thus I was very surprised to come upon Dr. Sturdee here, who is doing OR within Western Approaches command – based in Liverpool. That command, headed by Admiral Sir Percy Noble, is responsible for trying to win the Battle of the Atlantic – unquestionably the most momentous Battle of this entire war– notwithstanding the epic slaughter presently going on at the Eastern Front, and notwithstanding RAF Bomber Command's ambitious campaign to bomb Germany. If we lose the Battle of the Atlantic, Britain will starve and Russia will collapse. We are attempting to do our bit by helping Coastal Command to try and win the Battle of Biscay, a presently unsuccessful sideshow besides the titanic struggle to protect our shipping and in particular our convoys, from U-boats spread over no less than ten million square miles of Atlantic Ocean. There has never been a battle like it in human history. Make no mistake; on its outcome depends the future of civilisation."

" So Dr Sturdee here, and his colleague Lieutenant Loader, carry an enormous burden on their young shoulders. Admiral Noble personally sought out Sturdee because of something quite remarkable in the way of Operational Research which he did when he was only 14 years old, and a cadet at Dartmouth Naval College. He argued , even then, back in 1925, that the day of the battleship was over because of its vulnerability to the rapidly evolving dive- bomber. The battle of Taranto, and the sinking of the Bismarck, proved just how right, just how prophetic that boy was. The Royal Navy however didn't want to believe that its world dominance in battleships would end because of String-bags and so, thanks to Admiral Noble, Sturdee left the Navy and became a physicist. He had a distinguished career at first Birmingham, then Göttingen and Munich, before returning to Britain and working in airborne radar at Bawdsey Manor. That work, directed by Doctor E.G.. Bowen, lead to the formidable night-fighter force which is protecting us today, and has apparently put an end to the blitzes.

"Early this year, when Admiral Noble was appointed to head the Western Approaches command, with its colossal responsibility – as great as Nelson's in his day – he remembered the young Sturdee and persuaded him to come to Liverpool to help him. And, according to very fulsome letters I have received both from Admiral Noble, and his Coastal command deputy, Air Vice Marshal Robb, help he most certainly has. The work that he and Lieutenant Loader have already done will, I hope, eventually persuade my Lords of the Admiralty, that Operational Research is something which the Royal Navy – as a whole – needs. But that is for the future. When I met Sturdee a few weeks ago in Manchester I invited him to come down here so that we could , at the very least, exchange information. He said he needs other OR scientists he could talk to. And we, I believe, need to talk to an OR scientist like himself, who works much closer to the fulcrum of the real battle, than we do ourselves. So Sturdee, would you like to start things off."

Sturdee had a prepared talk but now he put his notes aside and spoke from the heart:

"I'd barely heard of OR, and had no intention of joining the Navy when Admiral Noble asked me up to see him in Liverpool. It didn't take long to convince me he faced, we all now face, a desperate situation in the Atlantic. It is so desperate that the government doesn't dare to tell the full truth of the matter. Germany is commissioning 20 new U-boats every month, And we are sinking one or two. To survive we need at least 1000 large vessels a month to unload their cargoes at our two last functioning ports – Liverpool and Glasgow. Yet Germany is sinking between 100 and 200 of our ships every month. The only defensive weapon we have is the convoy – which reduces, by a factor of about 20, the number of targets which U-boats can find every month. At present, convoys can melt into the vast empty spaces of the Atlantic Ocean, leaving most U-boats starved. But when, in about 12 months time, the Nazis can maintain, at all times, a cordon of 100 U-boats at sea, then even the convoys won't be able to escape. The battle will then reach some kind of climax leading to the defeat, the total defeat, of one side or the other. Which will it be?"

"At the present moment Admiral Noble and his men are putting up a heroic fight. None of our small number of convoy escort vessels were built to fight in the North Atlantic, because the Admiralty assumed, before the fall of France, that the submarine battle would be fought in the North Sea, as it had been in the First World War. Until I went to sea in a Corvette I had no idea of the appalling conditions in which our man have to fight , day and night, winter and summer, mostly up towards the Arctic Circle. Their clothes are always wet, and sometimes they have to go without hot food for *weeks* at a time. Weeks! Think of that. The seas are freezing, the between-decks where they are supposed to sleep in hammocks, are unventilated , soaking and so crowded that tuberculosis is rife. The winter nights are interminable, their radar and Asdics barely function, there are no ship-to-ship radios – they still use flags and signal lamps would you believe – and their weapons are more or less useless in the tumultuous seas. For instance depth-charges don't function below 300 feet while U-boats can dive to 2 to 3 times that depth. They even have to resort to ramming. The slowest escorts , the Corvettes, can't even keep up with a surfaced U-boat – while the fast ones – the destroyers – have such a short range that they must turn back to refuel before they even reach mid-Atlantic. And the weather– you can't ever imagine it – until you've seen a wave as tall as a block of flats, bearing down on you, it's crest curling as it is about to break. Even seasoned sea-captains look away, praying under their breaths."

"It would be easy to blame the Admiralty for our total unpreparedness but it was the politicians who refused the Navy proper escort vessels when they were asked for – and could've been built. And who could have foreseen the precipitous fall of France, which transferred the arena of the battle from the North Sea to the North Atlantic? The only thing that has saved us so far was that the Nazis were almost equally unprepared for this war – having put their resources into the building of dinosaur battleships like the Bismarck and the Turpitz. But they are building U-boats fast now and we are building weapons too. Who will have the right resources when the climactic battle comes in 12 months time, will decide the outcome."

"If Tony Loader and I have been able to help – and we have– it is mainly because our senior naval officers have been so harried by their unanticipated responsibilities – think of Dunkirk – that they don't have enough time to think deeply about the future – whereas we do. Admiral Noble has specifically charged us with that responsibility. There is no shortage of brainpower in the Navy but there is a critical shortage of time. Lieutenant Loader will tell you something about our detailed work– on depth-charges, on U-boat morale, and on Support groups, as Admiral Noble calls them. I'm going to talk about something more general, and more abstract , harder to grasp, but absolutely fundamental – and that is '*Concentration in war* '. I'd never heard of the concept until a few weeks ago when a historian mentioned it to me while we were washing up. Ever since it has haunted me day and night. It is to Operational Research what Pythagoras' Theorem is to mathematic. How many of you have heard of Lanchester's Equations?"

Nobody raised a hand.

" Very well then – I won't be wasting your time if I talk about Lanchester's Equations for thirty minutes. Later we could discuss their bearing on your Battle of Biscay , and on our Battle of the Atlantic."

As he continued the audience visibly began to sit up : some even took notes; he was interrupted with questions; Blackett's comment was "It is indeed surprising – and relevant; you weren't exaggerating about Pythagoras Sturdee'".

When he'd finished E.G.Williams, he of the shaggy eyebrows, asked about it's bearing on the Battle of the Atlantic.

"As it has developed" Sturdee replied. "We have been forced to concentrate our ships into convoys. And that has worked miraculously – or rather mathematically. Not many people, not all admirals , understand that we convoy for the very same reason that fish shoal and birds flock. Now Doenitz has found out that he has to concentrate his U-boats too, into wolf-packs."

Sturdee went into the mathematics of convoys and wolfpacks on the blackboard. He was going to stop because he'd use his appointed time but Blackett waved him to continue. After almost 100 minutes on his feet he drew to a conclusion: "So one can foresee the outcome as a series of climacteric convoy battles about a year from now. Each will be decided by the relative number of escort vessels to U-boats at each convoy. If there are too many U-boats they will overwhelm the Escort group and sink most of the cargo vessels in the convoy. It will be impossible to rescue the 4000 torpedoed merchant seaman and most will drown, leading to the rapid collapse of morale in the merchant marine as a whole. But if radar equipped, fast escort vessels comfortably outnumber U-boats then no U-boat will be able to press home a successful torpedo attack. Many will be put down and eventually destroyed by Support Groups with the time and the depth-charges to do so. The critical role of air power will lie with VLR aircraft that can patrol the convoy perimeter by day and night, putting down the shadowing U-boats, and preventing the concentration of a wolfpack of sufficient size to overwhelm the Escort group. It is this scarecrow capability of an aircraft, rather than its sinking capability that will matter, indeed will be essential, absolutely vital. U-boats give up and go away whenever continuous air patrol is present, and concentrate in areas where it is not."

To prove his point he showed several of Gwen's sinking-charts and finished on an apocalyptic note: "If, within 12 months, Coastal command has not been able to get its hands on four-engined VLR aircraft, able to patrol the Central Atlantic air gap, then gentlemen, we will lose the Battle of the Atlantic, and in losing that, lose the entire war."

Sturdee was succeeded by E.J.Williams who described the work he and his group were doing on the development of airborne depth-charges. Bitter experience had shown that the existing hundred-pound antisubmarine bomb was incapable of sinking U-boats. But there had been some, admittedly very limited success with dropping 250 - pound naval depth-charges. The problem lay in judging the depths of the U-boats. The only hope lay in depth-charging one while it was still partially surfaced. But the problem then was that naval depth-charges – to avoid blowing up the ships discharging them, had minimum depth settings of 50 feet, so they could not damage any partly surfaced U-boat. He had recommended that coastal command modify its shallow-depth settings, and this was in train.

Loader got to his feet at this point and commented:

"We have estimated that even an escort vessel located right above a U-boat, and fitted with active Asdic, will, because of the depth problem, require an average of one hundred 450-pound depth-charges, amounting in all to 20 tons, to sink a single U-boat. So it is no surprise to us that an aircraft with no Asdic, and with only one or two depth-charges, would be almost completely ineffectual, unless you catch it on the surface. What is needed, as Giles has pointed out, is an intelligent depth-charge, a smallish torpedo, guided by passive hydrophones, which could follow a U-boat's propeller-noise down into the depths and place a comparatively small charge in contact with the submarine's hull. Giles thought of it originally in connection with escort vessels and has even designed one. But it is *precisely* whatour aircraft need – as none will ever be able to carry 20 tons of depth-charges, or use Asdic. The Royal Navy has refused to develop it – short-sightedly so we believe. So why doesn't Coastal Command take it on as a matter of urgency?"

This led to an animated discussion which was cut off by Blackett in order to give Loader a chance to talk about the Western Approaches work on depth-charges, on merchant-navy and U-boat morale, on Support group logistics and on VLR aircraft.

The Walrus could only take off from the Thames in daylight so in early afternoon Blackett brought the formal talks of an end in favour of a general discussion. E.J. Williams got to his feet and turned towards Sturdee:
" Chiles I gather you think we are wasting our plutty time hunting subs in Biscay? Can you tell us why?"
Sturdee got to his feet, unsure whether to be tactful. He looked at his watch and realised there was no time for that, whether in minutes or years.. He looked at Williams' bucolic face: "To be honest I do – I think you are wasting your time. You can't hunt for submarines. There are too few in the vast ocean – far far too few. And there's no need to. The U-boats will come to you – all too readily – if you are in or near a convoy. And yet the fallacy of 'Hunting for submarines ' seems immortal. It nearly cost us the First World War. The Admiralty only introduced convoys at the very last moment. Now it has raised its ugly head again… in Biscay. People think it is aggressive and therefore commendable: whereas escorting convoys is defensive, and therefore reprehensible – not in 'the Nelson tradition'. But that is nonsense – on many counts. Nelson spent much of his life escorting convoys. He knew that sinking privateers was secondary to ensuring 'The safe and timely arrival of his merchant charges ': like-wise your U-boats. If you can prevent them from sinking merchantmen – does it matter how many there are? But anyway, if sinking U-boats is your ambition, the proper place to find them is within a few miles of a convoy. Yes they may be more concentrated in Biscay, on their way to and from their Brittany bases – but so they are in mid-Atlantic, but there they are thousands of times still more concentrated near a convoy. You can do the sums for yourselves. My opinion, and of many of my naval colleagues, is that the Biscay Battle is a double tragedy: first because it won't work; second, and far worse, because you're taking aircraft away from where they are most needed and from what only they can do – keeping U-boats submerged near convoys so that Doenitz cannot build up lethal wolf packs."
A long silence greeted Sturdee's reply, whether of antagonism or calculation he couldn't tell. He decided to go for broke:
"Such a campaign would never be allowed in our command. Apart from knowing it will be futile we have all absorbed the lesson impressed on us by Admiral Noble. Our paramount objective must be 'The safe and timely arrival of our convoys'. It

strikes me that some of the top brass in Coastal Command either don't understand, or don't agree with that dictum. Perhaps they believe that acting as scarecrows is beneath their dignity – won't earn so many gongs as sinking the odd – the very odd – U-boat? I hope I'm wrong, but I can think of no other rational explanation for what is going on. I hope you can persuade your bosses to desist." He sat down.

All hell broke out then. Blackett had to practically escort Sturdee and Loader from the room to catch a car back down to the Walrus. Far from angry he looked delighted:

"Well done Sturdee. You notice they are arguing more with one another then with you. They'll come round I think – they're damned good scientists. Now look – what I want you to do urgently is help me write a paper to my Lords of the Admiralty, strongly recommending that they immediately form an OR group of their own. Shouldn't take you more than a day or two – I'll do all the detailed drafting myself. If they swallow that, I'll offer them my own services – and that of most of my group. You're absolutely right: Biscay is a sideshow beside the big battle gathering out there. But Biscay is in Coastal command Group-19's area of command, not in 15's – which is under Noble's command. Unfortunately 19 Group doesn't have any aircraft with a range to get much further than Biscay. I'll be in touch."

"Sooner rather than later please. I'm planning to go to sea again fairly soon."

"Stout man. I'll make it a few days then, time is definitely not on our side." He shook hands with both men, and hurried off as Air Vice Marshal Robb arrived in the lobby.

CHAPTER 17

WORLD WAR

Sturdee was lying in bed reading Trollope's *Barchester Chronicles* for the n'th time, a wonderful way to forget the war and get to sleep, when there was a loud rat-tat on his door and Maurice broke in : "For God's sake man switch on your radio – History is being made !"

Sturdee turned on his bedside PYE , its big walnut cabinet almost perpetually tuned in to the British Home Service. The plummy voice of the newsreader swelled as the valves gradually warmed up:

".......... the pall of smoke over the burning harbour makes it difficult for observers to ascertain the exact extent of the damage, but two American battleships have sunk, only their super-structures showing above the shallow water while another has rolled over, showing its propellers and rudder above the water. We understand the main American Pacific fleet was in port and as there is no sign of any of its vessels making it to sea we must presume that the Japanese torpedo bombers and dive-bombers have sunk or severely damaged most of its capital vessels. It was at 7:30 am on a Sunday morning in Pearl Harbour, just outside Honolulu, the capital of Hawaii, when the Japanese squadrons swept in without any warning or US opposition. Most of the American sailors would have been asleep, enjoying their weekly lie-in far below decks, with little chance of escaping. Our correspondent reports that small rescue vessels are plying about in the harbour, looking for survivors, without much success. There is floating oil everywhere – much of it on fire. Being Sunday in a country at peace, Washington is closed down and we have been able to get no official reports from either the White House or the United States Navy, and it may be some hours before we do so. However the Japanese ambassador here in London has handed in a document containing an official declaration of war against both the British Empire and The United States. Our forces in the Far East have been alerted to the likelihood that they will be attacked within the next days or even hours. The Japanese have also declared war against the free governments of both France and Holland here in London. According to a spokesman for the Foreign Office a main objective of the Japanese forces will be the oil fields in the Dutch East Indies and in Burma. The prime minister is expected to make a statement in the House of Commons tomorrow afternoon. We repeat: Japan has declared war against the British Empire and the United States and has sunk much of the American Pacific fleet moored in Pearl Harbour..."

Sturdee switched off the radio as Joan came in to join them in her dressing gown .

"What do you think Giles?" Picton was obviously excited.

"I don't know Maurice" Sturdee got out of bed in his pyjamas as Joan handed him his own dressing gown: "Just a moment ago I was in Barchester listening to Bishop Proudie conferring with Archdeacon Grantley about Doctor Slope. Let's all go down to the kitchen – its warmer down there – and you can tell us what it all means."

"I'll go up and fetch Arfur" Joan said. "He'll want to know too."

They sat round the kitchen table drinking watery cocoa with the wireless on low volume in case of new developments.

" So what do you think Maurice? You are the bloody historian ?" Sturdee sounded irritable.

"What the Japanese must be thinking is difficult to fathom. In the long run they can't possibly hope to defeat America. They really need Far Eastern oil to make up for their American supply which Roosevelt cut off to force them to withdraw from China and Manchuria. He also warned them off the oilfields in Dutch Indonesia and French Indochina. The Japs must hope to capture them , then defeat China and Manchuria before America can recover. And they could succeed. It takes years to build new battleships. And by the time they succeed Japan will be an impregnable fortress with all the oil it needs, and in possession of virtually all the Far East."

"Including India?" Joan asked.

"Good question." Maurice responded. "Why the Japs would want India though, I can't think. It is a poor country and a drag around Britain's neck. But with the Mediterranean closed we are in no position to reinforce it – though I dare say Churchill will try. Because he served there as a young officer he's got a sentimental attachment to India as 'The Jewel in Britain's empire'."

"Damn India – what about us?" Sturdee wanted to know.

"Now that's interesting." Maurice sounded professorial: "It very much depends on Herr Hitler. If he's smart he'll declare war on Japan before Roosevelt can declare war on Germany. If he does Roosevelt would be paralysed. The Isolationists in America will keep him out of the European war and we'd have to keep on fighting alone – possibly with *even* less help from America then we are getting now. Officially speaking Germany would be an ally of the United States. And it wouldn't cost Hitler a halfpenny."

"Gosh I never thought of that!" Sturdee was bemused.

"But our friend Adolf is not renowned for his intellectual subtlety, whereas Roosevelt is itching to get into this war. If he can seize this moment to declare war on Germany, illogical as that may seem, then a Congress desperate for revenge on somebody, and impotent to attack Japan, might well get hoodwinked into war. And of course Churchill will be egging Roosevelt on – using his legendary powers of persuasion."

"You make it sound like children squabbling in the playground." Joan said.

"At emotional moments like this politicians rarely behave like statesmen. They can't resist a temptation to give a theatrical performance full of blood and thunder. So, my dear, you are all too right. The three gang-leaders Hitler, Roosevelt and Churchill can't afford to look weak in front of their own henchmen. They'll all try to outdo each other in threats and insults. I wouldn't like to predict the outcome."

The following day Japan attacked the British colonies Malaya and Hong Kong and a couple of days afterwards Hitler and Mussolini jointly declared war on the United

States. Joan was jubilant: "Everyone in the office was celebrating today. They say we are bound to win the war now."

"Hold your horses." Maurice demurred. "In the short term may be – but even that is not certain. America has never fought a foreign war of any consequence. Therefor its army , and in particular its navy, will be totally inexperienced and therefore probably incompetent. And how much of its military production, presently scheduled to come to us, will now be diverted to its own forces? So we might be worse off – much worse off temporarily. I understand there are 300 Royal Navy convoy escort vessels building in US yards; how many of those will come our way now?"

"And we desperately need them – desperately" Sturdee said.

"And in the longer run we shouldn't assume that the USA is any friend of ours. On the contrary. It was my distinct impression, when I was working over there, that America wants to take over our predominant position in the world. Yes they will support us temporarily, so long as it suits their purposes , but in the long run they'll bleed us dry, usurp our commercial position and undermine our empire. Even if we win the war, by 1950 we'll be a colony of the United States – not vice versa."

"Would that be such a terrible thing?" Joan asked

"In my opinion 'Yes.' " Maurice replied. "They have a materialistic culture and an appalling record on racialism and slavery. Compare what they've done to their native Indians with what we have done with our Indians in India ."

"What they done?" Arfur interrupted.

"Don't you believe what you see on those awful Hollywood films my boy. It wasn't the Indians who invented scalping – it was the White Man. He deliberately slaughtered the buffalo – the Indians' main source of food. He ruined him with gut-rot whiskey – even murdered him with blankets infected with measles and influenza."

"That's 'orrible." Arfur recoiled.

"Yes it is – and they set one tribe against the other by arming the weaker with rifles. The remnants were then driven into reservations which are little more than concentration camps in barren areas which nobody else wants."

"Are you sure?" Sturdee was incredulous.

"Of course I am. How else did Europeans come into possession of a whole continent in two or three generations? Their so-called 'War of Independence' was a bare-faced ruse to repudiate all the treaties signed by King George with the Indian nations, guaranteeing them rights to their territories in perpetuity. The Yankees weren't going to have that. All that self-righteous twaddle in the Declaration of Independence was to cover up the biggest land grab since Genghis Khan took Asia. Do you know Buffalo Bill– the 'Great American hero' – shot 5000 buffalo in one day – and left the carcasses out to rot on the plain?"

"What did 'e do that for?" Arfur asked.

"To starve the Red Indians, whose traditional food they were."

"It's hard to believe." Joan said.

"It's hard for *us* to believe." Picton continued "Because we are civilised. Because we will never do, have never done such a thing. And what infuriates me is the way that

Hollywood has been able to twist it into a heroic episode. Only the Russian occupation of the Caucuses at about the same time rivals it in hypocritical, cold-blooded, rapacity."

There was an unusual silence round the kitchen table.

"I'm sorry to sound so passionate," Maurice resumed. "But Joan did ask. If we abandon the truth for self-serving propaganda then we will be no better than the Nazis. If the Americans run the world in the aftermath of the war I cannot but feel it will be a distinctly backward step for civilisation – perhaps by two centuries."

"I don't see that Europe has any better claim to leadership – after two World Wars." Joan said.

"Europe no." Maurice replied. " But who mentioned Europe? I was speaking of Britain. We invented the modern world – not Europe; democratic government; trial by jury; the Industrial revolution; railways and steamships; the Abolition of slavery; sewage disposal; clean water; vaccination; freedom of the seas; public broadcasting; the middle-class; organised sport – the list goes on and on. They were all British developments, not European, and certainly not American."

"I think we should stop worrying about 'After the war' " Sturdee said "Until we've won this one – and that's very far from certain at present. If we don't get those extra escort vessels presently building in US yards, and we don't get VLR Aircraft, then I can tell you we will certainly lose the Battle of the Atlantic. And if we lose that it won't matter a damn what the Americans think or do afterwards because they'll be completely isolated. If Britain falls they won't be able to land troops in Europe. Hitler's Thousand years Reich might then become a reality. You should tell your colleagues Joan that it's far too early to start counting chickens ; we have to dispose of the foxes first."

On Captain McIntyre's advice Sturdee had postponed his second trip out to sea: "The best time to experience real convoy battles is spring and autumn. In the winter the weather is too vile and in the summer the nights are too short. If you went to sea now the odds are you wouldn't witness a single torpedo fired in anger."

In any case Sturdee was helping Blackett to draft the case for the Admiralty to have an Operational Research unit of its own. Drafts flew up and down the teleprinter lines between Blackett's secretary and Gwen. Blackett was doing most of the writing, Sturdee was supplying figures, instructive tables and examples, to colour and strengthen the case. In particular he presented an initial half dozen questions crucial to the upcoming crux battle which only an OR approach could hope to answer rationally. For instance: 'What was the ideal size for a convoy – if any? and 'How many escort vessels, and of what type, were needed to protect a convoy of specified size?', and ,in particular, he wanted to highlight the absolute necessity for air patrols, even in the mid-Atlantic, by questioning the minimum number of VLR aircraft required to fulfil that vital, literally vital task.

This work brought him into a closer contact with Wren Gwen. Hitherto he had regarded her mainly as Loader's ' bit of stuff', chosen more for her shapely bottom than her fine mind, while Gwen on her side, encouraged by Loader, had stood in awe of Sturdee's scientific reputation. The screwed up notes he threw into the wastepaper basket were often covered in patterns of Greek symbols which to her seemed like magic. When no one was looking she'd copy them out as if by doing so she might enter, like Alice, into a new wonderland. Sturdee – who was notoriously untidy on paper and couldn't spell, was mightily impressed by the neat and persuasive documents she made out of his crossed out, and crossed out again, scrawlings. She'd even rephrase his English, modestly enclosing her suggestions in faint pink pencil marks.

She went bright pink herself one day when he said spontaneously: "You know you are very clever young woman Gwen…" . When he looked up and saw her blush, he apologised:

"I'm sorry… that sounds so bloody patronising… it's just that I have so little experience of young women. I never had a sister or anything – and my mum died when I was very young."

"I know. And Tony… Lieutenant Loader I mean… said you never had a girlfriend."

Now it was Sturdee's turn to blush :"I'm afraid that's true. I grew up in an all man's world . You see there are no girls in Physics… and that's made me rather shy… very shy in fact. I so wish I wasn't…"

He was seated in his chair looking up at her standing beside him. Her blush gradually subsided, as she reached out her hand and rested it on his shoulder:

"There is no need to be shy you know sir… Women aren't all that different. I know lots of girls would find you attractive… wouldn't mind sitting on your knee."

"Is that so?" Sturdee sounded genuinely surprised.

"If you close your eyes, 'cos I'm shy too, I'll show you."

He closed his eyes and felt her gently settling onto his lap.

"There" she whispered in his ear "That wasn't too difficult was it? Now you can put your arms around me – in case I slip off onto the floor."

He did so, eyes still closed, but nuzzling into her hair:

"You've got a lovely smell."

"Have I? That's good. It means we are compatible like. You can kiss me if you like… Just in front of my ear. But you mustn't open your eyes yet – because I'm still shy. Promise."

"I promise." He gently kissed her cheek then found himself nibbling the lobe of her ear.

"Oh that's lovely… Don't stop… It makes me feel goose-pimply all over. Here…" She took his hand and placed it on her breast.

"My God…" he couldn't help himself.

"Isn't that nice?"

"It's… It's… it's beautiful. It's coming to life."

"Course it is. That's what breasts are for"

"… Oh God…"

"… Don't talk Giles. Can I call you Giles?"

"Of course you can."

"You want to try and make my nipple go really hard."

He must have been doing the right thing because the nipple stood up and out.

Her hand rested back on his:

" We ought to stop now Giles. If we don't, Tony might come back and find us naked on the floor."

She eased herself off his lap and stood up. He opened his eyes – as if waking from a dream. But she was real – smiling down at him. She kissed him lightly on the forehead: "There you see … nothing to be frightened of was it? Next time we might go a little further. I might let you to take off my bra. Now about the Battle of the Atlantic Sir…? "

Sturdee had been feeling depressed of late. It was all very well him analysing the battle to death but there was little he could do to influence the eventual outcome – which was approaching closer month by month and couldn't be much more than a year away.

The Navy desperately needed more and better escort vessels but whether they arrived or not or not depended on decisions made by politicians in London and Washington. He knew that battle would be lost unless the Air marshals also released some of their 4-engined bombers to carry out long range convoy patrols in the mid-Atlantic airgap – but there was no possible way for him to persuade them. Then there was the acoustic torpedo – the only weapon that would allow our aircraft to sink submerged submarines – the plans for which had been languishing in his files for months, and would remain there forever as long as the Admiralty research establishments stubbornly refused to have anything to do with it. He could only hope that Blackett would be invited, and invited very soon, into the councils of state that would be taking the big decisions. Six months from now would be far too late. It would take at least 12 months to design, test and mass-produce acoustic torpedoes, or 'FIDOS' as Loader had christened them ('For security old boy'). And even if they got four-engined bombers from the RAF– a diversion which probably only Churchill could enforce – it would take months to strip them down and re-equip them for long-range maritime patrol. Gun-turrets and armour plating would have to give way for extra fuel tanks while the old 1.7 metre radars would have to be replaced by the high precision 10 centimetre sets – also coveted by Bomber command who seemed to have a hold over Churchill. Things didn't seem to be going well for the British: he could only hope that Hitler was making as many cock-ups in Berlin.

Tony Loader tried to cheer him up, pointing out: "You weren't in Western Approaches 12 months ago Giles. I can tell you that nineteen forty one looked as if was going to be far far blacker than it has turned out to be. A handful of U-boats were running riot in the Atlantic, sinking up to 100 ships a month, and by April 41 it was 200.

Their numbers were increasing rapidly, the Navy couldn't sink them – defeat was staring us in the face by the time Sir Percy took over in February. Many of our senior naval officers were in despair. Then what happened? The sinkings fell away to a mere 35 last month – only 13 by U-boats, God knows why – and here we are, unexpectedly, in the pink. If you ask me old man our main problem from now on will be complacency; brass hats and politicians thinking we've got the U-boats licked – when perhaps Doenitz is simply biding his time, husbanding his resources for a decisive strike that will sink us all. That's what von Clausewicz teaches: the *Schwerpunkt* – concentration of forces for the mortal blow. How can we have mastered the U-boat – I can't see why or how – can you , when we are still only sinking 1 or 2 a month, while they're supposed to be building 20."

"McIntyre thinks that losing their three tonnage aces in March was a big blow. It has always been true that a small number of bold aces account for most U-boat sinkings ."

"Could be, but my money is on Sir Percy's reorganisation of convoy escort groups . Keeping them together. His 'Convoy Escort Instructions'. Training, training, training… Hitherto it was all a bit of a shambles with the Admiralty interfering at every twist and turn – diverting escort vessels away from convoys on wild goose chases following cold trails. Christ I remember it all too well. Sometimes there was only one poor bloody escort vessel left with a convoy. No wonder U-boats could rip them apart. And then we've cut down independent sinkings to a minimum – they were the jam for the Nazis, 20 times more likely to be sunk than the same ship in convoy. Don't forget that. That took a lot of brutal argument from Sir Percy – standing up to the shipowners, the Admiralty, even to the Prime Minister. We owe so much to him – so much."

"I certainly don't deny that Tony. You know that I am his number one fan – after you. All the same it's largely speculation. We don't really know what causes what in this beastly game – just as we didn't know that the U-boats could dive so deep. Something entirely unsuspected could be the cause of our present good fortune, something that could vanish overnight."

"Such as?"

"How would I know? Perhaps Hitler has ordered his U-boats to proceed cautiously for fear of antagonising the Americans and drawing them into the World War on our side."

"Bit late for that now."

"May be, but that could have swayed Doenitz this past six months. If so we'll soon see a huge increase in sinkings."

" I never thought of that."

"Then there's Sigint. – that enigma of the radio war. Perhaps they've lost their mastery of all our codes, or we have gained a mastery over theirs. By the way I had a message from George McVittie, my contract at Bletchley Park. He says there is only one chap there responsible for looking into the security of our own codes – which is ludicrous. And our Admiralty codes are, according to him and his cronies, pretty primitive. Therefor the betting must be that B-Dienst is regularly reading BAMS, our Admiralty code to all merchant shipping.”

“If that’s true, then no wonder they were finding our poor bloody convoys.”

“But again it’s all a question of effort – effort on the Nazi side this time. Yes they can probably break our codes in principle, given a few days or weeks. But can they break them quickly enough to make tactical use of them? Sometimes they might get lucky – sometimes not.”

“Our Sigint. is probably in the same fix.”

“Why not? We may just be going through a lucky patch. I’ll see if I can get anything out of Rodger Winn when I’m down in London next. He’s too wise a bird to commit anything to paper.”

Days after Pearl Harbour it was Britain’s time to mourn when *The Prince of Wales* and *The Repulse,* two of the Royal Navy’s proudest battle-wagons were sunk in the Indian Ocean by Japanese dive bombers.

“What they were doing out there without air support I cannot imagine.” Sturdee fumed.

“Apparently” Loader said. “They were supposed to have an accompanying aircraft carrier– *The Indomitable,* but it ran aground in the West Indies.”

Picton’s comment was: “What I want to know is why Churchill would send two of our most powerful ships to the Far East when we are fighting such a desperate war at home ? There can only be one answer. He knew about Pearl Harbour and the Japanese declaration of war against us, weeks, if not months ago.”

“Are you sure?” Joan asked

“One can never be sure in war – but what other explanation makes sense? And if Churchill knew, so probably did Roosevelt.”

“You’re not suggesting that Pearl Harbour was a put-up job?”

“That’s exactly what I *am* suggesting Joanee. I suspect Churchill persuaded Roosevelt into cutting off the Japanese oil months ago – knowing it would drive Japan to declare war. What other choice did they have? No proud race would pull out of its conquest of Manchuria after a public lecture from another power. Of course not. So the Japs began secretly planning attacks on Hawaii and Hong Kong – which the British Secret Service got wind of. So Churchill sends two battleships and an aircraft carrier to the Far East to protect our colonies out there. He certainly knew what was coming – even if Roosevelt did not.”

“You’re so cynical Maurice.” Joan was disgusted.

“I’m a historian my dear – as is Mr Churchill, though not a very good one – and historians know that nations have interests not sentiments. Both Britain and Japan have strong interests in the Far East – as do Russia and America. I’m rather glad Churchill is an historian. He was playing Britain’s cards as best he could – with mixed results. He’s got America into the war at the price of two battleships and 2000 drowned sailors. I’m sure he reckons that’s a very good bargain.”

Sturdee would have intervened to mention Sigint. and the likelihood that Britain, or America would have broken Japanese ciphers. But then he remembered, as he's had to do countless times recently, that he was sworn to secrecy. In compensation he got a brief note from Sir Percy:

'Giles, your schoolboy essay described the fate of Prince of Wales and Repulse almost exactly. Clever boy. If only the admirals had listened. Apart from the very sad loss of life we needn't be too disheartened though because a battleship nowadays is rather less valuable than a tiny corvette. In fact it may even be a liability. Best wishes. Percy Noble.'

Hitler and Mussolini duly declared war on the United States making Joan so certain of victory that she opened a bottle of her sloe gin so that everyone, including Arfur, could drink a celebratory toast. Sturdee almost refused, feeling it was bad luck, when the prospects for the year ahead appeared so grim wherever he looked.

The Duff House cabinet met every evening over dinner and after. At the moment it was trying to reach a decision over the fate of the three pigs, Damn Blast and Josie. Joan, and indeed Sturdee and Arfur had become so fond of the three animals that they were allowed into the house on cold evenings to toast their immense bellies in front of the Lounge fire. Maurice complained that most of the heat which didn't finish up heating the Victorian ceiling 12 feet above, was wasted on three enormous 400- pound porkers covered in thick blubber. He tried to argue that having the beasts in the house was insanitary, an argument Joan demolished:
"Look at them – Look how clean they are. They never roll in their own muck – like dogs do, then carry it into the house on their coats."
"They don't smell neither." Arfur added.
"They do when they fart." Picton objected.
"Well we all fart." Sturdee said.
"Don't be coarse." Joan admonished them. "But the fact is we don't have the food for them any longer. They are so big now that the swill from the canteen amounts to less than half the nourishment they need daily. They've been making up the difference with Windfall apples and whatever they can root from the paddock. And the cold is getting to them; Poor things need far more calories in winter. They look so pitifully at me when they've finished their pails of swill that I've been feeding them swedes– which we can ill afford. And then there are the debts that I've run up on their account – for instance a side of bacon for the canteen manager and dozens of pork joints to others for Christmas. God knows I love them , I really do. They've become friends to all of us…"
"Not me." Maurice said. "I knew we'd come to this awkward decision, so I've kept my distance. It's a problem as old as the domestication of animals. Around November they run out of feed and begin to starve . If you ask me they're losing weight already."
"They're not so." Arfur was sure

"Well they will soon. You don't want them to starve do you lad? What they'll do is escape in search of food – and be murdered out there for their bacon. Not humanely as we will do it but by having their throats cut – or worse. You wouldn't leave Gem out on a field at night would you?"

"No."

"Of course not. Even horse-meat is prized nowadays – for dog food if nothing else."

"What about the 'lectric fence?"

"That would never stop three strong beasts weighing more than half a ton between them."

"I'm afraid Maurice is right," Giles said. "Those fences are more a discouragement than a preventative."

So the argument rumbled on. In the end the three males left the decision to Joan: "After all" Picton said, trying to justify their cowardly behaviour "They're her pigs."

" Very well" Joan said next day looking grim. "I'll call the slaughterer in this coming weekend. But on one condition: you are here to watch and to help. I'm not having anybody eating meat in this house who's not prepared to take a role in what that means: killing animals, sometimes lovable animals who have as much right to live as you and I. All we can do is see that they don't suffer – don't even know what is to happen."

As the terrible Saturday approached Damn, Blast and Josie received even more affection than usual. Sturdee couldn't sleep on their last night and crept down to their sty with a torch. An hour later Joan and Arthur found him lying asleep in the straw with an arm over Blast's neck.

" He's been cryin'." Arfur announced, holding up the hurricane lamp.

"I want t to have a cry too." Joan replied, getting down beside Josie.

"Well I ain't going to cry" Arfur said. But he did – when all the lights were out.

Joan planned and commanded the operation, having rehearsed every detail in advance.

One by one the pigs were led into the yard by Arfur, using a swede as a lure . Maurice closed the gate behind and Arfur threw the swede down at the feet of the slaughterer . While they were eating, he shot them between the ears with his stun-gun. Sturdee and Picton then stepped forward, lashed the unconscious animal's rear feet and hoisted it upwards with a double block and tackle until it was suspended from the tripod sheerlegs with its snout several feet above the ground .

Joan placed a sterilised bucket under the nose and the slaughterer stepped forward with a butcher's knife and slit the creatures throat. Blood gushed out into the bucket while Arfur vomited noisily by the gate. Nobody said anything. Sturdee lifted the bucket when it was full, Joan replaced it with another. Sturdee went into the coach-house and tipped the bucket into a bin supplied by the butcher who was going to make black puddings out of the blood.

After the last of Damn's blood had throbbed out of into a bucket the slaughterer felt his ear for a pulse and quietly announced: 'He's gorn."

All three men dragged the massive body into the coach-house while Joan swabbed away any blood in the yard. The slaughterer had warned her that if the succeeding pigs got any wind of blood there would be hell to pay.

After the slaughterer had left with the carcasses the three adults gathered round the kitchen table:

"Where's Arfur?" Joan asked.

"I saw him leaving in the trap with Gem." Sturdee said "He looked dreadful – poor little chap ."

"Perhaps I shouldn't have subjected him to that? Wasn't it awful? I'll never keep pigs again." Then she burst into tears. Maurice tried to comfort her: "They had a bloody good life with us Joannie. Think of their fate if they'd been left imprisoned in a sty by some brutal farmer."

Sturdee said: "Well I feel like crying too. But if I did cry it would be for me – not for them. Because I've lost three friends. They were such characters – all completely different from one another. Do you remember that time they got completely sozzled eating half-rotten apples that had fermented?"

By making Joan laugh he hoped to coax her out of despair, and partially succeeded. Later , when Arfur failed to return from supper, she grew too worried about him to think about the pigs. By ten she was all for ringing the police.

"If you do" Sturdee pointed out "He might be taken away from us. After all, legally speaking, he has no right to be here. Anyway he'll be back. He knows old Gem wouldn't survive another winter out in the cold. And where else has he got to go to bed? I've got a long calculation to do. I'll wait up for them – and keep Arfur's supper warm."

The long calculation stemmed from the discussion they'd been having about the Russians holding out against Hitler: not many qualified commentators gave them a chance. And if the Russians fell, as they had in the First World War, perhaps Hitler would be able to concentrate his air force and his U-boats on the Atlantic– with dire consequences for Britain because no substantial help could be expected from America – not for 12 months at least.

Tsarist Russia had fallen not so much from military defeat as from aristocratic corruption and incompetence. For instance some officers sold their troops' ammunition to pay off private gambling debts. That would not necessarily hold under the Communists though Stalin was a paranoid tyrant who had, back in 1938, murdered most of his competent officer corps . Sturdee also knew that Wellington had defeated Napoleon's marshals one by one, then the great man himself, because he understood the importance of logistics – as they had not. So, at Maurice's instigation, he was calculating the logistic problem of invading as vast a country as Greater Russia. Like climbing a Himalayan peak or trekking to the Pole such an undertaking could only be carried out by staging, with pauses to consolidate and bring up new supplies. The 1924 Mount Everest expedition, which almost succeeded, had established seven

194

successively higher camps before attempting the summit. Soldiers , even German soldiers, could only fight for so many days before requiring rest, reinforcement and re-supply. A force fighting with tanks and artillery could move forward no more than thirty miles a day – and then for only 5 to 7 days –say 200 miles in a single stage. Assuming at least 10% casualties, 10 % to resupply itself, and 10 % to secure its lengthening corridor back to base, only 70% of the original force would be ready to fight the second stage of the battle – and so on. Thus pretty well all of the original fighting army would be expended well before it had advanced 1000 miles. And, no matter how he altered all his assumptions, the conclusion was clear– unassailable. Both Napoleon and Hitler would be defeated, even without the terrible agency of winter, by the inexorable force of logistics. The difficulty was that the logic was mathematical, a problem in exponentiation – beyond Napoleon's comprehension , beyond Hitler's apparently. If the Russians could only hold firm, not crack in their high command, then Hitler and all his men were doomed – sooner or later.

Sturdee was studying his figures in wonder, realising they promised almost certain deliverance , when he heard the clop clop of Gem's hooves in the yard. He glanced at his watch – well after midnight. He lit the gas under the boy's supper, noting with satisfaction that it contained no meat– just macaroni cheese.

When Arfur came in he looked blue and felt, when Sturdee put his arms around him, absolutely frozen. They hugged and Arfur sobbed briefly under Sturdee's armpit. Then he broke free and looked defiantly up:

"Yer wouldn't let them do that to Gem would you Giles?" Suddenly understanding the extent of the boys distress he gripped the skinny little shoulders and turned him around to face Gem's portrait on the wall: "He's your horse Arfur, and he is our friend. Honestly I'd rather eat Maurice than eat our Gem. Anyway we're going to need him and he's not going to starve 'cos of all the hay in his loft – which he mowed himself."

'Ee did didn't 'ee." The boy cheered up a little

"Well then" Sturdee released the shoulders : "Don't be so daft. Come and eat your supper and I'll make us some cocoa."

After Arfur had wolfed down his macaroni and was warming his hands in front of the stove he said: " It was seeing 'em die. I know they didn't suffer Giles – but they was gone so quick. It was like their lives meant nuffin'; weren't even real. I felt like nuffin' mattered no more, not them, not us , not Gem… not nobody. What's the point of living if we can all die as quick as that: one minute be full o'life and larfter, the next be nuffin' more'n pork…"

"That's the question men have been asking themselves for tens, perhaps hundreds of thousands of years, round Stone Age fires, alone in the pit of night. I can't give you a single answer Arfur – I would if I could. Some men, mostly weak man I imagine, turn to religion – to justify the suffering and disappointment of this world, by appealing to the next. Other men go to war because it gives them an immediate purpose – something to fight for here and now, without worrying about the longer term. And that's where I am just now. If we don't defeat Hitler we won't have a future to worry about. You know we all cried this afternoon in the end, even Maurice, though he pretended not to. Joan cried like anything…"

"I'm glad." Arfur said enigmatically.

"Don't blame Joan for goodness sake – she was just being grown-up and honest. She loved Damn and Blast and Josey as much as you and I did – perhaps more because she'd chosen them."

"I'm not blaming 'er Giles. I loved them pigs. It's just I don't want anyone, 'specially Joan, ter just forget 'em . Can't you paint 'em – like you painted Gem?"

"I suppose I could try: I've tried to sketch them often enough. But the buggers never stood still – not like Gem."

"Joan's got some photers."

"So she has. I'll see what I can do , probably in pen and ink."

"I would like to see one of Blast wiv 'is snout through the handle of a pail what 'e was goin' ter frow it up at the corrugated-iron ceiling of his sty."

"You fix that picture on your mind and perhaps you can help me."

"I don't want to forget 'em – never. And I ain't going to eat 'em, not even one tiny sossidge , not bacon, not rind, not nuffin'. Can you tell Joan?"

"You tell her yourself. She listens to you. Anyway, do you know what? I think you've grown into a man today."

Joan with her own logistic mind, quickly absorbed Sturdee's argument and was convinced: "Giles this is so important. It makes all the difference. The Nazis are surely doomed."

"Not surely – but probably I think. What do you think Maurice?"

"Stalin could crack – he is no soldier, just a bureaucrat – he kept the Party's file index I believe – which he used to blackmail and betray his rivals. But I understand he's so loathed and feared that he could never retire. Either he beats Hitler, or he'll be murdered."

"That's good then. No choice. What should our policy towards the Russians be?"

"Churchill loathes communists. But. We must make sure they win. Get them to do the majority of fighting; shed the most blood."

"You're a monster Maurice – you really are."

"Do you want our boys to bleed and die instead Joan? The Russians deserve everything they get. Didn't they join forces with the Nazis to invade Poland?"

"I suppose they did."

"Don't be taken in then by all that nauseous propaganda we now hear about pipe-smoking 'Uncle Joe'. He's at least as bad as Hitler– judging by his record. At least Hitler was a brave soldier, and a patriot. Stalin is neither. He's like a Cobra, hiding in the dark, ready to strike, because that is all he knows. He cares for nothing but his own survival – like a cold-blooded reptile."

"People like Bertrand Russell and Desmond Bernal are quite taken with him."

"Then they're fools– ignorant fools. Russell certainly is!" Picton was adamant: " He's all theory and no facts; a typical mathematician who should stick to his sums. As I understand it he even got those wrong."

"But he looks so clever." Joan said.

"Indeed he does. Because that's the whole secret of being a philosopher or a priest nowadays. You've got to look and sound the part. I suspect they hold beauty contest before selecting Archbishops nowadays."

"As usual we're getting off the subject." Joan said. "I think Giles's calculation is very very important. Everybody – just everybody ought to know about it. It might cheer us up, put heart into the Russians, and demoralize the 'Germans. Giles you ought to write a letter about it to the newspapers. And if you won't I will – or better still Maurice. He can sign it 'Professor… then more people might read it .'"

For security reasons a diplomatic bag with the highest secrecy documents travelled between the Admiralty and Western Approaches by car once or twice a week. By one such bag Sturdee received a note from Blackett:

' Dear Sturdee,

We're in! Sir Dudley Pound the First Sea Lord has asked me to set up an OR group within the Admiralty "With all dispatch". I hardly need say that your help, and the support of Sir Percy, were crucial. I will bring half of my Coastal Command group over with me and aim to recruit more personnel. Meanwhile you would do best to remain at Liverpool for now, closer to the action.

The immediate flap is of course Pearl Harbour and its long term consequences. Churchill is going to Washington in a day or two (consequently burn this letter immediately) and I hope to go as well to make connections with our American scientific colleagues. In particular I hope to interest their supremo Vannevar Bush in your FIDO and to recruit his support with regard to getting VLR aircraft in time for the big battle. If you have any other ideas forward them to me ASAP via the Admiralty, as we expect to be over there for 2 to 3 weeks.

On our return our immediate priority must be, as you suggested, to establish the optimum sizes for convoys and their escort groups. As you have been thinking about that for some time I suggest you urgently prepare a paper on it to act as a basis for discussion. Alas that fool Lindemann, (now Lord Cherwell) will have to be convinced (he knows nothing of naval matters and is egging the Prime Minister on to scatter more and more bombs harmlessly about the German countryside).

Best wishes

Patrick Blackett

Having burned the letter in the grate of Gwen's office upstairs, such a huge feeling of relief, almost exaltation, overcame Sturdee that he seized hold of Gwen and kissed her most lasciviously. Only the entrance of Loader whistling downstairs brought the discarding of clothing to a premature and frustrating conclusion.

From now on he could concentrate on what he could do best – Think, while Blackett would obviously take on the business of politicking in the corridors of power – about which Sturdee hadn't a clue.

CHAPTER 18
A WARM HEART AND THRUPPENCE

The death of the three pigs cast a shadow over Christmas at Duff House. Half of the meat had been donated to hospitals and orphanages, a quarter was used to pay off debts, the remainder was bartered with the butcher in return for large weekly joints of lamb or beef. Sturdee said: "I worked out Joan that you have provided the population with about three thousand satisfying, meaty meals which will do no end of long-term good; in sturdy children, in morale, in stamina to beat the Germans. And if they made us cry that was because the pigs brought extra love and laughter into our little world. So that's good too. You can have no regrets and I think we should get three more pigs next year."

"Thank you Giles." Joan smiled .

'What a lovely voice she's got' Sturdee thought 'When she goes I'll miss that almost more than anything.'

He felt something of a traitor to Joan nowadays because he was in an almost unbearable fever of lust for Gwen's provocative body. Loader was going on a course in Devonport just after Christmas and it was understood that Gwen would give herself entirely to Sturdee then. He could barely sleep, barely concentrate at the prospect. Fortunately Gwen was planning to go home to Wales for Christmas with her family, although the government was doing all it could to discourage unnecessary travel because the country's oil reserves had fallen to a dangerously low level – although they weren't   publicly admitting that. It turned out that Gwen had been on a dispatch-rider's course and could ride a motorbike. So Sturdee loaned her his, with enough petrol coupons to make the journey to mid Wales and back.

Gwen was thrilled but felt a little guilty too: "Won't I be a Squanderbug Giles, one that's wasting the country's war effort?"

"In normal circumstances yes. In the present circumstances no – very definitely no."

"Oh why?"

"Because I'm going to write an enormously important Scientific paper on convoying for the Admiralty. It could even alter the course of the war – and so long as your lovely body is just upstairs I can't concentrate even for a few minutes. Do you know I must undress you completely in my mind a dozen times a day?"

"Is that all?" She tinkled with laughter   "Well you are a cold fish Giles. I was beginning to hope as you was hot-blooded. I might have to change my mind now."

"If you did you could cost us the war."

"Well in that case Dr Sturdee I s'pose I'll have to do my duty… Close my eyes and think of England – isn't that what they say?"

"Yes it is. What Admiral Nelson really said was 'England expects every woman, and most especially every Wren, to do her duty…'"

"Go on there. I bet they never had Wrens in them days."

"Oh yes they did . What about Lady Hamilton? I believe she did her duty by Lord Nelson several times a night – and occasionally by day as well."

"You're having me on."

"Honest Injun. I read a book about it at University."

"In that case I s'pose I'll have no choice then."

"None whatsoever."

One of the most important innovations introduced to Western Approaches by Admiral Noble was 'The Table'. It was a war-games playing room in Derby House. Naval officers could rehearse the tactics to be used out there on the deep Atlantic. New escort-vessel commanders went on a training courses there to learn all the moves that would be expected of them when their convoys encountered enemy activity at sea; Escort Group commanders likewise, usually rehearsing with the captains under their command. And after a convoy battle all the senior officers would attend a 'Wash-Up' meeting to find out what they had done right, what they had done wrong, and how the tactics might be improved upon in future. Thus 'Western Approaches Convoy Instructions', the Allied blueprint for the whole battle, could be constantly tested and kept up-to-date. Since Loader usually attended these wash-up meetings on their behalf Sturdee hadn't previously bothered with them. The Table had seemed to him a matter for routine naval training: not a tool for analysis and research, but: "I was wrong" he admitted to Loader, "Totally and completely wrong. It's a brilliant idea that could mean the difference between defeat and victory. I've underestimated the Royal Navy once again."

"The best naval officers – and Sir Percy is one of the very very best –know just how important training is. Nelson impressed it on all his captains, indeed on all the officers under his command. They exercised their gun crews on a regular basis – using live ammunition, so that at Trafalgar our ships could fire two or more broadsides to the enemy's one. In effect it doubled the size of the fleet. Our ships of the line eventually battered theirs into splinters until the blood of their seamen was pouring out of their gun-decks reddening the sea. We lost 400 men, they lost nearly 4000, with 8000 captured. Although they had a superiority of 41 capital ships to our 33 they lost 22 to our none. If anything their ships were better and larger than ours and their crews outnumbered ours almost two to one. It was, above all, a victory for training – which the Navy has never forgotten."

"In modern circumstances, with far more sophisticated weaponry, I suppose training must be even more important?"

"When Sir Percy arrived here it was a shambles. Escort Groups made up of scratch vessels put to sea with no explicit instructions and almost no knowledge of each other's command personnel. Sir Percy's Table put that to rights in a matter of weeks."

The Table was not in fact a table but the wooden floor of a large office down in the bombproof depths of Derby House. Tiny model merchant ships, escort vessels and

U-boats were moved about by Wrens on their knees or by the command staff using long sticks. The pupils sat around the battlefield on movable chairs and were challenged to give appropriate orders as the battle developed. Donald McIntyre had told Sturdee that because at present most convoys crossed the ocean without encountering U-boats, he was more likely to learn about battle tactics at The Table than out at sea – and as usual McIntyre had proved right.

Admiral Noble now reckoned that the crux of the Atlantic battle would take place in the late winter or early spring of 1943 . Both sides had 12 months to get their crucial weapons not only in place but exercised. Nothing new not already on the slip-ways could be expected in time to affect the outcome. Aircraft, being mass-produced in factories , came in 100s or even thousands per month, but still took months to modify for the special needs of maritime war: folding wings, arrestor hooks and strengthened under-carriages to land on carriers at sea for instance. Thus Sturdee was very conscious that now was the last moment, almost the very last moment to get things right. To offer advice to Sir Percy and the other admirals, scientists like Blackett and himself needed to imagine the battlefield as it would become 12 months ahead – and imagine it *right*. And then, having done that, they would still have to persuade, and persuade quickly, commanders up to the level of the Prime Minister, to plan accordingly. That is why he had begun haunting sessions at the Table – to stimulate his imagination. Apart from anything else it was a good way to see into the mind of the enemy. He discovered that in a classical U-boat attack the submarine would, during the day, work its way ahead of the convoy using its extra speed and low silhouette to remain out of sight of the Escort group. Even the much improved 10 centimetre radar, the Type 271, now fitting, had a reliable range of only 5 miles so the U-boat didn't have to move too far to either flank of the convoy to remain undetected.

Once darkness had fallen , the U-boat could slow down and wait for the convoy to catch up with it until it was just far enough ahead to remain out of radar range. Then, when the commander was ready, he could turn his submarine through 180°, order 'Full speed ahead' and race down towards his potential victims at a combined speed of 25 knots , almost 30 miles an hour. At that velocity he would be within the Escort radar screen for a mere 12 minutes before he would be right in amongst the clumsy merchant ships which were his prey. He would then have only a matter of 5 to 6 minutes to pick a target, take several bearings of it for his attack computer to calculate the important aim-off angle, and fire a salvo of four torpedoes from his forward tubes. Then, still at a combined speed of 25 knots, he could be out of the convoy and way astern of it in a matter of another five minutes or less. The essence of success lay in speed of motion, speed of thought and speed of execution. Thus, under the cloak of darkness, a bold commander like Prien had been able to sink several ships in a similar way without ever being spotted.

But the bold commanders were gone – victims of their own temerity, and in any case radar was changing everything. The early long-wavelength sets had been crude, of limited range, and highly unreliable. The new short- wavelength sets now being fitted,

201

or retrofitted, to every escort vessel were a different matter altogether. With a range of 5 miles in most weathers, and a rotating aerial, they presented every Royal Naval vessel with a continuously updated map of the entire convoy and it's Escort Flotilla. Thus any U-boat which attempted to penetrate the radar-screen had to evade not just one set – but half a dozen or more. And it would have to continue doing so for about 20 minutes, long enough to penetrate the entire screen, and launch its torpedoes accurately.

Sturdee realised there was an entirely different way to look at a convoy battle – through the eyes of a U-boat commander. He had done so briefly when he was looking at the problem of U-boat morale: now he reanalysed the entire battle from the point of view of the German submariner. Naturally regarded as a villain by merchant seaman, and as a war criminal by the Allied Press, he was in truth an ordinary man trying to carry out an extraordinary difficult task calling for superhuman bravery. The British, not the Germans, had started the naval blockade on day one of the war, and were trying to starve his people to death, as they had almost succeeded in doing during the terrible 'Turnip Winter' of 1916/17. Having a surface fleet of nothing like the size and power of the Royal Navy, the U-boat was Germany's only hope of retaliation. But of its nature the U-boat was in no position to rescue the passengers and crews of the ships which it sunk – thus opening itself to the hypocritical charge of 'war criminality'. And the submarine commander was the loneliest figure in military history. Only one man could look through the periscope and make the decisions that would deal out death by drowning, burning and destruction and in the end result in the almost certain and horrible deaths of himself and all his companions down in the depths. If he didn't take great risks to fire his torpedoes he was a traitor. But if he did fire them he would almost certainly kill civilians.

With the introduction of effective British radar the U-boat commander, who was probably a relative novice by this stage of the war, had to hope he would avoid radar detection for 20 to 30 minutes. Each second he was within the screen decreased the fractional probability of his evading detection by a similar amount. Sturdee devised a simple Calculus equation to describe this declining probability with regard to a single escort vessel. Then, and this was a crucial step, he had to multiply the probability by the probability of simultaneously evading detection by all the other escort vessels. Thus if the probability of evading one ship was a half, the probability of evading six was a half, times a half, times a half, times a half, times a half, times a half or a mere 1 in 64 – almost an impossibility. The only hope for the U-boat then lay in distraction. If three U-boats attacked at once, only two escort vessels could concentrate on each U-boat at a time. Its probability of evasion rose from one in 64 to 1 in 4 and with three U-boats on the attack there was a 3 in 4 chance of a sinking.

Sturdee's new 'Convoy Equation', as he came to call it, was a real revelation. It was spare, elegant, remorseless and dramatic, like a bull-fighter's sword he thought. The message within it was merciless to both sides and would have pleased von Clausewicz. The convoy with twice as many well-trained escort vessels as attacking U-boats ought to crush the submarines and get away Scot free. The Wolfpack with as many U-boats as

201

escort vessels ought to cause havoc – sinking helpless tankers and cargo vessels to
right left and centre. The climax convoy battles that would determine the fate of the
Second World War, would, like so many historic battles, hinge on *concentration*.
Noble would need to build up his fleet of escort vessels per convoy; Doenitz to
concentrate his packs so as to overwhelm Noble's sheepdogs. The one sure way to
defeat U-boat concentration was the patrolling aircraft that could put the shadowing U-
boat down, and keep it down until it lost contact with the convoy – which would
meanwhile be taking evasive action.

True to his vow, Loader had been diligently studying Calculus under Sturdee's
tutelage. Now that study paid off. When Sturdee rushed into the office to show off his
Convoy equation Loader could catch a glimpse of what he was trying to say: " But hold
hard Giles. Let me take it home with me , mull it over, test it out with my slide rule.
You can't expect a poor bloody naval officer to become a genius mathematician
overnight."
   "Of course not. Take your time. But if I can't convince you what hope of I got of
convincing Noble, Lord Cherwell or, if necessary, Winston Churchill? If I'm right then
it's going to be absolutely essential that we prize four-engine bombers out of Bomber
command as soon as possible. And as a naval officer you are more likely to convince
admirals and the like than I."
   "I'm not sure about that chum. Humble lieutenants don't carry much weight at the
Admiralty. A civvy boffin like you might bamboozle 'em – blind 'em with science,
whereas they'd resent advice from a mere two - ringer like me."
   "I suppose that's possible – but you remember Noble listened to you Tony about
U-boat depths when he couldn't understand me."
   "And he fought the matter successfully up to First-Sea-Lord level."
   "This is going to have to go even higher – to the Chiefs of Staff. Air Chief
Marshall Portal, Chief of the Air Staff, is bound to fight bitterly against another
diversion of his bombers. If the Chief of the Imperial General Staff – that is Sir Alan
Brook – he's a soldier, doesn't take our side, then we are sunk."
   "There is still Churchill."
   "But we're getting ahead of ourselves ; way ahead. Before you go on your course
Tony I want you to decide on the validity of this equation for yourself – without any
further persuasion from me. Never mind the algebra so much – but does it make sense
in naval terms; does it predict outcomes that would seem reasonable to you and which
you can understand? "
   "Alright old man– but I hope you know what you're doing. I'd hate Christian
Civilisation to be lost over Tony Loader's fumbling Mathematics."

Neither of them need have worried. Loader had been pole-axed by the Convoy
Equation: "At first it didn't make much sense so I decided to work out several specific

examples with different numbers of Escort Vessels and U-boats, in each case first trying to guess the outcome without recourse to mathematics. And boy did it come up with the goods every time, though the outcomes in both senses were more decisive that I would have imagined. But in retrospect I could see why the equation was more likely to be accurate than I was. Bloody cunning, is all I can say."

"Not really. It was sort of a last resort – after I'd tried out everything else first. Over the last few months I must've thrown have away hundreds of pages of algebra away. That's how science generally gets done: more doggedness and perspiration that inspiration."

"I'll take your word for that Sturdee. There is however one snag – and a bloody big snag too"

"Oh? What?"

"Brilliant as it may be– it still remains a bloody equation which is incapable of changing the mind of a single brass-hat."

"I agree – I agree entirely."

"However I've got an idea."

"Go ahead."

"Why don't we test the convoy equation out on Capt Godfreys Table up in Derby house? We get our Admiral to invite an audience of salty sea dogs and then set up a series of exercises – as realistic as possible – with different numbers of escort vessels and U-boats, and find out what the outcomes will be. When all the exercises are over we'll compare the predictions from the equation – which have been sealed in advanced in an envelope and then, at the end, we open it and compare it with the outcomes of the battles on the Table. If they coincide the seadogs will be impressed – and will do our persuading for us. What do you think?"

"I suppose we could try that. Certainly I haven't got a better scheme."

As soon as Loader had departed for his course at Devonport Gwen invited Sturdee to her office upstairs:

"You haven't forgotten have you Giles?"

"I remember we were going to do something nice up here – but I've clean forgotten what it was."

" Oh have you? I'll see if I can jog your memory. Why don't you light the paraffin stove while I put some sheets on the mattress. I borrowed some from my mam while I was down home."

"Didn't she ask what they were for?"

"Didn't have to. She knows I'm a naughty girl. Now turn off the blutty light… That's better."

The window was boarded up so the only illumination was the flickering blue window in the stove. As his eyes adapted to the dark he could see Gwen grinning impishly at him. She came forward and rested a hand gently on his member:

"Well I never Giles: you're a fibber. Seems like you never forgot what you was coming up here for after all. You've been thinking wicked – next thing you'll be doing is taking off my blouse and my bra and kissing my nipples…"

He did so.

"Oh. …. there's lovely. You know how to make a girl happy… T'ud be better though if you was to fondle my bum at the same time. Arghh!…'

"You have got a gorgeous bottom Gwen."

"I know – at least all the boys says so. When I was 15 I used to charge the boys in the village 6 pence each for a look. None of the other girls got more'n tuppence."

"You're a wicked girl Gwen."

"I know. Mrs Owen at the sweet shop complained as I was ruining her custom.: 'None of the boys got money for sweets any more.' She said. Threatened to tell my dad so she did. So I lowered the price to thruppence."

"I've got thruppence Gwennie."

"It's a shilling now – it's much more beautiful – so they say."

"How will I know?"

"One fellow who had a good look – he was one of the boy's fathers – he said it was worth every penny of half a crown."

"Did he now?"

"Tell you what Giles. You put thruppence on the desk and I'll let you take my skirt down– in fact you can take it right off ."

Sturdee put down the threepence and Gwen offered her waist. He fumbled with the popper.

"I can see you never undressed a girl before Giles. You need to practice."

The black Royal Navy Women's Service skirt eventually yielded and Gwen stepped out of it. Her black uniform stockings were held up by suspender belt while her diaphanous panties left little to the imagination."

"My God!" His heart thudded, he could hardly breathe.

"Now you've got to be a good boy and wear one of these." She handed him a condom and turned discreetly away. He'd been practising and it slipped on effortlessly. She backed into him, waggling the cheeks of her bottom against his member.

After a decade and a half of frustration no young man could have restrained himself. His instincts overpowered him and overpowered the woman who was giving herself so generously. They both exploded in cries of ecstatic agony before collapsing onto the mattress, in one another's arms, panting. Neither said anything for a while as the sweat cooled stickily on their limbs. Sturdee removed the condom, wiped himself , then drew the sheets up around them:

"Thank you Gwennie " He kissed her eyelashes : "You're a lovely girl. I'll never forget that until the day I die. You know I've got the most wonderful feeling inside of me – as if I'm floating – as if I could go anywhere… do absolutely anything… I'm sorry if I was rough I…"

"Hush love" Gwen put a finger to his lips and sighed contentedly.

Half an hour later they climaxed again. This time hanging seemingly for ages on the crest before bursting down together in a perfect maelstrom of tumbling foam.

"It's better than I even imagined " He confided in her afterwards. "I'm sure it's because of you more than me."

"Was it worth waiting for so long then Giles?" She lent on her elbows, hair falling onto the pillow.

"No – I mean yes – you know what I mean…"

"I don't so. You have to tell me."

"Well it *is* wonderful Gwennie. I hope it's the same for a woman. But I feel such a fool now – waiting for so long. It wasn't really deliberate – I was terrified of being lured into marriage. It happens to so many young men – before their lives have even started."

"And young women – even more."

"I suppose so. One day I want to marry the right woman and have babies with her – not the other way round."

" Me too. As soon as Geraint gets back we're going to have three."

"Would he be jealous if he found out about us – about Tony….?"

" Do you know what he said to me before he went away?" Gwen sounded serious.

"No? What did he say?"

"He says ' Gwenny I love you, and I want you to be waiting here for me when I gets back – more than anything. I couldn't bear if you left me after we've been married like this.' You see we was very happy Giles, very."

"I can imagine."

" 'Well' he says because he is very clever,   'Well ' he says   'I know what sort of a young woman you are Gwenny – passionate and kind-hearted. If I was the make you promise to stay faithful to me you couldn't do it – not for all the tea in China. You're made for bedding Gwenny – you know it, I know it and so does everyone in the village. That's why they was so relieved to see us married.   So when I leaves I want you to leave here too. Go to the big city and bed other men if you must – but not where the locals will find out about it. Then when the war is over you and me will come back here to bring up our children in the village' ."

"Sounds a very clever man."

"Oh he is Giles, he is , and I love him . I have since he took down my knickers when I was 15 to have a look at to my bum."

" Did he have to pay??"

" No he didn't. But he threatened if I ever showed it to another boy in the village he'd tan it black and blue."

And did you?"

"Didn't need to did I. And if it wasn't for this blutty war no man but Geraint would have seen it since neither. No man – not even you."

" Well, I'm glad to hear it."

"That's why I prefer to go to bed with both Tony and you – because it seems like I'm being more faithful to Geraint. Does that sound silly?"

"No – in a funny way it doesn't. To sleep with only one would definitely to be unfaithful. Oh I love you Gwenny!"

They rolled about in each other's arms, giggling like little children.

" And I hope your Geraint comes home one day safe and sound, and loves you to death."

"Me too."

CHAPTER 19

THE LITTLE ENCHANTRESS

Sturdee's big ambition, ever since he left Dartmouth, had been to make an exciting scientific discovery , preferably in Astrophysics. Just prior to the war he'd been working on the problem or fuelling stars. For example how had the Sun gone on shining for a thousand million years without vast and mysterious sources of fuel? Sir James Jeans, the famous astronomer, had suggested that it was powered by radioactivity, by something like Marie Curie's Radium. Sturdee though, and his young colleagues out in Göttingen and Munich hadn't believed him. For a start Radium was an extremely rare element, almost absent from the Sun's spectrum – and from the spectra of all the other stars that had been measured. Jeans retorted that Radium was very heavy and would sink down out of sight in to the solar and stellar cores. Sturdee wasn't convinced though; it sounded too much like special pleading. Besides there was a vast variety amongst stars – from colossal Red Giants to tiny White Dwarfs with luminous pulsating Variables in between. Surely they wouldn't all bury all their Radium all the time. No, there had to be a far more powerful and far more natural process probably employing the common elements like Hydrogen, Carbon and Nitrogen. As George Gamov and others had pointed out in the 1920s such elements had the potential to release vast amounts of energy if only their atoms could somehow be fused together to form other elements like Helium. But there lay the fascinating problem: their nuclei were strongly charged with positive electricity which was repulsive and would prevent their fusing together. Sturdee, and like-minded physicists, had been hoping to find a way around this electrical barrier because they felt there had to be one, some little trick or channel which would allow the far stronger attractive nuclear forces to bypass the electrical repulsion. The mind that could find out that might harness the power of the stars for all mankind. But all that wondrous thinking had had to be laid aside to design radar antennae or scheme how to sink submarines. And by the time the war was over Sturdee's scientific mind would be past its best. They said that if a theoretical physicist like himself hadn't made it by the age of 35 he wouldn't make it at all – and he had only five years to go.

So at first it has been a considerable thrill to discover, or invent, the Convoy Equation , as sweet, as momentous a contrivance in its own way as Einstein's $E = mc^2$. Like the Oracle at Delphi, but without any riddles, it forecast the outcomes of encounters between the Escort Vessels in a convoy and any attacking wolfpacks which set upon them. There would be room for luck of course, but not very much. The sides that went into the encounter with slightly the wrong balance would lose, and lose most terribly. If there were less than twice as many competent escort vessels as U-boats then torpedoes would be fired in salvos; ships would go down, their bulkheads bursting, dragging their crews down into the deep; ammunition vessels would explode, blowing their hatches half a mile high; cargoes of precious aircraft, tanks, trucks, electronics, tractors, gas-masks, artillery and ambulances would never reach port; flour, meat, sugar, rice, cheese, bacon, eggs would feed only the fish while tankers abrim with Carib oil would spill it burning across the sea, illuminating the hapless ships for miles around. And seamen in their hundreds, perhaps thousands would die violent deaths — the lucky ones by blast, dismemberment or drowning, the less lucky by fire or bitter cold; and the least lucky from hopelessness after days or weeks of starvation, exposure and thirst. But if the balance tipped the other way the lot of the U-boats and their crews might be even worse. Picked up by radar well before they got anywhere near the cargo ships they would be hounded by destroyers, driven hundreds of feet down, there to be depth-charged by corvettes and frigates again and again and again until their hulls cracked , or their batteries leaked hideous poisonous Chlorine gas; or their crews went mad.

The Convoy Equation was pitiless, unforgiving. It's held out no hope for the incompetent the unlucky or the unprepared. Go into battle improperly equipped and you must sink and die. Two such battles not 50 miles, or six hours apart, might go in quite opposite directions simply because the local numbers decreed it so.

But was it right – that was the question? Sturdee knew from his scientific history about the hubris that sometimes impelled theoreticians like himself to fall in love with their own equations. The mathematics might itself be perfectly logical, but make a poor fit to reality, because after all, a mathematical model was just that, a deliberately simplified, perhaps oversimplified model of a much more sophisticated and interesting world. It was one of the tragedies, and also one of the comedies of Science. The more beautiful an equation was the easier it was to fall in love with it.

"I'm not going to do that." he announced stoutly to the Duff House cabinet after he'd showed off his beautiful baby to them for the third time. While Loader was away he explained their ideas to Sir Percy, and got his approval for an urgent test on The Table before an audience of Escort Group Commanders and ships' captains. Eschewing the temptation to meddle in the process himself he'd sketched out his ideas on paper and left it to Loader and Captain Godfrey– Lord of the Table – to fight the imaginary convoy battles he had asked for and to analyse the results.

"I didn't tell them about your Equation until it was all over." Loader explained afterwards. "And I didn't even know you'd predicted some of the results – until we opened all your envelopes together at the end."

"Well?" Sturdee was dying with impatience."

"By and large old cock it worked bloody well. Of course if the two sides were well matched chance and skill came into it. Some of the escort commanders were clearly better at handling a complex battle than others. But if there. was any significant discrepancy between the two sides at the start the equation not only got the outcome right but predicted the number of sinkings on both sides, uncannily well. Indeed some of the old seadogs felt there was some kind of a trick being played. I want you to come down tomorrow and talk with them; Noble's coming too. He wasn't present but he kept in touch via Godfrey. The biggest unknown, as I expected it to be, was the boldness with which different U-boat commanders played their hands in the game. But in practice it didn't make all that much difference. Either they had the time to make a successful attack or else they did not. How realistic that is I don't know. The aces like Prien....."

" All dead now" Sturdee reminded him.

"Were in a different class from the rest."

"In the end the whole thing was just a simple simulation, just a game . We shouldn't take it too seriously – but using the Table was a good idea of yours Tony."

"What would you have said if it had all gone wrong – if your equation had proved unreliable?"

"A very good question I have been asking myself. If we only had some really good data to test it out…"

"I've put Gwenny onto it, but don't expect much. The new 10 centimetre radar has changed things so much, that the older convoy battles are not relevant any more. . Of course in all our games our chaps have the new radar, the short-wave Type 271."

"We won't get anything better before the climax battle."

"That's okay. The chaps who've got it already rave about it; the ones who haven't – rave about the bloody shipyards. What are we going to do next Giles?"

"That depends. Blackett's away at present. When he gets back he wants me to go down to Whitehall and advise his new operational research group. Then I've promised the admiral we will look into Huff -Duff."

"High-frequency direction finding?"

"Yes. He hopes it's going to be critical – almost as important as radar. Then there is Sigint. To my mind the real question is 'Are more of our convoys being intercepted then we would expect – given the number of U-boats at sea ? If so it means our convoy communication system must be compromised – or if less, the U-boat signalling cipher has been broken by us. Everyone makes claims of course. No one admits to unpleasant truths. So it's bloody difficult to know what's going on."

"Bloody important though."

"Exactly. If we get that wrong we could lose the whole schemozzle."

"Talking of schemozzles ,what about the Yanks Giles?"

"We are going to see. My flatmate Maurice– a very wise old bird – thinks they're going to be a disaster – to begin with at least."

"Oh why?"

"They've no experience of proper war – 'Custer's Last Stand' for Christ's sake. According to him half of them are krauts or Ities – or worse still Irish sympathisers. But more particularly they are likely to requisition for their own navy all our escort vessels now building over there in their yards."

"My God!" Loader was horrified.

"We'd do the same thing wouldn't we ?"

"Maybe – but those escort vessels – we were absolutely counting on them – without them we'll be sunk."

"I suppose it depends whether they deploy them in the Pacific or the Atlantic. You can hardly blame them for trying to get their revenge on the bloody Japs first. According to Maurice it's all going to depend on the relationship between Churchill and Roosevelt. The Yanks hold all the bloody cards – money principally. We're doing all the fighting – as usual – apart from the Russians who haven't got much choice. The one thing we do know is how to fight a naval battle – but will they let us –the Yanks I mean? According to Maurice they are out to dish us – and steal our Empire into the bargain. We'll be supping with the devil–on very thin gruel indeed."

"We've been through two really bloody years Giles – we'll manage one more. Things look brighter now than they did 12 months ago with the blitz in full swing. At least that's over."

Loader spoke too soon. A few evenings later all three were working very late in the office when the dreaded moans of the air-raid siren chilled the blood. Loader rushed out of his room cramming on his steel helmet and clutching his gas mask:

"Get under the table Gwen," He yelled up the stairs: "I'm going out to my fire watchers post on the top of Derby House Giles. Get upstairs and look after Gwennie… It's too far from here to the air raid shelter on her own . Get in to bed with her . She'll be terrified poor kid. And switch off that bloody light on your desk!"

He opened the front door and they could hear the staccato drumming of anti-aircraft fire – big 5.5's by the sound of them. Then the throbbing of the Nazi bombers up in the night with searchlights darting about trying to pick them out in Half a moon. As the first bombs hit the dockland half a mile away he began to run toward Derby house. Giles slammed the door and ran upstairs.

As instructed Gwen had dragged the mattress under the bed and was lying under a blanket with only a torch on. Sturdee started to take off his shoes before getting in beside her

"No don't take them off Giles ; we might have to run."

He placed his arms around her, enfolding her like a child: "How are you?"

"Much better now you're here. I hate being in the bombing on my own."

A huge bomb went off somewhere near by shaking the foundations. A fire engine raced past, its bell clanging.

"Dammit. I forgot to turn off the gas at the mains. I'll go down. Here, lend us the torch

"Don't be long… Please."

As he ran back upstairs he thought of Joan, Arfur, Gem and Maurice up at Duff House. Would they be out in that awful Anderson shelter? As far as he knew it hadn't been pumped out for weeks. They'd all imagined bombing was a thing of the past.

Gwen shivered when he enfolded her again: "It's just lying here doing nothing that's so horrible Giles."

"I know"

"I volunteered to shoot an anti-aircraft gun, but they said I was too small. Why do you think they've started again?"

"God knows. Perhaps they've flown back from Russia because it's too cold to fight out there… engines won't start… guns jam."

"Do you think we'll get it night after night – like in May?"

"I doubt it. I have it on good authority that our night fighters are becoming so good that very few Nazi bombers which make it this far North will ever get home . By the sound of it there aren't many anyway – not like then. We had 300 every night for eight nights."

As if to contradict him a big bomb shook all the pots and pans in their kitchen next-door. Gwen gripped him more tightly:

"Are you frightened of dying Giles?"

"I'm frightened of dying having left nothing worthwhile behind. Are you?"

"Mainly about being disfigured."

"Having your bum blown off?"

"Maybe. And I don't want Geraint to come home, and me not be there to meet him."

"He's a lucky chap your Geraint. I hope he realises it."

" 'Course he does . And I'm a lucky girl."

The All-clear siren raised its long welcome moan: "Go and put the gas back on Giles. I'll make us some tea. Then we can go back to bed again. Tony won't come back tonight – he'll guess we're having a bit of slap and tickle."

"Okay – but I'll ring Joan first; make sure they're okay."

They were: "We went out to the shelter but it was so deep in there the water had reached the bottom bunks – so we all piled into Gem's stable. He was ever so pleased to see us. But no bombs came close. I was more worried about you."

Sturdee explained about the table.

"Are you coming home now?"

"I can't leave Gwenny here on her own obviously, and Tony won't be back until dawn, so I'll see you tomorrow evening."

There was something about the way Joan replaced the receiver which signalled her disapproval.

The final session at Noble's Table, with the Admiral himself in attendance, was interesting. Now that he had more escort groups Noble could allow them some leave in between convoys, leave that could be partially used for training. Thus there were more than a dozen captains and commanders fresh in from the Atlantic to take part. They listened intently while Sturdee explained the philosophy behind his Convoy Equation – the harassment of the U-boat commander's mind:

"He's only got five torpedoes loaded and only 14 to last the entire voyage. He can't afford to fire them off indiscriminately: they have to be carefully aimed off to allow for the motion of both the target and the U-boat – which means taking several accurate bearings whilst the U-boat is on a steady track – and feeding them into his on-board attack computer. I am estimating that is going to take between four and six minutes – particularly for the novice crews who must be in the great majority now. I assume that during that time they will be both vulnerable and nervous. If they get disturbed during that time I'm assuming they will break off and either go deep to escape depth-charges or drop out of the convoy altogether. Am I right?"

The discussion that followed was passionate if inconclusive. In his perceptive summary Sir Percy said: " We are perhaps not the best able to answer Doctor Sturdee's question. What we need are a few Royal Navy submarine commanders around this table with us to tell us how they would react. I should've thought of that before. I'll get in touch with Admiral Sir Max Horton C- in- C Submarines – and see if he can help. In the mean time I'd like to ask if there's anything new, any new tactic open to the enemy which we have to anticipate?"

One of the commanders asked: "Why does the enemy bother with aiming his torpedoes at all? Why aren't they simply directed to plough round and round in circles within the convoy until they hit something?"

Sturdee's response to that was: "Interesting, but risky because such a circling torpedo could also hit another member of the wolfpack. According to our calculations if that happened more than once in 20 sinkings then the U-boats would make a net loss."

In his own summary Sturdee said: "This equation is – just an equation. I can't see this it's going to directly affect you sailors at sea. Only it just might win us the battle on land that we have to win, that we *must* win first – for resources. In essence the equation is about the vital importance of concentration in battle. If you have enough radar-equipped escort vessels when U-boats are attacking you then you can prevent them ever firing their torpedoes. On the other hand if they can concentrate in large enough packs against you– ones containing more than half as many U-boats as escorts – they could swamp your defences and sink any number of ships. But to concentrate they need to shadow the convoy for hours – even days, and that is where VLR aircraft come in. Even one such can discourage shadowers from hanging on. We need four-engined aircraft capable of patrolling the mid-Atlantic air gap: they exist but at the moment the Royal Air Force , backed up by the government, simply won't let us have them. They say they are needed in their thousands to bomb Germany. We, gentlemen, need them in their dozens, to avoid losing the Battle of the Atlantic. And we need them *soon*. I am hoping that the Convoy Equation – if you endorse it – will persuade Air Marshals, Generals, Civil servants, and the politicians, to let us have both the VLR aircraft, and the extra escort vessels that we need to win this battle. The crux will come in about 12 months time when Doenitz has 300 U-boats, 100 on patrol at any one time. He will then be in a position to intercept every transatlantic convoy. Only if we have the right VLR aircraft, and the requisite number of escort vessels, will you be able to fight them through. It is, I'm sorry to say, as stark as that."

"But what can we do as individuals ?" An Escort Group commander asked.

"Not that much I'm afraid." Sturdee sighed: "But the more people who understand what we need, and why we need it, the better. I don't suppose the airmen and the politicians are being perverse. They just don't understand how a convoy battle can be won or lost – depending as it so dramatically does on the *local* balance between the two. If they can be made to understand that I believe they will give us the tools. But if they can't they won't."

Gwen was understandably proud of her body and welcomed any chance to show it off to an appreciative man and Giles was certainly that. At the age of 14 Gwen discovered that Nature had made her a gift it was a pleasure to share it with boys and men. She loved to disrobe and preen in front of the mirror and later in front of a male audience. Better still was to have a boy, preferably a boy much bigger and older than she, strip her naked either in front of the mirror, or in front of an audience of younger boys her own age. She knew this last was dangerous but you couldn't help herself. A body like hers had been designed by Nature to drive men wild. Over a dozen children in her village would never have been conceived if their fathers hadn't glimpsed Gwen's heavenly limbs minutes before.

"My god you are bloody beautiful Gwen!" Sturdee said for the dozenth time. She was sitting on the mattress naked, legs tucked under her, pinning her hair above her head. He was seated behind her drawing intently.

"My arms are beginning to ache Giles. I can't hold this pose for much longer."

"Just two minutes more. I so wish we had a mirror you could admire yourself in, then I could get your face as well – it's a classical pose."

" What you going to do with the painting when you finish it?"

"I thought one for me – and one for you. Then when I'm old I'll be able to look and think : 'That's gorgeous creature once gave herself to me.' And you'll be able to look up at yours and say: 'I was once as beautiful as Helen of Troy – I could bewitch any man — I was the divine enchantress."

"Go on with you. And what is Geraint going to think?"

"If he is the man I believe he is, from what you say, he'll be proud: 'That was my little Queen of Sheba' he'll say to himself , knowing that no other man in Wales had a wife, or a mistress, with a body like that."

"What about my children?"

"They simply won't believe it is you. You'll be a dumpy little thing by then – full the rabbit pies and treacle tarts. They'll say :'Who's that then Mam? And you'll say: "She was the most beautiful woman in Liverpool when I lived there. She kept up mens' spirits and so helped us to win the war. They say Helen of Troy launched 1000 ships but the Little Enchantress – for so she was called far and wide – helped men win the Battle of the Atlantic – and so saved Civilisation.' And when you die the picture will hang in the National Gallery in. London with a whole wall to itself . And people will come from far and wide to see 'The Little Enchantress.' "

"Go one with you Giles. What a fibber you are. But no one will know it was me." She sounded vaguely disappointed.

"Ah but they will. When the famous painter Sir Giles Sturdee dies, in his private collection they will find the identical painting – the gem of all the thousands he did. And on the back, written in oils by him: it will say 'This is my Little Enchantress a

Wren in the Royal Navy who helped win the Battle of the Atlantic. In civilian life she was Gwen Jones of Pant-bach in North Wales. No man who was lucky enough to see her in all her glory would ever forget Gwen. I have always intended to leave her painting to the Nation – which I do – on condition that it hangs in the National Gallery not many yards away from Admiral Lord Nelson on his column in Trafalgar Square. Trafalgar was a great naval victory; the Battle of the Atlantic a greater victory still."

"Oh Giles you are daft." She kissed him, tears running down her cheeks. "Anyone would think as you was Welsh."

"I am – half. Didn't I tell you? My mam came from Cardiff – but she died in the flu epidemic? You've got goose pimples. Better put some clothes on."

"It's not that. I am shivering inside."

"I'm shivering inside too. Do you know why? Because I'm terrified I'll never do your painting justice, never! "

"You've got to Giles, now you've promised. I'll dream of my picture hanging up by London. And all the boys will be able to see my bum then. Will it cost them?

"As I recall , entrance to the National Gallery is free."

"Well I think they ought to charge at least threepence to see my bum –sixpence actually."

"Very well, I'll make it a condition of my bequest to the nation."

In his life Sturdee had never attempted, let alone succeeded in anything so difficult as Gwen's painting. Her body was so exquisite, the human mind so aware of anatomy that even the tiniest mistake would show up as a disaster. But the small sketch went well and he managed to scale it up on the largest canvas he had in his studio at Duff House. But painting in her flesh-tints from memory was so hopeless that he recoiled in despair after the first disastrous attempt .

Gwen would have been happy to model for him in the studio he was sure, but he found himself reluctant to ask. 'Why?' he wondered. It didn't take long to find the answer: because Joan would disapprove.

Maurice, being elderly, tended to rise before dawn, and consequently go to bed early too, at much the same time as Arfur, whose official bed-time, had been laid down and enforced by Joan at 20.45 sharp. Thus Sturdee and Joan had the long winter evenings to themselves. Sturdee would light a log-fire in the study, the one room downstairs that was small enough to get warm, and there they would sit or lie with only the fire-light flickering up the walls to keep them company. Joan would often lie on the couch in her dressing-gown drying her long hair by the flames while Sturdee sat on the floor, his back against the couch, poking the poplar logs from time to time to bring them to life.

They talked about everything, they talked about nothing – for both it was the climax of their day, often the happiest moment, sometimes the only happy moment in their haunted wartime lives. Both had colossal, perhaps naïve expectations of life which they could share unashamedly with each other, but which they had not been able to share with anyone else. Joan's dreams were of travel to remote niches and corners of Europe and near-Asia, dreams which were fed with copious reading. She wanted to traverse Transylvania on horse-back, see the Sun rise over the Golden Horn, overwinter in Lapland, visit Termessos in the High Taurus, talk to the last Circassians left on the shores of the Black Sea, see Isfahan and Persepolis and stay in that 'Red-rose city half as Old as Time'. Whereas her practical brothers scoffed at such ambitions – asking where was the money to come from, who was going to protect her, how could she learn so many languages, Sturdee believed that if you wanted something enough, if your dreams were vivid enough, then you could bring them to life – sometimes. He poured over the old maps with Joan, shared her visions and had faith in her extraordinary abilities:

" I simply can't imagine you dosing sheep in Yackandanda or Maroochydore Joan. You'll pine away out there as all your dreams dry up in the burning Australian bush. You should live here in Britain, and write the most wonderful travel books that will be translated into a dozen languages."

Sturdee's own dreams , which he had likewise shared with no other, centred on the problems he would like to try and solve during his scientific career after the war: "I want to find out what keeps stars shining for several thousand million years – it must be something o do with Nuclear Physics, but how does it work. And then there are the Spiral nebulae – galaxies like Andromeda and the Milky Way. Do you know they are 100,000 light years *across* – and Light travels at 93 million miles *a second*. Can you imagine how anything so enormous came into existence Joan?"

"Or why?"

"And you know there are vaster structures still? Fritz Zwicky in California has discovered giant clusters like Virgo and Coma which contain hundreds or even thousands of such galaxies. And what about this? Each galaxy contains roughly a hundred thousand *million* stars! Isn't that astonishing?"

"Beyond imagination– almost. But what can you do about them Giles? Won't they always lie beyond our ken?"

"Man will never give up searching… wondering. It's not in his nature. We'll build bigger telescopes and put them high in the Andes – or the Himalayas. And we'll put television cameras on their eyepieces and see deeper and further than ever before. You know some astronomers believe the whole universe is actually expanding– blowing up like a colossal balloon in four dimensions. I want to teach students for my bread and butter but spend the rest of my days and nights wondering about the Cosmos."

"Would you travel?"

"I would hope so. Telescopes will have to be sited on remote mountain peaks – in places where there are no clouds, no people and no light pollution. In the Andes perhaps, or the high Caucasus, or possibly on volcanic islands in mid ocean. There's even a Rumanian fellow call Hermann Oberth who believes we could launch telescopes out into space on rockets. Out there there would be no atmosphere to interfere with the cosmic signals and we could see radiations we could never see from the ground – like the ultraviolet and infrared. That could be a total … total revelation."

And when they weren't dreaming aloud they switched on the standard lamp and read their favourite books to one another. Joan read *The Mill on the Floss* making Giles gag with laughter over the antics of young Maggie Tulliver. He responded with *Barchester Towers* and she read *The Reminiscences of an Irish Resident Magistrate*, that comic masterpiece by Somerville and Ross.

It was hard for Sturdee to imagine he could be more in love with anyone than was with Joan Duff. She provoked his mind, contented his soul and now his body lusted after hers. The affair with Gwen, far from satisfying his passions had roused them to such a peak of sexual excitement that he could barely think of anything else. And in his bones he sometimes felt that if he was forceful enough Joan would respond. She had a way of looking at him sometimes as no one had looked at him before – as if to say 'Take me – what are you waiting for?' But then she'd go all cold and practical, and talk about her fiancé Des, or worse still read out one of his witty letters.

Her brother John, who stopped by quite often when his Corvette *Pimpernel* was in Gladstone Dock said: "Joan's very moral: she gets it from our mother. Gordon and I are atheists, as I believe is Father – but he stays mum to keep the peace. But the priests seem to have a grip on the womenfolk in our family. It was always that way in Ireland – where our mother comes from. She'd have a fit if one of us was to marry a Protestant girl – or even a non-believer. She'd think of that as ' A Sin' – whatever that is. But mother, God bless her soul, is not very bright – whereas Joan – how can she believe all that primitive bog- side tripe I ask you? It beats us. But believe it she does – and acts upon it. The men have always swarmed around her – but she's never had a steady boyfriend – until she got Des's ring around her finger; and nothing will change her mind, not until Hell freezes over. I wish I could give you better news Giles – you're a smashing bloke – we would love to have you as brother-in-law. But she's signed a pact sanctified by the Holy Church. Our Joan – a bloody farmer's wife for Christ sake! We feel that will be the ruination of her. Mind you, Des is a really nice fellow."

This news made Sturdee bitter – he despised religion and all it stood for – and now he was denied his love because of it. He was of a mind to tackle her about religion – as a boy he had been a formidable philosophical debater on the subject – but then something more mundane happened. They were in the study one night, heads together reading one of Joan's hilarious poems, when Sturdee threw his arms about her :

"Oh Joan I love you."

It was an expression of natural human affection, with no romantic intention, but of course it ended in a passionate kiss. Then one hand swept up her thigh and on to her breast– which responded. He pulled her over on top of him, kissed her nipples and ran a hand over her thighs, drawing her dressing- gown high above her waist. In a moment he would have been inside her but suddenly, almost in horror , she broke free and ran from the room.

That was the end of their fireside chats. Nothing was said but thereafter Joan kept her distance and talked much about Des. Sturdee cursed himself for a clumsy fool – but he blamed Joan too. There was no doubt she was strongly attracted to him and shouldn't have let things go so far if she was going to brush him off. She couldn't keep him dangling – in case Des's bomber was shot down by the Japs.

So when the question of Gwen's painting came up he hesitated; he didn't want to offend either of Joan's romantic or moral sensibilities. But why the hell not? Her plans didn't include him – why should his include hers? Indeed it would be good to make her suffer a little of the pain she had inflicted on him.

"I've invited Gwen over this Sunday" he announced defiantly. "I'll take her up to my studio: she's agreed to pose for me in the nude."

"You can't do that…" Joan turned bright red.

" Oh – and why not?"

"Because… because it's immoral."

"Not by my lights it isn't. It's culture. Painting beautiful women naked has been a part of European civilisation since the 17th century. Look at the Rokeby Venus by Velasquez – which hangs proudly in the National Gallery, or the Naked Maja in the Prado."

"But she's married – Gwen, you said."

"What on Earth has that got to do with it? If I had a wife with a body as beautiful as Gwen's I'd want to have her painting hanging on the wall for all to see. I'd be proud of her – very. You should see Gwen's figure – it's magnificent… Superb… Unforgettable."

"Oh – so you've you been painting her already? Not here I hope."

"I've been drawing her – down in the office. But the windows are boarded up for the blackout. I need proper studio light to catch her flesh tents in oil paint."

"Well you can't bring her here."

"Oh yes I can. I pay rent. You can give me three months notice or whatever – but in the meantime I'll take whoever I want up to the studio and paint them with or without their clothes."

"No you can't. What about Arfur?"

"What about him? He won't see Gwen in the flesh – if that's what you're worried about — though it might do him a power of good. With no mother or sister, and living mainly with a horse, he probably has no idea of female anatomy."

"He doesn't need to – not at his age."

"You must be joking – you don't want him to grow up to be a catamite do you?"

"What's a catamite?"

Sturdee stared at Joan – who went bright pink.

"There you are Joan, you're far too innocent to supervise Arfur's boyish awakenings."

"And I suppose Gwen isn't?"

"If you insist I will lock Arfur out. Gwen probably wouldn't want him in the studio anyway."

"And he's not to see her painting."

"That I can't promise. It'll be hanging in my room – or in the studio."

"Then you're leaving this house at the earliest possible moment. I'm giving you three months' notice – from today. I'll put it in writing." And she flounced out leaving Sturdee with a vague sense of victory.

Maurice and Arfur were shocked by the rift and begged Sturdee to back down. But he wouldn't and Joan absented herself from Duff House when Gwen came. Sturdee became so absorbed in the difficulties of getting flesh tints right he forgot all about Joan – almost about Gwen herself:

"I could spend a lifetime painting this picture" He said to her: "I had no idea – no idea at all. If I had I'd never have started. Do you know your skin looks transparent Gwen? And yet it can't be. It changes colour by the minute . It's like the wind-ruffled surface of a tropical lagoon – only a million times more complex. If the light outside changes by 5per cent your skin changes by 50".

"Golly – I never knew – but thank goodness for the coal-fire Giles – it would be perishing up here without."

"Is your skin peach, or creamy, or tan – is it yellow, or orange or blue? They're all in there... terracotta, coffee- cream – or nacreous whitey green?'

"What's nacreous"?

"Like-Mother-of-Pearl. And do I *need* to be faithful to the tones? After all you'd look quite different by candlelight, or on a sunny beach. I barely know where to start. Some artists use only three flesh-tints – but Velasquez must have used a hundred."

"Who's Velasquez?"

"A great Spanish court painter. He painted one of the most famous nudes of all – The Rokeby Venus. It's in the National Gallery – very close to where your own painting will hang. It's still magic 300 years after it was painted."

"Can I see it?"

"I'll try to get you a print. And one of The Naked Maja by Francisco Goya. Then there's Manet's 'Olympia'. You've got the most beautiful body of the four Gwennie – but I'm much the worst painter. But that mirror makes a huge difference."

With Joan away he'd sneaked into her bedroom and borrowed her dressing mirror. Now, in addition to Gwen's back he could paint her front, and her face admiring herself in the mirror . But whereas Velasquez's Venus lay on her side, resting on an elbow– with her son Cupid holding the mirror up, Gwen was sitting upright, holding her auburn tresses up in a pile over her head as if wondering how to pin them.

Sturdee became obsessed with The Little Enchantress, inveigling Gwen to pose again by showing her the two partly painted copies. She was shocked by how good they were : "I never realised Giles what a wonderful artist you are ? I half expected you was having me on. Now I really want my copy. They looks almost finished to me. Are you sure you need to add anything?"

"That's a fiendishly difficult question to answer Gwennie: knowing when to stop. They say far more pictures are ruined by over-painting than vice versa. But I'm quite pleased. It's already better than my painting of Gem."

"Oh yes it is ! And that's lovely. Where is Joan?"

Sturdee explained.

"I'm sorry – perhaps she's jealous? You know Tony thinks she's sweet on you? He swears she is. He thinks she's bad for you – ' Holding Giles back in a state of suspended animation' – that's what he says."

"I know – he's told me so in no uncertain terms. He thinks she'd yield –if I jumped on her. But then he has no real idea about Joan – she's as formidable as Admiral Noble".

Gwen giggled, standing up to stretch her beautiful limbs: "I bet Arfur's had a peep through the keyhole to look at my bum – I'll have to charge him threepence."

CHAPTER 20
DISASTEROUS NEWS

The turbulence at Duff House was quickly overwhelmed by disastrous naval news for Britain coming from all round the globe. She was now fighting for her life not only in in the Atlantic but in the Indian Ocean , the Mediterranean and the Caribbean. Following the sinkings of the *Prince of Wales* and *The Repulse* – her two most powerful naval units East of Suez the Japanese had set about her merchant fleet in the Far East so successfully that the total of sinkings for December 1941 was 285 ship. Sturdee and Loader were shocked – as was everyone up to the Prime Minister. It was eight times higher than the previous month, and 3 three times higher than the average monthly figure over the previous year.

"Ten ships a day!" The normally ebullient Loader shuddered. "This can't go on – it simply cannot and if the Japs close The Indian Ocean how are we going to get our oil out of the Persian Gulf?"

In the Mediterranean the Führer had unleashed the Luftwaffe and more than a dozen U-boats in a frenzied attack on the Royal Navy all the way from Gibraltar to the Nile. He needed to get his supplies across the Med to Rommel's Afrika Corps fighting in the desert. Malta was being bombed into rubble, its air fields and its dockyards into impotent ruins. U-boats sank the famous aircraft carrier *Ark Royal* and the battleship *Barham* while Italian frogmen on human torpedoes had sneaked into the harbour at Alexandria, the Navy's main base in the Eastern Mediterranean, and blown the bottoms out of the battleships *Queen Elizabeth* and *Valiant*.

"Our Mediterranean Fleet is simply melting away" Loader literally wrung his hands: "And if that goes so will our Eighth Army and the Suez Canal."

Sturdee, who normally relied on Loader's resilience, grew rattled too. But then in mid-January 1942 things got worse still. News of British ships being sunk all down the American coast to the Caribbean began to come in every day. Oil tankers in particular, carrying the lifeblood of war , were going down like ninepins. With the Mediterranean closed, almost all Britain's oil had recently been coming from Trinidad, Curacao, Aruba, Venezuela and Texas. Now that was haemorrhaging too as Doenitz's U-boats exploited brightly lit waters all the way up the coast from Florida and the Carolinas to the Canadian border.

"Sinkings, sinkings. sinkings…" Gwen complained: "I can hardly keep up with my charts – 10, sometimes 15 ships a day. We can't go on like this can we Tony?"

"No we can't my dear. Something is going to have to change – and fast. But what? The aggressor usually gets the benefits of the early exchanges – we must hope that's the main cause – but honestly I don't like the look of things. We're besieged on all fronts and winning nowhere."

Professor Blackett, back from America, summoned Sturdee to London:

"I went over on the *Duke of York*, smuggled in amongst Churchill's junior naval staff. But as soon as we got to Washington I broke free and talked to as many senior American scientists as I could."

"You've heard about the awful sinkings?"

"Of course. 1942 is going to be a desperate year for us. As far as I can see the Americans are totally unprepared. Many of Churchill's hopes about them were based on wishful thinking – as is usual with him. They strung him along – had no intention of coming into the war. They wanted to keep out and hope we would win it for them – as we did last time. But there are some with their hearts in the right place. They've agreed to defeating 'Germany First' which is crucial; Japan will take second place. We have to thank Churchill for that. Although I loathe the man he's got Roosevelt eating out of his hand – for now. And then we've set up a plausible command structure for running the war – called The Combined Chiefs of Staff. In effect the senior military staff on both sides will sit round a common table every three months – to take the big decisions together – in place of the politicians."

"Why is that good?"

"It will be difficult, but all the alternatives were worse: Churchill meddling; the Americans– with no experience of serious war – going off on a tangent; or our own senior officers acting snootily. It could all yet go wrong. But with the immediate prospects so appalling perhaps good sense and good humour will prevail, at least for now. But that is all above our level. The good news is, on the scientific level, our level. I must say I was impressed Sturdee. Their senior scientific man Vannevar Bush is a brilliant appointment. An electrical engineer from MIT, he built Differential Analysers before the war…"

"I know – analogue computers."

"Exactly. Well fortunately for us he was in submarine detection during the last war – magnetometers. I gave him your Fido paper – he read it overnight – and came back next day with a gleam in his eye. I think you can take it that thousands of acoustic torpedoes will appear a year from now."

"Thank God!" Sturdee was elated: "More than anything else that used to keep me awake at night."

"Then he's heard all about our Operational Research. He's sending a couple of brilliant people over here to learn the ropes and take it back to America. You see he's got the self-confidence to learn More apparently than some of their admirals – who loathe the Royal Navy so I was told. And then there's radar; they're putting a huge effort into that: their electronic industry is far larger than our own. Your old boss E.G. Bowen is doing a great job there – teaching them all our tricks. They'll be concentrating on the high-frequency stuff – mass-producing precision sets by the tens of thousands. If we ever do get VLR aircraft they'll be equipped with 10 centimetre, or even 3 centimetre radar. Any U-boat that pops its head about the surface will be vulnerable from then on."

"Great."

" And finally I met some top-flight European scientists. I didn't realise how many had managed to escape at the last moment from the Nazis. Hitler has so denuded his whole scientific manpower – particularly of his most brilliant physicists, that it is bound to count against him in the long run."

"That's the problem isn't it? Will there be a long run? The way things are looking now – the rate we are losing ships, Britain may not get through 1942. We could be starved into submission before the year is out, and before America can have much positive impact. We've got 6,000 merchant ships altogether, and last month alone we lost 300."

"Yes. And so to work. Churchill – goaded of course by Lindeman – or Lord bloody Cherwell as he is now, is screaming for an urgent report on the optimum sizes for convoys. I understand you've been working on that?"

"Yes.".

"Well I have convened a meeting of my staff this afternoon. I'm asking you to kick it off. They've been so busy moving over here that they haven't had much time to think yet. Ideally we'll come up with some clear conclusions – because if we don't Cherwell will come up with some madcap scheme of his own. He nearly stifled radar you know by pushing his own totally ineffectual infra-red. We had to resign en masse and throw him off the Tizard Committee before we got radar through. He's hated Tizard and I ever since, and of course he's got Churchill's ear. So things could go very wrong if we don't have a clear and convincing case. Will you have anything encouraging to say?"

"Yes sir, I will."

Deliberately Blackett have left half his OR Circus with Coastal command, bringing the rest over to the Admiralty in Whitehall, where they were a mere drop in the ocean: "The difference in scale between the Navy and Coastal Command is vast" Blackett admitted. "And so is their outlook. Coastal Command is peripheral to the RAF – which itself is an infant organisation – with no history of success before the Battle of Britain. The Royal Navy on the other hand has been controlling the entire globe for 300 years, is vastly proud, highly professional and generally competent. They won't pay much heed to a few scruffy scientists. Do you know what Admiral Cunningham said after losing half his fleet evacuating the Army from Crete: 'It takes three years to build a warship, but it takes 300 years to build a naval tradition.' You can't but admire that spirit – but it means we'll be up against it sometimes. That's why I admire what you've managed to do at Western Approaches."

"Don't credit me Prof, credit Noble. I was his idea entirely. If anything gets done there it is because he's listening – listening to his sailors out on the sea, listening to his merchant captains, listening to his technical people like me. That's why, one and all, we are terrified that he might be replaced if things go badly – as at present."

"Even Churchill can't blame Noble for the Japanese invasion, or the loss of two battleships in the Indian Ocean."

"Maurice, a historian friend of mine who knows about such things, believes politicians like Churchill will do anything they can to steal the military glory from their own Armed Forces – but put all the blame on them when things go wrong."

"That's certainly true. Churchill has never accepted the slightest blame for Gallipoli – yet everyone knows it was his half-baked scheme from first to last."

"And he sacked Dowding after Dowding had won the Battle of Britain."

"That was shameful and should never be forgotten. He tried to afix blame for the Blitz on Dowding ."

"When my radar friends tell me that the new night-fighter command system which shot down most of last week's raiders, was almost entirely Dowding's idea."

"I didn't know that." Blackett said. "Alas Churchill is the only Prime Minister we've got, or likely to get. God knows I loathe his political philosophy – but we're going to have to work with him , bend him to our ideas when we can. Think of it this way Sturdee: we may have got Churchill – but they've got Hitler, and Hitler meddles in everything so I am told. At least Winnie is interested in science – for instance he supported Bacon's development of the tank within the Admiralty when he was in charge there during the last war. He deserves credit for that – but not half as much as he tried to steal afterwards. The real menace from our point of view is Cherwell. Cherwell has no standing – apart from his baleful personal influence over Winnie. We're going to have to undermine him if we can."

"Like murdering Rasputin?"

"Something like." A thin smile crossed Blackett's craggy face.

The two men were chatting over coffee before the convoy conference started in the Admiralty bunker. When a dozen or so scientists had settled, Blackett got to his feet:

"The next few months might make or break us, and far more importantly, make or break Britain. Over this last month we've lost nearly 300 merchant ships." There was a gasp from the audience.

"Yes – 'crisis' is a much over-used word – but if ever I have sensed a crisis this is it. I hardly have to tell you that every word, and I mean *every single word* that passes between us here today, is confidential, strictly confidential . You cannot even speak to your new naval colleagues for now – the time for that will come later. You see we have two wars to fight – one within the Admiralty, the other against the Nazis, and winning the latter will entail first winning the former. So *complete* security please."

"As you all know our chief weapon, almost are only weapon against the U-boat, is the convoy. If the convoy-system breaks down we could be vanquished. The Prime Minister therefore is urgently demanding a review of the convoy system, and in particular of the optimum sizes for them. At present the Admiralty is trying to impose an upper limit or 40 ships per convoy, mainly on the grounds that larger numbers are unmanageable. We're going try and come up with an answer, and one that will convince Lord Cherwell, the Prime Minister, and the Admiralty. That is a very tall order, considering that we've been in place for a matter of days only. Fortunately Dr Giles Sturdee has been in the thick of it for 12 months as scientific assistant to Admiral Sir Percy Noble commander-in-chief Western Approaches, who is responsible for the

Battle of the Atlantic. That's why I've asked him to kick this meeting off. Some of you will remember his fascinating talk about Lanchester's Equations a few months ago to Coastal command."

"Sturdee began by telling them about the climactic Battle for the Atlantic that Noble was expecting in 12 month's time when the Nazis had a hundred U-boats continually at sea.

"There will be no hiding then. Every convoy can expect to be spotted and attacked – not as now when 9 out of 10 slink successfully through. The whole point of the convoy will then switch from concealment to protection. What will the crucial factors be then ? Yes, I used and believed in Lanchester's Equations– which were provoking. But the problem will be – as there will be for any theoretical analysis – will be validating it, and convincing a committee of seamen. And what's the point if you cannot do that? Almost certainly huge changes will have to be introduced if we're going to win that climax fight – changes of weaponry, changes of tactics, changes of expectation, changes of command. So any theoretical analysis must be above all convincing: convincing enough to change minds *now*, and so to get things ready in time – for instance in order to build and exercise new weapons. The Admiral's belief is that once that crux battle is joined it won't last long – months at the most – with the issue being irrevocable. One side of the other will be strangled to death – and that will be that. So new weapons and new tactics that come too late – will come too late." He paused for effect.

"So *our* climax battle, the battle of the thinkers and theoreticians, is upon us *now*. If we can't convince our bosses to do the right things within the next few months we might as well give up. That's why we abandoned

Lanchester: we couldn't imagine The first Sea Lord Sir Dudley Pound , or the Prime Minister, undertaking a crash course in Differential Equations." The audience tittered.

"What we did instead was to try and see inside our opponent's head, get inside the mind of the individual U-boat commander as he tries to penetrate the convoy escort group, pick a target, take bearings, compute offsets, launch a salvo of torpedoes, and get away. This, it turns out, is entirely feasible because the commander has little time, very little room for manoeuvre, and few options. The vital result is, from our point of view, is that almost everyone who looks at the battle in this manner comes to the same conclusions. In other words it's an utterly convincing scenario. Yes it results in an equation, 'The Convoy Equation' as we call it , but that is not what matters. Seamen can readily see what the equation implies, what has to be done now, and done then."

Sturdee went into the derivation of the Convoy Equation, its implications, and the recent tests that had been made on the Training Table in Liverpool .

"But you haven't explained" someone said. "It's implications for the optimum size of convoys – which is what I thought we were discussing?"

"Fair enough – but I thought the conclusion was obvious. The more escort vessels there are per U-boat, the less chance that U-boat will have of firing its torpedoes. Now the bigger the convoy the larger the complement of escort vessels you can have to accompany it. So the larger a convoy the safer it will be: and not just a bit safer but a lot safer. Thus if you double the number from 40 to 80 ships it is safer by a factor of exponential 2, or a factor of 7 ! And it hasn't cost us a single extra escort vessel. The smaller convoy might have 6 escort vessels the larger 12. There will be twice as many escort vessels per U-boat but no more per cargo-vessel – and that is the vital point."

The scientists appeared to be convinced: "But what's the obvious counter-measure?" Blackett wanted to know, "There usually is one in war."

"The enemy must increase the size of his wolfpack. Remember that it is the *ratio* of U-boats to escort vessels at the convoy which matters. If he can double his own number he also increases his chances by a factor of seven. It is a *deadly battle of concentration*–' Getting there fustest with the mostest ' As Gen Ulysses C. Grant used to say in the American Civil War."

" And how do we prevent them concentrating – U boats I mean, into larger packs? "

"Sturdee went into his argument about the vital need for VLR patrol aircraft to keep shadowing U-boats submerged, and thus unable the call up reinforcements.

Blackett had to leave to attend another meeting, so one of his assistants summed up at the end:

"You must understand Sturdee that we are almost complete novices to the field of convoy battles and Escort groups. We've been working for the RAF on bombing tactics against individual U-boats crossing The Bay of Biscay – which is scarcely relevant. Until we arrived here a few days ago I had never met a naval officer, so it would be entirely inappropriate for any of us to express opinions on questions of convoy battles – yet."

There were murmurs of agreement from his colleagues.

"We've got to be careful since this is our very first venture into Operational Research for the Navy. Get this wrong and we'll be discredited for good . Personally, I was very taken by your account of trying to see into the mind of a U-boat commander, and the elegant Convoy Equation which results. It certainly settles the question of optimum convoy size in the most conclusive way – 'The bigger the better'. But I have no way of knowing whether your picture of the average U-boat commander's mind is a sound one. Perhaps only another sub-mariner could comment authoritatively on that. I believe we should consult some forthwith. In the mean time I really believe we should get Patrick to stall the Prime Minister. It will be in no one's interest for us to deliver premature, unsound advice. Admittedly we have very little time, but we have to come to our own considered, independent view of the matter."

With that, Sturdee had to be content, but he did manage to see Blackett briefly once more before returning to the North:

" A good talk Sturdee. Just what I wanted. You almost convinced me but, as Adrian pointed out, we're going to need time to come to a considered view – time we really haven't got. I've already contacted Admiral Sir Max Horton, commander-in-chief submarines, and he's going to send a couple of his chaps down here to give us help. But suppose you're right– what's our next move? Do we write a very comprehensive report spelling out the full implications of your Convoy Equation, or simply respond to the question of optimum convoy size – leaving the VLR aircraft situation to another day? And do we expose your equation to the full glare of Cherwell's diseased mind, or keep it concealed below the surface as a secret weapon to be used in dire emergency only? Obviously it will mean nothing to Churchill."

"I can't comment Professor – except to say that Admiral Noble has to be at the table when these matters are decided. He's the commander on the spot, and in my experience he's always got his finger on the pulse of this fearsomely complicated and ever-changing battle. In the mean time I want to do two things: look into the technical aspects of VLR aircraft; if we leave it to the RAF they might bamboozle us. And into Huff Duff – High-frequency Direction Finding. If by chance we don't get VLR aircraft in time: Huff Duff may be our only last hope for locating shadowing U-boats to prevent the growth of huge, virtually invincible and unstoppable wolfpacks."

"Very well. Do you need any help ? You don't have to work on your own any more Sturdee."

"Can I come back to you on that sir?"

"Of course. But if I do have to go before the Prime Ministers Atlantic Committee I may ask for you to be at my side as an expert."

CHAPTER 21

GOING WEST

Back in Liverpool Loader, Sturdee and Gwen were compiling and analysing the latest sinkings. Loader was less despondent than he had been:

"Yes the loss of 285 ships in December was shocking and unsustainable, but things could've been worse. Firstly it was mostly composed of coastal traffic sunk by the Japs from the air in the Far East. That's reflected in the tonnage lost, only 580,000 tons."

Sturdee whistled.

"I know; had those vessels been transatlantic freighters the figure would've been over one million tons, so thank the Lord for that. And it probably is a one off: unescorted tramps sailing close inshore among the islands and straits of Malaya, Indonesia and Hong Kong where even a light aircraft can reach and sink them. We've lost the Far East anyway so those losses shouldn't recur."

"I suppose not ."

"The good news is that U-boats claimed only 26 sinkings in December and lost 10 of their own."

Sturdee whistled again.

"Wonderful isn't it? The first month we've got over 5. And 8 of those sinkings were to escort vessels, so we must be doing something right at last."

"They can't keep losing 10 U-boats for 26 sinkings. That'll be a huge dent in their morale. Anything below 20 ships sunk per U-boat is a victory for us remember. So 2.6 is a huge victory !"

"But don't get carried away old boy . Whenever Doenitz loses he switches his point of attack. Starting on January 12 about half a dozen U-boats appeared off the US coast and began sinking two or three of our vessels a day, particularly tankers. And the situation could get much worse because we've got no convoy system in place over there and there are no means of starting one. It's up to the Yanks – and from what I hear they are hopelessly unprepared. They don't even understand the purpose of convoying apparently – not according to one of our staff who went over there with Churchill. And even if they did understand, they don't have the escort vessels. So, as far as the U-boats are concerned it must be like shooting fish in a barrel. They sleep on the bottom by day, surface at night and pick off our poor bloody ships as they pass in front of the seaside illuminations. Do you know those buggers refuse to dowse their lights because 'It might interfere with our tourist trade'. They have no idea about war Giles– no idea. And it's not as if it was just their ships going down. Oh no! All our trade coming up from the South Atlantic, from South America, from the Caribbean and the Gulf of Mexico, and of course the Panama Canal must pass up the Carolina coast before convoying across the North Atlantic. This is building up towards a real disaster. The worst is to come. "

"How are the U-boats managing to sustain themselves so far from home?"

"We've all been asking that. Their larger longer-range type IX U-boats are coming into service. But probably the secret is refuelling, either from surface vessels or submarine tankers."

"That could make them vulnerable."

"It would if we had any escort vessels or aerial reconnaissance over there – but of course we haven't. It's entirely up to the Yanks. They won't let us in."

"And at the moment, they are obsessed with their war against the Japs in the Pacific. You can't blame them for that."

"It's not a matter of blame Giles ; it's a matter of bleeding to death. If our oil reserves fall too low neither the Royal Navy nor the RAF will be able to keep on fighting."

"What are our reserves?".

"Nobody knows; somebody suggested that 'It was for the Prime Minister's eyes only'. "

"Doesn't sound good. That poor bugger. Think what he's got on his plate – and he's nearly 70: The Battle of the Atlantic. The Japs over-running the Far East – the fall of Singapore and Hong Kong…

"Supplying the Russkis via Murmansk…"

"North Africa and Rommel…"

"The Mediterranean from end to end– especially Malta, which could fall any day."

"Keeping the Americans on the rails…."

"Oil…"

"Food…"

"Munitions…"

"Bombing… both of their side and ours….."

"Keeping the Empire on side – especially India and South Africa. Even the Australians are panicking and want to go back home…"

"You can't blame them."

"I don't. But it doesn't help."

"And then there are a whole lot of issues that are probably secret – but just as vital. For instance Spain Tony."

"Spain?"

"Yes; why doesn't Spain come into the war on the Nazi side? After all Franco is a fascist, and almost a Hitler puppet. If they came in we'd almost certainly lose Gibraltar – and with it the Mediterranean and North Africa. Churchill must be doing something to keep them onside."

"How does the poor man sleep at night – or sleep ever? Brandy and cigars won't do it for long – not at his age."

"How does he keep his temper I'd like to know?"

"Most of us would blow up like an over pressurised boiler. Perhaps he does."

"Yes perhaps he does. You know I might see him soon."

"How come Giles?"

"Blackett may want me to give evidence to the Battle of the Atlantic Committee. Churchill chairs that himself."

"About what? "

"About convoy sizes."

Life at Duff house was miserable. Joan would barely look at him, let alone speak. Poor Arfur was distraught, as any child would be whose parents had broken up. He tried his little best to heal the breach – only to have his head bitten off:

""I wisht you'd never painted that pitture Giles – even if it is smashing."

"So you've seen it?"

"Course I 'ave. Seen 'em bofe sitting in your studio. She's beautiful in't she?"

"I think so. I had to paint her … I couldn't help myself… I hope you didn't tell bloody Joan you'd seen them."

"No I 'aven't."

"Well don't."

"Why not?"

"Because she'll think I've depraved you."

"I don't know what 'depraved' means."

"It means turning you into a half mad monster who can't think about anything except naked women. Do you feel like that?"

Arfur blushed up to the roots of his hair – a very rare phenomenon.

"Well, go on boy, tell the truth. I used to dream about naked women when I was your age – much younger."

"What age?"

"Five or six, as I recall."

" Gor…"

"What does that mean?"

" It's younger than what I done." Arfur flushed again.

"Well there's nothing wrong with it." Sturdee took pity on him. "All normal boys and men do it. And when you grow up you'll sleep in bed with naked women. That how babies get conceived."

"I guessed – I seen horses do it. And them ducks on the lawn never stop. Nor them 'ens."

"Exactly. It's called 'Sex'."

"So why 'as Joan got so angry?"

"Ask me. Tell me honestly Arfur does Gwen's picture make you feel sexy? Make you feel you want to do things to girls ?"

Arfur flushed again.

"OK, so it did. But has it changed you much?"

"Not really Giles. Some of the boys down in London 'ad dirty pittures – we all seen them. And some was filfy. Turned me stomick. But Gwen's picture is lovely, makes me want to smile inside – makes me 'appy. I didn't know anyfink could be so… So… Loverly. I wisht I could see something so beautiful as that one day. There is nuffink dirty about it is there?"

"Of course there isn't – on the contrary. A woman's loveliness is one of the greatest gifts that life can give us. You know– I'll let you into a secret Arfur– but you mustn't tell anyone ever. Until Gwen let me see her body just a few weeks ago I'd never seen a naked girl – or slept with one."

"Cor!"

"I'm so grateful to her. It was an act of the greatest kindness and grace. She felt sorry for me – because I was so innocent and ignorant. And it was wonderful, beyond all my wildest imaginings. I will be grateful to her for the rest of my life. Look – there are tears in my eyes: tears of gratitude. It was partly from a desire to give something back that I wanted to paint her. That's why there are two pictures – one for her, and one for me, so never feel anything for Gwen but the greatest respect. She shared her loveliness with me when I needed it."

"Then why is Joan so mad?"

"Ask her."

"I did – and she got really angry. Told me never never to speak of it again, so I ast Maurice."

"And?"

" He said as I was too young to understand – but I might one day. Ee's miserable too about you and Joan falling out. Scarpers off to his bedroom all the time. I got no one to talk to now– 'cept Gem. And he can't read to me at nights."

"Poor Arfur" Sturdee put his hands round the boy's shoulders.

"Are you going to leave Giles…" the boy broke down "…. yore my best friend… after Gem." He began sobbing loudly.

Sturdee knelt down and folded Arfur in his arms, hugging tightly, tears rolling down his own face too.

"Somehow Arfur we're going to stick together, me and you. I don't know how for now. But you're my best friend too. We can't split up now can we?"

The boy shook his head.

"When I leave here I'll try and find lodgings just round the corner – then I can come and see you and Gem all the time. We could meet in his stable – or down the paddock. I'm sure Joan wouldn't mind."

"What about up in me room too?"

"I'm not sure about that– but you could come round to my place – any time. We might even try to get a spare room there – why not?"

"You mean it Giles?" The boy drew back to stare at Sturdee, his miserable tear-blotched eyes wondering whether he was really being told the truth – or being lied to by an adult yet again.

Sturdee could see the boy desperately needed reassurance. Too many things had gone wrong for him of late:

"Look at it this way. I am almost as alone as you are in this world Arfur. So I can't afford to lose you can I?"

The boy shook his head.

"Well then – I don't know how we'll manage to stick together; I really don't. But somehow we will – because we both want to."

The boy nodded thoughtfully. Then he said:

"I don't want to lose Joan neither. I love her too…" his eyes filled again .

" I know you don't . But Joan's going off to Australia one day to marry that fellow Des. And she wouldn't be able to take you – even if Des would let her."

"But that won't be for years – she said…"

"Who knows? Joan can't promise. If her fiancé sent for her she'd have to go. Girls do you know. That's life; they can't help it – however much they love their friends. Joan's got to have babies of her own. Its Nature."

Sturdee went down to Farnborough for a week to consult The Royal Aircraft Establishment about very long-range aircraft. At Sturdee's request Blackett had made the arrangements in double-quick time: "You've been assigned the full time of a Dr Andy Reece, an expert on large aircraft, for one week exactly. I think that's very generous considering, so suck him dry. And leave your coordinates with my secretary in case I need to call you up here at short notice."

Reece was a gangly enthusiast who strode about restlessly, usually with a long pencil behind his ear. His office was full of model aeroplanes hanging from the ceiling and photographs of birds in flight: "They tried to find you lodgings at short notice Sturdee."

"Call me Giles."

" But they are chock-a-block down here right now – as you can imagine. You can have a bed in a Nissen-hut with a couple of dozen erks, or you can come back to our place: your own room, 15 bob a night full board – no questions asked – but bring your ration book."

"That's very kind; I'd love to."

" Suits us too. It's fresh company– and the odd bob comes in handy. Be be warned we've got two young kids, Rosemary and Orville, five and three respectively. Noisy in the morning – but in bed by seven. You can change your mind."

"It will be a pleasure."

"Good. Then we can natter day and night – though not over dinner. Margaret has strict rules about aeronautics over the dining table."

"I should think so – with a son called Orville."

Reece laughed : "She knew what she was getting into when she married me. Insane about planes – that's me. So what can I do for you?"

Sturdee explained about the mid-Atlantic air gap and the urgency of solving it. Reece, who was the same age as Sturdee, listened intently, occasionally removing the pencil to scratch into his thatch of curly hair.

"Would it help Giles if I started off with a little seminar on flight design in general?"

"Go-ahead." Sturdee took out his notebook as Reese rose to his feet:

"Well the first thing to learn is that there is nothing magic about aerodynamics – if beetles can fly so can practically anything. The truth is that it's engines which fly. Tack on a couple of wings, any old wings, to your engine, and a control system, and Bob's your uncle. Right?"

"If you say so."

"The second thing to note is that scale is vital. Double the length of any flying machine and its weight goes up by 8 but its wing area by only four. That's why bugs can fly but pigs cannot."

Reese strode about the room counting off points on his long bony fingers: "Thirdly every aircraft or indeed bird design is a compromise. If you want one thing you can't have another. It's either speed or its range."

"I can believe that."

"This compromise thing is both a curse and a blessing. Once you recognise that you can often get what you want by throwing something else away. Snip off the ends of a Spitfire's wings and it will go faster – but lose manoeuvrability at high-altitude. A successful design is rarely inspired – it's a matter of choosing the right combination for the task desired."

"Fourthly, as I said, it's the engine that really matters. The Wright brothers got the glory but it was their engineer Charlie Taylor who got them into the air."

"I didn't know that."

"Engine designers rarely get the credit – because it all goes on out of sight, under the bonnet. Did you know we've got the Jerries on the run right now – would you believe it, because of much superior engine design."

"I didn't know."

"Some humble little fitter up in the Midlands came up with a dead simple idea which enables all our engines to produce 30% more power than the Jerry's."

"What is it?"

"Obviously I can't tell you. It's the most closely guarded secret in the air-war – and long may it remain so. Jerry aerodynamicists are generally better than ours, but we can still trump them with raw power nowadays, and thank God because you can convert that power into any number of advantages, depending what you want – extra speed, extra payload, extra armament, extra range, extra height – or whatever."

"Thank goodness for the little fitter then."

" And my last general point is 'Induced Drag'. It's the drag you unavoidably generate when you generate lift. Lift arises from diverting air downwards. Now diverting air downwards requires power, and that power has to come from somewhere. That somewhere is extra drag on the wings – it's like a propeller pointing in the wrong direction. We call it Induced Drag because it's the drag induced by creating lift . Gottit ?"

"I think so. I flew in a glider in the Alps once and read about gliders afterwards. As I recall, their aerodynamics are dominated by Induced drag?"

"Exactly so. The only way to reduce it is to have long thin wings – like a glider or an albatross. The longer the span the more air you can push downwards. The more you can push down the slower you can push it down to provide the desired amount of lift. And the slower you push it down the less kinetic energy you use up in doing so – in other words the less Induced drag you generate."

"Ah – now I see!" Sturdee was delighted with the explanation. No esoteric aerodynamics was involved.

"Just look at birds". Reece continued "Birds' wing configurations reflect their life-styles and their sizes. If you want to go a very long way, like a Great Wandering Albatross, then you need very long narrow wings – 12 foot span. If you want to dart about in the forest– like a Jay, go for the shortest ones – and so greater manoeuvrability."

"So what about Very Long-Range Aircraft?"

"Yes well now we're coming to it Giles. You can probably guess what I'm going to say?"

"Very long narrow wings. Most of the carrying capacity in fuel; light weapons-load – concealed inside the fuselage; no gun turrets sticking out into the airflow; all extraneous weight – like armour plate, thrown away? "

"Yes, that's pretty much it. And you'll get a very long-range aeroplane capable of great endurance – but little else. For instance you won't be able to carry many depth-charges and therefore won't be able to sink many submarines. Can you put up with that weakness? You can have endurance, or you can have depth charges – but you can't have both."

Wondering whether to tell Reese about FIDO Sturdee decided it was not something Reese ' needed to know' in order to do his job, and therefore, on security grounds, he shouldn't be told. But he found it a loathsome decision to have to make .

Until Reece invited him home Sturdee had never experienced the fun of giving little children a bath, putting them to bed and telling them a story. Rosemary and Orville's eyes opened as wide as saucers when Sturdee told them the story of how puzzled and hurt the little earthworm was when his friend the caterpillar turned into a butterfly one day and flew off.

"Did he come back again?" They asked.

"Yes he did. He came back every day for tea to tell the worm about all his adventures in wonderful places and about the amazing people he had met."

"Why didn't the worm go with him?" Rosemary wanted to know.

"Well you see he never grew any wings."

"But that's not fair!" she responded.

Taken aback Sturdee had to think of an answer: "Well you see when the winter came the poor little butterfly died. It was so cold, and there was no more honey for him to eat. But the little worm burrowed deep into the ground where he was as snug as a bug in a rug."

As they were eating supper with Reece's wife Margaret there came plaintive calls from upstairs. She returned with a fiendish grin on her face, directed at Sturdee:

"They wanted to know why the little butterfly died when his friend could've taken him with him down to his nice snug home. I said I had no idea but I'm sure Uncle Giles has, so I'll send him right up."

She and Andy laughed aloud:

"You might be some time. I'll put your supper in the oven Giles."

Reece was a true fanatic when it came to anything that flew– from a Pterodactyl to a Messerschmitt. He seem to know the detailed performances of anything that flew and could pluck wingspans, top Speeds, lift coefficients and horse-powers effortlessly out of his head. He was confident though:

"Given time to make the mods there are two or three aircraft out there which would meet your requirements– namely to patrol the air gap for about four hours at over 200 knots before returning to base."

"What's the choice?"

"My first choice would be the Consolidated B 24. Its an American bomber with a high aspect-ratio wings."

"Like an albatross?"

"Like an albatross – designed for high altitude bombing at 25,000 feet or more. Apparently it's a swine to fly– you need wrestler's arms. And it's unpopular with crews because it kills them."

"How come?"

"Well it's got a high wing. If they crash-land the wing comes down on top of them and crushes them, whereas in our Lancs for instance, the wing and propellers are underneath and protect the crew."

"I can see their point."

"Then they are complicated, hence bloody expensive, half as much again as a Lanc., and therefore costly to maintain ."

"You're not putting a strong case."

"Well I am in a way because if the bomber boys don't like them, and they don't, the more chance for you seagoing types to get your hands on a squadron or two. You'll never get them to part with their Lancs , I can tell you."

"Is that so?"

"Just try. But now for the positive side. That lovely clean Davis-aerofoil wing generates the minimum of induced drag– it will go on and on and on and on . Chuck out the gun turrets– you're not going to need 'em out there, the heavy armour plate – you don't need that either, nor the heavy superchargers for high altitude performance, and one and two other goodies– like self- sealing tanks, and then swap bombload for extra tanks and she is your bird. I estimate you'd get comfortably over 4000 mile range and 19 to 20 hours endurance, but with less than a ton of weaponry."

"Sounds ideal."

"Nothing that flies is ideal remember Giles, but this might do the job you want – get a radar set out and over the mid-Atlantic, and keep it patrolling a convoy at the right height and speed, with just enough explosives to keep the U-boats down."

" That could win the battle– and indeed win the war. How easy are they going to be to get hold of?"

"I'm afraid procurement is not my speciality. How many would you want? And when?"

"About 200– in less than a year from now."

"Then you could be in luck. They've set up a production line at Ford's biggest motor plant at Willow Run in Detroi t– 10 or 20 aircraft per day I believe. A fortnight's production would do you."

"How long would it take to modify them for Maritime use?"

"Difficult to say. It's mostly a case of taking things out. If you could persuade the yanks to build a batch without gun turrets etc in the first place you'd be halfway there."

Reece read one of his many files: "Hello look at this: apparently Coastal Command's got some Mark Is already. Calls them Liberators. Only nine mind you – good for evaluation purposes but scarcely enough to do serious battle. They flew themselves over here in September and have been assigned to 120 squadron in Northern Ireland. But they're having serious problems with spares apparently and they are largely unserviceable already in consequence. Perhaps that's why you haven't heard of them: the RAF is keeping mum to hide its embarrassment. Doesn't mean to say it's not a good aeroplane though: they should have ordered more spares."

"Perhaps the spares were torpedoed en route?"

"Happens all the time. Shows the importance of secure convoys doesn't it.".

"I feel awful not knowing about them."

"You did 't know about their special characteristics until about 10 minutes ago Giles."

"I suppose not . But whose fault is that?"

"Working on your own must be bloody difficult. In any case aircraft performance characteristics are highly classified. You'd have to have winkled them out of the RAF."

"I'll soon be part of a large team at the Admiralty. But if I give you a ring from time to time will you be able to help?"

"Of course old boy."

"You can't imagine what a relief all this is Andy. It's been keeping me awake for months. I was beginning to think that we were doomed – really. Do you know our poor ships we going down at more than 100 a month? But that is highly confidential. Perhaps I shouldn't have mentioned it. Forget I ever said that. Can we draw up a technical paper for my bosses?"

They set to work with Reece proudly showing Sturdee round Farnborough in spare moments. A hub of the war , thousands of scientist and technicians were working day and night, often in the open, to take a lead over the Luftwaffe. They saw wind-tunnels, high altitude chambers, engine testbeds, stress analysis, parachute design, radar installation, test flying , undercarriage development, weapons evaluation… Sturdee was particularly impressed by a film they were shown of tanks being destroyed by rockets fired by Hawker Hurricane fighter planes:

"You get one hell of a punch from a small aeroplane" the scientist in charge explained ; "A few bob's worth of rocket can brew up a 40 ton leviathan. The armour hasn't been designed that could resist one of our lethal little beauties."

"Do you think they could penetrate a submarine pressure-hull?"

"How thick?"

"2 centimetre"

"Like an assegai through a kid's blancmange."

"Honestly?"

"You give me a submarine and we'll demonstrate. But don't expect to get much of your toy back."

"Are they accurate?"

"Deadly."

Sturdee made a detailed note. A light but deadly antisubmarine weapon was the very thing needed by shipborne aircraft or flying boats. Depth charges were far too heavy whereas machine guns were ineffectual; but the rocket……:

"Have the Fleet Air Arm shown any interest?" Sturdee asked

"Not to my knowledge old boy. They're very new and hush hush. So don't go blabbing about them round Whitehall."

"I'll be very careful I promise. But if rockets could turn the tide against the U-boat, and they might by the sound of it, then surely the Navy needs to know?"

"I suppose. That's the problem with secrecy. It may act more against your own side than the enemy's . God knows how one tackles that."

"By snooping around like me. Don't be surprised if the Navy descends on you next week. One of your nasties could blow the entire conning-tower off a surfaced or submerging U-boat."

"I won't old boy. New customers are always welcome here."

"I'd be a bit cautious Giles." Reece warned him afterwards: "I didn't trust that chap. Far too sure of himself and his weapon. If you noticed most his so-called 'tanks' were very light, Bren-gun carriers more likely. And I doubt that rockets could be deadly accurate."

"Now you mention it…"

"There are all too many shysters about like him… with miracle weapons for sale. One learns to be cautious…"

"I'll remember. But we'll look into it at least."

In coming to Farnbiorough Sturdee had hoped to meet up with Hanbury Brown his close colleague and friend from their Bawdsey Manor days in Suffolk, but unfortunately Hanbury was flying around Fighter Command analysing the results of the recent mini-blitz. Luckily though he'd made it back to Farnborough on Sturdee's last day and they spent an afternoon together, and an evening in the pub. It was fortunate, not only from the point of view of their friendship, but because Sturdee was to pick up a clue , barely noticed and apparently irrelevant at that time, which was eventually to affect the whole battle for the Atlantic.

Hanbury was jubilant over his night fighters' success. : "You'll be pleased to know Giles that very few of the blighters which bombed Liverpool ever got back home. We picked them up before they got to the Midlands on the way in and harried them mercilessly to the target and then back East as they tried to escape over the North Sea. More than half our chaps claimed kills, some made two or three."

"Congratulations! You and Taffy Bowen started out on airborne radar back when?"

"1936 at Bawdsey."

"It must give you great satisfaction to know you've placed a shield over Britain."

"Yes it does actually – considering our primitive beginnings – literally a man and a boy– with me being the boy – just out of university. Taffy was the one with the vision and determination."

"But you finished it off Hanbury –when Taffy flew to the States with the cavity magnetron."

"Me and a horde of other people. Dowding, head of Fighter Command, was crucial. It was the last thing he did before Churchill sacked him for winning the Battle of Britain."

"That was disgraceful."

"Yes it was – more than that. I hope restitution will be made one day. Dowding should be on a national plinth– up there with Nelson and Wellington."

"Why was he sacked?"

"God knows . Perhaps somebody else– one can guess who– wanted his glory. Or it might have been in-fighting within Fighter Command itself. We've got a frightful little shit called Trafford Leigh Mallory throwing his weight about now though Sholto Douglas in command now. I know Mallory did his best to undermine Dowding because Dowding rejected his ridiculous Big Wing Theory. And thank God he did. If he hadn't we'd have lost the battle comprehensively."

"So the Failures rise to the top?"

"It seems so Giles. But I hope that's not going to be a trademark of the Churchill government. It's important to get the right people at the top at crucial moments. I mean look what Dowding did for us in this night fighter business.?"

"What?"

"Well there are three phases to catching night-bombers. First you catch them coming in, usually over the coast in a big formation, using our coastal Chain Home radar. Last you have an individual night-fighter up on patrol, which picks up an individual bomber from a mile or so astern, and which then homes in using its on-board radar and blasts it out of the sky with cannon- fire. But in between is the vital second stage of GCI or 'Ground Controlled Interception. Inland radars pick up the bombers, *and* the night-fighters, and direct the night-fighter to within a mile of a bomber, otherwise there will be no interception. Taffy and I realised that from the beginning, but for some reason Watson-Watt wouldn't buy the GCI stage. Thought it was unnecessary. But by God it is necessary. It was Dowding who put things right just-in-time God bless him. And it works like a charm It's turned Prime Minister Baldwin's dictum that 'The Bomber will always get through' completely on its head. From now on – thanks to radar, bombers will hardly ever get through – or if some do get through their casualties will be frightful."

"Thanks to the cavity magnetron I suppose?"

"No – that's the thing Giles, we've done is all with valves. The magnetron would've been better, much better – but those sets didn't arrive in time."

Sturdee was sorry to leave Reece and his little family behind when the Shagbat came down from Liverpool to collect him:

"I shall miss Orville especially."

"He'll miss you. You're an ace with stories. You'll have to have a couple of kids of your own one day Giles."

"I'm determined now. But I've got to find a wife first."

"That's the hard bit, especially for types like me and you. Good luck old man."

CHAPTER 22
IN CHURCHILL'S LAIR

As the February sinkings began to come in, two things became apparent. The focus of U-boat activity had moved conclusively from mid- Atlantic to the American coast and the Caribbean. And secondly the total figures were going to be frightening. The jump from 35 ships lost in November to 285 in December could largely be attributed to Japan's entry into the war – a one-off event which wouldn't recur. Even the 106 lost in January could partly be explained by the same cause but by mid February things were looking dire :

"Seems like we're going to lose 150-plus this month" Loader predicted "A number only exceeded once before – in April 41. And February is usually a goodish month for us – the weather is too foul for the Huns up in the far North, but now they're sunbathing in the Caribbean, or off the Carolinas, picking off our poor bloody merchantmen like clay pigeons – especially oil tankers – our most valuable ships carrying our most precious cargo. You know we lost 6 out of 8 tankers in a single convoy? I don't like to be defeatist Giles but that's a recipe for defeat if ever I saw one."

"What can we do?" Gwen asked.

" It's not obvious. All, or nearly all our antisubmarine resources are on this side of the Atlantic, while Doenitz's seem to be on the other, in what he calls 'Operation Drumbeat' apparently. Normally our defence would be convoy – there really is no other, but we can't organise convoys right over there from here. Even if we had the resources to do it – which of course we haven't – the Yanks wouldn't let us. They're very prickly about that sort of thing. They 'Don't need the goddamned Royal Navy to tell them how to fight a war' – or so they say. The fact is they know bugger all about antisubmarine warfare – and have apparently made absolutely no preparations to fight such a battle. At least we had corvettes and destroyers when we started out – while Doenitz was pretty starved of U-boats then. Now he's got about 200, with 20 more coming into operation every month. And if he can keep even 20 over there on the other side one daren't think of the consequences. If they pop to the surface after dark, wait for a cargo vessel to pass in front of the holiday-resort lights they could each bump off 2 or 3 vessels a night. That's 40 a night, 1200 a month, a fifth of our entire worldwide fleet." Loader ran a finger across his throat – the kind of melodramatic gesture he despised and wouldn't normally make:

"And do you know what's worse? They're not using any fuel. They can wait for our ships to come to them like sitting ducks. So they can go on until they run out of torpedoes – and they carry 14 each. And they're getting so brazen that some of them aren't bothering with torpedoes any more; simply coming to the surface and sinking our boys using bloody gunfire. One round from an 88 will send a 16,000 ton tanker and its entire poor bloody crew to kingdom come."

" There must be *something* we can do?" Sturdee sounded desperate.

"We could assassinate Admiral Ernest J King, Commander in Chief of the United States Navy. He is responsible for leaving the lights on. He is responsible for not introducing convoys. He is responsible for not assembling temporary escort vessels – quite small ships would be adequate so close to that coast. He's the fool that hates the Royal Navy more than the Germans. He is the one in a blazing temper all the time. Who won't take any advice. Who is drunk apparently most of the time."

"Why won't he convoy?"

"The fool apparently doesn't understand convoy – can you believe it in this day and age? He thinks convoys are for fighting, not for concealing your ships."

"How do you know all this?"

"Mansfield, Noble's Chief of Staff told us. The Admiralty is blowing its top – but can do nothing. Some of their people were over in the US with Churchill in December– but King wouldn't listen to them. Apparently he served briefly with the Royal Navy in the First World War and has born a grudge against us ever since. Now is his chance to get his revenge – and by God he's getting it."

"But that's appalling!"

"Somebody said, Lloyd George probably, that there's only one thing worse than having allies in war and that's…"

"… not having any." Gwen jumped in.

"Exactly. Trust a Welsh girl to know her Lloyd George."

"It sounds" Sturdee said "As if this is yet one more problem only poor old Winnie can solve. He has to persuade Roosevelt to sack King."

"What a way to start an alliance."

"Can you think of any alternative?"

Life at Duff House was no fun any longer. Meals passed in silence. There were no pigs to provide light relief. There was always silence when Sturdee and Joan were in the same room. There seemed no point in lighting a fire so everyone sloped off to their cold and lonely rooms at an early hour. Every other evening Arfur came to Sturdee's room for his bed-time read, alternating with Joan:

"I wisht you and 'er 'ud make it up."

"You heard her Arfur – she threw me out. It's gone too far now anyway. I have started looking for other another place. But it's not easy in this neighbourhood; all these big houses round here don't take lodgers, they're too posh. I've even been going up to their doors and knocking. It's embarrassing."

"What we going to do wivout you Giles ? Sawin' wood; building fings like the pigsty, and the 'lectric fences ? And what about your motorbike; Joan 'll nivver be able to run 'er market garden wivout that?"

"You should be asking her those questions – not me. I don't want to leave. I was happy here. I'll miss you, Maurice and Gem. Then where am I going to get another studio? I'll probably never paint another picture until after the war. But that's the trouble with war – it's disrupting. Everyone has to move on as the circumstances change. You could say we were lucky to have as long as we did together. If my boss Admiral Noble moves, I'll have to leave too. As a scientist I am officially an employee of the government – like a soldier or a sailor. I could be transferred to London tomorrow– or the Outer Hebrides. Even abroad; there are a lot of British scientists going to America just now."

"What for?"

"All manner of things – mostly secret."

"Would you like to go Giles?"

"Wouldn't mind – but only if I was in the thick of the scientific battle. Poor old Britain is going through a hard time at present. Nobody can slack off. We're like two bare-knuckle pugilists slogging it out, toe to toe. The first one that flinches will be socked to defeat. Right now I'm doing a pretty good job here – but that could change – I may be needed more in London soon."

"I don't want you to leave."

"Me neither."

Sturdee was planning another convoy passage – this time with an Escort group Commander to see how a real battle was run. Captain McIntyre had invited him to come with his Escort Group to the MOMP or Mid Ocean Meeting Point where McIntyre would turn back. Sturdee then hoped to transfer to a Canadian Escort Group and continue all the way to Halifax, Nova Scotia.

"After all " he explained to Loader "The poor bloody Canadians are bearing almost half the burden with even less resources than we have, little tradition, and even fouler weather."

"How could you help them?"

"I don't know – until I've had a good look. Anyway it might be the other way around – I might pick up a tip or two that could be useful to us."

"I doubt it old boy. The general impression is that the Canadian effort is a bit of a shambles – not surprising when they put to sea with almost no training. Heroic yes – but effective no."

"We'll see. The Royal Navy is inclined to be a trifle arrogant. We were a shambles ourselves not so long ago."

Loader was going to protest but grinned instead: "I suppose."

But before Sturdee could put to sea Blackett called him down to London:

"Churchill has called a meeting of his Battle of the Atlantic Committee for three days time. The latest sinking figures have sown panic in the corridors of power."

"I'm not surprised. We feel pretty helpless up here too. What's the agenda?"

"Not finalised yet. Probably talking about convoys and long-range aircraft I believe. The First Sea Lord Admiral Sir Dudley Pound will attend and he's asked me to be there in support in case scientific matters come up . I told him I'm not up to steam yet but you are – so you're invited too. Probably neither of us will have to speak– but you never know. Cherwell will be there forcing his pseudo-scientific ideas on Churchill, so we must be ready to counter if necessary."

The idea of speaking in front of the Prime Minister made Sturdee so nervous he barely slept in his hotel the night before. In the morning he went over to Blackett's new office in the Admiralty and together they made their way along Whitehall to the underground bunker near Downing Street where the meeting would be held. Having passed through several security checks a young civil servant took them down in the lift and into the Prime Minister's conference room: "You're early" he said, seating them along one wall: "If you are asked to speak, step forward to the table over there" He gestured. "The PM hates mumbling so better to speak too loudly than the converse."

"If I want to intervene" Blackett asked "How should I indicate?"

"You can't, not directly. Whisper in your boss's ear, and if Sir Dudley approves he'll raise his hand for the PM's attention."

"Is there an agenda?"

"It's just being roneoed off. I'll see you get one in a moment. These things, important though they are, tend to be rather informal: generally don't last long. The PM's got a War Cabinet meeting at 11."

As people began filing into the room Blackett said: "This will be a good experience for you Sturdee – if nothing else. If you do get called stick to what you know – and you'll probably be the best informed man in the room – on that specific topic. But if you wander off and offer more general opinions you can be chopped into little pieces. Remember, every one round this table will have a very sharp axe to grind."

Most of the men seating themselves round the table were civilians in dark suits, men of 60 years of age or more. One exception was the First Sea Lord, Admiral of the Fleet Sir Dudley Pound, covered in gold braid and almost bald, he nodded to Blackett and sat down with his back to them. Opposite him in the uniform of an Air Chief Marshall sat a distinguished looking man with a long thin nose. Glancing at his agenda Sturdee guessed he could only be Sir Charles Portal, Chief of the Air Staff, Pound's counterpart in the Royal Air Force.

Suddenly everyone stood up, and there was silence for a moment. When they sat down again the Prime Minister was sat at the head of the table almost opposite Sturdee. He was a little man, far smaller then Giles had imagined, but with a powerful stillness about him which left no doubt as to who was in charge. He wore a frockcoat and glasses on the end of his nose, secured by a chain running around his neck:

"The latest shipping figures I think gentlemen first." he growled.

A staff captain unfolded a chart from the wall which much resembled one of Gwen's charts back in Liverpool. It showed the Atlantic with a rash of black dots running down the American coast into the Caribbean, showing Allied sinkings. There were murmurs of dismay from round the table as the captain went through the figures.

"And how many U-boats sunk?" Churchill asked.

"Two Sir."

"As against?"

"Three last month, and ten the month before – December."

"And what have you got to say to that Admiral?" Churchill looked and sounded ferocious, as if it was all Pound's fault.

"No one can pretend Sir that 150 ships lost against two U-boats sunk is not an augury of defeat, because it is. But the whole situation has changed and is largely beyond our control. Nearly all the sinkings are now taking place in American waters where we have no influence at present, and very few escort vessels. The sinking are so high because the Americans have not and will not introduce a Convoy System: nor will they dowse their coastal lighting. We have made representations to Admiral King about both of these matters , on several occasions I have to say, to which he has turned a deaf ear. But unless both these measures are instituted the sinkings can only get worse, possibly much worse. We all know how vulnerable independent ships are, and out there they are triply vulnerable. Their route is largely preordained and therefore approximately known to the enemy, they have no protecting escort vessels, and they are backlit by the shore lights. So far as the Hun is concerned, it is a turkey shoot. We are sure that Doenitz is in a position to move many more of his U-boats over there and he's no doubt doing so at this moment. I hardly need to say the situation is very grave – the gravest we have had to face in this campaign so far."

" Have you no recommendations for us?" Churchill looked furious.

"I wish I had Prime Minister. Unless we can get the Americans to do the right things, and to do so very soon, we are helpless. I can even foresee advising you to halt all sailings from the Caribbean northward. That would include ships coming through Panama, ships coming up the coast of South America, and the ships that come across the South Atlantic from the Cape and then come home via the Caribbean. The most immediate and serious impact would be in loss of oil – almost a complete termination of our supplies – without which we cannot fight. I must remind the committee that our total oil reserves at present will last for less than three months. All of our oil presently comes from the Gulf and the Caribbean; all of it."

"But surely there must be other routes?" someone protested

"Yes there are." Pound agreed. "The obvious one being directly out from the Caribbean across the Atlantic towards Gibraltar and then North from there. But we do not have escort vessels at present with the requisite range to cover the transatlantic leg, because we do not possess bases down there. Thus in mid-Atlantic ships will be unescorted and consequently vulnerable. We made a trial crossing with eight tankers in convoy and six were torpedoed, as you just heard. We are making every effort to introduce the refuelling of escort vessels at sea. That is promising in the much calmer waters down there. It will certainly come, but it will take 3 to 6 months to come into full operation because so many ships have to be been fitted with special gear. If and when convoy escort carriers come into commission, they should be especially effective in the clear skies down there. But they are being built in United States yards and are even further off. I'm sorry to say Prime Minister that the only remedy we can see at present is to galvanise the Americans into sensible action before this battle, and consequently this war, in lost."

If Pound was hoping for effect, he got it .There was complete silence in the room, with everyone looking towards Mr Churchill for leadership.

The Prime Minister, who looked smaller and tireder than ever, lit an enormous cigar as if sparring for time:
"Well Admiral", he growled with a bleak smile "You've certainly spelled things out. Has anybody got a suggestion?"
Silence ensued.
"Can we, for instance, offer the Americans any support to get things going over there? Yes Admiral?
"We've looked into that Sir. Between us and the Canadians we could offer a dozen corvettes immediately, either manned or unmanned, indeed we have done so already. A dozen trained corvettes could get a convoy system up and running almost immediately. But Admiral King turned us down. He maintains that weakly escorted convoys are worse than no convoys at all."
"Is that true?"
"No sir; on the contrary. Even a weakly escorted convoy of 50 ships cuts opportunities for interception by a factor of at least 25. That is our experience, both in this war, and the last."
"So" Churchill scribbled notes: his cigar in his mouth: "There is a remedy to the crisis, but it will involve me persuading the president to do the right thing , and to do so immediately. That is not always easy. I shall want a two page note from you Admiral, with all the facts and figures, particularly the gravity of the situation. I also command you to keep those dozen corvettes in readiness to get things started right away when I get the Presidents agreement."
Sturdee noted that he didn't say 'If'.
There was a palpable sense of relief around the table as if defeat had been faced down yet again, as it had been so many times over the past 18 months, and in this very room – over Dunkirk, over the Battle of Britain, ... over the Blitz...
Churchill glanced up at the clock on the wall:
"We have time for one more item. What is it to be?"
Pound was the first to raise his hand.
"Well Admiral?"
"The provision of very long-range aircraft for maritime patrol. I'm sorry to monopolise the committee's business, but this is urgent too." Churchill looked around the table. Nobody demurred.
"Very well. Go-ahead. We can spend 20 minutes on this."
Pound rose to his feet and went over to the wall chart being displayed by his Staff Captain:
"In both wars we have found that convoys protected both from the sea and the air rarely lose vessels to U-boats. As you will see from these six-monthly sinking-charts the progress of this battle has been almost perfectly marked by the extension of our aerial reconnaissance further and further out to sea. As we have spread outward so the

enemy has retreated seaward. At the beginning of the war he was picking off our ships in the South-Western Approaches and the Channel. As we patrolled those he retreated to the North-Western Approaches. Now he makes very few sinkings within 500 miles of our islands. But our outward progress has come to an end for lack of the aircraft with sufficient range. Our Wellingtons and Whitleys can get out to 300 miles, our Sunderlands to 450, and our Catalina flying-boats , operating out of Loch Erne in Northern Ireland, out to 600 miles. Beyond that, at present we cannot go. But there is no reason that we cannot patrol the entire North Atlantic and so bring an end to U-boat sinkings on our main maritime artery – the one to North America."

He paused for effect . 'What a fine looking man' Sturdee thought, an eagle among the undistinguished hens looking up at him. Even Churchill looked insignificant by comparison.

"Coastal Command has a handful of four-engined bomber aircraft, B 24 Liberators, that presently have a range of 2700 miles and an endurance of 14 to 15 hours, but they could easily be modified to do much better. I'm told that with extra fuel tanks placed in their their bomb-bays they could go out to 4000 plus, and remain in the air for over 20 hours."

"Now 4000 miles gentlemen is a crucial figure. An aircraft with a range of 4000 miles plus could entirely close the Atlantic Air Gap, the 600 mile wide gap in mid-Atlantic in which U-boats are presently free to roam without any hindrance from air patrol from our side, or from Canada. If we can close that gap *in time* the Battle of the Atlantic will be half won."

He paused again for affect:

"I said 'In time' gentlemen, and deliberately so. As you know Doenitz is building up his U-boat fleet by roughly 20 new boats a month. By the end of 1942 he should have enough boats out there to draw a cordon completely across the North Atlantic. At present most of our convoys slip through between his wolf-packs and get across scot-free. By the end of this year perhaps, none of them will. That's when we expect the Climax Battle that will decide the outcome of this war, to take place. If we cannot win that we will be forced to capitulate."

Again he paused:

"And where would it be fought? In the mid-Atlantic Air Gap of course. That is where Doenitz will reckon his best chance to be. There he will concentrate his cordon of 100 patrolling U-boats; there he will try to form wolf packs of two or even three dozen submarines each to attack our convoys as they attempt to make the three-day passage of that fateful bit of sea. There will be fought a battle far more fateful than Trafalgar or Jutland. In all our long naval history only the Spanish Armada will compare. We have got to be ready gentlemen, we have to be. Those of us sitting around this table have to bear the heavy responsibility to our citizens, to our descendants, and to those slaving under the Nazi heel in Europe, who can only look to us for help."

"The old boy is really going it " Blackett whispered, "Not like him at all."

"As to numbers, let me remind you. We have 20 fifty-ship convoys sailing West every month and 20 sailing back East. Since a transatlantic voyage takes roughly 15 days that means 20 convoys at sea at any one time. Since the air gap is 600 miles wide, or one fifth of the entire voyage: that means there will be roughly 4 convoys attempting to cross the gap at any moment, two going West and two coming East. If we are to provide each convoy with only one aircraft on patrol night and day then we need 200 4-engined patrol aircraft and we need them soon. We need them soon so that they can be extensively modified to attain the necessary range and endurance. Gun turrets and armour have to be stripped out, the engines modified for low-level performance, and extra fuel tanks fitted. In all, I am told, that should take 3 to 6 months. We've only got nine months in all. That is why this is of the utmost priority. The present onslaught on the American coast may seem bad gentleman, but just wait until we get to the Battle of the Gap– if we are not prepared. So, in sum , I am asking that Coastal Command get 200 four-engine bombers: preferably Liberators or Lancasters, with almost immediate effect. I am informed that we are already producing 500 such aircraft a month, so we are asking for, at best, two weeks supply."

He walked back to his chair.

"Well gentleman?" Churchill looked round the table. Eventually he called: "The Paymaster General".

Blackett whispered: "That's Cherwell's official title."

"I must say Prime Minister I find the admirals plea utterly unconvincing; utterly."

By craning forward Sturdee could see the speaker, a bald, severe looking lman of about 60, with a toothbrush moustache; he looked more like a country solicitor with dyspepsia than a scientist:

"The First Sea Lord is asking for, nay demanding a significant part of our whole heavy bomber supply just at the moment when Bomber Command is building towards a decisive onslaught on Germany's heartland. Air Marshall Harris is promising 1000-bomber raids in a matter of weeks. It is by those very numbers he hopes to overwhelm the enemy's defences. Start frittering our bombers away here and there in mere defence and we throw away the one offensive weapon we have, our dagger pointed at Hitler's heart."

Sturdee could now detect the faint German accent. Before his ennoblement Cherwell had been Frederick Lindemann who had grown up in Baden Baden.

"As to the 500 bombers a month, I am sorry to say that they are almost, if not quite entirely, a figment of the good admiral's imagination. I think he is referring to the entire Allied production of such aircraft. The great majority are being produced in American factories and do not belong to, and cannot be assigned by us. And even our own production of Lancasters is only just starting. Even if we denuded Bomber Command entirely – which in my opinion would be an entire repudiation of our long agreed offensive war strategy – we couldn't supply him with as many as 100 aircraft, and more probably with less than half that number."

"Now consider our contemplated 1000-bomber raids upon Germany. The casualty figures over heavily defended targets like the Ruhr or Berlin can safely be anticipated as 5% or more. Each such raid will therefore require 50 or more replacements when the admiral is asking for 200 immediately. We might as well call off our bombing strategy altogether. And what will Stalin say to that?"

He left the question in the air before resuming:

" But put the matter of Bomber Command to one side and consider the Admiral's case for the aircraft. It hinges on the anti- correlation he has shown us between sinkings and the presence of aircraft patrolling with convoys. Now we have a very important saying in Science: 'Correlation is not Causation'; let me repeat that phrase gentlemen: 'Correlation is not Causation'. What does it mean? Let me take a famous example that has been recorded in this century: an almost perfect correlation between the average size of Chinese women's feet, and annual United States steel production. Both have risen dramatically in lockstep with one another – but no one asks us to believe that one is the proximate cause of the other. It would be madness to suppose so, as I am sure you will all agree. But Admiral Pound is asking us to swallow an almost identical argument with regard to maritime aircraft patrols. Yes he has demonstrated a correlation, or rather an anti-correlation in this case, between sinkings and the presence of Allied aircraft, but he hasn't presented, or even pretended to present, a causal connection between the two. It could be, as it was in the case of the Chinese ladies nether regions, entirely coincidental. I am afraid he will have to do far better than that – at least to persuade a scientist like myself. Why Admiral, do maritime patrol aircraft – which carry very few bombs, because they need most of their load capacity for extra fuel – and which in consequence rarely if ever sink a submarine, how do they, and more importantly why would they, turn the entire course of the titanic submarine battle in mid-Atlantic? He doesn't make any sense to a scientist, no sense to me at all."

"Admiral?" Churchill called on Pound to reply.

Pound stood up:

"No one can see into his enemy's mind – not with any certainty. I do not know why U-boat commandos retreat in the face of airborne patrols , and it is not necessary to know. I could speculate – as could we all– but there is no need. The fact is they do retreat – they have always retreated – and that should suffice for us around this table. Psychological speculation is no part of my job. And as for the Chinese ladies – they sound more like red herrings to me. This is no time or place for philosophical digressions, or debating points."

"Good for you Admiral" Sturdee hissed, louder than he had meant to. He'd been infuriated by Cherwell's assumption of the Scientific cloak, as if only he had a capacity to think straight.

"Sir Charles Portal" Churchill called up the chief of the Air Staff. "They're your bloody aeroplanes in the end. What do you want to do with 'em?"

Portal strongly supported Cherwell:

"We don't want to cripple our bombing campaign before it has started Prime Minister. We should stick to our plan. By the time of Admiral Pound's climactic battle we may have already beaten Nazi Germany to its knees. Imagine 1000 heavy bombers converging on London to drop nearly 10 tons of incendiaries or high explosive bombs each. We all experienced the Blitz. This will be ten times, no fifty times worse. Can you imagine any civilian population sticking it out?"

The discussion became general. Only the First Lord of the Admiralty – Pound's civilian counterpart – supported the First Sea Lord, as he was bound to do. To Sturdee's amazement Admiral Pound himself went to sleep in the middle of the debate, and had to be discreetly woken by Blackett just in time to hear Churchill summing up:

"As usual we are faced with an acute lack of resources and difficult, very difficult choices have to be made. The First Sea Lord has made an eloquent bid for 200 bombers to fight his climax battle in 12 months time ; the Chief of the Air Staff argues that they would be much better employed in the huge bombing raids he intends to launch against the heartland of the Nazis in a few weeks time. It is future d-defence against present offence . The majority sentiment around this table is quite clearly offensive. So Admiral Pound's request for very long-range aircraft is refused – at least for the present."

Back in his office Blackett smiled at Sturdee's impotent fury:

"That's how it is Sturdee We scientists can only advise, not decide – it has to be so in any democracy."

"That swine Cherwell…" Sturdee spluttered.

"Don't tell me. We had to put up with him on the Tizard Committee for several years. He assumes the cloak of Science but in reality he hasn't done any real science for quarter of a century But he impresses the politicians through his 'Oxford Professorship and his dogmatic air while his recent peerage places him on a level with Lord Rutherford – in their eyes. And he employs superficial little tricks to great effect."

"Like that 'correlation versus causation' nonsense ."

"Exactly: that bamboozled them . More usually he blinds them with a firework display of mental arithmetic. They imagine a great scientific brain is at work, a brain that cannot possibly be wrong."

"But… but he's a charlatan,… a witch-doctor… another Rasputin…"

"I sometimes wonder myself if he isn't a Nazi agent – he so uniformly advocates policies inimical to the British cause. He almost succeeded in preventing the development of radar. The Tizard Committee had to resign en masse, and then reform itself with no Lindemann – as he was then – on board."

"What are we going to do? Without the aircraft in mid-Atlantic we can only lose."

"As to that, the battle is not entirely lost – not yet. I am still feeling my way, but I suspect real power in this war lies not in Churchill's committees – but in the Chiefs of Staff . I don't think he would over-rule them on a purely military matter – which this is."

"Who are the Chiefs of Staff?"

"Pounds representing the Navy, Portal the Air Force, and they are chaired by General Sir Alan Brooke representing the Army. They meet nearly every day and take all the key military decisions . Churchill frequently interferes but Brooke usually manages to see him off . But the recent decision in Washington to vest control of the

Allied war in the *Combined* Chiefs of Staff, that's the British and American chiefs of staff meeting in conclave, ought to boost Brooke's standing vis a vis the Prime Minister's. But that depends how Brooke gets on with his Washington counterpart, General Marshall."

"It's all so complicated…"

"It's bound to be, in an alliance between two democracies. But it could work. Take this business of the 200 long-range Liberators. If Pound could convince Brooke, and Brooke could convince Marshall we could get our Liberators within a fortnight. I'm told the Americans are already turning out 500 or more a month. Cherwell will count for nothing then – after all he is a nonentity on the international scene. His power lies solely in the personal influence he asserts over Churchill – which is immense . And as Paymaster General he worms his way into almost every high-level government meeting."

"How are we going to defeat him?"

"How do you think Giles?"

Sturdee was taken aback by the question: "I… I suppose we have to undermine his scientific pretensions… in front of the politicians, and in particular in front of Churchill himself?"

"Go on." A bleak smile appeared on Blackett's face.

"I suppose we have to try and set him up. Get him to declare himself on an issue of importance; beguile him into using his dirty little tricks to bedazzle politicians, then blow him clear out of the water: demonstrate conclusively that he is talking scientific nonsense?"

"You've got the makings of a politician Sturdee. But don't think it hasn't been tried. Where his own reputation is at stake Cherwell brims with low cunning. To operate the trap-fall beneath his feet, we need the perfect issue to snap his neck before he can even squeak. Let me know if you come up with something."

Back in Liverpool Sturdee shared as much of the bad news as he dared with Loader.

"What are we going to do Giles?"

"I've no bloody idea."

"We've got to get aircraft out to mid-Atlantic – we absolutely have to. If we can't fly them out there, they have to go out there on the deck of an aircraft carrier."

"Wasn't there some scheme…"?"

"Yes Giles, Escort Carriers , big merchantmen modified to carry and fly-off half a dozen smallish aircraft. Better than nothing though."

"I seem to remember something?"

"HMS *Audacity*, she was the first one, commissioned last September. And she made a great job protecting convoy HG 76 from a wolfpack as it steamed home from Gib. But then the Germans picked her out and picked her off, and the carrier went down with the loss of several hundred lives, and all her planes. Escort carriers are a damn good idea if you ask me – but they're bound to be conspicuous . We've got quite a number building in American yards – which should commission in time."

"They may be our only hope now. Find out what you can about them. Meanwhile I'm going out to sea with Donald McIntyre. It will be good to get away from politicians. You know they make me feel literally dirty Tony. They seem to enjoy fighting one another – forgetting the Germans."

"I hate to stick up for them Giles, but somebody's got to do it. War is all about priorities. Somebody's got to choose 'em."

"I suppose"

"You're a lucky devil. I wish I was coming with you Giles."

"You look after our Gwenny Loader… somebody's got to do it."

"I suppose."

CHAPTER 23
HURRICANE

The one thing Sturdee was dreading about the trip was another bout of seasickness. When consulted Loader was unhelpful:

"Some, including Nelson, get the vomits every time they put to sea, but that's unusual. It depends on the individual… and the ship. Corvettes are notorious for rolling, But you're on a destroyer this time. They roll alright – but not so violently. They are plungers and whippers, and bloody wet, often going through the crests of the waves in a big storm. We lost one Captain recently when a wave broke through his forrard sea-cabin and washed him out."

"Well thanks for the good news."

"You're welcome, but destroyers have proved to be more robust than expected. We haven't lost one so far, not even up in the far North Atlantic – for which they were never designed."

Donald McIntyre's ship '*Walker*' was a small First World War destroyer designed to protect battleships from small fast Motor Torpedo Boats in the inshore waters of the Channel and the North Sea. To catch the MTB s she was nearly all boilers and turbines which generated nearly 30,000 shaft horsepower, enabling her to reach well over 30 knots in calm water – a sea condition she was most unlikely to meet in the North Atlantic. But looking down at her from the Gladstone Dock Sturdee saw no erstwhile greyhound of the sea but a battered veteran of many a storm, obviously adapted and modified over and over again to fulfil her present role as convoy Escort Leader. Most of her guns and torpedo tubes were gone; her after-deck was a mess of depth-charge rails, depth-charge throwers and drum shaped depth-charges themselves. Her upper works were a tangle of aerials while her bridge was surmounted by a large opaque drum which Sturdee guessed must house her rotating radar scanner. She had two oddly assorted funnels, one abaft the bridge, a smaller one aft. Most noticeable to a man who was about to embark on her was how narrow she was, less than 30 feet across, he guessed: "How the hell do a hundred and thirty men squeeze aboard that?" he wondered aloud.

"With difficulty!" A cheery voice answered from behind. "By your bag you look to be coming with us?"

Sturdee introduced himself.

"Ah yes", the cheery young midshipman said: "The skipper told us about you. A real brainbox. What do you think of her?"

" A trifle… spartan."

"She is the best Sub killer there is. *Walker*'s got three certain kills already – including an Ace . I'm the midshipman. Everybody calls me 'Midi' " he shook hands. "We may not be the Queen Mary but we're a happy ship."

"Where are the life boats?" Sturdee asked.

" Mostly swept overboard in storms. But we've got life rafts instead – see one slung abaft the funnel?"

"The black-and-white camouflage is odd isn't it?"

"All the fashion. Damned effective at sea. Breaks up our profile. U-boats don't see us coming until we are on 'em. Could have rammed one blighter last trip – but we're not allowed to any more – too expensive."

Captain McIntyre could only see him briefly: "I'll be verra busy the first couple of days. There won't be any action for a while because we've got continuous air cover out to 450 miles. Inspect the ship though from truck to keelson – we've got a lot of new and vital equipment on board. I told the midi to show you round. But when things get serious you can come up to the bridge and shadow me. We should have plenty of time to talk then. The main concern at this time of year is the bluidy weather. It looks okay now, but the glass is falling fast."

They were a cheerful lot in the wardroom , a mix of Regular, Reserve and hostilities-only RNVR officers who had sailed many times together. He was surprised how confident they were:

"We've got the measure of Jerry now." The First Lieutenant said "He hardly stands a chance against our new radar. We are on him like a shot and down he goes. He's too busy dodging depth-charges to get off a torpedo . And when he does come up…"

"*If* he does…" someone interrupted

"Yes, *if* he does the convoy is long gone on a new course. In the last eight convoys we've lost only one ship – and we sank the blighter that did it ."

"They're getting more scared of us then we are of them." someone added: "That's why they skedaddled off to the American coast."

Sturdee explained his reasons for coming to sea and they all promised to show him their new toys.

Fortunately the sea was fairly calm so although the *Walker* dashed about at high-speed shepherding the ships into convoy pattern, heeling steeply as she turned, his stomach felt fine, so he decided to start with the radar after supper on their first night at sea.

The midi, with whom we were sharing a tiny cabin under the bridge superstructure, took him aloft to the radar hut behind the bridge itself . Despite his background in radar, he could scarcely believe the improvement. The beam rotated slowly around on a circular screen picking out all the ships of the convoy and its Escort Group as individual bright green dots which slowly faded. But before they disappeared altogether the beam returned and painted them bright green again.

"This PPI or 'Plan Position Indicator' has transformed everything" the radar officer explained: "We can see the whole battlefield at a glance, day or night, fair weather or foul. Station keeping is a doddle. That releases the Watch to look out for U-boats."

"What's the maximum range?"

"Set at 8 miles right now. We can usually pick out U-boats at four or five . To be honest the old radars weren't much cop, but these new Type 271's work like a dream – powerful, accurate, reliable… We can't imagine life without them. If you ask me Jerry's had it. The skipper insisted that the whole crew come up here one by one to see it working. It's done no end of good for morale. Everyone feels we're going to win now. You're a boffin aren't you? Well thank those boffins who made it."

Up on the completely darkened bridge a quarter moon was drifting in and out between six- eighths cloud. The convoy must have been astern because all Sturdee could see were the wakes of an escort vessel to port and another to starboard, each about a mile away. Occasionally one would move into a shaft of moonlight enabling him to pick out their sleek low-slung profiles, quite different from the bluff and bulky cargo vessels.

As usual in darkness his ears became more sensitive. There were the regular pings of the Asdic coming from its cabin. He could clearly hear the wake rushing out to either side of the bow directly beneath. The funnel seemed to be vibrating with the effort from the powerful turbines below. Then he thought he could hear aircraft engines, radials by their soft sounds, probably four . He turned to the midi interrogatively and pointed up. " White Crow" the midi whispered "Sunderland flying boat."

As his eyes accustomed the figures on the bridge began to stand out against sea and sky: the port and starboard watchmen, the Officer of the Watch occasionally giving orders to the quartermaster on the wheel one deck below, and someone else hunched in a chair, looking out to sea with glasses, presumably Captain McIntyre.

Every few minutes the destroyer executed a sharp turn, presumably a zig-zag to prevent any enemy getting an easy torpedo shot. A voice came briefly through on the intercom; McIntyre replied.

"That's new." Sturdee said: "They used to use semaphore lamps."

"TBS" the midi explained "Talk Between Ships". New American gear. It's very high frequency, short range wireless. Won't go further than the horizon so won't give our positions away. A miraculous improvement they say. The escort commander can really control all his ships from here now, and they can tell him instantly if they've got a radar or Asdic contact. How the hell we ever did without it…"

Sturdee glanced over at McIntyre, hunched in his duffle jacket, looking bloody cold. So much responsibility on one man's shoulders: seven escort vessels comprising five destroyers and two corvettes; 50 odd cargo vessels of all nationalities, but predominantly British, and something like 5000 souls. And cargoes of course. Britain was still exporting desperately to pay for its imports, though God knows what the island had to spare in the middle of a war: probably coal and Scotch whisky… He must ask Joan. But then he remembered – Joan wasn't for the asking any more. He felt miserable every time he thought about her. The sooner he moved out of that house the better.

Fortunately McIntyre called him over:

"All quiet you see. It's the weather that's worrying me. The glass is low and dropping like a stone. Can you feel a wee bit verra long swell? That's the outrider of a big storm if I'm no mistaken. We're making Northing, but whether we'll escape……."

"Can the convoy hold together in a storm?"

"Mebbe, mebbe not . It's those Greek ships I worry aboot: few of them really fit for these seas; no rescue equipment, poorly trained, poorly paid crews. But it's no the convoy I worry about so much as these five destroyers. We've barely got the fuel to get us t' Iceland in fair weather. If we get hove to in a hurricane for several days we might have to desert and head for home. We've got a refuelling tanker with us but refuelling at sea needs fairish weather. No chance in a storm. It's shortage of fuel which gives escort commanders ulcers. We leave port with 450 tons each which will give us 2000 miles at 15 knots. But wi' all this zig-zagging and chasing down contacts at 30 knots that can all be gone in eight or nine days. And once   the destroyers have left, the puir bloody corvettes wi' a speed of 16 knots are no match for a surfaced U-boat wi' a speed of 17 and a half. That's why refuelling at sea is so bluidy important, why Noble pressed for it so hard. Wi' destroyers an escort group is usually a match for any wolf pack; without 'em the struggle can go either way. *Walker*'s lost only one cargo vessel when her convoys have been attacked."

"And sunk three U-boats?"

"Aye"

"What about the modified depth charges?"

"Already arrived. Huge improvement. On our first discharge pattern we set one to go off verra deep. Then the U-boat commander realises there's no safety any more doon there, and up he comes, tipping the odds verra much in our favour."

McIntyre broke off to answer a voice query that came through on the TBS. Sturdee moved to the wing of the bridge from where he could look astern and see column by column of black freighters ploughing across a partially moonlit sea in their wake. How vulnerable they would look to any U-boat which managed to penetrate either the radar screen on the surface or the Asdic screen beneath the waves. The Battle of the Atlantic had truly become the battle for the dark.

Sturdee returned to McIntyre:

"So you think we're getting on top sir ?"

"Ay and noo . If two U-boats attacked us now we would see them off for sure. We might just be able to handle three – with five destroyers , but four would be too many. They would overwhelm the screen and get amongst the columns of ships. It's all about concentration in war – once again. It was true in Drake's day, it was true in Nelson's and Jellicoe's, it's true in Noble's and Doenitz's. Now Doenitz is concentrating off the American coast and reaping the rewards; and we canna follow him .The Americans must learn their own hard lessons."

"With our ships."

"Aye, wi' our ships – and that's the agony of it. Are we getting on top?' We are in the Eastern Atlantic, but we are now losing in the West. And Doenitz is building all the time . The real issue will be decided in mid-Atlantic in about 12 month's time. The side with the concentration there and then will win. Each convoy will be a concentration battle between us and them – don't you agree?"

"I do. That's why we're fighting – and losing the battle for very long range aircraft."

"It was a foolish mistake to put Maritime control into the hands of the RAF. Controlling our sea lanes was always the Royal Navy's task, whether by sea or by air. To split it between two rival forces could lose us this battle , and so this war. Makes my blood boil . What does that Portal fellow care about our ships? He's left Coastal Command a dumping ground for obsolete aircraft and second-rate commanders. Churchill should gie that laddie the boot. If he does na do it soon we could all go down a year from now."

"Portal believes bombing Germany is our first priority."

"How can he bomb Gairmany if he's nae got fuel? He'll ha' thousands of the four- engined bombers sitting on the tarmac for lack of it when all we want is two hundred now to win this battle out at sea . Afterwards he can have all the fuel he needs. Did you feel that long period swell?"

"Yes I did."

"That means we've got 24 hours before the storm hits. So if you want some sleep or hot food laddie I should snatch it now. Could be a week before you get another chance."

The Captain was right about the storm. While he was still asleep Sturdee was hurled from his upper bunk into the door face first. Shocked, stunned and in agony he tried to gather his wits in the partial darkness. The plunging and rolling left no doubt that he was at sea. The blood pouring out of his nostrils, and the pain in his entire face from forehead to upper lip confirmed that he must have been catapulted headfirst into the door. The door thank goodness was of flimsy wood: had he hit the solid steel bulkhead he would have fractured his skull.

To staunch the bleeding he knew he would have to sit up or stand . Easier said than done with the cabin plunging and rearing like a wild buckaroo. He got hands on the edge of the lower bunk, tottered to his feet and was promptly slammed backwards into the door again, his shoulder blades and the back of his head taking the impact this time.

"This is serious" he thought. "A few more of those and I'll be killed."

The destroyers bow rose and Rose until she she was almost standing on her propellers. Sturdee slithered down the cabin floor, away from the door towards the deadly steel bulkhead. Realising his danger he managed to jam his feet against the steel and his back against the bunk while he clung on to a piece of the locker.

Water roared down the deck just outside as the ship burst through the crest of what must have been a giant wave, and crashed almost vertically down the other side, all of its rivets groaning under the strain.

"Christ, she'll never to stand much of this!" He cried aloud to nobody, feeling very afraid.

Sheer terror drove him to his feet and into the middi's unoccupied lower bunk. He'd noticed two ropes dangling from the upper bunk and he secured them to cleats on the lower, imprisoning himself as if in a rope cage. When he got hurled sideway again they would arrest his trajectory. It was a trick he had learned aboard his little cruiser in the Thames estuary, but he'd never been in a storm remotely like this. He jammed himself in, bracing himself between the footboard, and the sideboard of the bunk , with one hand clinging to the safety rope, the other splayed across the inner wall. He decided that nothing would move him there, short of a sea bursting into the cabin. He would rather bleed to death than face being broken into pieces like a felon on the Wheel.

Once he was braced his brain began to experience the full fury of the storm. First there was the noise, the shrieking and moaning of the wind in the superstructure, the crashing of seawater against the hull or rushing along the deck, the creaking of rivets, the rattling of equipment that had broken loose. Then, loudest of all, was the occasional slamming of the ships bottom as it fell off a wave into the trough below. It travelled through the whole destroyer rattling drawers in their shelves, shaking ammunition in its lockers, even the teeth in a man's head.

"Dear God" he thought aloud "How long can this go on?"

His mind travelled around the ship, thinking of all the crewmen who had to be sticking to their tasks to keep the old vessel from foundering.

Out on the open bridge, soaked to the skin, and blinded by driving spray, would be the officer of the watch conning the ship to keep her head into the oncoming seas. He'd be calling out, more likely screaming out, orders to the quartermaster who must somehow be braced to spin the steering wheel. If either of them made a single mistake her head would fall off and she'd be rolled over, capsized , taking them all down. He found himself, for the first time in his life, saying a prayer for them . John Duff had told him : "There are no atheists in a big storm at sea."

And what about the poor devils down on the boiler and engine rooms? Sturdee could feel the engines constantly surging and falling back, in train with the colossal waves. Probably she couldn't hold herself head to wind by rudder power alone. The officer of the watch was probably calling down for more or less power from either port or starboard propeller every five seconds.

And how could the poor stokers down in the bowels of the ship brace themselves , let alone give precise turns to pressure valves without being scalded or breaking their bones?

He thought about the forecastle, the liveliest, berserkest part of the little ship, up in the plunging bow where the majority of the crew would be rolling about in their hammocks with sea water squirting through the deck rivets immediately above their heads.

The Walker twisted and shuddered: executing a manoeuvre she had surely never been designed for, one designed to tear her plates from her frames and send her to the bottom.

'I am terrified' Sturdee thought'. 'I never envisaged this . No one could imagine this ordeal ashore. And yet this is the lot of these men, storm after storm, winter after winter. I must calm down, I must calm down, I must calm down….. I must not panic. Presumably the ship has survived many storms before . She's the descendant of ocean going vessels going back to the time of Drake . You wanted to be a Royal Navy officer Sturdee, so here you are sharing their lot. Why do you think they are admired all over the world? Not because of their plain uniforms, but because they are as tough as teak'.

Gradually he bullied himself into some kind of calm, leaving the ship to look after herself. He couldn't recall an instance of a destroyer foundering at sea, so why should the *Walker*?"

"My God you look a mess"

Sturdee woke to find the midi standing over him. He tried to rise:

"I'm sorry I'm in your bunk."

"Relax old chap. I can use the upper if I get a chance– which is not likely .Can I get you an aspirin or something? You've got two colossal black eyes and there's dried blood all over the shop – most likely from your nose. I should have warned you to lace up but we weren't quite expecting this."

Sturdee could feel that the storm was more violent than ever:

"Is this normal?" He asked

"From late September to late March we get some real blows up here. Pinger just came off watch. he said it's storm force 11, gusting 12. So that's a real hurricane. You'll be able to brag about that when you get ashore."

"I won't feel like bragging – more likely thanking God for deliverance. I can feel my atheism shaking a bit at the knees already."

"You haven't got your sea legs – that's the problem . We get used to it, can sense every motion of the old tub before it happens. But that is why I've come down here with strict orders from the skipper . You are confined to your bunk– My bunk – until further orders. I've brought you some biscuits and two bottles, one to drink from; one to pee in. If you have to do the other – not recommended though – use the bucket in the locker down there. Now strict orders mind. The Skipper seems to think you're a pretty valuable chap and he's made me responsible for you. If I lose you he's threatened to see I never get another seagoing berth. So I'm relying on you Giles to do the decent thing."

The midi nearly fell over as Walker corkscrewed and dived over a cliff until such light as there was went out.

"By God we're submerged." the midi yelled.

The bow climbed and climbed, Sturdee hung on like grim death until light leaked back into the cabin again through the shuttered porthole grating.

"Phew – that doesn't often happen. The old girl is really going it today. Hope we don't lose our radar scanner. Toodaloo old chap: I ought to get back up on the bridge. We're doing half-hour watches at present, and no one, absolutely no one is allowed on deck."

And he was gone, slamming the infamous door behind him.

Only after a begging note to McIntyre was Sturdee allowed on the bridge 48 hours later: '*Captain, a major part of my reason for coming to sea in midwinter was to experience the effects of rough weather on the battle in all its aspects. I appreciate your solicitude……*'

The wind dropped from Hurricane strength to Storm force, but the waves were enormous, quite terrifying in fact .The midi had lashed him to a stanchion at the back of the open bridge where he could brace himself between two vertical steel surfaces.

The only two men beside him on the bridge were the Officer of the Watch in oilskins yelling soundlessly down to the Quartermaster at the wheel on the deck below, and his assistant who was working the two telegraphs, or throttles calling for more or less power from each propellor. Both were dressed in black oil skins and Sou'westers which flapped and shuddered in the storm. `Sturdee's own sou'wester blew away in seconds, leaving his face the target of flying spray which flayed his skin like a firehose.

The grey sea was everywhere streaked with long skeins of white foam blowing downwind towards them, but Sturdee had no eyes for anything but the colossal wall of water bearing down on them from ahead like a toppling cliff. More than twice the height of the Walker's topmast and vertical, it was more terrifying than a childhood nightmare. Wanting to scream, Sturdee forced himself to look as the Walker's bow began to rise and rise until he was almost lying on his back, with the crest of the monster blowing off above his head. Somehow the little destroyer, a mere 1500 tons or so, burst through the crest under throttle and dived over the monster on the far side, only to be assaulted by its successor.

Almost more terrifying than being on the bridge was looking to starboard and seeing a Corvette in its own mortal battle with the storm. At times its hull was almost entirely out of the sea, at others buried up to its funnel in foam.

For years afterwards, even after the war, Sturdee used to have nightmares about that hurricane. Even McIntyre admitted afterwards that he sometimes felt mortally afraid when he saw an enormous wave bearing down on his ship : "Ye' need to have the fear of God in ye to take all the precautions we need. There's noo many atheists out here on the vasty deep. There's more prayers going out from this wee ship right now then any cathedral in the kingdom."

"Gosh it makes me admire you all. If only our citizens knew what you lot are going through out here to keep us in food and supplies, no one would waste a thing, throw away a crust or a rind . Black marketeers would be strung up from the nearest lamp-post and every striker kicked to death – or better still sentenced to come out here and experience Hell for themselves."

"Ay that would be better" McIntyre agreed. "But every man has only got so much stamina, so much strength. Fortunately Noble knows this. He rotates men around, gives us leave when he can. After three or four trips a man is completely bushed. I know I canna keep thinking for a whole convoy if I haven't slept for a week. Every man I have ever met has got a breaking point. Get some sleep yourself laddie while we gather the flock together. We may get some action after that. The U-boats have been riding comfortably half a hundred fathoms down. Now they'll pop up and find some poor battered ship and her exhausted crew to blow apart – but no if I can help it. But I'll need the guid Lord's assistance."

"In what sense?"

" A sea calmer than this and soon; we need to refuel at sea."

"I want to see that."

"Not as much as I do laddie. That storm cost Walker 150 tons of fuel, and some of the other four destroyers more. We'll be bone dry unless we get a sip before we get to Reykjavik."

"Did everyone survive – the storm I mean."

"Every ship did – but no every man – alas. A corvette lost three men overboard whilst they were trying to lash down a depth charge that had broken adrift. A suicide job I'd say: volunteers only."

"My mate lost his hand the same way."

"Loader? Some of the bravest men in this Navy serve down on the depth-charge deck. I've seen them up-to-their necks in Arctic water hoisting 450-pound charges into the throwers wi' little care for either life or limb. Loader was a guid officer. He'd surely have got his own command."

"He might yet. The medicos say he is making great progress with his wooden arm."

"Guid for him. We canna afford to lose his like. Yes, and two freighters lost men overboard – both Greek of course. We shouldn't charter them – not fit for this trip."

"What about before the war?"

"They didn't come up this far North. In fact nobody did. The weather is too foul for peace time. Look, I've got an interesting chart."

Out of the drawer in his day cabin McIntyre drew a small chart showing the main trade routes into Britain in times of peace. Sturdee was intrigued because it was nothing like Gwen's sinking charts back in the office. There were five braids of shipping converging on their island: one through the Mediterranean coming mainly from Asia via Suez; another up from the Cape and round the bulge of Africa; a third out from the bight of South America, mainly from the River Plate and the Amazon. The thickest braid seemed to come in straight from the Caribbean and Panama, making past the Azores. The last thick braid came up the American coast and headed East from the Saint Lawrence Seaway, never making it further North than the Clyde.

"So this Great Circle route coming far North towards Greenland and Cape Farewell is a purely wartime institution?"

"That's right " McIntyre agreed. "The great liners might take it to save their time– it *is* the shortest – but most were put off by the fate of the Titanic. Anyway fee-paying passengers don't like to get sea-sick. So this is a desolate stretch in peacetime. Only the shearwaters and whales bothered to come up here. Everybody sensible steered clear to Southard."

"After that hurricane, so would I."

" Aye; you are a bit of a mess laddie . Don't let your best girl see you wi' a face like that. Looks like you collided with a steam hammer."

Travelling at right angles to the hurricane's track they quickly left its wake behind. The sea abated and the Sun emerged to paint the water a sparkling Prussian Blue. Sturdee wished he'd brought his paints, if only to catch the colours.

"Come on deck" the midi bid him "We are about to oil at sea. We'll be in the way on the bridge, so I'll take you aft , up on C gun-deck. It should be reasonably dry up there."

"I haven't been dry since my trip to the bridge"

"There are not many dry men on a destroyer Giles. I'm sometimes soaked for weeks. Hazard of the trade I fear."

" Sturdee was shocked by how little freeboard the destroyer had aft. The ocean flew by seemingly only a foot or two below their feet.

"When I say, run like hell, and grab a stanchion if you hear a sea coming."

From C Gun deck Sturdee saw that they were rolling along beside a smallish tanker that was providing lee a mere tennis lawn or so away, the two ships masts rolling giddily together and away from one another. A line-throwing gun cracked from the tanker's bridge and a rope soared over the destroyer's deck where it was grabbed by her crew. The Walker's crew started hauling back, drawing a tall derrick out from the tanker with the oil-hose suspended from it in a large loop. The Walkers drew the hose on board and connected up.

"Looks tricky to me." Sturdy shouted.

"It is. It's our job to keep exact station, the tanker's to let in and out the loop to prevent the hose snapping. Look – they've started pumping. Everyone will be holding their breaths while this goes on."

"Aren't we vulnerable?"

"More than usual yes. But we are in the heart of the convoy. A U-boat is unlikely to get in here, while another destroyer is standing by."

"How long?"

"About an hour to fill our tanks: 400 tons. Then we can get all the way to Canada if ordered. It's a real revolution this refuelling at sea. Virtually doubles our effective destroyer strength."

With all of his destroyers re-bunkered MacIntyre relaxed:

"Let 'em come. We're ready. We've long lost our air escort of course. But we'll see how our new toy performs – Huff-Duff."

"High-frequency direction finding"

"It has been some time in gestation – but now they say it really works. What did you think of the refuelling?"

"If it really doubles the size of our destroyer fleet – then it's a battle winner I'd say."

"We can't survive without fast escorts. You've got to chase these buggers down: put them under, depths-charge and dept-charge them, then race back to the convoy. Corvettes can't do that and even these new frigates with their 22 knots will be marginal. But a 30-knot destroyer should put the wind up any U-boat commander. If we can afford to stay over a submerged U-boat for long enough we are bound to crack him open in the end. And by the way these refuelling tankers can also resupply us with depth-charges so we don't have to be mean."

When the news came through that the Escort was going straight on to Halifax Nova Scotia instead of turning back at Iceland everyone was delighted:

The midi explained: "We can take supplies to all the folks at home as well stuff ourselves with steak-dinners."

"What sort of supplies?"

"We've all got lists from home: there's food : decent leather shoes, cosmetics and silk stockings are very popular: fancy under-clothes, cigars, Scotch would you believe. Strictly speaking it's illegal, clogs up the ship– but any skipper who didn't look the other way would have a mutiny on his hands. It's almost the only perks we ever get. I intend to buy toys– makes me the most popular uncle in the land. The skipper I know always goes for a sack of onions. Turkey is a must be Christmas-time. Oranges. And what a girl will do for some frilly knickers…"

"I get the picture."

"You should make up your own list Giles. They'd never forgive you if you got back empty-handed."

"I've never thought…"

"Well start! A whole lot of new shops have sprouted just for the likes of us. You should hear them arguing in the wardroom about the best things to take home."

Sturdee always found McIntyre worth talking to. He was interested in the big picture, planning to study History after the war. Most of his naval career had been spent in the Fleet Air Arm but he'd had to give up flying for medical reasons. It was so cold on the bridge that they retired to McIntyre's Day cabin.

The ex-flyer wanted to know about the VLR aircraft problem which was still preying on Sturdee's mind:

"It was always fuilish to put maritime patrol in RAF hands. May as well have handed over our guns to the army, and asked soldiers to come aboard and fire them. Now our destiny, and the destiny of Britain, lies in other hands wi' other priorities. I'm surprised Churchill canna see what a folly it a' is."

Sturdee told him about Cherwell.

"Sounds like an old fuil. But he can't be entirely so. As a pilot I shall always be grateful to him for stopping the spin. But what makes anyone think bombing will bring Gaimany to her knees? Didn't bring us. Once we knew it was coming we went underground like rats."

"I don't know. They seem to take it for granted."

"Aye. That's often the way wi' untried weapons. They seem like miracles – until ye put them to the test in battle. Think of poison gas, or dreadnoughts. Both turned out to be duds. Ay, and what about Asdic? That was supposed to put an end to the U-boat – and Here we are 20 years later fighting for our lives. I never believed in that dictum of Baldwin's – what was it?"

" 'The bomber will always get through' ?"

"Aye. Where the hell did that come from? Seems to me a bloody great four engine bomber lumbering over Germany at barely 200 knots for hours on end will be easy meat. Jerry is nay fuil: if we can develop radar– so can he. And their fighter planes are equipped with cannons– unlike ours. One squirt wi' those and you're gone, so my pals in the Fleet Air Arm tell me. They should know; they've been up against them in the Med. It sounds very dicey to me. And for that we are to get nay long range aircraft for the Atlantic?"

"Apparently."

"If you ask me laddie – that's where you should attack them – Churchill, Portal and all…"

At that moment the intercom sprang to life: "Captain Sir. Radio officer here. We've just got a strong Huff-Duff signal from the starboard flank of the convoy. Definitely U-boat traffic: sounds like a sighting report."

"I'll be on the bridge immediately. Follow me Sturdee."

Before the Captain reached his station the TBS broke in: "Walker from Volunteer. We have strong Huff Duff signal bearings 347 degrees. Probably U-boat traffic" .

"Volunteer from Walker. We have Huff Duff also. Chase down bearing immediately. Navigator to plot an estimated range."

"Captain from Navigator. Wilco."

"Hydrangea from Walker : Close up to starboard flank position immediately. Replace Volunteer."

"Wilco from Hydrangea: Close up to Starboard flank immediately; replace Volunteer. Wilco."

"Captain from Navigator. Poor range estimate: 12 plus or minus 4 miles, 12 plus or minus 4."

"Volunteer from Walker. Range estimate 10 plus or minus 4 miles from your original position."

"Call action stations!"

A bell shrilled out and men poured out of the hull like ants escaping from a nest. From the wing of the bridge Sturdee watched the afterguard close up on the afterdeck around the depth-charge rails and throwers.

" Captain to crew. We have picked up a U-boat Radio emission from 12 miles to starboard. Volunteer is investigating."

McIntyre muttered to Sturdee as he focussed his binoculars on *Volunteer* rapidly disappearing in a cloud of spray: " Our first Huff Duff attack."

Apart from the steady ping of the Asdic the ship's company relaxed in to suspenseful silence, waiting for news from Volunteer.

"Any minute now." McIntyre muttered.

"Walker from Volunteer: surfaced U-boat 4 miles ahead."

A ragged cheer went up from Walker's crew.

"Walker from Volunteer: range 5,000 yards. Preparing to open fire."

"Will he hit it?" Sturdee asked.

McIntire shook his head: "Verra unlikely from that range. He'll probably try to close some more . Type VII U-boats can submerge completely in under 50 seconds."

"Walker from Volunteer: range 4000 yards."

Looking round at the weather-beaten faces Sturdee detected signs of silent prayer.

" Range 3000 yards: opening fire!"

"Walker from Volunteer: U-boat diving."

"Vanoc from Walker : standby to join Volunteer"

"Bluebell from Walker : Close up on Vanoc's station."

"Asdic contact! Walker from Volunteer. Asdic contact 1000 yards."

" Vanoc from Walker: join Volunteer immediate."

"Commodore from Walker: standby to execute Raspberry."

McIntyre explained: "We must assume the U-boat got our position and course away to Brittany who will now be directing other submarines to intercept us. So now our U-boat is submerged we'll execute a drastic change of course to put them off.

The Commodore at the head of the convoy will direct all ships by flag and semaphore. The freighters don't have TBS but we must keep radio silence at all costs. And in a few minutes Volunteer will be out of TBS range. But he knows we are going to Raspberry, so he should catch us up in due course."

"How long are you going to leave them out there on top of the U-boat?"

"If I called them in by wireless – which I would do in an emergency – I would give the convoy's position away, so this is where the Western Approaches Convoy Instructions come in . The senior officer out there will abide by those rules and return to the convoy accordingly. In the old days there'd be a bugger's muddle of radio traffic flying all over the place , most particularly to Doenitz's headquarters in Lorient. Now he'll be in the dark, and hopefully we'll sneak away."

" And what are the chances we'll sink the U-boat?"

"If they remain out there two hours: they'll make four attacks each per hour, dropping eight depth-charges per attack; that's 128 depth-charges. You can make your own guess."

"Better than even!" Sturdee exclaimed.

" Aye, that would be my guess too."

While they were all waiting for news Sturdee went into the wireless office to get a briefing on Huff Duff:

"The clever bit" the wireless officer explained "Is the bird-cage shaped aerial at the top of the mainmast. Without rotating it can still tell from which direction the signal has come. The problem up to now has been a shortage of time. The U-boats only transmit for about 20 seconds – which was too short for us to do much. But this new box of tricks does it all, more or less automatically." He put his hand fondly on an electronics rack about size of a bedside table:

"If she picks up a signal she rings an alarm bell. Now this cathode ray tube acts as the recorder. It's got a long-persistence phosphor. The signal appears as a glowing streak, like a compass needle on the dial. The point is it remains there long enough for the operater to read off the bearing on the compass rose. And that's basically it,; bobs your uncle. If you go racing down that bearing you catch your U-boat with his pants down."

"Range?"

"Early days yet. Depends on the atmospheric conditions. We often get two waves coming in – one direct, one reflected off the ionosphere. But pretty much any U-boat close enough to do us harm or report our position is going to give its own position way."

"This can change the whole course of the battle couldn't it?"

"We are hoping – we're certainly hoping. It's been years in development apparently. But when every escort vessel is fitted with one it could be a winner. We could then take cross bearings and get a precise position. We won't be so dependent then on aircraft to put out the eyes of the shadowing U-boat."

"Well thank you. It was worth coming all the way out here just to see this."

"Fingers crossed. Let's wait and see if Volunteer and Vanoc get the spying blighter. I wouldn't like to be inside his hull right now. A real underpants job I'd say."

There was a real sense of triumph throughout the fleet, particularly within the Escort group, when Volunteer and Vanoc screamed back to rejoin them ,Victory penants hoisted.

"I think we've seen a wee bit history Giles" McIntyre remarked, back in his day cabin: " Thank the Lord the Navy can find its own U-boats at last, wi'out the bluidy RAF."

CHAPTER 24

IN THE DRINK

Despite the terrors of the hurricane and the excitement of the U-boat chase Sturdee's mind had never strayed far from that fateful Atlantic Committee meeting in Churchill's bunker. They were to have no volunteer aircraft for the approaching showdown battle in mid-Atlantic, all because that Rasputin Cherwell had blinded Pound and Churchill using a cheap pseudo-scientific trick. Motivated as much by hatred as dismay Sturdee's brain had ever since been searching for a stratagem to show the man up, preferably in front of his all-powerful boss. There had to be one, he felt sure. Any man as sure of himself, and as superficial as Cherwell must be vulnerable to entrapment. But as Blackett had put it they needed to find a stratagem 'To snap the man's neck before he could squawk.'

But quite apart from Cherwell, whose cold black eyes, bald head and toothbrush moustache haunted his dreams, Sturdee felt very strongly that an idea, vital to the Battle of the Atlantic, was drifting about it in his head just below the level of consciousness. It was an experience, not uncommon among scientists who had spent months or even years struggling with some intractable problem. He felt both excited and infuriated. He was sure his mind wasn't playing a malicious trick. It knew something momentous that he didn't. More probably it had sensed the connection between two ideas or two facts that had entered his head from different sources. He'd been talking to and interrogating so many different people of late: Donald McIntyre, Patrick Blackett, Tony Loader, Andy Rees at Farnborough, Admiral Noble, Hanbury Brown, George McVittie, Rodger Winn .... Two previously disparate ideas had made a perfect contact deep in his brain, sending out powerful signals everywhere but to his conscious mind. Given time, years perhaps, the truth would become apparent, stealing into his mind , or in a flash of blinding insight. But time he did not have. All was converging towards the great 'Showdown Battle' as it was coming to be called, either in late 42 or more probably early 43. But the great decisions which would dictate the outcome would be made long before then, in the next few months or even weeks: 'What was it, what was it , what was it... .....?'

He was torn between two utterly opposing instincts: to relentlessly hunt the puzzle down, or to forget it altogether in the hope it would make itself known in its own good time. Given that his preoccupations of late had been the Convoy Equation, VLR aircraft and Fido – the acoustic torpedo – he suspected that the elusive connection must concern at least one of those and so he began a list of every item that had preoccupied him concerning them. But it didn't work.

'I might have guessed' he almost spat at himself in frustration.

" You aren't half talking to yourself when you're asleep." the Midi reported.

Sturdee explained the situation in detail, hoping thereby to release the dam – but that didn't work either. They were actually entering the harbour at Halifax Nova Scotia, with Sturdee on the bridge beside the captain, watching the preparations on the deck below to go alongside the quay when enlightenment struck him like an executioner's axe:

"My God – I must get back immediately!"

"What's that?"

"I'm sorry sir, I was talking aloud . But I've got to get back to Britain right away."

"I thought you were going to look at the Canadians?"

"I was. But I've had a really crucial idea and not a moment is to be wasted if we are going to exploit it. Not a moment. It could make all the difference."

"To what?"

"The Show-down battle."

"Well in that case… you are welcome to come back with us, but we're all hoping for a few days leave here first. Some of us haven't slept for a week… No one's had a bath in three weeks, and I don't know anybody in the entire Escort group with a shred of dry clothing. The Royal Canadian Navy are kindly putting us up in quarters ashore. And of course we've all got to do our shopping… Our families would never forgive us."

"Don't you worry about me sir, I'm sure I'll scrounge some sort of an early lift back home."

"With a face like that Giles , I wouldn't be so sure. You look like a real ruffian . I'll give you a note to the Port Captain which might help. Meanwhile you'd better come ashore with us. *Walker* will be completely deserted and under guard."

The pleasure of a hot bath and a seemingly enormous bed which didn't pitch and roll, of salt-free skin, of clean dry clothes, of hot food with fresh fruit and vegetables and of endless quiet, quiet, quiet… made Halifax Nova Scotia seem like the anti-room to Paradise. Sturdee even locked himself in the lavatory for half an hour to experience the forgotten luxury of solitude. When he went for a walk he lurched from side to side, anticipating Atlantic rollers that never came. He went shopping with Ralph, as the midi consented to be called while ashore, and bought silk underclothes for Gwen, an air rifle for Arfur to shoot the rabbits in the paddock, a Harris Tweed sports jacket for Loader, a roll of silk for Jean , and two bottles of his favourite Islay whiskey for Maurice, and for himself a pair of real leather shoes, a new slide-rule and some half decent paint-brushes. Ralph agreed to smuggle them back in the *Walker* and deliver them to the dry-cleaning shop. In return Giles drew a large cartoon of all the faces in the wardroom. Everybody laughed when they saw it and had copies made:

"I'll treasure it all my life" the midi said "You can't imagine. You know Giles, you're completely wasted as a boffin. We all think so."

"I will be if I don't get back to Blighty – and soon."

The Port Captain's Office sent for him where a harassed young man said:
"The best we can do for you Dr Sturdee is a berth on the Royal Canadian Navy corvette
the *Moose Jaw* leaving at 6 AM tomorrow morning, part of an Escort group to an East
bound convoy. They'll be going as far as the mid ocean meeting point then turning
back. The captain of the Moose jaw will do his best to transfer you to a Royal Navy
escort vessel going on with the convoy to Liverpool. But of course transfer will depend
on the weather. If the worst comes to the worst you could find yourself back here in
two weeks time."

"Okay, I'll have to take that risk. Many thanks."

They were a friendly lot aboard the *Moose Jaw*, and almost impossibly
young; even the skipper Jasper Mckendrick was younger than Sturdee: "Most of us had
never seen the sea until we took to it." he explained.

The *Moose Jaw* was a carbon copy of the *Pimpernel*, but built in Canada.
Too many Britons forgot that the Canadians had in both wars been their first and most
faithful allies. With almost no ships and no navy of their own to speak of, they had
built 50 Corvettes in tiny yards designed to turn out fishing vessels, and manned them
with green sailors and almost green officers. Somehow, with minimal training and
minimal equipment they had managed to take over the escort duties in the Western
Atlantic when the Royal Navy was so hard pressed in the East and in the Western
approaches. With none of the tradition or infrastructure of the Royal Navy it was almost
impossible for them to give their sailors anything more than a rudimentary training,
while their Asdic, their depth charges, and their radar– when they had any– was of the
most primitive kind.

Having little else to do Sturdee spent much of the time on the *Moose Jaw*'s
bridge as she fussed around her deep-laden convoy, loaded down to their plimsolls with
goods desperately needed by Britain. He spotted oil tankers from Trinidad who'd
managed to escape the slaughter off the American coast; refrigerator vessels from
Argentina and New Zealand, presumably carrying meat; Canadian grain carriers loaded
with the hard Manitoba wheat which the Britons favoured in their white bread; low
slung ore carriers with barely any freeboard; Americans with their decks loaded with
armaments, including tanks and aircraft.

"Pray they get through." The captain said.

"Amen to that."

"What's it like over there? Really like?" The Canadians all wanted to know,
preferring personal testimony to the so obvious propaganda of the broadcasting media.

Sturdee found himself struggling for a coherent reply: "I suppose we've all
got used to the war now. People do. We've defeated the bombers. There's just about
enough to eat. We are determined to get our own back on the Germans and defeat them
one day. Nobody knows exactly how, or when, but there's a widespread feeling that we

will. People work all hours of the day and night– with a sense of common purpose that we never had in peacetime. This is a good war with a moral purpose – not like the last. And that's bloody important. So we work like demons, including women, eat what we can, sleep when we can, listen to the news on the radio and generally follow Churchill's dictum 'Keep buggering on'– and thank God we are an island. The government isn't too bad– though they don't always tell us the truth. This Battle of the Atlantic for instance. Few people realise how desperate it is, or how much worse it could get. The Nazis are adding 20 new U-boats every month and we are sinking only two or three."

"Don't tell us. We can't sink a single one over this side. And the Yanks seem to be making a complete hash down South. Our admiral told us that Ernest J King – The Yankee admiral – is an unutterable bloody fool. Doesn't believe in convoy, pig ignorant of submarine warfare – and worst of all, won't take advice. A bloody know-all wasting away men's lives by the thousand. They say he's in drunken rage most of the time. And he absolutely hates the British."

"We've heard that too."

"In the pubs around Halifax there's talk of mutiny among some of the merchant seaman. Why should they sail with no escort, and with the bloody shore lights still all on? If enough of them refuse to sail, we're done. You can't make them. They're civilians. Half at least foreigners, Lascars, Dagoes, Portuguee, Greeks, Swedes...... it's not their war is it?"

"I wonder they've been so patient so far. I suspect it's mainly because most convoys still cross undetected. But that's not going to last – not with increasing numbers of German U-boats. This coming year is going to be desperate I reckon– especially for us Brits. We're very grateful to Canada for coming into the war so early. You didn't have to. Not like the Americans......."

"They're only in it for themselves – like as always. We are used to them. My folks left Pennsylvania after that so-called War of Independence and settled up near Lake Erie. We think of them as traitors. They was after Indian land assigned to the Indians by King George in return for the Indians' help against the French. It was land theft and treachery pure and simple, and they dressed it all up in bullshit as per usual. The 'Declaration of Independence'. .. bloody hogwash!... Hell – look at that fogbank rolling in."

Sturdee had seen nothing like it before . A white cloud swept up on them from the port side, swallowing the convoy, ship by ship, column by column. Fog horns began to blast all around them as vessels tried to locate one another in the whiteout. The *Moose Jaw* was soon entrapped, even her bow disappearing from sight from the bridge. The sound of fifty foghorns booming and echoing from all directions was terrifying. Wherever Sturdee looked it was easy to imagine a colossal oil tanker looming out of the sea-smoke to slice the tiny corvette in half. Eventually his nerves could stand it no longer. He descended to his bunk, put on his lifejacket, stuffed his ears with cotton wool and tried to sleep. He would rather have run the gauntlet of a wolfpack. The Newfoundland Banks were notorious for fog, which was one of the reasons U-boats tended to stay clear of them: the other being the intensely cold water coming down from the Arctic, which must have made life miserable for any sub-mariner immersed in it.

By the time the convoy emerged from the fog banks, everyone's nerves were shredded. Sturdees admiration for the cheerful young Canadian seamen who'd got them all through without a single collision was unbounded. He vowed to do everything he could to see that every Royal Canadian Navy Escort group was fitted with at least one Type 271 radar as soon as possible and urged the *Moose Jaw*'s officers to start campaigning volubly for them at once. The authorities, be they Canadian or British, had obviously decided that the Royal Canadian Navy was only fitted to perform one of the two roles of convoy escort – namely Concealment. The other – Protection–it was neither equipped nor trained to perform. So long as the U-boat cordon was sparse most Canadian-led convoys would sneak through it successfully, and the Canadian operation was very valuable. But once that cordon thickened up and wolf packs could be assembled, Sturdee could foresee slaughter on the Canadian side of the Atlantic on a massive scale. That day was approaching fast and the only practical remedy that he could see was very long range aerial support. Even with a wealth of professional officers it had taken the Royal Navy years to lick Escort groups into shape. It was too late now for the Royal Canadian Navy to follow suit – likewise the Americans.

It was absolutely essential for him to get back to Britain with all speed – so he decided to confide in Jasper McKendrick skipper of the *Moose Jaw*: "You've got to get me back onto a British ship when you turn round at the mid ocean meeting point" He insisted. "Even a two-week delay could be fatal."

"I understand" McKendrick said. "But it all depends on the weather. And for Christ's sake Giles we are getting close to the Arctic Circle in February. If the weather is really good we'll launch a boat naturally… more likely we will need to use a Breecher's Buoy – know what that is?"

"Not in detail".

"The British ship, which will be upwind, will fire a rocket line down over us. They haul it in dragging over a stronger cable from which you will be suspended in a kind of round lifebuoy-shaped chair. In you gets and they drag you across. In theory you will be well above the water. In practice you are likely to be dunked in the sea several times. And even that means moderately good weather because both ships will be rolling and pitching alongside one another, broadside on in heavy seas."

"And failing that – moderate weather?"

"If you are absolutely desperate you jump for it – into the sea downwind of the potential British rescue ship. She drifts down on you with scrambling nets over her side, and in theory you will eventually grasp one of those nets and climb aboard her. But rather you than me."

"Why?"

"Christ man, this isn't Brighton beach. That water down there is basically melting ice – zero degrees. You have about 3 minutes to make it across before you begin to pass out. And even if you grasp the net you may be too weakened by cold to climb. I have seen the poor devils from shipwrecks just clinging there struggling against cold and gravity before snuffing it. I try not to look any more. So near and yet so bloody far."

"Well I may have to try." Sturdee said

"What about your wife and family?"

"I don't have any. Anyway this is war. Everyone else is risking their lives – just because I'm a civilian doesn't make me exempt. Look at those poor buggers on the CAM ships. They're catapulted into the air in their Hurricanes to go and shoot down the Focke-Wolfs, but there's nowhere for them to land back afterwards, except in the drink.. How many of them ever survive?"

"Are you quite sure all this is so bloody urgent Giles?"

"I'm afraid it is. Yes it is. Look, I don't want to risk my life Jasper. Maybe I haven't got a wife and family – but there's things I want to do after the war."

" I guess we will have to pray for you Giles– Or better still pray for unseasonal weather. Hell, I'm the captain aren't I? I can hold a Sunday service... a bout of hymn singing always goes down well at sea."

True to his word Lieutenant McKendrick held a sabbath service on the afterdeck in amongst the depth-charge throwers. Such men as could be released from their duties sang 'Onward Christian Soldiers, 'Abide with me', and that most moving hymn of all 'For those in peril on the Sea' . An elderly stoker read the Lesson and the captain concluded by praying 'For the Weather and for the life of Dr Giles Sturdee our English guest on board the *Moose Jaw* who is soon going to risk his life by swimming across to a British vessel at the Mid Ocean Meeting Point." Everyone glanced briefly at Giles, who despite his atheism, had been singing with the best of them, then looked quickly away. The Service finished with a stirring rendition of the Lord's Prayer, which, like their hymns, carried across the grey seas to the crew of a British freighter nearby, some of whom joined in.

Despite their exhortation, the short days grew shorter and the winds and seas rose as the ships made their way North and East towards the Mid Ocean rendezvous. Sturdee wrote a long letter for Blackett which he gave to McKendrick to post in case he didn't make it.

With 24 hours to go, the encoded forecast from Iceland arrived:

"I'm afraid it doesn't look good Giles" McKendrick said." I've telegraphed our squadron commander about your predicament. As soon as the two convoys are within semaphore range he'll try to get one of the British ships to stand by to pick you up. Hopefully they'll have a proper rescue vessel with medical personnel on board."

"They usually do."

There was considerable debate in the wardroom as to what Sturdee should wear. Some clothing would definitely slow the process of Cold Shock and hypothermia but wet clothing could be very heavy and could make it impossible for him to climb the scrambling net. A compromise was agreed on ; they gave him a life jacket and plenty of advice. Being Canadians they knew about cold: "Whatever you do keep your mouth out of the water Giles . Many overboarders simply drown. The cold shock alone will make you gasp and suck in water."

"Should I swim ?"

"You'd use precious energy."

"But it will keep his circulation going, especially in his arms and legs and fingers. He's going to need those in the scrambling net."

"In the wind the boat will drift down on you far faster than you can swim. But swim anyway – for the circulation."

"We're going to make him a harness with a shoulder ring. If he's too weak to scramble up they may get a boathook in to it and haul him aboard."

"How strong are you Giles?"

"I've done a hell of a lot of wood-sawing of late. That should help."

"Should do."

"Make sure to grab the net at the bottom of the roll. If you try in mid -roll it will rip your shoulder sockets out."

"No you shouldn't. You should grab it on the down role ."

"Don't be a fool – he will be dragged under."

"Not for long."

"But he might be dragged under several times."

"I suppose."

"So it's the bottom of the roll Giles, and get your feet onto it, as well as your arms. And be prepared for a violent jerk and lift.".

"You're all making it sound impossible."

"They will try and fire a line from their ship. If they can we'll attach it to you. Then they can haul you across and up. Easy beezy."

"Let's just wait and see fellas. It's no good anticipating too much."

Sturdee didn't sleep much the night before the rendezvous: partly it was natural nervousness of the perilous transfer, but in addition he wondered whether he was being altogether sane. Would two weeks more or less make any real difference to the outcome of the war? Like many young men exempt from active-duty he felt strong twinges of guilt – and here was a chance to show his mettle – more to himself than to anyone else. But why did he need to? He was normally brave: if nothing else his climbing exploits in the Bernese Oberland had demonstrated that. There was no need to test himself again. And what if he drowned? At this stage of the war he probably knew more about the infant subject of Naval Operational Research than anyone else on the Allied side. Wasn't it foolish, indeed criminal to put it to unnecessary risk? Round and round the arguments went while another part of his mind was monitoring wind and sea.

He was on the bridge with McKendrick when the convoy spotted smoke on the Eastern horizon. They had a westerly gale behind them and a steep following sea. The freighters were hobby horsing up-and-down and rolling considerably.

"Are you still determined to go?" McKendrick yelled against the wind. Giles nodded.

"Not much chance of a Breeches Buoy in this. Look, you can see the mastheads of the British convoy when we're on the crest of a wave."

At a combined speed of 16 knots the horizon quickly filled with a total of 100 cargo vessels and over a dozen escort vessels.

"There is a semaphore message coming in for us from our escort leader Giles. It's probably about you." McKendrick yelled above the wind

The signalman presented his pad to McKendrick: "Yes it is. Transfer permitted. Sturdee. Moose Jaw close up on Royal Navy Rescue vessel 197 to centre rear Eastbound convoy. Moose Jaw to rejoin Westbound at 13:20 hours."

A pit opened up in Sturdee's stomach.

"Go below Giles and get your gear on. Keep warm and I'll send someone to your cabin when it's time." He held out his hand : "Good luck."

"Thanks for everything Jasper."

" We will try to get a line across– but in this wind…"

After what seemed like an eternity an able seaman came to get him. The ship was rolling hideously, obviously beam on to wind and sea. Out on deck they clung to the windward rail. To windward of them was a vessel larger than the Corvette, and moving in parallel, rolling hideously too. She looked like one of those Scottish inter-island ferries, all along her side were what looked like thick fishing nets dangling into the sea. About 50 yards of grey heaving sea separated the two vessels. The rolling was so violent that it took all of the strength in his arms merely to hold on and inch aft in pursuit of the seaman.

A loud crack drew his head up and he saw a line flying towards them in the wind from the other ship and over their heads. The seaman lumbered across the deck to retrieve it , signalling Sturdee to carry on aft.

Another burly seaman joined them and between them they secured the end of the line to the stainless steel ring on Sturdee's harness. Then the AB shouted in his ear: "Now sir, over the rail and face this way."

Somehow with one seaman holding the rope and using the brief intervals between rolls, they got Sturdee over the rail on his stomach and facing inboard, feet braced wide apart on the ships gunwhale , hands locked to the upper rail.

The AB yelled at him again: "When you're ready, at the bottom of the roll, take a deep breath and leap outwards and back. Get away from the ship as fast as you can. They will haul you in."

Sturdee nodded, trying to collect himself, struggling not to let go with either hand or foot because then he would be dashed face-first into the rail or into the hull. His upper arms needed every ounce of their strength.

Up, up, up they rolled, gravity pushing him inboard staring at the two sailors facing him but hanging backwards from the rail. They poised briefly at the top with scarcely weight enough to keep his feet in place, then down, down, down with momentum pulling out at his arm sockets, until they briefly stopped, seemingly just above the reaching waves.

Up, up again they went for the last time, poised in the air, and as they swung back Sturdee took breath, waited for the roll to stop, and leapt outward and back from the *Moose Jaw*.

Because of the salt in them polar waters can drop well below freezing point and as they closed above his head Sturdee almost screamed at the agony. But not quite. He knew the danger of sucking in seawater and waited to surface before gasping in air. Fortunately the cork lifejacket had prevented him going deep but he certainly screamed when he came up – as much in terror at the sight of the *Moose Jaw's* colossal hull hobby-horsing inches away from his skull, as at the biting cold. He turned away and struck out frantically for the other ship.

After a few strokes which scarcely got him anywhere he saw the orange line going taut and felt a steady pull acting on his harness. They were reeling him in. A rush of water went right over his head but he fought successfully not to swallow any. He took in as much air as he could, to make his body more buoyant, raising his mouth a vital extra centimetre or two above the surface, at the same time he tried to lean backward in his life jacket to the same purpose. The agony had gone out of his lower body; presumably the pain nerves had numbed off. His feet indeed didn't seem to exist. He could still move his fingers but it couldn't feel them much either. He'd need those. He held them up a trifle, trying to keep them out of the freezing water.

The rescue ship, which looked absolutely enormous, was bearing down on him rapidly. He twisted his neck and saw that the Moose Jaw was some way off and forging ahead. He turned back and, knowing he would need to think while his brain was still warm enough to do so. What had they said? Two or three minutes of consciousness in Arctic Waters. He must have lost more than a minute already. He struck out with both arms and both legs to maintain the circulation for as long as possible
.

There were men up there on the rail looking down at him, waving encouragement. But he was beginning to feel faint; he wanted to vomit. It was getting calmer though, he was in the lee of the rescue vessel which was like an enormous rolling cliff above his head. His orange line was climbing out of the water pulling him upwards. towards the wet black scrambling nets. He put out a hand and nearly had   his arm wrenched clean out of its socket. The pain in his shoulder was agonising. He did vomit. What was it the Canadians had said? 'Bottom of the roll !'. That was it: "You must grab the nets with both hands *and* feet at the bottom of the roll." He felt really faint now like when he was a boy that time. Yes , now he could see the scrambling was racing up and down as the ship rolled her guts out.

Up and down. Up and down. He didn't feel he could do it. His feet had disappeared. His hands were weak. He wanted to sleep. But what about Arthur… Joan… and Gwen/? He ought to try just for them. Down the net came with a rush into the water beside him. It stopped. He reached out and felt it. The orange line went rigid as a bar, forcing him into the net. Then up it went , with him hanging on by his good arm and one foot stuck in a rung..

"Get your other foot in !" Somebody's screamed, and he managed to, taking some of the weight. But before you they could rescue him the ship rolled back, and down he plunged , taken underwater by the net. Then up again bursting for breath, then down, then up then down until he let go and the lights went out.

"Close run thing" Joan said. Or was it Joan. It couldn't be Joan she was in Duff House and he was here. But where was here? It wasn't Halifax, and it wasn't the *Moose Jaw* .

"Body temperature's up to normal Sir."

"You know I've seen this fellow before somewhere – and not so long ago."

"Rescued him before ? It happens."

"I don't think so. Do you know anything about him?"

"Only a name." The sick-berth attendant looked at the bed head: "Dr Giles Sturdee."

"Good Lord! I do know him. Giles. Of course. He's a lodger in my sister's house in Liverpool."

"Joan." Sturdee said it in a whisper.

"My dear chap. How do you feel? I'm Gordon Duff – do you remember?"

"Where am I?"

"In the sick bay of her majesties Rescue Vessel the HMS *Carmarthen Bay*. I am the medical officer aboard . We hauled you out of the sea yesterday: more dead than alive. Only the herculean efforts of Able Seaman Cully Jones saved you for posterity. How do you feel?"

"Got a nasty pain in my left shoulder."

"Dislocation probably. We'll look at it later ."

"Why am I so warm?"

"Warm water- bottles. You had hypothermia. We thought we'd lost you ,didn't we Evans?"

"We did sir. Like a ham just out of a freezer-chest you was."

"How long was I unconscious?"

Sturdee had opened his eyes and could see they were in an all-white, well-equipped sick-bay. He recognised Gordon Duff.

"I don't think you were really truly out, not for long. Mostly sleeping, recovering from shock."

"Will I have suffered any brain damage?"

"Ah yes you're a boffin as I recall. Joan told me. Rather unlikely I'd say. Do you remember what happened?"

Sturdee responded by explaining aloud in mind-numbing detail. Gordon Duff declared his brain to be in perfect working order.

"Where are we bound?" Sturdee asked next.

"You'll soon be tucked up in bed in Duff House, Liverpool."

The following night a loan U-boat managed to penetrate the convoy's guard from astern and sink three ships, including an ammunition carrier and an oil tanker, with a single salvo of torpedoes.

The fearful detonation of the ammunition ship drew everyone on the *Carmarthen Bay*, including Sturdee with only one working arm, on deck. By the brilliant white light of dozens of snowflake rockets and parachute flares they watched the ghastly spectacle in horror. The front of the ship had vanished, presumably in the initial detonation, but the stern was burning fiercely, setting off explosion after explosion which blew huge chunks of wreckage high into the sky.

"Look ,look, look…there's poor bastards on the afterdeck trying to launch a boat."

"They're jumping over the sides…"

"Oh my God…"

"Christ, the forrard davit has gone … they're falling into the sea."

"We've *got* to go and rescue them…"

"It's too bloody dangerous with all that falling debris…"

"We can't leave them to die…"

"I can't look…"

"Those murdering fucking German swine…"

" Oh NO!… Please god… Oh no…"

Sturdee was horrified by what he saw that night, permanently scarred in his memory. He begged aloud for the men on the ammunition ship to die as quickly and mercifully as possible. He stood by the scrambling nets later when the *Cardigan Bay* rescued most of the 50 or so crew of a grain ship from the lifeboats they had managed to launch. Worst of all was the burning tanker who's crew, swimming for their lives, were overwhelmed one by one as the escaping oil caught fire and spread outward across the sea. The captain risked the *Cardigan Bay* by dashing into an embayment within the burning oil to snatch the last half a dozen swimmers before the oil got to them. Crewman leapt overboard to help the weakest swimmers into the scrambling nets. They retched as they were hauled over the rail, choking with the foul smelling crude oil they had ingested in their desperation.

"Many of those poor sods will die on board." Somebody whispered in Sturdee's ear "I've seen it all before."

"We must be visible here from miles around." another of the crew said: "I hope the skipper doesn't hang around much longer."

Sturdee, who had been moved into a two-berth cabin by himself , couldn't sleep that night. The horrors he had seen and heard and smelt had no explanation, no redeeming feature, no quittance, no consolation, not even the promise of an eventual end. The Germans would go on torpedoing as long as they had a U-boat left afloat. We would go on depth charging them until the last U-boat man was crushed by the depths of the ocean. And in the mean time husbands, fathers and sons would drown or burn or freeze , sobbing for their mothers , and cursing their pointless fate and God as they died.

At breakfast Sturdee sat opposite an exhausted looking Gordon Duff.

"How do you stand it?"

'Stand what?"

"The sights we saw last night."

"I didn't see them. One night on deck in a burning convoy was more than enough for me. I lost my religious faith there and then. There is no god. There cannot be. Joan was shocked and so was our mother. Now I wait down in the sick bay and do my best to save their lives or at least ease their suffering at the end. I pump them out, dress their burns, give morphine, and tell them, honestly or not, that they are going to live." He glanced at his watch: "In an hour's time there will be at least three burials at sea. But I won't be there. That's the Padre's job, poor devil."

"I'm sorry Gordon, I shouldn't have asked. I'm not trying to pry. I guess I'm asking for help – or for hope. Can one forget – or ever sleep again?"

"Most people do. Eventually. My advice to you Giles is force it out of your mind as soon as possible. Lock it out. Pretend it was a nightmare. I know that's not fashionable in Freudian circles – but what the hell do they know?"

"Has that worked for you?"

"Yes…. yes it has. I never talk about it. I walk away when anyone else tries to. That enables me to get on with my job – which is not entirely pointless."

"Of course not."

"We manage to save a few fathers, husbands and sons down there in the sickbay. Try this marmalade. What were you planning to take back to Joan from Halifax?"

Sturdee explained about his consignment on the *Walker*.

"Isn't she wonderful – Joan?"

Sturdee didn't quite know what to say.

"We're hoping she's not going to marry that fellow Des. Nice enough chap – admirable in fact. But Joan's extra ordinary. She needs a chap with an imagination as big as she's got, another dreamer of dreams. John and I think she's sweet on you, only she doesn't realise it."

Sturdee shook his head negatively.

"Well, you'd be the last to know about it Sturdee – except her. She's one of those who can't see the trees for the forest – if you know what I mean: a big heart, a colossal brain but defective specs. That's what our bigger brother David always says. Have you met him?"

"Not yet, but Joan often talks about him."

"She idolises Dave. He says she is not fit to find a husband for herself – we'll have to find one for her. God knows we tried before the war. But she's looking for some demi-god."

"She's a bit of a goddess herself" Sturdee said, trying to smile: "You've got to admit."

"Well exactly. Tall, gorgeous, with a mind of her own. Where are we going to find an equal – or better still a superior? And what's worse is that she's always preferred strong men – like Dad – or Dave. Men who won't take any nonsense from her."

"Well, you are you asking for an impossible combination I'd say."

"Don't we know. But Joannie is someone very special Giles. She deserves somebody very special – and in her heart she knows it poor thing. She wasn't brought on Earth to be ordinary, or to lead an ordinary life. You know she's knocking thirty ? She'd make an amazing wife and mother – if ever she can find a mate."

"She's found him – the bloody War Hero."

Gordon laughed: "You know what she sees in him? He's not there. He's a god-pilot in the sky, thousands and thousands of miles away. She can imagine him doing impossibly heroic and god-like deeds. When she sees him picking his nose – or worse still washing the car of a Saturday morning, poor old Des will crash and burn – in Joan's estimation. She wants someone who will make her think, make her change her mind, surprise her, shock her even. She 'd prefer a chap who'd give her a black eye to one who would bore her, or act too predictably. I'd say you are far more her cup of tea than Des is Giles – but she's too much of a bloody dreamboat to see it."

Sturdee explained about the nude painting.

"That's interesting" , Duff nodded: "Joan is a bit of a prude; gets it from Mum. But she hardly ever loses her temper. Did you sleep with the girl?" Sturdee nodded.

"Well there you are Giles " Duff broke into a big smile, reminiscent of his sister's: "She's plain bloody jealous, that's what. Women can sniff out these things a mile off. And do you know what? I've never known Joan to be jealous before. She's not that type. She's always thought she is more attractive than any other woman. Now she's not so sure."

He stood up, looking haggard once again.

"I'm going below to see how my surviving patients are doing. If you haven't seen a burial at sea you should go out on the afterdeck in a few minutes. I find it very moving. After hundreds of years of practice His Majesty's Royal Navy knows exactly how to order these things."

CHAPTER 25
A CHANGE OF HEART

Dressed as he was in in odds and ends from the slop-chest of the *Carmarthen Bay* Sturdee took a taxi from the Gladstone Dock directly to Duff House. It was mid-morning but fortunately Arfur was home to let him in:

"Cor Giles, what you dun your fice – an' yer arm?"

"I've been fighting."

"Anyone can see that. An' your cloves?"

"They're mostly on a Canadian Corvette called the *Moose Jaw* about 3,000 miles from here. That's why I've come home to put on some decent clothing. I'm going to go to London in an hour or two."

"Oh no! You been away so long."

"I'll be back."

"She's forgive yer."

"Who has?"

"Joan o' course."

"Good Lord… Why? "

"I made her come up to your studio and look at the pitture."

"Good heavens!"

"Are yer angry?"

"No; why? What did she say?"

"Nuffink. She just stood and stared at it Giles– wiv 'er marf open. Then she sat on the bed and cried. I never 'eard 'er cry before … not like that….. sobbin' an all."

"She must've said something."

"When she stopped – an' blew 'er nose an' that , she said: 'What a little fool he must think me Arfur. He is much bigger'n me isn't ee?' I didn't know what to say Giles. Then she says, fierce as anything, like it was all my fault: 'We've gotter make 'im stay Arfur. You go to, 'cos he listens to you.' And I do want you to stay Giles. You know that. We was all so happy before this 'appened…". The boy left the question hanging in the air.

"I'll think about it. I hate being bossed about though, or controlled. We were happy though – you're right."

"Shall I tell Joan?"

"No!" Sturdee snapped "Don't even tell her we talked about the picture. But you did the right thing Arfur – taking her to see it. Clever lad."

"I fort you might be cross?"

"Well I'm not."

"She said it should hang up where everyone can see it. 'It'll be famous one day' she says. She even brought Maurice up to see it."

Sturdee laughed. "What did he say?"

"He gorped at it – like what she did. Then 'ee says, snooty like: "I rather fink my deah, clever though he undoubtably is , that young Sturdee is in the wrong perfession.""

"Cheeky old devil. Now I must pack. You can help me. I can only use the one arm. I'll be back in a day or two."

Blackett saw him first thing in the morning: "You *have* been in the wars Sturdee"

"Mainly hurricane damage sir."

"So why the extreme hurry?"

"I think we've got them – Lord Cherwell and the Bomber boys."

"Go on."

"I feel such a fool. It was in my head all the time; I just didn't make the right connection."

"Happens all the time."

"Do you remember that mini blitz back in January?"

"Vaguely."

"The Germans sent a smallish force against Liverpool – amongst other places."

"Oh yes. It was never repeated."

"And do you know why? Because virtually all their bombers who came in any distance from the South Coast were shot down by our night fighters – either on their way in, or more often on their way back out."

"Were they?"

"My ex-colleague Hanbury Brown developed the night-fighter radar system under Dowding, and he analysed the results afterwards. Chain-Home radar picked up the incoming bomber streams well before they crossed our coast. Then more precise ground-control-interception sets further inland selected out individual bombers and guided our Bristol Beaufighter night-fighters onto their tails. When they were within 2 miles the night fighters' own radars took over. They then sneaked up from behind and below and opened up their four Hispano-Suiza cannons from close range. With 20 mm shells exploding on contact the bombers simply disintegrated. It was slaughter. According to Hanbury most bombers could never have known what hit them."

"I see. But I'm not sure I get your point Giles."

"Don't you see – Cherwell, Portal and Churchill are all assuming that our bombers will get through and wipe out Germany. But they won't! If our night fighters can slaughter their bombers – as they can now, then the reverse will soon be true."

"But they don't have the Cavity Magnetron."

"Exactly what I thought. But here's the rub. Hanbury's system – I worked on it myself – was developed *before* the magnetron. It uses valves entirely. And the Germans are still aces at valve-based radar. If we got ahead of them temporarily it was only because radar is primarily a defensive weapon, and we were defending whilst they were attacking. Once the boot is on the other foot you can be sure they'll develop valve-based airborne radar as good as anything we've got. It was Heinrich Hertz remember who first developed radio back in 1877, and they haven't lost their touch."

"Are you telling me Sturdee that our bomber offensive is doomed?"

"In the long run yes. Long flights over enemy held territory to targets like Berlin will be suicidal . All the Germans have to do is relocate their vital industries, such as aircraft production, further East. If you ask me our four-engine long-range night bomber is another one of those untested miracle weapons like the super-battleship. Harris, Churchill, Portal and Co are ignoring their own night fighting lessons. They are hypnotised by a shibboleth. Bomber Command could easily lose more four-engine aircraft in a single sortie to Berlin then we need to win the entire Battle of the Atlantic."

"You put it dramatically."

"It is dramatic – in my opinion Sir. That's why I raced back across the Atlantic."

"Have you any idea how we could change minds?"

"Politics is not my strong suit…"

"But…"

"Portal is the crucial link. As the Prime Minister said, you remember :   ' They're all your bloody aeroplanes Portal – what do you want to do with 'em?' "

"I remember."

"And Portal shouldn't have a prejudice against Coastal Command. He's in charge of it after all – as he is in charge of Bomber Command. He ought to be able to take a dispassionate view on the disposition of aircraft between his two commands. It's not as if he's battling the Navy."

"True."

"And if we can turn Portal then we've won. Pound would of course support him and we'll have the majority of the Chiefs of Staff."

"And General Brooke would probably support them – making it unanimous."

"Would the PM overrule them?"

" That I cannot say. I'll try to find out. The immediate question is how do we turn Portal? Remember Giles I carry no weight in the Air Ministry any more. Indeed, so far as they're concerned, I'm now part of their mortal enemy – The Admiralty."

"If it's to be an inside job then someone from Night Fighter Command should approach Portal. Hanbury-Brown, based at Farnborough, would be superb. You have to meet him immediately sir. Then he might persuade Portal to carry out an exercise where a portion of Bomber Command tries to penetrate our own night fighter screen. If they fail we will have a very strong case."

"You've thought of it all haven't you Sturdee?"

"I've just seen three of our ships being torpedoed." He relayed the ghastly scene to Blackett in some detail, not knowing that Blackett had witnessed similar horrors in the First World War.

"That swine Cherwell should take a trip on a convoy rescue vessel." he concluded bitterly.

Despite his hopes expressed to Arfur, Sturdee remained for over two weeks in Whitehall. The Admiralty was close to despair over the totally unnecessary haemorrhaging of its tonnage off the American shore. Blackett's Circus wanted to hear about the impact of the Type 271 Radar and Huff Duff on the convoy battle. And in turn Sturdee tried to influence some top brass into equipping the Canadians better.

Sturdee eventually scrounged a lift back to Liverpool in the Walrus, arriving back at the house at noon when only Arfur was home. He'd dispensed with his sling and as Arfur instantly pointed out:

" Your fice is nearly normal again Giles."

Apparently Gordon Duff had been staying with them for the past fortnight before going back to sea again:

" 'e said you'd been an 'ero an' jumped in the Arctic Ocean and nearly froze to deff."

"Nonsense: that was the only way to transfer from ship to ship."

"Well 'e said so, an' ee should know 'cos ee was there."

"I was there too don't forget."

"No you wasn't cos you conked out. Gordon said some sailor 'ad to dive in the sea and fish you out, 'more dead 'n alive' he said. And look at them kitbags – arrived for you yesterday."

"Good Lord – the *Walker* must've got back from Halifax. There's a present in there for you Arfur."

"Cor."

After lunch they took the 22-calibre air- rifle down to the paddock where Arfur duly shot a rabbit. By the time Joan and Maurice arrived back from work a rabbit casserole was bubbling gently in the oven."

"Heavenly!" Joan said, lifting the lid and taking in the aroma: "You seasoned with parsley and thyme – and if I'm not mistaken with a rasher of bacon."

"I shot it and skinned it an' paunched it meself." Arfur boasted: "Giles taught me. And we can have one every week can't we Giles?"

"As long as the poachers don't find out. Don't tell a soul about our rabbits – not a soul."

" Bless the Lord God of hosts!" Maurice, still in his raincoat, had lowered his bony knees to the kitchen floor and was clasping his hands theatrically to Heaven.

"What on Earth are you doing Maurice?" Joan sounded like a headmistress.

"For his servant has seen the promised land – or more to the point – if he is not deluded – he has seen a bottle, nay two bottles of the finest Laphroaig Whiskey from the blessed Isle of Islay."

"No he's not deluded." Sturdee laughed. "Furthermore they've sailed all the way from Scotland to Halifax Nova Scotia and back again, escorted by the ships of His Britannic Majesty's Royal Navy. And they are both for you."

"Dear boy! Help me to my feet Arfur – I must hug my deliverer."

When that was done Arfur insisted on showing off his air rifle by firing a shot and hitting a tree trunk in the darkening garden.

Joan barely looked at Sturdee, but blushed when he gave her the roll of pale blue silk.

"Whatchyer going to do wiv it Joan?"

"Never you mind you nosy devil. And get me some potatoes out so I can peel them. We're going to have a feast to celebrate. How about a stewed-gooseberry pie with custard?"

"I prefer raspberries."

"I wasn't asking you, I was asking Giles. He's our returning hero."

It was quite like the old days, that evening round the kitchen table. The rabbit casserole was declared to be delicious, the equal if not superior of their harvest festival feast while Maurice made a great fuss over his Laphroig, an opinion from which the other three dissented: "It smells like bloody seaweed." Sturdee complained.

"It's meant to!" Maurice was indignant.

"I'd rather have a glass of Joan's sloe gin."

"Me too." Arfur agreed.

"You'll be lucky my lad."

"He can share a sip of mine."

" What's he doing here?" Maurice pointed to Higgins who had just leapt up onto a nice warm shelf above the Rayburn stove.

"Ee's allowed." Arfur was indignant. "Isn't he Joan? But I puts 'im out last fing and he sleeps wiv Gem. Feeds hisself 'e does – on mice. And he's a good ratter. Caught a big un in the chicken house 'e did – was likely eatin' our iggs."

Of course they all wanted to know about Sturdee's voyage. He did his best to convey the awesome nature of the hurricane, realising as he did so that it was impossible:

"You know the worst thing in retrospect wasn't the monstrous waves curling, toppling miles above the ship as they rolled towards us, even Captain McIntyre had to look away sometimes – nor was it the violence which did in my face – and you should see the black and yellow bruises on my back – no it was that noise – the demented, moaning, malevolent screeching of the storm as it howled through the rigging and battered the superstructure. You can't imagine, and I cannot describe how threatening it was, hour after hour, day after day; night after night, higher and ever higher in pitch , promising you personal destruction. It was.... vindictive... Like a torturer determined to break your very soul..."

" I hope it doesn't put you off sailing dear boy."

"I thought about that too Maurice. Let's hope. Time heals they say."

He had to tell them about his swim, recalling above all how tiny he had felt between the two oceangoing vessels: "Ships don't usually remain stationary beam on to a big sea, and you can see you why. They literally roll their guts out from almost capsizing one way to almost capsizing the other. I could see their slowly turning propellers, and the red lead paint on their keels. It was mad. You think 'I'll never grab hold of that scrambling net – it will tear me into pieces..' And it nearly did. If they hadn't tightened the orange lifeline at exactly the right instant I'd have had my left arm literally torn out of its socket."

"Don't Giles please. It makes me feel sick." Joan had closed her eyes and was shaking her head.

"Sorry. I got carried away. It's all coming back now that I'm comfortably at home. Perhaps I shouldn't tell you about the torpedo attack? That was much worse."

But they insisted, even Joan whose four brothers were all at sea, potential victims of just such an attack themselves.

Recalling that Arfur's father had been lost at sea on a tanker Sturdee left the burning oil tanker out. He said a few words about the exploding ammunition ship, concentrating mainly on the evacuation of the grain ship where everyone was rescued.

"Most people *are* rescued." he tried to reassure Joan. "After all the merchant seamen are all civilian and could refuse to put to sea. And the escort vessels and the rescue-ships which your brothers serve on are too small and too nippy for the U-boats to fire at."

"My eldest brother Dermot is the captain of big freighter."

"I'd forgotten him."

"He's supposed to be passing through the Panama Canal with a cargo of Australian wool."

"Christ" Sturdee said, but beneath his breath: "He'll just be running the gauntlet off the American coast."

Sturdee was lying in bed, preparatory to going off to sleep when there was a timid knock on his door:

"It's me Joan. Can I come in?"

He told her sit on the end of the bed because his chair was covered in clothing and he didn't have any pyjamas on.

She sat sideways onto him, looking at her knees:

"Please don't say anything Giles. This is going to be very painful for me... I don't know if I can go through with it..."

" I'll look the other way if you like..."

"Yes ... yes do... please."

"Go on."

"I've come to ask you to stay here with us... And to apologise for my appalling behaviour."

"Joan..."

"Hush Giles... You promised!"

"I did."

"I don't know what came over me. I feel bitterly ashamed now. I go red every time I think about it. I behaved like a spoiled teenage frippet."

"Joan..."

"Hush!" Then she went on: "The truth is – as I can see now– is that I was jealous. I... I tried to cover it up with a hypocritical show of prudery, but the truth was that I didn't like to think of you being in my house with a naked woman. Now I've said it !"

She let out an immense sigh as if she'd lifted a heavy weight off her chest. It was some moments before she resumed:

"I would never have been forced to see the truth if Arfur hadn't begged me to look at your painting. I don't suppose you realise Giles how wonderful it is. How could anybody imagine – even for a moment, as I wanted to imagine – that you would paint anything smutty. Anyone would be proud to be portrayed as you have painted Gwen. Of course you... you've slept with her – that's obvious. But why shouldn't you? What business was it of mine to think otherwise? You were saying thank you to her in the very best way that a highly talented painter could. You immortalised her for giving you an overwhelming gift that you will never forget, her body and with it her blessing and affection. I think the painting will be famous one day – and so does Maurice. Why? Because it is the tribute of every man to every woman who has shown him, out of the goodness of her heart, the way to earthly paradise. I think Gwen must be the very first woman you've slept with. No you don't have to answer Giles. And you know she slept with you more for your own sake than for hers, and you found the experience sweeter than you ever imagined... Overwhelming. And your painting is an inspired gift of thanks. You'll probably never be able to paint another as powerful as that – because you'll never be able to feel quite the same again – not even after your wedding night."

"I don't know…"

"I felt so small when I saw your painting Giles, so mean, so bourgeoise, so insignificant, so second rate. Who was I to pass judgement on you – or Gwen? I've made so many people miserable too – you, Maurice and especially Arfur. I wanted to rush straight to my Confessor– but then I thought. 'That's too easy Joan; you've got to confess to Giles!' So here I am."

"Okay but…"

"I haven't finished. I've been rehearsing this for days. Please let me say it all…"

"Very well."

"Of course it means something doesn't it? Obviously I wanted you for myself. I was jealous. And that's wicked. I'm engaged to Desmond. I love him and we will certainly be married one day when this wretched war is over."

"Joan I don't want to…"

"Let me finish Giles! You promised… so I want you to stay here… for all our sakes. We did have a happy little family here didn't we… before I spoiled it all? Our home from home out of the war. I was happy I know. You were happy Giles – admit it . Maurice was happy – and what about Arthur? If only for his sake we should stay together. Poor little mite, he cried his heart out. Where is he to go if not with us? He trusted us and I've betrayed him."

"But Joan I'm in love with you."

"I know" she turned towards him: "I know. And I must be a little bit in love with you Giles – otherwise I wouldn't have behaved so badly would I?"

"I suppose not."

"So what I'm saying is that if you can bear to live with with me, I can bear to live with you, both of us being a bit in love with one another, but knowing it must come to an end one day. There is nothing unique about us: nothing new. Millions of couples have had to put up with situations like this over the centuries. Secretaries in love with their happily married bosses. Unhappily married husbands besotted by their attractive sisters-in-law. Close friends in love with each other's spouses. It's one of the oldest stories in the world. Civilized people can manage it, have managed it for the sake of harmony and happiness, other peoples' as well as their own. Maybe it's bittersweet – but bittersweet is far better than nothing at all – at least I think so Giles . I will be much happier here if you are here too. I hope you'll be much happier here than alone in some wretched digs. We *are* close friends – even if we can't be lovers?"

"Yes. I missed you like anything."

"And I was desolate. If you'd been drowned I would have felt like a widow – and if that's wicked I can't help it. Please stay Giles, please."

"Okay – for now anyway."

"Oh Giles…" She threw yourself on top of him: "I can hug you can't I?" She didn't wait for permission.

"No kissing…" He laughed, half smothered: "Anything two men can do we can…"

"I'm so happy Giles I could cry."

"Permission granted. But wait a mo' there's one strict condition."

"What?" She sat up, sounding alarmed.

"I don't want to hear one bloody word more about Des. If you want to talk about him talk to Maurice or Arfur – but not in my presence. And don't read out any of his blasted letters in my hearing. Is that agreed?"

Joan nodded – biting her lip:

"Only in return will you do one thing for me Giles?"

"Depends."

"Not painting Gwen without her clothes on in our house. I'm not trying to stop you sleeping with her elsewhere. I have no right. And you probably should. It will be better… better for us."

He didn't say anything. He wasn't going to give up painting nudes – not even for Joan

"Giles" Joan had turned bright crimson and was looking at her knees again. "Yes?"

 "I know you can't give up painting. You shouldn't anyway, it would be a crime. If you want to paint a woman in your studio you… you can paint me. I'll take off all my clothes if you want to want me to – everything."

He didn't know what to say.

"Please say something Giles."

"It's a very handsome offer Joan. And I shall certainly think about it. When I can get my hands on a large enough piece of canvas I'd like to do a life-size replica of the Rokeby Venus – Velasquez's masterpiece."

CHAPTER 26
ACROSS THE POND

The comfortable old life at Duff House resumed. The family all lingered around the kitchen stove in the evenings after dinner talking, while reading aloud to Arfur later on became a communal activity in which even Maurice participated – although he did tend to break off and deliver himself of overlong learned disquisitions. Sturdee and Joan kept a studied but comfortable distance apart, avoiding the too intimate tete-a-tetes which had contributed to their recent crisis. And as the evenings lengthened so the garden became once again a market garden. Two new young Saddleback porkers, Ceasar and Augustus took up residence in the pigsty while Joan was raising a tiny piglet called Bodicea on the bottle in the house. Gem and Arfur were slowly ploughing up more of the paddock in hopes of an even greater harvest of onions. Joan's job, and Maurice's were vastly easier now that bombing had ceased and the transport infrastructure had largely been repaired:

"I'm getting quite bored." Joan complained. "With no blitzes I'm becoming dispensable. Do you think they'll resume Giles?"

"I'd lay 50 to 1 against. The RAF has licked the German night-bomber using secret weapons. Baldwin's dictum that 'The bomber will always get through' has proved to be a shibboleth – thank goodness."

"No doubt the Germans will develop secret weapons of their own." Maurice commented.

"Yes – I suppose so. Perhaps I'm being too sanguine. Say 30 to 1 against then."

"So, I'm going to concentrate on the garden." Joan said: "I hate to think I'm not contributing to the war effort when our brave sailors are still drowning in their thousands out at sea. I 've heard rumours that we lost 300 ships in December. I worry about my oldest brother Dermott – whose ship is in transit from Australia right now."

Sturdee was confident that he understood the Battle of the Atlantic at last. That Britain *could* win it he was pretty sure. The Type 271 radar had robbed the submarine of its chief weapon – darkness. Noble's Support Groups, armed with the new deep-setting depth charges would be able to sink U-boats because at last they would have the time and the weapons to do so, while Huff- Duff would greatly assist them in finding victims. Doenitz's only hope lay in overwhelming convoys with huge wolfpacks. But concentrating those large packs would mean U-boats shadowing a convoy for days while constantly using radio. VLRAs could put an end to that – provided they were made available in time. And that was the big doubt so long as Bomber Command, with its promise to reduce Germany to rubble, hogged the Prime Minister's imagination, and consequently the supply of four engined aircraft.

Modern warfare was so much a matter of measure, countermeasure and counter-countermeasure Sturdee reflected , and that in turn relied on the flexibility of government. If a government could learn quickly, then alter its stance intelligently, it had so much the better chance of winning. When it came to Britain versus Germany he was confident that Britain would hold a big advantage in that department. The proliferation of scientific committees, and the influence they carried in Whitehall, was testament to that. Victory in the Battle of Britain was a direct consequence of the Tizard Committee's recommendation to develop radar fast, and the willingness of politicians and service chiefs to listen and to promptly act. But could they be made to change their minds over the provision of VLRAs in time for the climax Battle of the Atlantic? He was fairly confident he'd done all he could in that direction. He'd raced back to Britain, convinced Blackett, and now Blackett was working on Air Chief Marshal Portal through Hanbury Brown. If Hanbury couldn't swing it then who could?

In future though unilateral decisions by the British government would count for much less than joint decisions reached between Britain and America, with the preponderance of power increasingly on the American side, through sheer weight of numbers. How would that work he wondered, and decided to ask Maurice:

"In my experience Giles every democracy has the worst government it can afford. It only pulls itself together when challenged. Louis the 14th, the Fire-wood crisis, Napoleon, the Kaiser, all proved existential challenges to Britain, all of which we survived – eventually. Consequently we're comparatively well governed – if a little rusty. America though – that's a different story altogether. Geography, History and the British Empire have between them entirely insulated America from serious external challenges. It hardly had to fight for its independence, its written constitution is a recipe for paralysis, while it displaced and exterminated most of its native peoples, rather shamefully I have to say. So you can expect a pretty appalling government – an expectation confirmed by their performance in the First World War – when they arrived at the Western Front far too late and with no artillery. Though I suppose you could explain that as low cunning."

"If you're right Maurice we could lose the Battle of the Atlantic – and with it the war."

"Maybe. If so we will have to run the show ourselves while leaving the Yanks to think they're in charge."

"Is that feasible?"

"We'll have to see. Lloyd George could certainly have pulled it off, while Churchill is no mean illusionist, not to say a self-delusionist."

Blackett summoned Sturdee up to London urgently, explaining after he arrived:

"The sinking figures – they're causing real panic in the Admiralty. You probably only know the North Atlantic challenge – but we're haemorrhaging in the Indian Ocean and the Caribbean simultaneously. Do you realise that between us and the Americans we are losing one big oil-tanker every single day! If that goes on we'll lose the war by midsummer. Now that Singapore has fallen the Japs are concentrating on cutting off all trade between India, Ceylon and the Cape. And they're moving on the Persian Gulf to cut off the oil we need to fight in North Africa. Obviously we've got to divert escort vessels and maritime patrol aircraft out of the Atlantic where we are desperately short-handed already."

"My God."

"Worse still we've got 300 escort vessels on order in yards in America – which the Americans could requisition tomorrow. If they were employed in the Atlantic well and good – but they could finish deep in the Western Pacific."

"I thought it was agreed: 'Germany first'?"

"So it was – before Pearl Harbour. But war sets its own agenda."

" What can I do?"

"There is a plan afoot to send a naval delegation to Washington – with the intention of persuading the Americans to introduce the convoy system off their East Coast immediately. As you know it is a complete shambles at present."

"I know."

"For some reason they're refusing to do anything about it. We've got to find out why and persuade them to change their minds at once. The Admiralty are assembling the delegation right now and they want a knowledgeable scientist. I suggested you."

"I see."

"I know you've just come back Sturdee – but you are the only one with the antisubmarine background, and the seagoing experience. The Admiralty agrees: you could tip the balance."

Sturdee looked dubious.

"And there's another thing. Vannevar Bush, their top scientific man, is really interested in Operational Research and wants to get it going inside their forces immediately. He wanted me to go over to give a lecture tour round some of the big universities and scientific establishments. But of course I can't leave the Admiralty just to present– not when we're bedding in. But you Giles would be the very man."

"Me?"

"Who else? You've been up to your neck in it – and very successfully too. You know how to liaise with commanders, you've got a strong background in radar– and of course your recent German university background is fairly unique. They'll listen to you – their top scientists I mean – and join the cause. When I mentioned you Bush jumped at the idea."

"Isn't he the one who took up acoustic torpedoes?"

"The very one…"

"I could at least find out how they are progressing. How long will we be away?"

"It's difficult to say quite honestly. The Washington meeting shouldn't last beyond a week. But in your case it might depend on how many people Bush wants you to talk to. We can't afford to upset him. He is a very big wheel indeed. We don't have his equivalent over here. He's a bit like Lindemann, Tizard and myself rolled into one , a sort of President of wartime science over there."

"Very big then."

"If you can get his ear who knows what might eventuate? I daresay he could conjure a couple of hundred VLRAs out of thin air. The scale of things over there is gargantuan. For instance they are setting up a radar lab which will eventually house 5000 scientists."

"5000! That's hard to believe. In numbers at least they'll overwhelm both us and the Germans put together."

"That's their intention I believe. Bush is planning for America to become the scientific super-power after the war– when Germany, or us — whoever wins – are both on our knees."

"By the way how's the VLRA thing going?"

"Slowlee slowlee catchee monkee. Your Hanbury Brown certainly convinced me. Excellent choice of yours Sturdee. He'll be seeing Air Chief Marshal Portal next week. He's itching to set his night fighters at Bomber Command. Harris will refuse of course but Portal can overrule him. Machiavelli would've been proud of you Giles."

"It was all obvious really."

"Um . We can argue about that."

Duff House was dismayed when Giles announced his imminent departure – doubly so when he couldn't tell them where he was going or when he would be back. The farming side of the enterprise would suffer without the use of his motorcycle side-car so Sturdee taught Maurice how to ride it after Joan had refused.

"He don't look safe to me." Arfur averred.

"I'll just have to take the risk." Maurice retorted. "At my age one doesn't care so very much. I dare say I will be in a good deal less peril than Giles. And don't forget the whisky near boy– if you are going to where I suspect you're going."

Gwen gave him a passionate send of, Joan and Arfur a tearful one:

"It's not the same wivout you Giles. Gem, he knows it and even 'iggins."

"What about me?" Sturdee replied. "I won't have anybody I know. So you can bet I'll come home just as soon as I possibly can. I'm relying on you to look after Joan Arfur. You know Maurice – he's too absent-minded."

The Royal Navy delegation were ordered to the Clyde where they embarked on a vast troopship which they recognised, under her wartime grey camouflage, as the Cunarder *Queen Mary*. Her luxurious fittings had all been removed to make way to accommodate 15,000 troops but she was practically deserted as they set sail under cover of darkness. On deck in the morning Sturdee found her alone on an empty ocean, relying on sheer speed to escape the attention of U-boats. He amused himself by calculating her chance of being torpedoed as about one in fifty on a single transatlantic voyage.

Admiral Ferry, in charge of the delegation, called them together for a briefing: "This is likely to be an extremely tricky undertaking. I hardly have to tell any of you of our present catastrophic shipping losses off the Eastern seaboard of the United States. Our task is to find out why the United States Navy hasn't taken steps to stem the bleeding, and in particular why it hasn't introduced convoying. We are authorised to offer help with this, including 10 Corvettes immediately, with or without trained crews, as desired.

"At the same time the First Sea Lord has emphasised the extreme need for tact. The U.S. Navy has virtually no experience of modern warfare, apart from its humiliating defeat at Pearl Harbour. That's likely to make it *less* receptive of any advice from Royal Navy, especially if it is perceived to be of the patronising kind. I should emphasise that this mission was not sought by the Americans, but rather forced upon the U.S. Navy and its commander-in-chief Admiral Ernest J King, after our Prime Minister had persuaded President Roosevelt. We cannot afford to antagonise the U.S. Navy at the very beginning of an alliance which we hope will last for several years, and we are very much in their hands for now. Their present commitment to Germany First and to the Atlantic over the Pacific, is by no means written in stone. And they have 300 of our escort vessels, the ones we are relying on to win the climax battle in the Atlantic later this year, building in their yards. And last but not least, our best hope of obtaining VLRAs before that same battle, lies with the American B- 24 Consolidated Liberator which they are manufacturing at a rate of a hundred and twenty a week! So we have many reasons to be tactful gentleman. I beg you to watch your tongues at all times, to be sparing with the drink, and to advise your colleagues if you think they are overstepping the mark. Our potential for causing harm can hardly be exaggerated."

He paused for some time to let this warning sink in:

"At the same time I don't want to paralyse you. We simply cannot go on as we are. All our oil, all of it at present – comes up from Trinidad, Venezuela and Texas by the Eastern seaboard route – where we are losing a large British oil tanker every other day. Doenitz knows he has us by the throat at last and isn't going to let go. The remedy– the only remedy – as we know from bitter experience – is convoy."

"It's all too easy to get angry with the Americans for failing to do their job – even contemptuous – but it is worth recalling our own behaviour in the First World War. The Royal Navy resisted convoying until defeat was staring us in the face. All manner of extraneous objections were raised against convoying : it wasn't offensive enough; merchant ships would never be able to keep station; we didn't have the escort vessels; it would dramatically hinder trade… and so on and so on. And last but not least — no one, absolutely no one, foresaw the dramatic effectiveness of the convoy tactic – until it was actually tried. Even after the war few historians were able to explain why it worked so well. It wouldn't surprise me to find out that the present US Navy command is unpersuaded of the effectiveness of convoy. It's our job to change their minds, and change them fast. If we can do that without causing offence we will have fulfilled our mission."

He paused again for thought:

"Far be it from me to offer what will in effect be psychological advice. However it is my experience that strong commanders can quickly change their minds, whereas weak ones cannot. Their frail egos, and their vanity, interfere with their judgements. So seek out the strong, whatever their rank, and try to persuade them. If you can do that they will persuade the rest of their colleagues later on. As for the weak, don't press your point, use flattery, and retire. Above all try to talk to as many American naval officers as you can, be it in cocktail parties or formal meetings. Most men are not fools and can see the truth when it is presented aright. And after all the truth is on our side."

The only other civilian in the delegation was Rodger Winn from the Admiralty Tracking Room. The fact that such an indispensable character had been released from his responsibilities to come, underlined the importance of their mission. Winn took him aside:

"The fact is that Bletchley Park has lost touch with Shark– the Nazi U-boat cipher."

"Oh no!" Sturdee found it difficult to stifle a groan. On top of all the other disasters – the sinking of the *Repulse* and the *Prince of Wales*, the fall of Singapore... this could prove the final straw.

"It happened in February. All their traffic became opaque overnight. We can no longer divert our convoys away from wolf packs with any certainty, because we're not getting the gen. We can use traffic analysis – that's all. So expect even heavier casualties."

"What happened?"

"We can only surmise that the Germans have finally decided to utilise the fourth wheel in their Enigma cipher machines. It was always on the cards, and they must have grown suspicious at their lack of success in finding our convoys. Things are now far far more difficult for our codebreakers. There's no certainty they'll ever break back in. I don't have to tell you how serious this could be."

"No – of course. I suppose Noble knows?"

"Yes. I don't know how that poor man ever sleeps?"

"Me neither. I think he consoles himself by imagining the pickle his chief antagonist is in."

"Doenitz?"

"Yes."

"Then there's not much consolation to be found there just now. I was looking through the broken U-boats messages before we lost our 'in'. Some of the U-boats off the US coast are lying on the bottom asleep by day then surfacing at night. Means they're burning no fuel. And using guns to do their sinking, rather than torpedoes, thus avoiding the need to return home to replenish. Even worse, they've brought two of their Type XIV submarine tankers into commission. They can each carry 700 tons of fuel across the Atlantic and replenish a dozen ordinary U-boats."

"So I heard. Do you think our shipping losses are mounting for lack of breaks?"

"Not so far I believe Giles. At present Doenitz doesn't have to look for his prey – it's steaming in plain sight through the Caribbean and then up close to the East Coast. Things will get serious when he is forced to move his packs back into the mid-Atlantic."

They also talked about Admiral Ferry's speech: "Yes he is an intelligent man." Winn agreed: "He knows we'll have a job on our hands. I've been sent over as 'The

Man with the Golden Tongue' – professional barrister and all that. My Lords of the Admiralty have touching faith in my powers of persuasion. They believe I will be able to lull grouchy American admirals into doing the right thing."

"I hope they are right."

"So do I Sturdee – so do I."

The Mary was so big that she barely felt the ocean swells and so fast she could avoid most storms by outrunning them. The resulting comfort on board was ludicrous by comparison with Sturdee's recent voyages aboard the *Walker* and the *Moose Jaw*. The Ocean raced by a world below them – almost an irrelevance to the passengers on board who expected to be at sea for only five days.

Having nothing better to do Sturdee composed the lecture he would be giving at various American scientific institutions. He realised it was important because good scientists could mostly choose the kind of work they would do and Operational Research hardly sounded glamorous – not by comparison with aerodynamics, radar, or weapons design. In fact it sounded distinctly boring whereas he had found it anything but. He decided to discuss three examples from his personal experience: the depths submarines could reach; the importance of VLR maritime air reconnaissance, and the origin and implications of the Convoy Equation. There were, he realised, important security implications; it wouldn't do for the Royal Navy's thinking to get back to the Germans but Blackett had reassured him that attendance at his lectures would be 'by invitation only', a precaution to which Vannevar Bush had readily agreed.

But good scientists look beyond particular instances to more general considerations. What, for example, were the qualities a trained scientist could bring to the business of war? The first quality, Sturdee had no doubt, was Cultivated Curiosity. Good scientists pose questions which others let pass by. Why: for instance, did U-boats dive to depths of no more than 100 metres – as the depth- charge designers had assumed ? Or how long would a U-boat commander need to press home a successful torpedo attack? Within that question lay the seeds of the Convoy Equation. Sturdee agreed with Voltaire who had written : 'Measure a man by the questions he asks, not by the answers he gives.'

The second obvious quality was dispassion – a dispassion you could hardly expect of a serviceman fighting for his life. Noble's recognition that protecting convoys and sinking U-boats were two entirely distinct activities, calling for different attitudes of mind, and indeed different task-forces – Escort Groups and Support Groups – was an example of dispassionate thinking – though it came from an admiral in this case, and not a scientist.

Thirdly came Scepticism – a tendency to question received wisdom. His own scientific career had begun when, as a boy, he had questioned the invulnerability of battleships to aerial bombing.

Finally came Calculation, a habit of mind physical scientists were trained to employ. Many military questions could be answered only in quantitative terms. Convoying, for instance, only made sense because it reduced the chances of a ship being found by a U-boat so much more than it increased its vulnerability when it was. Military men who were not trained to think thus, needed scientists to compliment them.

Intelligent Americans would also want to know what were the prime difficulties of Operational Research. Those Sturdee found it harder to identify. Picking the right question came high on this list. Should you be content to answer questions posed by commanders, or should you try to identify those questions for yourself? Both of course, but with the latter more likely to be fruitful. But that raised the tricky matter of ignorance. A scientist in a laboratory, remote from battlefield experience, however brilliant, was hardly likely to identify the most vital questions. In his case going to sea and flying out on a Catalina patrol were stimuli which imagination couldn't have done without. Then there was Tony Loader who acted as his naval alter ego and indispensable critic, who always forced him to defend his ideas in terms an admiral or air-marshall would readily appreciate. Brilliant Operational Research was pointless if it wasn't put into effect. He had been immensely lucky because Percy Noble had chosen him personally. Had he been foisted on Western Approaches by the Admiralty his efforts would probably have counted for nought. When Sir Percy was replaced he might have to go too.

So fast was the great Queen, and so occupied was he by his reflections, that they were alongside the terminal before his lecture was complete.

His overwhelming impression of New York was rush and noise. Ships' sirens, tugs' whistles, taxis honking, police sirens all echoing off the concrete canyon walls all chased them from the terminal to Penn Station. Alas there was no time to enjoy the flesh pots of Manhattan, or even to see them ,before their train pulled out, southbound for Washington.

The conference, for such it turned out to be, convened around an enormous table in a room with no windows and very little air – and that seeming of great age. The British delegation of a dozen sat at one end , the American of twice that number, some distance away, at the other. The US chairman, apparently a very junior Admiral, mumbled through the introductions before delivering his bombshell:

"I am sorry to say that Admiral Ernest J King – our Commander in Chief – will not be attending. He has sent a message to say he has half a dozen more important conferences dealing with the dire situation out in the Pacific. We have to draw up a list of recommendations for him today, and if he has the time, he'll look it over tonight. At some point tomorrow he will certainly drop by to announce his reactions and deliver his contingent decisions."

"One day?" the British delegation looked at one another. Surely – this couldn't all be decided after one day?'

"Now Admiral Ferry it is for your side talk and for us to listen."

Astutely Ferry moved halfway down the table so that he could be heard by both delegations. He then delivered a succinct address emphasising the desperate nature of the situation from the British point of view and the great importance attached to this meeting by both the Prime Minister and the President, who had planned it in conference by telephone. He went on:

"Gentlemen we have come all this way to bare our hearts. We have come through Dunkirk and the Battle of Britain but never have we been in more peril than we are now. These are not my words but those of Mr Churchill. We are an island nation whose very survival depends on foreign-trade. In peacetime we import 100 million tons a year – two tons for every man woman and child – including most of our food. If we make great sacrifices , as we are doing – you wouldn't want your children to live on what we can afford to feed our own – then we may survive on half that amount – and fight back against the Nazis with the eventual hope of rescuing Europe – and with it most of Christendom. But if our imports are halved yet again – which is the situation facing us right now – largely due to the sinkings going on off your East Coast, then we may be doomed. Even to tell you about our parlous situation is to take a desperate risk. The Nazis must never know how close they are to strangling us right now. Our own people are not being told for fear of the truth getting back to Germany. Thus I must ask you gentleman, as our friends and allies, not to even breathe a word outside this room of what you are about to hear – or even to write it down."

Sturdee looked at the members of the US delegation and could see that Ferry's words had had their intended effect.

A Captain from the Supply Division showed lengthy tables of tonnages required, tonnages arriving – and the consequences of the shortfalls: oil, steel, wheat, copper, chemicals, medicines, timber, sugar, cotton, tobacco… he ran through them all, underlining the strategic importance of each. Even Sturdee was shocked to learn how close they had cut to the bone already. Any sophisticated artefact like a fighter plane required hundreds of different raw materials, many of which had to be imported. For instance the supercharger on the Rolls-Royce Merlin aero-engine, which powered most of our warplanes, required a rare metal mined only in Northern Rhodesia. It had to be shipped around the Cape then right up the Atlantic on one side or the other. With a lesser substitute the loss in performance of the engine would mean that the Spitfire would no longer be able to fight with the Messerschmitt 109 on equal terms.

The Supply captain was succeeded by Commodore Mansfield, Admiral Noble's Chief of Staff at Western Approaches. He gave a detailed account of the British and Canadian convoy system as it had developed and succeeded in the North Atlantic. We had been getting on top of the U-boatss, he said, until Germany declared war on the United States in December 1941. Then Doenitz had moved his U-boatss to the US East Coast and the monthly tonnages spoke for themselves:

Month	Tonnage lost	Ships sunk	To U-boats alone
Oct	218 th.	51	32
Nov	104 th.	35	13

Dec	583 th.	285	26
Jan	420 th.	106	62
Feb	680 th.	154	85
Mar.	834 th.	273	95

So far as it went Mansfield's presentation was fine, but it did assume that the American naval officers knew is much of the history and philosophy of convoying as Mansfield did himself. But the many questions asked made it clear that this was far from the case. Sturdee reflected that this was to be expected since both sides in the naval war employed secrecy and propaganda; there were no impartial observers of a sea battle, so losers could get away with falsely claiming that they had won as the Germans had done after Jutland in 1916.

The final British presentation outlined a barebones scheme for convoying off the US coast based around two dozen escort vessels, half supplied, with their trained crews, by Britain and Canada. It should reduce sinkings by three quarters so he claimed – provided it was implemented at once and the shore lighting – which backlit the vulnerable cargo ships – was turned off

Many of the Americans were not convinced and most of the afternoon was taken up with wrangling over the detailed list of recommendations which Admiral King had demanded.

Next morning King kept them waiting. And waiting. And waiting. The British took Ferry's advice and mingled one to one with the Americans, who were individually friendly and forthcoming – surprisingly so in some cases. They were all evidently terrified of King:

"He came out of nowhere" one officer explained to Sturdee.

"Worse than that" another intervened. "He came out of the 'Elephants Graveyard' , where our unwanted admirals are put out to graze until they can be decently retired."

Another said: "He's held no seagoing command – aside from a submarine supply vessel, which hardly ever puts to sea."

"I thought he was a naval aviator." Sturdee said.

"Rumour has it that he made one solo flight, though he's boasted of many more."

"How come he's risen so high?"

"Well sadly, after Pearl Harbour , all our senior commanders, including Betty Stark, our commander in chief, were tainted with the blame. They were all shouldered aside and the President plucked King out from obscurity. With the President behind him, and no credible rival, King wields a hell of a lot of power."

"And by God he's keen to see everybody knows it. That's why he's keeping you guys waiting. It's part of his Big Act."

Suddenly everyone stood up:

"Admiral Ernest J. King Commander-in-Chief United States Navy." The chairman piped.

As it happened Sturdee was only a few places away when the great man strode in , tossed his gold encrusted hat onto the table and sat down. You could have heard a pin drop.

The next few minutes made Sturdee so angry that he couldn't sleep for 48 hours. King set out to antagonise the British – and succeeded. Some of what he said then etched themselves so deeply on Sturdee's mind that he would recollect the exact words perfectly for decades afterwards.

With burning black eyes King cultivated the manner of an angry, bullying, petty-officer. Picking up the folder of recommendations they had so carefully prepared yesterday, he banged it contemptuously on the table:

"This list of demands is way off the wall. There is no way in Hell I'm going to authorise them."

" Our Navy is in the Pacific. And so long as I am in charge it's going to stay in the Pacific until the last Nip admiral is feeding the fishes one thousand fathoms down…… I have told the President that the U-boats are your problem. It's up to you Briddish to bomb the goddamn hell out of German shipyards and U-boat-pens. If necessary we can ship our own trade North and South by rail-road. The U-boats are your goddamn problem – not ours. If you can't handle the Krauts then you shouldn't have taken them on. Even if I wanted to I don't have the escort vessels to run a convoy system. You should know that. All our shipyards are occupied building escort vessels for you, and not a one for us. And you should know that inadequately escorted convoys are worse than no convoys at all. Much worse. It's handing over a whole mess of helpless merchant ships to be shot like fish in a barrel. My Gahd I would've expected you Limies to have learned that lesson by now… … And I'm not going to order coastal cities to turn off their lights. That would kick the hell out of their tourist industries and I'd have half a dozen governors on my tail…… Germany first? It was easy for the goddamned Congress to sign up to that horse-shit a year ago – but they didn't give us a single dime to make any sense of it . No sir, our priorities are all in the Pacific. If we lose the war to the Nips the President will be impeached within the week – and he knows it. This… This…" and he banged their list on the table even harder "Makes no goddamned sense to me and I'll see it makes no sense to the President either. You've come all this way on a wild goose chase. But we didn't invite you, not the U.S. Navy. No sir that's for sure…"

He glared around the room. Most of the Americans looked uncomfortable while the British, including Sturdee, had their mouths open.

King put on his hat, looking even angrier than ever and stood up. The Americans stood up. He strode to the door then turned dramatically:

"My advice to the Royal Navy gentlemen is simple. Next time you pick a fight, pick one with someone your own goddamned size, not with the big boys."

Ferry called a council of war in the delegation hotel:

"A mixture of intimidation, ignorance, callousness and treachery." he said. "Admiral King is trying to scare us away. He is so ignorant of convoy that he probably couldn't spell the word. He's a traitor to his president – who genuinely supports 'Germany First', and he is utterly insensitive to the lives of seamen, including American seamen , being carelessly lost just miles away from here, because of those city lights ."

"If you ask me," someone said "He's seen too many cowboy films."

"If you ask me" Commodore Mansfield retorted "King is absolutely terrified; he's in a blue funk. He is trying to conceal the fact that he has no idea how to run a Navy."

" I'd heard that the US fleet was at Pearl Harbour expressly at Roosevelt's command, and against the direct advice of all his senior admirals. He's trying to avoid the responsibility by sacking them, and appoing this King creature in their place."

"All this may well be true gentlemen," Ferry said "But what are we going to do? What can we do? I'm not even sure if this conference is still in session, or has it been disbanded already by Admiral King? The First Sea Lord – and the Prime Minister– will have to be informed, and in graphic terms , at once. We will need to compose a cable which will go out via the British Embassy this evening."

They were in the middle of writing that when Ferry was called out. He returned with a senior member of the US Navy delegation, now dressed in civilian clothes:

This is Captain Walter Gilkey" Ferry announced. "He has kindly come of his own volition to say something to us which may be of the greatest assistance. I hardly need tell you that what he has to say must never leave this room. Captain Gilkey…"

Looking sheepish the American started quietly, but his words gathered volume and conviction as he spoke:

"We – that is to say I – didn't want you to leave with the impression that we totally agree with Admiral King… with what was said this morning. Convoy is the only solution to the turkey shoot which the Nazis are conducting off our beaches right now. And with your generous offer of corvettes with trained crews we could pretty much get it started next week. But now King… the admiral – has spoken his mind, he won't change it… he can't . That, he would conceive, would weaken its position within the Navy, and more importantly within Washington. It would be hopeless for us to try – you saw what he can be like – and quite hopeless for you. He is acting the part of the stubborn, patriotic old seadog – as he imagines it to be. And no crack can be allowed to show in his make-up – even if unnecessary lives are being lost to maintain his act."

"But don't despair!" Gilkey looked round from face to face, his own burning with conviction:

"You have to understand how things are done in our democracy. The Press rules the country via the president. King is President Roosevelt's man. President Roosevelt is a Democrat while the Press is by and large Republican – and they don't like him– no sir. They think he dragged us into this war – against the wishes of the American people."

He paused:

"Now here's the deal. If we can convince the Press that good American boys' lives are being unnecessarily lost off our shores because of President Roosevelt's incompetence there will be hell to pay. Pictures of burning and dying sailors on the front pages and on cinema newsreels; Mom's and sweethearts crying… fatherless kids… you name it. The president would be made to seem like a heartless son-of-a-bitch – just what the Republican press- tycoons would love. Within the hour Roosevelt would send for King and bawl him out. And three days later the convoys would begin to sail."

There was a long silence, while the British naval officers digested Gilkey's plan. The American continued:

"The Royal Navy needs to keep out of sight. All most Americans know is that you guys helped to burn down Washington in 1812. What you can do though, through your embassy press attache , is supply our reporters with as much gruesome photographic material as possible… exploding ships, burning oil, dying seamen… you know what I mean. Rely on our fellows to feed them the dope on convoys, and how they could save the day. You watch it. A week from now Kings arse will be roasting over a griddle. The only way this would go wrong is it if it is found to be a stitch-up between our two navies – yours and ours. Now gentlemen I must sneak out the kitchen entrance…"

The delegation was ordered to remain in Washington, but Ferry allowed Sturdee to go off North, so long as he remained within 24-hour recall.

Following Blackett's orders he entrained for Boston to call on Vannevar Bush the US scientific supremo, who maintained offices both in Washington and at his home institution MIT, The 'Massachusetts Institute of Technology' in Boston, where he was at present. Bush , who must have been a very busy man, kindly agreed to see Sturdee at once. He turned out to be a twinkly pipe smoker who seemed to know everything and everybody – and to keep it all in his head: "We will arrange for you to give a talk here Friday Sturdee. About 100 fellows from here, from Harvard and from the Radiation Lab should turn up and I will ask for senior representatives from the three services . Later, if you have the time, we'll fly you to Chicago and then to California to do the same. It's important to do this quick. We don't want all the brightest fellows lured away to work on other projects before Operational Research gets its fair share. That wouldn't do. So it's up to you to pull them in. Your fellow countrymen Taffy Bowen has been doing a great job luring the brightest and best from all over the States into our new radar lab. I anticipate they'll win us a few Nobel prizes one day. So you've got some tough competition."
"I used to work for Taffy."
"Great man. A very great man. Now I understand you want to look into our work on acoustic torpedoes? Professor Blackett hinted that you had much to do with their conception?"

"The idea was obvious. Can they be made practical in time? That is the question."

"I completely agree". Bush pressed a bell and a tall bony man in a business suit came in: "This is Dr Bill Worthmann, an old PhD student of mine; Bill will shepherd you around while you're in the States. I understand they're putting you up in the Faculty Club; isn't that so Bill?"

"Yessir. And I'm taking him over to the Harvard underwater test tank this afternoon. They'll demonstrate their Type 24 Mine."

"Thank you for coming Doctor Sturdee." Vannevar Bush transferred his pipe into his left hand to shake hands: "What you have to say could make a real difference. Not , so I understand, for the first time in this war. See you Friday." And he twinkled outrageously.

'Type 24 Mine' was the codename given to the US Acoustic Torpedo to conceal its real nature. Sturdee was taken by the scientific team to see it performing in the largest aquarium in the world , on the campus of Harvard University:

"We've got a real tight skedule" the young team leader explained: "Bell Telephone – electronics, us – Acoustics and Western Electric – propulsion and explosives – started work in December. We are aiming to get a firm order for 10,000 from the government in June for operation by March 43. So the baby you're going to see today is a test vehicle only, built to develop the guidance and control system – which we reckon is the tricky part."

They were standing in semi-darkness looking up into the huge tank. Sturdee could easily imagine himself a diver 50 foot deep in the open ocean, with sunlight filtering down into the green depths. He half expected a shoal of fish to swim into vision:

"The black barrel 15 foot long they're lowering into the water now is the simulated U-boat. It's got two screws, and is fully manoeuverable up to 4 knots." Sturdee nodded.

"The yellow guy at the far end of the tank is our Mine – We call it The Hound-dog. It's 7 foot long like the intended weapon and you will notice it has four sonar sensors bulging out from the belt around its waist. They are deliberately set back so that the nose can block sound signals from the U-boat unless the Hound is pointing straight at the Sub. Those four sensors are connected to the four rudders at the stern , two vertical, two horizontal, via the electronic brain, which operates using valves and relays . So let's see it in action."

The team leader bent over his control console:

" Okay, the Hound is now active, its sonars are listening at 24 kilohertz. But as yet there is no signal from the Sub. Now watch:"

The Hound began to circle slowly in a complex rolling spiral:

" That trajectory, which is programmed, enables it to listen for signal economicaly in all directions. Now I'll switch on the Sub's propellers:"

After a while the hound stopped in the water– as if sniffing. Then it turned towards the submarine and began diving towards it.

"Now I switch off the Sub so."

The hound drifted for a while then entered it's original corkscrew searching-mode again.

"I turn on the submarine's propellers again."

This time the hound picked it up immediately, pointed at the U-boat , halted for a while as if checking, then closed in on its prey.

Nothing had excited Sturdee more since he had joined the Navy. He was allowed to manoeuvre 'The Submarine' but nothing he did could shake of the deadly bloodhound.

"The operational model will have 4,000 yards endurance at 12 knots. That means a U-boat could outrun it on the surface. But we can't manage any faster with the battery drive. That means the U-boat must never find out he has the little bastard on his tail. The plan is to drop it only after a U-boat has submerged."

"So it is aerial?"

"Yep. Will weigh only 700 pounds, so pretty much any patrol plane could carry two or three of them."

"How much explosive?"

"Ninety pounds of Torpex, right up the front behind the contact detonator."

"That should do for any U-boat. But would it be robust enough to withstand an air-drop?"

"We'll have to see. But the specs call for launch from up to 300 foot altitude and at 110 knots. The valve people swear they can withstand that while, for the drop, the fins and rudders will be protected by a disposable sabot."

Sturdee shook his head: "You know this weapon could win the war? You can't imagine what it will mean to the poor devils out on the ocean. U-boats were practically unsinkable. Now they will become coffins."

"Yeah, and the great thing is these babies are passive. They don't give off any sonar to speak of. So counter measures are practically impossible. An' you know what? They'll cost only 1800 dollars each. Your Admiral Doenitz has had it."

Sturdee slept better that night than he had done for months. His dreams were full of yellow Hound-dogs following U-boats down to their dooms in numinous green depths. Life was suddenly precious again.

Vannevar Bush was mightily pleased with Sturdee's talk:

"Just what we needed. Some really smart people are interested in OR already. I can see this catching on in a big way over here. Even Admiral King might approve." He twinkled knowingly.

"Not if he finds out its British roots."

"I understand he served for a few weeks aboard a Royal Navy warship in World War I. Apparently it bruised his ego."

"Well it's certainly recovered since Sir."

Bush laughed aloud: "You know the president says that Admiral King must shave with a blowtorch, whilst his daughter told the Press he is the most even tempered man in the Navy — that is to say that he is always in a black rage."

Taffy Bowen, Sturdees original boss back at Bawdsey Manor, now eminence gris in the Radiation Lab down the road, entertained him to a magnificent dinner in a Boston restaurant:

"I dare say you haffn't had a decent blow-out for ages Chiles. Today is my treat boyoh. These Yankees really know how to feed themselves. We'll start with a Maine lobster – each. Then a ribeye steak big enough to last the whole blutty war. We'll even stretch to a bottle of French Beaune."

Taffy looked sleek and happy:

"They appreciate me over here; not like that blutty Watson-Watt. "

"You're more Welsh than ever." Sturdee laughed.

Taffy winked: "They are a bit in awe of the English over here – think we Welsh are colonials like themselves. They don't realise we Welsh have been running England since Tudor times. And we're not giving them their independence back. But we've got to settle these blutty Germans first. Now tell me Chiles – what is Hanbury up to?"

Taffy Bowen had pioneered airborn radar back in 1936, and it was his valve-based system, as refined by Hanbury Brown, that had recently seen off the night time Blitzes.

"It's a shame you weren't there to take the plaudits Taffy. They ought to give you a knighthood."

"The wife would appreciate that: Lady Bowen of Swansea." He laughed at the idea: "I'd haff to buy a cap and pretend to be her chauffeur."

"Aren't you sorry you left Britain?"

"You must be joking boyo. Taffy is very well suited here – in all sorts of ways" he winked again, this time lasciviously: "You won't beleef what's building in our Radiation Lab – the whole future of electronics. Unlike the Brits who only educate a tiny elite – two per cent maybe , the Yanks educate 10 times as many. Combine that with a three times bigger population and they'll dwarf Britain – and Germany combined, after the war. Poor old Britain – she's giving her Crown Jewels away to the Yanks for practically nothing. Look at the Cavity Magnetron which I brought over here. That should have been our big earner in the 21st-century, like steam in the 18th century, and railways in the 19th. Now the Yanks are getting it for free – like the jet engine. We may beat the Germans – but we'll lose to America – we haff already. And they all work so blutty hard over here."

"Why?"

" Frightened you see. The Depression was terrible over here – 30 per cent unemployment – worse even than in our valleys. This war has been a godsend to them. They'll come out on top, with Britain on her blutty knees. You know they've got two thousand PhDs working just on solid-state amplifiers over here while Britain has got just one, that brilliant fellow Skinner at Bristol University."

"I'll worry about all that Taffy – after we've won. There's no guarantee of that right now." He gave Taffy the monthly sinking figures and Admiral King's reaction.

Even Taffy looked grave after that.

CHAPTER 27
HORRIBLE OLD MEN

Sturdee gave his talk at the University of Chicago but received an order to board the *Mary* in New York before he could go on to California. Far from empty this time the great ship had embarked 4000 very young but cheerful Canadian volunteers to fight at Britain's side. To Sturdee they looked like boys: he prayed that fate would be kind to them. He had to share a cabin with two other members of the delegation but there was still room to pack in plenty of presents for the folks at home. He himself had been to visit the Metropolitan Museum of Art in Central Park to pick up some tips on painting nudes, and to buy a big enough roll of canvas, with spreaders, to last a year or two. He was determined to get started on his Rokeby Venus.

Everywhere the war seemed to be going from bad to worse. In North Africa Rommel was in the total ascendant; in Russia the fighting season had just started, but no one was giving the Russians much chance of lasting through it. And in the Far East the British army had been humiliated time after time by small numbers of Japanese troops who, unlike the British, seemed to relish fighting in the jungle.

At the Dry Cleaners he was greeted by Tony Loader and Gwen with the total sinkings for April – 674,000 tons, 132 ship sunk to the bottom, 74 of them by U-boats.

"How does that compare with last year?" he asked

"The tonnages are much the same, but last year we lost only 58 to U-boats." Gwen said.

"And about 100 sinkings is the critical figure – the difference between victory and defeat by the Nazis." Loader said . "Right now, having sunk 132, they're winning handsomely."

"And it's our fault, or rather the fault of Admiral Ernest J King of the U.S. Navy…" Sturdee reported what had happened to the Royal Navy delegation in Washington.

"But surely that can't go on…?" Loader was horrified.

"You tell me Tony. What happens when we get a truly incompetent Admiral in our Navy?"

"Generally he'd be sacked or replaced by the First Sea Lord."

"But what if he actually *is* the First Sea Lord, or the U.S. Navy's equivalent? Which is the case here."

"The nearest parallel I can think of is Jellicoe. He was exhausted by 1917 and was shoved sideways – it is widely believed by Lloyd George. The Prime Minister is the only one who could do it. The equivalent in the United States would be the President I suppose."

"Unfortunately King is Roosevelt's own chosen creature – recently appointed, and Roosevelt apparently fancies himself as something of a naval strategist. All I can say is that King obviously hates the British far more than he hates the Germans – that's plain. But what's the point of worrying when we poor devils can do nothing about it? The American Press is our only hope apparently."

"Have you heard Tony's great news?" Gwen interrupted " Go on tell him Tony."

"The medical board have passed me fit for active service at sea again."

"No!" Sturdee threw his arms round his comrade.

"And Noble has promised me a seagoing command. A corvette – or even one of these new frigates."

"Congratulations! It's everything you been praying for. You've got your dreams back... How wonderful Tony... How wonderful..."

"I will be at sea in time for the climax battle."

"And he'll get a half stripe and be a 'Lieutenant-Commander'." Gwen looked as proud as if she was Tony's wife.

"But what will we do without him?" Sturdee was suddenly dismayed, recognizing the consequences: "You know you've done an amazing job here Tony?"

"Well thank you. But we all know it's been a team effort. Your brains, my knowledge and Gwen's evident good sense..." he patted her on the bottom, "To say nothing of Admiral Noble. Like everything else good in this battle we were his idea in the first place. How lucky Britain has been in his appointment – but how long will that last? If these big sinkings continue they'll sack him – even though it's none of his fault."

"How unfair!" Gwen was indignant.

"Someone has got to take the blame sweetie. It's never the men at the very top."

"Tony is right" Sturdee agreed. "They even sack the most successful because some one else covets their glory. Look at the Battle of Britain – our only real victory so far. It's only too obvious that Dowding and Park won that. Then what happened? Within weeks they were both sacked without recognition and replaced by two Cocktail Party creatures – Sholto Douglas and that odious Trafford Leigh-Mallory. According to Hanbury Brown the men who actually fought in that battle are seething with resentment."

"How can we ever win then ?" Gwen despaired.

"Because the other side often pick leaders who are even worse." Loader responded: "Look at friend Adolf for a start; I bet he's no strategic genius. And fatty Goering. And look at that idiot they had in the First World War."

" Hindenburg you mean?" Sturdee asked.

"No the other one."

"Ludendorff?"

"Yes. He pretended afterwards, to protect his military reputation, that his army hadn't been defeated fair and square – which it had been in August 1918 at Amiens – but had been 'stabbed in the back' by their own politicians. And that is why we are fighting this second bloody round."

"It's not all bad news you know" Sturdee intervened "We're going to win this war, one way or the other. Listen..." He told them about the acoustic torpedo – swearing them to absolute secrecy. Then he went on:

"If all else fails we will mass-produce our way to victory. Or rather the Americans will. I went up to Baltimore to see the 'Liberty Ships' program. It was our idea but this organising genius Henry Kayser is revolutionising shipbuilding. They prefabricate sections of the ship and, then when that's done, weld them together, not rivet them . It's more like a Ford car assembly line than a British shipyard. Hardly any skilled craftsmen are needed, so you can put a huge workforce, including women, to work in no time. And you know how long it takes them to put a 7,000 tonner together, and ready to go to sea? Guess."

"Six months?" Loader ventured.

"42 days. Six weeks."

"My God!"

"Kayser reckons that if necessary they could turn out 8 to 10 million tons a year."

"By God!" Loader exclaimed "That's more per month than the Jerries have been able to sink."

"Exactly. So in the long run – if is there is a long run – Admiral Doenitz cannot hope to win. My worry is that he may win in the short run; and he probably recognises that. If he can go on sinking a hundred ships a month , as we know he is now, then some of the merchant seamen will refuse to sail – particularly the many foreigners. Why should they risk their lives in a war that is not their war? Once the sea lanes are cut Britain will have to capitulate within three months – or starve. So somehow we have to get through this next 6 to 9 months – *and* win your climax battle at the end of it. And to that end we're going to need VLRAs. I'm off to find out how that is going. Time is running out in that direction."

After spending a single night at Duff House the Walrus dropped him at Farnborough. Hanbury Brown greeted him by tossing the day's newspapers across his desk : "You obviously haven't seen these" :

'THOUSAND-BOMBER RAID ON GERMANY'

the headlines blared. The RAF had last night apparently mounted an overwhelming attack on the city of Cologne in the heart of the German industrial Ruhr, practically wiping it out.

"Note anything fishy Giles?"

"It does seem a trifle early to know the outcome."

"Precisely. Those headlines were probably being run off when our bombers were still in the air. They're based on an Air Ministry press release –propaganda pure and simple. Bomber Harris is determined that his boys, his command, will win the war on their own."

"And will they?"

"God knows. But he is determined to frustrate any attempt to prove otherwise. He's given us no chance to show that our radar equipped night fighters – and thus their German equivalents – could shoot his bomber streams out of the air , as I'm pretty sure we could."

"But I thought…"

"Yes, his boss Portal agreed that the test should be made – but I suspect Harris has got friends in higher places– Lindemann for a start – and perhaps even Churchill."

"I must say these headlines make gory reading ."

"Of course they do. The Brits want their revenge for the Blitz – why not? Don't you… I do."

"But not if it costs us the whole ruddy war at sea."

"Exactly. If we have to capitulate through starvation you can bet Adolf will make us pay 10 – no 100 times over – for any petty revenge we can exact now."

" 'Thousands of fires were started… their Fire Brigade was overwhelmed… a fire-storm was started which took thousands of lives as factory workers fled their burning homes…… the entire population of 700,000 fled the ruined city…… the effect on German war production will be devastating…'. "

"Those are exactly the thing the bomber fanatics want us to believe – but whether they're true is another matter altogether – I have no way of knowing. As I recall the Blitz over here never made any dents in British aircraft production. I mean I wish Bomber Command all the best Giles. If they can win the war on their own then God bless 'em . They may or may not have got through to the target last night… it's a good idea to use overwhelming numbers… but in the longer run radar equipped night-fighters armed with explosive cannon , and travelling much faster, will get the better of them. Look at what we did to the Nazi night bombers back in January."

"I know– when I was hoping to hear we were getting somewhere with the supply of VLRAs to Coastal Command. If I'm reading you aright the answer is 'precisely nowhere ' ? "

"Not quite . After my long talk with him Portal accepted that tests using British night bombers against British night fighters will definitely have to be flown. I'm sure that that was news to him. Also I think he now realises he could lose the is war by mis-allocating his precious supply of four-engined aircraft. In other words he's now got an open mind. He is no longer entirely in Bomber Harris's pocket. Now tell me what Taffy is up to in America."

The situation sounded so grave that Sturdee went straight up to see Blackett instead of returning to Liverpool. Like everyone else Blackett was poring over the results of the Cologne raid:

"Make no mistake Sturdee – much will hinge on its success – its *substantial* success I mean – not this newspaper puffery. I'll know more tomorrow when the results of today's photo-reconnaissance flights have been analysed. Meanwhile you can brief me on your American trip."

They want on talking far into the night, both of them bunking down in the Admiralty air-raid shelter. Blackett was as excited by the news of FIDO, the acoustic torpedo's name inside the Admiralty – as Sturdee:

"You realise what this means Giles – once its operational – and if it is a success then aircraft will become the main U-boat sinkers, not ships. As it is they can't carry enough depth charges, they merely find the U-boats – then have to call up escort vessels to actually sink them. FIDO will change the entire psychology of our higher command – don't you see?"

"No"

"At present Coastal Command is seen by everybody from the Prime Minister downwards as a poor relation. Why? Because it has no real offensive capability on its own. Unlike Bomber Command – or the Royal Navy– it can only assist the Navy in its defensive role. When everybody is eager to strike the heart of Germany, why divert resources away to a mere handmaiden? Now think of one of these long-range Liberators equipped with centimetre radar and half a dozen of your Fidos Giles. Why they could locate and sink several U-boats on every sortie in protection of a convoy."

"Yes I can imagine that."

"Now look at it from Portal's point of view! His four engined aircraft could be winning the war at sea – not the Admiralty– and that's often what matters to these brass hats. With FIDO in the offing I can see Portal going in bat for VLRAs in a very big way. We've got to get the idea into his mind right away. He won't take it from me – the Air Ministry and the Admiralty are at daggers drawn right now: you know we refused to let any Coastal Command aircraft go on the Cologne raid – and Harris is fuming . Write me a short anonymous report on FIDO right away and I'll see Portal gets it through an appropriate channel."

Sturdee wrote his report before breakfast and got it typed before he went to see Blackett: "Thank you Giles. The Photo reconnaissance results are in. But first I should give you the background. Have you heard of the Butt Report?"

"No."

"Last year a civil servant called Butt was asked to report on the effects of earlier Bomber Command raids on Germany using all the subsequent photo-reconnaissance and other intelligence. The results were shocking. Only one in five crews who thought they had hit the target had got within 5 miles of it. Tizard concluded that this war cannot be won by night-bombing – it's far too difficult and inaccurate – and said so – only to earn the undying enmity of Lindemann. And Butt'sanalysis was subsequently confirmed by looking at the after-effects of Luftwaffe night raids on Hull and Birmingham. Much was made of them in the newspapers – but in reality the effects on our war effort were negligible – even counter-productive because they stiffened our determination to fight back. In short bombs blow in windows, blow off chimney pots and start the occasional fire."

"… and kill people…"

"You'd be surprised. The Germans have dropped 50,000 tons of bombs on Britain but killed only 40,000 people so far, rather less than the number who die in road accidents in peace time. The dent in our war production has been negligible – less than the effect of single bank holiday."

"Good Heavens – why don't they let those figures out? It would cheer everybody up."

"Perhaps we don't want the Germans to know? Perhaps we want them to go on wasting their resources in vain. One of their twin engine Dorniers or Heinkels can drop only one ton of bombs and so kill on average only one civilian. And now that your Hanbury Brown can shoot them down they could lose more precious aircrew then we lose random civilians. It's a fool's game."

"… But… But…"

"What I think you're struggling to say Sturdee is then 'Why on earth are we so anxious to bomb them?' "

"Exactly!"

"We'd be falling into the very same trap we trying to set for the Luftwaffe. And, into the bargain, depriving the Royal Navy of the long-range aerial support it needs to protect our trade and win the Battle of the Atlantic!"

"Of course."

"So you see why I'm finding it hard to sleep just now Sturdee. Your Admiral King may be a fool – he certainly is – but right now our own high command seems intent on committing ritual Hari Kari . Harris, Portal, Lindemann… Churchill… the Press … as far as I can see they are all so consumed by the spirit of revenge that they can't see defeat staring them in the face. It's our job as scientists to throw cold water in their faces – and make some of them think. It won't be easy. So long as they've got Lindemann on the other side they can say 'The scientists are divided'. I sometimes think that man is a traitor. You know he was Germany originally? He might be a great German patriot."

"It doesn't bear thinking about."

"No it doesn't. It's sometimes difficult to retain a sense of balance in wartime. But if people like you and I can't do it Sturdee, then who can? We've both lived in Germany and admire German culture – just as we hate the Nazis. You know there are plenty of Nazis on this side of the channel – more properly called Fascists – our upper classes for a start? Nazism is a little too lower class for our huntin' shootin' set . But of course they don't think of themselves as such – as Fascists I mean . Provided it is covered by a figleaf of patriotism fascism is very okay by them. They're animated more by hatred of the British working class than by anything positive. However… I shouldn't be talking politics. For all I know you may be a scion of the nobility."

Sturdee laughed: "Definitely lower deck I'm afraid."

"Someone defined Operational Research as 'Trying to prevent a war from being prosecuted by gusts of emotion ' and right now that's our job – most particularly Henry Tizard's and mine. Somehow we've got to prevent the understandable desire for revenge from clouding the minds of our war leaders. And it's not just revenge but desperation; at present Britain has no other direct way, apart from strategic bombing, of striking back at the enemy – which we need to do, if only to relieve pressure on Russia. But it's difficult with Lindemann standing in the doorway. With his country house background he regards Tizard and I as no better than Commies – at least that's how he apparently portrays us to the brass hats. Anyone who offers a rational argument has, he says: ' Been listening too much to Tizard and Blackett' ."

"So you haven't got a chance?"

"That remains to be seen. Not everybody is as taken in by Lindemann as Churchill is. His schoolboy facility with mental arithmetic doesn't impress everyone. Now to this Cologne Raid."

He turned the photos on his desk round for Sturdee to see: "Despite the Admiralty's refusal to help, Harris managed to send over 1047 aircraft – though many were obsolescent light bombers capable of carrying only a few bombs. Some were from training squadrons flown by trainee pilots:

"They dropped less than 1,500 tons of bombs , two thirds of them incendiaries. They did set off a large number of small fires which, as you can see, burned 600 acres of mediaeval wooden houses near Cologne Cathedral – which was hit several times– but survived as you can observe. We have no precise idea of the casualties– but if our experience is anything to go by they probably amount to about 500 dead – only one in 1400 of the city population. That's hardly likely to undermine morale – any more than they did in Britain. The large modern industrial buildings are not, and were not vulnerable to incendiaries – which are easily put out by fire-fighters."

"What were our casualties?"

"We lost 43 aircraft – that's about 200 aircrew– about half the number of civilians lost by the Germans . Given that fit man of fighting age make up about a sixth of any population that means we made a net loss in fighting personnel on this raid."

"There must be some gains surely?"

"Yes there were. The accuracy was impressive with over 80% of them dropping their bombs over the Cologne area, including the suburbs. That's a big gain over the Butt report. They used Gee – a form of radio navigation which alas does not extend much further into Germany. And their concentration was impressive. The whole bomber stream was in and out within 90 minutes– the idea being to completely saturate any defences – in particular their Kamhuber Line of radar controlled night fighters. Hence the comparatively modest 4% losses. So it wasn't a shambles – as it would've been six months ago. But as a contribution to winning the war… negligible. It was only a gesture; a sort of propaganda stunt which will fool nobody – except possibly our own Press and the Prime Minister. Whose morale it will stiffen most – ours or the German's – is a good question."

"And who will learn the vital lesson?"

"Exactly. At least it shows Germany is not entirely invincible. And it is some kind of response to the Communists who wants us to 'Open a Second Front now.' – which we are in no position to do – not without suicidal consequences."

"How many four engine bombers did we lose?"

"About a dozen I believe."

"A dozen VLRAs would double– more than double the aircraft we could operate in the mid-Atlantic."

"That is what we have to impress upon our Chiefs of Staff. Admiral Sir John Tovey, Commander-in-chief Home Fleet was so angry when he heard about this raid yesterday that he urged the entire Board of Admiralty to resign forthwith unless we get proper support for the U-boat war immediately. He's reported to have said 'It's difficult to believe that the population of Cologne would notice much difference between a raid by 1000 bombers and one by 750.'"

"250 VLRAs with FIDOs would finish the U-boat war in weeks – no days."

"Pray tell that to the Prime Minister– if you should meet him Sturdee. I doubt he will listen to me – or Tizard – not with Lindemann standing over him like a guard dog. There is none so deaf as those who will not hear."

Before returning to Liverpool Sturdee called in on Rodger Winn , last seen during their terrible encounter with Admiral King in Washington:

"You worry too much Sturdee. You know what Bernard Shaw said: 'Britain and America are two nations bitterly divided by a common language' and for once Shaw was right. I was partly educated at Harvard and Yale where I learned that truth from painful experience. Educated Britons often demur at calling a spade a spade whereas educated Americans may prefer to call it a 'goddamn fucking shovel'. It's just our different mannerisms."

"I don't think King was acting" Giles retorted. "He really hates us."

"A couple of days after the contretemps I was sent into bat by the First Sea Lord to negotiate with King. But King wouldn't see me – only his deputy Ingersoll would. So when he tried to peddle the same line as King I exploded, I even used some home-spun Texan patois. I said

"What a crock of shit! I don't care what your incompetent admirals do to your own ships or your seamen, but by God they're not sinking and drowning ours." The twisted little cripple grew visibly before Sturdee's eyes.

"Gosh…"

"It's only a trick" Winn laughed "I had a famous Shakespearean actor teach me. Believe me sometimes it comes in useful in the court of law… legal histrionics."

"And?"

"Well Ingersoll laughed . That's how he would've expected an American in my position to behave. Cold disdain would have choked him up. So he trusted me after that. Got me into see King himself – and we did some sensible horse-trading. I made him see the sense of gathering all submarine intelligence under his own command in Washington – like we do here. And I offered him some worthwhile inducements – which I am not at liberty to disclose – to get convoys going pretty quickly."

"It's hard to believe…"

"You just watch. King will pretend it was all his own brilliant scheme – but who cares so long as it's done?"

"I wish I had your… gift of the gab Rodger."

"It's no gift. It's a carefully nurtured skill based on training and practice. With a crooked spine and twisted limbs like mine you need compensating weapons."

"I'm sorry… I didn't mean to sound patronising."

"I'm sure you didn't. But you innocent scientists have far too much faith in the bare facts. Facts aren't arguments – which is what you need to change men's minds. I'm afraid your Professor Blackett – however clever he may be – doesn't understand that at all. That's why that unpleasant man Lord Cherwell is running rings around him at present. It's no good sounding vastly knowledgeable and superior – as Blackett is inclined to do. He needs to do something more – be something more – to convince men like Churchill – who is every bit as clever as he is, but in a different kind of way."

"Blackett despises Churchill – and Cherwell."

"Doesn't it show? Unless he changes his manner he could lose the war for us – at least for the Admiralty. You're close to him Sturdee ; can't you drop a hint?"

"I'm terrified of him – like everybody else."

"This is war time Giles ; terrors are there to be conquered."

There was much for Sturdee to think about on the long railway journey back up to Liverpool. The passengers, whether in uniform or not, were all cheered by the news that Britain was getting its own back at last and that 'The Jerries were getting a dose of their own medicine' . Wildly inaccurate – indeed wilfully inaccurate newspaper accounts of the Cologne Road were handed back and forth with approval. From them it would appear that Germany's industrial might had been reduced to rubble overnight. At times he found the urge to cry out "But it's not true!" almost irresistible – but of course he couldn't say a word. Anyway, and after three years of almost unrelenting defeat, Britons deserved some comforting consolation – even if it was based on delusion. He reflected how easy it was for a wartime government – any wartime government – armed with the weapon of secrecy – to control its population through propaganda. No doubt very few ordinary German citizens had any idea what a storm of hatred and revenge their own government's activities were stoking against them in Britain – or the terrible price they would eventually have to pay in consequence. According to the Air Ministry's latest triumphal bulletin the main mission of Bomber Command – which couldn't achieve much else – was now 'To destroy the morale of the German people by de-housing their entire industrial workforce'. 'It's just another bloody pathetic slogan' he reflected. Blackett had been far ruder:

"I'm told at Oxford dons think it a sign of weakness to change their minds in the face of fresh evidence. So with Lindemann. Instead he is changing the objectives of Bomber Command to suit its limited – its very limited capabilities. And of course it panders to his apparent hatred of the German working-class."

CHAPTER 28
ESCORT CARRIER

With so much going wrong, and with nothing he could do to put it right Sturdee was relieved to get back to Duff House and put his back into the mundane tasks of running a market garden in May. Onions, seemingly millions of young onions had to be transplanted, weeded, and protected from birds and marauding pigs. The three new ones christened Caesar, Augustus and Bodicea by Joan, were just as ravenous, assertive and amusing as their predecessors. Pig-swill had to be boiled and carried, electric fences had to be moved to give the pigs enough room to root – but not enough to escape. Two more old poplar trees had to be brought down and sawed up to dry for the following winter's firewood. The Anderson shelter had to be pumped out and dried in case it was needed again. The duck pond had leaked and needed re-puddling. The big old house needed constant maintenance which only he was capable of supplying : slates and windows damaged during the blitz; gas, electrics and plumbing… craftsmen had all but disappeared, either into the forces or in to vast new wartime factories. Maurice was hopelessly impractical while any spare time Joan had was taken up with all the bartering required to keep the business running. Thank goodness Arfur and his mate Gem were quick learners, hard at work from dawn until dusk. They patrolled bombed out areas , looking for timber, slates, glass, bricks, roofing-lead and sandbags.

Thus employed Sturdee sometimes wondered if his time should have been better employed in winning the war. But, like many scientists, he found that physical labour was actually a stimulant to hard thinking, whereas sitting in an office was stifling. Anyway Tony Loader was much away on courses preparatory to going back to sea. Over lunch Sturdee approached Admiral Noble about a replacement:

"It won't be easy Giles. With all of our new escort vessels coming off the slipways we need every decent naval officer we can find. And a dug-out wouldn't be any good I imagine?"

"No Sir."

"What I might do is second to you – on a temporary basis– officers out of the Escort fleet enjoying a spell of rest ashore. I try to give my valuable commanders – and indeed everyone I can spare – intervals to recuperate ashore. The stress out there guarding convoys is more than any human can endure for more than so long."

"I know." Sturdee acknowledged. "Captain McIntyre told me how invaluable your rotations are. Frankly I don't know how some of them stick it. Commander Gay was on the bridge for 72 hours continuously whilst I was on *Bluebell*."

"I doubt Giles whether the Royal Navy – for all its illustrious history – has ever asked so much of its men – from Commanders down to ratings – as we are asking of them out in the Atlantic now. Ultimately it is their courage and endurance pitted against the courage and endurance of the U-boat men – who for all they are our enemies – are very brave too – which will decide this issue. You know Sturdee I draw such courage as I have from them? On the rare occasions I am able to go to sea I always make a point of visiting the ordinary seamen and stokers in their mess decks. People think I do so to boost their morale. In truth it is the other way around; they are boosting mine. When I'm losing some beastly battle down in Whitehall I think: 'No I'm damned if I'm going to let them down'. And that gives me the grit to stick it out. I only hope that when they have won our war their countrymen will have the grace – and the imagination – to realise who won it for them. Yes the Battle of Britain boys were heroes – they stuck it out for three weeks. Our stout lads will have to stick it out for at least three years of sheer hell."

Despairing of VLRAs, Sturdee had set Loader the task of looking into the only possible alternative – Escort Carriers. As a desperate last resort the Admiralty had ordered some merchant vessels to be fitted with flight decks that would enable at least some air patrolling above convoys running the gauntlet of the Air Gap in mid-Atlantic.

Loader's report was equivocal: "We have only ever had one in commission, the *Audacity*. She was a converted German cargo vessel we had captured in the West Indies. She was a bloody abortion if ever there was one." The photograph he handed to Sturdee showed a very strange contrivance – the ship had had its entire superstructure removed to make way for a featureless flat deck: " As you can see – even the funnel's gone: they must have vented her smoke sideways. She's got no lifts and no hangars. The only six aircraft she carried – Grumman Martlets – had to be parked out on the open deck – as you can see. And somehow they had to take off and land over one another. But she did protect convoys against long-range Focke-Wulfs – indeed shot down two in September last year off Cape St Vincent. So then the Admiralty included her in a homebound convoy of 32 merchantmen from Gibraltar – HG 76. By all accounts they had one hell of a battle. They sank five U-boats and shot down several aircraft– for the loss of only two merchant ships. But then there was a big cock up as a result of which *Audacity* was torpedoed some 500 miles off Cape Finisterre."

"What sort of cock up?"

"The captain of the *Audacity* – McKendrick – was senior to the commander of the Escort group – Johnny Walker. Despite being requested to remain within the convoy perimeter – where he would have been protected from U-boats – McKendrick insisted on sailing independently at night– where of course he was a sitting duck. McKendrick and 500 of his crew lost their lives unnecessarily, and we lost our only Escort Carrier. But the Admiralty were mightily impressed – and so they should've been: five U-boats sunk for the loss of only two merchantmen. So they ordered 30 more conversions – almost all from American yards. The first ones are just coming into commission."

"They must be very vulnerable. I mean they look so obviously different."

"Not if they can stay inside the convoy. Unfortunately they have to sometimes turn into wind to fly off or land their aircraft."

"That sounds dicey."

" It does . But we'll just have to suck 'em and see. Beggars can't be choosers. If they can cover the Air Gap for us when the Crux battle comes they will be worth their weight in gold; no in diamonds! Sir Percy is very anxious to get aboard one and observe it in action."

"Do you think there's any chance I could go out with him?"

"I can only ask; the old man's got a soft spot to you. But don't count on it."

In spare moments Sturdee built the frame and stretched the canvas for his Rokeby Venus. It was over 6 feet wide and four tall. Joan was a big girl and he wanted a full-sized painting.

"Wossit for?" Arfur – who helped him – wanted to know.

"It's a secret." Sturdee replied.   "You'll find out when it's finished – that's to say if I'm satisfied with it."

"I betcher goin' to paint Gwen again?"

"I'm tempted – but no. That first one was blind luck. Its good isn't it?" he said, admiring the two copies drying against the studio wall.

"Bloody... marvellous" Arfur agreed.   "I reckon they get better every time I looks at 'em. Me and Maurice sometimes sneaks up 'ere to take a peek."

"Do you, you little devil. Well no more peeks please: not while I've got my secret project on. If you want to see Gwen ask me and I'll let you in after I've covered the new picture. From now on I'll lock the studio."

"You don't trust me!" Arfur sounded hurt

"It's not that, honestly its not. It's just that this one is going to be so bloody hard; I'm superstitious. Silly isn't it for a scientist? But that's how I feel. It's like going into open the batting at school. I always had to wear somebody else's pads – for good luck."

Arfur appeared to be satisfied with that lie – which was just as well because obviously Joan wouldn't want Arfur to know she was lying naked up in Sturdee's studio.

It was all very well stretching canvases – or reading about Velasquez – but how to approach Joan herself? Did he appear matter-of-fact and say 'Oh , by the way, I'd like to start that painting this afternoon. If you wouldn't mind popping up at two and taking all your clothes off..."

He wouldn't be able to do that that – not even for all the VLRAs in Bomber Command.

 He considered what he imagined would be the professional approach. He'd casually show her the excellent print of The Venus he'd managed to buy at The Metropolitan Museum of Art in New York and say: "Do you think you could manage a pose like that?"

But he blushed to even think about it.

He put off approaching her for days, then weeks. He thought of asking Gwen instead – that would be so much easier. But he'd promised Joan not to paint Gwen again in Duff House and anyway Joan might be very insulted. Having her tremulously made offer turned down in favour of another woman would be as good as, or as bad as, being told her body wasn't beautiful enough.

The longer he delayed the more momentous the difficulty seemed to loom. He longed to share the decision with somebody else– but who could he ask – only Gwen. But he gibbed away from doing that because he knew that if Joan ever found out she'd be livid.

So he procrastinated. But he couldn't go on doing that forever. What would Joan herself be thinking – as surely she must be thinking of the matter?

He was beginning to lose sleep – too petrified to move, too nervous to remain still. But what was he hesitating for? He couldn't lose Joan – because she wasn't his to lose. She was Des's fiancé and would one day disappear with him deep into the Australian bush. As far as he Sturdee was concerned she was just an artist's model. If it had been peacetime he would have been paying some young woman half a crown an hour to pose for him – with no awkwardness on either side.

Weekends were becoming a nightmare. After all Sunday was the obvious day to start the painting because they were both free all day. Sturdee would screw up his nerve – and then find some urgent task to excuse the confrontation.

He was saved by Loader who turned up one Thursday evening when they were in the middle of supper.

"Sorry old man" he apologised when they were alone. "But this can't wait and I can't risk the phone. The Admiral's flying out to HMS *Biter* tomorrow at 3 PM. He's going in the Shagbat and he's agreed that you can go with him. They'll fly to Loch Erne in Northern Ireland tomorrow. Then, weather permitting, they'll fly on out the following day to rendezvous with the incoming convoy which *Biter* is escorting."

"So, how long do you think?"

"Several days I should imagine. Sir Percy is anxious to see the *Biter* in action."

"Me too. Thanks for organising this Tony."

"You won't when you're in that perishing draughty Shagbat trying to land on a minuscule aircraft carrier half the size of the real thing, and with no arrester gear. You'll probably disgrace yourself in your trousers – and then what will the Admiral think of you?"

Little did Loader know that Sturdee would far rather have disgraced himself in the Admiral's eyes than in Joan's. Now that confrontation could be postponed for yet another weekend.

It was fine May afternoon when the staff car deposited them at the airfield next to the Supermarine Walrus as the Shagbat was officially called. The pilot and navigator saluted the Admiral smartly, the two passengers climbed into the two rear seats and the aircrew into the two front. Knowing how draughty the Walrus was Sturdee had his pyjamas on under his ordinary clothes. Admiral Noble inserted plugs into his ears, thus permitting Sturdee to do likewise. The rear-facing Bristol Pegasus engine clattered into life above their heads, a seaman pulled out the chocks and the Shagbat waddled out to the runway.

Looking down from 2000 feet they could see the Mersey and the Irish sea beyond almost choked with shipping. Concentrated as he was on the military side of the struggle Sturdee could only wonder at the logistical battle which Joan and her colleagues had to fight. Most of Britain's ports had been closed by German bombing so virtually all of her imports and exports , a million tons or so a week, had to squeeze in and out now via either Liverpool or Glasgow – which meant turning around 250 oceangoing cargo ships a week: unloading them onto outgoing wagons, reloading them from incoming wagons; getting the right items into the right wagons and then assembling those wagons into trains that would carry them on to their final destinations all over the United Kingdom. Thank God the blitzes were largely at an end because it had brought the railway system to its knees. Before the war the British had been importing two thirds of their food: no wonder they had been forced into rationing and cultivating every patch of half-fertile soil. He watched an incoming convoy of 50 ships being deserted by its Escort group who were making for Gladstone Dock and some well earned sleep.

And what about the Germans ? The Royal Navy had imposed a complete blockade on Germany from the very first day of the two and half year old war. No wonder she had had to strike out East in search of alternative supplies. Maurice was right; this was a war of Blockade with both sides' fingers grasping the other one's throat. It was ruthless, merciless, indiscriminate and uncivilised. The helpless would starve first – the old, the weak, the conquered. With no fuel, particularly in Russia and Eastern Europe, citizens were freezing in millions – no tens of millions. The fighting men would get priority, the honest would suffer with their followers – whilst the parasitical rich would thrive, as they always did – like worms in a plague. The only way the whole pointless catastrophe could end was if one side or the other could be strangled into capitulation. But could they be? In a Total War, deliberately poisoned by propaganda, both sides came to loathe one another . Bombing in particular fuelled hatred and a fierce determination not to lose. Certainly the British wanted revenge on the Germans – and were now doling it out , one thousand bombers at a time. But perhaps all they were doing was steeling the Germans' determination to retaliate ? And they would retaliate – with their U-boats at sea. The poor British public, kept from the truth by their politicians, had no idea of the desperate crisis they were about to face in mid-Atlantic. It wasn't even clear that those very politicians understood themselves – otherwise why would they refuse Coastal Command the very long-range aircraft needed to close the Air Gap South of Cape Farewell?

These gloomy thoughts were terminated when the Walrus crossed the coast of Northern Ireland – now dressed in the brilliant emerald green of May – the very picture of peace and tranquillity. Was there a greener, fairer spot in all the world Sturdee wondered? After the war he would come over here, set up his tent, and paint and paint and paint. He watched the sun flashing off lakes and rivers as they flew Southwest into the province of Fermanagh. They began their descent over Enniskillen which he recognised from its site on Loch Erne. On Lower Loch Erne the white Catalinas and Sunderlands were swinging at anchor as they had been on his previous trip, noses to the Southwest prevailing wind, groundcrews visible here and there on the wing surfaces, servicing engines . They landed into the Sun, raising a cloud of spray which, for a moment, generated miniature rainbows. A launch towed them to their buoy while Sturdee flexed his frozen legs, trying to get the circulation back.

Everybody wanted to see the Admiral – after all he was their Commander-in-Chief – while nobody was interested in Sturdee. So he slung his pack over his shoulder and walked to the Officers Mess, revelling in the silence and scent of summer grass. Looking out onto the loch he could see F for Freddie riding to its anchor. It was quite possible therefore that he would run into Fox and his crew, and indeed, with a couple of dozen other aircrew, they were sprawled in armchairs enjoying tea.
"Blow me down if it isn't Giles" Fox rose to greet him, his boyish face wreathed in smiles: "Come and join us – and tell us who's winning the war. Bloody Jerry seems to have deserted our bit of the pond. Have we won or something?"

Sturdee did his best to inform them, but wary at every turn of what he could and could not reveal. In particular they would have been jubilant over FIDO – which would absolutely revolutionise their lives one day – but he couldn't breathe a word – for it was Top Secret for now, and would remain so even after it came into service. He concentrated on the VLRA problem – which they had done so much to stimulate – but of course the news was bad – which made them very angry:
" All I can say chaps is 'Don't blame the Navy'. They've done everything they can to get their hands on more Liberators. It's your bloody Air Force that's hogging them for Bomber Command. Save your anger for Air Chief Marshal Portal – he could change the situation overnight, if he wanted to. If he would side with Coastal Command against Bomber Harris, we could solve this problem in time for the Climax Battle. As it is…". Sturdee shook his shoulders. He went on to apprise them of the horrendous tonnage losses off the American coast, and the refusal of Admiral Ernest J King to do anything about it. By dinnertime all were seething with anger. Perhaps some of that anger would eventually get back to Portal. The RAF was not known for subservience towards its senior officers.

For the Walrus, which was not fitted with radar, to fly out into the waters of the Atlantic in search of a convoy continuingly zig-zagging to avoid U-boats, would have been a suicide mission – a totally unwarranted risk of Admiral Noble's invaluable life. The plan was therefore for the Walrus to follow a radar-fitted Catalina which would hopefully locate their convoy before continuing on to its own mission much further out into the ocean.
"It all depends on us being able to maintain visual contact with the Cat" the pilot explained as he made his final checks. "If we can't I have strict orders to turn back Sir. In any case we must turn back when my fuel gauges fall below 50 per cent. Given a

predicted West wind or 30 knots that should give us adequate margin to get back. And obviously we don't want to land in the Republic of Ireland and have our Commander-in-Chief interned for the duration of the war. And even if we find the convoy we've still got to land an aircraft with no arrestor hook on an undersized carrier. Provided the seas are not too bad I'm confident we can do that. All the same Admiral this is going to be a dicey trip. My first concern must be for your safety Sir and as commander I must maintain the right to call it off at any stage if I feel the odds are against us".

Noble nodded: "That is understood lieutenant . I shall not at any stage attempt to interfere with your command of this aircraft. But if we can manage to land on the *Biter* that could have long-term benefits for the course of the larger battle."

As soon as there was enough light they taxied out onto the loch and took off. There was five- eighths cloud forecast which should thin out once they were out over the sea. The Catalina, burdened with tons of fuel, staggered into the air below them and set off West along the Donegal Corridor. The street lights were still on in Donegal town and Killibegs Harbour as they droned out to sea at 120 knots, keeping low to avoid the stronger headwinds expected higher up. Sturdee, who was nervous about the rendezvous, was glad to see that the cloud had indeed thinned a bit and , as instructed by the pilot, kept his eyes on the Catalina because three pairs of eyes ought to be better than two. The admiral, plugs in his ears, worked on papers spread out on his lap.

After two hours the fuel gauge was down to 60 per cent, which meant they had utmost 30 minutes more before turning back. The Catalina began to climb, presumably to increase the range of its radar. Below and ahead the sea, which was gaining colour as the sun rose behind them – was streaked with foam. Force five Sturdee reckoned; probably ideal for a carrier landing. He was nervous about that – especially in an aircraft with no arrestor hook. He'd seen too many films of aircraft over shooting – and finishing in the drink. It was true they had flotation jackets but the sea down there looked perishingly cold. He might last for twenty minutes but the Admiral, who must be close to sixty, and carried no spare flesh, wouldn't last ten.

"We've found them!" the Navigator turned excitedly in his seat. The Catalina had turned 20 degrees to port and was wagging its enormous wing in an elephantine way. They all peered ahead, even the Admiral, and caught a glimpse of smoke blowing towards them before seeing the ships themselves.

"There she is ! "Sturdee exclaimed excitedly, sighting the unmistakable flat top of a carrier in the midst of the convoy. The Catalina stood off to port, no doubt telegraphing his number to the Escort commander. They didn't want to be shot down by their own ack-ack.

The two seaplanes parted company, the Walrus dropping steeply and throttling back. The navigator used his binoculars and to read off semaphore signals to the pilot, who relayed them on to the Admiral::

"They've got a stern wind Sir. *Biter* has been ordered to drop back and turn to wind'ard for us to land on. But first they are going to launch a Swordfish."

As they passed down the side of HMS *Biter* Sturdee took a good look at the strange vessel – which might be the Navy's last hope of winning the Battle of the Gap. Ugly she certainly was, the handiwork of clumsy surgeons who had excised her entire upper structure and replaced it with a giant wooden table a hundred and fifty yards long. A small 'island' had been grafted to the starboard side hanging out over the sea. The bow and stern projected out from beneath the table carrying what looked to be 4-inch guns. Down either side of the flight deck further ack ack guns could be seen on excrescences stuck out into space. The only aircraft on deck was an ancient booking biplane being made ready to take off. Painted entirely in black-and-white camouflage – a scheme devised by the painter and sailor Peter Scott, from sea level HMS *Biter* certainly didn't look like an aircraft carrier– which presumably was the whole idea. U-boats wouldn't be able to pick her out as readily as Sturdee had feared.

They made a low circuit of the convoy – a large one by the look of it with a dozen columns of four or five ships. Two tiny looking escort vessels, destroyers by the look of them:, dropped back with the *Biter* as she made her risky turn into the wind.

" Eyes skinned for U-boats gentlemen please" the pilot ordered: "Now is their chance – if ever."

Turned into wind and sea the escort carrier was forced to travel in precisely the opposite direction to the convoy – obviously not a desirable situation.

The Walrus banked sharply and raced back towards the head of the convoy, then banked steeply again to station itself down wind of the carrier. The engine note dropped; Sturdee's stomach began to churn.

"They've catapulted off the Swordfish" the navigator announced "Now it's our turn."

Unfortunately Sturdee couldn't see much ahead but now they were low down, not more than a couple of hundred feet, the waves looked much larger than they had done from high altitude. That meant the carrier deck would be pitching up and down.

He glanced at the airspeed indicator – only 60 knots. If the wind was blowing 30 and the carrier was doing 15 that meant the Walrus was coming in at only 15 knots, say 20 miles an hour relative to its intended destination. That didn't sound too bad.

Glancing over the side they seemed only feet above the sea now which was white with *Biter*'s wake. He raised himself in his seat trying in vain to see ahead over the pilot's shoulder. His heart leapt as the aircraft bumped and lurched , then bumped violently again. Thank God he hadn't strapped himself in. The engine coughed and died. If only he'd painted Joan……

"We are down gentlemen." the pilot calmly announced "On HMS *Biter* if our navigator hasn't cocked up."

To his amazement Sturdee saw a man in helmet and goggles staring at him through the window from not 3 feet away.

From the tiny glassed-in bridge of the *Biter* they watched as the Walrus was manhandled astern, it's wings folded back to look like a giant locust, then disappeared down by lift to the hangar-deck below.

"In principle" the captain of the *Biter* explained. "We can carry a dozen aircraft – depending on type. Right now we are carrying six Fairy Swordfish and three Grumman Wildcats – Martlets as they used to be called.

"Aren't they obsolete– the Swordfish I mean ?" Sturdee asked.

"Any aircraft that can cripple the *Bismarck* isn't obsolete." The captain glared at Sturdee: "Handsome is as handsome does in this game. We've got two up right now and no U-boat has dared to surface anywhere near this convoy – and we are all the way from Baltimore."

"I'm sorry sir, I didn't mean to impugn your air arm. But isn't there something more modern in the works? I mean a biplane in the 1940s…"

"For convoy escort duties in mid-Atlantic the Stringbag is fine; she'll take off and land in pretty much any weather, has an endurance of 5 ½ hours carrying a torpedo and three crew. The only thing she lacks is a decent antisubmarine weapon. The 3 hundred-pound bombs she carries are useless. Once the Jerries get wise to that they'll call our bluff and refuse to submerge. Then we'll be in trouble. It's not the aeroplane you need to blame – but the fools who sent them to sea unequipped to sink submarines."

"Make a note of that Sturdee." The admiral said : "That sounds serious."

Over the next 48 hours , as the convoy zigzagged its way towards Londonderry, the admiral, accompanied by Sturdee, inspected every corner of the strange vessel , watched all its main systems in action, and talked to many of the 500-odd crew. She carried two radar systems , one for air defence, and a 10 centimetre anti-submarine set like the other escorts, while a Huff Duff aerial like a parrot's cage was perched atop a special mast forward of the Island:

"That's a good idea" Noble said "She can find her own targets" . He was even more enthusiastic about her huge bunkers carrying 3000 tons of oil:

"She's got a range of more than 10,000 miles" he explained "That means she can stay out near the Air Gap for weeks, passing back and forth from convoy to convoy. Half a dozen of these vessels might make all the difference."

"Couldn't they also refuel other escorts?" Sturdee asked.

"That's in hand. Later models will be fitted with refuelling gear."

Down in the hangar they got to see the Grumman Wildcats, short stubby monoplanes like flying barrels.

" They're the convoy's air protection." The captain explained "Very effective on the *Audacity* where they shot down several Focke-Wulf Condors. But we haven't seen any Jerry aircraft so far – and are not expected to."

When they got to the Swordfish the captain, who'd obviously taken a dislike to Giles said:

"I suggest Doctor Sturdee takes a flip in one himself. How else could he appreciate it's sterling qualities?"

"I don't think that will be necessary." The Admiral intervened.

"Oh, but I'd love to Sir!" Giles replied, only half sincerely. He was damned if he'd let some RN bully put him down. Anyway it might stimulate his scientific imagination as that Catalina patrol had the previous year.

He was intrigued by huge rolls of canvas suspended from the hangar ceiling.

" Fire curtains." the captain explained "We carry 30,000 gallons of aviation fuel. One shell through this thin-skinned hull and we'd have an inferno. Those things might help, but I doubt it."

At dawn next day, swaddled from tip to toe in allegedly windproof clothing, Sturdee found himself in the Observer's cockpit of a Fairy Swordfish waiting to be catapulted over what looked like a storm swept ocean. Without goggles he would have been blinded by the storm-force wind of 60 knots generated partly by the elements, partly by the *Biter*s motion, but mostly by the propeller screaming around in a blur ahead of them. The pilot in the open cockpit in front of him raised his hand and Sturdee felt his head being wrenched off his shoulders backwards. The plane seemed to briefly fall then buck again upwards . The horizon ahead tilted and suddenly they were racing backwards alongside the *Biter* which was battering its way through a head on sea in waves of spray.

When Sturdee thought back on the war years afterwards that flight in the Swordfish always featured. Any terror he felt on take-off and landing, and he certainly felt that, was overwhelmed by the memory of noise, freezing cold and helplessness. The wind roared through the struts and wires which held the wings together. The 650 Horsepower 9-cylinder Bristol Pegasus motor completely unsilenced, hammered at his eardrums. And yet he was supposed to concentrate, having displaced the official Observer. Were he to miss a U-boat on his starboard side sector, men could lose their lives by fire, oil or freezing. And knowing he couldn't pee, of course he wanted to. Nobody had told him about that, or indeed about the duration of his penance, but throttled back as they were in spotter mode, the Stringbag could manage six hours.

It came to him, as it had aboard the *Bluebell* and the *Walker*, that the Battle for the Atlantic was above all a war of endurance. Two sets of men, rather three when you counted the Canadians, had to endure cold, wet, discomfort and danger not for four hours, not for four weeks, but for years and years. One side was bound to crack in the end. What qualities: what discipline, what belief- system would cling on the longest? The Germans were tough, would face death for the honour of their Fatherland. What, if anything, could keep the British going that extra bit longer? He had no idea.

There was an intercom that allowed the three-man crew – for there was a wireless operator/rear gunner in the cockpit behind him, to communicate, but they rarely did so. The main purpose of the earphones built into his leather helmet was the reduce the noise level from the wholly unendurable to the barely tolerable.

The pleasure of staring at grey wave-tops and grey tramp steamers quickly wore off. Refusing to ask how long his penance would continue Giles had to pee in his pants after four hours. The immediate relief to his bladder was rapidly forgotten as urine froze round his thighs and down his trouser legs. He just hoped the captain wouldn't notice his disgrace – or construed it as a sign of fear – which it certainly was not. By the end, all he could think of was cupping his fingers round an immense mug of hot tea.

HMS *Biter* never made it to Londonderry. She was ordered to turn around at sea and accompany an outgoing convoy bound for Halifax, Nova Scotia. The Walrus, loaded with only a small complement of fuel, soared off the little carrier's deck like a gull, and bore them back to Derby House. In his report for Noble, which he showed first to Loader, Sturdee wrote:

'The Escort Carrier is by no means a satisfactory alternative to VLRAs. Although it has the range its low speed of 16 knots means it cannot be despatched at short notice to meet an emergency. Its aircraft are primitive and do not carry radar, and worse still are wholly unequipped with weapons capable of sinking U-boats. Their fragile construction and vulnerability to fire means that escort carriers cannot be risked within range of enemy aircraft – indeed they should largely be operated from the coast of the Americas. The High Command should be discouraged from imagining that Coastal Command no longer has an urgent need for VLRAs because, given the vulnerability of Escort carriers, it's not hard to imagine U-boats evolving tactics, for example shelling, to destroy them.

Having said all that, Escort carriers do, with certain provisos, offer us some hope of winning the Climax battle even if proper VLRAs turn out to be few and far between. Those provisos are: (a) the urgent fitting of U-boat-lethal weapons to their patrol aircraft. The aircrew themselves suggested rockets – and I agree, though whether such can safely be fired from fabric-covered Swordfish I do not know; (b) the fitting of 10 centimetre radars on some patrol aircraft on every carrier and (c) there be enough Royal Navy and U.S. Navy Escort carriers in commission by the end of this year for a total of at least six to be continuously deployed within a few hours sailing time of the central Air Gap.'

Loader's comment was:

"Trenchant stuff Sturdee. You don't need me to edit your prose any longer. Whether it is sound overall I cannot say. But every point you make obviously deserves consideration. I wouldn't spray it around though if I was you. Were Lindemann to get his hands on it, or Bomber Command, we could kiss goodbye to VLRAs for good and all."

CHAPTER 29
TERRIBLE SECRETS

Whenever Sturdee experienced the hardships and dangers of the seamen serving out on the Atlantic, he came back a braver and more impatient man. He couldn't let them down , and he was damned if he'd let anyone else get away with the same crime. He loathed all profiteers and lost his temper more than once with dunghill cocks who used the war to build their little empires in despite of all the country's desperate needs. But most of all he grew angry with himself and his own weaknesses – in particular his tendency to daydream and procrastinate.

'I'll tackle Joan about the Rokeby painting immediately I get back home' he vowed to himself on the *Biter* 'And I'm going down to London to tackle Blackett. He's got to change his manner towards Churchill and Lindemann… '

Easier said to himself than done. The whole atmosphere back at Duff House had changed with the arrival of Joan's much older brother Captain Dermot Duff on his ship from Australia, where he now lived. Sturdee was astonished by his effect on Joan. Normally witty and irreverent she was quiet, almost cowed in Dermot's presence. A large loud-mouthed man who was used to laying down the law in his own watery demesne, he continued to play the tyrant captain ashore. Many years older than Joan, he thought of her as an irresponsible, not very bright flippitygibbet. For a start the idea of her taking in male lodgers like Maurice and himself – when she was supposed to be looking after him and his three brothers – evidently irritated him, an irritation he made no attempt to conceal. He interrupted Maurice whenever he expressed an opinion and looked down on Sturdee from his six foot four as obviously a shirker and probably a coward. He snapped at Arfur and put an absolute ban on the three pigs entering the house any more:

" It's completely unhygienic!" he snapped at Joan "It's a wonder you haven't got TB."

"I 'ates 'im" Arfur confided to Sturdee "An so does Gem an 'iggins; 'Iggins won't come in the house no more. I've a mind to scarper meself – back again to Gem's old stable."

"Don't do that. He won't be here long. His ship will have to go back to sea."

"I hope 'e gets torpedered. 'im and Maurice had a terrible row while you was away Giles."

"What about?"

"About Joan."

"Go on."

"Dermot told Joan as her mum and dad would be 'shamed of 'er. Oughter join the Wrens or the Women's Land Army – an 'pull 'er weight proper'."

"My Gosh!"

"You should 'ave heard Maurice. I never knowd 'e could get that angry. Gor' Giles you should've 'eard 'em bofe. Nearly blew the kitchen winders out shouting. Maurice told 'im as he was 'pig igorant! 'Your sister' 'e says. 'Is worf more to the war effort that 'alf a dozen battleships – 'an an aircraft-carrier an all. She does more ' he says 'For the British war effort every week than 50 ships captains like you will do in this whole ruddy war.' "

" 'And 'ow would you know you old drunkard?' says Dermot– loud enough to lift the roof off – cos he's tried to stop Maurice drinking 'is whisky. Says it's evil."

"I'll tell you 'ow I bloody knows ' yells Maurice 'Cos I work wiv er and for her – like hundreds of uvver 'ighly ejjicated civil servants at The Board of War Transport. And as for taking in lodgers where do you fink that bacon and egg come from what you're a-stuffing yer fice wiv? Lookin' at the size of your belly Captain Duff you haven't been living on thin rations for three years like the rest on us . You know you're taking protein what rightly belongs to that poor boy' – an' he points at me 'Wot lost his dad in the war.' "

"Good for Maurice" Giles laughed.

"Ar, but that weren't the end of it. Dermot ordered Maurice out of the house 'This very moment'. 'I will do no such thing' says Maurice . 'I pays me rent' he say. 'And what are *you* paying may I ask? Sponging off your poor sister I dare say? And eating rations what properly belongs to Arfur and me?' "

Giles, who'd taken an instant dislike to Dermot, cried with laughter, which set Arfur off giggling as well. When they'd recovered he asked about the outcome.

"Well Joan said as Maurice would 'ave to take 'is meals in the scullery. 'I'm damned if I will' says Maurice. 'Tell you what I will do though, I'll toss for it , and if your bruvver is a man ee'l accept. And so they tosses and Dermot loses and 'ad to eat his meals in the scullery for two days – until Maurice says he could come back in the kitchen again – 'pervided he stops bullying 'is sister.' "

"I wish I'd seen it." Sturdee said, giggling again.

"You 'ang around long enough Giles and they'll be at each uvver's frotes again. They 'ates one another like cat and dog they does."

And Arfur was right. That very evening as they all sat down to supper Captain Duff launched into a lengthy grace phrased in Latin.

"If you don't mind." Maurice interrupted loudly.

"What did you say?" Duff opened his eyes and glared in astonishment at the mutineer.

"If you don't mind Captain I'd rather you kept your religious sentiments to yourself. I happen to be a respectable Atheist. And anyway God had nothing to do with this excellent repast, nothing whatsoever. Joan got the liver from the butcher in exchange for our home-grown pork. The onions came from our garden and I dug up the potatoes myself – didn't I Arfur? And Giles sawed up the tree to cook it with. So you see God was entirely superfluous – as she usually is!"

It took the combined efforts of Joan, Sturdee and Arfur to broker a peace. Sturdee offered to light a fire in the desolate dining room where the three lodgers finished their supper.

"Sanctimonious bloody fool." Maurice growled as he masticated the last of his now cold repast.

"What I can't understand is why Joan defers to him." Sturdee replied, "She's gone right down in my estimation."

"Perfectly natural." Old Picton replied. "She was a little girl, probably no more than five years old, when Sanctimonious first went away to sea , so their relationship got pickled in aspic. She's not like that with her three other brothers is she; not even with David – who is also older than she is ?"

"On the contrary; she bosses them all about..."

"There you are then. I dare say that when she's seen enough of dear Dermot at close quarters she'll see through him, stout though he is."

"God forbid..."

"After Dermot was born, Joan told me, their mother underwent a religious conversion – became a devout Catholic..."

"That explains a lot..."

"And he's got a chip on his shoulder about the Royal Navy. Apparently he was turned down for Dartmouth as a boy."

"I'm not surprised. He's too bloody stupid for a start."

"But right now he's got wee Joan completely under his thumb. If you want to keep in her good books Giles, you'd best be polite. In my experience family loyalty can exert an all-too- powerful influence."

Realising that Joan certainly wouldn't want her Big Brother to know she was posing nude in front of one of her despised male lodgers, Sturdee procrastinated yet again. To vent his spleen on Dermot he wore his Royal Navy uniform at breakfast next day, despising himself as he did so. Dermot glared at the wavy Lieutenant's stripes on his arms – with a mixture of astonishment and indignation, before sticking his face back into Maurice's newspaper.

That weekend Maurice unburdened himself to Sturdee as they worked side-by-side on their knees weeding carrots:

"The oil situation is getting desperate. Britain needs at least 1500 tanker loads a year to fight this war. We can't get oil via the Mediterranean any more so it is all having to come from Texas and the Caribbean – principally Aruba in the Dutch Antilles, Curacao, Trinidad and Venezuela. And that means a lot more tankers, particularly as they can't sail direct but have to be convoyed up the East coasts of America and Canada and then across the North Atlantic. Right now we're lucky if we can get five round trips a year out of a single tanker. So even without sinkings we'd be desperate."

"I can imagine."

"We only get by because the Dutch and Scandinavian tanker fleets fell into our hands after the Nazi invasion. And when Roosevelt cut-off Dutch East Indian oil from the Japanese the Yanks were bound to take some of that themselves – leaving more Texan oil for us."

"I saw American tankers in our convoy last week."

"Now everything is changing. No more Dutch East Indian – or Burmese oil – the Japs have commandeered all that: and the Americans are going to have to fight a huge naval war all over the Western Pacific – requiring every drop of oil they can pump out of Texas and California for themselves – and every tanker they can lay their hands on. So that leaves us with Caribbean oil only– and a totally inadequate tanker fleet which is being torpedoed out of existence right now off the coast of the Carolinas."

"Don't I know… and that incompetent fool Admiral Ernest J King didn't even order the shore lighting turned off until mid April… 'because of the tourist industry'. And there is so little in the way of convoy escort that U-boats surface at night and use gunfire – they don't bother with scarce torpedoes. A single 88 millimetre shell can turn a 15,000 ton tanker into a blazing inferno. And it's all so bloody unnecessary. The coastal waters down there are mostly too shallow for U-boats to operate comfortably. They can't dive deep enough to avoid depth-charge attacks. Even quite small escort groups could put them to flight – but oh no! Do you know King doesn't even understand what convoys are for?"

"We need 300 oceangoing tankers but even with our allies we've got access to only 200 at present ,while this last six weeks we've lost twenty in the Caribbean trade alone."

"My God!" Sturdee stopped in his tracks.

"Doenitz is concentrating on tankers of course. Very easy to spot – and even easier to sink. If he can sink a dozen a month, and he is well ahead of that schedule, we'll be finished by Christmas."

"But surely we've got reserves Maurice?"

329

"Three months supply, that is all. And the Admiralty has got more – but only for its fighting ships."

"We might not even last until the Climax battle at the end of the year then?"

Picton kneeled up to ease his aching back. Then he looked at Sturdee:

"I never thought we'd lose this war Giles – but now it's within Doenitz's power to win it. You remember that paper you wrote on merchant seamen's morale?"

"Of course."

"I looked up some facts and figures on that – from the last war. Do you know that in 1917 – during the worst of the crisis – over 600 merchant crews refused to put to sea?"

"My Gosh."

"As you say. Now apply that to oil tanker crews alone..."

"You couldn't blame the poor buggers – it's hard to escape from a burning tanker. I'm still haunted by what I saw earlier this year – men swimming for their lives – only to be overtaken by burning oil."

"If Doenitz ordered his men to machine gun all escaping oil tanker crews – and his men obeyed – many oil-tankers would refuse to sail – especially those from neutral countries. That would be curtains for us."

"I hadn't thought of it like that Maurice."

"Nor me – until a couple of weeks ago. I haven't been sleeping well of late. Do you think Doenitz's men would machine gun sailors helpless in the water? You are the German expert here."

Sturdee looked back to his time in Germany:

"We are bombing them out of house and home. That's Bomber Command's declared policy right now – they call it: 'De-housing the civilian population'. Well if my family had been 'De-housed' I dare say I'd kill Germans – in cold blood if necessary. And don't forget we started this blockade business long before they did. If the only way to protect my kids from starvation was to machine-gun enemy sailors I wouldn't hesitate. Not for a moment."

"Are you sure Giles?"

"I might hesitate – but for a few seconds that's all."

"Then why should we expect German sailors to be any more scrupulous?"

"So you think we are actually facing defeat – right now?"

"Yes – particularly if we persist in this bloodthirsty policy of bombing German civilians. Why shouldn't cornered Germans strike back ?"

Sturdee didn't sleep well himself that night and next morning went into the dry-cleaning shop to examine the latest merchant shipping losses. A grim looking Loader was helping Gwen compile her final sinking charts for May.

"Over 700,000 tons old boy, or 150 odd bloody ship – 125 of them to U-boats. You know I'm not the despondent type – but we can't go on like this. And look where they are." He pointed to the Atlantic chart on the wall :

"Almost no sinkings round our shores – and only a handful in the North Atlantic – we appear to have licked them there – for now. But all down the American coast from Maine to Florida – particularly around Cape Hatteras…" he pointed to a thick rash of crosses, like a military cemetery .

"Worse still though they are now creating havoc in the Caribbean." Loader picked up another cardboard chart which he put on Gwen's desk to rest against the wall:

"We needed a larger scale chart" Gwen explained "There are so many islands and penisulas out there Giles."

"It's a bloody paradise for U-boats as it was for pirates." Loader pointed to dozens and dozens of grizzly crosses:

"You see the shipping is forced into narrow channels between Cuba and Florida, or this between Cuba and the Yucatán Peninsula coming up from Mexico. Then there's the Wind'ard Passage leading down to Jamaica and the St. Vincent Passage between all these piddling islands here. The sun is out all day and any U-boat commander worth his salt can see for bloody miles and miles."

"What's this huge rash of sinkings round here?" Sturdee pointed to an area off the coast of Venezuela.

"You may well ask old boy. That's where our most strategic cargoes come from. Big oil refineries in Trinidad, and on Aruba here , an island in the Dutch Antilles– and here in Curaçao – to say nothing of Venezuela itself. Apparently it's one great pool of oil. They say Curaçao and Aruba refine half a million barrels of oil a day. And just here: a little bit West in the Guianas up the Demerara River is where half our bauxite comes from. The rest comes from Jamaica."

"What's bauxite?" Gwen asked.

"It's the mineral we smelt to make aluminium – mainly for aeroplanes."

"So that's why the government was asking housewives to hand in any aluminium saucepans they could spare?" Gwen said

"Yes honey. We desperately need every ounce of aluminium we can lay our hands-on – and so do the Russkis. I happen to know we're sending some of our precious supplies round the North Cape of Norway to keep their aircraft industry going. And what happens when one of those bauxite freighters sticks its head out of British Guiana here? He's sent straight to the bottom by a Jerry submarine. And as for our oil tankers coming out of Trinidad and Curaçao…"

"How many of these sinkings are tankers? Sturdee wanted to know.

"They don't always tell us what kind of ship goes with what name." Gwen explained. "But you can often guess can't you Tony?"

"Yep. And of course if it goes down off Aruba or Galveston what else would it be? We estimated, didn't we Gwenny, that 55% of our tonnage lost this month is in oil tankers ."

"How many's that ?"

Gwen picked up the slide-rule Sturdee had taught her how to use. The two men watched her. She stopped and looked up:

"Tony told me that the average tanker weighs about three times as much as the average cargo vessel. If that's so then we've been losing about one tanker every day."

"Are you sure?" Sturdee asked.

Gwen looked at Loader for support:

"Well we can't be certain" he said. " We could find out though– give us a few days. But it smells about right. I know we lost 6 out of 8 tankers making a dash for Gibraltar – hoping to avoid the carnage off the Carolina Capes. Its slaughter out there right now."

Sturdee, feeling the need for support, sat down in Gwen's spare chair.

"Are you all right Giles?" Gwen put an interrogative hand on Sturdee's shoulder.

"No, to be honest I'm feeling shaky – for the first time in this war." And he described to them the conversation he'd had with Maurice Picton the previous day.

"So you are saying" Loader summed up "That we've got access to less than 300 tankers – and we're losing roughly one-a-day– mostly in the Caribbean where at present we can do fuck all about it?"

Sturdee closed his eyes and nodded.

"And that, long before we actually run out of tankers their crews will mutiny and refuse to put to sea?"

"Yes – if Doenitz orders his men to machine-gun tanker lifeboats."

A tangled discussion ensued it which Sturdee was inclined to blame the American Navy, Admiral Ernest J King in particular.

"Won't wash old boy. It was never the Yank's job to protect our sea lanes in the southern Caribbean. The truth is we never expected Jerry U-boats to get as far as Trinidad and Curaçao – so we never made any preparations. Now we are paying the price."

"Well how do they get there?".

" Good question – they must be refuelling – either at sea or from bases ashore."

"Where for instance?"

"God knows – but Hitler has plenty of Fascist friends in Central and South America. They're all dictators aren't they? I was reading about Anulfo

Arias, President of Panama – he loves Hitler apparently. And then there's a lot of anti-American sentiment – the aftermath of that ridiculous Spanish-American War of 1912 – started by that monster William Randolph Hearst to increase the circulation of his newspapers."

"Is that true?"

"Yes it is." Gwen intervened" I was reading about this beautiful castle he's done up on the coast of Glamorgan – it's for his girlfriend from Hollywood, Marion Davies – she's Welsh."

"Why not" Loader said "But I put my money on refuelling at sea. We're doing it– why not them? They don't even need special U-boat tankers. One U-boat could steam steam slowly and economically out to the Caribbean, transfer its fuel oil to another U-boat on active patrol, then steam slowly back to Brest . It's so calm in the Sargasso you wouldn't even need special gear."

"It'd halve their number of effective U-boats." Sturdee pointed out

"True enough but who cares when there are targets a'plenty – as now? He may need only half a dozen U-boats actually on station."

Sturdee decided to go down to London to beard Blackett. The matter was now extremely urgent if they were to have any chance of getting VLRAs in time. Anyway he was doing no good in Liverpool, while Dermot Duff would obviously try to drive a personal wedge between him and Joan.

"Good idea" Maurice had approved. "I suspect that Joan has been quietly supporting you – which only inflames his suspicion that she's become sweet on you."

"Which she hasn't."

"I wouldn't be so sure of that Giles. Of course she's loyal to Desmond – that's in her nature – but she's a warm blooded creature is Joan. And you're here whilst Desmond is half a world away."

"But he is a war hero."

"You're getting to be a bit of a hero yourself lad, what with flying off aircraft carriers and jumping into the Arctic."

"Oh that…"

"Joan was very upset about that. Didn't sound at all like a landlady I can tell you."

Sturdee hadn't exaggerated when he'd told Rodger Winn that he was terrified of Blackett. Blackett was a terrifying sort of man. Tall, grim of visage, formidable of reputation, he embodied both the Admiral the Fleet and The renowned Professor of Physics in one persona. Who else in Britain was actually contemptuous of Winston Churchill and made no bones about it? But that of course was the trouble– as Winn had pointed out. Unless he could somehow engage the Prime Minister's attention, then Lindemann and his bombing strategy would continue, denying the Atlantic the long-range Liberators it so desperately needed.

Joan had made a typically perceptive remark regarding Blackett:

"It seems to me Giles that his reputation is so great because he has *two* reputations, one as a naval officer, one as a scientist, and that combination probably *is* very unusual. But being unusual doesn't necessarily make you outstanding does it? Beethoven may have been unusually good at tennis, but we wouldn't remember him today for that if he hadn't been an outstanding composer as well. If you ask me Giles you should look into your Professor Blackett's separate credentials. If he was neither an outstanding naval officer nor an outstanding scientist then he is no better than he should be."

With Loader's help he found Blackett had been naval cadet at the outset of World War I and had served at Jutland – but in a very junior capacity as an artillery spotter locked up in a gun turret. He had been gazetted lieutenant by the end of the war but had held no distinguishing command nor won a decoration for gallantry– as Tony Loader had.

"He might have become a senior naval officer if he'd stayed on – or he might have been axed by Geddes, as so many were in 1926 – but he left the Navy in 1919 to go to Cambridge."

At Cambridge, so Sturdee found from his Cambridge colleagues, Blackett had eventually become a graduate student of Ernest Rutherford who truly was a genius and the moving spirit behind Nuclear Physics. Indeed, working at Manchester University in 1913, if was Rutherford who discovered that atoms have nuclei . Rutherford had set Blackett the task of developing the Wilson Cloud Chamber as an instrument for studying nuclear reactions and Cosmic rays. This Blackett had very competently done and as a result he and Occilianni had discovered a new atomic particle called the 'Positron'. However, due to over-caution on Blackett's part they were pipped at the post and the resulting Nobel prize had instead gone to Anderson in the United States . Everyone said it was damned shame – but then that was science – the most competitive business in the world. Rutherford had been furious and Blackett had left for Birkbeck College in London.

So Joan had been right. Blackett had been a junior but unexceptional naval officer and later a very competent experimental physicist – one of 'Rutherford's boys' – but by no means a genius. Despite that reasoning Sturdee was still very nervous when he walked into Blackett's Whitehall office. There he sat looking far more like a genius than Lord Rutherford – who resembled the potato farmer he once had been.

"An unexpected surprise Sturdee." Blackett remarked from his desk – and an unwelcome one by the sound of it. However when Giles handed over his report on Escort Carriers the great man looked interested and put aside the paper he was working on and began interrogating Giles about his experiences aboard *Biter*: " I must say you have a rare talent Sturdee for being in the right places at the right times. And that's invaluable! This…" He tapped Giles's report "May supply the very ammunition I need to fend off the Paymaster General – or Lord Cherwell as we must all remember to call Lindemann now. As I understand it you're saying escort carriers can never be an adequate alternative to VLRAs – only very poor stopgaps?"

They went into the technical details and then, as if to dismiss him, Blackett said: "You might give a short talk on escort carriers to my boys tomorrow before you leave."

"Sir – there is one other thing I have to talk about… Why I came to see you in person today." Giles felt and sounded terrified.

"Well…?"

Giles dried up.

"Go on Man. Spit it out…" Blackett glared at him as if he were a naval rating who'd come aboard drunk and disorderly. The opening words that Sturdee had so carefully prepared had vanished from memory.

"Well…?"

"It refers to you sir. I mean I've been asked to say… well people in the Admiralty have asked me to approach you… and… and… point out that you might be losing the war for us… unintentionally of course…"

"It's nice of them to add the excusatory adverb." Blackett put down his pen, as if ready to do battle. "And quite what am I accused of, may I ask?"

Giles took a deep breath, before charging into the fray:

"It's your manner Sir. You frighten people… you can't help that… but you also show your contempt at times. That doesn't go down with admirals – and it only confirms Mr Churchills belief that you are a Bolshevik. As things stand you generally antagonise him when you speak, when of course we all want you to persuade him…"

Blackett stood up, all 6 feet plus of him. He walked behind Sturdee and stared out of his office window. There was a long pause when neither man spoke. Then Blackett said, in an unexpectedly low voice:

"This couldn't have been easy for your Sturdee."

"No sir."

"So I must be grateful to you – whether you are right, or whether you are wrong…"

"My view hardly matters. I'm only acting as a messenger…"

"Yes I see… And one with just the right degree of detachment."

There was another long pause before Blackett came back and sat matter-of-factly down – the hint of smile on his normally thunderous visage:

" Cheer up man, I won't hold it against you. You are only doing your duty. We won't speak of the matter again. But I assure you I will think it over most carefully. I'll do anything I have to to win this wretched war – even it means buttering up little Winnie."

After Blackett, Sturdee went to see Rodger Winn to report that he'd done his duty.

"We are relatively becalmed here" Winn said, "Not much going on this side of the Atlantic. Doenitz's moved his submarines to the far shore – where they're creating havoc. It's caught the Admiralty on the hop – as well as the Americans over there. They never expected U-boats would have the legs to get so far."

"Refuelling?"

"A very good question indeed. You recall we have lost our break into Jerry ciphers?"

"Back in February."

"Well we still haven't got back in. All I have to work on is traffic analysis – 'where are the U-boat radio-signals coming from?'. You can often glean a lot from that. Well there are hints , no more, that U-boats are rendezvousing with one another far out to sea. In particular several other U-boats rendezvousing with a single one remaining almost stationary . What else could that be but for re-supply?"

"Couldn't we bump them off?"

" We could if there were VLRAs in the western hemisphere and they were fitted with effective anti-submarine weapons. Presently we have neither. Anyway it's a game that we could play only once or twice before the Germans caught on. I mean you don't turn up at a remote rendezvous by chance do you?"

"I suppose not."

"And if we do break back into Shark we don't want them to suspect that we've done so. So we can't just turn up out of the blue. Our watertight rule must remain: 'Never use Sigint. information unless you have a plausible alternative cover story.' And quite frankly it's hard to manufacture one in a case like this. It would be foolish to give our whole Sigint operation away for the sake of a single supply-vessel."

"I can see that. But we're worried to death about the Caribbean." Sturdee told Winn of his fears over tanker men's morale. Winn listened attentively before replying:

"You're not the only one losing sleep over that. I was at a recent Atlantic Committee where contingency plans were put forward to deal with it."

"What could we do?"

"If forced to, the Admiralty could requisition the entire tanker fleet and treat it as a branch of the Royal Navy. Any crewman who refused to sail could then be treated as mutineer who was deserting in the face of the enemy. And you know the penalty for that?"

"Death by firing squad. Seems a bit drastic."

"Not if it is the only alternative to capitulation. We wouldn't hesitate, nor should we in my opinion."

"So the tanker men are in everybody's crosshairs? Doenitz's and ours."

"They know that. Even their union leaders understand that therefore they are far better off as they are – very well-paid incidentally – than subject to military pay and military discipline."

"Poor devils. I saw some of them being burned to death in the sea off Iceland."

"I'm surprised, with all their money, that the oil men haven't found ways to safely evacuate their ships – inflammable motor lifeboats for instance."

"You always cheer me up Rodger."

"If I do it's because I've trained myself to always look at the other side of the hill. We are in dire straits no doubt– and things will get worse if we lose the Mediterranean – which we're just about to do if Malta falls."

"I didn't know that."

"You wouldn't. The government is determined to conceal how desperate the situation out there is –it's highly classified by the way – but unless we can relieve Malta in the next week or two, North Africa will fall – and with it the Suez Canal and the Middle East. The Prime Minister and the First Sea Lord can't waste their time on the Caribbean while they're struggling with that. We could lose half a million men in Egypt alone."

"My gosh! Do you think we can – relieve Malta I mean?"

"Scuttlebutt has it that we must land 50 Spitfires on Malta right away or we are sunk. The Americans are kindly lending us a a big carrier to fly them off but the Royal Navy has to fight that carrier, and our own carrier *Eagle*, deep into the Med, then back out again while Hitler is throwing every bomber and every U-boat he has got at it. If we can't get those Spitfires in then Hitler has as good as won the war. The great prize of the course is Middle Eastern oil. With that in his grasp Russia would eventually fall – and India."

"What about the other side of the hill now ?"

"Touché. Well just think how desperate the Germans must be getting. They haven't been able to important a thing for 2 ½ years. Imagine living without coffee, or decent tobacco , not even cotton for a change of under-clothes for all that time, never mind fighting a war on two fronts with only dribbles of oil. The Luftwaffe is practically grounded, their tanks short of fuel, the battleship *Turpitz* can barely leave port. If you think we've got supply problems Giles, they've got nightmares. They're having to manufacture much of their petroleum out of coal , produce inferior ersatz rubber and they've got no tin whatsoever . We're both of us strangling the other – it's a question of who chokes first."

"If only we could win in the Caribbean."

"Yes, well I've been looking into that. Come and have a dekko at the Chart." Winn hobbled into the next office and pointed up at the wall:

"At first sight it looks like an ideal hunting ground for U-boats – all those restricting passageways where they can lurk in wait for the strategic shipping to come to them. No wonder they're creating mayhem."

" But look a little closer Sturdee. If you ask me it's ours for the taking. Doenitz is winning because we were unprepared. Now that we recognise our peril we should, with a little organisation, be able to turn the tide."

Sturdee stared up at the huge chart, realising he knew next to nothing about the historic Caribbean Sea.

"Notice it is almost completely enclosed by a ring of islands running first East in a quarter circle down from Cuba then South almost to Trinidad off the coast of Venezuela. We could run our ships all the way up that island chain from South to North West without them ever being out of range of air patrol using quite short-range aircraft. And we've got bases on almost all those islands . Many belong to us – didn't you collect British Empire stamps as a boy?"

"Briefly."

"Look at the names…". Winn read them out as he traced the island chains from East to North West with his walking stick: "The Grenadines… Saint Vincent… Martinique… The Leeward Islands … The British Virgin Islands , The US Virgin Islands… Puerto Rico is American… Hispaniola is independent – as is Cuba – but both are terrified of the Americans – who even have a huge base there at Guantánamo covering the Windward Passage. And look at the inter-island passages within that chain. None is more than 100 miles across – they can all be crossed by cargo vessels in broad daylight in a single day. Once we organise our shipping and air-cover U-boats won't stand a chance. Besides, much of the water is too shallow and too clear for submarines to hide in it comfortably. The good visibility should be more to our advantage than theirs . When they surface at night to attack shipping our ships will be safely sheltered at anchor in shallow bays. And as long as we've got short range patrol aircraft, which the Americans can mass-produce in scads, we won't need precious escort vessels – or not many."

"Gosh I hope you're right Rodger. I was beginning to think we might lose this war."

"We still could . If we don't get those fighter planes through to Malta we're done for. So keep your mouth shut Sturdee. How I hate this secrecy – but it's absolutely essential."

" Yes it's beastly. I can't even speak to my close colleagues without first weighing every word I say: 'Can I tell them that – or is it classified ?', and one forgets – and so becomes overcautious – which itself becomes counter-productive – especially if you are a scientist like me. We work by associating ideas – but if we can't talk about them……"

"It's the same for them – the Germans. Since their successes in France and Russia too many over here are inclined to regard them as Supermen. They simply stole a march on us, that's all. If we can scrape through the next few months, they are doomed. We hold too many good cards. There is a saying in the Army apparently 'There are no such things as bad soldiers – only bad officers', and our commanders are far better than theirs – man for man: Churchill versus Hitler; Alan Brooke versus Keitel; Pound versus Raeder – though people reckon Pound is a sick man; Dowding versus Goering…"

"…Noble versus Doenitz…"

"And leadership counts for much in war. Look what our Admirals have achieved with their backs to the wall: overcome the magnetic mine; evacuated Dunkirk and Crete; prevented a cross-channel invasion; cleared our Western Approaches of U-boats; held the Mediterranean so far – against enormous odds in the air…

"And most importantly kept our sea-lanes open…"

"… Whilst ruthlessly blockading Germany and so driving Hitler into the Steppes of Russia."

"Where, if my calculations are right, he will perish."

"No, it doesn't do to think of Germans as the Master Race. If anything they're weaker than we are – tho' good at concealing it. Their High Seas Fleet never came out after Jutland, tho' they claimed to have won it. And their airmen were cowardly."

"I didn't know that."

"Surely you have heard about Baron von Richthoffen's Flying Circus?"

"Yes but… I thought he was the great aerial ace. Didn't we bury him with full military honours?"

"Yes we did. We wanted to encourage their Ace system. But you should read 'Winged Victory by Victor Yeats, an RFC pilot at the time. Von Richthoffen avoided battle by lurking way behind his own lines , under a huge umbrella of protective fighters. He only accepted battle when the odds were overwhelmingly in his own favour. Instead of doing his job of establishing air superiority over the battlefield – he was simply burnishing his private reputation – at the cost of losing the war for Germany. He should have been shot as a coward – not worshipped as a hero."

"I never knew that."

" That's why Dowding suppressed any talk of Aces in Fighter Command – which is probably part of the reason Churchill – who was after all a newspaperman – sacked him. Churchill admires Aces– but Dowding knew better, thank the Lord."

"I always learn something new Rodger, when I'm with you."

"We Kings Norton boys must stick together. Now I want to talk about something completely different."

They went back into Winn's office where Winn shut the door:

"Cipher breaking. I'm beginning to suspect the Germans have broken ours . I can't be sure but there are too many instances when a German wolfpack turns up right on our planned course. Naturally nobody believes me."

"Why not?"

"Because changing all our codes and ciphers would be enormously inconvenient and time-consuming. And in the mean time we'd be almost deaf and dumb. That's something no Admiralty could afford for a moment."

"But…"

" 'But *not* changing our codes and ciphers could be catastrophic' – you were going to say?"

"Yes."

"So everybody is seeking an alternative explanation for omniscient wolf-packs. The favourite at present is improved Hydrophones. This is where I want your advice Sturdee Could Jerry have developed hydrophones capable of picking up a convoy as much as 100 miles away? Because that is the suggestion. What is your opinion?"

"I'd need to think about it."

"Naturally. In the mean time, I would like you to teach me something. How do I calculate the Odds on a U-boat turning up by chance at an awkward place for us, at an awkward time. I'm no mathematician but surely it can't be all that hard?"

" You are a lawyer – that's a good start."

"How so?"

"Well it was a French lawyer called François Viete´ who invented algebra in the first place – back in the 16th century. It was natural for someone dealing with 'The party concerned' to replace it with X – and that's what happened. Viete´ was an amateur mathematician but his 'Unknown quantity X'. completely revolutionised mathematics. Descartes adapted algebra to do Geometry, and that lead to Calculus."

"So I've got a chance?"

"I don't see why not. I will train you how to use 'The Gamblers Secret' – otherwise known as 'Bernoulli's Theorem' – but not the mathematical reasoning behind it: that would take too long."

"Is it helpful?"

"You bet – as the Yanks say. Once I learned it at University my poker improved out of sight."

"Well I want to play Atlantic poker– the chips being ships and the cards U-boats."

"Let's go."

Winn , being a keen bridge-player, proved to be a quick learner so by lunch time he was juggling Probabilities and Combinations with some ease. Over lunch, in the canteen, they returned to the matter of code breaking:

"If we can do it," Winn whispered. "Why can't they? We don't have the monopoly of logical brains do we?"

"On the contrary. The University of Göttingen is – or was – The world centre of Mathematics and Theoretical Physics."

"You were there weren't you?"

"For 12 months. We don't have anywhere quite like that in Britain."

"What about Cambridge?"

"While Rutherford was alive they were aces at Nuclear Physics– which he brought with him from Manchester University. But he died back in '37 and the Germans in Berlin quickly overtook them. Germany has a far better university system then we have. Ours was, and still is, badly diseased by The Church."

"So there's every chance Jerry will be as good at code-breaking as we are?"

"Potentially yes – better even. But, as I understand it, that all depends on which side of the hill you are fighting…"

"I don't follow."

"The stronger party, the one holding the initiative, hardly cares what the weaker party is up to. But the weaker party desperately needs to know where his enemy will strike next. It is his only the hope of avoiding annihilation. Up to now Hitler has always held the initiative – so I suspect we put a much larger effort into code breaking than he has. But the tables could easily turn."

"Perhaps they have already."

"And Effort is absolutely vital. I don't have to tell you that the quicker you can break a message the more useful it can be. For instance you can take a evasive action in time."

"Don't I know." Winn agreed.

"But you shouldn't be asking for my help Rodger– You should be asking the Station X people."

"They don't have much time for us matelots – arrogant dons most of them."

"They should be able to tell – from the traffic they've broken, whether our own codes and ciphers are compromised. At least I would have thought so. For instance an accurate direction to intercept one of our convoys which has just been rerouted by radio – would surely give the game away."

"But maybe they use cunning cover-stories like I do?"

"I wouldn't have thought they'd have the same scope for that that we have. They don't have aircraft, or surface vessels out there to put the blame on."

" No you are right Giles."

"But one thing I'm sure of Winn– you shouldn't be trying to solve this problem on your own– or relying on me. You need direct access to Station X yourself."

" Little chance of that. Those boys are above the law and, even – dare I say it – above the Admiralty. Churchill calls them 'My Golden Geese'– because they lay the golden eggs that give him so much power."

"Well if I can beard Blackett surely someone in the Admiralty can beard Churchill. We'll definitely lose the battle if our convoy codes cannot be made secure."

"You don't need to tell me that!"

"Sorry".

On the train, a very slow train back to Liverpool, Sturdee had so much to ponder and confide to his latest research notebook: cipher breaking; the islands of the Caribbean; Hydrophonics; Baron von Richthofen; Blackett; the Fall of Malta; oil tankers; seamen's morale; the safe evacuation of burning tankers; the Carolina Capes; Port-o'Spain Trinidad; bauxite supplies; VLRAs; U-boats machine-gunning tanker crews ; escort carriers; loss of the Middle East; and Joan..... Joan.... Joan... he was going to paint her – as soon as brother Dermot put to sea again. But in the meantime what about U-boat hydrophones? He picked up his fountain pen and began to calculate.

From time to time he looked up at the innocent faces of the other passengers in the railway compartment around him. How lucky they were not to know all the terrible secrets that he did. But no doubt many of them had agonising secrets of their own. 'Poor devils' he thought, biting on a stale fish-paste sandwich.

CHAPTER 30
THE CODEBREAKERS

An uneasy truce had settled upon Duff House. Dermot no longer came down for the family breakfast in the kitchen, but ate his own later, while supper was a subdued affair from which the three lodgers retired as soon as the dishes were washed, leaving brother and sister together. Sturdee could see that Joan was very uncomfortable:

"'They 'as argyments." Arfur reported darkly.

Breakfast was a key part of the family's day. Joan maintained that the war would be won or lost depending on what the contestants had eaten for breakfast, and tried her best to ensure that they started the day with something more than the dreaded Milksops – bread soaked in warm milk – to which so many had been reduced in 1941. In addition to porridge and toast there was either a fresh egg, depending on the hens and ducks, and a rasher of bacon, or at the very least a bit of Spam.

"Why do you think we've beaten the French, the Spanish the Dutch , the Germans and the Russians in every war for the last 300 years? It's because of the good old English breakfast. They are just as brave as us and can fight as hard, but by mid-afternoon their strength gives out. You can't fight all day on croissants and coffee now can you? But with a belly full of fried bread and bacon one is ready to go on fighting – and win the day. Isn't that so Maurice?"

"If Gibbon had heard of your theory my dear I am sure his masterpiece would have concluded differently."

" Oo 'was Gibbon ?" Arfur fell into the trap.

"Edward Gibbon my boy wrote "The Decline and Fall of the Roman Empire '– the second greatest work of prose in the English-language – blaming the whole catastrophe – as he thought of it – on the rise of Christianity. But had he had Joan's knowledge of nutrition he'd probably have blamed the Fall on the decline of the Roman loaf."

"Well I 'ates our new bread!" Arfur pointed with disgust at the beige object on its board on the kitchen table: "What they call it?"

"'It's 'The National Loaf' " Joan explained "We've got to eat it because it will win the war for us."

"Why?" Arfur sounded angry : "Even Gem turns 'is nose up at it."

"Because it contains all the goodness we need to survive: proteins, vitamins, calcium…. Whereas that artificial white bread the British got used to in the 19th century had all the wheat germ milled out of it. You wouldn't catch the Germans standing for things as stupid as that would you Giles?"

"Indeed not. Their bread is practically black. That's why they don't have to import two thirds of their food like we do."

"And that's why they were winning." Joan added "But now we've discovered their secret, they'll lose."

"Which reminds me" Maurice said, looking at his watch, "It's time for the 8 o'clock News". He turned on the big Pye radio in its Walnut cabinet and tuned to the

BBC Home Service. As the valves warmed up the plummy voice of the newsreader Alvar Lindell swelled. There had been more Baedeker bombing Raids upon Exeter and Bath overnight with several dozen civilians killed. The Japanese were being held at the border with India by British and Indian troops ; fierce aerial fighting continued over Malta; the British had managed to fly off over 70 Spitfires from two aircraft carriers approaching from Gibraltar and land them on the embattled island.

"Thank God!" Sturdee exclaimed with evident relief.

The siege of Tobruk was holding out against Rommel in North Africa. The British invasion of Madagascar was continuing. The Nazis were advancing in Southern Russia.

"Why is Malta so important?" Joan asked Giles

"It's the key to North Africa and thus to Suez , the Middle East and Persian oil. If our aircraft and submarines based there can prevent Hitler and Mussolini supplying Rommel we can hold out in the desert. Right now we are in headlong retreat. Our tanks don't seem capable of standing up to the Germans."

"It really is becoming a World War isn't it?" Joan said, clearing up the porridge dishes. "It's scrambled egg and fried bread next."

"Not dried egg!" Arfur groaned.

"Half and half." Joan said.

"And you are lucky to get it you ungrateful little urchin." Maurice said. "I'm sure Giles will eat your portion?"

" Of course I will."

"No I'll 'ave it."

"Well don't grumble then ." Joan took the fried bread out of the Raeburn oven, added small portions of scrambled egg from the saucepan on the stove, giving herself much the smallest share. Automatically Giles and Maurice added portions of their own back on to her plate when her back was turned. Arfur looked guilty.

"So what on Earth are we doing in Madagascar?" She asked Maurice, pouring strong tea out of the pot in its knitted cosy.

"It's a Vichy French colony." Maurice explained: "Churchill's worried the Nazis – or more likely the Japs – might use it as a submarine base to cut off our shipping to Egypt , coming up from around the Cape."

"And that would be fatal." Sturdee added " At the moment we can't supply our forces in Egypt's through the Mediterranean. It's the Cape or nothing."

"Aren't we winning anywhere?" Joan asked plaintively.

Apart from the sound of fried bread being crunched there was only silence in response.

"Right, well, " Joan said briskly getting out the thick black notebook she called her 'Farm Diary' and looking at it: "The main thing at the moment is weeding and hoeing. All the indications are that we going to have a wet summer – a very wet summer – which is good neither for onions nor potatoes."

"Our two main crops." Maurice added gloomily.

Joan continued : "I got the list of the worst weeds to look out for from the Ministry of Agriculture and given it to Arfur. Have you got it?"

343

Arfur took it down from a shelf and began reading a list of the offending plants : "Docks; Groundsel, Thistles, Goldenrod, Couch Grass and Charlock." He turned the paper towards them showing drawings of the criminals.

"I want you all to familiarise yourself with them" Joan said "And to root them out wherever you find them. They could easily reduce our yield of food by half. Don't let them seed – that's the main thing. Get them before they do. And even more important I've got a list of animal pests to look out for: Wire Worms, Leather Jackets and Slugs. Apparently they can wipe out one's entire crop in a week. You must familiarise yourselves with the earliest signs of them – particularly in our spuds"

"What abaht Rooks? We got 'undreds of them."

A heated debate followed. Sturdee was of the opinion that Rooks were insectivores and therefore friends to the farmer – but the other males were against him. Joan decided in Sturdee's favour and the rooks were spared – " 'For the moment: innocent until proven guilty' ." She pronounced. "Now I must rush – did you pump up my bike Arfur?""

"Yus"

"Thank you."

"Weeding then, every spare moment – all of you. And Arfur try and shoot a rabbit – for tomorrow's supper." And she was gone.

"I prefers to snare 'em." Arfur opined, getting up to start his working day. "Saves ammo. Toodle-oo. Gotter feed the pigs."

Loader was jubilant about Malta: "Those Spits will give us a chance. The poor old Valetta docks were taking a real pasting from Jerry bombers. We've even had to move out our flotilla of submarines which was sinking so many German troopships. The Navy is helpless nowadays without some air support."

"You served out there didn't you, before the war?" Gwen asked

"Indeed I did: the Mediterranean Fleet, everybody's favourite posting. What a time we had! I was in a Tribal class destroyer, the *Gurkha* – based at Alex – Alexandria. Racing up and down to Gib, the Adriatic, the Greek islands; it was like one long yachting holiday. All the sun you could want; everyone in white ducks; jaunts ashore in Venice and Rome. Wine for dinner… those were the days! And I've got a lot of shipmates – lucky devils – out there still. But it's no picnic nowadays. Our boys are being bombed to bits by the Luftwaffe. That's why we need air bases in the desert. But our bloody pongos don't seem able to take Rommel on"

"Don't they call him 'The Desert Fox' ?" Gwen asked

"Yes" Giles answered "Because he turns up out of nowhere at exactly the wrong place and exactly the wrong time for us. Sounds like Sigint to me.". he added, before biting off his tongue.

"What is Sigint?" Gwen asked.

Loader hastily changed the subject: "We've been looking into the building programme for Escort Carriers, as you asked Giles. Not easy: there's so much building going on – on both sides of the ocean. And sometimes it's not clear who is getting what

– with this Lend Lease business. As you know we built the first one, *Audacity*, but she was sunk in 1941. Now we've got *Avenger* and *Biter* in commission – *Dashe*r Is coming next month and *Activity* in September – all carrying a dozen aircraft – mostly Swordfish and Wildcats. But then in October US yards are due to deliver the first of whole new class of no less than 50 slightly bigger vessels, the *Attacker* class with 20 Aircraft each – Grumman Wildcats and Avengers, a speed of 18 ½ knots , two lifts and one catapult each. Think of that – 50 carriers – mostly for the U.S. Navy– but a dozen are assigned to us.

"They could make a difference to the Atlantic air gap – if we get them –but you know us – always the Cinderellas."

"Well they won't be much use for anything but Anti-submarine warfare. Too slow and far too fragile for fleet protection. You need something like 30 knots for that – and extensive compartmentalisation. One shot from a 4- inch shell and any Escort carrier could go up in flames."

Sturdee went to his office to think about Rodger Winn's worries about the Admiralty's Convoy Code being broken. That could be catastrophic . If Doenitz's wolfpacks could knowingly lie in wait for convoys the Allies could lose the war in in a matter of weeks. And why not? If cipher breaking was primarily a matter of mathematics – as people appeared to think – then there could be no doubt that in this field the Germans were supreme. Sturdee thought of their towering mathematical giants like Carl Friedrich Gauss, Bernhard Riemann and David Hilbert and could find no Brits since Isaac Newton who could match them.

But how to *prove* that Admiralty Cipher Number Three had been broken – that was the question . Sturdee could understand that admirals would be reluctant to replace the whole system aboard hundreds of ships, if not thousands worldwide – one they had replaced only last year. No wonder they would prefer to attribute the odd wolf pack turning up mysteriously to improvements in U-boat hydrophonics.

Hydrophones: Sturdee knew little about them. He thought back to his trip on the *Pimpernel*, and listening through the Asdic earphones to the weird sounds that had come up from the deep: hushing sounds that the operators had attributed to 'Wave Noise'; Wake sounds from the Asdic dome itself butting through the sea with the ships motion; Clicks allegedly from shrimps; Asdic returns from distant fish-shoals perhaps; reflections off the interfaces between layers of water with different salinities and different temperatures; whales calling to one another from far far away – noise … noise… noise. It was a 'Signal-to-Noise' problem – a problem familiar to him from his radar days.

"Signal-to-noise!" He seized his pen and began to write out some algebra. The signal from a convoy would fall off as a square of the distance away from the U-boat, because the signal would spread out in all directions over the surface area of a hemisphere . The noise however would come from all sorts of distances: most of it from nearby. And anyway it wasn't the noise itself which was a source of confusion for the observer , or the listener in this case – but the *variation* of noise level from moment to moment. One could hear signals above steady noise , but not above noise which was continually changing . So it was something like the square-root of the noise level which entered the signal-to-noise equation. Then there was the sensitivity of your detector – in this case your hydrophone. It might amplify the signal by a factor of 10 say, but it would amplify the noises too, by the same factor.

In a few moments Sturdee knew the answer to his question, to Winn's question, in the form of an equation. It told him that the maximum distance that a hydrophone could pick up a signal would rise with only the quarter power of its sensitivity. In other words for U-boats to detect convoys at 100 kilometres instead of 10, as Winn's admirals were supposing, their hydrophones would have to be no less than 10,000 times as sensitive! And that was an impossibility; engineering evolved by increments not by steps of that dramatic size.

He stood up with a sigh of satisfaction. Theoretical Physics was such a beautiful subject, both simple and yet profound. In only a few seconds he had arrived at an insight that had evaded Roger Winn , brilliant though he was and would have evaded any seaman until eternity. But what did it mean? It meant that if Winn was right – if wolf packs were turning up where they had no right to be, then B-Dienst in Berlin had broken Admiralty Cipher Number 3 already. Winn needed to know – and at once.

He didn't dare to speak of such a sensitive matter over an open line but arranged to meet Winn at Station X in George McVitties office at Bletchley Park and got a staff car to drive him down to Hertfordshire.

They met in Hut 8 where Sturdee briefed the two older men about hydrophones. McVittie, a physicist himself, agreed that Giles's argument was 'Ingenious but not absolutely conclusive'."

"And that's the problem," Winn said "My admirals won't act until we present them with pretty conclusive evidence. You can't blame them, because changing ciphers throughout a worldwide fleet is a hell of business."

"And what would pretty conclusive evidence amount to?" McVittie asked.

"A broken cipher message from Doenitz to his U-boat commanders ordering them to intercept a convoy that has just been rerouted over the wireless, using Admiralty Cipher Number Three."

"No chance old boy. You know we lost Shark in February when the Kreigsmarine introduced a fourth rotor-wheel into their Enigma machines."

"No progress?"

"We are working on it like mad. But one more rotor makes everything 26 times more difficult – because of the 26 letters in the alphabet. Our electro- mechanical bombes are just too slow to cope. Nobody is very hopeful I'm afraid – Alan Turing and Hugh O' Donnel Alexander – our two resident pundits. don't believe we can hope for an imminent breakthrough; anyway cipher breaking is not like that – inspired leaps of imagination – it's more about hard grind – and right now we can't grind any faster."

"What are you going to do?" Sturdee asked Winn afterwards.

"I'm damned if I know Giles. I've been using your Gambler's formula to calculate the Odds– and once or twice it's come up up with highly suggestive answers. But they're not going to convince the Board of Admiralty. I suspect the Germans have indeed broken in. All we can do is be damn careful not to signal our intentions in advance – not unnecessarily."

"But that defeats the whole point of Admiralty surely?"

"Of course. We'll have to think of something. If they can survive after having their own ciphers broken then so can we . I hope."

"It feels to me that we are gradually losing this battle and losing this war…"

"But you must remember the Germans are losing it too Giles. It's all a question of who gives in first. They are desperately short of oil, aluminium and rubber; their casualties on the Eastern Front must be horrendous; their Italian allies have proved to be useless – or worse; the Americans have come into the war against them, and helpless though the Americans are at present they will, I suspect, eventually pull themselves together, especially when it comes to industrial production . Their shipyards alone can produce vessels faster than Doenitz can sink them. Then look at Doenitz himself; doesn't he remind you of von Richthofen?"

"I don't follow."

"Richthofen , the Red Baron, lurked behind his own lines, waiting for easy victories – when he should've been much further forward fighting for No Man's land ; remember I told you? And Doenitz is doing the same. He's opted for easy pickings off the US coast, and in the Caribbean, instead of fighting it out toe to toe with us in mid-Atlantic. If he did that – and won, we'd be finished. What does he do instead? He retreats. Whenever we put up a serious fight he retreats. First from the Channel, then from the South-Western Approaches, then from the North-Western Approaches – now he's deserted the mid-Atlantic for the American coast. Does he look to you Sturdee like a man who is confident of victory?"

"I hadn't thought about that. I supposed he was waiting to build up his U-boat fleet for the climax battle?"

"Two can play at that game. We could be building escort vessels faster than he can commission submarines. If you ask me he's trying to save his own skin. If he lost too many U-boats he'd lose influence with Hitler, who is known for playing off his subordinates, one against the other. Our admirals, by contrast, don't mind losing their ships – when our strategy demands it. Do you know what Admiral Fraser said after he'd lost half a dozen valuable ships off Crete evacuating our army last year?"

"No."

"He said. 'It takes three years to build a ship, but it takes 300 years to build a naval tradition' ."

"Gosh, I like that."

"It's fine isn't it. At heart the German admirals must be terrified of the Royal Navy. Who wouldn't be? It is the most invincible fighting force in all of history. Even the Roman Army couldn't compare. Our seamen don't lose wars . The idea of defeat is unthinkable to them – unimaginable. And hostilities-only auxiliaries – people like you and I Sturdee – must be the same. We are not going to lose ! Yes ,we might go on taking it on the chin – but in the end we'll win; it's just a question of how and when. Well I must be off. Thanks for your hydrophone stuff. You convinced me: all I have to do is convince my admirals. That's another matter entirely."

The little cripple turned on his heel and hobbled off down the corridor of Hut 8 , relying heavily on his walking stick

.

CHAPTER 31
THE VITAL INSIGHT

It was Arfur's duty, as part of his education, to read out articles from the newspapers, selected by Maurice, to his fellows at the breakfast table after the morning BBC news bulletin:

"It sez 'Baedeker raids resumed on Torquay and Oxford. Over 70 dead, and historic buildings destroyed or damidged. Cats Eyes Cunningham and his gallant night fighter crews shot down a dozen bombers. "

Sturdee laughed sardonically.

"What's so funny Giles?" Joan asked.

" 'Cat's-Eyes-Cunningham'! What a load of codswallop…"

"It sez here as our pilots git extra carrots to eat, so they can see in the dark."

"That's even more ridiculous. Whoever manufacturers such piffle, and expects the British public to swallow it? The Press ought to be ashamed of themselves – let alone the government."

"Well how *do* they see in the dark?"

"Radar of course. I used to work on it before I came up here to Liverpool. It's supposed to be hush-hush and the government thinks it can feed the Nazis with this childish propaganda. But the Germans know about radar; they invented it back in 1920. The only novelty is squeezing it inside an aeroplane. It was bound to come – and evidently has. That's why there are no more serious blitzes."

"What are Baedeker raids then? " Arfur enquired.

"They are night raids on our beauty spots." Maurice replied. "Our bombers burned down the beautiful old wooden city of Lübeck a few weeks ago. Hitler was so enraged that he's threatened to destroy all our beauty spots which feature in the Baedeker tourist's guidebook. It's tit-for-tat."

"How sad." Joan said. "What possible good would that do to anyone – on either side? And why did we burn Lübeck? That's just savagery. We can never rebuild a mediaeval city. The war will be over one day – and then we will all regret it. Might as well burn down the Louvre — or the Uffizi Gallery."

"I agree." Sturdee said "Churchill has appointed this bloodthirsty blimp Bomber Harris to run Bomber Command and about all his aeroplanes are capable of right now is burning down wooden cities."

"Is that really true?" Maurice asked

"I believe so."

"Churchill normally has more sense – warmonger though he is." Maurice replied "I suspect he was pushed into this by Stalin. It's either that to help the Russians – or, God help us – opening a Second Front in mainland Europe – which we are in no position to do at the moment."

"But burning down medieval cities isn't going to help Russia." Joan protested

"No it isn't." Sturdee agreed. "I suspect it's got more to do with inter-service rivalry. The RAF wants to be seen as winning the war, rather than our army or navy."

"It's a tragedy then." Maurice said.

"We need some of those long-range bombers to defend our convoys, but Bomber Harris – and ultimately Churchill– won't let us have them."

"I stand corrected." Maurice responded. " It's not a tragedy – it's a catastrophe."

"Next article Arfur." Joan ordered, taking the vacuum seal off a bottle of her last year's gooseberry jam and sniffing it.

"Restront meals to be restricted in price to five shillins."

"Now that's a good idea!" Sturdee exclaimed "Stop all those spivs and plutocrats gobbling up all our scarce luxuries – fish for instance."

"Do you know Icelandic haddock is four shillings a pound?" Joan said. "If you can get it – four times the price of rationed meat."

"Gosh I'd love some smoked haddock with poached eggs." Maurice's eyes gleamed "With fresh garden peas."

"Followed by a suet pudding with hot treacle and custard." Sturdee added.

"I want Apple pie wiv ice cream."

"You can't have it." Maurice sounded cross. "It's suet pudding and custard isn't it Joan?"

"Dreams… dreams… dreams boys. If we could afford a bit of fish – which we can't – I'd prefer cod with parsley sauce…"

"… And Pembrokeshire new potatoes." Sturdee added

"… served with fresh runner beans like my dad used to grow at Leigh-on-Sea ."

"What about broad beans?" Maurice suggestion. ''Young ones swimming in farmhouse butter…"

"We're doing it again" Joan said "Fantasising over food we probably won't have for years and years. I know everybody does it but I don't think it helps. Sometimes I can't get to sleep at night – dreaming about the impossible – like fresh Leigh-on-Sea cockles from my home town – with brown bread and butter."

"Yore doing it again."

"I know. Let's change the subject. Anyway it's your fault Arfur. Read another item from the newspaper."

"'It's the Gazalla campaign: British forces advancing into Cyrenaica. Where's that?" Arfur looked up.

"Eastern Libya" Maurice replied. "North Africa – the Desert War , though I don't think the press, or anyone else for that matter, really knows what's going on. First we advance, than they do: back and forth like yo-yos. I suspect it's got more to do with supplies than actual fighting. We can supply our boys from round the Cape via Cairo. Hitler's trying to supply Rommel across the Med – from Italy and Sicily. Rommel needs a forward supply port, Tobruk preferably. That's why we've been clinging onto it so desperately for almost a year. If Rommel can capture Tobruk he could cut his supply lines by 1000 miles – putting Suez in jeopardy."

"He seems to be a brilliant general." Joan said

"So they say– but I'm a historian; I'm always suspicious of brilliance – it's always too facile an explanation. There's usually some more mundane underlying cause. Perhaps his tanks are better than ours? What do you think Giles?"

"I know nothing about tanks. But it could also be Intelligence. It's highly suspicious if you always turn up in the right places at the right times. There could be a spy in our Cairo headquarters – after all the Egyptians are no friends of ours."

Sturdee felt abnormally frustrated. Since evolving his Convoy Equation he felt he knew what was needed to win the Atlantic battle – bigger convoys, more escort vessels, new Support groups, and VLRAs , but he could do nothing more to bring any of these necessities into being. Admiral King's ignorance of anti- submarine warfare, and Bomber Harris' intransigence over long-range aircraft were, in particular, inviting defeat. Rodger Winn was right: it was no good knowing what had to be done if you couldn't persuade the key people. Persuasion, persuasion, persuasion… that was the problem with mathematics – you couldn't use it to persuade those who didn't understand it. And of course mathematics *was* quite often wrong , though usually it wasn't the mathematics itself – but the necessarily simplified models of the real-world upon which the mathematics operated. There was a disastrous instance of that in history. The cruel workhouses, the Common Land Enclosures Act, the forced emigration of so many Victorian Brits had all been justified using Thomas Malthus' mathematically based, but totally ill-founded *'Essay on Population'* published in 1798. People often had an illogical reverence for things they didn't understand – the basis for fraudulence in finance, medicine, politics – and above all religion. So leaders like Churchill were entitled to be sceptical of mathematical arguments – which might be nothing more than bamboozle, the modern equivalent of witchdoctors' bones.

How, Sturdee wondered, could he make his Convoy Equation more persuasive, something more than that very 'Slide rule strategy' which so many commanders distrusted, so many politicians despised?

Sturdee's most precious possessions were his Research Notebooks, a dozen records of his scientific thinking which he'd started back to his undergraduate days at Birmingham University. He confided in them , communed with them, used them as a constant source of reassurance and inspiration. He'd even compiled an Index of their contents which he kept in a precious scarlet leather diary . He consulted them now to find out where exactly the Convoy Equation had come from.

The actual mathematics of the equation was trivial for anyone acquainted with the Theory of Probability. Thus it could hardly be wrong – even Tony Loader had quickly acquiesced to that. The insight came from looking at a convoy battle from a U-boat commander's point of view. And that was surely the right perspective because in war the attacker always held the initiative . He it was who located the prey, called up reinforcements and decided on when to initiate an attack, how long to persist with it, and when to break it off. And the truth was that once battle was engaged the commander had very few options. Because of the relative speeds of convoy and U-boat in the invariable head-on night attack, the time needed by a submarine to submerge, choose a target, aim off and launch its torpedoes was limited to a very few minutes. It had only one chance before it was out of the back of the convoy, and effectively hors-de-combat, unable to make a second attack until it had worked its way right round to the front of the convoy again , an exercise which could take all of the following day, and which could be frustrated by any patrolling aircraft.

No seaman, particularly an experienced escort vessel commander, disagreed with any of this – the wisdom of bitter experience. Thus, so far as Sturdee, and indeed Loader could see, the Convoy Equation was inevitable, indisputable, inflexible, and all the evidence from mock attacks on the Derby House Tactical Table backed it up.

Sturdee stared at the equation:

$$P = e^{-E/U}$$

knowing that it held the secret to the Battle of the Atlantic – and thus to the whole world war. In the far-off days of Thucydides and Xenophon kings and commanders went to consult the Oracle at Delphi before risking war or concluding peace. But here was an Oracle any war leader capable of decrypting it would do well to consult, for it held their fate in its hands. The problem with Pythia the head priestess at Delphi, and with this equally beautiful equation, was that both were inscrutable to those who most needed to know. What would Churchill make of it– or Hitler – what Doenitz, or even Lindemann?

What *are* we going to do with our beautiful equation Tony ?" He consulted his oppo in the next office.

"What do you mean?"

"It's so beautiful, so true, so momentous – but inscrutable."

"Yes I know old boy. I had a hell of a struggle to get the hang of it. Why don't you offer to give Winnie a short course in algebra?"

"Don't be an ass."

" Hold on, I've just had an idea." He stood up and yelled up the stairwell:

"Gwennie come down here. We want your opinion – and bring your slide rule."

Gwen came down looking puzzled.

"See this equation here? It gives the probability P that an individual U-boat can sink a ship in convoy when there are E escorts and U U-boats. Do you follow?"

"Yes."

"Okay, well do a calculation. Suppose there are 6 escort vessels present – which is typical, but only one U-boat, what is the probability of him succeeding in an attack?"

"What's 'e' ?"

" You don't have to know the exact value, about 2.7 " Sturdee replied "Because its marked as 'e' on your slide-rule."

"Oh yes I see it. Give me a pencil and paper."

The two men watched her at work.

"I can't believe this." she muttered " I'll do it again."

They waited.

"I don't think I've made a mistake." – she looked perplexed.

"Go on darling – what's your answer?"

"About one in 700."

"Bang on you see ? Loader was excited : "About 1 in a thousand . Or a thousand to 1 against. No sensible commander is going to take on odds like that ."

"I see." Gwen looked at Sturdee who nodded

"Now what if he calls up two of his pals by radio so there are three of them attacking at once. What are his chances then? You've got six escorts and three U-boats now."

Gwen worked her slide rule: "P has gone up to 1/9 or about 11%."

"What about 4 U-boats?"

"P is 1/5.".

"Now you're talking. A U-boat commander with any guts is going to take his chance then. He's got a one in five chance of making a sinking, and as things stand alas, a bugger-all chance of getting caught. You look perplexed girl?"

"Yes, but there are four U-boats now. Won't they all have the same chance ?"

"Yes, I suppose you're right. Don't we just multiply things by four? They'll get 4/5 of a U-boat between them. Is that right Giles? It does sound a bit daft..."

There was a silence while the other two watched Sturdee. Eventually he reached out for Gwen's paper and scribbled out a formula which he turned around to show them...

"This is Bernoulli's Theorem, sometimes known as the Gamblers Secret. If I know P, which we've already calculated, I can use this formula to calculate the probability of one sinking, of two and so on."

"Rather you than me old boy", Loader looked puzzled. "Why don't you have a go?"

Sturdee sat down, took the slide rule and began calculating. The two others awaited in silence.

" The chance of zero sinkings with 3 U-boats is still quite high – 73 percent. That makes sense because each lemon has only a 20 per cent chance of success. The chance of exactly one sinking is 24 percent, the chance of 2 only 3 percent."

"That comes to 100 percent in all ." Gwen said, rather dubiously.

"So it should do " Sturdee responded " Because the chance of 3 sinkings is neglible."

"That's much better than I would have thought– from our point of view I mean," Loader added" But what happens when they call up that other slimy bugger – four U-boats in all?"

This time it took longer for Sturdee to announce his result:

"The probability of zero losses is still 41%. The probability of exactly 1 loss is also 41%. The probability of exactly 2 is 15%. So , by subtraction the probability of three or more sinkings can be only 3%."

"Those are the kind of figures commanders need to know about before they reach decisions."

"I agree." Sturdee said. "I should have thought to work them out before. Well done Loader , and you Gwennie, it was you two who provoked this calculation."

Gwen surprisingly blushed.

"What I'd like to know old boy is what will happen if a Wolfpack attacked – with six U-boats say, or even nine."

"That will take me an hour or two. I'll give you both a buzz when I've finished."

It was almost lunchtime before Sturdee could announce his results:

"This makes for a very interesting story. First of all the number of sinkings has *nothing* to do with the size of the convoy. I never realised that before – but it's obvious when you look at the convoy equation. It contains only the ratio of escort vessels to U-boats – nothing about convoy size."

"I see what you mean. But my Lords will need some convincing. Convoys of more than 40 are anathema to them."

"Why?" Sturdee sounded pugnacious.

"I'm not sure. Part of some ancient doctrine perhaps?"

"If we're right the bigger the convoy the better– because it can afford more escort vessels – which *is* the vital number."

"Got you !"

"The other point," Sturdee continued. "Is the catastrophic effect of allowing packs to grow or even exceed the number of escort vessels. For instance with 6 EVs and 9 U-boats I estimate a 75% chance of six or more losses!"

"Gosh!" Loader sounded impressed for once.

"And what is the only way they can raise a pack of nine – and how long would it take?"

"The shadowing U-boat must call up his mates by radio – and, as I recall, if they're are spread out optimally we calculated that only one new one could arrive per hour."

"So it's going to take 8 hours or more to assemble a devastating Wolfpack. And that's where your VLRA will come in. If it can only put the collecting U-boats down for a few hours a day they will never make it! No effective pack . Virtually no losses. An unanswerable case for more VLRAs in mid-Atlantic?" Sturdee sounded triumphant.

"By Jove I think it does." Loader squeezed Gwen round the waist: "I believe our golden boy has done it again – won the war – in theory!"

"And you can go to Hell too Loader."

"I shall certainly be going. No popsies in heaven – so they say."

"But seriously. This is a theory we can test. It predicts, rather improbably, that losses will be independent of convoy size. And that is something we can test, or Gwen can test by looking at the existing figures – can't you Gwen ?"

"I think so. Convoy size is usually recorded alongside casualty numbers."

"And if that proves out it'll be hard to argue with us. And now we can see exactly why air patrolling is so damned decisive– and its lack so catastrophic. By submerging the U-boats during the day– and thus preventing the gathering of a sizeable pack before nightfall, they render U-boats more or less impotent."

Sturdee was so excited he couldn't sit down.

"Steady on old chap – I suspect you're right – but you've still got to to convince the brass hats. If they can't understand your Convoy Equation you can't expect'em to digest your Gambler's secret – or whatever you call it."

"Bernoulli's Theorem."

"Mussolini's Theorem sounds like."

"Jacob Bernoulli was a Swiss – who taught Maths in Holland 250 years ago – and wrote the first decent book on betting odds."

"Still won't wash."

"But don't you see Loader , it's not MY equation this time, it's not like the convoy equation. It's is as old as the hills, like Pythagoras' Theorem, so even if they don't understand it, they can hardly argue with it can they? They can't blame it on me– or Blackett or Tizard. They'll just have to accept it – and its consequences."

"Nice try old man but in matters of life and death commanders won't be convinced by sums, nor should they be. They need convincing in their bones."

"I read somewhere that Nelson chose to cut the enemy line at Trafalgar on the basis of a calculation."

"Is that so? I read somewhere else that he was copying a tactic employed successfully 30 years earlier by Rodney at 'The Battle of the Saintes'."

"It seems I can't win."

"Yes you can – you've just got to be more convincing and less airy- fairy. Come on, it's time for lunch. They say it's whale-meat mince today with mashed parsnips."

"Ugh ! I only hope the Nazi commanders are reduced to the same disgusting grub as we are."

"No chance old boy. They'll be living off the fat of the land – the fat of France in particular. Doenitz is probably this minute enjoying a first course of Pate de foie gras with one of those delicious French baguettes, followed by a Châteaubriand Steak washed down with a magnificent bottle of Beaune, a sliver of Roquefort cheese, and Eclaire au Chocolat to finish with."

" I hear they've run out of cocoa. We've cut them off."

"Then they'll just have to make do with a Tartine au framboise sauvage , deluged with clotted cream from Isigny."

"You swine. I hope you choke on your whale mince!"

CHAPTER 32
YANKS.

The Derby House canteen was buzzing with rumours just in from the Pacific. It appeared that an American carrier fleet had inflicted a devastating defeat upon the main Japanese Carrier fleet off Midway Island to the West of Hawaii. All four Japanese fleet carriers had been sunk: "Caught them with their pants down apparently" Loader relayed the news to Sturdee – "Their own planes were refuelling and rearming on deck when the Yank dive-bombers caught them."

"That was lucky."

"More likely it was Sigint. I'm sure we've broken the Jap codes. How else would Winnie know to send *Repulse* and *Prince of Wales* to the Indian Ocean well before Pearl Harbour?"

"I don't know. It didn't do us any good."

"No but this time it's wiped out Admiral Tojo's entire carrier fleet. That's *finis* for them." Loader sounded jubilant.

"What does it mean for us ?"

"I'm just trying to think." Loader pushed his minced whale aside, unable to stomach it's fishy odour: "For a start it might give the US, and Admiral Ernest J Bloody King, some self-confidence . And boy do they need it. Up to now he's felt too inferior to take any advice on anti-submarine warfare from us. Now he might – and that could transform the situation off the American East coast."

"Gosh I hope you're right!"

"And the Yanks can relax a bit over the Pacific now.. They must have been terrified the Japanese carriers could do to San Francisco and Los Angeles what they had done to Pearl Harbour. Out of the question now I would think. I'd be a surprised if they've got any fleet carriers left. In the long run they've had it now. American shipyards will simply overwhelm them. This treacle tart isn't half bad by the way. And India's probably secure now."

"I don't follow."

"Without carrier support the Japs won't be able to resupply a massive army in Burma or India."

"That's amazing – such long-range repercussions."

"That's naval warfare for you Sturdee. He who controls the oceans controls everything in the long run. How do you think we came by our empire? It simply fell into our hands. The Spanish and French colonies were completely cut off from Europe . No, the whole Pacific will become an American lake. It's the best news we've had for ages. Good on the Yanks! Here's to them!" Loader lifted an imaginary toast.

Blackett, it appeared, nurtured no hard feelings against Sturdee. He telephoned to say: "I have got Philip Morse talking to my boys right now. He is the head of the new ASWORG in America. Does that ring a bell?

"No."

"Antisubmarine Warfare Operational Research Group ."

"Never heard of them."

" But they've heard of you Sturdee. Indeed it was those talks you gave over there which encouraged them to set it up. Apparently they think of you as the bee's knees. So I'm sending them up to you for a few days. It's absolutely vital we impress them . Where King may not take advice from the Admiralty direct he might take it from his own scientists. They're both aces by the way. Morse is a full professor at MIT– an expert on acoustics. His assistant William Shockley is a star at Bell Labs."

"What about their security clearances?"

"You can tell them anything– except Ultra of course." Sturdee took this to mean SIGINT from Station X which was always labelled 'Ultra-secret' .

Philip Morse was a dapper moustachioed little man 10 years older than Sturdee. His first words were : "It was hearing your talk in Boston which made me want to set up our own group within the U.S. Navy."

"How did you get over here?"

"By a very roundabout route didn't we Bill? Pan Am flying boat from New York to Bermuda, on from there to Lisbon and from there to Loch Foyne on the West coast of Ireland. We transferred to Shannon airport and caught a flight from there to Bristol – then on to London by train."

Sturdee took an instant liking to Morse. He was modest, eager to learn and very well read :

"I am no scientific genius I'm afraid: neither in theory nor experiment – not like Shockley here. But I try to learn a bit about everything – everyone says unbridled curiosity is my worst fault."

"That's a distinct advantage in OR " Sturdee replied "You've got to poke your nose into everything. You can't wait for the servicemen on the spot to always tell you what they really need. After all they can't always know – because they don't know enough science."

Morse, being an expert on acoustics, Sturdee tried out on him his argument about U-boat hydrophones and their necessarily limited range, though careful not to mention its implications for SIGINT. After a lively discussion Morse eventually concurred with Sturdee's analysis.

Then they went on to talk acoustic torpedoes. Morse reported: "As I understand it our Navy has just ordered 10,000 'Type 24 Mines', as we are calling them, for delivery early next year."

Sturdee was so thrilled he had to go and inform Tony Loader at once:

"I told you Giles we're going to win this ruddy war – in the end. We always do you know. It's a difficult habit to lose."

"And to acquire. Come and meet our Yanks. We've got to show them everything – especially the Convoy Tracking room and the Exercise Table at work. They could act as our way into influencing U.S. Navy tactics."

William (Bill) Shockley was a foxy-faced expert on radar and an ex PhD student of Morse's. For some reason Sturdee couldn't like him – if only because of his constant complaints about British food:

"My Gahd they only had one urn for tea and cocoa at the St. Eval base. We had cocoa flavoured tea for breakfast and tea flavoured cocoa for supper."

"You want to try whale meat with parsnips," Loader said "Then you 'll have cause to complain."

"Or what about Mock Crab?" Sturdee added, keeping a straight face: "They say that it's made up of minced German prisoners of war. Can't get enough of them unfortunately. But we are sending out raiding parties. Of course they don't tell you, but that's what our Commando forces are mainly for."

When Shockley went off to Farnborough Sturdee asked Philip Morse, after consulting Joan, to stay at Duff House. Dermot had at last thankfully left for the Argentine.

"He won't have a ration book." Jane explained "But those Yanks have loads of cash".

"I can't ask him…"

"You can't but I can. Then we'll all feed like fighting cocks."

And so it was arranged. Morse, eager to find out what life was really like on the Home Front settled into Dermot's room. Joan produced meals from the home farm supplemented by certain off-the-ration luxuries such as Icelandic cod. Morse got on well with Arfur, helped with the sawing and weeding and was vastly entertained by Maurice:

"That guy's a walking faculty of history" He said, pulling on the other end of Sturdee's saw: "You know what he said to me yesterday?"

"Go on."

"He said there are really two world wars going on right now: a minor one between Britain and Germany, and a major one for world supremacy between America and Britain post-war"

"That sounds like Maurice."

"He said you'd win the former, but lose the latter to us. What do you think Giles?"

"I'd have to think; but in my experience Maurice is often right . He's trained himself to see the big picture – without taking sides. It's certainly true that Churchill has rather foolishly handed over all our scientific Crown Jewels to America : the Cavity Magnetron, the Jet engine – and there are rumours about Atomic weapons."

"Yes, I've heard them too. We got a lecture from a Professor Oliphant from Birmingham University about it. He said we should take it up because it was unsafe to build atomic factories in Britain – because of the bombing. Several of our faculty members disappeared shortly afterwards. We suspect they have been assigned to some atomic project."

"If we'd given the steam engine away to say Prussia – which was then our ally – in 1810, we'd never have led the Industrial Revolution, or built up our vast Victorian wealth. So Maurice is probably right. He says Churchill is half American anyway. His mother was one of those American heiresses who sold themselves for a British title. His dad was a bloody Lord."

"I never knew about his American side."

"What do you think Philip – about Maurice's theory?"

"It was a total surprise to me: I come from Ohio but I've been settled in Boston for 10 years. Boston, so they say , is the biggest Irish city in the world and Irish-Americans are no friends to Britain."

"Don't we know. Your ambassador here, a gangster called Joe Kennedy, wanted us to cave in to Hitler."

"There's a lot of envy of the British Empire – and the British Navy– in my country. Our Commander in Chief Admiral King hates you."

"I detest that man!" Sturdee resumed sawing: "He's such an incompetent. How did he ever get promoted?"

"Quite simple really. All our senior admirals were blamed for failure to anticipate Pearl Harbour. King happened to be the senior admiral not so tainted. He had no part in it .Indeed he had no part in anything worthwhile. He'd been put out to grass – as incompetent."

"He's certainly that. He's losing us the Battle of the Atlantic right now – and God knows how many unnecessary lives – American as well as British."

"Obviously I've got to be careful what I say Giles. But what about Midway?"

"Yes we can't begrudge him that. A titanic victory by all accounts. Tony though attributes it to code breaking – not good Admiralty."

Loader managed to get Morse in to see Admiral Noble for 10 minutes. Sir Percy had given him some trenchant advice: "Giles' strongest card is that everybody trusts him, ; they know he's not snooping on them , or reporting on them to me, or to the Admiralty, behind their backs. So they're glad to have him aboard – which has proved to be vital. Vital. His work on rescue ships, on U-boat depths and on long-range aircraft is changing the course of the battle . Whatever you do Professor earn and retain your Admiral's trust. Without that you will be superfluous, 'Surplus to requirements' as we say."

"I'll take that lesson to heart Giles." Morse said on his departure back to London, and thence back to Washington where he was moving ASWORG headquarters from Boston: "Come over and see us in the Navy Main building near the Capitol. More important, send us all your reports, addressed personally to me and I promise absolute confidentiality. And I will do the same to you. Right now we can't contribute much – but eventually I hope to build up our staff to the size of Professor Blackett's."

"Joan will be sorry to see you go Phil – we all will. No more fish pie or salmon soufflé."

"I've promised Joan. My wife has already dispatched her first food parcel to Duff House."

"We'll pay you back after the war."

"Just win this one for us. That will be payment enough."
"If you can educate Admiral King, we will."

CHAPTER 33
VERY LAST CHANCE

Tobruk had fallen and once again Britain's Desert Army was in headlong retreat before Rommel's Panzers. Loader was furious:

"Can't the buggers fight? What's wrong with them? There are 450,000 of them, twice as many as The Afrika Corps. They've now fallen back on a place called El Alamein – practically in the suburbs of Cairo. What infuriates me is that Jerry can now build air bases within easy bombing range of all our poor bloody ships in Alexandria. Why the hell couldn't they hold on to Tobruk? The Australians held onto it for almost a year?"

"They've gone back to Australia to defend their own country against the Japs. In my newspaper it says defence of the town was handed over to the South African Division – and they didn't put up much of a fight."

"Why would they? Those Boers are no friends of ours. But you can't blame Boers; you have to blame the general who put 'em there. What's his name?"

"Auchinleck."

"Churchill should sack him and put someone else in charge, someone who can fight."

"I think it was Churchill who personally appointed Auchinleck only a few months ago."

"Oh God! Our ships in the Med are being bombed to bits for lack of air protection, all because our army is so pathetic. Too many old Etonians and guardee officers if you ask me. St. Vincent expelled that kind of parasitic trash from the Navy nearly 200 years ago. They are a throwback to the Cavaliers who got smashed by the humble Parliamentarians in the Civil War."

"Cromwell's Ironsides?"

"Now there was a real man. He did so much to forge the Navy too."

It took Gwen but a few days to establish that convoy sinkings were indeed independent of convoy sizes. The overwhelming number of sinkings at present were among independents in areas were the allies were failing to convoy.

Sturdee was jubilant. There were two implications of this result. Firstly convoy sizes should be increased, even doubled immediately. An 80-ship convoy with a dozen escort vessels would be almost invulnerable to submarines. Since wolfpacks of more than a dozen would be almost impossible to assemble' in a day, large convoys would stand a good chance of getting through unscathed even without air cover. And with a modest amount of air cover they would be virtually impregnable. The second implication was that the Convoy Equation, and all it implied, was almost certainly right. It was conceivable that another theory but Sturdee's could explain Gwen's result but , as even Loader conceded, that was highly unlikely. The burden of proof now lay upon those who wanted to disagree with Sturdee's Mathematics.

Sturdee and Loader now compiled a paper summarising all their thinking about the coming Climax battle for the Atlantic:

WAR IN THE ATLANTIC: THE APPROACHING CLIMAX
BATTLE.
by
Operational Research Group, RN Western
Approaches Command.
16 June 1942

Abstract
We will probably lose the Battle of the Atlantic in Spring 1943 unless, as a matter of urgency, we supply Coastal Command with 3 dozen modified Liberator bombers to patrol the Mid-Atlantic Air Gap.

Painful though it has been – with occasional monthly sinkings of more than 100 of our merchant ships, and with the loss in 1941 of two thirds of our required imports – the contest has been but a skirmish so far, preliminary to the decisive battle. The Nazis entered the war with only 50 U-boats, far too few to mount an effective blockade but they are now commissioning 20 a month while we are sinking only 3 or 4. With 300 they will be able to keep a cordon of 100 continually at sea, able, if spaced 10 miles apart, to intercept every convoy we despatch. The comfortable days of our concealment will be over. Every convoy will then have to fight its way through that cordon, defended only by its own Escort Vessels (EVs) and such very long range (VLR) air support as we can muster. We are facing a climacteric battle which could decide the outcome of the entire war.

As in most such decisive battles, viz Trafalgar and Waterloo, concentration will be everything because the power of a fighting force then increases with roughly the *square* of its numerical size. Why so? Because a unit in the numerically inferior force will generally be subject to a larger barrage of incoming fire and so will survive to fire its own weapons for a correspondingly shorter time. Half as many soldiers or ships, each with lives half as long, are, ceteris paribus, only a quarter as effective. Donitz already knows that one or two U-boats have little chance of launching their torpedoes successfully against a convoy with a typical escort group of half a dozen radar-equipped EVs. They are trained therefore to shadow the convoy on the surface and call up reinforcements by wireless. Given the average spread of the cordon they can reinforce at a rate of no more than one U-boat per hour of shadowing. If a dozen reinforcements could gather before nightfall they could attack en masse that night with, as we shall see, every chance of inflicting catastrophic losses. If, on the other hand, aircraft can patrol the convoy for much of the day, U-boats will be kept submerged, impotent to summon reinforcements, impotent even to keep up with our ships, for their submerged speeds are too low. If Donitz can concentrate he will win. If we can prevent him he will lose. We are facing the classic "battle of concentration" known from Thucydides to von Clausewicz.

To think in context put oneself in the mind of a U-boat commander hoping to launch a convoy attack. He will have been trained to get ahead of the convoy by day, using his superior surface-speed (17 knots as opposed to about 8 for merchant ships in convoy) then attack at full speed from ahead at night, submerging only when he is forced to do so by one of the EVs. If depth-charged he will have to dive too deep to take further part in the action. If not he will need some time to trim to periscope depth, select a target, take enough bearings on it to aim off accurately, and launch his salvo.

From his point of view time is of the essence, and in very short supply. At a combined approach speed of 25 (17 +8) knots he will be in range of the escorts' modern radars for 12 minutes even before he can get among the merchant ships. After that, now probably submerged, he will need a further 15 minutes to fire his salvo. The chance of finding all that time without being intercepted will be rather small – unless the escorts are distracted by other pack submarines attacking simultaneously. Knowing the above timings it is straightforward to calculate his chances of success. Table 1 shows the probability (in per cent) of launching such an attack against a convoy with 6 EVs (typical), given different numbers of submarines N(U) in the pack:

TABLE 1 Percentage chance of individual U-boat success

N (U) (U)	1	2	3	4	5	6	9	12
P (%)	0.1	3	10	20	25	30	50	70

We see the insanity of launching an individual U-boat attack. With less than 3 or 4 companions even bold captains might hesitate, and remember that today, in his rapidly expanding fleet, most of Doenitz's commanders will necessarily be inexperienced. On the other hand within a largish pack of 9 every U-boat has a 50 per cent chance of success. Concentration, concentration, concentration: with it Doenitz stands to win; without it to lose.

Now look at the same battle from the Admiralty's point of view. They will want to estimate their expected losses, and in particular their percentage chances of getting through unscathed L(0) (zero losses), of a 'tragedy' (3 or more), or of a 'catastrophe' (6 or more). Again it is straightforward to calculate such chances as the pack-size N(U) grows (Table 2 where blanks connote less than 1 per cent).

TABLE 2: Probability (%) of various losses as function of N(U)

N(U)	L(zero)	L(1)	L(2)	Tragedy	Catastrophe
1	100	0			
2	95	5	1		
3	70	25	3		
4	40	40	15	3	
5	20	40	30	15	
6	10	30	30	30	
9		2	5	90	75

Again the implication is crystal clear. At all costs we must prevent U-boat concentration. Once the number of U-boats first equals and then exceeds the number of EVs, catastrophe first becomes likely, then inevitable.

What can we do? The obvious remedy is to increase the number of our EVs per convoy. That is however difficult and expensive. The enemy will always hold the initiative as to where he will concentrate his U-boats, and that is what he has done so far throughout the war: first in our South Western Approaches then in our North Western before being pushed far out to sea by air patrols mounted from the British Isles, and latterly from Iceland. He also moved U-boats with predictable success to unpatrolled areas off Gibraltar and West Africa. Now he is concentrating off the Carolinas and in the Caribbean with distressing consequences for our merchantmen. But the general point is that increasing our EVs everywhere will never be economic when the enemy can concentrate wherever he will.

Admiral Noble is proposing to partly meet this threat with the introduction of Support Groups, the first of which are forming now. These groups of fast EVs will be stationed where they can best be sent to the aid of besieged convoys. By temporarily doubling the number of EVs in that convoy they can partially offset the enemy's advantage from concentration. Even so ships have only limited speeds and so Support Groups might take 12 or more hours to arrive – by which time it might be too late. Much faster respite is called for, and that can only come from the air. An aircraft can transfer from one convoy to the next in less than an hour.

Where and when will the climacteric battle be fought? One can hope that our troubles in the Western Atlantic will soon be remedied by convoy and air patrol. Doenitz will then be forced to move most of his U-boats back to the Mid Atlantic Air Gap, his last remaining hope for a decisive result. Intelligence estimates he will have sufficient U-boats (300) to completely close his cordon by Xmas 1942 and will have everything to lose by delaying the confrontation any longer. Allowing for atrocious winter weather out there to abate a little the command at Western Approaches anticipates that the decisive battle will start in early spring 1943 and because of the concentration factor, be over shortly thereafter, one way or the other. Either sea- transport into Britain will break down entirely – in which case we will starve; or the U-boats will be defeated. The mathematics of the situation allow of no intermediate result. After one side or the other gains the upper hand the outcome will likely be irreversible.

So what are our chances? The battle will be fought in a square roughly 700 miles on a side centred 700 miles south of Cape Farewell, the tip of Greenland. It is defined by the inability of our existing aircraft based in Britain, Iceland or Newfoundland to reach it. This inability is not absolute however because there is a single squadron (a dozen) of special Coastal Command 4-engined Liberators which can get to it. Stripped of all unnecessary weight and drag and equipped with extra fuel tanks they can remain aloft for more than 20 hours and patrol the critical area with high definition radar. At 200 knots they can circle a convoy every 15 minutes. Experience shows that any U-boat detecting their approach will submerge immediately and remain submerged for at least 30 minutes. Too slow to keep up, the submerged submarines may lose the convoy. In any case the assembly of a lethal wolf-pack will be prevented.

The diminution in sinkings due to so many hours of air-patrol per convoy can straightforwardly be calculated (Table 3):

TABLE 3:Probable loss rates (%) as function of air-patrol time.

H(Hours/day)	Zero losses	Tragedy	Catastrophe
0		100	85
2		95	30
4		75	6
6	9%	30	
8	50	3	
10	90		
12	100		

(Assume 6 EVs as before and N(U) =12 minus H(hours).

The figures are dramatic but entirely expected given the vital importance of Concentration. Once Doenitz has 100 U-boats in the Gap his packs can build rapidly during the day and strike lethally the following night. But if they cannot build, because of patrolling aircraft, they will be ineffective.

How many VLR Aircraft will be needed to win the Battle of the Atlantic? Not so many it turns out; less in fact than are lost in a single 1000-bomber raid over Germany. We have 20 convoys crossing the Atlantic at any moment with a fourth of them – say 5 – in the Gap at any one time. If each were to get 8 hours of air patrol (Table 3) a day that requires 40 hours per day in all. Given that a Liberator requires 16 hours to get out to the Gap and back that allows it 4 hours patrol time per sortie. So 10 Liberator patrols a day could win us the looming Battle of the Atlantic. Supposing a plane/crew could fly out every 3 or 4 days this calls for barely more than 3 dozen aircraft, of which we have a dozen already. In the context of 1000-bomber raids this number is minute. Recall though that these are not production- line machines. They have to be stripped of much unnecessary equipment and reequipped to hold the extra fuel for 20-hour patrols. We know they can do it because 120 Squadron based in Northern Ireland does so already.

Because they cannot carry sufficient weight of explosives to be generally lethal our maritime patrol aircraft have had to act thus far more as scarecrows than U-boat killers. That is about to change. The submerged U-boat cannot still its propellers for long because it needs way to operate its hydroplanes. That will make it peculiarly vulnerable to the acoustic torpedo which can home in on its propeller noise, follow it down into the depths, and there send it to its watery grave without human intervention. The US Navy, following a RN initiative, has just ordered 10,000 of these 'Type 24 Mines' for delivery by Jan. 1943. Fitted with 3 or 4 of these light weapons there is no reason why VLR Liberators should not sink at least one U-boat on every mid-Atlantic sortie. Had we a few dozen in time, such aircraft could win the battle out there within weeks.

In summary the approaching climax battle of the Atlantic will be lost if Doenitz can concentrate his 100 U-boats on station in the Mid Atlantic Air Gap. However we can prevent him doing so by equipping Coastal Command with no more than 3 dozen 4-engined Liberator bombers. We will need 3 months to modify them and two more to train their crews. We have 7 to 8 months before the battle commences. It won't last long; either way. But the result will probably be final.

P.S. Our calculations depend on two kinds of assumptions. The mathematical assumptions (see Appx. A) which led to our tables are unexceptionable and can be checked by anyone with a High School Certificate in Mathematics. The tactical assumptions (Appx. B) are more questionable but they have been formulated and tested not by us but by Western Approaches Command, a body with more practical expertise of Anti-Submarine warfare than any other on the planet. All we have done is bring the mathematical and tactical assumptions together to work out the numerical consequences using arithmetic which has been checked by several independent operational research scientists. To dismiss these arguments, however unpalatable they are, is therefore to dismiss the experience of the very Escort Group commanders who have been fighting this war successfully for two years.

P.S.S. Could these conclusions be nullified by the possible effects of cipher-breaking by either side? No. Cryptanalysis cannot much effect the Climax Battle because Doenitz's 100-boat cordon will locate all our convoys without it, whilst we will be unable to avoid them because there will be no gaps through which to pass.

P.S.S.S. Will Escort Carriers (ECs) be able to supply the necessary air patrols in the Gap if VLRAs are not made available? Perhaps Yes, perhaps No. ECs are highly recognizable as such, thin skinned and extremely vulnerable to fire. Moreover they must turn out of a convoy into wind in order to fly their aircraft off and on. At such moments they are vulnerable to torpedo attack. *Audacity*, our first EC, was very successful while she survived, but was quickly sunk by a U-boat when outside the convoy perimeter. Do we risk the entire Atlantic war gambling on ECs?

Both Admiral Noble and Air Vice Marshal Robb countersigned the paper which was rushed by dispatch rider to Blackett and to the highest echelons of the Admiralty in London.

It must have had repercussions because Blackett reacted with an encoded reply only three days later:

"Great paper Sturdee. My boys have been all over it and we concur. More importantly The First Sea Lord wants a one-page version he could take, at an appropriate moment, to Churchill at short notice. Could you send me a draft? I'd do it myself but very short papers, as you will find, take much longer to write, if they are to be effective. Anyway Churchill would be more likely to react favourably if it came from your group, and not mine, though Admiral Pound will most likely sign it as his own, and submit it to the Chiefs of Staff also. Good luck.'

Sturdee was both thrilled and terrified. Getting the wording right or wrong could mean the difference between victory and defeat. Unfortunately his chief wordsmith Tony Loader had deserted him with only a brief note:

"Sorry boss, temporarily gone to sea with convoy for Russia. I have to get my sea legs back before I get a command of my own. In any case we need first-hand experience of this Murmansk convoy business because it's taking away so many of our precious Escort Vessels. Back in about a month. PS the old man approved it."

The next 48 hours was a nightmare as, abetted by Gwen, Maurice and Joan, Sturdee came up with the one-page, 500 word edition:

THE APPROACHING CLIMAX BATTLE

From
First Sea Lord to Prime Minister.
June 1942

We will probably lose the Battle of the Atlantic in Spring 1943 unless, as a matter of urgency, we supply Coastal Command with 3 dozen more Liberator bombers to patrol the Mid-Atlantic Air Gap. They will require 6 months to modify for this role.

With 300 U-boats Doenitz will be able to keep a cordon of 100 continually at sea, able, if spaced 10 miles apart, to intercept every convoy we despatch. The comfortable days of our concealment will be over. Every convoy will then have to fight its way through that cordon, defended only by its own Escort Vessels (EVs) and such very long range (VLR) air support as we can muster. We are facing the climax battle which could decide the outcome of the war.

Concentration will be everything. Doenitz already knows that one or two U-boats have little chance of launching torpedoes successfully against a convoy with a typical escort group of 6 radar-equipped EVs. They are trained therefore to shadow the convoy on the surface and call up reinforcements by wireless. Given the average spread of the cordon they can reinforce at a rate of no more than one U-boat per hour of shadowing. If a dozen reinforcements can gather before nightfall they could attack en masse that night with every chance of inflicting catastrophic losses. If, on the other hand, aircraft can patrol the convoy for much of the day, U-boats will be kept submerged, impotent to summon reinforcements, impotent even to keep up with our ships, for their submerged speeds are too low. If Doenitz can concentrate he will win. If we can prevent him he will lose. We are facing the classic "battle of concentration" known from Thucydides to Nelson.

The Gap is defined by the inability of our existing aircraft to reach it. This inability is not absolute however because a single squadron (Number 120) of Coastal Command Liberators can already get to it. Stripped of all unnecessary weight and equipped with extra fuel tanks they can remain aloft for over 20 hours and patrol the critical area with high definition radar. At 200 knots they can circle a convoy every 15 minutes. Experience shows that any U-boat detecting their approach submerges immediately and remains submerged for at least 30 minutes. Too slow to keep up the submerged submarines may lose the convoy. In any case the assembly of a lethal wolf-pack will be prevented.

Based on experience the diminution in sinkings per hour of air-patrol per convoy can be estimated :

Probability of different loss rates (%) as function of air-patrol time.

H(Hours/day)	Zero losses	Tragedy (>3)	Catastrophe(>6)
0		100	85
2		95	30
4		75	6
6	9%	30	
8	50	3	
10	90		
12	100		

[assuming a typical 6 EVs in convoy; where >' is 'more than' and blanks denote zero %. The dramatic differences are to be expected when there can be no sinkings with 12 hours of patrol.]

In summary the approaching climax battle will be lost if Doenitz can concentrate his 100 U-boats on station in the Air Gap. However we can prevent him doing so by equipping Coastal Command with 3 dozen more modified Liberator bombers. We have 7 to 8 months before the battle commences but 6 months will be needed to modify them and train their crews. It won't last long. But the result, either way, will probably be final.

Thinking was one thing, trying to persuade innumerate but very powerful old men was quite another. By the time the paper finally went off to London Sturdee was both mentally and physically on his knees.

CHAPTER 34
IN THE NUDE

As soon as he began to draw Joan's naked body Giles knew he'd made a serious mistake. It wasn't her figure, which was very beautiful – though not quite as perfect as that of the Rokeby Venus – according to some experts, that of an 18-year-old model. Nor was it the awkwardness both of them had felt acutely at first, Joan specially, who had blushed crimson. They'd overcome that. He'd promised to look away while she adopted the reclining position, resting a cheek on an elbow, displaying her wasp waist and long legs to sensual effect. But the Rokeby was all about the bottom, the proudest, the most exquisite, the most unforgettable bottom in all of art. In over three centuries since Velasquez had painted it, no artist had remotely approached the perfection of that bottom. And now Giles was challenging himself to succeed where so many other greater artists had failed. He felt terrified, embarrassed and foolish all at the same time. Worse still, as soon as he begun to draw he knew he couldn't do it. The large 7-foot canvas he had prepared was so large he couldn't take in Joan's figure all at once and get her proportions right. Either her head came out too big, or the legs too short , or the shoulders too narrow or the bum too large. Artists loved caricature but you couldn't caricature perfection.

He'd borrowed Maurice's gramophone and Beethoven's triumphant Seventh , which had been thundering throughout his misery, had come to an end.

"That was lovely." Joan said, the first utterance by either of them since the sitting had begun.

"Would you like a rest? Are you warm enough? I could stoke up the fire a bit more."

"No, I'm quite comfy for now . Choose some more music – but don't tell me what it is."

He put on Handel's Water Music and glared at a drawing which was hopelessly wrong, irredeemably so. And he knew why. He was standing too close to it to take it all in. But how had Velasquez overcome the same problem? The solution came in a flash. He must have started with a much smaller drawing – then scaled it up. He glanced at his watch. Only forty-five minutes of the agreed sitting time left. Perhaps.

At the end of the Water Music and the pizzicato movement from Schubert's C major quintet, Joan said she had to go.

"Can I see ?" She asked, tying the belt of the dressing gown which she'd made from the silk he had brought her back from America.

"Certainly not. No self-respecting artist would show his work before it was finished."

"Are you pleased then?"

He had to think about that:

"Let's say it would be easier if you weren't so bloody beautiful."

"Like most people, I've never seen my own behind."

"Take my word for it."

"No; I'll wait until I've seen your painting. How long will it take?"
"At least three more sittings."
"Sitting!" She laughed, "That's the one thing I won't be doing. Not in that pose!"

Sturdee was excited by his smaller drawing Probably because he'd rushed it , using the absolute minimum of line and shade, it 'looked right'. Anything more added would only detract. Perhaps because she really was, his Venus looked unattainable ; mortal man could gaze upon her – but never touch. Velasquez had enhanced that effect ingeniously by having his model gaze into a mirror, hypnotised by her own beauty, uncaring of what any other voyeur might think.

Joan's one great fear about the painting was that Arfur would find out about her posing in the nude for Giles before the picture was finished. But at the moment he was away in Hampshire – on a visit to Maurice's cottage with Maurice. They had departed in Sturdee's motorcycle sidecar partly to do maintenance on the old building – which had been left vacant since the beginning of the war, but mainly to console Arfur for his 'terrible tragedy'. Almost entirely on their own Arfur and Gem had turned one third of the paddock into a flourishing potato plantation. They had ploughed, ploughed again and harrowed, planted and weeded until furrows fifty yards long and straight as a die sprouted dark green plants which promised to keep more than 40 people in calories for a year. Arfur was immensely proud of his plantation: the first earnest of his elevation to manhood. He had become intensely patriotic, never missing Mr Churchill's speeches, and regarded the flourishing crop as his contribution to the war effort. He had felt inadequate knowing that everyone else at Duff House, even Joan , was fighting in the war against Germany. Now he too was making a manly contribution.

Joan, the only one of them who knew anything about horticulture, and that garnered mostly from Ministry of Ag. pamphlets. had told him to dig up one of his plants from time to time to see how the tubers underneath were getting on. Lovely white-skinned globes, they swelled week by week fuelled by the summer sun on the leaves above. Arfur counted, Arfur weighed , Arfur calculated . A harvest of one and a half tons he reckoned: roast potatoes to go with the Sunday joint; mashed potatoes to go with sausages and peas; new potatoes swimming in butter and parsley; potato cakes for breakfast; rissoles; onion and potato pie, bubble and squeak; fried potatoes with bacon; leek and potato soup; potatoes baked in the bonfire – and above all chips: chips, chips, chips. Arfur could eat chips every day, all day. Big chips cooked in beef dripping sprinkled with Oxo and seasoned with salt and Vinegar. He would stand looking over his domain, imagining so much happiness spread far and wide.
Then disaster. One sunny day he knelt on hands and knees to dig up a lusty looking plant with his bare hands, soil sticking in his nails . Horror! The swelling white globes had turned into empty skins, rotten- looking , yellow, diseased. In a panic he dug up another. The same . He ran down to the field on the far side. Worse if anything. Even the centre of the field was infected . There was scarcely a healthy potato left. In a

matter of days everything had gone. He howled, he wanted to cry, he was wretched. Every skin had been penetrated by something evil, and consumed from the inside out.

"Leatherjackets". Joan pronounced after comparing the disgusting remains with a pamphlet from the Ministry illustrating the pestilences and parasites to which potatoes were heir.

"It's not your fault Arfur." she tried to console him afterwards , reading out her pamphlet aloud: 'Leatherjackets are the grubs of Crane-flies, more often called Daddy Longlegs. They lay their eggs in grassland in late summer; they lie dormant in winter but the following growing season they can attack root-crops , particularly potatoes and carrots. For that reason it is unwise to plant root crops in newly cultivated grassland. Better to leave the tilth unplanted for a year, which gives the birds, particularly rooks, a chance to clear the land of such grubs which can grow up to 4 inches long. If an infestation is discovered, plough the land immediately to prevent the grubs pupating and turning into flying insects which will spread their eggs elsewhere."

Maurice exclaimed: "My gosh we could lose our onions!".

"I don't think so." Joan replied. " Onions have their own pests – but not Leatherjackets apparently. But we mustn't take any risks. Can you start ploughing tomorrow Arfur?"

"Ar, I can. Shouldn't be 'ard.. The soil's soft now – not like it were in February. Could be done in a day if we started early."

"I'll get up at dawn" Giles offered "At about five. Get your breakfast while you're harnessing Gem. Didn't I tell you rooks are good news?"

"And with a bit of luck," Joan added "That land will be clean next year – just right for a new crop of spuds."

"It just shows you" Maurice said "Farming is a skilled business. We amateurs are bound to make mistakes."

"I feel 'orrible abaht it." Arfur looked like crying.

"Well don't." Joan said. "If anyone is to blame, it's me. But potatoes have always been an unreliable crop. Look at the Irish Potato Famine."

"Was that Leatherjackets?"

"No that was Blight " Maurice explained. "A fungus brought over from America on the first transatlantic steamships in the 1840s."

"I didn't know that." Sturdee said.

"It wasn't the only hideous disaster inflicted on Europe by the steamship. Phylloxera came over at much the same time too. That was an American beetle that wiped out 99.9% of all the Vines on the Continent . It completely ruined the peasant classes of France and the Mediterranean countries. Only mass emigration saved many from starvation."

"How did they wipe out the beetles?" Joan asked

" They didn't. You can't. They had to graft European Vines on to American rootstock – which is impervious to the beetle."

"You'll feel better Arfur, " Giles encouraged. "Bringing all those horrible grubs to the surface tomorrow where the rooks will eat them."

"I wish't I knowed more abaht farming. To think as I put up scare-crows to frighten off the bleedin' rooks. Perhaps if I hadn't…"

"If I got you some books on farming would you read them?" Joan asked.

" 'Course I would."

Knowing that the moment Arfur returned Joan's sittings would end, Sturdee transposed his sketch onto the much bigger canvas. Velasquez' genius lay not so much in the drawing as in the small number of flesh tints which had enabled him to breathe so much life into the body underneath. He was tempted to copy Velasquez's tints exactly, but there were arguments against that. Firstly Velasquez 's Venus had a marble white sheen . Upper-class Spanish women of the time had prided themselves on the ghostlike palidity of their skin, doing everything to protect it from the sun . Joan however had no such pretensions. Her flesh had the peach-like complexion of a woman used to cycling, gardening, even carrying buckets of pigswill. So he mixed a large kitchen bowl of oils to achieve a neutral flesh tint matched to Joan' colouring. He could do so easily because she didn't have to pose in the nude for that. Then he subdivided the neutral mix into six cups, also purloined from the kitchen, and tinted each very lightly , according to Velasquez's prescriptions: one with a hint of a burnt sienna; one with warm red; one with purple; one with Ochre; one with a precise combination of cold red and cold blue, which he had been taught made perfect shadow; finally one with a strong mixture of whitest white to capture those parts of the body reflecting the most light. Thank goodness he thought, artists no longer had to employ raw lead in their white pigments. Poor Goya had been rendered stone deaf by that poison.

Next he made a rough copy of the original small drawing and tried out his tints on it. They were nearly all too strong so that Joan turned out looking blotchy. He thinned and altered , hoping that the final result would dry with the same blush they had been painted . As the court painter, Velasquez had been careless of the cost of his model and had probably painted thin glaze upon thin glaze to achieve perfection. Sturdee would be lucky if he got 5 to 6 hours altogether, depending on Arfur's return. Certainly there would be no opportunity for correcting mistakes. For the second sitting Joan brought a book and chose the music in advance. There was no uncomfortableness on either side. On Sturdee's recommendation she was reading. ' L'Oeuvre' Zola's masterpiece, closely modelled on his boyhood friend the painter Ce´zanne.

Having blocked in the large painting in his neutral tint Sturdee immediately went to work on Joan's bottom. If he couldn't get that right the rest of his painting would be superfluous. The cleft had to be perfect ; he scarcely dared to to breathe while he shaded it in with the lightest, lightest touch. Phew! Then the merest hint of pink, particularly where she was resting upon the dark drape which she herself had made in imitation of the Rokeby one by dying an old bedsheet.

Needing to relax he then worked his way up the spine in the merest ghost of a shadow, expanding outwards between the shoulder blades using the ball of his thumb , and two brushes , one between his teeth. More than anything it felt like one of those face climbs he'd done in the Bernese Oberland. You looked and looked, weighed and measured , but then you had to commit yourself, going fast because otherwise calf and fingertip could give out before you reached a safe stance. In both pursuits there were passages with scarcely time to take breath: then a ledge with a crack above in which you wedged a hand securely enough to blow like a breaching grampus.

"I never realised painting was such an athletic activity." was Joan's comment in between Rossini pieces.

Sturdee never replied because he was too committed to realize there was anyone else in the studio. He now had one brush for light shadow, one for light itself which picked out Joan's calves and shoulder blades. The gramophone ground to a hideous halt without him noting. He had turpentine burning in his mouth, paint on his chin, both cheeks ,and in his hair.

"Giles!" Joan's shouts eventually drew his attention.

"Wind the gramophone for goodness sake, and stoke up that fire. I'm all over goose-pimples, even if it is summer time. A girl's not supposed to lie naked and unmoving for nearly two hours, not if she's alive"

"I got carried away."

"So I could hear from all your blowing and ranting."

"Was I swearing?"

"You certainly were – and in no gentlemanly way. My mother would have had a fit if she'd heard some of the words you used, words not used among polite society in Leigh-on-Sea."

"I don't believe you."

"Cross my heart and hope to die."

"I'm in another world when I paint . There is just me, this beautiful body mocking me, the canvas, and a sardonic Velasquez looking over my shoulder. Okay, the fire's roaring again."

"I can feel it thank goodness."

" Here goes Signor Rossini. It's 'The Italian Girl in Algeria' ."

"My favourite."

"Can you last another hour?"

"No , but I might manage half. And don't neglect me so entirely. I'm not being paid you know. A girl like to know she's appreciated."

"If I can just get this painting right you'll become immortal . You can't be more appreciated than that."

Arfur and Maurice returned from Hampshire in very different moods. Arfur was full of the wonders of country living – which he had never experienced before – and announced that after the war he was going to become a farmer. Maurice, as he confided to Giles over a late whiskey, was sad:

"I visited my poor wife's grave. The cottage is no longer the home she made for us both any more – it's just a dwelling now. And I could see my lonely and pointless old-age stretching out before me. This is far better. Here we are struggling to achieve something worthwhile . We may fail but we're at least putting everything of ourselves into it. My life has meaning here: so has yours; so has Joan's and so has Arfur's. And that means so much. I am glad to be back. So did you bed Joan?"

"What do you take me for?"

" A healthy young man much in love with a young woman who is in half a mind to reciprocate. More than half."

"Then you're wrong. She thinks so little of me that she agreed to pose in the nude and I painted a not half bad picture of her."

Maurice wanted to see it, after being sworn to secrecy:

"It's not quite finished." was his first comment.

"It's only background stuff – and her face of course."

" But it's bloody powerful. It draws the eye at once. One can't take one's eyes off it. Especially that bum. What does Joan think of it?"

"She hasn't seen it."

"Good heavens. Perhaps that's as well."

"What do you mean?"

"Let me look at the Rokeby picture."

Giles handed him the print.

"Yes, I thought so. Whereas Velasquez's Venus is unattainable – admiring her own beauty in the mirror, your young lady flaunts herself. Her bum sticks out towards you that tiny bit further. 'Here – take me if you can' she's saying 'I'm ripe for love'."

"It didn't feel like that at the time."

" Oh didn't it ?" Maurice sounded sceptical.

"No it didn't."

"Nevertheless, that is how you have painted her Sturdee. It's a magnificent piece of pornography. To a high class madame it will be worth a thousand guineas – or more . She'd hang it prominently in her salon so that her rich clientele would look at it and reach for their wallets at once."

"I never meant…"

"Never mind what you meant– it is what you have painted. Do you want my advice?"

"That depends."

"Don't let Jean ever see that filthy lovely painting."

"Why not?"

"Because it will make matters even more awkward between the two of you. She'll be furious. You're claiming she has surrendered to you when– by your own account – she has not . In other words you've raped her on canvas, for all the world to see. Tell you what."

"What?" Giles felt sick.

"Give her that sketch you've done. It's lovely – moreover you can't recognise Joan's image. Finish the big painting – but then dispose of it for 30 years. Joan might love it as an old lady – whether she's married you by then or not."

Sturdee must have looked devastated because the older man put a consoling hand around his shoulder:

"You know Velasquez might have preferred your painting to his own; but he would never have got away with it in those days. But Giles I don't want you to lose her unnecessarily. Our Joan is a marvellous mixture of scullery maid and empress . And I care for you both. You're the only family I might ever have. It would be too risky to show Joan your painting, fine though it is."

Maurice was right of course. Sturdee stared at his handiwork after the older man had gone. Yes it was pretty filthy – if looked at in a certain light, though he hadn't felt it at the time. But he was loth to destroy it after putting so much of himself into its creation. In its way – as a piece of pornography – it was bloody good. He finished it off with a good likeness of Joan's face and hair both in and out of the mirror. But he omitted Velasquez's Cupid – resisting the temptation to insert a wicked-looking Arfur instead.

As soon as it was dry he removed the canvas from the stretcher , and reversed it, varnishing Joan before hiding her from sight. All the expert eye would see afterwards was a brand new canvas , stretched and ready to paint. He even prepared it with fresh white gesso so there was no chance whatsoever of Joan's silhouette showing through. He had a professional frame the smaller drawing which he presented to Joan in private.

"What about your big painting?" She asked

"Destroyed it. Took it down the garden and burned it when no one was about. All the proportions were bloody wrong. Couldn't bear to have it around – reminding me what an amateur I am."

"I'm sorry. For you I mean Giles. You sounded as if you were trying so hard."

"I was. I was. But trying and succeeding are not the same. That was my last nude. I'm just not good enough. I'll stick to sailing boats and horses in future. We all have to learn our limitations."

The two of them never mentioned the painting again. Sturdee found himself relieved . It had been Joan's idea – not his own. On the fresh canvas he started a painting of the Shagbat taking off in a cloud of spray, throwing rainbows up into the sky. Arfur loved it. He begged Giles to leave it hanging on the studio wall.

CHAPTER 35
CRACKING UP

When Loader came back from his Murmansk convoy he was exultant:

"Never had any problems with my tin flipper. Confident I can do Escort duties – though not handling depth-charges in heavy seas – I wouldn't be doing that any more anyway. All I've got to do now is convince the sawbones."

"What about the convoy?" Sturdee asked.

"That's another thing altogether; I'm just finishing my report. Nothing like the Atlantic. Do you know that daylight up there lasts practically 24 hours. So no good for U-boats. Never got a sniff. But didn't the bloody Luftwaffe come after us: wave after wave out of Norwegian bases. I never want to see another Junkers or Heinkel in my entire life. Low-level attacks – you could practically see their pilots' faces. Us firing ack-ack: pom-poms, Oerlikons, 4.5's, – empty shell-cases rattling all over the deck. I thought we would run out of ammo. Even the merchant vessels were spraying machine gun fire all over the shop, sometimes in our direction."

"Any luck?"

"You won't believe how hard it is to hit fast-moving aircraft from the deck of a rolling ship. But on the other hand I would say only one of their bombs in 50 hit our ships. They got three ships out of about 30: one sank; two limped on to Russia. We shot down half a dozen Jerrys."

"Sounds like a pretty fair return."

"Depends how you do the calculation."

"How do you mean?"

"Do you realise Giles there was practically one escort vessel for every cargo vessel whereas here we are having to work with only one for 10! We are getting the hind tit as usual."

"Bloody hell." Sturdee was furious

"Echoed old man. Echoed. But think on this. There is a whole extra source of escort vessels in the North Sea which we could call upon if things get nasty in the Crux battle."

"Good point. I suppose it's a matter of priorities – supplying Russia to keep it in the war – or supplying ourselves. So things might change if we start losing in the Air Gap?"

"Exactly. So I think we should be generally cheered up Giles. My God but those Russkis are mean devils. Do you know they wouldn't allow us ashore, not even for a stretch or a drink after bringing them all those goodies at the risk of our lives. Understandably our matelots hate them."

"I suppose we are supplying them for our good, not for theirs . The longer they keep fighting the less fighting we'll have to do. No suicidal Second Front for instance."

" Or some kind of deal drawn up between Winnie and Stalin."

" Same thing isn't it?"

" Do you know about our latest sinkings?"

"You'd better go and see Gwen. She's upstairs. I can't bear to look at them any more."

"Have you been keeping her warm Sturdee?"

"You mind your own business Loader. I'm a gentleman."

"Whatever *that* means."

Sturdee received a note to go and see the admiral. Nobody would think that Noble carried upon his shoulders the burden of the biggest battle in history:

"I don't want to lose you Giles. We all know what a contribution you've made: but I've been getting reports that you are suffering from nervous exhaustion."

"May I ask who from Sir?"

"No you may not. But sources I respect, and more than one. Therefore I am putting you before a medical board. They may order an interval out of the line of fire. All I ask of you Giles is to be totally frank with them. We all need you back here – but only in sparkling form. That's what makes you different: seeing things the rest of us are too exhausted to see. There is no shame in mental exhaustion. All my escort crews get regular leaves. I insist upon it. And you will do the same. No man who ever lived could do without it – me included. Interview over. When you are properly fit I will want to see you immediately again."

Back at Dry Cleaning Sturdee wondered if the reports were true. Who might have informed upon him – Loader, Blackett, Winn... there weren't many alternatives. But did it matter? It was true he couldn't sleep properly any more: he still went to bed exhausted then woke two hours later, heart pounding. Then he would lie restlessly for hours seeing that monster Ernest J King throwing away the war for the sake of his petty ego. Or the awful sinking figures rolling round and round like a nightmare in his head .

The board of five doctors, including two civilian psychiatrists, asked some probing questions. Sturdee decided to reply with honesty as Noble had asked him to .They called him back afterwards:

"We are not used to dealing with scientists like yourself Doctor Sturdee – but you are exhibiting all the classical symptoms of nervous exhaustion or 'neurasthenia'. Not surprising after what you been through this past 14 months. Have you got a home to go to?"

Giles briefly described Duff House.

"Ideal." The chairman said: "It's market gardening for you the next three months. You are excluded from Derby House, entry to your office, or contact with your naval colleagues as from the end of this week. Until we clear you for duty again. We understand that Admiral Noble relies heavily on your judgements. You are in no condition to give him sound advice at present. Back here in three months."

Sturdee was looking gloomily at the sinking charts on the wall, wondering where he had gone wrong, when Loader burst in waving a scrap of paper:

"I've got it Giles, I've got it. A seagoing command: one of those new River Class Frigates now completing her fitting-out on the Clyde. We may well form part of one of Noble's new Support Groups in time for the Climax battle!"

Gwen ran downstairs and flung her arms around Loader's neck.

"While I've been chucked out." Giles grunted.

"I know Sturdee. Mansfield told me. Best thing for you old boy. You're knackered. You'll be back. Just look at me."– he waved his tin flipper in the air : "Where are we going to hold the party? I know where to get the booze . But we ain't got much time. I am off in a couple of days."

It had to be Duff House of course, despite Loader's wariness of Sturdee's landlady. For her part Joan was sure it must be Loader who had turned Giles in, and was consequently grateful and forgiving. What was to have been a drunken carousal turned into more of a Midsummer celebration with food as well as drink.

"What the heck am I going to do for three whole bloody months?" Sturdee complained a couple of nights later over supper. "I've never been idle in my life."

"And you're not starting now." Joan said "What about our other potatoes up here in the garden? We should start lifting them pretty soon. No sign of Leatherjackets in them so far, not yet but…... But the sooner we start lifting them out of the ground the better. There must be about a ton and a half, all to be lifted by hand. Backbreaking work – I was wondering how the Dickens we'd manage. And what about cooking and heating this winter? I see there's not much left in the woodpile."

"True enough."

"And we could make a fortune out of bundles of kindling-wood. People are desperate to light their coal fires while firelighters can't be had for love nor money. Arfur could sell them on his stall. And most importantly, you can now run me to some of the markets and market towns. You know what bargains we sometimes pick up. That reminds me. We've got to lay our hands on a chemistry set for Arfur."

"A chemistry set?" Sturdee sounded amazed

"Every boy had one before the war: all my brothers had. How is he going to become a proper farmer if doesn't know chemistry? I'll advertise. There must be hundreds lying about forgotten. Half a saucepan of onions will winkle them out . Then you can teach him while there's a chance."

"You get me the set and I'll teach him. Make sure the instructions are inside the box though. My chemistry is rusty."

After Joan had gone up to read to Arfur, Sturdee asked Maurice:

"Do you think I'm exhausted? "

"Come to think of it, you have been gloomy of late. Despondent about the war . None of that old Giles sparkle. I'd say you were becoming convinced we are going to lose. Is that true?"

"I must admit I can't see our way through this coming winter and spring. It is all so out of our hands now – and in those of horrible, selfish, innumerate old men – King, Lindemann, Bomber Harris. And there's all that tripe about in the newspapers...."

"Then I can see you wouldn't be much use to your Admiral any more Giles. The last thing he can want is a defeatist at his headquarters."

"But I'm not a defeatist...."

"Sounds like it to me. Let me tell you something to cheer you up. Ever heard of Cryolite?"

"Nope."

"I thought not. It's one of the rarest minerals in the world. There's only one mine producing it on the entire planet – and that's at some godforsaken place in West Greenland."

"So?"

"How important is Aluminium to the war effort?"

"Bloody vital – especially in aircraft manufacturer."

"Do you remember that call over the BBC for all of us to hand in spare aluminium pots and pans to make Spitfires?"

"I do. We went down to the police station with one or two of our own."

"But how do you make Aluminium?"

"Out of bauxite ore as I recall– which we get from either the Caribbean or Canada. We get bauxite-carriers in our convoys."

"Then what?"

"I have no idea."

"You've got to smelt the ore at extremely high temperatures – nearly two thousand degrees. Costs a fortune in coal. Unless?"

"Unless what?"

"You add a pinch of the Greenland Cryolite. Brings the smelting temperature down to under one thousand degrees."

"My gosh that must make a difference to the cost"

"It does. It does,. And where do you think Mr Hitler gets his Cryolite from?"

"No idea."

"He doesn't. Hasn't had any for years and he'll never get his hands on any . We'll out-produce him in aircraft production 10 to 1..."

"I never thought of that."

"Ever heard of blockade Sturdee? Blockade, blockade, blockade! That's what this war is all about lad. Has been from the very beginning. You worry we're not getting some of our convoys through. Hitler hasn't had a *single* convoy through since 1939 – nearly 3 years ago. And you talk about defeat staring us in the face"

"I didn't."

"Yes you did. And Cryolite is only one tiny item. There must be literally hundreds like it . You've lost your sense of balance Giles. Think of the other side of the hill – it might cheer you up again. Mr Hitler's had it. Unless he can get to Caucasian oil before this winter he's finished. And he's hundreds of miles short of the Caspian Sea isn't he? Soon he won't be able to fly the aircraft he's got. Aviation gasoline must be costing the Germans more than good Schnapps a pint. Which reminds me. Why don't you snitch us a glass of Joan's Sloe Gin? I'm sure she'll forgive you – in the circumstances. Nervous breakdown and all that."

"I'm not having a nervous breakdown."

"Of course you are. They don't hand down three month holidays lightly. Go on, be a sport. That Cryolite story was worth a gin any time."

"Oh alright. Joan's in a good mood now I can run her to markets regularly."

"Make it a big one then. We might not get another chance like this."

Now that he didn't have to get up early Sturdee often sat up late talking to Maurice. A favourite topic of conversation was Joan :

"She'll make you a wonderful wife Giles."

" It may have escaped your notice Maurice that we are not married and that she's engaged to somebody else – a certified war hero."

"Pshaw."

"And she's a staunch Catholic while I am an equally staunch Atheist – no more inclined to give up my belief-system than she is."

"But she loves you my boy. Why else would she be so jealous of Gwen – or pose for you in the nude?"

"We've discussed that. We *are* mutually attracted – but it can become nothing more. She's plighted her troth and that's that. In a sense I admire her for that."

"But you know why she's plighted her troth?"

"Presumably because she loves Des."

"No, it's because she's been brought up to be a doormat for other people. First some dirty priest got at her when she was a wee girl. Her duty was to sacrifice herself for others: for her mother, for her younger brothers, for the Church of course , but never for herself. Fancy missing a monster brain like hers and turning her into a typist at age 15. That's akin to female mutilation – as practiced in darkest Africa. Her body is simply a vessel appropriated by the Pope to bring forth a very large brood of voting Catholics."

"Well I'll have no part of that!"

"Deep down I believe Joan's beginning to doubt too. She's slowly emerging from her childhood chrysalis – and goodness knows what magnificent creature will finally emerge. She could become anything – run a university for instance."

"Not challenging enough."

"But she needs a consort as bright, if not brighter than she is herself , and where's she going to find him? You're that man Giles. Of course you are. Every week is bringing her closer to acknowledging that you are her one real chance of fully realising herself . She's almost like a daughter to me and I can see the transformation."

"I'm afraid it's too late now."

"What?"

"Can I tell you something in strictest confidence Maurice? Strict mind you. I may not be around for long. My background is really Nuclear Physics. Most of my former nuclear colleagues seem to be disappearing from Britain. I suspect something big in the nuclear way is going on in Canada, and Scientific Manpower will post me out there soon too – like it or not. If Noble's s not here to fight for me I'll be gone like a shot – likely for years. And Noble can't last forever. He must be utterly exhausted – never mind about me. He almost hinted."

"Our little family will be heartbroken – me, Arfur, but Joan especially."

"Bloody hazard of war. We've been lucky so far – apart from Arfur losing his dad."

"I'll miss you Giles. Always pined after a son of my own."

"I am beginning to hanker a little myself. Suppose it's my age. But I'd have to go. There's hardly anyone around with more experience of German nuclear physics than me."

"But couldn't you take Joan? If you were married I mean?"

"Hardly likely. It'd be Top Top Secret; probably in some godforsaken out- of- the-way weapons' establishment. Families would be as welcome as they would be aboard a submarine. Anyway it wouldn't be fair on Joan. Here she's something. There she would be regarded as an encumbrance."

"She'd probably end up running it." Maurice laughed hollowly, clearly disappointed.

"How are you sleeping now Giles? I noticed your light on at 3 AM."

"Not well. But my Ernest J King nightmares are becoming less frequent. I still wake up heart hammering – but can't recall why. I'm reading Van Gogh's Letters and painting whenever I can. That really helps – as if it occupies an entirely different sector of my mind – to the exclusion of all else – even this bloody war. Your portrait's next."

"Not in the nude I hope."

"God forbid – but if you're offering…"

Joan was the next victim of 1942. She was sacked. Her boss had been posted to Washington to haggle with the Americans over shipping space for British imports. His successor, a stickler for the proprieties, was horrified to find a mere typist holding a position of such responsibility. Despite the pleadings of all the people who knew what she'd achieved in the dark hours of the blitz, they were ignored and she was demoted back to the typing pool.

Maurice was incandescent ; he'd had a blazing row with the new man – and lost:

"By God Sturdee I'll get her a gong if it's the last bloody thing I do. That little pipsqueak…… Now he wants me out too. But they can't sack me. I've got a contract for the duration."

Some kind of accommodation was reached eventually in which Picton agreed to move out of his management role into a new one that he'd invented for himself – consultant on the effects of the blockade upon Germany:

"It's vital when you come to think of it Giles. Remember that Cryolite story I told you? If we can discover Hitler's exact pressure points we might strangle him in months – weeks even. It might be some obscure chemical feed-stock. For us in the First World War it was nitrates to make explosives – that's how the Jews got a homeland in Palestine."

"I don't follow."

"There was a Zionist chemistry professor at Manchester University called Chaim Weizmann who promised to synthesise all the nitrates we could no longer import from elsewhere – at a price – a home for the Jews in Palestine. He and Lloyd George did some kind of underhand deal which Britain couldn't wriggle out of afterwards".

"Strewth – but you never hear about that nowadays."

"Who wanted to crow about it? But it worked beautifully for both sides. We got all the shells we needed to defeat the Kaiser's army in 1918. The Jews finally got a home, and in Palestine too, where they really had no right to be. Only the Arabs lost out. But you can't make an omelette without breaking eggs; like Churchill sinking the French fleet in this war to stop it falling into German hands"

"Your intellectual will never understand omelette arguments."

"So long then they will never be fitted to govern."

"But what about Joan?"

"Sorry dear boy, I digress. I've partially outwitted our pocket Napoleon – persuaded him I need a good library, which I do. So they've given me a cubbyhole in the University. Joan comes over to help me three days a week, providing she goes back into the typing pool for the other two. It's the best I could do."

"What does Joan say?"

"She's been asked to keep mum for now . Unless the blitzes resume…"

"Which they won't…"

"There's no longer any need for her special skills. At least the little shit was right about that. If Joan and I can make a little breakthrough at the University he can take the credit and I'll bag Joan full time. I suspect she'll be great at library research."

"Cross referencing in that great memory bank of hers?"

"Bloodhound Joan."

"The trouble is Maurice you know nothing of the cutting-edge technologies where Hitler's real pressure points may lie : the Rare Earths for instance . If I was allowed to work…"

"Which you are not."

"I'd put you in touch with Professor Blackett. One of his boys could provide you with up to date info. from our side."

"Relax dear boy. I can make that contact myself – now you've given me the tip."

"I suppose you could."

Joan allowed Gwen to come over to see Giles, on the strict condition there was to be no shop – and with Maurice to chaperone them:

"Any news of Tony?"

"He managed to give me a phone call from Scotland – and he sounded just thrilled. Says he's got a very young wardroom with hardly anyone over 20 – but he thinks he can lick them into shape when they go out for sea trials in a few days time. He asked after you and left a message. Said it was he who 'ratted on you' to Captain Mansfield. And is happy to hear he was right."

"I suspected as much – who else could it have been?"

"How are you Giles? You look ever so brown and fit."

"It's all this farm labouring. Lifting tons of spuds by hand. I spent all day yesterday sawing wood with Arfur. Look at my hands. How's Geraint?"

" He's fine– according to his letters. But we can't say much – with all the censors. Sometimes I think it would be better with no letters at all."

"It must be ghastly. What mob is he in?"

"Royal Engineers."

"I always meant to ask what he did in civvy street."

"Electrician – our local electrician. He'll take over his Tada's business after the war."

"Good luck to him Gwenny – and to you both."

"But are you really getting better Giles?"

"We'll see. Have they replaced Tony?"

"I suppose there's no harm in answering that, " she flicked a glance at Picton: "Yes, it's a Lieutenant Tom Phillips. Very quiet like. Seen a lot of action at sea – but he's recovering from shellshock."

"Poor blighter."

"Gets the shakes sometimes. They warned me. He goes to all the Washout meetings like Tony did – and helps me prepare the sinking charts – but I'm not telling you about those."

"Is he looking after you properly?" Sturdee raised a conspiratorial eyebrow.

"You mind your own business Doctor Sturdee. And anyway I don't need looking after any more. I've been promoted. I'm Leading-Wren Jones now."

"Congratulations – about time!"

"And I have been seconded to Captain Mansfield's Derby House staff. So now no one can snitch me away to drive a lorry or anything."

"By the time I get back you'll be a Petty Officer."

"The war will be over before then. Seriously Giles – you don't look right. I can see you are not sleeping properly. Now can we go upstairs and see my painting again?"

"As long as Maurice comes too."

"Of course."

1942 wasn't finished with Joan – not by a very long way. With her onions she was one of the wealthiest barter traders in Liverpool. For instance she purchased a lorry-load of seaweed from the coast to go on the onion crop ('We'll be able to sell them at a premium as Breton Onions' she said) and a proper two-man saw for Sturdee and Arfur to saw up the 'fallen' poplars. So in the long June twilight she was sometimes out until 10 PM on her bike making bargains. On one such night, after the others had gone to bed, only Maurice was still up, with one eye on her supper keeping warm on the stove:

"Thank goodness, I'm ravenous Maurice! " she said, blazing through the scullery door. "By the aroma it must be one of Arfur's home-made rabbit casseroles. Goody goody."

"Dead right! That kid gets better and better. And there's even more good news. A letter from Des– apparently in Australia by the postmark. So he must be safe."

She snatched it from him: "I was getting really worried. You know I haven't heard for seven weeks."

She sat down at the kitchen table and carefully cut the pale blue airmail letter open with a knife.

Picton was taking her dish off the saucepan when he heard the gasp.

" What's wrong?"

"He's had a bad crash and is in a Brisbane hospital."

"Is he okay?" He turned with plate in hand .

She choked , head in hands covering her face, the letter on the table beside her.

"What's wrong…?"

"Joannie what's wrong?"

She was shaking head slowly back and forth as if she couldn't believe.

"What's wrong Joannie?"

She took a deep stuttering breath, indicating that he should read the letter.

He's sat opposite and did so, noting that the handwriting was all over the place as if written by a badly injured hand:

' Dear Joannie, I know it's a long time since you got a letter but there are reasons. We crash landed in secondary jungle in PNG in March. I was badly injured and Wally the co-pilot bought it. But thank God the observer– you remember Frank, survived and dragged me out of the kite just as it was catching fire. Anyway they got me to a casualty clearing station in Port Moresby PDQ, from there on to a hospital ship and here I am recovering in a large military hospital in Brisbane with lots of other poor sods wounded in PNG. They set my arms and legs and operated on my caved-in breastbone and fizzog. Looks like I'll be AOK eventually, but even uglier. So don't worry about old Des – the devil looks after his own. But it's the end of the war for me so the medicos say.

The other reason is I was married two weeks ago in the hospital chapel to Molly Roscoe. By God I feel a ****. But it's happened. She was an old flame from college days, quite by chance working as a volunteer nursing aide in another ward. We almost got engaged before I came to Britain.

The fact is Joannie I couldn't recall your face or your presence any more. That's probably my dim imagination. And then I was getting the wind up. All your letters only show what a wonderful and special person you are while, truth be known, I'm a very ordinary bloke – probably finish up as an estate agent or a dirt farmer scratching a living out there in the dusty West. And you're far too good for that. If I'd lured you here and dragged you down I would never forgive myself. Then my own life would have become a purgatory. I could see all your brothers thinking the same thing, and they were *right. You are too special for me Joannie. All that war hero rot will wear off. I'm no hero believe me – not beside what I saw some blokes doing out in PNG.*

Maybe I'm making excuses. I don't mean to. I don't want you to feel I'm 'Doing the right thing'. Not a bit of it. I'm only doing what I feel is right for me. Molly is an ordinary sheila and doesn't expect more from an ordinary cove like me that I can easily deliver. And you must do the same thing Joannie. Right now I'm all washed up. If there hadn't been a bloody war things might have turned out different. But then we wouldn't have met. Girls used to make heroes out of pilots – but we are very ordinary joes these days. We don't fly – the aeroplane does that. We are just bus drivers. Farewell and good luck. Des.

Picton couldn't restrain himself:

"The letter of a gentlemen! Des was always that. And wise beyond his years."

"What am I going to do Maurice?"– she was staring at him, face white with shock, pupils dilated.

"Do you trust me lassie?"

She nodded slowly several times.

"When you gather yourself a little, you go quietly upstairs, open Giles's door and creep into bed with him. He went up exhausted after all his lumberjacking."

She took another deep breath and exhaled it slowly:

"What am I going to say?"

"Not a thing do you hear Joannie – not a single word. Don't turn on the light either. Just slip in beside Giles and put your arms round him. He will be fast asleep. Mother Nature will take care of you both."

"But …"

" We both know, and all your friends and brothers know, even he does, that you have been in love with Giles for more than a year. Now stand up. I want to see you steady on your feet."

"She did so."

"Take off your engagement ring."

She obeyed like a puppet.

"Now go upstairs lassie and go to the husband your God made for you."

CHAPTER 36
ARMAGEDDON

A month into his 'holiday' Sturdee received a summons, accompanied by a third - class railway warrant, to attend an interview at the Office of Scientific Manpower in London. Seeing they were his ultimate employers and paymasters he was bound to go. He was interviewed by small man in large thick horn-rimmed glasses who looked like an owl. He introduced himself:

"Charles Snow – in better times a physical chemist at Cambridge. What have you been up to at Western Approaches?"

Sturdee briefly recounted his work on depth- charge settings , on Merchant Navy morale and rescue ships, acoustic torpedoes, Support Groups, VLRAs and convoy tactics, and on his recent contact with Blackett. A shorthand typist was busy in the background.

"You know you disappeared off our books when you absented yourself from Bawdsey?" Snow sounded like an irritated housemaster : " Highly irresponsible. We had a Dickens of a business locating you. You do realise I hope that scientific manpower is one of our scarcest resources ?"

Sturdee explained about Noble.

"Yes yes – we know now of course. But at the time it was as if one of our destroyers had disappeared without trace. Make sure it never happens again. Apart from anything else it's not productive – or healthy as you've now found to your cost, we have your medical records, for a scientist to work so utterly alone as you were . But we left you in place because, at the time, you were the *only* scientist doing operational research within the entire Navy. The Board of the Admiralty were actively resisting it at that point. It was only thanks to your personal acquaintance with Admiral Noble that they allowed you in. Thank goodness the Board has finally reversed its traditional position – indeed the First Sea Lord regularly consults Professor Blackett now. You should regard Blackett as your superior from now on and inform him of all your movements. How long you will be allowed to remain with the Admiralty remains to be seen."

When Sturdee started to protest Snow was impatient:

"This war, as you must surely understand by now, is all about priorities – and priorities change. Once it was all about radar – so we posted you pro tem to Bawdsey. But on our books you are down as 'A Theoretical Nuclear Physicist'. Would that be accurate?" Sturdee nodded.

"Let's go into your background." Snow consulted Sturdee's file:

"BSc Physics, Birmingham University; PhD there under Professor Oliphant on 'Quantum Tunnelling'. Then twelve months at the University of Göttingen in Germany when you removed yourself – you seem to make a habit of it – to the University of Munich."

"I wanted to work with Professor Arnold Sommerfeld and his group there."

"Which you did for 18 months before returning to Britain in early '39 and signing on with us. You realise that your German Physics background makes you a pretty rare bird

Sturdee? Potentially it could be very valuable – if exploited wisely. What do you know about the Uranium Bomb?"

"Very little. Of course, like everybody else in Nuclear physics, we discussed the possibility at Munich as soon as we heard about Hahn and Strassman's discovery of the chain reaction in Berlin – that was 1938."

"And what was the general reaction?"

"Intellectually or emotionally?"

"Both."

"As you can imagine the emotional response depended very much on people's politics. Sommerfeld for instance, being Jewish: was preoccupied with finding a way for himself and his family to escape from Germany. And many others were in the same boat. Naturally they were horrified at the prospect of Hitler possessing a Terror Bomb that might have led to Nazi world hegemony. Though a few – very few – were delighted by that prospect. Naturally the two sides hardly mixed or talked. They were becoming mutually suspicious."

" And scientifically?"

"Again very mixed. Nobody could work out the minimum mass of Uranium 235 that would go critical. Guesses ranged between a few grams – which would have been useless – to tens of tons – which would have been impractical as a weapon – and extremely dangerous. Then nobody seemed to know if there were any worthwhile Uranium deposits in Europe. We knew that the Joliot-Curies in Paris had got theirs from the Belgian Congo. Then everybody quickly realised the real problem would be separating the active Uranium -235 isotope – which is very rare, from the much more common but inert Uranium-238 isotope. As I recall most of us thought of it as a remote possibility – which might take decades, even if it was pursued at high priority. Some idealists thought of the eventual possibility of unlimited cheap Uranium power for civilian purposes."

"And you?

"I was far too obsessed with nuclear Astrophysics to bother much. But I recall meeting a Hungarian – Leo Szilard, who was obsessed about the Uranium bomb. He thought it might change the course of history."

" Ah, Szilard." Snow perked up: "Do you realise he took out a patent on the Uranium bomb in 1935. And he gave that patent to the Royal Navy – in the hope that they would develop it before Hitler. There some fool filed it away without realising its enormous significance – just the ravings of another mad inventor."

"'Understandable I suppose before we knew about the Chain Reaction. You must remember that came right out of the blue. None of the theorists predicted it – not even Heisenberg or Schrodinger or Pauli. Right out of the Blue. Szilard's ideas, as I recall, didn't convince anybody at Munich."

"Well things are very different now – did you ever go back to see the Birmingham group?"

"Yes I went back to see Professor Oliphant – sniffing for a job. He it was who told me to apply to your Scientific Manpower. He didn't have anything immediately to offer himself. All his funds were going towards employing refugee physicists from Germany."

"Wise man. Do you know he's turned the Physics Department of Birmingham into the hub of western Physics? Thank God for our colonials. When Rutherford died the Cavendish laboratory more or less collapsed at Cambridge. Oliphant went to Birmingham, Blackett to Manchester, Chadwick to Liverpool. Since than Birmingham has produced the Cavity Magnetron…"

"Randall and Boot."

"Yes, but now Oliphant's showing the way to the Uranium bomb too. Thanks to your very high security clearance I can share some details – but as you can imagine they must remain ultra-secret. Ultra!"

"I understand."

"We think we are in a possible race with the Nazis – with the odds on them winning – given that they had a potential head start – and the high quality of their physicists. Well, Rudolf Peierls and Otto Frisch at Birmingham worked out the critical mass of Uranium 235 in 1940 – which, if they are right, makes a Uranium bomb highly feasible and extremely dangerous: the equivalent of 2000 tons of TNT. So one bomb could destroy a city. 10 could bring about the capitulation of your enemy. So everyone will be after it."

"I can imagine."

"So of course we set up a committee to look into feasibility, called the Maud Committee – Blackett is on it . It hasn't yet reported officially but its main conclusions are known."

"What about isotope separation?"

"They've worked out how to do that using gaseous diffusion."

"But that would be incredibly slow."

"It will take thousands of stages in a factory bigger than any presently in Europe – and more electricity than we could ever spare. Professor Simon's people are working on it frantically at Oxford. But we could probably separate enough Uranium- 235 to manufacture several tens of bombs a year. Churchill is very keen to drop one on Berlin – believing it would end the war overnight. But it really can't be ready before 1944 at the earliest."

"By which time the Russians might have collapsed — or we might have lost the Atlantic battle."

"Is that likely?

"50-50 unless we get those VLRAs immediately."

"As bad as that is it?"

"I think so – but then I'm regarded in some quarters as a 'defeatist' "."

"Blackett doesn't think so. As we speak he and Admiral Pound are fighting Bomber command over your Liberators. Apparently it's all a question of convincing the Paymaster General."

" Bloody Lindemann."

"Lord Cherwell now. He has the PM's ear – which is what matters. Now back to the bomb. Cherwell is all for it – but he wants it manufactured here in Britain – where the plant would be vulnerable to a single Nazi bomb. So we are siting it in Canada – Chalk River, Ontario. Got oodles of cheap hydroelectric power. The challenge then would be to find enough scientists to design and build the bomb itself – for when the active Uranium-235 becomes available. That's where you come in. The Canadians are woefully short in that department."

"I can imagine. But surely not just me."

"Good Lord no – George Thompson is already over there leading a British delegation – but it's all hands to the pumps. The PM's so anxious about it that he shared the secret with Roosevelt, which may seem rash. For some reason the President is mad keen to take it up in America."

"That's good."

"But is it? There are two schools of thought on that. One school, led by Oliphant, thinks American industrial might will be essential to get the bomb before the Nazis. The other , led by Cherwell, suspects the Americans of wanting the bomb to run the world after the war – and cut us out entirely."

"Having met Admiral Ernest J King I can see his point. Some Americans, Irish Americans in particular , absolutely loathe us ."

"So we're finding out – rather painfully. It's tough having allies isn't it? Very cool heads are needed to deal with the Americans. After all what do they know about war – beyond exterminating their Indians?"

"That's a bit harsh isn't it?"

" They're not my words – but we're wasting time. Negotiations are in hand to move the bomb project from Canada to the United States, so be prepared to go there instead."

"Will I be able to take my wife – I've just got married?."

"Good heavens no – if only for security reasons. Security is on the stratospheric level. If Hitler finds out we are stirring he could accelerate everything on their side."

"Couldn't we bomb his diffusion plant – if he builds one?"

"That is the hope. But you know Bomber Command. They can barely hit a large city – never mind a single factory – however large. Then they might come up with a quicker method of isotope separation."

"Some people in Munich talked about centrifuging."

"Anyway the decision will be taken at the very highest level – whether to bring the Americans in . Formally at the Chiefs of Staff level; actually between the Prime Minister and the President. The PM. apparently thinks he's got Roosevelt in his pockets at present. It certainly looks like that. But Roosevelt is a tricky devil so they say. Never really commits himself I'm told; his left hand doesn't know what his right hand is doing . He might have got the measure of Churchill. Certainly Churchill needs him more at present than he needs Churchill. What are Roosevelt's real war aims – as opposed to what he tells his public – or us? If you ask me it will end in a murky compromise – as always."

"What sort?"

"The Americans will come in on the bomb, even building it down there. But we will have a big enough scientific presence to make sure they can't 'snitch it from us' afterwards – that is how Cherwell put it. So every damned nuclear physicist we've got will have to go over there for the sake of his country."

"But if we lose the Atlantic…?" Sturdee left the question hanging

"Yes well… but what can you do about that now? By the time you're fit for duty again it will be far too late for you to make a difference – even frontline OR people like yourself. Leave Blackett to fight your battles in the corridors of power. If he can't win them, you certainly cannot. In my opinion – for what it's worth – we are bound to win the Atlantic battle sooner or later."

"Why?"

"Because we have to , and Germany does not. We simply cannot afford to lose it, and they can – at a pinch. Their priority surely has to be their army on the Eastern Front. And then what about all the new American cargo-vessel construction? The so-called Liberty ships. They are on target to build 1000 this year."

"We knew the plan but whether it's feasible…"

"That's 7,000,000 tons worth this year alone, With even larger numbers in 43. Lord Lithgow our minister of shipping dismisses them as 'welded tin cans". But if they last the war who cares? Maybe they won't last as long as riveted British-made ships but we'll be so poor after the war we may not be able to import much any more . Liberty ships were designed over here, by the way. Yet another British idea taken up in America."

"What about American Lend -Lease?"

"A mere drop in the ocean – so my economist friends tell me, but we'll be on our knees according to Keynes – and he should know. But for now, according to the PM America is "The arsenal of democracy". The Americans are flattered by the title. But what I suspect is that the PM means that they are the Arsenal, we are the Democracy. But we must move on. There's one more thing you may not know – with all this bloody secrecy – of course it's necessary – which might cheer you up – your acoustic torpedo – what do you call it?"

"Fido."

"Well it passed its final tests last week in America with flying colours. They have ordered 10,000 for delivery by this coming January. Some may be ready for your climax battle – that's the idea anyway. Turning them out like Ford cars. But very high security classification for now. Only Noble knows about them in Western Approaches and only Blackett and the Board at the Admiralty. Do you think it will make a difference?"

"It could be absolutely critical. It means our aircraft will be able to sink U-boats at last."

Snow glanced at his watch: "Only a few more minutes before I must see the next man. I always ask if people have any vital tips they want to hand on. With all this secrecy important connections get missed. With my position here at the heart of things and in touch with all the scientists, I can sometimes pass on a tip to the crucial ear. But we need to be quick."

"First of all our Night bombing will fail in the long run. Forget the cavity magnetron: even with valve- based technology we built a night fighter force using ground control interception, or GCI, which brought an end to the Blitz. The Germans will certainly do likewise. They'll build up a night fighter force that will blow Harris' s bomber command to bits. Air Marshall Portal has to understand this – and of course Churchill. Hanbury -

Brown at Farnborough is your man to prove this. After all he developed our night-fighter radar system." Snow made a note: "And your second tip?"

"I am 95% sure our Admiralty Convoy codes have been broken. Too many U-boats turning up when we divert convoys to doubt this. Rodger Winn at Admiralty Intelligence in Whitehall is your man there. He sniffed this out, I just confirmed his suspicion. Somebody's got to change the bloody codes – and fast . Otherwise we could go on losing thousands of ships and lives – quite unnecessarily."

"Why are they reluctant to change?"

"Because they believe some myth that U-boats must carry sonar detectors that can pick up our convoys from 50 or more miles away. That's impossible – I have found a simple signal-to-noise argument against it. Detection distances rise only with the quarter power of sonar sensitivity. But that's not an argument that will convince an Admiral, only a scientist. Somehow the Navy Board has to be persuaded. Both Blackett and Winn have my argument."

"I hope they can persuade the First Sea Lord – even Churchill. What you're saying about our ciphers being broken sounds very serious to me. Be sure I'll pass that message on to the appropriate quarters. Any last question?"

"When do you think I'll have to go – to the States I mean. I've only been married a fortnight."

"Congratulations. I can understand your reluctance to leave then. But you won't be going immediately. Too many things are up in the air for now . It's not even certain we'll bring the Americans in. Probably not before Christmas. It may be early spring. But we'll send you at the earliest possible moment that we can. So hold yourself in readiness."

"Is there anybody I can talk to about this bomb thing. I'm so out of date."

"As it happens there is. The man who discovered the Neutron – which is what this is all about apparently, is James Chadwick who'll obviously be going too – when the moment comes. In a very senior capacity no doubt. He was only complaining to me last week he's got no one up there at Liverpool University to talk to. You know he's the chair of Physics there. Now, with you, he will have. Can't sleep apparently, worrying what the Nazis are up to. If anyone should know about that, you should."

"I'll go to see him the moment I get back."

"I'll send him a note about you Sturdee. But one last word before you leave . You seem to think you've failed at Western Approaches. That may or may not be true, I'm in no position to judge. But Blackett is certain that it's thanks to you , more than to anyone, that the Admiralty has finally come to see that Operational Research has to play a central role in all its future plans. That doesn't sound like failure to me. On the contrary. Now get well as soon as you can, and go to see Chadwick. He'll be expecting you."

On the interminable train Journey back to Liverpool, sustained only by a meat paste sandwich so stale that the corners had turned up, Sturdee began to think about Nuclear Physics again for the first time in three years. None of the servicemen crammed into the carriage with him would imagine that the seedy looking man in the corner was trying to work out the critical mass of Uranium needed to make an Atomic bomb. But so he was, and enjoying every single moment of it. Physics had always been his passion since boyhood – it flowed in his veins. For all too long it had been dammed back by the necessities of war. Now it flooded back in again, perfusing all the organs of his being, bringing it truly back to life again. Thinking about what he really loved thinking about was a far better cure for his wounded spirit than sawing wood, lifting potatoes – or even making love to Joan. Having a very visual imagination, which was probably why he enjoyed painting, he imagined himself a tiny neutron trying to escape from inside a block of Uranium. From his perspective each Uranium atom around him appeared like a single frogspawn – a large wholly transparent blob of protoplasm, with a tiny opaque black nucleus at its core. So long as it didn't hit a nucleus dead centre the neutron could easily stream out through the protoplasm and escape off into empty space. Obviously the larger the total mass of the frogspawn there was, the harder it would be to entirely escape. If that mass was supercritical the neutron would more than likely hit a nucleus and that nucleus would split up, releasing two further free neutrons which in turn would probably hit and split another two more nuclei, setting up a so-called Chain Reaction which would destroy the entire mass of Uranium, releasing a vast amount of energy in a so-called 'Nuclear Bomb'. The question was, and it was a mathematical question, just how much frogspawn, how much Uranium, would be needed to prevent most of its neutrons escaping, and thus fizzling out like a damp firework. By the time he got to Crewe Junction – where he gave up his seat to a fat lady with an enormous shopping basket, he had the answer – or a sort of answer – and very intriguing it was. The critical mass depended on no less than the 12th power of the ratio of the area of the Uranium atom to the area of its nucleus. Sturdee had never before encountered anything in Mathematical Physics that depended on the 12th power of any quantity . The implication was that the Uranium bomb would only work if the ratio of the atomic to the nuclear area was *precisely* right. If it was one and a half times too big the bomb would be too expensive to make, too heavy to transport, and too dangerous for Man to ever use. On the other hand if the ratio was a mere 1 ½ times too small, the bomb would be no more lethal than a firecracker. That meant that if Peierls and Frisch at Birmingham University has got their sums right the Creator was playing a hideous trick on humankind. He was providing Man with just the kind of lethal toy he needed to blow himself and all his kind to smithereens!

So it was in a sombre mood that a few days later he called on Professor Chadwick at Liverpool University. Sturdee knew that Chadwick had been a protégé of Rutherford at Manchester University when Rutherford and Geiger had discovered the atomic nucleus there in 1913 – one of the epoch- making discoveries of all time. When Rutherford had later moved to Cambridge he'd taken Chadwick with him, where Chadwick, following up one of those hunches for which Rutherford was famous, had, in 1932, finally pinned down the elusive Neutron in an experimental tour de force admired by everyone. Sturdee's friend Hans Bethe, in his famous review article, had called the discovery of the Neutron "the true beginning of nuclear physics" because, together with the proton and electron , it appeared to control the whole of physics on the atomic and subatomic scale.

Sturdee had of course heard Chadwick talk at conferences but never spoken to him man-to-man. Chadwick was a tall figure with a beaky nose– and the air of an anxious heron:

"Welcome, welcome" he broke into an unexpectedly friendly smile "I got that note about you from Charles Snow who seems to know everybody and everything. To tell the truth I'd very much value a chat from time to time. My own senior people are neither of them British citizens, which means I can't share confidential matters with them,while most of the rest are too young." Chadwick looked to be a man in his late 50s, but much under strain. Sturdee had read that internment in Germany during the First World War had ruined his health:

"The fact is I can hardly sleep these days – knowing the bomb is a virtual certainty – it's just a question of who and when. Why are we dithering when the Germans certainly won't be? I understand you have misgivings about working on the project?"

"Not so much that – but going to America – when I still have so much to do here. And is the bomb really feasible ?"

"I had doubts myself initially. Even after I saw the Peierls-Frisch calculation I still wasn't convinced – but then we used our cyclotron to make some cross-section measurements ourselves. There could be no doubt after that – none whatsoever. A critical mass of about 10 kg of Uranium 235 is right! And if we can find that out so can everybody else – the Germans, the Americans– even the Russians or the Japanese. It's simply a question of who is going to move first. All the frightening possibilities go round and round in my head. That's why I've been on sleeping pills for two years, every single night. It will be a race against time. If the Americans come in with us, as seems to be the present plan, it will be your duty – and mine– to go over there and speed things up if we can. The bottleneck will be a shortage of trained people like you and I. We are as scarce as hens' teeth ."

"But I'm so out of date. I haven't read a nuclear journal in three years."

"Then get up-to-date. Make free with our library. I can point you here and there. But of course most of it's going underground now, but you'd be surprised at how much remains unclassified. For instance just last month two irresponsible American chemists published their finding that Plutonium may also undergo a chain reaction."

The very nuclear physics that kept Chadwick awake soothed Sturdee to sleep at last. There were no storms at sea, no cipher-breaking, no wolf-packs, no deaf committees, no irate American admirals – just beautiful mathematical physics, and the wonderful scent of Joan asleep with a naked thigh over his . He squeezed her bottom; she sighed contentedly, but didn't wake.

CHAPTER 37
HANGING ON

After some half-hearted attempts to prevent him from hearing the BBC News or from listening to Arfur reading selected snippets from the newspaper, Giles was allowed access to as much news as the British public were allowed to hear.

By August he was feeling much more robust, sleeping well, eating like a horse and working hard in the garden and sawmill. Marriage suited him, as it suited Joan. With one notable exception they were temperamentally, physically and intellectually well-suited to one another. The frustrated sexual passions of two healthy people who had remained virgins almost into their 30s burst like a dam, changing both their personalities for the better. Joan quickly overcame her inhibitions , especially after they were married . Even Arfur noted a change in her mood with wonder:

"Why doesn't she never get cross wiv me no more?" He asked Maurice late one night.

"I dare say she gets cross with Giles instead. That's what new husbands and wives do. But you notice they're always laughing together?"

"An' arguin' a lot too."

"That's also what new husbands and wives have to do. Battles have to be fought which may settle issues for a whole lifetime."

"Fr' instance?"

"For instance…" Picton looked back at his own marriage… "Well for instance who is going to be in charge of this, who in charge of that. Money for instance."

"That'd be Joan."

" Then who is going to work, and who is going to stay at home and look after the children."

" Giles will always be a scientist, ee told me, but our Joan won't just stay 'ome and do nuffin' else will she? When will they 'ave kids?"

"Fairly soon I would imagine."

"I can't see Joan wiv a baby."

"I can. She'll treat it just like she treats all the rest of us in her big family."

"Like me?"

"And Gem, and Dam and Blast… and me. She's a natural mother. She'll take a baby in her stride– and still work as hard as ever. Joan's a natural dynamo."

"Will she boss Giles around?"

"Bound to – but we'll have to see. Giles is no pushover, not when he's interested. Look how he refused to be married in church."

"Joan was very cross about that."

"She was. It never occurred to her that anyone could hate the Catholic Church as much as Giles does."

"What made 'er give in?"

"I don't think she had much choice. It was either a civil wedding or no wedding at all. And all her brothers were on Giles's side , except for Dermot, and he wasn't here thank God. The real issue will be their children. Her priest wants Joan to promise that they will all be brought up in the Catholic faith and Giles refuses. He says Joan is entitled to tell the children anything she wants about religion, provided he has a right to do likewise. And he is an Atheist."

"There might be a big fight?"

"There might. But it's years away. By then they'll have been married for ages – and be able to put things into perspective ."

"Why do people argue?"

"Arguing is good – at least I think so. Joan is a very clever person – and so is Giles. That's part of the reason they married one another. Both would have been bored with a spouse who couldn't argue with them on equal terms. Haven't you noticed how we all enjoy arguing round the supper table in the evenings?"

"Yuss …" Arfur sounded uncertain

"That's how people come to understand things – and sometimes change their minds. Argument is really thinking aloud. Argument helps us all to grow up – even old fellows like me. I love a good argument. What about you?"

"I didn't used ter."

"Why not?"

"Made me feel like everyfink was falling to pieces."

"I can understand that. But changing and adapting – that's what all successful people – and animals – have to do. Look at you – think how you've changed since you lived on the Isle of Dogs with your mother and father. It hasn't been very long has it? What was the hardest bit?"

"Learnin' to trust people. How was I to know Joan wouldn't fro' me aht – or Gem if he didn't earn 'is feed?"

"So why do you trust her – now I mean?"

Arfur thought hard before answering: "I s'pose it's cos Joan is prahd of herself. She'd niver do nuffin' to let herself down: nuffin' mean: nuffin' like tellin' lies…". the boy struggled for an analogy: "She couldn't let me dahn any more than I could let Gem dahn. If I ever did I'd feel mean and dirty inside. I'd rather starve again than feel like that…"

"A highly percipient answer – in one so young."

"What does 'percipient' mean?"

"Sorry – I'm wandering off into academe again. Percipient mean 'wise', 'penetrating'…. You are saying Joan is a woman of principle just as you are 'a man of principle'– always have been. Do you remember you refused to come and live with us – unless Gem could come too? You'd rather have gone on starving in that wretched stable. That's what Giles called you even then: 'A Man of Principle'."

" D'you fink Joan is like she is 'cos she goes to church every Sunday?"

"She believes so. She's been taught to believe she'd be a wicked woman if the priests hadn't saved her for God. I think they stole the credit for Joan's conscience Arfur. Can you imagine Joan being wicked?"

"O' course not."

"No more could I. Priests are like doctors. They often steal the credit – and the money – even when people would get better anyway. It's a shabby confidence trick if you ask me. I can't make up my mind whether they are more fools or rogues – priests I mean."

Arfur wanted to change the conversation before Maurice strayed off on one of his diatribes:

" Joan nor Giles'd ever let me dahn ; I knows that. That's why I was planning to go an' live wiv 'em – arter the war . But it don't seem nat'ral like – if they got young kids of their own."

Maurice could see Arfur was troubled : "I can see your point. But by the time the war is over and Giles is back from wherever he's going to go – you'll be a grown man – at agricultural college at least. Even if you had natural parents you'd only see them from time to time. You'd have flown the nest."

"Like them young jackdaws what was the nesting in our chimbley."

"Exactly. Anyway I was planning to ask you. You know I've got no wife or family. I'll be very lonely on my own after the war. If you – and Gem of course – came to live with me down in Hampshire, I'd be highly honoured. And there's a famous agricultural college, so I'm told, not 30 miles away. And I'm sure we could rent a field, or part of a field, for Gem."

"We'd atter build a stable Maurice. E's too old to stay out in the winter."

"We would. But there's plenty of room in the garden."

"And I'd atter learn bricklaying too — which'd come in 'andy when I'm a farmer."

It was early October before Sturdee was cleared to resume full duties . He made a beeline for the Dry Cleaners where he found Gwen , and Loader's replacement Lieutenant Tom Phillips, compiling sinking charts . Phillips was a quiet RNVR man with a slight North Wales lisp. It was hard to imagine anyone less like Tony Loader . The only thing they shared was a Distinguished Service Cross, that highly prized Royal Navy decoration for gallantry.

Sturdee's eyes shot to the wall where the monthly sinkings were displayed:

Month	Tons	Ships	To U-boats	U-boats sunk	By escort vessels
June 1942	834,000	173	144	3	1
July 1942	618,000	128	96	12	6
Aug 1942	661,000	123	108	10	4
Sept 1942	567,000	114	98	11	4

"Phew!" He exhaled an audible sigh of relief:

" You can't know how I've been waiting to see those They're not bad at all .What's the explanation?"

"The Americans finally introduced full convoying down their East Coast in July," murmured Phillips "And we did the same for the Caribbean. "They even turned off the shore lights that were back-lighting our poor vessels , specially tankers. In August Doenitz ordered his U-boats out of the area and back into mid-Atlantic."

"And I see we're even sinking U-boats at last. What brought that about?"

"It's mostly aircraft – not our escort vessels." Phillips replied. "The U-boats don't seem to get any warning of their 10-centimetre radars . They get caught on the surface – both by day and night, and destroyed either with bombs or shallow-set depth-charges. But then there are hundreds of them swarming out there – nearly 300 altogether they say. Bound to be more U-boat casualties – wouldn't you say?"

"I suppose so. But it's disappointing that our escort vessels aren't doing any better."

"It's the usual problem – Escort commanders are reluctant to detach escort vessels for sufficient time to do the sinking – not in the face of the enemy."

"But I thought that was going to be the task of the Support Groups – the special 'sinking groups' Loader and I used to call them?"

"It was, and it is. But as soon as Admiral Noble assembles and trains a Support Group it is spirited away to support someone else – the Malta convoys in the Mediterranean, the Arctic convoys round the North Cape ..."

"My God – that's a scandal! Hasn't Churchill got *any* idea where our our true priorities lie?"

"They say," Gwen interrupted: "We'll be lucky if we land thirty percent of our precious tonnage of imports this year."

"That's a recipe for defeat – surely!" Sturdee was despairing: "Dammit, even a politician should see that. Where *is* Churchill's commons sense?"

"Hold hard." Phillips intervened quietly: "We *had* to reinforce Malta – otherwise we'd lose the Mediterranean – and with it North Africa and the Suez Canal – as we still might. And as for the Russians – they're still fighting aren't they – against everyone's expectations? Surely we can't let them down when they probably need every ton of armaments we can ship them."

"I suppose so," Sturdee conceded: "But if we lose the Atlantic, neither the Med. nor Russia will matter a damn."

"Granted. But poor Winston's got to juggle all the priorities. With Stalin and the Bolsheviks screaming for a Second Front; our airmen begging for more bombs and bombers to bomb Germany; Admiral King wanting to move the entire U.S. Navy to the Pacific to fight the Japs; Roosevelt as usual playing a double or even triple game of his own.... everyone yelling about our oil supplies from the Middle East; the Governor General of India yelling for support in the Indian Ocean.... and who can blame any of them? Even Winston Churchill can't summon new escort vessels out of thin air , can he? So whenever he sees one spare he throws it into the breach. I don't know how that poor man sleeps at night – if he ever does."

"I suppose you are right." Sturdee didn't sound convinced.

"Anyway things aren't all bad . The admiralty has given permission to double convoy sizes – which will mean far more escort vessels per convoy – and release some for new Support Groups."

Sturdee nodded: he'd argued strenuously for that. Blackett had obviously carried the day with the Navy Board and the First Sea Lord, Sir Dudley Pound.

"The other good news Giles, " Gwen broke in "You know you told us to keep a very close eye on the losses of merchant seaman…"

"That's right," Sturdee explained to Phillips: "Because if merchant seamen think it's too dangerous to sail – don't forget many of them are not British but Dutch, Norwegian, Danish, Greek, American, Indian lascars, Portuguese… – they won't sail and the whole enterprise could collapse. Sorry Gwenny, I interrupted…"

"Well I've found that the average loss is five crewmen per ship torpedoed – when the average crew size is about 80. So that's only one in 16. "

"When, as I recall, the critical figure we estimated was one in seven. If more than one seaman in seven was drowned following a torpedoing then the merchant marine would eventually mutiny – and we'd lose. But the figure is now only one in 16. Great news Gwenny . Well done! That's Admiral Noble's doing of course."

"And yours Giles; you were the one who persuaded the Admiral."

"We all did, but he didn't take much persuading."

"And why don't we tell Giles about the exciting construction figures, especially in America?"

"I've heard. Almost miraculous. 140 new 7,000 tonners a month."

Looking at the wall chart he could see that sinkings had only exceeded 140 in June. The Merchant fleet was actually expanding for the first time since 1939.

"Despite all, perhaps we're actually going to win this battle" He said, more to himself than to the others.

"I don't believe Doenitz is capable of winning it anyway." Phillips said quietly

"Why do you say that?"

"I sat in this office staring at the sinking maps for month upon month with not much else to do: charts going right back to the beginning – and one thing stood out. Doenitz is a retreater. He never stands and fights us toe to toe. When the going gets tough he always retreats . He's only got a stomach for easy pickings. He drove us out of the South-western approaches – the Irish Sea and the Bristol Channel, back in 1940, so we retreated to the North-west Approaches – Liverpool and Glasgow basically. If he had bottled us up there we'd have been finished – wouldn't we?"

"Of course. And we bloody nearly were."

"But instead of sticking it out and taking the casualties , what did he do instead – retreated out into the Atlantic. Then further out to the Air gap. And later down to the Azores – and off Freetown West Africa. Each time we took him on he retreated even farther. Lately off the East coast of America and the Caribbean; then in August he retreated back to mid-Atlantic. He's obviously not willing to face the U-boat losses which a decisive victory might entail. That tells you something doesn't it Sturdee?"

"So what does it tell us?"

""I suspect Doenitz is not fighting to win this war; that he's fighting some internal battle within the Nazi hierarchy; against the Wehrmacht perhaps, or the Luftwaffe. Or perhaps to curry favour with Hitler. Big tonnage is what he's after – when he was always going to lose the tonnage-war in the end. And now he has. Why didn't he fight it out when he had the chance? I don't believe he's got the confidence to win the crux battle."

"That's an interesting point of view," Sturdee admitted. "I hadn't thought about it like that?"

"Napoleon said 'Battles are won and lost in the minds of the opposing commanders.' "

"Don't say you're another historian?"

"Hardly that. But I used to be a history teacher in a grammar school in North Wales." Sturdee caught the slight North Wales lilt.

"Good Lord you'll have to come over to our place and argue with Maurice, our resident historian. He's got an outspoken opinion about everything."

"Thank you, I'd like that. The other good news is refuelling at sea. They've solved the hose problem – changed to rubber hoses from canvas ones . Now every Escort group is accompanied by a refuelling tanker which means our fast escorts, particularly destroyers, can refuel in all but the foulest weather. They can now go right across from Liverpool to Halifax – and not detach at the height of a convoy battle."

"That'll will make a huge difference."

" It will, particularly as Escort group commanders don't mind detaching fast escorts for long enough to sink U-boat contacts – because, travelling at 30 knots, they can rejoin quickly enough to avoid more sinkings – particularly now Huff-Duff is working so well."

"What about VLRAs?"

"I'm not the person to ask about that but Air Vice Marshall Robb told us recently that it looks very sticky. The Americans are keeping their Liberators for themselves, and those they do leave us are filched by Bomber Command – That's my understanding."

"Giles". Gwen interrupted "You know Tony's escort group is based in Gladstone Dock. They're due back in within a few days."

"How's he getting on?"

"He loves his frigate doesn't he Tom?"

"And got a confirmed U-boat last month – running down a Huff-Duff contact."

"And how is Geraint?" Sturdee asked Gwen.

"No news at all. Not for weeks."

"That must be worrying."

"Perhaps it's because the Eighth Army has retreated so far – almost all the way to Cairo they said on the BBC."

Duff House was all agog to know how the Battle of the Atlantic had progressed whilst Sturdee was on sick leave:

"What about your Climax battle?" Maurice asked.

"Still to be fought – probably in the spring now . But their numbers are building up dramatically – 300 commissioned U-boats already. Technically speaking we're slowly getting on top of them but our leaders appear to be as scatter-brained as ever. They haven't given us any VLRAs and it looks as if we'll never get any in time now."

He told tell them about Tom Phillips and Joan asked: "Do you think he'd be interested in your old bedroom Giles?" Joan wanted a replacement tenant to help out with the heavy labour after her husband left. Giles had had to tell her he would be gone soon.

"No idea. We can only ask. Let's ask him over for Sunday lunch and you can all chat with him. He can see my old room and make up his mind if he could stand Maurice."

"Thanks. Not to mention the heavy labouring." Maurice riposted.

"You're spoiled Maurice , but you don't realise it." Joan said. "When he gets a whiff of our Sunday joint roasting in the oven he'll sign on straightaway. You'll see."

CHAPTER 38
SACKED

Sturdee was in his office workng on the VLRA paper when Tom Phillips came through the street door:

" He's gone. We've lost him!"

"Who's gone?"

"Admiral Noble. They've just announced he is being sent to Washington as head of the British Naval Commission over there – with immediate effect."

"My gosh!" Sturdee was devastated. They all knew it would come some day – but just before the Crux Battle…?

"Are you sure Tom?"

"I am afraid so,. And they've announced his replacement. Everyone was gathered around the notice in the lobby at Derby House : Admiral Sir Max Horton: Commander-in-Chief UK submarines' ."

A warning bell rang somewhere deep in Sturdee's memory… 'Horton… Horton…where had he come across the name before?': "Do we know anything about him?"

"Apparently he was a distinguish submarine commander in the last war."

"Things have moved on…"

"Yes well… I suppose the general idea is that an ex-poacher might make an effective gamekeeper."

"What about poor Noble? I suppose Churchill's sacked him like he sacks all his best commanders ."

"It all depends on this post in Washington I suppose. If it's a sinecure then he *has* been sacked – but it might be pretty important: persuading the Americans to do the right things at sea , convoying and such…"

"That's true. Perhaps he's been sent there to try and control that fool Ernest J King… If anyone could Noble could … you know King is rabidly anti-British, and terrified out of his wits? Roosevelt unaccountably dragged him out of what the US Navy calls its 'Elephant's graveyard'. Can you believe that he's never held a seagoing command – not even a minesweeper."

"Then no wonder he's terrified. In the circumstances so would I be. But all that can be of no concern to us."

"I suppose not. But Admiral Noble's disappearance could entirely do for us – I mean you, I and Gwenny . I have no idea what Admiral Horton's ideas are on Operational Research… but I've come across his name somewhere before; find out as much as you can about him Tom – and pronto– you are the Naval officer here ."

The first news of Horton– and it was rather shocking, had came back from a Washout meeting– that is to say one of those meetings held at Derby House amongst the escort crew commanders following the completion of their convoy.

The idea of the meetings was to find out if any lessons could be learned for the benefit of future convoys.

"He's turned them into Courts of Inquiry," Phillips, who had attended it, was almost in tears : "He's a tyrant and bully. He's always looking for someone to blame. And most of the time we doesn't know what he's talking about. He assumes every decision taken by a commander during a wolfpack attack in the middle of the night should be faultless."

"My goodness."

"He keeps on prating about training as if Noble hadn't done his best to train us all. He had the nerve to say: 'Nobody should make mistakes at sea. All your mistakes have to be made here during training sessions ashore.' Some of the commanders were seething, absolutely seething. It's amazing someone didn't blow up. One of them finally invited him to go out to sea and observe a real convoy action. He could hardly refuse in public could he? Perhaps that will kick some sense into him If he turns Washout meetings into Courts of Inquiry everybody will naturally clam up."

"And then we will learn nothing from our mistakes."

"Exactly."

"But surely he can't be all that much of a fool? Surely he must know a lot about submarines at least ?"

"That's the joke apparently. He's been C in C UK submarines since the beginning of the war. But we have hardly any submarines based in the UK. Most of those we have are out with the Number 10 Flotilla in Malta – and they are under C in C Mediterranean. So Horton's been occupying a cosy little sinecure over here – with almost no experience of real convoy work in war."

"My gosh! He seems like a disaster."

"Not necessarily. Almost all commanders in chief start green. Noble did . The question is 'Can he learn' ? Is he big enough to accept advice from those who know far better than he does? Or will he go on posturing like a pocket Napoleon?"

"Like Admiral Ernest J King…"

After Tony Loader had attended the Washout meeting which followed the arrival of his convoy from Halifax he came over from Gladstone Dock to see Giles and Gwen:

"My God what an awful little shit Horton is . Captain Mansfield – who was there – even protested: 'Finding scapegoats isn't helpful ' he said, and all of us echoed 'Hear Hear' loud and clear. You could see Horton didn't like that, not one little bit . There are all sorts of rumours going around about him: how he keeps his staff up half the night playing bridge. And have you heard about the bloody golf clubs?"

"No."

"He invited – practically ordered one of his Staff to play a round of golf with him. The chap said he'd left his clubs at home in Surrey for the duration; so what did Horton do? He commandeered a Royal Navy car and driver and, at a time of desperate fuel shortage, ordered it down to Surrey and back to fetch the bloody clubs."

"Are you sure that's true?" Phillips began shaking, as he still did sometimes under stress.

"Apparently there can be no doubt about it. Mansfield refused to sign the driver's chit – and there was an almighty row. Mansfield will be out next – you watch ."

"I wish you hadn't told us that Tony." Giles said. "Noble was our shining inspiration at Western Approaches – the best reason to believe we would win in the end. And now we've got this... this…….. abomination."

"Don't take it too much to heart old boy. As a naval officer one has to put up with good commanders and bad. The Navy's spent 300 years learning how to deal with the failings of mankind. One bad egg can't ruin a ship's company. And the worse the egg the sooner it begins to smell – and the sooner it gets tossed overboard. One little shit can't ruin Noble's convoy escort system built up over two years. If Horton can give up his golf for long enough to come out to sea with us he might learn a thing or two. Aparently he plays a complete round almost every day at Hoylake golf course. Now I want you all to come , Gwenny included, to see over my lovely Frigate. We'll win the War for you – Horton or no bloody Horton".

They had a conducted tour of the Frigate HMS *Wye* with Loader proudly explaining at every turn:

"She's just what we needed all along. We've got the legs of the surfaced U-boat and yet, unlike a destroyer, the endurance to get all the way to Halifax – and more if necessary. We've got two engines and two screws instead of the corvette's one – and we're 300 foot long instead of two. We don't carry all those ridiculous boilers built into a destroyer, nor all those bloody gun turrets. The one we've got up forrard will deal with any U-boat. Without all those unnecessary boilers this girl's got plenty of space – for fuel, for men, for all sorts of electronic equipment and for depth charges, for an amazing 10 cm radar and for Huff Duff . We've got extra depth-charge throwers and it's rumoured that in January we'll get Hedgehog– which, according to reports, will simply exterminate U-boats. If you haven't heard about it Gwenny it's very hush hush. It's a sort of mortar which fires 24 shaped depth charges in a pattern far ahead of the ship. There is no dead time between a contact and firing, and there is no bloody nonsense about trying to guess the U-boat's depth. The nasty little things simply explode on contact, and it's 'Good night Fritz' ."

"Can they really split a U-boat hull ?" Giles sounded surprised.

"They couldn't – but they can nowthey've changed the explosive to Torpex"

"So we're going to win the climax battle?"

"Yes – but only if we get enough of those of these babies – and VLRAs in the mid-Atlantic Air Gap. Somehow you have *got* to close that Giles. Its Doenitz's only hope."

"I thought escort carriers were supposed to do that."

"They were – and they still could do. But guess what's happened to them? They been snatched away from us to protect some big operation in prospect."

"Oh 'Operation Torch' you mean?"

"I believe so. So our seamen have got to go on dying out there so Generals and Air marshals can claim they've won the bloody war on their own. There's a rumour going round that our senior admirals, Tovey and Co, have threatened to resign en masse unless we get some air-support in time. You know what the real trouble is don't you? There isn't a single war correspondent out there in mid-Atlantic to watch us dying. They're all based in bloody London where they can't get seasick. Or in the desert with the other Brylcreem boys. The British public doesn't really know where the real fighting and dying is going on – so our politicos don't care so much. That's a blind spot that could lose us the war you know."

It didn't take long for Sturdee to find out what the new Commander-in-Chief thought about Operational Research. He was summoned to Horton's office and immediately recognised the man from a previous encounter when he and Tony Loader have been trying to convince the Admiralty that U-boats could dive below 600 feet. Horton, who had been called in as an expert witness, had positively laughed at the idea and poured scorn on what he'd called 'slide rule warfare'. No British submarine had dived below 300 feet – and that was that.

As he described the encounter to Jean afterwards

"He doesn't even look like an Admiral. He's more like someone associated with the unsavoury side of the horseracing business, perhaps a bookie's runner. For a start his uniform is far too big – looks as if he's been invited to a fancy dress party and couldn't get a proper fit."

"You shouldn't judge by appearances Giles. They say Nelson looked like a boy not an admiral."

"I suppose not… But after Noble he looks laughable."

"And he's probably aware of that fact. But what did he say?"

"He said. 'I've got no time for slide rule warriors'. "

"To which you replied?"

"I didn't say anything at first. But then he added, as if I was a naughty schoolboy 'What have you got to say for yourself?'"

"Gosh. Did you react?'

" I said "Thank you for being so frank with me Admiral. I'm sure you won't mind me be equally frank in return. We have met before – at a meeting to discuss U-boat depth capabilities. You actually laughed at the idea that they can go below 300 feet. And that is why our depth charges were so ineffectual. They can actually reach 900 feet – as we proved. I suggest you stop fighting the last war – and try to learn about this one. Good day to you."

"Oh Dear. Now you'll have to leave Liverpool…." Joan was obviously very upset.

"I suppose I should have tried harder – especially over Gwen and Tom Phillips. But I've got my pride. I'm damned if I'll smarm up to a little squirt like Horton – war or no war."

Joan didn't persist because Sturdee had had to tell her before they got married that he   might not be around for long – though neither had expected a rupture to come so soon. She was desperately hoping to get pregnant before he had to leave.

Blackett ordered him down to London where he stayed in a boarding house in Bayswater. From there he could walk to work along the Serpentine, across Green Park and through St James's Park, crossing Horse Guard's parade to the Admiralty. There were sandbagged anti-aircraft guns and barrage balloons everywhere.

"Now that Charles Snow has briefed you," Blackett said "We can talk Uranium bomb. And we desperately need people like you Sturdee, the Americans are starting almost from scratch – though they have bagged a few top European emigres – Enrico Fermi for a start, and Hans Bethe."

"Gosh. Hans was a good friend of mine. I wondered where he'd finish up. He simply disappeared from Germany without warning. I'd love to work with Hans again."

"They've put Robert Oppenheimer, an American figurehead, in charge. Have you met him?"

"Briefly in Göttingen."

"The politicians don't quite know why the Yanks are so eager to have the bomb. Our intelligence suggests it can't possibly be ready before the show here in Europe is over. So what could they possibly want it for?"

"So why are *we* so keen?" Sturdee asked .

"I wish I knew the answer to that. I suspect it's because we don't trust the Yanks with sole possession of the bomb . They might try to dominate the post-war world."

"Never!"

"Why not? They have an extraordinarily rapacious history so far. If you ignore all that self-serving window-dressing– The Declaration of Independence and so forth – they've devoted themselves to clearing out the entire Western Hemisphere and stealing it for themselves – The Indians, the French, the Russians, the Spanish and of course the Mexicans .They proudly call it 'The Monroe Doctrine'. It's Hitlerism, Hollywood style . They would have taken Canada too in 1812 if we hadn't stopped them. Perhaps that's why we don't intend to let them have sole possession of the bomb – our bomb really. That's where people like you come in. You'll be over there in the very thick of it. Able to bring any 'secrets' back here, if necessary."

"When will I have to go?"

"No earlier than May I imagine. They are planning to build some highly secret establishment to develop it in. That will take months at least. And in the mean time what are we going to do with you? It's getting late in the day to do much about your Crux battle. Come to our Group meeting on Thursday. Maybe we could decide after that."

While he was waiting he went over to see Rodger Winn in Admiralty Intelligence. He wanted to know if Bletchley Park had broken back into Shark.

"I'm afraid not." Winn said. "Not a single dickie bird for eight months. But I'm now practically positive the Germans are reading our convoy traffic on an hourly basis."

"My gosh!"

"Yes it's an absolute tragedy. It was always suspicious how often they turned up when we diverted a convoy."

"What makes you so certain now?"

"Well first of all I used that betting odds stuff you taught me. But now we're sending out false messages and seeing how long it takes for U-boats to react."

"Couldn't you use that to trick them – and let our convoys slip through?"

"We could, and we might have to do if things get desperate. But we don't want them to know we are on to them so that when we do change our ciphers they will go completely blind."

"Are we going to change?"

"It's taken a devil of an effort to convince my Lords. For one thing they're reluctant to admit we've been so completely out-smarted. We like to think of ourselves as being the smart ones; you know Room 40 and all that in the First World War.."

"But surely they can't argue with U-boats rapidly reacting to false messages?"

"They had assumed that Bletchley Park would let us know if the Germans had broken our Ciphers."

"But if we are out of Shark…"

"I suspect this has been going on for years. Someone has badly fouled up – either here or at Bletchley Park. We are going to change Admiralty Cipher number three and BAMS."

"How quickly?"

"Months unfortunately. You see every ship has to be issued with new cipher and code books all over the globe. There are no short cuts."

"My God! The Germans could be reading our mail throughout the Crux Battle?"

"I'm afraid that's a possibility. But we are working as fast as we can. Depends when that battle begins. Meanwhile we're completely blind to them."

Sturdee wasn't able to sleep that night for the first time since his breakdown. He tossed and turned and peeped between the blackout curtains at the search lights in Hyde Park criss-crossing the sky, wishing he was back in bed with Joan at Duff House. He missed her now, almost every moment of the night and day. He had become, so he realised, a properly married man, no longer an individual but part of a duo facing the world together… he ached for her company and advice. How could he survive in America without Joan for possibly three whole years? How he loathed the bloody war.

Blackett had delivered a masterly survey of the current situation to his assembled Circus of two dozen scientists:

"I am learning my way about the Byzantine corridors of power here in Whitehall. Though gentlemen, we must continue to rely on scientific arguments and reliable evidence , because that is our unique strength, but when we come to writing papers, it will be as well to know our audiences, be aware of their particular prejudices, preoccupations and preferences."

"So far as I can see, the real power in the land, when it comes to running this war, lies within the Imperial General Staff. That consists of three men, Admiral Sir Dudley Pound the First Sea Lord, for the Navy; Air Chief Marshal Sir Charles Portal for the RAF, and, General Sir Alan Brooke for the Army, who is their chairman, and CIGS, or 'Chief of the Imperial General Staff'. Unlike all the other committees it meets every day for several hours and takes all manner of decisions from allocating resources to appointing and dismissing commanders in the field. When they are in agreement – and I emphasise the 'when' gentleman, the Prime minister is apparently reluctant to overrule them. So long as the fiction is maintained that he is running the war on a day-to-day basis he supports almost all their most important military decisions – as, in my opinion, he should.

Mr Churchill now finds himself in an alliance with two absolute dictators Stalin and Roosevelt – for make no mistake, in all but name, the President *is* a dictator . So when our PM sits down with them , as he will shortly be doing at Casablanca, he needs to show he carries the same heft as they do – though, in reality this country is still a democracy, even in war, which their countries are not."

"The Prime Minister's particular obsession is 'Offensive Action.' He will support practically anything, however hare-brained, if it can portray itself as 'offensive', backpedal on anything which he sees as purely defensive. That's why he's so keen on the mass bombing of German cities – even if it makes, so I believe, no real military sense. Likewise, although he talks much about 'The Battle of the Atlantic'– a phrase he himself invented, he never gives it full-blooded support, because he sees it as a predominantly defensive operation."

"Churchill's views on the scientific aspects of the war are, of course, heavily influenced, if not entirely controlled – by his scientific amanuensis Professor Lindemann, now Lord Cherwell – the so-called 'Paymaster General'. Make no mistake he is an extremely important and somewhat sinister figure – the Rasputin in Churchill's court. But whether we like him or despise him, as I do, we have to make the best of him . Once upon a time, some 25 years ago, he did some first-rate science on aircraft control, so somewhere in his muddled brain there must be some respect for rational thought. But, as I have slowly come to understand him his great weakness is his insecurity. He's like a mistress; his power depends entirely on Churchill's favour. Were he to lose that favour he would be as nothing . So he has to seem, in the PM's eyes – a sort of scientific magician. That places him open to manipulation gentlemen. If Lindemann can seize one of our ideas – but portray it as his own, he might push it for all he's worth. I ask you to remember that when writing papers for the Prime Minister."

"Of course that won't often happen . Our day-to-day target, outside he Admiralty, must be the Imperial General Staff . Of them Pound is certain we are going to win the war – because the Navy has won all its wars going back to King Alfred. Therefore he under-represents the Navy's needs – and is apparently asleep much of the time during meetings. By contrast Portal is very much aware that the RAF has no tradition and must earn its spurs – otherwise it could go into liquidation. The Americans for instance do not have a separate air force, it is simply a. branch of their army. In short the RAF wants to be seen as winning the war on its own – hence the nonsense of these 1000-bomber raids. General Brooke plays his cards close to his chest. The Army is currently in a weak position , having left all its heavy equipment at Dunkirk – and doesn't currently have a main battle tank capable of taking on the Panzers – viz the rout in North Africa . Apparently he sees his main role as restraining Churchill's wilder excesses. But I emphasise this : all three of them are capable of reading, learning and changing their minds. And that must be a blessing. Our job is to occasionally change their minds – if we can – by rational argument."

In the short run it was decided that Sturdee would lead a small group of three or four and train them to understand the intricacies of convoy tactics, and in particular the Convoy Equation and the consequent Sinking Tables : "When you leave for America my staff here need to be as competent as you are in all those arcane but vital matters. And that includes of course the argument for more VLRAs."

It was wonderful sharing an office with other really smart scientists again – though Sturdee guessed is wouldn't be for long. They challenged everything he said or claimed . On the first day one of them, Frank Sutcliffe said: "I find it difficult to believe these Sinking tables of yours Sturdee are right. They're just too damned dramatic. And if I can't believe them, and I'm a physicist, how on Earth do expect brass hats and politicians to believe in them? They just smell wrong. And you agree don't you Harris?"

"I'm afraid so Sturdee. I went and asked Patrick Blackett if he'd checked them and he said. 'No, I had no time'. So it is your word Sturdee against everybody else's Common Sense."

Sturdee was about to respond robustly but quickly thought better of it :

"Well go on and work out the theory for yourselves. I'll write down all my basic assumption and you can work out the mathematics on your own . I found the results pretty hard to swallow myself – at first. But that's precisely why they are so damned important. The side which first understands, and follows their implications, will win. It had better be us."

He had a good deal of amusement sitting quietly at his desk listening to them fumbling argumentatively towards the convoy equation for almost a fortnight – as once he had had to do himself . Then they got stuck on 'Bernoulli's Theorem' – because the large Bernoulli family of mathematicians had so many theorems named after them. He had to give them a hint.

When they did finally get to the Sinking Table they were even more astonished than he, Loader and Gwen had been when they had first worked it out between themselves at the Dry Cleaners in Liverpool.

Sutcliffe said: "Mathematics is incredible sometimes isn't it ; I mean literally. I remember my maths master proving that if you take one step, then half a step, then a quarter of a step and so on you'll never get as far as two-steps, even if you go on walking for eternity."

Harris, obviously an ex public-school type added:

"I read somewhere that because the ancient Greeks couldn't solve Zeno's Paradox – you know the one about the hare never being able to catch the tortoise, they lost their faith in Logic and thus self-confidence in their whole Civilisation. And so the Romans defeated them."

"Bit far-fetched for me." Sutcliffe responded

" You two didn't believe in our Sinking Table stuff did you?" Sturdee interjected

" Touche´"

"I spent two years in Germany, just before the war. And my experience was that they are very much better educated than we are – not least mathematically."

"And so they might get to your Sinking Tables first … and we could go down the same way as the ancient Greeks you mean?" Harris asked, and Sturdee nodded.

"That's something to keep a man awake at night."

"It nearly drove me around the bend – literally." Sturdee admitted, but he didn't tell them about his breakdown.

"But how the hell are we going to convince the brass hats – if we found it so fiendishly difficult to convince ourselves?" Sutcliffe sounded worried .

"That's going to be your job chaps." Sturdee said cheerfully "I've done my bit , without much success I have to admit. I'm handing the job on to you. And you could lose the war, all on your own. Good Luck."

Faced with a wet weekend alone in the boarding house in London at a time when the city was almost entirely closed down because of the war, nearly drove Sturdee mad. He took a train down to Farnborough to see Hanbury – who was his usual ebullient self:

"Don't tell me about boarding houses, or RAF messes Giles. If I have to eat another sheep-less Shepherds' pie or another semolina pudding I will assassinate somebody. It seems to me that you have been living high off the hog – quite literally– with your new wife. Sounds quite a girl – I'd like to meet her."

Giles – especially because he was hungry– described Joan's horticultural and culinary skills: "Do you know we have rabbit stew once a week with streaky bacon– and our own herbs…"

"Please, I beg you Giles, I'm drooling already…"

"And a roast joint every Sunday…"

"You're bloody war profiteers."

"No we aren't – we are actually feeding about 30 people with produce."

"Now I'm beginning to hate you ."

"Sorry old man. It's just that I'm hungry myself. Do you know we had a bloater for supper last night. It was ghastly, absolutely ghastly."

"I'm glad to hear it. Very glad indeed; you'll get no sympathy here."

"I suppose I've had a cushy number. But it's all over now." Sturdee described his ejection from Western Approaches and his present preoccupation with VLRAs : "It's finally come to me that the only way we are going to get anything in time is to change Air Chief Marshal Portal's mind. Do you remember that scheme we thought up involving an exercise between Bomber Command and your night fighters?"

"Vaguely. It didn't come to anything as I recall – because Bomber Harris refused to play ball."

"I've been thinking about it again. It may be the best way– indeed the only way to change Portal's mind."

"Remind me."

"It was actually your idea Hanbury. If one night we could fly a whole formation of British bombers against your night fighter defence – we could portray it entirely as a way for testing and exercising our fighter defences. Nothing need be said of the fact that we would, at the same time, be testing the ability of Bomber Command to penetrate a defence system equipped entirely with valve-based radar – which the Germans have already. If, as you suspect, bomber command suffers unacceptably high 'losses', that would undermine their whole case for the area bombing of German cities wouldn't it? And, more to the point, that might leave Portal free to release Liberators for VLRA duties with Coastal Command. The only new thing I'm suggesting is to portray it entirely as *an urgent and necessary test of our night fighter capabilities.* There's no need to alert Bomber Command. And that way we might actually get it done."

"Yes I remember now Giles. And it might bloody work. We have enough experience already to know that those big four engine crates are sitting ducks for our Beaufighters. But we've never had a proper exercise – formation against formation– not one-on-one– because Harris argues his 1000-bomber raids overwhelm the German defences – by sheer weight of numbers."

"And he could be right of course but it ought to be tried out shouldn't it? After all we might be sending the flower of our youth to be slaughtered over Germany – as we did on the Somme in 1916."

"So there's much more to such an exercise – than the mere filching of Liberators . By Jove we've got to do it Giles! For everybody's sake. Let me have a word with my boss, Sholto Douglas, the Head of Fighter Command. I bet he'll be all for it. We need all the realistic exercises we can get. Flying conditions on the Eastern front in midwinter must be foul just now. It might make sense to Hitler to bring his bombers back to France and have another crack at us. Sholto said as much the other day."

" But does he carry any weight?"

"How do you think he managed to supersede Dowding at Fighter Command after Dowding had just won the Battle of Britain? Our Sholto is a cocktail party warrior of the most lethal sort; a poisoned stiletto against Bomber Harris's bludgeon – leave him to me."

And so it was arranged, though the exercise couldn't proceed until the dark of the Moon in January. Hanbury promised Sturdee a ringside view– in the cockpit of a night fighter. "… but wear every damned item of clothing you can get – including your wife's drawers; it can be bloody freezing up there. People have got frostbite."

Back in Whitehall Blackett sent for him: "We had a Maud Committee meeting yesterday; things are moving fast. They've identified the site – a place near the Sangre De Cristo Mountains down in New Mexico – Los Alamos as I recall the name . So I hope you like desert scenery Giles. It could be ready as early as May. And I talked with Chadwick about you. We agreed you are wasting your time in Operational Research now – you should be getting up to speed on the Maud Report and all its technical appendices – and the best place to do that is at Liverpool University with Chadwick. After all you'll both be going to New Mexico – and if we can get Charles Snow's approval we'll get you posted as Chadwick's Theoretical assistant at Liverpool."

And so it was arranged – but with one technical hitch. Every train seat over the Christmas period had been booked for service personnel going on leave. The woman at the booking office stared at Sturdee as if he was a cretin. A Christmas of bloaters in Bayswater sounded appalling . Joan it was, who saved the day in an act of spectacular bravery:
"I'll come to get you Giles."
"How on Earth…"
"On your motorbike of course."
"But you can't ride."
"I'll learn tomorrow and come down the next day."
"That's madness Joan…"
"I'm your wife now aren't I?"
"What's that got to do with it?"
"If you can jump into the frozen North Atlantic to do your duty then I can surely learn to ride a motorbike…"
Nothing would dissuade her – not even the fact that she had neither licence nor insurance, nor that the bike's lights didn't work: "If I leave at dawn I should be in London before dark – if I don't get lost."
But she did get lost – in the Northern suburbs of London , but she did manage to find her way to Paddington Station from where she rang Giles's landlady.
It was dark by the time he found her– shivering with exhaustion, hunger, cold and shock:
"Oh Giles" she burst into tears in his arms, the first time ever: "I do so miss you…"
He pushed the bike round to his lodgings and bribed his landlady into providing a hot bath for Joan. They slept in one another's arms, properly man and wife at last.

Christmas at Duff house, probably the only one they would share together, perhaps for years, was a cosy affair. With all Giles's logs the fires roared day and night. The latest generation of pigs had made the final sacrifice so there was meat and plenty to spare. Joan's seaweed-fed 'Breton' onions had sold for a king's ransom and had paid for enough Sloe gin to keep even Maurice contented. Arfur, visibly matured and almost burly of build, now thought of himself as a farmer while Joan invited a dozen orphans to share Christmas dinner which included a black market goose , and an undeniably Giles-like Father Christmas. Even the BBC News wasn't too bad: the Eighth Army had attacked at El Alamein and was driving Rommel's Afriks Korps back into the desert. On the Eastern front Hitler's armies appeared to be stalled at a place called Stalingrad while the Americans had successfully landed in North Africa. Mr Churchill claimed to see some hope:

"Not the end, not even the beginning of the end, but perhaps the end of the beginning."

Sturdee reversed the canvas in his studio, framed the painting and hung Joan's Rokeby Venus on their bedroom wall while she was out at work. Her astonished and passionate reaction to it was everything an artist and an ardent husband could have wished.

CHAPTER 39
NIGHT FIGHTER

Although Sturdee was now officially out of the loop, some of his old contacts in Liverpool and London kept him up-to-date with the Atlantic picture. For instance Rodger Winn managed to tell him the wonderful news that Station X had broken back into Shark in December . It was thanks to two very brave British sailors Fasson and Grazier who had clambered down into the hull of a badly damaged U-boat sinking off Alexandria and recovered its codebooks before the two men were drowned. There was every hope the break would last – perhaps right through the Crux battle.

Then Air Vice Marshal Robb, who remained at Derby House in charge of Coastal Command in the Western Approaches, had come round to Duff House in civilian clothes to speak to Giles:

"Admiral Horton may think Operational Research is worthless but I certainly do not agree. So why don't you come and work for me – for us. The VLRA problem is key to the approaching Crux battle – and you've made yourself the expert on that."

"What about Horton?"

"Whether we get any more VLRAs or not will have nothing to do with him. That struggle will have to be won at a far higher level than Western Approaches – at the Imperial General Staff level – or even the War Cabinet."

"Horton's a fool!"

" Admiral Horton has indeed had a very bad start – I'd say he's now got to learn very fast or …… Now what about that job Sturdee?"

Giles explained his new situation, outside operational research altogether, but he also described the night flying exercise between Bomber command and Fighter command which he and Hanbury had cooked up. Robb was excited:

"That's *exactly* what we want. Exactly! The man we have to impress is Air Chief Marshal Portal. He is so mesmerised by the bombing of Germany he can't even see the Battle of the Atlantic as being more fundamental – even to that. What can I do to help?"

" You can get Coastal Command to see that the results of the exercise– supposing them to be favourable – are not supressed, as were the earlier conclusions of the Butt Report into the wild inaccuracy of our bombing campaign."

Robb came up with a good idea: "Any decent war exercise has official umpires. They are there to see fair play – and more importantly to see that the right conclusions are drawn. Clearly they can't come from either Bomber or Fighter commands in this instance. The logical place for them to come from is therefore Coastal Command. I'll see what I can do Sturdee . The other two commands will surely be in a weak position to resist."

Robb had lent Sturdee his Anson to fly down to Farnborough for the exercise. Hanbury Brown was excited:

"It's all set up for tonight Giles. No moon. Five Eights cloud forecast at 10,000 feet. Do you really want to fly in a night-fighter?"

"You promised."

"I know I did – in a rash moment. I hadn't thought about the practicalities."

"Which are?"

"Our most effective night fighters are the two-seater Bristol Beaufighters. But there's only room for a pilot in front with the radar operator right at the back in the rear. There's no room for an observer like yourself – unless you're prepared to take a real risk – which a married man like you shouldn't. Why don't you come up to Fighter Command HQ at Bentley Priory with me. We'll see far more of the exercise developing from there anyway. You may go up all night and be unlucky – see absolutely Damn all .. indeed that's quite likely."

"But Hanbury...... I've got all worked up for this. I've brought two pairs of pyjamas, a balaclava, and special socks knitted by Joan to keep me warm. You remember you warned me!"

"I did. What I'd forgot to mention – what slipped my mind at the time, is that you'll be flying in a potential death trap. If your Beaufighter gets into trouble, engine failure for instance , the pilot can bail out through his own hatch, the radar operator through his rear hatch, but there is no way out for the observer. That's why they're generally not allowed to carry them. But I had to have one aircraft fitted so I could monitor the whole setup myself – when we were developing it. And that's the one you would have to fly in I'm afraid – but I wouldn't recommend it. It's the one in which I lost my eardrum when my oxygen supply conked out and we had to dive from 20,000 feet. I thought that was a necessary risk we had to take at that time. But I don't want to stand side-by-side with Joan at your grave next week."

"Can't you see – I can't back out now. I've told Robb, I've told Joan, I have told Blackett – this could mean the difference between us getting VLRAs or not. People like Churchill and Lindemann are impressed by people who take personal risks. Perhaps they shouldn't be – but they are."

They wrangled for ten minutes before Hanbury, always a man of his word, gave in :

"Very well Giles. I knew you'd bloody insist. I'll take you out and show you the kite. The crew are waiting for you. They want to take you up for a test flight in daylight."

The Bristol Beaufighter night fighter was a sinister looking beast. Painted matte black apart from its roundels it had two gigantic radial engines sticking out in front of the wings with triple-bladed propellers which almost reached the ground.

The pilot, who look like an undersized sixth former, introduced himself with a grimace as 'Boy' and took him around the machine:

" Two supercharged Bristol Hercules 14-cylinder radials – giving us 3000 horse power altogether. Don't be fooled by how quiet they are. More powerful than Rolls-Royce Merlins – but they've got sleeve valves instead of poppets. They'll give us about

320 miles an hour or 280 knots at 20,000 feet. Comfortably faster than any bomber – Jerry or otherwise."

"This herringbone thing" He pointed to something sticking out of the plane's grotesquely stubby nose: "Is the transmitting antenna for our Type IV radar."

"Working at about 1.5 m wavelength." Sturdee recalled his radar days.

"The receiving aerials" the pilot continued "Are these sticklike things on the front of the wings just outboard of the landing lights."

"Big lights."

"Yep – we need them because we have to land in the bloody dark; we can't illuminate the airfields for fear of being strafed by Jerries. That's the trickiest job actually: getting the crate down in one piece. We've survived so far… Just."

The pilot bent under the nose: "There are our four Hispano-Souiza cannons that do the business .They can brew up any bomber in no seconds flat. Can fire 20-millimetre explosive rounds at 750 rounds per minute each. Belt fed ; 250 rounds per gun."

"Ever fired them in anger?"

"Once. Got a Heinkel back in May. One press of the tit and the poor bugger disintegrated . They don't come over any more. Very boring job this. Hopefully we'll get some action tonight. No live rounds though. We don't want any accidents do we ? Either way. This is a Spider." he introduced a slightly larger sixth former:

"Spider's going up into his cubbyhole to play with his box of tricks."

Spider climbed up into the rear fuselage, until his head appeared in a tiny blister canopy on top of the aircraft:

"He is miles behind you?"

"Yep, because there's no room in the cockpit for two. They had to bloody amputate its nose."

"Why?"

The skipper shrugged: "Follow me."

They climbed another stepladder projecting down from behind the cockpit; Spiders feet could be seen above and behind them.

The pilot demonstrated the straps , the radio intercom and the oxygen supply: "Don't touch that box of tricks over there. That duplicates Spider's displays. He'll switch it on and off for you when you want to see exactly what he's seeing up there."

"Would I be able to see a bomber visually – if we find one ?"

" Only if you crane round my shoulder and look up through the canopy while I try to creep up on the bugger from below– so he can't spot us . We don't want a squirt of machine gun fire do we ? At least I don't."

Several hours and a test flight later Sturdee found himself in complete darkness within the Beaufighter's bowels. Uncomfortable but not yet cold, thanks to his extra clothing, his apprehension had given way to boredom. It was hard to believe that what was to happen over the next few hours might settle the Battle of the Atlantic – even the war itself.

"Bloody boring this job" the skipper commented over the intercom. "We can't even read. No lights. We have got to protect our night-vision. Spiders box of tricks will only get us within about 250 yards. From there we've got to home in on visual. And if his rear gunner sees us before we see him he'll open fire at point blank range."

"Is that likely? I hope you've had your extra carrots."

" Can't stand the bloody things. Haven't had one since I left school." Boy Laughed. "But seriously, if we creep up gradually from below; that's the dodge . He is looking down for us against the background of the Earth. We'll see up at him against the stars – if there are any– which there might be tonight. It'll be my eyes again Jerry's. Spider will be blinded – as you will be – by staring at those cathode-ray things, whatever you boffins call 'em. `I've got to glance at my instruments from time to time– though we've had them dimmed to the absolute minimum. But I need to watch my engine temperatures, my ASI, the artificial horizon, and the altimeter."

"How long might we be here?"

"Could be hours. Could be all night. Could be off in seconds. The fighter command controller will give us the nod."

"And in the meantime?"

"We talk. There's nothing else to do. I have heard all Spiders bloody stories– and he's heard all mine. So it's up to you chum . Sing for your supper. Give us a yarn; anything… at least we won't have heard it before."

Sturdee decided to tell them about a weekend he'd spent climbing in the Bernese Oberland with his friends from Munich. About an hour into his account the intercom, over which he had been speaking , crackled into life:

"Turtle, Turtle, vector 30, Angels zero Niner."

"Here we go chaps . Turtle vector zero three zero; Angels 090. Wilco Roger Turtle ."

The starboard engine broke into deafening life with a loud cough, and then the port. The whole machine shook and trembled as the pilot throttled up.

" Chocks away."

They bumped over the field. Sturdee could see nothing though there was a dim glow from the instruments in the nose.

They swung round on one brake as the engine noise rose several octaves:

"Here we go chaps – hold tight."

In a matter of seconds the two big Hercules engines had dragged them into the sky, he felt them bank, heard the undercarriage clunk into place and wondered yet again whether he was being a fool. Boy had made the situation plain :

"There's no point in giving you a parachute chum, you'd never get out of the crate from there. I've not got much chance either. Escape for the aircrew is the last thing bloody aircraft designers think about . The very last. I have to hang from there by two bars, kick my hatch out and drop through it . In straight and level flight maybe I'd stand a chance. In any other attitude, like a dive or spin – no bloody chance. So don't worry too much chum . If we get into trouble I'll do my damnedest to get the crate down . Spider can bail out though."

At 9000 feet they got new orders:

"Turtle we have a bandit for you. Possible formation. Vector Six zero, retain attitude , range 15 miles."

"Turtle Wilco Roger. Switch on your box of tricks Spider."

Two cathode ray tubes came on, one vertical, one horizontal, and began glowing and flickering to Sturdee's left front. They were repeaters of Spiders display.

"Turtle Vector 57. Range 12 miles."

The engine note dropped.

"Turtle Vector 48, range nine nautical miles."

Sturdee tried to peer forward through the canopy but he could see only upward . One or two stars would be seen. It was becoming freezing cold.

"Turtle, Vector 43, Range six , Angels Zero Niner."

"Ground control can see both them and us, using separate radars," Spider explained "We should pick something up on the displays any mo' now."

Sturdee stared at his tubes, one showed a flickering vertical line – presumably height, the other a flickering horizontal line – presumably direction right and left. Because their antenna set-up was so horizontal the altitude information would be rather crude.

"Bring us in well below him Spider. I'll throttle back so we can creep up below his belly."

" I've gottim!" Spider was excited.

On his horizontal repeater Sturdee could see a marginal bump in the noise to far right.

"Range 4.5 miles. Right and down a bit."

"We've got 5/8th cloud above us."

"Looks like more than one target Boy. Range 3.7."

Sturdee could see that the target, now showing on both displays – was indeed fuzzy.

"Left... Left... Straight... 3.2 miles. Speed up Boy."

"We're in thick cloud now."

"2.5 miles. Right a bit ... Straight..."

"Out of cloud. How high?"

"He's up 500."

"Good." Keep us there.

"We're closing fast , 1 point 3 miles."

"Bits of clag."

"Closing in fast. He's still high."

"My God I can see him. Four Lancs by the look of 'em– in diamond formation. Lean over my right shoulder Giles and look vertically up. You can see their exhaust flames."

Sturdee could see very little that made sense but he did see one set of bright Rose-orange stars they could only have been Boy's exhausts.

"They haven't seen us – I'm right underneath. Well done Spider."

"How do you know they haven't seen us?"

"They've been ordered to switch on their landing lights if they spot us . Us likewise. Now comes the dicey bit . Standby. I'll climb up, under the rear Lanc's tail, open my airbrakes then 'Lights on'."

Sturdee felt the nose come up.

"Gottem by Christ. See 'em Spider?"

"Of course. Ruddy great monsters."

"If we could open fire now– bloody mayhem. Christ……..we're into clag !"

The nose went up sharply and the Beaufighter pitched about in the wake of the great bombers before breaking free and banking to starboard.

"Turtle to control. Interceptions successful and complete. Four four- engine bandits ."

"Control to Turtle . Acknowledge four times four bandits. We have a new target for you. Vector 270 Angels 12. Range 30 miles."

"Turtle to Control; Roger Wilco: Vector Two Seven Zero; Angels Twelve, Range Three Zero. Speed Two Six Zero knots. Turtle Out "

They made two more successful interceptions that night, but lost a third bandit in thick cloud at low altitude before Boy announced they were getting low on fuel.

"Now for the dicey bit Chaps: landing in the bloody dark."

They had to go around twice with the undercart and flaps down before Boy was satisfied. Even so it was with a very hard jolt before the brakes squealed, seemingly just inches away from Sturdee's head.

When the engines died and with the Intercom dead, the silence was deafening. Sturdee unplugged his oxygen and took off his helmet. His throat was dry, whether from the altitude or sheer fright he wasn't sure. His lips were numb with cold. He'd have to try and ring Duff House and tell Joan he was safe.

When he got back from fighter command headquarters Hanbury was jubilant:

"We successfully intercepted over 40% of the formations detected by Chain Home. And even if we knocked down only half of those, that would still imply that Bomber command suffered 20 percent casualties. Ruinous. Quite ruinous. And look at the map of Europe Giles."

He pointed to the one on his wall:

"The Jerries can install their radars and their night fighters well forward of the German border – in Holland, Belgium and Northern France. Their night fighter defence should thus become even more effective than our own. In the long run Bomber Command should be smashed."

Then he looked serious:

"I don't know why I'm so happy. Maybe all this will help you get your Liberators. But what this really means is the slaughter of our young men in the air. We're sending them to their pointless deaths – as we did in Flanders during the last war . What do you think – how was your night?"

"Valve-based or not your radar system seems damned effective. Boy – our pilot – thought we might have shot down half a dozen Lancs in a live show. The poor buggers are virtually blind and defenceless from below."

"I know. Once Jerry gets his system sorted out we'll be slaughtered in the air. Very few of our airmen will complete a Tour of Duty; that's 30 Ops you know Giles. We're sending them to almost certain deaths. For what, I ask you?"

"Blackett reckons it takes a ton of high explosives on average to kill a single civilian – very often a woman or child. But you'd think from reading our newspapers that Germany is already on its knees."

"I know Giles. Spectators are always much blood-thirstier than combatants. That sickens me."

"We're not going to deflect Churchill or Lindemann from mass bombing. But once Portal realises that eventually he'll get the blame for needlessly slaughtering our airmen , he might change his mind sufficiently to give us those Liberators . You've got to give us the ammo to write an effective – a devastating report."

"Whose name will it go forward under?"

"A very good question. You could write a report crowing about Fighter command's success. I'm hoping that Air Vice Marshal Robb will put his name to one retailing Bomber Command's complete bloody failure. Mind you we'll need chapter and verse for every line, every table, every claim. If Portal won't buy it himself it might go all the way up to cabinet level. Once ministers realise they are knowingly sending our young men to certain and futile deaths, some of them may kick up a fuss."

As usual talking to Hanbury cleared Sturdees head. For a start Hanbury was smarter than he was and had a more common-sense point of view. He was continually building things with his hands instead of going off into mathematical pyrotechnics as he did himself. 'Hanbury is a proper scientist' Sturdee reflected 'He should be going out to New Mexico – not me.'

"You forget," Hanbury said: "I spend most of my time with these RAF types. There's a deal of insecurity among their senior officers with regard to the Royal Navy. They've lost the Fleet Air Arm to the Navy quite recently, now they've lost the operational control of Coastal command to the same enemy . No doubt they suspect this call for 'their' Liberators is another bid to undermine their very existence."

"How ridiculous!"

"Not at all. The Admirals look down on the Air Marshals as scarcely better than mechanics – after all they weren't at Trafalgar."

"What are you saying?"

"I suggest we play down the Liberator angle – it's too sensitive. Prioritise the slaughter bomber command is bound to suffer over Germany. If this exercise is anything to judge by casualty rates of 10% or more per raid can be expected. Come on you're the mathematician – what would that mean to surviving a tour of 30 Ops. , which is what our air crews are supposed to do?"

Steady reached for his pocket slide-rule: "My God… 10% casualties per sortie implies Odds of 24 to 1 to 1 *against* surviving a tour of duty."

"What if it's 15% ?"

Sturdee manipulated his rule:

"130 to 1 against survival."

"So as I see it our Air Marshals are behaving like those 'Chateau Generals' in the First World War who were accused of sending their own men over the top to certain death while they sat in comfort and safety manoeuvring for personal glory."

"Sounds like it."

"Then surely that's the angle we should play Giles? Make the Air Marshals feel guilty about squandering their young air crews over Germany –especially if they have an alternative way out – by sending them out to patrol your Atlantic Air Gap instead."

So as his swansong in Operational Research Sturdee wrote a report regarding the recent night exercise, the heart of which read:

"In 1941 Bomber Command was forced to give up daylight raids over Germany as being too expensive in casualties. The writing is now on the wall for the night-time raids as well. The recent exercise reveals that if the Luftwaffe has only valve -based radar, which it certainly has, its' pilots will intercept a large proportion of our bombers even before they get to the German border . Since our heavy bombers are obviously blind and helpless to night fighter attacks from below we can expect regular losses of 10% – or even more per sortie. Then the implications are unavoidable. A 10% casualty rate implies that only one crew in 25 will survive a tour of duty of 30 sorties. Commanders and politicians must either accept that they are sending our men on suicide missions over Germany or find some entirely new tactic for foiling the Luftwaffe's night fighter force as it develops. Sending our young man to their almost certain deaths to de-house a few civilians in Germany is reminiscent of the slaughter on the Somme and Passchendaele in the First World War.

"Many in Britain assume that RDF or radar is a solely British weapon. It is not. It was the Germans who pioneered radio in the first place (Heinrich Hertz, Karlsruhe 1877) while the first radar was built in Germany in 1920 to guide vessels into port in thick fog. However radar is a defensive weapon . We used it to defend ourselves in the Battle of Britain, and more recently to curtail the night-time blitzes. We can certainly expect that the Germans will be able to defend themselves just as effectively against night-time RAF attacks. Indeed, because they can site their radars and fighters in Holland, Belgium and France, well forward of their own borders, they should be doubly effective. Horrendous loss rates as high as 15% or 20% per sortie are not out of the question while 10% is quite likely. Given the information already available History cannot but hold the Air Staff mainly responsible for such an avoidable tragedy. In a democracy wildly inaccurate and bloodthirsty newspaper headlines surely cannot be a basis for directing this war."

It was all too easy for Sturdee to write so dogmatically, something he would come to be ashamed of later, for after all his name wouldn't be on the paper – he was hoping it would be Air Vice Marshal Robb who would have to beard the wrath of his superiors in the Air Ministry. Great moral courage was required of any professional serving commander who put the lives of his men above the dictates of his seniors. Obedience was almost everything in a professional military force, but obedience without moral courage was surely a recipe for every kind of catastrophe – and indeed war-crime. How many recent British commanders , Sturdee worried, had lost their posts for speaking truth to power. Obviously Dowding for a start, and probably Wavell.

Blackett of course was delighted with the draft of Sturdee's report for he was at the same time trying to undermine Bomber Commands claims to be having a decisive effect with its massive raids. To his fury he had discovered that Lindemann had completely twisted the facts of an Inquiry into the effects of German bombing raids on Hull and Birmingham earlier in the war. Professors John Bernal and Solly Zuckermann, who had led that inquiry had actually written: 'In neither town was there any evidence of panic resulting either from a single raid or from a series of raids . In both towns raids were, of course, associated with a degree of alarm and anxiety– which in no case was sufficient to provoke mass antisocial behaviour. There was no measurable effect on the health of either town."

But Lindemann had used that very same report to write for Churchill that: " a force of 10,000 bombers – which should be available by mid 1943, could drive the great majority of the population in 58 German towns to: 'Flee their houses and homes' . Bombing on this scale, he surmised 'Would so damage morale as to break the spirit of the German people.' The Air Staff , including Portal, had found this twisted report: 'Simple, clear and convincing.'

" But it's dishonest nonsense!" Blackett raged over the phone, and in a report copied to Sturdee wrote: 'From the effectiveness of air cover it could be calculated that a long range Liberator operating from Ireland and escorting convoys in the middle of the Atlantic would save at least half a dozen merchant ships in its service life of some 30 sorties . If used for the bombing of Berlin, the same aircraft could drop less than 100 tons of bombs and kill no more than a couple of dozen men, women and children and destroy a number of houses. No one can dispute that the saving of six merchant ships and their crews of about 400 men and cargoes wasn't of incomparably more value to the Allied war effort then the killing of some two dozen enemy civilians, the destruction of a number of houses, and a certain very small effect on production. The difficulty will be to get these figures believed when Lord Cherwell is using the very same evidence to paint an entirely contrary picture."

"He sounds more like a traitor to me." Sturdee had replied.

"I suppose he could be – after all he spent his first 30 formative years in Germany. But I fear it's much more than that. You know Lindemann is at Oxford?"

"Yes."

"Well, Maurice Bowra, a certain Oxford don much about in the corridors of power, told me, with approval : 'In Oxford we regard it as a weakness to change one's mind'. "

"But surely changing one's mind is the very hallmark of a civilised and intelligent being…"

"Not in Oxford apparently."

Finally before leaving operational research entirely Sturdee wrote yet another draft of his report on VLRAs. Mindful of his new colleagues' remarks that the very calculations which convinced scientists were the very arguments to which non-scientists objected – perhaps feeling that the wool was being pulled over their eyes, he rewrote that earlier report with nearly all the numbers excised . Churchill was rumoured to insist that papers on which he would have to decide should be no longer than half a page at most. He tried to write it with Churchill in mind:

THE APPROACHING CLIMAX BATTLE

From
First Sea Lord to Prime Minister.
1942
(First draft prepared by OR group Western Approaches)

We will probably lose the Battle of the Atlantic in Spring 1943 unless, as a matter of urgency, we supply Coastal Command with 3 dozen more Liberator bombers to patrol the Mid-Atlantic Air Gap. They will require 6 months to modify for this role.

With 300 U-boats Doenitz will be able to keep a cordon of 100 continually at sea, able, if spaced 10 miles apart, to intercept every convoy we despatch. The comfortable days of our concealment will be over. Every convoy will then have to fight its way through that cordon, defended only by its own Escort Vessels (EVs) and such very long range (VLR) air support as we can muster. We are facing the climax battle which could decide the outcome of the war.

Concentration will be everything. Doenitz already knows that one or two U-boats have little chance of launching torpedoes successfully against a convoy with a typical escort group of 6 radar-equipped EVs. They are trained therefore to shadow the convoy on the surface and call up reinforcements by wireless. Given the average spread of the cordon they can reinforce at a rate of no more than one U-boat per hour of shadowing. If a dozen reinforcements can gather before nightfall they could attack en masse that night with every chance of inflicting catastrophic losses. If, on the other hand, aircraft can patrol the convoy for much of the day, U-boats will be kept submerged, impotent to summon reinforcements, impotent even to keep up with our ships, for their submerged speeds are too low. If Doenitz can concentrate he will win. If we can prevent him he will lose. We are facing the classic "battle of concentration" known from Thucydides to Nelson.

The Gap is defined by the inability of our existing aircraft to reach it. This inability is not absolute however because a single squadron (Number 120) of Coastal Command Liberators can already get to it. Stripped of all unnecessary weight and equipped with extra fuel tanks they can remain aloft for over 20 hours and patrol the critical area with high definition radar. At 200 knots they can circle a convoy every 15 minutes. Experience shows that any U-boat detecting their approach submerges immediately and remains submerged for at least 30 minutes. Too slow to keep up while submerged, submarines may lose the convoy. In any case the assembly of a lethal wolf-pack will be prevented.

Based on experience, the diminution in sinkings, per hour of air-patrol per convoy, can be estimated :

Probability of different loss rates (%) as function of air-patrol time per convoy per day:

H(Hours/day)	Zero losses	Tragedy (>3)	Catastrophe(>6)
0		100	85
2		95	30
4		75	6
6	9%	30	
8	50	3	
10	90		
12	100		

[assuming a typical 6 EVs in convoy; where >' is 'more than' and blanks denote zero %. The dramatic differences are to be expected when there can be no sinkings with 12 hours of patrol.]

In summary the approaching climax battle will be lost if Doenitz can concentrate his 100 U-boats on station in the Air Gap. However we can prevent him doing so by equipping Coastal Command with 3 dozen more Liberator bombers. 5 months will be needed to modify them and train their crews. That battle won't last long. But the result, either way, will probably be final.

Robb had accepted his night fighter report but was understandably cagey about the actual wording and Sturdee was never to be certain which version, if either, Portal would actually get to see. However things were actually moving in the Highest Command Stratosphere. While he was flying in the Beaufighter Churchill, Roosevelt and their Combined Chiefs of Staff – both British and American, were meeting in Casablanca to decide on future strategy for the rest of the war . And finally someone, perhaps it was Churchill or Pound, persuaded them, at the very last moment, to see sense. They agreed, despite all that Admiral King could do or say that: "The threat of the U-boat menace should be the first charge on the resources of the United Nations" , and their planners confirmed that: "At least 80 very long-range bombers would be required to cover the Atlantic Gap ; half should be *delivered* to Coastal Command by the beginning of April, the rest before the beginning of August."

When Sturdee heard this via Blackett his only comment was:

"They may be just too late."

By now Sturdee's mind was largely taken up with the bomb . Someone ingenious had suggested that if the fissile uranium 235 could be compressed in the midst of a conventional explosion, the critical mass would be much reduced, while the efficiency of the chain reaction would be much higher because free neutrons wouldn't be able to escape so easily with all the uranium nuclei crowded together. It was a very clever idea but the calculations needed to actually confirm that it would be feasible were very challenging – very, but just up his street. He was able to combine his "Frogspawn Approach" with his experience of calculating the effect of depth- charge explosions on U-boat hulls to get an approximate result which looked highly promising. Chadwick urged him to persist and refine it :

"After all it could reduce the time to get to the first bomb by at least a year. We'd need to separate much less Uranium 235."

Now that Sturdee was destined to lose it, married life at Duff House seemed infinitely sweet. He and Joan never stopped talking but their marriage hadn't upset the balance of the household as a whole. Their contentment reassured Arfur while Maurice felt he had fostered a great marriage which might otherwise have never happened. As Joan reported to him one day when the others had gone:

"Life's so much more exciting since we got married – and I'm not just talking about you-know-what. Giles is so interesting. He knows so much more than I do. You know the other night we were up until three talking about – guess what?"

" I have no idea ."

"The Roman Empire. He's reading Tacitus's '*Annals of Imperial Rome*' and reading extracts aloud to me. All those murdering poisoning empresses like Messalina and Agrippina. Its enthralling. And then we argue about it – for hours. I never imagined marriage was going to be like this. He is so… so… stimulating. It's as if I'm coming to life for the first time; opening like a flower."

"I'm sure he feels the same way my dear ." Picton replied "Indeed he said so – 'A marriage of true minds' as he put it. But I'm going to take a little bit of the credit for that. You've got such a big brain Joannie – you simply had to find someone else who could keep up with you…"

"It's more than that, I realise how uneducated I am."

"Not your fault."

"I could've read a lot more than I did… Now I feel I'm going to go on talking and learning and listening – and arguing, all the days of my life. And it's wonderful! I feel like Alice when she'd fallen down that burrow and woken up in Wonderland. I can't bear to think of losing Giles – even for a year."

"At least he'll be safer over there my dear."

"I suppose so."

"Safer than going out into the Atlantic on corvettes and seaplanes."

"But if I know Giles he'll take up mountaineering, or something else equally dangerous , as soon as he gets to the kind of wild place they may send him to."

CHAPTER 40

THE SAINT PATRICK'S DAY MASSACRE.

At the beginning of March Joan announced triumphantly that she was pregnant, though the baby wasn't expected until September, by which time her husband would be long since gone.

"Tadpole" was the name Giles had decided to call the foetus:

"Maybe she'll be two or even three years old by the time I get back. Do you think she'll bond with me after all that time?"

" He," Joan replied, for she was determined on a boy, "Will no doubt have bonded with Arfur instead and will look upon you as an interloper. So you'd better get back as quickly as you can."

" At least I wouldn't have lost a foot like poor Geraint."

He was referring to Gwen's husband who'd been blown up while clearing a minefield at El Alamein and who was expected back in Britain at any moment.

"You know Gwen is applying for a compassionate discharge. She's hoping to go home, have babies, and help Geraint restart his electrician's business."

"What's she going to do with her painting?" Joan asked

"She's asked me to hang onto it until Geraint 'is ready to see it' as she put it; which could take years."

"What's Tom Phillips going to do without her?"

"He'll get a replacement I suppose. You know he's failed his medical again?"

"I'm glad. It means he can have your old room here – after you've left –and help us with the heavy gardening.".

"You'll need a lot more help now. You'll really have to ease off Joannie . Let Arfur take charge – even of the marketing. Don't take any bloody risks! I might not be back for three or four years."

"Don't say that!"

"It's out of my hands. We've got to win this bloody war first. And you've got to bring up our family – we may never have another baby. We'll both in our mid thirties.".

"My mother had babies until she was almost 40."

"But she started young."

"Don't be so negative Giles. I want at least four children."

" 'I want' and 'I can' are two different things here." He changed the subject:

"Blackett tells me I'm going to be replaced by at least four chaps here – whether Horton wants them or not. It's now Admiralty policy to have Operational Research in the front line. He wants me to sort of introduce them to Western Approaches. They're going to have a proper office within Derby House and a confidential phone-link with Blackett's office at the Admiralty."

" But if Admiral Horton doesn't want them…?"

"Exactly. It will be interesting. But Horton has made so many enemies already he might have to accept. Captain Mansfield, Noble's Chief of Staff, has gone. After he refused to sign Horton's golf-club chit he was made persona non grata at Derby House. He's been promoted Rear Admiral instead and has gone to Washington with Noble. So Western Approaches is left without its two abiding spirits – just that barrow-boy Horton in charge. God knows what will happen. And just as we face the Crux battle. It's a catastrophe."

"Now stop grinding your teeth Giles. You can't do anything about it can you? I dare say the Germans have got idiot admirals too."

"They say Hitler's just axed his chief admiral – Raeder, and replaced him with Doenitz. So they'll put all their eggs into U-boats now. I'm told they are commissioning five new U-boats every week! We'll have to sink 20 a month just to keep up – and we are lucky to sink half that number – less than half. The Battle of the Atlantic is turning against us. We could be starving in six months – no three."

" You know only 25% of our required imports got through last year? Joan replied " But nobody is supposed to know. Bad for morale so they say."

The Uranium compression calculation went well. Sturdee realised he was likely the only person in the world with the improbable mixture of experience needed to crack it so easily– nuclear physics, explosives and hydrodynamics. They were so promising that he did the calculation in two entirely different ways as a check.

"I'll forward them to Oppenheimer in the States." Chadwick said "This could significantly shorten the war you know."

"I hope we never drop the bloody things. If we're right we could kill a hundred thousand people in an instant."

"Presumably the threat alone will bring about capitulation."

"Presumably."

When he'd finished that calculation Sturdee grew restless again. The Crux Battle was about to start and he, who had schemed then planned so long for it, was left on the side-lines. He would call in at the dry-cleaning shop to chat with Tom Phillips and Gwen , or in the hope of meeting Tony Loader on a rare spot of leave. He gathered that everyone at Western Approaches, from the most senior Escort commanders, to the most junior Wrens were fed up with Horton and his bullying manners – not to say his ignorance of modern antisubmarine warfare. He was still playing golf most afternoons on the Hoylake course.

"Though he's not getting his own way entirely any more." Phillips reported "Apparently Captain McIntyre and some of the other senior Captains put him in his place after a recent Washout meeting. They threw us tiddlers out of the room first , but apparently you could hear them shouting behind closed doors."

"Good. The little shit deserves taking down several pegs."

"And another thing Giles – a Captain Nevil Cave was asking after you. He is one of the new Duty captains brought in by Horton – ex-submarine commanders and all that. He's been reading all your stuff on Support Groups and the Convoy Equation. He's running a war game every day to test it out – which the wrens call 'Caves Folly' because it involves so much extra work. Apparently Horton has tasked him to find the best way to deploy Support Groups once they are trained. You know we've got five now – but he hasn't released them from training."

"Oh Christ, we did all that testing back in the summer."

"I know – but Horton won't accept anything from the days of Noble – without testing it for himself."

"I suppose that's reasonable. What does Captain Cave want?"

"He wants you to go and see him ASAP." Phillips consulted the schedule on his wall: "He's got the 10 PM to 6 AM Watch at present."

" I'll come in at sparrow-fart tomorrow - get me a pass in will you. It will be March 15."

"The Ides of March" Phillips recalled "The unlucky day they assassinated Julius Caesar."

"Maybe we can assassinate Horton – another dictatorial swine in the same mould."

"Now now Giles." Gwen intervened. "Don't forget Captain Cave is one of Horton's boys. If you talk like that he won't listen."

Sturdee was as usual awed by the Operation Rome when he arrived at 5 am next day. The huge wall-chart stretching from Cape Farewell, at the southern tip of Greenland at the top to Newfoundland and Cape Cod in the west , down to the Azores – and then over to Gibraltar , Cape Finisterre and Ushant on the East, was busy with activity. A Wren atop a very tall ladder was moving a U-boat symbol Southwest towards an Eastbound Slow convoy SC122 which had come out from New York and was now turning Northeast off Cape Race - the western tip of Newfoundland. He was relieved to see , following the death of a young woman, that she was now wearing a safety harness as was a WAAF up another ladder moving a Coastal command aircraft symbol towards a landing at Reykjavik in Iceland. At desks below them on the floor Navy and Air Force officers sat at desks taking in and recording messages coming in on their phones, and handing them to messengers. Up above at the rear in theatre-like boxes, where they could survey the entire scene and give commands, were the Duty Captain RN the and the Duty Group Captain for RAF Coastal command. Sturdee was relieved to see no sign of Horton who had a flat in the building and who was rumoured to turn up at awkward moments in his pyjamas.

Sturdee made his way up to the Naval box and introduced himself to the man who was presently responsible for the whole Battle of the Atlantic on the Allied side:

Cave gave him a penetrating look, patted a seat beside him, and resumed some business with a messenger. But eventually he turned to Sturdee and shook hands:

"I'm grateful to you for coming in. I have been catching up on the work that you and Loader did on Support groups and want to pick your brain if I can. But first let me fill you in on the present rather tense situation" He pointed out at the huge plot:

"We've got two eastbound convoys about to enter the Air Gap. Fast convoy HX 229 out of New York with 40 ships, and slow convoy SC122 originally with about 52, which left New York two days earlier. The weather has been appalling – even for the North Atlantic in winter. You know a very large cargo vessel with the convoy commodore on-board simply capsized with the loss of all hands last month?"

Sturdee tried to imagine such nightmare conditions.

"Then – very bad news, we lost Shark five days ago when the Germans changed their weather codebook and Station X has not yet broken back in , so it's difficult to divert convoys when we don't know exactly where the wolfpacks will be. But from the signal traffic there must be three large packs out there, one at the western margin of the gap lying in wait, and two more actually in the gap to the North-east sweeping down to catch the convoys if they manage to get pass the first."

"How many?"

"Rodger Winn reckons at least 45 U-boats. In three packs of about 15."

"And the escorts?"

"SC122 has been joined by Ocean escort group B-4 out of St John's Newfoundland – that is headed by Commander Boyle with two destroyers, a frigate, five corvettes and a rescue vessel to look after 52 merchant vessels. HX 229 on the other hand has only a very weak Escort group of four ancient Town class destroyers and one Corvette under the command of Lieutenant Commander Luther who has made only one ocean crossing."

"My Gosh . What about a rescue vessel?"

" None, I'm afraid."

"But that's suicidal! At least one escort will have to detach to do rescue work leaving only four escort vessels to face more than a dozen U-boats. Surely there must be a Support group on its way?"

"Afraid not. Admiral Horton has retained all of them in the UK for further training. You know he's a terror for training?"

Sturdee was at a total loss what to say . It seemed like utter madness.

"What about air cover?"

"As you can see," Cave pointed up towards Iceland "120 Squadron based in Northern Ireland have detached two Liberators to stand by at Reykjavik . But the weather is so foul up there that they may not be able to take off, let alone find the convoys if they do."

When their Watch was over Cave asked Sturdee back to his office:

"The Admiral has tasked me to look into the deployment of mobile support groups – once they are completely trained. Everyone said I should read the paper that you and Loader wrote on it last summer. Pretty strong stuff – though I can't understand where your figures come from. However I've been running a war game based on it – and I must say that so far it backs you up remarkably well. Can you explain the basis of this convoy equation you mention. It will be anathema to the admiral who – as you know – abhors what he calls 'slide rule warriors'. However that doesn't mean to say he's right.

I'm open to new ideas, and if you can convince me I may be able to convince him – eventually. I gather Support groups were your idea?"

" Not at all. They were Admiral Noble's, and his alone. He simply asked us to look into the numbers – and in particular how many extra escort vessels would be needed to form them. A remarkably small number as it turned out."

Sturdee spent the morning going through the whole Convoy Equation business with Cave – who was a good listener. As an ex submarine-commander from the First World War he immediately appreciated Sturdee's approach of looking at the battle from the point of view of a U-boat commander hoping to penetrate the escort cordon and then to find the time to launch a salvo of torpedoes accurately.

By the time they parted at lunch Cave was willing to concede that though he didn't, and never would, understand the Convoy Equation, it seemed to be based on sound Common Sense:

"It won't impress the old man though. For a start he likes to think that Support Groups are his own idea – and certainly not Noble's."

"But but …" Sturdee bit his tongue.

"And equations are anathema to him. But he does believe in war-games, hence my exercises."

"But we did all those war-games last summer… it was Loader's idea."

"I know you did – now. But the Admiral's got to see them play out for himself."

Cave might have winked at this point – but it was so subtle that Sturdee couldn't be quite sure.

"Can I come up to the Ops room again tonight.? It seems we are facing the Crux Battle at last ."

"Yes of course. Both convoys will be crossing into the Air Gap tonight or tomorrow morning. Why don't you join me at 10 PM tonight and watch all the fun."

Fun wasn't the operative word he would have chosen and so Sturdee went to his tiny office in the University and worked out the likely chances of the fast convoy HX229, which had such a weak escort, and an inexperienced commander, and worst of all no rescue vessel. The results were as ominous as he had anticipated. He wondered whether Cave or Horton had any idea of the catastrophe awaiting the poor devils out on the storm tossed Atlantic who they were practically sending to hideous and unnecessary deaths. He couldn't bear to go home and face Joan. He dossed down for a few hours in Gwen's empty bed at the dry cleaners, so as to be fresh for the approaching Night watch.

At 10 pm Cave greeted him cheerily in the the Ops room which, as usual, was a scene of silent but efficient activity. Up on the giant green wall chart the tapes denoting the two convoys' progress had moved a couple of feet North East during the day. He was relieved to see no sign of sinkings so far– which would be denoted by upturned red cargo-vessel signs. But the ominous numbers of black-and-white U-boat crosses, black for guessed positions from Winn, white for position fixes using U-boat radio signals . Sturdee had never seen so many – he counted four dozen at least , just waiting for their more or less undefended prey to approach.

"Storm's abating out there." Cave announced. "But full Moon and visibility 10 miles. Slow convoy SC 122 with 52 ships and seven escort vessels has crossed into the Gap, while fast convoy HX 229 with 40 ships and five escort vessels is astern 100 miles West So' West of them, and is just entering. They are both keeping radio silence so as not to give their positions away. But if you ask me the Jerries know exactly where they are."

"Winn and I are pretty sure B-Dienst has broken the Admiralty Convoy Code – so they knew the poor bugger's routes even before they left New York."

"Are you sure?"

"No , but look at those wolf packs – they're right in their tracks."

"More like they're shadowing astern and calling up reinforcements. There's been a lot of U-boat radio traffic during the day– but unfortunately Bletchley Park still can't break it. And we're pretty darned thin on the ground here at Derby House with so many of our senior chaps away at this Convoy Conference going on in Washington."

"Perhaps that's why they've allowed SX 229 to sail without a rescue vessel? That should never happen, never! We worked out all that back in 41."

"We've got a new Watch on duty now."

"Obviously…" Sturdee was going to say more, but bit off his tongue with a cough.

Cave was busy for some time getting messages from the floor, and making decisions:

"I'm also worried about refuelling. None of those poor old World War One destroyers in the fast convoy can make it across without re-bunkering. They've got the equipment but the weather is far too bad for it: mountainous seas apparently. They were supposed to try on HX229 but I doubt they managed it. If they don't succeed, the poor merchantman could be left with a single escort – *Pennywort*. Sounds pathetic doesn't it? Forty merchant ships up to 15,000 tons each , being protected by a tiny corvette called *Pennywort* weighing less than a thousand . What do your equations project for tonight?"

" They predict a 75% percent chance of more than five torpedoings in HX 229 alone and a 60 percent chance of more than six."

"I find that hard to believe."

"I hope I'm wrong of course , but how will we know – if there's complete radio silence?"

"They'll break it once they are in certain contact with the pack. What's the point of silence thereafter? The buggers already know where you are."

"What about the prospects of air cover? That could make an enormous difference."

"Best go see the Coastal Command chaps in the box next door."

Sturdee did so and introduced himself to the Group Capain on duty, whom he'd met before:

"All we can do on the West side of the Gap, which they're entering now, is fly a couple of Liberators from 120 Squadron in Northern Ireland up to Reykjavik Iceland – which we've done already. Otherwise there is not a single long-range antisubmarine aircraft on the entire Eastern seaboard from Nova Scotia to Florida."

"But what about the Combined Chiefs of Staff conference at Casablanca in January? I thought they made VLRAs for the North Atlantic the Allies' absolutely top priority."

" So they did. But they reckoned without Admiral Ernest J King, Commander-in-Chief of the entire U.S. Navy. He is fighting his own private war – and not against the Germans apparently, but against us Brits. He's got at least 120 VLRA Liberators, but he's posted them all to the Pacific. A dozen in Newfoundland would make all the difference. Wouldn't be an Air Gap then. We'd have closed it from both sides."

"So he is disobeying the Combined Chiefs of Staff, both American and British – to say nothing of his own president?"

"Apparently so. They say he's in a drunken rage – or a drunken funk most of the time."

"I saw him in action once. Couldn't sleep for nights afterwards."

"All we can offer these poor chaps tomorrow are 18 precious Liberators from Northern Ireland – where they are supposed to be stationed to protect the Eastern Atlantic. So the two up there in Reykjavik are due to take off eight hours before dawn Convoy -Time and arrive with them at first light. But the latest Met report from Reykjavik is horrific. They've got a Force Seven gale on the runway itself. Those poor buggers are so loaded with extra fuel that, even in good conditions they can barely stagger into the air. Some of them fly for 20 hours you know, risking their lives when their tanks run dry. We've lost two crews that way already."

"All because of that swine King."

"As you say. But the world is full of swine. You just don't promote them to run your entire Navy. Blame Roosevelt."

"But how can a politician sensibly pick an Admiral ?"

"A very good question– probably as old as the ancient Greeks wouldn't you say? Our own Prime Minister isn't a good picker of commanders is he? Look at the Dardanelles and look at Norway. Anyway why blame the Americans ? We've got masses of potential VLRAs – Lancasters, Halifaxes… Sterlings. Bomber Command just won't let us have them. Or rather, Air Chief Marshall Portal – he is our top boss – won't give any to Coastal Command. That could change now though ."

"Why?"

"We've got a new chief at Coastal Command – Sir John Slessor. He's a real bruiser if ever there was one – flaunts a badly broken nose from his boxing days – to let everybody know who's coming. I think he might get us some VLRAs. And things are gradually improving. We're forming a second squadron of Liberators at Aldergrove – Number 86. We should have over 40 machines by April."

"What support can you give those two convoys from there?

" As soon as they cross the middle of the Gap we ought to be able to reach them from Aldergrove, so we're planning several hours of aerial protection each day. But they have to reach that point first – about a thousand miles out from Northern Ireland."

When he got back to the Navy box Cave was preoccupied:
"HX 229 has just broken radio silence. He's been attacked by a big pack and lost 3 merchant ships torpedoed. We're just decoding their identities from their convoy numbers…" he gestured to a naval lieutenant at his side. Later he read out:
"*Elin K* , Norwegian, 40 crew , tonnage unknown, cargo of wheat and Manganese."
"*Zaanland* , Dutch, 7000 ton refrigerator ship, Meat, wheat, Zinc."
"*James Oglethorpe*, American, 7000 ton Liberty ship. Wheat and sugar, About 60 crew,"
"*Pennywort* and *Beverly* detailed to try and pick up survivors."
"That leaves only three escorts with the convoy."
"Exactly. And all three are tiny World War I destroyers running out of fuel. *Mansfield's* radar doesn't work and there;'s only one Huff Duff set in the entire escort group. You obviously need two."
"Yes I know. Usually the other set is on the Rescue vessel. But there isn't one."

An hour after midnight – 22 hours local convoy time, there was a lot more bad news:
"*William Eustice* , American , 7000 tons of sugar, has been hit. Sinking. *Volunteer* attempting to pick up survivors. *Mansfield* away following a U-boat contact."
"But that means there are no escorts left with the convoy."
"What else could an escort commander order? Leave the seamen to drown? Apparently other cargo vessels are not stopping to recover their fellow seamen."
"Why not?"
"You tell me. Funk probably. They'd be sitting targets when they stopped."

Three hours later:
"*Harry Luckenback*, American , torpedoed, 6000 tons, 54 crew."
That made five victims in all, and it was still only 1 AM out on the ocean.

At 3 AM, shortly after *Volunteer* had returned as an Escort there was disaster:
Caves' assistant decoded the incoming messages:
"*Irene DuPont*, American, 12,000 tons, general cargo, torpedoed, sinking."
"*Nariva,* British , 9000 ton refridgerator ship carrying Argentine beef. Torpedoed. Sinking slowly.
"*Southern Princess*, British oil tanker carrying 12,000 tons of fuel oil. Ablaze and illuminating the whole convoy. Crew of 100, including rescued British seamen returning from New York."

At 6 AM Cave was replaced but Sturdee remained to follow the awful tragedy, although he was exhausted. Someone pointed out that it was Saint Patrick's Day.

Attention now switched to slow convoy SC122 steaming 100 miles ahead of HX229. Although it had a relatively powerful accompaniment of seven escort vessels and a rescue ship it was, according to the chart, running slap into two large wolfpacks. At dawn local convoy time, the slaughter started:

"*Kingsbury*, British, 5000 tons ; Soya, bauxite, timber, crew over 50, torpedoed, sinking."

"*Aldermin*, 8000 tons, Dutch, Oil-seed, general cargo, crew of 80 plus . Torpedoed."

"*King Gruffydd*, Welsh, 5000 tons of Tobacco, steel and explosives. Sank rapidly."

"*Fort Cedar Lake*; British, new ship, 7000 tons, general cargo, 50 plus crew. Torpedoed. Sinking"

Sturdee, had also done a calculation of the prospects for this slow convoy, which wasn't so bad, seeing as it had seven escorts and a rescue vessel. Even so he found it had a 60% chance of losing more than four ships – which it had already, and a 16% chance of losing more than six."

Next, 'The St Patrick's Day Massacre', as it came to be known, switched to the ill-escorted fast convoy. In broad daylight, 11 am convoy time, the messages came in and were decoded:

"*Terkoelei*, Dutch, 5000 tons, about 60 crew, cargo wheat and zinc, torpedoed, capsized."

"*Coracero*, British , 7000 ton refrigerator, meat, Donaldson Line, torpedoed, sinking rapidly. Destroyer *Mansfield* directed to pick up survivors."

That was 10 ships torpedoed in HX 229 and Sturdee anticipated more. There then followed direct cries for help from Lieutenant Commander Luther, the inexperienced escort commander, who had been put in an impossible situation with such a weak escort. The first one read:

'HX229 ATTACKED. REQUEST EARLY REINFORCEMENT OF ESCORT. 51,45 N: 33,36 W."

The second, 90 minutes later, obviously in response to the Admiralty:
"HAVE BEVERLY AND MANSFIELD IN COMPANY, PENNYWORT AND ANEMONE OVERTAKING ASTERN WITH SURVIVORS. PERSISTENT ATTACKS WILL NOT PERMIT REFUELLING OF THE DESTROYERS AND SITUATION IS BECOMING CRITICAL. HFDF AND SIGHTINGS INDICATE MANY U-BOATS IN CONTACT."

"My God!" Sturdee couldn't help exclaiming "Now that whole convoy could be lost. Isn't there any help on its way?"

The Duty captain responded:

"*Highlander* , a Havant class destroyer is on its way from St John's Newfoundland trying to catch up, but it's not due until tomorrow afternoon or evening. It was supposed to be part of the original escort group, and its captain Commander Day was supposed to command that group – but they had boiler trouble and couldn't leave St John's with the rest."

Over in the RAF office the Group Captain was rather more positive:

"Two Liberators have just made contact with that faster convoy, one from 120 Squadron and one from 86, both based in Northern Ireland. They are attacking surfaced U-boats already. If nothing else that should keep them down and they may lose contact. But the Liberators are right at their extreme range and won't be able stay around for long."

"What are they armed with?"

" Depth charges of course. But only four each." The Group Captain looked at Sturdee quizzically.

"I only ask because you're supposed to have a new airborne anti submarine weapon on the way."

"That's very hush hush."

"I know. But I designed the bloody thing: an acoustic torpedo. They were supposed to be ready in January. They could save our bacon now. Every U-boat sighted by a Liberator could be sunk."

" So I believe. Yes they've been delivered to Coastal command from America – I thought they were American. But we simply haven't had the time to fit them and train the crews . With one squadron to cover the entire Atlantic we didn't dare to take a single aircraft, a single crew out of service. "

"I see. Understandable I suppose."

" They will come soon, but not in time for these poor devils". and he pointed up at the chart, where the two convoys , leaving behind a scattering of red sinkings, were wallowing towards their approaching fates.

'The Charge of the Light Brigade in slow motion' Sturdee thought. There were about 2000 men out there in each convoy, and perhaps most of them were facing appalling deaths. Only the lucky ones would die quickly.

He couldn't drag himself away. Here was a struggle more fateful than either Trafalgar or Waterloo and yet almost nobody on dry land knew about it, or what the outcome would be. In the words of Churchill, speaking on the BBC last year: 'The very survival of Christian civilisation' might depend on the next few hours.

Early in the afternoon, and after the slow convoy had lost yet another ship – the *Granville*, registered in Panama but manned from Britain – Captain Cave came in looking rarely flustered. He gestured Sturdee to follow him to his office:

"The Prime Minister is absolutely furious. He's just got the latest sinking figures and has called a Battle of Atlantic committee meeting for tomorrow morning . Admiral Horton has been summoned to attend – it could mean the sack for him. Apparently Admiral 'Betty' Stark , head of all US Naval forces in Europe, will also attend . I have had a thought and I want you to help."

"Go-ahead."

"This may be the *ideal* opportunity to present our case for more escort vessels and more VLRAs. Horton wants me to prepare a case on paper which Churchill will read. So it can't be much more than one side of paper apparently. And you're the very man to write it Sturdee."

"Thanks a lot. But Horton will never take my word…"

"He may have to now – to save his skin. But we needn't put your name on it. I'll front it if you like, but the Admiral will have to take the responsibility."

"Of course I'll help. What are you thinking of? "

"Just a short précis of that paper you wrote in June with Loader – showing how small increases in escort vessel numbers per convoy can lead to a dramatic fall in sinkings – your Convoy Equation stuff. But for heaven's sake don't mention equations, just put in tables. I'll back it up with stuff from my war-game. Isn't HX 229 a perfect example of a convoy with a too-small escort suffering appalling casualties. What are the figures now?"

"10 torpedoed for sure. One US vessel has romped ahead – and so will almost certainly be sunk as an independent. And the *Clarissa Radcliffe*, British, is straggling behind due to mechanical problems, and is probably doomed with 40 or more U-boats out there. So that's 12 lost out of the original 40 and there's at least another night and day before they're across the Gap."

"So let's get to work. The admiral's catching the night train for London and we need to be finished by 7 PM at The latest. That gives us about four hours. Can you do it?"

"We can only try– but we'll need the best typist in Derby House. Can you please summon Leading Wren Gwen Jones. She knows my awful writing."

As he explained it to Joan afterwards:

"I hardly know what we wrote now. There was so much to say, it was so important, but the challenge was to cram it into so few words. Impossible really. But Churchill won't read anything long they say . He can't have the time poor devil. Cave was damned helpful and Gwen was a brick as always. Somehow we did it and Horton apparently approved the result because he took it with him to London.

Exhausted though he was Sturdee couldn't bear to sleep knowing the next few hours were critical. He sat next to Cave during his watch, crossing his fingers and toes as the various reports came in:

"Both convoys report mountainous seas, Snow showers, but the `North- nor-east gale is abating. Full Moon but a lot of low cloud."

"Slow convoy SC122 attacked. Two ship torpedoed and sinking:
Port Auckland, 9000 ton refrigerator ship, British, carrying meat. Crew number 70, and *Zouave*, 4000 ton British carrying iron ore . Sank immediately crew of 40 men."

"SC122, rescue vessel *Zamelek* is still detached far astern trying to pick up survivors of *Granville* and other ships torpedoed earlier. So corvette *Godetta* detached to try and rescue survivors of latest sinkings."

"That's seven ships gone in SC122 and 12 in HS219" Sturdee counted aloud.

He tried to imagine how a tiny corvette could squeeze a potential 220 rescued seamen on board.

Just before he went off duty at 6 AM Cave handed the phone to Sturdee:
"It's a Professor Blackett calling from the Admiralty for you:"
Blackett had been ordered by Admiral Pound, The First Sea Lord , to attend Churchill's Battle of the Atlantic committee with him to provide scientific backup if it was needed:
"What can you tell me Giles?"
Sturdee reported the stark numbers and said he'd fax a copy of the Cave report immediately.
Blackett said: " There's some panic at the Admiralty. Some are even suggesting we will have to abandon Convoys altogether."
"No! No!" Giles was adamant. "This whole disaster is the result of massive incompetence here under Horton. Too many experienced staff away at the Convoy conference in Washington. HX 229 should never have sailed into the Gap with such a weak escort and no rescue vessel. Repeat: no Rescue vessel! Worse still Horton's got all five Support Groups over here in the UK undergoing even more training. That's sheer madness! Those two convoys were like lambs to the slaughter. Then of course there are still no VLRAs on the Western Atlantic seaboard. That's entirely Admiral' Kings fault. He's disobeyed the Casablanca Conference. If there were even a dozen we wouldn't have a bloody Gap. Finally our escort carriers are still on the Mediterranean supporting Operation Torch which finished weeks ago! It's not the convoy system itself that's at fault. It's the present bloody idiots who are running it – on both sides of the ocean – since Admiral Noble left. Make absolutely sure Pounds knows those facts before he orders the convoys to disperse. Horton probably won't admit his own errors because he doesn't understand antisubmarine warfare. I believe he had a round of golf

at Hoylake this afternoon. He's not fit to take the responsibility if you ask me! If the ships do disperse we could have another catastrophe on the scale of PQ 17. If those Support groups were out where they should be – in the Gap – this would never have happened. Never never never!"

Blackett promised to ring Sturdee after the meeting ,to let him know what had transpired . Gwen had brought him a blanket from the dry cleaning shop so he bedded down on the floor of Cave's office for a few hours of desperately needed sleep.

Miraculously the next night passed without further sinkings. Sturdee could only suppose that the mountainous seas following the gale had made life almost impossible for the U-boats. With conning towers only a few feet above the water visibility, even survival for their lookouts , became marginal. They tended to dive to fifty fathoms and sleep peacefully– but it meant they would lose contact with the convoy , even a slow one moving at six or seven knots.

"And don't forget there was some air cover yesterday." Cave pointed out. "That usually scares the buggers off."

Sturdee was dying to hear about the outcome of the Battle of the Atlantic Committee but before it came in there was more bad news:

"Fast convoy HX 229. Destroyer *Mansfield,* running short of fuel , detached at dawn to try to reach Londonderry at slow speed."

"That leaves only four escort vessels – and effectively three, with no rescue vessel."

"None of the five Liberators out from Northern Ireland have managed to find HX229 – but they have found the slow convoy SC122 about 100 miles further East."

"My God."

"It's not easy. Apparently *Volunteer* is not responding to their call signs for fear of giving his position away."

But that didn't work. At 2 PM local convoy time:

"HX229: Fatal U-boat attack. *Canadian Star*, 90 crew, torpedoed and sunk."

"*William Q Grisham*, American Liberty ship, 69 crew, torpedoed , now sinking."

That was 14 ships lost out of the original complement of 40, with God knows how many merchant seamen drowned or dying of exposure on open life-rafts.

Blackett finally got through in the evening: "Churchill was furious. He seemed to think it was all Horton's fault: "What are you going to do about it Admiral ?" he demanded.

"Give me 15 more destroyers and we will beat the U-boats." Horton replied.

Churchill banged the table and said: 'You admirals are always demanding more ships but when you get 'em things get no better' ."

Thereupon Horton handed the Prime Minister Captain Cave's report. The Prime Minister temporarily adjourned the meeting so that he and Admiral Stark, Head of U.S. Navy operations in Europe, could read it. Then he reconvened the meeting. He then turned to Horton and said:

"You can have your 15 destroyers – I'll take them out of the Home Fleet. That means stopping all our Russian convoys for the present. You can imagine how angry that will make Marshall Stalin – to say nothing of President Roosevelt, who had promised him succour. Our oil reserves here in Britain are getting desperately low – less than three months left."

"So Horton got away with it?"

" Yes he did. He's an unprincipled street fighter like Beaverbrook – or Churchill himself. But I admired Churchill today. He was put in a beastly situation and he did the only thing he could. He'll get *all* the opprobrium. That was real moral courage"

"Was anything said about VLRAs?"

"A little. Stark was very surprised indeed to find that Admiral King hadn't supplied any of the promised U.S. Navy Liberators to Newfoundland. He said he'd get onto General Marshall, the US Chief of Staff today, and even the President directly – that is today US time. There may be repercussions."

"And what about our Escort Carriers?"

"Apparently they are already on their way from the Mediterranean."

"There was no talk of abandoning the convoy system altogether?"

"Thank goodness no. I briefed Admiral Pound privately along the lines you suggested. I think he realises just who has cocked up – but of course he wasn't going to say that at the meeting He must really have felt a fool having his ships re-dispositioned by the Prime Minister, when it was really his responsibility."

"Was Air Chief Marshal Portal there from the Air Staff?"

"No, but the new Head of Coastal command was: Sir John Slessor. He pointed out that unless oil supplies come across the Atlantic, Bomber Command's campaign over Germany would have to be halted for lack of aviation fuel. I think that made a hit with both Churchill and Lindemann."

"So this whole bloody unnecessary tragedy could do some good in the end – and those poor devils dying horribly out there right now might not be dying entirely in vain , or so that Horton can enjoy his daily round of golf ? "

"One can only hope so."

"It sickens me to think that Horton of all people will come out of this smelling of roses."

"That's your fault Giles , you shouldn't have written such a convincing report. But seriously, Horton may not be such a disaster in the long run. The problem with both Pounds, and Noble if I may say so, though I know he was your hero, is that they are gentlemen – through and through. Churchill wouldn't know a gentleman if he had one served on his plate for supper. He is more inclined to listen to loud-mouths like himself, like Lindemann, like Beaverbrook – and like your Horton. When all's said and done Western Approaches got 15 modern destroyers today, that's three more Support Groups.

With Noble sitting on the committee today I doubt that would have happened. He'd have taken the responsibility, and the blame."

"But this disaster would never have happened in the first place ."

"I dare say. It sometimes takes a disaster to wake the British up : Islwanda in the Boer war ; the Somme in Flanders."

"Now it's 'The Saint Patrick's Day Massacre'. "

"Perhaps. We'll have to see. Will the right lessons be learned by the right people? That's how wars are won and lost."

CHAPTER 41
CRUX BATTLE

At the beginning of April 1943 Sturdee was put on short notice for his departure to the States. He had orders to report to an office in Washington from where 'you will be transported to your final destination'.

"It sounds like a death sentence" Maurice remarked.

"Shush! Don't let Joan hear. She's already nervous enough about me going. Anyway Chadwick knows – our final destination is at Los Alamos in the wildest wilds of New Mexico. That's top-secret by the way – in fact you didn't hear that; it slipped out. They'll probably send us across the Atlantic by high-speed liner – one of the Queens probably – far too fast for any U-boat to target. But we are to go by separate boats – just in case."

"You are becoming a valuable property Giles. Pity you can't take Joannie."

"I hate to leave here to have the baby on her own. You will look after her won't you Maurice?"

"My dear boy… like a daughter– which she sort of is to me now. What other family do I have, apart from Arfur. He'll miss you too."

With departure at hand Chadwick sent Sturdee up to Birmingham University to check his compression calculations with the people up there who had proposed the compression idea in the first place. Joan of course didn't want to lose the last few days of his embarkation leave but Chadwick explained:

"If that compression idea is right it could shorten the war by at least a year – at least. And with 10 million lives being lost every year we simply can't afford to muff it."

Put like that he could hardly refuse.

Before he went however Loader came into Gladstone Dock with his escort group and invited Sturdee over to his wardroom 'For a few pink gins and a natter.'

In wonder Loader showed Sturdee the storm damage to his frigate – solid steel stanchions inches thick swept away; a massive depth charge projector simply torn out of the deck like an uprooted oak:

"I had to send half a dozen of my chaps straight to hospital – broken limbs, cracked ribs – one with a fractured skull. Fortunately no one was swept overboard – but one of the corvette's depth-charge hands was lost. How the hell their crews stand it I simply don't know. Every one of them deserves a decoration if you ask me. The North Atlantic has been in a fury all winter. Even the old hands have seen nothing like it. Hurricane force winds, titanic seas… I once saw an old V-class destroyer standing vertically on its stern. I couldn't believe it. Then of course the storms break off the ice and send it into our tracks and then the ice causes fogs .We lost an oil tanker to ice last trip and one of the escort vessels had its propellers ripped out and had to be towed into St John's. In such weather it's almost impossible to keep the convoys together. Some of the old merchant ships, particularly the Greek freighters, were never built to take weather like this. Life boats and life rafts get swept away. We hoist some of ours high into the rigging to try and save them from the seas – but when you're rolling almost 90° either way it's almost impossible. Fortunately we haven't lost our radar or our Huff Duff or our Hedgehog so far."

"I meant to ask you about your new miracle weapon. "

"The crew don't like it much. No big satisfying bangs astern like the old charges. But I like it. The 24 projectiles hurtle into the air with a noise to wake the dead , then fall into a circular pattern a few hundred feet ahead. Then down they plummet into the depths – until they hit a U-boat hull and explode on contact . But no U-boat, no bang. But we did get one last trip. We could hear it break up on our Asdic. Then lots of oil and grisly bits of flesh came to the surface. You know we have to net them to show the intelligence wallahs – otherwise they don't believe any sinking claims. Let's go over for a gin in the wardroom. I want you to fill me in on the big picture. At sea the horizon is the limit. Sometimes I can't see even one other escort vessel, just rusty old freighters hobby-horsing up and down amidst bleak grey seas."

Sturdee told him about the Saint Patrick's Day Massacre, and his anger at Horton . Loader however demurred :

"I dislike the little turd as much as anyone. But you've got to remember the extraordinary weather conditions out there this winter Giles. You can't blame Horton for those. Do you know why there was no rescue vessel at St. Johns for your HX 229?"

"Incompetence I would suppose."

"Then you would suppose wrong. It was off Greenland on its previous trip when Ice began building up on its superstructure and rigging. The comparatively small crew they carry couldn't keep up with chipping it away – and it capsized under the top hamper. All were drowned. There was no other rescue vessel to rescue them."

"Poor buggers!"

"Have another gin. Here's to wives and sweethearts – may they never meet!"

"Then why were there no Support Groups in the Gap?"

" A good question – with a fairly good answer. Every commander has to strike a delicate balance between the training of, and the active deployment of, his forces. The Royal Navy is, quite rightly, obsessive about training. Trained crews are many times more effective than untrained ones. At Trafalgar our gunners could fire three broadsides in the time it took the French to fire one – because the French had been blockaded in port where of course they couldn't fire live broadsides and exercise – like our chaps out at sea. And as navies and weapons become more complex so training becomes ever more essential. Doenitz is a fiend for it apparently. His crews spend six months exercising together before they are allowed out on patrol. Noble was hot on training – as you know. But the poor Canadians – being so green, are barely trained at all. That's why they lose so many freighters in convoy – compared to the RN. So Horton's obsessive about training. He wouldn't allow his Support Groups into battle before they'd been thoroughly trained . It was a risk of course and we had to pay for it on Saint Patrick's Day. But who are you – or anyone else – to say that in the longer run Horton was wrong? He's set up his new 'Battlegroup School' at Larne , and every Escort group has to spend two days there just before it joins its latest convoy. We like it. We then work so smoothly together out at sea that everyone knows just what to do in practically every emergency. Horton's often out there at Larne in the tutorship HMS *Filante* driving us on. We'll have to see – take a longer term view than just one battle – however disastrous it was. You boffins sometimes forget: 'The best laid schemes o' mice and men gang oft agley.' Horton may not be quite the villain you think Giles. Admittedly he's more like a drill sergeant than a proper Admiral like Noble . But give him a chance. How would you like to succeed Sir Percy as our Commander-in-chief; how would you like to fill such a great man's boots ? I wouldn't, and I couldn't."

Loader's remarks, as usual, left something for Sturdee to ponder over while he was in Birmingham. Being a scientist, and not a naval officer, there were many aspects to fighting a war, which was certainly far more complex than doing science – with which he wasn't familiar. It was so easy to be dogmatic when you were ignorant. He knew all about the *science* of the Atlantic battle almost nothing about the real war. What did he know of guts , or drowning, or fear , or of the determination of two fine groups of men to outlast one another in an awful struggle where the losers' families could be starved into submission?

While he was at Birmingham University Sturdee mused upon its role in the war . If the Allies were to win the Science War – which they would certainly have to do before victory could be secured , they would owe most to a tiny group of people in the Physics Department of Birmingham University – the ultimate unfashionable redbrick university. Here in 1940 John Randall and Henry Boot had devised the Cavity Magnetron, a source of microwaves 1000 times more powerful than any previous device, and a wonder that was revolutionising radar – and much else besides. The Americans were building up the Radiation Lab at MIT , with 5000 PhDs simply to exploit it. Its literally astonishing transmitting power at very short wavelengths meant compact and effective radar sets could be installed even in small ai,rcraft. And so high was the precision at those wavelengths that it permitted operators to 'read' the ground beneath them, as if they were reading a map: individual buildings, roads, factories all showed up while it permitted a Liberator crew to find convoys at night and in storms , and pinpoint every U-boat in the vicinity. As Hanbury Brown put it : 'The Cavity Magnetron has completely removed the cloak of darkness.'

Even so the magical Magnetron was the lesser part of Birmingham University's contribution to winning the Science war. Two refugee physicists there, working for Mark Oliphant – Rudolf Peierls and Otto Frisch – had made the first calculation of the Critical mass of Uranium 235 needed to make an Atom bomb. It might have been 1000 tons or 1000 micrograms – in both cases rendering such a weapon quite infeasible, but it was actually about 10 kg, promising a hideous weapon small enough to be carried in a baby's pram, yet lethal enough to wipe out an entire city, with most of its inhabitants, in a flash. Professor Oliphant, head of the Birmingham Nuclear physics group, had then gone around on a crusade to convince first the British government, and later the American, that such a weapon could and should be made – in case the Germans, with their superior nuclear pedigree, got one first.

' All this in one tiny, unfashionable physics department' Sturdee mused, feeling proud to be an ex-student. But thanks to an outrageous propaganda campaign the British public had been convinced that all great British science went on at either Oxford or Cambridge – a total fiction. Physics of Oxford was presided over by Lindemann – who hadn't done any science since the First World War, while Physics at Cambridge have been entirely built around Ernest Rutherford , who they had poached from Manchester University, and who had suddenly died back in 1937, leaving an unfilled, and perhaps unfillable vacuum.

The discussions over the Uranium detonation were so intricate that it was the end of April before Sturdee made it back to Liverpool where he went straight to see Captain Cave at Derby House to find out how the battle was progressing.

"Well the Saint Patrick's Day Massacre certainly put the fear of Godt into all the top brass. That by the way is a feeble pun. Captain Eberhard Godt, Doenitz's Chief of Staff, is now running the day to day U-boat campaign on the German side. Doenitz has left for Berlin."

Sturdee didn't laugh.

"Well we got our 15 Home Fleet destroyers. Fine vessels, except for their niggardly range – but how useful they will be with crews largely untrained in anti-submarine warfare, is debatable. The Admiral is working them up as hard and as fast as he can. But have you heard the latest shock from your friend Admiral Ernest J King?"

Sturdee shook his head, dreading what might come next.

"He's completely withdrawn the United States Navy from protecting any and all Atlantic convoys!"

"What?"

"Unbelievable isn't it. The Americans are supposed to be sending millions of men and hundreds of millions of tons of supplies across the Atlantic to fight Hitler , and yet they're refusing to protect a single bloody ship."

"What on Earth…"

"It's staggered everyone. He suddenly announced it , without warning, explanation or excuse at the Washington Convoy Conference in March."

"But I…"

"Don't ask me to explain his action Sturdee. One School has it that he hates the British so much that he refuses to undertake combined Ops with us. Another that he's lost his nerve entirely and is permanently drunk – which seems more likely to me. Then there is a third school who see it as a cunning ploy worked out by Sir Percy Noble, now head of our Naval Mission in Washington, with the connivance of both Roosevelt and Churchill – to tactfully bypass a total incompetent in running the most crucial theatre of the war."

" Do you believe that?"

"I don't know. But the point is that the decision has been taken – and we have to live with it. The Americans are now out of the Battle of the Atlantic, leaving it entirely up to us – and the Canadians of course."

"My God – and we were struggling already – with at least 100 U-boats out there on patrol all the time."

"Don't tell me…"

"And if we do finally land back on mainland Europe the required tonnage of extra supplies to be transported across will be vast. The Americans surely want to help protect their own men and their own munitions?"

"It seems not. It seems Admiral King has ducked that responsibility entirely. Perhaps he was frightened by the disproportionate American casualties on Saint Patrick's Day."

"What do you mean?"

"Abandoning a ship after it's been torpedoed is a highly skilled business – as you might well imagine – particularly getting the lifeboats launched and safely away from a listing vessel in heavy seas. Well these new Liberty ships with absolutely scratch American crews often didn't manage it. Either they abandoned too quickly, leaving their code books behind – or left it too late – when most of the poor devils drowned . Perhaps King doesn't want to face the music when the American Press finds out. This way he can blame it all on the British. "

"Which is what you might expect of such a weakling."

"What's the point of crying over spilt milk. The Admiral thinks we can handle it. He has ordered the Canadian escort group over here for proper training and moved the Royal Navy's responsibilities far to the West, almost all the way to Newfoundland."

" Stretching us even thinner than ever."

"But that's only temporary. Once the Canadians are properly trained they'll take over the entire sector formally patrolled by the Yanks. And we'll give them better equipment – modern radars and Huff-Duff for instance. They've been making do with our out-of-date cast-offs."

"I know. What about VLRAs then? Surely the Americans aren't abandoning that obligation too?"

"They say not. But so far not a single United States Liberator has appeared over the Atlantic. King's even removed the few he had operating over Biscay and sent them to Morocco of all places – to a special 'Morocco Command' he's created there for himself."

" 'They're my toys, and if I can't be in charge, nobody else is going to play with them.' How absolutely pathetic. Contemptible. "

"It sounds like it. On the other hand Air Chief Marshal Portal has finally changed his mind – or come to his senses. He's re-assigned no less than 120 Liberators that were formerly going to Bomber Command to Coastal Command instead – if and when they arrive from America. And they'll all be converted to the VLRA role. And in the mean time we've given the Royal Canadian Air Force six of our own eighteen precious Liberators to operate out of Gander, Newfoundland as an interim measure. They will do something to close the Air Gap from the Western side – our greatest vulnerability for now."

"That could make a difference – even if it's only six aircraft."

"Then the American Army, and even the U.S. Navy, have been ordered by the Combined Chiefs of Staff to station some of their Liberators in Newfoundland too."

"We've heard that before."

"We have. Let's wait and see. But in the meantime – if the weather improves– which surely it must since it's nearly May already, our Escort Carriers , which have finally arrived back from North Africa – might be able to fly off their aircraft in the Gap, denying it to Doenitz once and for all. HMS *Biter* and HMS *Archer* are out there with Support Groups already, while HMS *Dasher* is on its way. And the one tiny concession King has made is to leave his escort carrier USS *Bogue,* with its escort group, out in the Azores area, which might make it possible to run our oil tankers direct from Dutch oilfields in the West Indies and Venezuela, direct to Britain."

"That could be valuable."

" It could; if it works."

"Let's see."

"There are however two bits of *really* good news. Station X has broken back into SHARK – and the hope is it may be more permanent this time. So we sometimes know where the wolf packs are assembling , and can divert *some* convoys, though we don't always get the information in time; it's often far too late to be useful. Even better, we've now changed our own convoy code books at last, and the Jerry appear to be very confused. It does suggest that indeed our codes were broken."

"That could be absolutely decisive: far more so than Shark."

"Let's go and have a dekko at the plot ?"

They stood in the Navy box, behind the on-duty Captain, while Cave whispered:

"We've got a big slow outbound convoy ONS-5 bound for Halifax Nova Scotia, going via the far Northern route, which looks from the chart, as if it's going to have to fight its way through the Gap in the next couple of days."

As always Sturdee was moved by the huge green chart of the Atlantic with it's Wrens on high ladders moving symbolic U-boats, convoys, stragglers, and 'Independents' – merchant vessels hoping to sneak across because of their extra speed – unseen.

" A mug's game." Cave commented. "According to Rodger Winn there are at least 45 U-boats up there in the North, including three large wolfpacks. Only really appalling weather is preventing mayhem. Last we heard from ONS-5 they had Force 11, that's Hurricane force winds, and mountainous seas. That makes it almost impossible for a merchant ship to keep station. So they're scattered all over the show like a dogs breakfast."

"What's the Escort?"

"It's B7 , commanded by Commander Peter Gretton in the destroyer *Duncan*, with another destroyer, a frigate and four corvettes."

"Rescue vessel?"

"Two Rescue trawlers."

"I'd hate to be out there in a trawler in a hurricane."

"Tough chaps. But there's ice as well. After all they are only 30 miles South-east of Cape Farewell, the southern tip of Greenland."

"My God! Ice – and a hurricane. Why go so far North?"

"To avoid even more wolf packs. They've only been attacked once so far – but the Escort beat them off."

"I bet the U-boats have gone deep now for a spot of peace and shuteye. What about their air support?"

"A Liberator out of Iceland 1000 miles away is due to meet them tomorrow – weather permitting."

"Poor devils indeed. No wonder the Yanks want no part of this fight. Only seamen made of teak will survive out there."

Sturdee was drawn back to the Operations Room next day to find that the convoy, hove to in the hurricane , had lost one ship to a torpedo. The real worry now was that the weather was preventing any chance of refuelling the two destroyers which might then have to leave the convoy. Cave said: "Horton's ordered Support Groups 3 out of St John's to reinforce them: five of those Home

Fleet destroyers led by *Offa*. But they'll take two days to reach them in such of awful weather conditions."

On the following day there was both pack ice and icebergs within sight from the convoy, which was now scattered into helpless little groups out of sight of one another. The first of the Support Group arrived.

On the first of May a Liberator all the way from Iceland, found the convoy, and helped the escort commander to both shepherd the scattered fleet together, and direct it away from the most dangerous ice. The wind was still blowing hurricane force preventing all thought of refuelling the escorts at sea.

On the following day the Escort Commander Gretton in destroyer *Duncan* was running so short of fuel that he had to reluctantly depart for harbour, leaving Lieutenant Commander Sherwood RNR in the frigate *Tay* to take over his duties. Fortunately the five destroyers of Support Group 3 arrived – but they were short-range vessels too, which couldn't stay long without refuelling.

Sure enough two days later three of the Support group destroyers had to leave again due to fuel shortage. Two wolfpacks were detected dead ahead and the situation looked critical to Sturdee. Joan tried to dissuade him from visiting the Operations room:

"You'll have another breakdown Giles if you're not careful. There's nothing you can do to help, absolutely nothing."

"But one can't draw one's eyes off the contest. It's like a mongoose tackling a poisonous snake."

"Is it that awful man Horton's fault again? The Wrens can't stand him you know because he shouts at them as if they were dogs – never bothering to use their names."

"No, it's probably not his fault this time. It's just that the weather out there is unseasonably awful. Fortunately the nights are getting shorter and shorter, because they are almost up on the Arctic Circle."

"Why does that help?"

"U-boats usually attack only at night."

Sure enough, the following night the storm abated and two Wolf packs attacked and sank five cargo vessels. Worse was to come the following night with a loss of seven ships in convoy which had now lost 12 out of the original 40. It looked like the beginning of another St. Patrick's Day Massacre. Fortunately the two rescue trawlers did sterling service, so the loss of life was nowhere as bad as it might have been. And The Germans lost one U-boat to a Royal Canadian Air Force Catalina flying out of Newfoundland , still 650 miles away, whilst the corvette HMS *Pink* sank another with depth charges.

When, despite himself, Sturdee returned to the operation room the following night Cave looked more cheerful:

"Fog has come in Sturdee. That alters the Odds completely. The U-boats can't see us while we can pick them up on radar. Now it's our turn."

And Cave proved to be right. Without any outside help Sherwood's diminished escort group managed to sink no less than four U-boats inside 24-hours , an unprecedented feat which led to cheers breaking out in the normally sober Operations Room.

"That'll give 'em something to think about" Cave said. "And support group 1 is on its way from St John's to help, with three frigates and two sloops. They've got much longer endurance than most destroyers."

Sturdee was too busy preparing to leave for the States to hear Convoy ONS -5's eventual fate . He had to clear all his books and belongings out of his bedroom so Tom Phillips could move in in mid-May. Then Sturdee had to train Tom in all the practical duties he would be taking over, including wood-cutting, pig feeding, onion farming, electric fencing, motorcycle maintenance.........

He finally got the order to sail from the Clyde on the Queen Mary in late May. Joan decided to hold a farewell party for about a dozen friends which revolved around a whole roast leg of ham, half a dozen bottles of Sloe gin and three of Elderflower champagne. Maurice got pickled and made a speech awarding Sturdee the laurels for practically winning the entire war single-handed. Eventually Giles had to cut him off:

"It's very kind of you Maurice –but it's all complete stuff and nonsense. I have never fought in a war, never risked my life, never taken the responsibility for a single military action, never had to make an agonising moral decision about who to save and who to let die; never killed an enemy or a friend, never had to survive month after month, year after year, storm after ferocious storm in a hammock slung from the leaking foredeck of a tiny corvette that was never designed to survive the winter hurricanes of the far North Atlantic. It's all too easy for us civilians, warm and dry and largely safe at home, to imagine that because we are doing our best that we are winning the war. That's especially true of academics and scientists like myself who make deep analyses and offer smart ideas. But we never have to make the awful decisions, or take the final responsibility. If we win this war – and that has to be decided – we will have to win the Battle of the Atlantic first. And that is being won and lost out there on the vasty deep by humble seamen, most of them amateurs, living in conditions so appalling and dangerous that most of us ashore cannot even imagine them, and which would give us nightmares if we could. I have been privileged to see just enough of those horrors both on the surface, and in the air above, to know that I am not man enough to have stuck it for very long, as they do uncomplaining, totally unheralded by the British Press, who, like me, are too lilly-livered to go out there into the stormy wastes – and report what it is really like. Indeed there's only one person here qualified to talk about the Battle of the Atlantic – because he has fought in it for over two long years, and that's Tom Phillips. Tom would you like to say something?"

Philips looked alarmed. He was quite unprepared. He grimaced unconsciously, while the hand holding his Sloe gin trembled so badly that he had to put the drink down before getting slowly to his feet:

"Giles I… Giles I… don't know what to say. B..b..b.b.. but yes it's horrible out there – probably as b.b.b..bad for the German seamen as it is for us. We should think of them too. They are mostly amateurs as well – husbands and fathers and s.s..s..sons, only doing their best , risking horrible deaths in the cold black deep, far below the surface. W..w..what a horrible way to……
d..d..d.d..die "

Phillips stood there silent for so long that some in his audience became uncomfortable:

"B..b..b.. but… I'll tell you what. I believe we are going to win. They are cracking for the first time. W… we've outlasted them – somehow. I don't know how – b..b…but we have. They've lost over 40 U-boats in the last month – and seem to have vanished from the mid-Atlantic. I know it is h-hard to believe – I certainly find it so… But I think we m..m..may have won."

CHAPTER 42
1954: EPITAPH AND MEMORIAL

The idea of the memorial and an accompanying ceremony exactly 10 years after the tragedy was Maurice Picton's idea. Sturdee , who wanted to forget the whole ghastly war, hadn't wished to go but he felt he had to in the circumstances, as well as contribute substantially to the cost. As a full professor of Physics at Swansea University he might not have been rich but he was certainly better off than Maurice, who was retired, or Loader who was a happy but impecunious maths-teacher.

The detonation of the atomic bombs over Hiroshima, and then Nagasaki, had sickened Sturdee, as it had so many of the scientists who had worked with him on the Manhattan Project. As far as they had been concerned building a bomb had been a precaution – just in case the Germans, who had been leading nuclear research prior to 1939, looked like getting the bomb first. After it became clear that Germany had been completely outdistanced in the atomic race, the whole need for such a bomb, so far as Sturdee and his like were concerned, evaporated. He'd stayed on for the Trinity test in the Alamagordo Desert because he had played a key role in the project. But after that, without letting anyone know, not even his boss and friend Hans Bethe, Head of the Theoretical Division at Los Alamos, he'd made off westward through Arizona then California up to Vancouver where he'd caught The Canadian Pacific Railroad to Ottawa. From Canada he' d gone on to Newfoundland where Loader had arranged a berth home for him aboard a Royal Navy vessel.

Charles Snow and the Scientific Manpower Commission hadn't been best pleased to see him back in Britain – but when he agreed to write a very detailed report on the Uranium bomb design they'd agreed to go on paying his salary until such time as he found a university post , which he very quickly did at Swansea . He found he dearly loved teaching Theoretical Physics but nearly died of double pneumonia in the terrible winter of 1946-47, being saved, literally at his last gasp , by the newly available wonder drug Penicillin. While convalescing in a sanatorium in the Black Mountains he'd made close friends with a fellow patient Ifan – an anthracite miner from the Llanelli area to the West of Swansea. Ifan had taken him down the pit – an experience which horrified Sturdee even more than the winter hurricane he had survived, strapped to his bunk in a destroyer in the North Atlantic. Anthracite is highly compressed coal, the result of the squeezing and folding over geological time, of the western end of the horizontal Welsh coal seam. Miners there had to lie on their sides in the extremely narrow seams to hew out the coal by hand, and mostly choked to death of "dust", or Silicosis, in middle age. Sturdee couldn't comprehend that any man could take up anthracite mining in the first place, or endure it for long.
"We starts it when we're poys see," Ifan had explained, "When it seems like the manly thing to do. Pesides – what else was we to do in the Thirties in Wales?"

It was inconceivable to Sturdee that civilised Europeans should be expected to spend their entire lives tunnelling like blind worms hundreds of feet beneath their normal habitat out in the sunlight and fresh air. There had to be an alternative – there had to be! And there was – nuclear power. This had been vaguely talked about among scientists pre-war, and later more specifically among the physicists at Los Alamos. Minute concentrations of radioactive minerals heated the entire molten Earth – why should not they , in greater concentration, power the steam turbines that generated mankind's electricity? Uranium was one possibility certainly – but there were others such as Thorium or Plutonium. Fired up by his detestation of what he had seen, first down the pit and later in the Silicosis clinic at Swansea hospital, Sturdee became one of the first physicists in Britain to seriously look into the possibilities of nuclear power. Apart from anything else it helped to assuage his conscience after Hiroshima. Britain was now building a Bomb of its own , for which purpose it would need Plutonium-producing uranium reactors – so why not modify them to produce electricity as well? He had built up a thriving nuclear power group at the university and served on any number of government committees dealing with the subject. Ifan, who was invalided out of the pit, became his enthusiastic amanuensis, tasked with bringing the Welsh miners over to the idea of nuclear power. Pioneering nuclear-power was far more worthwhile, and even more exciting, than sinking U-boats or building a nuclear bomb. The Labour government were all for it, and soon the coal miners themselves joined up, unwilling to see their own sons follow them down the pit. So the last thing Sturdee would have the time or inclination for was mourning the cruellest tragedies of war.

So absorbed had he been in his other activities, which included boat- building and painting, that Sturdee almost forgot the war until 1948 when a parcel had arrived from Maurice Picton now living back in Hampshire. It contained a book entitled *The History of US Naval operations in World War II, Volume I , The Battle of the Atlantic, September 1939 – April 1943'* by Professor Eliot Morison of Harvard University. The front piece was a full-sized photo-portrait of Admiral Ernest J. King in full uniform and brass hat, looking as if he'd just won the Battle of the Atlantic single-handed. And dipping inside the text it appeared that indeed he had . According to Professor Morrison the U.S. Navy – having cleared the Atlantic of U-boats, had gone on to escort millions of American servicemen and all their supplies across that ocean on their way to liberate Europe.

At first Sturdee imagined it was some kind of practical joke – for instance there was absolutely no mention of the fact that King, without warning, explanation or excuse, had actually withdrawn the United States Navy entirely from the North Atlantic in March 1943 – weeks before the Crux battles of April and May, leaving the Royal Navy and its Canadian allies to suddenly fight the Germans alone. But reading on, it appeared that Professor Morrison was actually claiming to tell the truth. In a rage, Sturdee, who couldn't sleep that night, had rung up Maurice first thing, foaming with indignation.

It took some minutes before Picton could break in:

"Dear boy – I'm sorry, I should have warned you. But one has to expect this sort of thing – especially from the Americans. It's how American history has always worked."

"But…….." And Sturdee had broken into another diatribe…

"Calm down Giles. Of course you're right – but its rather amusing in this case – even pathetic…"

Sturdee foamed again before Picton could resume:

"Morrison got his 30 pieces of silver from King. Why else would you write such a farrago of lies ? King appointed Morrison to be a Rear Admiral – an academic who'd never been in action; apparently the fool struts about the Harvard campus, even giving his lectures in full Admiral's uniform with braided hat, to the amusement and derision of his colleagues. And no doubt there's a very handsome pension attached."

"But it's dastardly theft… it…it's… it's all b..b. bloody lies!" Sturdee ran out of expletives.

"Of course it is. Almost every word. And Roosevelt probably connived in it: excused his extremely foolish appointment of King. But surely you know the aphorism: 'History is written by the winners'? "

"Of course. But the Americans didn't win this bloody battle! They fled."

" They did. But Morrison has inverted the aphorism to read: ' The winners are crowned by those who get to write the history'. Look at our historians here in Britain – many are so-called 'Regius professors' – that is to say: 'Appointed to tell the story from the Kings point of view'. That's why our greatest Englishman, Oliver Cromwell, gets such a bad historical press. It's just that American historians are particularly shameless. They've had to be – look at America's ignoble birth – all that hypocritical nonsense in their 'Declaration of Independence' ."

"I don't get you."

"You don't want a history lecture now Giles do you – remember you're paying this phone bill. But the truth is that the American colonists refused to pay their fair share of the cost of ejecting the French from North America which the British and the Indians had just done in The Seven Year's War. And the Yanks wanted to pinch the Midwest which had been promised by King George to the local Indian Nations for their crucial help in that war. The Declaration of Independence was simply a dirty trick for abrogating those solemn treaties and pinching all that territory – to which the American colonists had absolutely no moral or military right. They even tried to pinch Canada behind our backs in 1812 while we were fighting Napoleon. Yes it's a very ignoble tale which has had to be covered up – all too successfully I have to say. Admiral Professor Morrison is in that same dishonourable tradition."

"It's all above my head Maurice and…"

"No it isn't Giles; is beneath your dignity, as an honest man and scientist."

"But why are they lying now about the Second World War? That's got nothing to do with the bloody War of Independence?"

" A very good question , to which I can only ask you a question in return."

"Go on."

"Why have the Yanks thrown us out of the Manhattan Project, and why are they building thousands upon thousands of Atom bombs?"

"Yes that does worry me."

"It should worry us all."

"But what can we do now – about King and Morrison I mean?"

"I'm going to write my own history of the Atlantic campaign. And you can be sure that in my version, both of those clowns will stink."

"Promise."

"If it's the last thing I do. Rest easy Giles. The true story will emerge in the end , but it may take me three years to winkle out the necessary facts. So pray for my continuing good health."

"I will, I will."

"We don't want another world war do we, based on a lie? The Second World War was caused by Ludendorff's Lie – that his army hadn't been thrashed at Amiens in 1918. Hitler and the German people chose to believe him and so they tried again in '39. Lies can be lethal. The lie that America won the war could lead to all sorts of mischief."

"Well puncture it then!"

"I'll do my best. But I'll have Hollywood to contend with. Tens of thousands of picture houses around the world pumping out heroic tripe every evening. I doubt that a shabby old professor like me can win that one."

"But you've got a *try* Maurice!" Sturdee had begged.

That had been back in 1948, but it took six years for Picton to make good on his promise to Sturdee, and it was only weeks before the Memorial ceremony in 1954 that Sturdee got to see a pre-publication copy of his book at the old man's club in London where the two had dinner together to celebrate. It had taken so long partly because Maurice had decided to include the U-boat- mens' story too. As he explained:

"It's fashionable to portray them as crazed, fanatical Nazis. They were mostly ordinary men too, not even volunteers, fighting to protect their own families from starvation, from the ruthless blockade imposed on Germany by the Royal Navy from the very first day of the war . Three quarters of those U-boat men went to terrible graves in the North Atlantic. In the big picture, in the long run, they deserve their memorial too. They may have been our opponents , but they were gallant men in their black iron coffins, as brave as any men who ever put to sea."

They both drank heartily to that, and Picton had outlined some of the U-boat men's stories which Sturdee had never heard before. That took so much time that Sturdee suddenly realized he would have to rush for Paddington if he wasn't to miss the last Swansea train:

"I must dash Maurice but before I do what briefly were the factors which you feel turned the battle so quickly and so decisively in our favour in April and May 1943? Remember I only witnessed a part of it before leaving for the States in mid-May."

The historian ticked off the key points with his fingers:

"One – changing our own convoy codes in April, thus depriving Doenitz of his chief source of intelligence, one on which he had probably relied for so long. He never changed his own codes, not radically. So you can put that down to our less rigid system of government and admiralty."

"Two: Noble's Support Groups. Once Horton stopped mucking about with them they enabled us to concentrate superior numbers at most convoy battles, and thus to overwhelm the German wolf packs. Your Convoy Equation got it right. It was Thucydides all over again."

"Three: Closing the Air Gap at last, with increasing numbers of VLRAs and Escort Carriers. And arming them with acoustic torpedoes meant that, for the first time, they could sink U-boats all by themselves – and so they did. They sank over half of the 40 U-boats lost in May."

"Four Huff-Duff which gave escorts a way to find U-boats…

"Sorry Maurice – I've got to dash– See you at Duff House in a fortnight… I'll have read your whole book by then."

Solemnly standing round the edges of the Memorial pond, the Liverpool drizzle fell gently onto their hats and clothing. Here in the paddock where once Joan's pigs Damn and Blast had rooted, they looked back 10 years and remembered. There was Maurice Picton, a little shaky on his legs now, using a stick and clutching the notes of the address he was about to give. There was Tony Loader wearing, for the very first time since he had left the service in 1948, his Commander's naval uniform with the ribbons of his DSO, DSC and bar, along with his sword as a mark of respect for the dead. There was Gwen, now a dumpy little figure holding hands with her youngest daughter Caenwen who was holding another sister who was in turn holding her big brother holding the hand of their father Geraint – a tall man in his Sunday best suit. Then the forlorn figure of Tom Phillips' widow Freda in her mourning suit with a widow's black hat and veil. After her two elderly folk, husband and wife, who had always owned both house and paddock and who had agreed to have the memorial pond on their property. Sturdee, who had forgotten to bring a raincoat, and was getting wet in consequence, was holding the hand of his son Percy – named after Admiral Noble – who in turn was holding onto his mother Joan – who was holding on to young Arfur – barely old enough to stand on his own feet. A little squall ruffled the pond, sending wavelets to die away among the reeds. When they were all silent and still, Picton raised his quavery old man's voice :

"Friends, we are gathered here to honour and remember three other gallant friends who cannot be with us today. On this very spot ten years ago to the day, in October nineteen hundred and forty four Arfur Sugden, and his old mate Gem, were blown to bits when their plough set off an unexploded bomb which must have dropped much earlier in the war. It must have been a very big bomb because it hollowed out a crater 15 feet deep – which became the foundation for this pond, leaving nothing of our two friends to be found. Arfur was barely 15 years old while Gem was believed to be well over 20. They were ploughing this ground to grow potatoes for our war effort, having harvested over 5 tons of the same crop over two previous seasons – a remarkable achievement considering their respective ages – and a substantial contribution to winning the war."

"For those of you young ones who were not then here the two heroes were very dear to us. Arfur was an orphan when Joan found him living with his friend Gem , in Gem's stable not very far from here. We adopted him and more importantly, he adopted us: bringing with him – he insisted upon it, his four-legged friend Gem. Had things worked out differently……" the old man fought to keep his voice from breaking… "They were to come and live with me after the war – as a sort of honorary grandfather to Arfur, because Joan and Giles were Arfur's adoptive mother and father."

"Arfur…" and the tears ran down the old man's cheeks, mingling with the drizzle "Arfur was a great little chap, stout-hearted, principled , clever and brave. Had he lived he would have become a fine farmer – for he loved the land – and raised an even finer family. As for Gem – what can I say of an old horse who was a true gentleman, whose beauty and character shine through in the inspiring portrait which Giles painted of them both together, and which I now possess. One day we hope it will hang in the Municipal gallery of this fine city which played such a crucial, crucial role in the war. Without the Liverpool Docks , without the Gladstone Dock where Commander Tony Loader and his comrades in the Royal Navy escort fleet were based, without the hinterland of railways and marshalling yards which Joan so expertly scheduled during the Blitz – and for which she has never been justly recognised, this country – and our civilisation – might have lost the war; for the Battle of the Atlantic had to be won both on the land and on the sea."

"We are equally here to honour Lieutenant Tom Phillips, Distinguished Service Cross, of the Royal Naval Volunteer Reserve, or RNVR, our very dear friend, who took his own life shortly after the war ended. I am so glad his wife Mrs Freda Phillips can be with us today." He turned towards the widow, in case anyone didn't know who she was:

"Tom served out in the Battle of the Atlantic for no less than three years before his tiny corvette was torpedoed. Somehow, through superhuman courage and endurance he survived in an open lifeboat for many days after the last of his companions had died of hunger, exposure or despair. A very tough man was Tom Phillips, a true hero among many other heroic sailors. It must have been an unimaginably horrible experience , from which, unsurprisingly, he never recovered. It is amazing to me that he battled on as long as he did. Yes a very tough man was Tom Philips, though you would never have guessed that from his gentle manner. He covered up his wounds and did sterling service at Western Approaches Command in Derby House until after the war, and he lived here with us, doing the hard physical labour which Giles, and young Arfur, had left behind. As a result he and Joan fed I don't know how many vulnerable people who otherwise might have half starved – old people, hospital patients, and orphans especially. So Tom Phillips was twice a hero, once at sea , and once on this very earth now beneath our feet."

"With the kind help of Mr and Mrs Fairbridge, the owners of this paddock, and their fine house above – in which most of us lived throughout the war – we called it Duff House then, after Joan Duff our boss – though it's true name is 'Adleboden' after the Swiss spa – we have had this old crater transformed into a pond which we hope will become a joy to the wildlife hereabouts in years to come. Here wild ducks will come, perhaps to raise their ducklings among the reeds. Here herons will come to fish – certainly gulls. Here tits and sparrows and chaffinches will come to drink at dawn and dusk. And here will fall the peace which Arfur and Tom and Gem fought for and so deserved, but which they never lived to enjoy. May they now rest in that eternal peace which passeth all understanding."

"There are many things I could say – but I won't. They were, in different ways, all casualties of the greatest battle ever fought , the Battle of the Atlantic. So we will end our little remembrance with a few words from Captain Stephen Roskill, the official historian of the Royal Navy's role, and the Royal Canadian Navy's role, in that battle, and then conclude by singing what I hope will be a rousing rendition of a great Hymn.

The old man looked down at his notes for the first time and read from Roskill's *'The War at Sea'*:

"... the U-boats and the convoy escorts would shortly be locked in a deadly ruthless series of fights in which no mercy would be expected and little shown. Nor would one battle , or weeks or months of fighting decide the issue. It would be decided by which side could endure the longer; by whether the stamina and strength of purpose of the crews on the Allied escort vessels and aircraft, watching and listening all the time for the hidden enemy, outlasted the willpower of the U-boat crews , lurking in the darkness or the depths, fearing the relentless tap of the Asdic, the unseen eye of the radar and the crash of the depth-charges. It depended on whether the men of the Merchant Navy, themselves almost powerless to defend their precious cargoes of fuel, munitions and food, could stand the strain of waiting day after day and night after night throughout the long slow passages for the rending detonation of the torpedoes, which could send their ships to the bottom in a matter of seconds, or explode their cargoes in a searing sheet of flame from which there could be no escape. It was a battle between men, aided certainly by all the instruments and devices which science could provide, but still one that would be decided by the skill and endurance of men, and by the intensity of moral purpose which inspired them. In all the long history of sea warfare there has been no parallel to this battle......"

As his last words died away old Picton held both hands out to Joan for her to lead the way. In her stout contralto she broke into the opening bars of the old Seamans' Hymn :

"Eternal Father strong to save, Whose arm does bind the restless wave....."

Gradually, one by one, the other voices joined in: Maurice's wavery tenor, Geraint's booming Welsh bass, Gwen's soprano, Loader's quarterdeck baritone, Sturdee's whisper, Percy's choirboy alto.....

Who bids the mighty ocean deep
It's own appointed limits keep;
O hear us when we cry to Thee
For those in peril on the sea.

O saviour whose almighty word
The winds and waves submissive heard,
Who walked upon the foaming deep,
And calm amid the rage did sleep;
O hear us when we cry to Thee
For those in peril on the sea.

O Holy Spirit, who did brood
Upon the waters dark and rude,
And bid their angry tumult cease,
And give for wild confusion peace;
O hear us when we cry to Thee
For those in peril on the sea.

O Trinity of love and pow'r,
Your childrens' shield in danger's hour;
From rock and tempest, fire, and foe,
Protect them where-so- e'er they go;
Thus, evermore shall rise to Thee
Glad hymns of praise from land and sea

As they sang , the drizzle , which had restrained itself for so long, turned into heavy rain which raised rings all across the quiet pond, rings which spread out and joined one another in a sort of endless cadence of their own.

THE END

—

Printed in Great Britain
by Amazon

82455600R10264